WILLIAM WELLS

HOPE'S ROAD

NOVEL

»vantage»
POINT

Vantage Point Books and the Vantage Point Books colophon are registered trademarks of Vantage Press, Inc.

FIRST EDITION: April 2012

Published by Vantage Point Books
Vantage Press, Inc.
419 Park Avenue South
New York, NY 10016
www.vantagepointbooks.com
Manufactured in the United States of America

ISBN: 978-1-936467-29-7
Library of Congress Cataloging-in-Publication data are on file.

0   9   8   7   6   5   4   3   2   1

Cover design by Victor Mingovits

For Mary, of course

King Mykerinos's Daughter

*But while Mykerinos was acting mercifully to his
subjects and practicing this conduct which has been
said, calamities befell him, of which the first was this,
namely that his daughter died, the only child whom he
had in his house: and being above measure grieved by
that which had befallen him, and desiring to bury his
daughter in a manner more remarkable than others, he
made a cow of wood, which he covered over with gold,
and then within it he buried his daughter who, as I
said, had died.*

—Herodotus, "An Account of Egypt:
Being the Second Book of His Histories,
Called Euterpe," paras. 40–59

1:   REQUIEM: LOSING HOPE

LIKE A SPOTLIGHT discovering a player on a stage, the first light of a June Saturday morning illuminates a man as he sits on a wrought-iron patio chair in the backyard of a stately red-brick Georgian colonial on Maitland Avenue in Edina, Minnesota. Above him, a grey squirrel with an acorn in its mouth scrabbles along a branch of a gnarled oak tree. A bird finds its morning song from somewhere higher up. Three deer, a doe and two spotted fawns, wander into the yard and pause. The doe considers the man, who is too preoccupied with his thoughts to notice; then she turns and leads her family to the safety of somewhere else.

The man is Jack Tanner, a fifty-two-year-old tax attorney with the largest law firm in Minneapolis. He is of average height and weight, with dark brown hair, hazel eyes, regular features, and medium build: a perfect thirty-eight regular, like the male models in the Brooks Brothers catalogues that arrive at his house quarterly.

Jack Tanner: devoted husband to his wife, Jenna; adoring father to their daughter Hope; Eagle Scout; dean's list; good son; solid, civic minded citizen who serves on committees and charitable boards; good neighbor; recycler of refuse; reasonably generous tipper if well-served; Republican with a social conscience; payer of taxes; registered organ donor; eighteen handicap; good as his word; reliable as the sunrise; salt of the earth.

Jack has been sitting like this for more than an hour, arriving before dawn just as one of the sprinkler system's backyard zones swooshed on. He had to move his chair because one of the heads had become misaligned and was spraying the section of patio where he sat. This reminded him of a scene from one of his favorite movies, *The Firm*. One of the characters, a lawyer upset by the death of a partner, which he knew to be a murder, was sitting in his backyard just as Jack is now, so distraught that he was oblivious to the fact that he was getting soaked by his sprinkler system. A powerful scene, displaying without dialogue the man's inner turmoil.

Jack is distraught, too, but even *in extremis* he remains a practical man. So he moved the chair. He is wearing striped cotton pajamas, a Christmas present from his daughter, and tan deerskin slippers, a birthday gift from his wife. Against the chilly morning air, he has made a shawl of a plaid woolen stadium blanket taken from the mudroom closet on his way outside. If Jack had planned to sit a while out in the yard, he might have shrugged on his thick white terrycloth bathrobe bearing a blue Ritz-Carleton Chicago logo, purchased from the hotel during a business trip. Jenna had accompanied him on the trip and gotten a robe, too. They stayed the weekend, saw *Jersey Boys* at the Shubert, and dined at Charlie Trotter's. A nice memory.

Jack has been up since two a.m., when a dream startled him into consciousness. In the dream, the Tanner family was asleep when Jack was awakened by a loud noise downstairs. He heard the tread of footsteps coming up the front stairway. He tried to get up, but some force was holding him down on the bed as the danger approached.

This dream is typical of the ones he has been having for the past year. When they involve great men and grand events, he is always a supernumerary, factotum, spear-carrier, servant at the feast, voyeur at the bacchanal, wedding guest, rear-echelon warrior. Nothing is expected of him. When in a dream story it is time for him to act, he cannot.

He must have called out in his sleep because Jenna awoke, poked him, and went back to sleep. He got up, checked the hallway and Hope's bedroom, and then began roaming through the big old house, knowing there was no intruder, and finally ended up in the backyard. He doesn't know why he's out there; maybe he finds his house to be oppressive somehow.

He hears a voice. After a moment he realizes it is

his own. Or maybe thoughts so vivid they only seem to have been verbalized. Either way, it is some kind of monologue—or is it a prayer? Jack has never believed in prayer. However, he reflects, this would be a perfect time to discover that he is wrong about the religion thing. If there *is* a God, then there is someone to petition when bad things happen to good people, a cosmic appellate court, which would be nice on this, the second worst day of his life. But to Jack, any view of history would suggest that such appeals merely rise up into the black void of the universe, either unheard or ignored, *certiorari* neither granted nor denied. Of what relevance is a Prime Mover who does not intervene in human affairs? Jack has always wondered. Of what use is a Supreme Being who allows wars and pandemics and tsunamis and the death of innocents? Did Jews lose their faith as the Zyklon B gas came hissing out of the showerheads at Auschwitz-Birkenau and Treblinka?

"Hey up there, anybody home?" Jack asks the morning sky. Of course, he does not expect an answer, and gets none. The yews do not ignite. He is not struck by lightning. There is nothing up there for him but the void of deep space. He knows he is not himself this morning, because the normal Jack Tanner does not ponder such deeply philosophical questions as the existence of God, and he certainly does not sit in the backyard at dawn talking to himself and to the sky above. But if religion is truly the opiate of the masses, well, maybe he can will himself to believe just enough to ease his pain and to maintain some level of functioning today. Is he losing his mind? If so he must resist that, if only for Jenna's sake, because she may be losing hers, and there is not room in the Tanner family just now for another lost soul.

The first worst day of Jack Tanner's life came exactly one year ago, on the day that Hope, a luminous, lovely, smart, and beautiful young woman, disappeared after leaving her off-campus apartment at the University of Wisconsin in Madison late one evening.

When Hope was a sophomore at Madison, she told her two roommates she was going to her boyfriend's apartment, and might or might not be back that evening. The boyfriend, Slater Babcock, told the police she never arrived. Why hadn't he become alarmed when she didn't arrive? Because he didn't know she was coming, he told his Madison police department interrogator; they often surprised one another by just showing up, he said. It was one of their things. "A surprise date," they called it. Hope's roommates confirmed this. Phone records showed that Slater had called Hope earlier that evening, but that was not proof that he was lying about not knowing she was coming. They might have been talking about anything.

So Hope Tanner was simply gone, without a trace, as if a person could somehow be misplaced, and a year later she remains unfound, despite the efforts of the Madison Police Department, the Wisconsin State Police, the FBI, and a private investigator Jack hired a month after the disappearance, when the official search seemed to lose momentum, as least in Jack's opinion.

Hope is an only child. Jenna's pregnancy became

high-risk when she developed high blood pressure and diabetes. A first pregnancy was ectopic; the fetus did not survive. Jack and Jenna had made a list of boy and girl names, which they saved. But when Hope was born as a healthy baby, and Jenna was fine too, she told Jack she wanted to name their daughter Hope. This name was not on their list, but when the newborn was presented to the parents in Jenna's hospital room, Jenna said, "Oh Jack, she is everything I hoped for." Jack took the infant in his arms and said, "Hello Hope, nice to meet you."

To mark today's sad anniversary, Jack and Jenna have invited a group of family and friends to gather at the First Lutheran Church. The gathering was the idea of First Lutheran's minister, the Reverend Lars Johansen. Lacking a body, it is not a funeral. In fact, the precise nature of the gathering has not been made clear to the guests. No one has asked Jack or Jenna for an explanation, which Jack appreciates. Unable to admit that Hope is dead, Jack refuses to think of this as a memorial service. Lacking Hope, it is certainly not a celebration.

The invitations, which Jenna ordered printed on creamy vellum by Anna's Stationery in downtown Edina—the place where Jenna would have ordered Hope's Save the Date's and wedding invitations—describes today's event as "a coming together in fellowship of Hope Tanner's family and friends." (Lars Johansen's suggested wording, whatever it means.)

This left attendees unclear about what their attire should be. The black of mourning? The bright spring colors of an Easter service? Most guests chose a middle ground: sports coats and slacks, dresses and pants suits, in the muted tones of business casual that left their options open, depending upon what turn events in the church might take.

Jack and Jenna attend Sunday services at First Lutheran just often enough to maintain their status as "social Lutherans," meaning that they came on Advent Sunday, Christmas Eve, Easter, and one other Sunday every month or so. These occasional drop-ins are a harmless hypocrisy to Jack. The Tanners are reasonably generous with their (deductible) contributions. Apparently, the Lutheran God requests ten percent of total income— gross or net? Jack has wondered (the Tanners are in the three percent range). Jack considers church membership analogous to belonging to the right clubs in terms of business networking—the Minneapolis Club, the Edina Country Club, Jenna's Junior League, the Minnesota Horse and Hunt Club, where Hope took riding lessons and he shot the occasional quail and pheasant.

Some of Jack's legal clients are First Lutheran congregants. Although he cannot prove that he's gotten any new business directly from the pews, he knows that showing his firm's flag at First Lutheran can't hurt. In fact, the Hartfield, Miller, Simon & Swensen business development committee keeps a checklist to ensure that all important clubs, charities, and Western religions are covered.

Hope attended First Lutheran until she was sixteen and told her parents she didn't see the point. Jack couldn't argue with that conclusion, in fact he admired the fact that his daughter was a free thinker, and Jenna didn't object.

First Lutheran will be a nice location for today's gathering, Jack reflects, even though there will be no religious service. The church's white clapboard structure is distinguishable from the homes of its mostly upscale parishioners only by its white wooden steeple, by the sign on the front lawn which announces the topic of the Reverend Johansen's Sunday sermons (he has chosen "The Basis for Belief" for tomorrow) and the list of events for that month, and by the heavy mahogany double front doors from which issue every Sunday morning a throng of smiling worshipers. Otherwise, First Lutheran looks right at home in upscale Edina. It was the architect's intent to create a structure to contain a faith that fit the neighborhood. The parishioners agree that he succeeded.

Just like his church, Reverend Johansen fits nicely into Edina. He is a graduate of Breck, the prep school where many of his congregants were classmates, Dartmouth, and the Yale Divinity School. He has a six handicap (obviously, a minister has more time than a lawyer to work on his game, Jack has concluded), is an oenophile, drives a black Lexus LS460 sedan, and is married with children. Rumors that he is gay matter not a whit to the community. Lutherans pride themselves on their inclusiveness; their faith is a big tent.

For the past year, Reverend Johansen has been "ministering" to Jack and Jenna. He is good at it, so good that the Tanners have hardly noticed they are being watched over by this good shepherd via his invitations to Jack for the occasional round of golf, to Jenna for coffee at Starbucks, and to both of them for dinner with him and his wife, Margaret. Once, over lunch at the Edina C.C. clubhouse after playing a round, Jack surprised himself by asking the reverend if he believed in God. Reverend Johansen considered this for a moment, as if he had never thought about it. Then he said, ""I believe in the *idea* of God, Jack. If there is not a God, then there should be, because so very many people need that idea to hold onto."

""So you decided to work for someone you aren't sure exists?" Jack asked.

The reverend smiled. "Divinity school was easier to get into than law or medical school."

Jack felt certain that this good man's belief went far deeper, and that his flippant manner was something he could put on like the Polo golf shirts he wore when dealing with agnostic parishioners like Jack Tanner. Those who wanted the full tilt theological boogie got it. The rev knew his audience.

So there were no home visitations after Hope disappeared, or hand holdings, or hugs, or tears, or suggestions that now, after a year, it is "time to give closure" to their suffering, as if it is a surgical wound that can be sutured. No assertion that "time heals all things," which, the reverend knows from long experience, it sometimes does not. But his experience has also taught him that the heavy weight of grief can be borne better when it is shared communally. One person cannot carry a coffin. He believes that today's gathering will remind Jack and Jenna Tanner that they are not alone in missing Hope.

JACK AND JENNA are riding in their silver BMW 750iL sedan *en route* to the church, Jack at the wheel, as always. They are decades away from that age when the woman takes over the driving and the man, whose genes dictate faster decay, rides a grumpy, disappointed shotgun.

Jack is concerned that Jenna seems oddly disconnected from the events of this day, even more so than she has been over the past months, as the investigation into Hope's disappearance dragged on, then slowed to a stop never officially declared by the police. Little by little, Jenna has been slipping away from him, and he is at a loss over how to save her. He wonders if she thinks that about him too. He knows that he has become disinterested at work and socially reclusive. How could he not? And how could Jenna be her old self when so much of that self revolved around her motherhood?

"Oh look," Jenna says as they pass a tan stucco Mediterranean with a builder's sign on the front lawn. "It looks like the McPheeters are finally doing the new kitchen they've talked about for years. I wonder why Grace didn't mention it to me." Jack right now does not give a flying fuck about Brad and Grace McPhetters' new kitchen. How could Grace mention the project when Jenna hasn't been seeing or taking calls from her friends?

It is nearly ten a.m. as they reach First Lutheran and swing into the parking lot. After being awake most of the night, Jack had lost track of the time, and Jenna seemed to have completely forgotten about the gathering -- she'd scheduled a hair appointment and seemed vexed that she had to cancel it -- so they both had to dress hastily and are inappropriately late to their own event. The invitation said to be at the church at nine-thirty.

Walking up the aisle to the front row of pews with Jenna on his arm, Jack sees that everyone they've invited seems to have shown up. Jenna is wearing a pink linen suit with a white blouse and white platform shoes; she is smiling and nodding at the guests as if they are all here for Hope's wedding. This was all a big mistake, Jack concludes. Jenna has apparently lost her faltering grip on reality altogether, pushed over the edge by Reverend Johansen's stupidly insensitive idea. Jack should have understood this and called it off.

Jenna's parents, Arthur and Ann Waverly, had driven in late last night, too late for a get-together, from their home in McLean, Virginia. Ann had once been a passenger on a 747 that made a "hard landing" at Richmond International; after that she was finished with air travel. Jenna's brother, Ethan, a professor of history at Georgetown, is here with his current wife, Diane. Jenna's sister, Elizabeth, flew in with her husband, David, and their twin sons, Peter and James, from Boston. Jack's father, Russell, a prominent attorney who served two terms as Minnesota's Attorney General, is not present, but he has an ironclad excuse; he died three years ago from a stroke while playing golf with his longtime pals at Minnekhada Country Club. At Russell's funeral, everyone told Jack that, if you had to go, that was the way to do it: suddenly, without pain, among friends, doing something you loved. One member of the foursome, Lonny Schuster, handed Jack the scorecard from that last round, showing that Russell Tanner had completed fourteen holes at nine over par. "He was the playing round of his life," Lonny said. "It's such a shame he couldn't finish." Jenna thought this was bizarre and morbid, but Jack explained that it was a guy thing, and meant as a kindness. Jack still had that scorecard in a cardboard box in the attic, along with other mementos of his father's life.

Jack's mother, Lucia, still lives in the Tudor on Lake Harriet, within the Minneapolis city limits, where he was raised. Lucia drove to the church with her sister, Alice, and Alice's husband, Frank, a wealthy industrialist in Waseca. Frank is majority owner of the Minnesota Timberwolves professional basketball franchise, an expensive indulgence, Lucia always says, a solid investment, even if they're not winning just now, you'll see when we sell the team some day, Frank always counters. Jack has courtside season tickets, perfect for client entertaining.

The pews are filled out with various nieces and nephews, friends and neighbors, and Jack's partners from Hartfield, Miller. In the balcony, in a section reserved for them, are selected representatives of the local and national news media, with their notebooks, tape

recorders, and TV cameras at the ready. Jack decided
to allow these "pool journalists"—he learned that term
during the initial news coverage—inside the church on
the advice of the public relations agency on retainer
to his law firm. The agreed upon strategy is to "take a
proactive stance" to avoid having the guests harassed by
a snarling pack of reporters waiting outside the church
doors after the service.

The news media have agreed to Jack's rules: no flash
photography, shoot video with natural light, do not ask
anyone for comments. Hope's disappearance was, for a
two-week cycle, a major national news event, especially
for the insatiable 24/7 cable-TV news programs. Now,
everyone is apparently doing year-later-whatever-
happened-to follow up stories, occasioned by this
gathering (a second reason, Jack realizes, why it was a
bad idea).

He wonders if anyone, other than the people in this
church, will be interested in news about Hope, a year
later, not being found. Whenever he and Jenna heard
about a family tragedy like theirs, they of course thought
it was terrible, and then they, along with everyone else
not directly affected, promptly forgot about it. They
were busy and had their own lives to lead. Everyone is
always so very busy, too busy to wonder what happens
to a family like the Tanners when they are no longer
breaking news.

Jack does not know how the reporters found out
about this service. There was no public announcement.
No press release. No press conference by a "family

spokesperson." Perhaps one of the journalists is a member of the First Lutheran congregation and saw the item about the Tanner event in the church bulletin. Or maybe a congregant or family member or friend decided to alert the news media. Some people gain a sense of importance by trying to attach themselves to important events, like barnacles on a ship's hull.

Cued by Jack and Jenna's arrival, Reverend Johansen, wearing pastoral casual—an open collared white shirt (Brooks Brothers Oxford cloth button-down), blue blazer with brass buttons, khaki slacks, and Gucci loafers—enters from stage left, clears his throat to test the microphone, and begins to speak, in his deep, resonant, amplified voice, about the joys of family love and the importance of drawing closely together as a caring Christian community during trying times. The *Book of Ecclesiastes* is quoted, as is Proust's *Remembrance of Things Past*, Shakespeare, and T.S. Eliot. The reverend likes scholarly quotations. Some think this a Yale affectation.

Jack finds he is barely listening, picking up only occasional fragments of the minister's remarks. He hears: "To everything there is a season, and a time to every purpose under the heaven." And he wonders why Reverend Johansen is quoting lyrics from a Pete Seeger song.

Jack reaches over from time to time to squeeze Jenna's hand, which she accepts with a pleasant smile. He wonders if his wife will be able to hold it together through the service. At least they are not having everyone over afterward for one of those post-funeral-type brunch buffets of spiral-sliced baked ham and beef tenderloin served on dinner rolls with salads and Jell-O molds and relish trays. That would have been the polite thing to do, but Jenna didn't suggest it, and Jack didn't think she could pull it off.

In closing, Reverend Johansen mentions First Lutheran's need for a new wing to be used for potluck suppers, bridge club, casino nights, and other special events. He says that anyone who is interested can see blown-up architectural rendering of the proposed structure mounted upon a tripod in the kitchen on their way out; there are coffee and cookies, too. Donations can be made to a fund established for this purpose.

Jack asks himself if he is bothered by this bit of churchly commerce, but concludes that he is not. There is no charge for the use of the building this morning, so go ahead and turn Hope's service into a fundraiser; you scratch my back, and I'll scratch yours.

As the reverend sits on a throne-like chair on the far side of the alter, four of Hope's high school and college friends walk up individually to the podium to read poems, Bible passages, and, in one case, the opening lyrics of the Bette Midler song, "Wind Beneath My Wings." They struggle not to cry. One of Hope's former Madison roommates, Patty Pinckney, comes to the transept and, *a cappella*, sings the Sarah McLachlan song "Angel" in a pristine soprano that could shatter a crystalline heart. All of this does seem funereal, but Jack forgives the girls. They are young and sad and do not know how to behave at this unusual event any more than everyone else.

To end the service, it is time for Jack to speak. Jenna had planned to speak, too. She spent a week writing notes on three-by-five note cards. But she casually informed Jack during the drive here that she has changed her mind. "You do it, dear," she said brightly, patting his arm. "You'll be fine." As Jack stands, Jenna looks up at him and says with a smile, "Break a leg."

He is wearing his lawyer's uniform: navy blue pinstripe suit, white shirt, red tie, and black tasseled loafers. He steps to the podium, adjusts the microphone up to his six-foot height, withdraws a folded sheaf of yellow legal pad paper from his suit coat pocket, spreads it out on the podium, and reads silently to himself the words about his daughter that he had composed in longhand at four a.m. this morning while seated at the desk in his study, before wandering out to the back yard.

A moment passes, no more than ten or fifteen seconds. To the assembled multitude, Jack is aware, it must seem an eternity, as they wonder when he will begin or if he will break down. He wonders along with them. A breakdown is exactly what the news crews up in the balcony would dearly love: the "money shot" of a grieving parent tearing up. This would guarantee that the footage would make the local and national newscasts and be positioned page one above the fold in the local newspapers.

But, as he stands there scanning his text, which praises his daughter's intelligence and compassion and wit and many interests and extra-curricular activities, it occurs to him that, despite the fact that he has kept everything in the present tense, this is all a transparent fiction. This "coming together in fellowship" is in fact a requiem for his poor lost daughter.

He refolds his notes, puts them back into his jacket pocket, and hears himself say, "Jenna and I and Hope thank you all for coming." Then he walks down the altar steps to the front pew and offers his arm to Jenna, who stands as if they had rehearsed exactly this conclusion. As they walk down the aisle, the congregation sits frozen as if uncertain about what is appropriate for the awkward and unusual moment. Finally, Jack's mother stands, and then everyone rises and follows Jack and Jenna out of the church in a silent and solemn recessional.

HOME AGAIN, STANDING in their own recently remodeled kitchen, with its polished black granite countertops and large center island with a black wrought-iron pot rack suspended above it holding a too-good-to-be-used array of copper cookware from Williams-Sonoma, Jenna says to Jack, "I think I'll have a cup of tea. Would you like one too?"

"You know I never drink tea," Jack answers quietly, then instantly regrets saying this. Who knows what Jenna knows anymore?

She puts the teapot on the Viking gas range, draws a glass of water, and uses it to swallow two Xanax capsules prescribed three months ago by her psychiatrist. Then she goes to the laundry room and puts a load into the washer, forgetting to add the detergent, Jack notices as he watches from the kitchen. He wonders again how to help her, and again cannot think of how, except to do a better job of being there for her, which he vows to do.

He walks down to the basement, pausing at the bottom of the stairs. He cannot remember why he has come down here. To get a tool? To change the furnace air filter? He doesn't need any tool, and he changed the filter last week. He goes back up to the kitchen, then up the back stairway to the second floor, pausing outside Hope's bedroom. The door is closed. Ever since "the disappearance," as Jack and Jenna have always referred to the event that has irrevocably altered their lives, Jack has kept opening this door because Hope always had it open, even when she was sleeping. This habit began when she was very young and imagined that some fearsome creature was lurking under her bed, or in her closet, or on a ladder just outside her window, ready to snatch her when the lights went off. When she cried out for her parents, one of them would pad down the hallway and sit with her until she fell asleep, or they would take her into their bed, assuring her that she was safe, and believing it then. Whenever Jenna passes the open door to Hope's bedroom now, she closes it. Jack does not ask Jenna why she closes the door because he does not want to hear her answer.

Jack opens the bedroom door and enters, saddened again by the usual accouterments of a happy, well-adjusted young woman's life: the frilly canopied bed, covered with pillows and stuffed animals; her field hockey and lacrosse sticks; the cork board mounted on one wall, displaying concert ticket stubs, dried wrist corsages, and photos of herself with friends mugging for the camera; Edina High School and University of Wisconsin banners; and all the other artifacts of the living Hope. Already, he thinks, his daughter's bedroom is taking on the look of one of those period rooms, preserved in a museum, where no one has ever lived. Maybe he should string a velvet rope across the doorway.

He moves to Hope's bed, draws back the spread, and touches her pillow, maybe, irrationally, hoping to find it warm. He walks over to the window and looks out at the oak tree in the back yard. Hope's bedroom is not the largest of the four in the house. Other than the master, one of the other rooms has quite a bit more square footage, and a bigger closet. Jack and Jenna chose this as Hope's nursery because it's closest to their bedroom. Later, they asked if Hope wanted to move into the larger bedroom, with more closet space, but she said no, she loved the view of the backyard with that big oak tree. She named the squirrels, pretending that she could distinguish one from another, and that they were a family, and also a woodpecker that took up residence in the tree.

Then Jack sighs, replaces the spread, and leaves the bedroom, pointedly leaving the door open. He pauses in the hallway, unsure of where in the house to go next, or what to do when he gets there. He wonders what can possibly come next for him and Jenna, other than to keep on waiting for Hope to reappear in some form or other, so they can either celebrate the miracle of her safe return, or hold a real memorial service and then try to get on with their lives, whatever that means. Please, let all this be a dream and let me wake up now, he thinks. If I promise to believe, will You do that?

He hears the clink of dishes being put away in the kitchen. He had stacked the dishwasher with last night's dinner dishes early this morning, just for something to do. It was not full enough to turn on, meaning that his wife is putting away dirty dishes. He goes into the master bedroom and over to his highboy dresser, opens the top drawer and withdraws his Browning .380 automatic pistol in its black leather holster, feeling its weight in his hand. He had bought the gun just after Hope was born, to protect the household. He has never fired it and never really imagined he would have to. It was just one of those things a man with a family should own, like a tool set and a ladder. The home's alarm system and the 911 operator are the primary lines of defense.

Except for his neighbor, Hank Whitby. Hank owns an insurance agency. He is in his fifties, balding and somewhat overweight. He does not look like the warrior he was in his youth and, it turned out, still is. Hank served as a Marine platoon leader in Vietnam. When a burglar made the mistake of entering the Whitby home at three in the morning six years ago—the only break-in that anyone knew about in the neighborhood for as long as the Tanners have lived there—Hank came downstairs, in the nude, a detail that somehow got around the neighborhood, and put three .40-caliber, hollow-point rounds from his Smith & Wesson semi-automatic pistol into the burglar's chest, killing him before he hit the floor. The deceased turned out to be a career criminal with no history of violent acts, unarmed except for a Swiss Army knife. Nevertheless, the Edina police detective investigating the incident, a former Marine himself, found the shooting to be a justifiable homicide, and no charges were filed. The *Star-Tribune*, in its story about the break-in and shooting, noted that Minnesota is one of the states with a "castle law," which gives a person wide latitude in defending his home from an intruder. All letters to the editor that the paper printed agreed that the burglar had it coming. An editorial stopped short of saying that, but did support the castle law and the Second Amendment.

There would be no question, Jack feels certain, about what Hank Whitby would do if his daughter was harmed, and the police had a prime suspect but lacked sufficient evidence to make an arrest. Hank would relentlessly track down the person he believed was responsible and mete out vigilante justice. But Jack Tanner is not Hank Whitby. Will the Tanner family ever find, if not Hope, then justice, vigilante or otherwise? Jack is left wondering as he puts his pistol back into the drawer.

2: JOY RIDE

TWO YEARS LATER

A RED-TAILED HAWK rides the air currents rising off the vast rolling undulations of Wisconsin farmland on this June morning. The rich black soil, muddy from last night's hard rain, is just beginning to push up a nature's bounty of corn, soybeans, and alfalfa.

The hawk banks right, its intense gaze painting the landscape like laser beams from a warplane's weapons system as the predator scans a field of stubby rows of ruined cornstalks, looking for breakfast: perhaps a rabbit, or a mole, or a snake. Absent that, road kill will do. The hawk wheels left, making a pass over the six-lane concrete ribbon of Interstate 94, which runs from Minneapolis to Milwaukee, and where sometimes these tasty, flattened feasts can be found, pancakes of fur and meat, blood, bone, and gristle.

But this morning, there is only the flow of shiny shapes moving at high speed: nonfood things of no particular interest to the hawk. One of these shapes is the figure of a man, dressed in black leather hides, bubble-helmeted, booted, streaking toward the sunrise on a motorcycle. Glancing upward, Jack Tanner notices the hawk. Alternating his attention between road and sky—carefully, for he is new to this two-wheel business, and a Harley-Davidson does not come with training wheels—he watches the hawk drift away from the highway and pass above a white clapboard farmhouse squatting behind a windbreak stand of jack pine.

Near the house is the ramshackle skeleton of a red barn with a peeling, faded Mail Pouch Tobacco sign ("Chew Mail Pouch Tobacco/Treat Yourself to the Best") painted on its side and, beyond that, a newer outbuilding constructed of corrugated metal. Perhaps a son, Jack imagines, has inherited this spread from his father and, unlike most rural sons, decided to remain on the land, declaring his commitment with the new structure. I bet there's a good country breakfast being served in that house, Jack thinks: steaming stacks of blueberry pancakes, a platter of fried eggs, link sausages, bacon, home-fried potatoes, strong coffee, and sweet rolls still warm from the oven… Or is that vision of farm life as outdated as the Mail Pouch sign, with this spread gobbled up by an agribusiness giant like Cargill or Archer Daniels Midland, and an MBA overseer inside starting the day with an espresso and egg white omelet before setting (undocumented?) migrants to work?

THE SUN HAS now risen above eye level. Jack flips up the tinted plastic bubble of his helmet and feels the rush of wind in his face. Powering up a long uphill grade, he comes up behind an eighteen-wheeler rig with a "How Am I Driving?" sign on the back and an 800 number to call if you care to answer the question (does anyone ever?) or apply for a driver's job. The truck must have a full load; it can only make fifty up the grade, so Jack guns the Harley and leans left into the passing lane. The cycle engine emits a rumbling, percussive, percolating sound: "potato-potato-potato" it seems to be saying, this exhaust note so distinctive, Jack once read in a law review article, that the Harley-Davidson Motor Company of Milwaukee tried unsuccessfully to trademark it.

Jack runs up beside the semi and sees it carries the name and logo of the Green Giant Company. It's a refrigerated truck, called a reefer, he knows, hauling frozen vegetables, peas, Brussels sprouts, corn, green beans, or lima beans, from a processing plant in LeSueu, a small town in Minnesota farm country south of Minneapolis, to grocery wholesale warehouses somewhere or other. He knows all this because, over the years, he has posted hundreds of billable hours against his law firm's Green Giant account.

The driver is a cowboy type with a face nearly as weathered as that Mail Pouch sign. He gives Jack a thumbs-up salute. Jack answers with a grin and a nod, not wanting to try to drive one-handed. This exchange pleases him. It is exactly the sort of fellowship of the open road he'd hoped for when he took delivery of the Harley. You pay your money, just south of twenty thousand dollars, you join the brotherhood of the open road. As a man gets older, Jack reflects, he needs to compensate for shrinking muscle mass and plummeting testosterone levels with valves and pistons and fuel-injected carburetion. That's why you see so many men his age driving Porsches, motorcycles, bigass SUVs never taken off-road, and tricked-out pickup trucks whose rear beds never see a load. The fortunate few ride the really big iron: Gulfstream Vs, Cessna Citations, and Hawker 1000 private jets, and motor yachts the size of Navy destroyers. But for Jack's purpose, this Harley will do just fine.

He feels good. He is on the road.

NEARLY EIGHT A.M. now, still not warm enough to unzip his jacket. What's that joke? Summer in the Upper Midwest is six weeks of poor ice fishing. But Jack is prepared; along with the motorcycle, he purchased a complete riding ensemble: helmet, black leather jacket with enough zippered pockets to stow a hundred dollars in coins, black leather chaps to wear over his jeans, and matching black leather boots. Checking himself out in his full-length bedroom mirror earlier this morning, he'd decided he looked more like the biker character in the Village People than an authentic Harley guy. Well, you play the hand you're dealt.

THREE DAYS EARLIER, Jack had purchased his motorcycle at Hog Heaven, which is what the locals call the Harley-Davidson dealership on Broadway in Minneapolis. "Hi there!" a woman called out as he entered the showroom. She walked over and offered her hand and a smile. "I'm Brenda and I'll be your server today," smiling at her joke. Jack too.

"Hi. Jack Tanner," he answered, taking her hand.

Brenda was pretty enough until Jack got close and noticed the lines in her face, and that her shock of short blond hair didn't likely come from her DNA. She was probably in her mid-to-late forties, but she still had a good body, an asset that could trump her flaws, especially if the bar was dark and you'd had a few beers. Jack reflected that an unkind soul might conclude that Brenda had a lived-in look to her. Miles of hard road on the odometer. Rode hard and put away wet. Well, she wasn't selling cosmetics in Neiman Marcus.

"Feel free to look around and let me know if you have any questions," she told Jack, then went over to the parts counter, where she had a cigarette going in an ashtray. A flagrant violation of the Minnesota Clean Indoor Air Act, Jack amused himself by thinking. But this was clearly not the place to make a citizen's arrest.

Brenda and two other sales people had watched from
the front picture window as Jack rolled into the parking
lot in his new BMW sedan, slid out of the soft leather
cockpit, hit the remote lock, and headed for the front
door. Predators salivating at the approach of fresh meat,
Jack thought: middle-aged man in his forties, nice car,
fits the Harley demographic as calculated by marketing
back at corporate in Milwaukee, Jack had read in some
men's magazine while waiting for a haircut.

One of the other sales people was called B-School
because he had an MBA. He was a jowly man about
Jack's age, sporting a ponytail and duded out in a leather
Harley vest with no shirt and a full complement of
biker tattoos. B-School had founded and then sold a
software firm; he was doing this job as a goof. He'd sold
a Fat Boy that morning—how fitting, fat boy selling a
Fat Boy, Brenda had amused herself by thinking—to an
orthopedic surgeon. He should know better than to ride
a cycle, B-School had remarked, heh heh, later in the
break room. Jesus H. Christ, hadn't this doc cobbled
enough Humpty Dumptys back together after they'd
dumped their bikes on gravel or wet pavement, or been
dumped by drivers who didn't see them or just didn't
like to share the road with bikers?

The other sales associate was Rick, a blade-thin kid
in his twenties with a shaved head and nose ring who
walked with a limp and showed the scars of skin grafts
on his arms; he was a cycle racer on weekends who
thought the bone surgeon looked familiar. The previous
afternoon, Rick had unloaded a traded-in, fully tricked-

out (it even had an *air bag!*) Honda Gold Wing GL1000 on a soybean farmer from Blue Earth who didn't want to give his business to the nearby Faribault dealership because it was owned by a guy who'd dated his wife in high school and still had a thing for her.

BRENDA WAS UP, so B-School and Rick drifted off as Jack wandered around the big neon-illuminated showroom, admiring the rich, lustrous paint jobs and glistening chrome of the inventory. Just sitting there, resting on their kickstands, they positively radiated kinetic energy. A full quarter of the floor space was devoted to Harley-Davidson merchandise, with racks and stacks of leathers and denims and sports clothes, helmets and boots and saddlebags, and every manner of Harley logo items: coffee and beer mugs, baby clothes, metal-studded belts, dog collars and leashes (think pit bull), jewelry, coffee table books displaying sexy glamour shots of the bikes ... Welcome to Harley World, Jack thought, it's not just a ride, it's a cult. Scientology on wheels. Do I really want to drink this Kool-Aid? he asked himself as he took it all in. Maybe it's too over-the-top for a guy like me. Except I don't *want* to be a guy like me anymore.

Brenda finished her cigarette and stubbed it out in a Harley-logo ashtray on the counter (Harley dealerships were one of the few public places still having ashtrays inside —*you can pry my Marlboro Menthol out of my cold, dead hand, motherfucker!*) and found Jack checking out a sleek, black, low-slung model displayed on a raised platform.

"So, Jack, any of these got your name on it?"

Jack looked around. "Maybe."

"Ever had a bike before?"

"Not since my Schwinn," which made her laugh.

"Okay. We got Softails, Dynaglides, Road Kings, Electra Glides, Sportsters, and the V-Rods. A ride for every occasion."

"I'm not sure what kind I want," Jack admitted.

"Not a problem," Brenda said. "How ya gonna use it? Maybe take the wife to Dairy Queen on weekends?"

"I'm planning a trip down to Florida."

Brenda looked impressed. "Hey now, we got ourselves a player here. Follow me." She led Jack to one of the rows where the biggest cycles were displayed.

"You'll want one of these heavy-duty touring models for a long haul like that, say a Road King or Electra Glide. That way you'll arrive with your kidneys intact."

Jack walked over to one of the bikes. It was blue, his favorite color. This seemed as good a way as any to choose.

"That'd be my choice too," Brenda said. "The Road King Classic. Sweet as they come. Big enough to eat up the interstates, but less bulky than the Electra Glides, which the cops favor."

She patted the leather saddle. "Mount up, cowboy. Let's see how she fits."

It fit just fine.

Jack was startled a few minutes later, just after he"d

signed the sales contract and handed over his credit card, earning him lots of airline miles, when Brenda gave a thumbs-up to the guy behind the parts counter, and the guy began ringing a big brass ship's bell bolted onto the wall: BONG! BONG! BONG! BONG!

When the ringing stopped, all available dealership staff shouted out, "Another Harley owner! Welcome to the family!" This reminded Jack of those T.G.I. Friday's kind of restaurants, where the wait staff surrounded your table to sing happy birthday. Surveying the showroom crew and the other customers who were roaming around, Jack felt it was maybe more like the Manson family to which he was being welcomed. Still, he was excited to be the owner of such an exotic piece of machinery. He arranged with Brenda to pick his bike up the following morning.

"You'll need some leathers and a helmet, too," Brenda said and led him over to the apparel section. Before they were done, these items, plus a pair of boots and fingerless riding gloves, were piled on the checkout counter, barcode tags being scanned. Jack had said no to a coffee mug, key chain, and sleeveless T-shirt. As a cute little blond in a tight T-shirt and jeans was bagging up the gear, Brenda told Jack, "You can stop at the DMV on your way home and get a cycle license learner's permit. Then you practice driving until you're ready for your road test, which consists of driving around cones in the DMV office parking lot, no problem, and they'll add an endorsement on your driver's license."

Jack hadn't even thought about that. Fine. He'd

drive to Florida on the learner's permit. That would be his practice.

"I can go with you if you want," Brenda added.

"To the DMV?" Jack asked.

She grinned. "No, to Florida."

Jack laughed as if he knew she was kidding, which he did not.

CRUISING ALONG I-94, Jack is thinking about the time he arrived home from the office and found Jenna in the kitchen, washing lettuce in the sink. Her shoulder-length strawberry-blond hair swirled sexily as she turned to greet him, smiling, like a model in a TV ad for a hair-care product. She was wearing a white cotton turtleneck and black jeans. The turtleneck stretched over her breasts, her nipples visible through the thin fabric. She crossed to the pantry on some invented errand so, Jack knew, he could see her fine little bottom move under the denim like a sack full of cats on the way to the river. Jenna the tease. He walked up behind her, pressed his body into hers, caressed her breasts, and kissed her neck. She said, "Hey sailor, whatta ya got in mind?" And then it was shore leave time, right there in the kitchen.

He wonders if he should remind Jenna of moments like these when he stops to see her in Virginia. Would she remember? He's never certain, on his way to these visits, whether she wants to remember anything about her past life …

Suddenly he hears a high-pitched, pulsating noise.

What's that? The engine blowing up? No, it's a siren, behind him. In the rearview mirror he sees the flashing lights of a Wisconsin State Patrol cruiser, coming up fast. He checks the speedometer. Christ. Daydreaming and doing eighty-six. He eases off the throttle, pulls onto the gravel shoulder, kicking up stones, pushes down the kickstand, and carefully eases the weight of the big cycle onto it. It is a heavy mother. If it tips over, he may not be able to pick it up without help, which would be embarrassing.

He turns in the saddle and sees that the trooper is still in the cruiser, probably running the cycle's license plate through the onboard computer. After a moment, the trooper gets out, puts on his Smokey the Bear hat with one hand and, standing behind the car door, lets the other rest on his holstered pistol. They love to get all duded up in those hats and boots and tight jodhpurs, looking like a cross between a Canadian Mountie and the Lone Ranger, Jack muses, awaiting his fate, a speeding ticket, his first in years. Now his insurance rate will go up.

From behind the car door, the trooper calls out in a loud, clipped, no-nonsense voice, right on the edge of courtesy, but not to be disregarded: "Please. Step off. The motorcycle. Sir."

Jack hesitates, wondering if they are always this cautious in Wisconsin on a traffic stop. Then he remembers he is not his usual, respectable, solid-citizen self, the tax-paying tax lawyer in a Brooks Brothers pinstripe suit, driving a German automobile costing more than the trooper's annual take-home. Now he is a law-breaking motorcycle guy in leathers, potentially dangerous. He does not want his trip to end here on the gravel shoulder of I-94 somewhere in Wisconsin with a bullet hole in his new leather jacket, which cost him four hundred forty dollars. Or spread-eagled on the ground with his face in the gravel getting his arms cuffed behind his back. He swings his leg over the gas tank, dismounts, and stands facing the trooper. Even though he hasn't been told to, he keeps his hands in sight, which, he knows from cop shows, they want you to do.

"Thank you, sir," the trooper says, stepping out from behind the cruiser's door, his right hand still on the pistol. "Now please lean forward against the seat with your feet spread wide."

Again, Jack hesitates. This entire situation is so utterly unfamiliar. The trooper says, more sternly, with no "sir" attached this time, "Do. It. Now."

Jack leans forward, resting his hands on the saddle, his legs a yard apart, the limit of his range of motion these days. Just like in the movies, he thinks. The difference being that, in the movies, the trooper's gun is loaded with blanks.

Jack hears footsteps on the gravel, then he's being patted down. "That's fine, sir," the trooper says when he's finished, a degree of professional cop-courtesy returning to his voice, now that he hasn't found the .380 Browning semiautomatic pistol that is back in Jack's dresser drawer at home. "You can stand up, please, and remove your helmet."

"I'm a lawyer," Jack blurts out as he removes the helmet, and then instantly regrets it. To a law enforcement officer, it's probably better to be an outlaw biker than one of those scum-sucking, bottom-feeding attorneys who subvert justice with their courtroom tricks.

"I'll need to see your driver's license please," the trooper says. His gold nameplate reads, "Cpl. Jensen."

"Sure," Jack answers, as cooperatively and unthreateningly as he can. "No problem, officer."

To Jack, Cpl. Jensen looks like a teenager, barely old enough to drive, let alone enforce the traffic laws, the same way the Minnesota Twins starting lineup and summer interns at his law firm now look to him.

Jack balances the helmet on the saddle. It slides off onto the ground, one hundred eight dollars worth of shiny black polycarbonate shell with anti-fog face shield and removable, washable, antibacterial lining, now scratched by the gravel. He unbuckles one side of the black leather saddlebag.

"It's in here." He smiles, so that the corporal will not think he is reaching in for the Browning pistol that is not there. He fishes out his wallet. He also knows from cop shows that he should take the license out and not hand over the wallet, lest it appear a bribe is being offered. He does this now.

Cpl. Jensen takes Jack's Minnesota driver's license, looks at it and says, "Please remain here for a moment, sir." He goes back to the cruiser, gets in, and begins typing on the keyboard, running Jack's name through his onboard computer, looking for outstanding warrants.

Then he slides out, ambles back over to Jack and begins the usual dialogue of the routine traffic stop, the kind of stop that does not involve a shoot-out:

"Do you know what the speed limit is here, Mr. Tanner?"

"Seventy, I think?"

"And do you know how fast you were traveling?"

"No," Jack fibs.

"I clocked you at just a hair under ninety at the top of that rise back there."

"I guess I wasn't paying attention."

Jack knows better than to speed on interstate highways in Wisconsin, where traffic fines are a big revenue source for the state. But he's been on an adrenaline high ever since pulling out of his driveway in Edina. He needs to dial it down a notch and keep his head in the game.

But mercy, unrequested, is granted. Instead of writing a citation, Cpl. Jensen touches the saddle of the motorcycle, as if petting a horse.

"A Road King," he says. "Nice bike. Had it long?"

"Not too long," Jack answers.

"I see you're riding on a learner's permit." He pauses for a moment, then says, "Okay, Mr. Tanner, this is a warning. Slow down. I've had to clean up after more than a few accidents involving motorcycles coming up against cars and trucks, and the cycle *always* loses."

Road kill for that hawk I saw, Jack thinks.

Cpl. Jensen nods, and strides back to the cruiser, opens the door, then turns back to Jack and asks, "By the way, Mr. Tanner, where are you headed?"

"Oh I'm just out for a joyride," Jack answers.

But he is actually headed for Key West, Florida. Land's End. The southernmost tip of the North American continent. Because Key West is where Slater Babcock lives.

JACK HAD BOOKED himself on a Delta flight to Miami and reserved a rental car for the three and a half hour drive to Key West. But then he had an epiphany of sorts. He'd arrive as the same man who boarded the flight in Minneapolis. And that man, he concluded, wasn't man enough to do what needed to be done, whatever he decided that was. It was clearly not what he'd done over the past three years, which was to let Slater Babcock, the man who almost certainly murdered his daughter, enjoy his life in a world that no longer included Hope. Jack needed his trip to somehow be transformative. He needed new experiences. So here he was, a middle-aged tax attorney riding a motorcycle intended to be his Rocinante, the horse another deluded knight-errant rode in search of adventure.

3: A SLACKER IN THE HORSE LATITUDES

A SNOWY EGRET high-steps on spindly legs up the coquina shell driveway of a pink clapboard cottage with a green tin roof and white wooden hurricane shutters at 311 Admirals Lane in Key West. The bird flaps its wings and hops atop a white Bentley Azure convertible parked with its top down, half on the driveway and half on the Bermuda-grass lawn. It perches on the driver's seat headrest, its delicate talons making indentations in the interior's hand-sewn hides, normally a creamy maize color but now darkened by the water of the lawn's sprinkler system, which turned itself on a few hours earlier and gave the Bentley's interior a good soaking.

Inside the cottage's master bedroom, the sub-tropical

sun filters through wooden shutters, cutting across the
face of a young man lying on his back in bed, mouth
open, adenoids rattling. The sunlight causes the man to
stir, and regain semi-consciousness from his boozy sleep.
Although awake, he does not immediately open his eyes.
Instead, as is his habit, he takes mental inventory of his
good fortune before facing whatever fresh heavens and
hells may await him during this new day.

First of all, he, Slater Allan Babcock, at the age of
thirty, has it, by his accounting, made in the shade. He has
his health, despite a regimen of physical debauchery that
he has followed for the past eight years. Slater had been
in boot-camp shape while attending the University of
Wisconsin, where he was a starting long-stick midfielder
on the lacrosse team until he used up his four years of
eligibility without earning enough credits to graduate.

Second of all, he is now living the life he always
imagined for himself, that of raconteur and slacker in
the horse latitudes. His monthly trust-fund checks are
supplemented by income from the Rusty Scupper, the
bar his father bought for him.

Third of all, he'd just spent the night playing hide
the salami with a woman who is another man's wife,
which he prefers, along with women who are divorced,
or single, or underage, or, if they have taken good enough
care of themselves, overage. Jail bait to cougar, and the
full range in between, is his target market.

He opens his eyes, blinking at the sunlight, props
himself up on one arm, and reaches for the Oakleys on
the bedside table, which he keeps there for just such a

time: awakening when the sun is high and his head is higher, which happens just about every morning. This small movement causes the woman sleeping beside him to roll over on her back and drape a slim, tanned arm over her eyes against the sunlight.

Slater studies her as her shoulder-length hair, cut and colored a shade of tawny blond, fans across her pillow. The satin sheet slips down below her waist, revealing a tanned body, obviously toned by hours of workouts. Slater finds a small hand mirror on the bedside table. On the mirror are three lines of white powder left over from last night. He inhales a line into each nostril, gallantly saving one for his guest. The drug begins to activate that part of his frontal lobe where memory is stored. He recalls meeting this comatose, nude blond at his bar, the Rusty Scupper, last night. He flops back down, enjoying the rush, and more details come to him. Her husband is some sort of big-shot real estate mogul from Chicago. She traveled with him to Miami, where he had business. She finds her husband's business to be a bore, so she rented a car and drove down U.S. 1 until the road ran out.

He noticed this striking blond sitting alone at the far end of the bar. A number of other unaccompanied women were at the bar, too, as always. Many of them had good bodies and pretty faces, too, at least in the dim light of the barroom. He focused on this particular woman because, unlike the others at the bar, she wasn't drinking some touristy concoction like a Tequila Sunrise (spare me from the relentless onslaught of Parrotheads, Slater often thinks) or Cuba Libre, Hurricane or, a big seller at the Scupper, A Day at the Beach (1 oz. coconut rum, ½ oz. Amaretto, 4 oz. orange juice, ½ oz. Grenadine). This woman's drink was the only one without a little parasol in it.

Pineapple, the three-hundred-pound Samoan bartender on duty this shift, informed Slater that she was drinking Black Jack rocks. Slater instantly liked her for that. She was wearing a form-fitting white shift and wedge heels; she was *not* wearing a puka-shell or shark's-tooth necklace, an automatic disqualification, but a tasteful string of pearls with matching earrings.

Decked out in a white linen suit, black raw silk shirt, Gucci loafers without socks, and a Panama hat, a cheroot dangling from his lip, Slater strolled over to the woman and leaned on the bar beside her.

"You are, hands down, the hottest female in the place," he said. "I suppose you hear that a lot."

"Yes, I do," the woman said, not looking at him.

"And I suppose men are always trying to buy you a drink."

"That too," she said. "Whenever my husband is not with me."

"Well, I'm not going to buy you a drink," Slater said. "I can do much better than that."

She looked at him and arched one eyebrow.

"From this moment forward, whenever you come to Key West and visit this establishment, all your drinks, and any food you want, are on the house. The hot wings are excellent, and the Scupper Burger is to die for."

She looked at him with a slight smile of amusement. "So they sell gift cards here, like at Starbucks?"

"No, but that's an idea to consider," he said. "I happen to be the proprietor of this place, and I'm putting your name on the comp list."

"Why do I think that's a long list and all the names are female?"

Slater shrugged.

"Not that I don't appreciate the thought," she added, sipping her Black Jack. "But it's unlikely I'll ever be back here. So many bars, so little time."

"Then we should take full advantage of this fortuitous moment," Slater said, sliding up onto the stool beside her. He motioned to Pineapple, who, knowing the drill, was keeping an eye on them. He ordered another drink for her, a Ketel One vodka rocks with a twist for himself, and a double order of the hot wings, "inferno" style.

"Would you care for a burger?" he asked.

She smiled. "No, let's wait for breakfast."

Bingo.

Twenty minutes later, they were in the Bentley out in the gravel parking lot and Slater was enjoying a world-class blowjob, noticing through the fog of booze and fellatio that her hair matched the car's leather upholstery. There were more drinks at his house and Cirque du Soleil style sex in his bed until they both dozed off. All in all, a most acceptable evening. Slater liked to say to his buddies that he'd never had a bad round of golf or bad sex; it was great just being a part of the game.

Slater remembers all this, but still not this woman's

name. He sits up. His head is spinning, his temples throbbing and his stomach churning, all of which produces a disoriented, semi-nauseous condition he had come to know as "morning." He puts his head back on the pillow and notices the pink areolas of the sleeping woman's perky breasts. The sheet over him forms a little pup tent. He briefly considers waking her for more sex, but that would invariably lead to conversation, and he isn't one for morning-after chitchat. So he carefully eases himself out of bed and shuffles, still naked, to the kitchen, where he finds a bottle of Advil in the cabinet above the stove and downs four caplets with orange juice straight from the carton, his usual breakfast.

Slater gazes out the kitchen window. The palm fronds are rustling in the breeze. It's a perfect morning for a boat ride. He keeps his fifty-three-foot Carver, the *Bachelor Pad*, moored at the Key West Yacht Club. Yes, that's the ticket, he thinks. I'll take the boat out, maybe troll for a red snapper or a pompano for dinner, and when I return, that no-name blond will be gone.

When Slater Babcock is done with a woman, he is done.

4: 310 HIAWATHA STREET

DOWN THE HIGHWAY another twenty minutes or so, Jack spots a sign at the Eau Claire exit promising "Food/Fuel/Gas/Lodging." He leans to the right, taking the exit ramp feeding him onto a two-lane road lined with gas stations, fast food restaurants, and chain motels: McDonald's, Burger King, Arby's, Pizza Hut, Sunoco, Mobil, Red Roof Inn, Comfort Inn, Days Inn, Marriott's Residence Inn, a Holiday Inn … The kind of ubiquitous neon strips that have replaced small town Main Streets, Jack reflects. Anywhere, U.S.A., no sense of place anymore, when every place looks alike.

However, this particular road does hold a special place in his memory bank. One long-ago Christmas Eve morning, when their world was new and anything seemed possible, even lifelong joy, the Tanners stayed at the same Holiday Inn he is now rolling past. On that trip, Jack and Jenna had been arguing in code, to avoid upsetting Hope, who was six. She sat in the back seat of their tan Volvo 240 DL station wagon, the family runabout of choice during those years in suburbs like Edina, playing with her Barbie doll. Today, a six-year-old girl would be texting friends on her iPhone, Jack reflects. Cookie, their Bichon, was asleep on the seat beside her. The cargo area was piled high with Christmas presents for Jenna's parents and three sisters.

Jack thought they should not risk driving to Milwaukee that morning for the traditional family gathering at Jenna's parents' house because an early morning snowstorm was building in intensity, the farmland covered with a glistening coat of rime, layered on like butter cream frosting on a devil's-food cake. The Volvo did poorly on slippery pavement, even with snow tires. They made it as far as Eau Claire after creeping along over black ice, past cars that had slid off into the farm fields. When state troopers directed them around a jackknifed semi, Jenna finally agreed that they should stop and find a motel.

They chose the Holiday Inn, because it advertised a swimming pool under a luminous green geodesic dome, which they knew Hope would love. Christmas Eve dinner was cheeseburgers, milkshakes, and fries from the McDonald's drive-thru, eaten in their room, with a plain burger for Cookie. The desk clerk waived the hotel's no-pet rule for these orphans of the storm. They watched an

Andy Williams Christmas special on TV and were as cozy and happy as they'd ever been on Christmas Eve, Jack and Jenna agreed. By morning, the snowstorm had ended. They arrived in Milwaukee late Christmas morning, buoyed by the common adventure they'd shared.

That drive to Milwaukee had been scary. As protector of the family, Jack had managed the situation badly by yielding to Jenna, he felt, putting them all at risk. Upon returning home, he traded the Volvo for a Toyota Land Cruiser with full-time four-wheel drive. Still, it was an adventure they never forgot. Hope, as oblivious to the danger as she had been when she left her apartment that last, sad night of her life, Jack thought, mentioned it every Christmas Eve for years afterward: remember when we drove to Grandpa's and Grandma's in the snow storm and stayed at the hotel with the pool? Wasn't that fun? Can we do that again this year?

Cruising the Eau Claire strip, Jack notices a large number of trucks parked at a Happy Chef restaurant. According to the mythology of the open road, this is a good sign, so he pulls into the parking lot. He hasn't yet discovered, but will before this trip is done, that the vehicle count outside a truck stop can say more about the adequacy of the parking lot for semis and availability of showers for the drivers than about the quality of the food.

It turns out that the Happy Chef is a bright, warm, and crowded refuge from the chill of highway travel on a motorcycle. Roger Miller's "King of the Road" is playing on the sound system. Not yet, Jack thinks, but stay tuned. Everything on the menu looks good: Eggs "any way ya like'em," pancakes (plain or blueberry), waffles (plain or pecan), biscuits with sausage gravy, sides of bacon, sausage (patties or links), hash browns, and, even at this early hour, rib-eye steaks, pork chops, creamed chipped beef on toast, hot turkey sandwiches with stuffing and mashed potatoes, burgers, corned beef Reubens, and more.

Arteriosclerosis be damned. Jack orders the Open Roader, a stack of three buttermilk pancakes with two fried eggs, choice of bacon or sausage (on a mad impulse he gets both), hash browns, and toast. This kind of breakfast, the kind that he had imagined being served in that farmhouse on the hill fifty miles back, he has avoided, for health reasons, ever since he turned fifty. Special rules on this ride, meaning, no rules at all.

A man seated at the counter beside Jack says, without looking up from his meal of fried eggs and biscuits with sausage gravy, "So, you're on a cycle?" Jack's helmet is under the counter between his feet and he's wearing the leathers. "What kind?"

The man has on a denim jacket with Peterbilt and American flag patches and worn jeans, both faded from long use, not stone-washed at the factory, and cowboy boots with silver toe caps. He adds, "I'm Ray. Ray Price."

"A Harley," Jack says, proud he can tell this guy wearing the flag that he's bought American. He swivels on his stool, offering his hand, which Ray takes. "Jack Tanner."

"Had me an Electra Glide once. Sold it for more than I paid, and then bought a Fat Boy, which I dumped on the way home from Sturgis when some jackass in a Mercedes heading the other way swerved to avoid a deer and ran me into a ditch. Now I got a stainless steel plate in my hip and I stick to the eighteen-wheelers."

Ray takes a bite of eggs. "So where you heading, pard?"

Jack looks over at his counter-mate. He is tempted to blurt out the truth to this guy, perhaps to impress him, or maybe for the relief of telling someone. Maybe Ray will know what Jack should do about Slater Babcock. But instead Jack answers casually, "Oh, you know. Mid-life crisis. Buy a motorcycle, take it out on the highway to see what it'll do, and get some breakfast."

Ray downs the last of his coffee, stands, tosses a ten on the counter, touches Jack on the shoulder, smiles and says, "Had my own midlife crisis some years ago. My buddy Jack Daniels helped me through it." He pays his check at the cashier stand and heads out to his rig.

Jack's plate is clean. He reflects that his trip is just hours old, but already he's seen a hawk, had an encounter with the law, eaten a real man's breakfast, and had a chat with a knight of the open road. Nothing transformative yet, but it's a start. He stands, leaves a ten-dollar tip, and has the cashier add a packet of Mylanta chewable tablets to his tab.

TRAFFIC IS HEAVIER now, especially the big semis, which always frustrated him in a car, riding right up his tailpipe when he was in the slow lane and then popping out behind him when he got into the passing lane, pushing him to speed. But on the cycle Jack has found that he can bob and weave through traffic. He notices the disapproving looks he gets from some of the drivers of cars and minivans, as if he is some badass, non-conformist outlaw. Good. I'm a mean motherfucker—for all they know. Lock the doors and hide the women.

A gap in the traffic now. He powers up a rise, the highway bordered on the left by the limestone cliffs of the Wisconsin Dells and open farmland on the right. He checks his watch. About another half an hour to Madison, his first stop.

JACK AIMS THE cycle onto the Highway 30 exit and turns left toward Madison. He rolls down Johnson Street, Lake Menona on his left, Lake Mendota on the right, enjoying the panorama unobstructed for the first time by the confines of a car. Madison is a little gem of an All-American college town, Jack has always thought. But ever since Hope disappeared, the town has taken on the stark grimness of a crime scene.

He veers right onto University Avenue and turns through the main gate of the University of Wisconsin campus. Students strolling across the quad turn at the sound of the Harley. The engine noise also attracts the attention of a security guard on a university motor scooter, the kind with an enclosed cab and small truck bed on the back.

Campus security, what a crock, Jack thinks. The campus police protect the buildings and grounds, and follow up on crimes against persons after the fact. But he can't really blame them. If you are targeted by evil, you are not safe anywhere in this world, including bucolic Madison, Wisconsin.

He feels the urge to drive through the campus shouting a warning to every co-ed he encounters: *Be careful! Don't go out alone!* Of course this would be madness. These girls would just stare at the lunatic on a motorcycle, maybe call 911 on their cell phones. He'd be the one who would frighten them.

He notices a couple walking on the sidewalk with their backs toward him: a girl with shoulder-length blond hair, wearing jeans and a sweatshirt, and a tall boy in khaki slacks and a varsity letter jacket. This is a Division I school, Jack knows. Big-time athletics. This boy must be good at whatever sport he plays.

From the back, the girl looks like Hope. All of these college girls look like Hope to him: beautiful, smart, happily oblivious of the true nature of the world; on their way to class, or their dorm rooms or apartments, or Starbucks … On their way to their futures: careers if they want, husbands, first houses, children … They can have it all, they are certain. Let them think that as long as they can. Jack will not tell them otherwise.

North along Campus Drive, then right onto Highland Avenue, which runs along the western boundary of the campus. He reaches Hiawatha Street, with its rows of student rental apartment buildings: converted Victorian houses, cinder block and brick mid-rises, ranch house style duplexes. Oaks and maples line the street, their spring buds coming out.

He pulls in front of 310 Hiawatha, the four-story, tan brick, 1950s apartment building where his daughter had lived. Last lived. Sitting astride the cycle, he watches students with backpacks, most of them plugged into iPods or chatting on cell phones, pass in and out of the building. He thinks about that late August day three-and-a-half years ago when he pulled up to this building in a U-Haul truck, with Jenna, Hope, and Cookie all jammed onto the front bench seat with him, the truck loaded with furniture and clothing. Hope was excited to be moving off campus after a year in the freshman dorm.

One night, during final exam week at the end of her sophomore year, Hope had gotten a cell phone call, then left the apartment she shared with two other girls, telling them she would be back in an hour or so. She didn't say who called her or where she was going. It was about ten p.m., one of her roommates told police. No, it was more like eleven, the other stated. Hope was wearing jeans and a tank top, one said. No, it was shorts and a tee shirt, the other said. Other recollections didn't match either, even though only one day had passed.

Thus were Hope's roommates eliminated from the list of suspects. Everyone involved with the victim of a crime, or suspected crime, goes onto the list, Jack was told by the lead investigator, Detective Lieutenant Vernon

Douglas of the Madison Police Department, even two sweet girls like Maureen Fox from Fargo, North Dakota, and Sherry Silverman from Plainfield, New Jersey. But when two or more people invent a story, Douglas explained, that story is identical. Honest recollections by witnesses almost never match. Vernon Douglas was a tall, muscular, middle-aged black man who looked like he could have played football for a Division I school. He seemed smart and competent, Jack told Jenna, and this provided some small comfort.

The next morning, Maureen and Sherry discovered that Hope wasn't there and that her bed did not appear to have been slept in. Hope frequently spent the night at her boyfriend Slater Babcock's apartment (something Jack and Jenna did not know, but who cared about that now?). She had taken her cell phone and keys, but not her wallet or any overnight gear. Her yellow VW Beetle convertible was still parked on the street. When she didn't return to the apartment by the following night or answer her cell phone, the roommates called campus security.

Jenna answered the call from the dean of students. In a panic, she called Jack at the office. Two hours later, they were on a flight to Madison. The Madison police, it quickly became clear, had no solid leads. A convicted sex offender lived two blocks from Hope's apartment, but he was in the hospital for an appendectomy on the night in question. Jack angrily asked the dean, Winston Toller, when they met in the dean's office on Jack and Jenna's fourth day in Madison, how in the hell a sex offender could be allowed to live in a neighborhood near the campus. Were there others the parents and students didn't know about? How about other felons? Murderers out on work release? Armed robbers wearing ankle bracelets?

Dean Toller, an affable, portly man in his sixties, who always wore tweeds and bow ties, was a professor of economics who had held the dean's job for the past six years. He said that his office was notified about the man, but the law allowed him to live where he wanted. He had not been notified that any other "convicted offenders" now resided anywhere near the university.

And why weren't the parents of students told about things like that? Jack demanded to know. I'm an attorney, Jack said, and I will certainly look into the possibility that the university has some liability for what's happened—illogically, he knew, because the sex offender was not a suspect. But *someone* was responsible for Hope's disappearance, and Dean Toller, who was responsible for the safety and well-being of the university's students, was a handy scapegoat.

Toller, much accustomed to dealing with angry parents, responded by saying that no one yet knows if any crime has occurred, and we're all hoping for the best, but the university will certainly review its policies on such matters. "I'd rather you keep track of your students than review your policies, Dean Toller," Jack said as he left the office.

Hope and Slater Babcock had been dating for about four months, Maureen and Sherry told Douglas. Slater was a "spoiled rich kid from Connecticut," they said, but, as far as they knew, he had never threatened or harmed Hope in any way. He didn't seem like that kind of person. They didn't think Hope was very serious about him; she just enjoyed his company.

Questioned repeatedly by Douglas, and also by a state police investigator and an FBI agent from Milwaukee, over a two-week period, Slater never wavered from his story. He'd spoken with Hope by cell phone on the night she disappeared, but they hadn't talked about her coming to his apartment, which was a half-mile away from Hope's. Whenever they spent the night together it was at his place, because he lived alone. Sometimes she came over unannounced to surprise him. She often walked instead of driving, because his building had no visitor's lot and finding a parking spot on the street at night was difficult, and Hope liked the exercise.

Slater's father, Charles Babcock, a New York investment banker, hired a Milwaukee criminal lawyer to represent his son as the questioning continued. This was not at all unusual, especially among the ranks of the wealthy and powerful, Douglas told Jack. Such people tended to "lawyer up" whenever they felt the least bit threatened, Douglas said. It was not an indication of guilt. Jack told Douglas that he wanted to confront Slater Babcock. Maybe a father could sense something that the police could not, or make a persuasive appeal. He just wanted to talk to the young man. Jack didn't really believe that he could get any more out of Babcock than could the police. If he was innocent, there was no more to get. If he was guilty, he certainly wouldn't admit it. But Jack felt he had to do more than just sit on the sidelines while no one was finding his daughter.

Douglas for the first time hardened his expression and sternly ordered Jack not to talk to Slater, not to get anywhere near him, because Jack might say or do something that "could be prejudicial to the case, and also get you into a great deal of trouble."

Douglas reported that Charles Babcock, through his lawyer, had already advised the Madison chief of police, as well as the offices of the Dane County prosecutor and the state attorney general, that he was ready to do anything necessary to "protect his son's legal rights and prevent any slander of his character."

Jack felt a great weight on his chest when Douglas said "the case." She's no longer Hope Tanner, she's just a "case," a police file number.

During one conversation on the second day after Jack and Jenna arrived in Madison, Douglas asked them both if Hope had any history of "going off on her own" without telling them. It happened, Douglas said. It was a possibility he had to explore. Two years ago, a female student went to Cancun with friends during spring break after telling her parents she had to stay on campus to study for exams. The parents found out when they decided to drive to Madison from their home in Green Bay to surprise their daughter with a care package of her favorite goodies and take her to dinner. Douglas tracked her down.

Douglas should have had plenty of time to look for

Hope, Jack discovered by checking the city's crime rate on the Internet. Although Douglas was the city's sole homicide detective, there were only four murders in Madison in the previous two years—"only," Jack caught himself thinking. That statistic would be of no comfort to a victim's friends and family. Jack did not say this to Jenna, but he was greatly troubled that a *homicide* detective was assigned to the case. There was no body. She was officially a missing person, and Jack clung to that fact. Jack asked Douglas about this.

"Yes, we do have two other detectives," he responded. "One specializes in thefts and robberies, the other provides general backup wherever he's needed. It was the chief's call. He picked me, I think, because I've been around the longest, and finding your daughter was … *is* the department's top priority. Believe me, we're doing everything that can be done. With the assistance of the FBI, we're monitoring her credit cards for any usage. We've looked at her Facebook page, e-mails, blogs, and Tweets for anything that looks suspicious. So far, nothing from those avenues. But we're not stopping."

On their third day in Madison, Jack insisted that Jenna return home, convincing her that she should be there in case Hope called or showed up, although he did not think either of these possibilities likely. Jenna was mainly staying in their hotel room anyway, and was becoming increasingly frantic. Before she boarded an American Eagle turboprop for Minneapolis, at the Dane County Regional Airport, Jenna said to Jack, "She's gone.

I know we'll never see our daughter again, and our life will never be the same." Jack told her that it was too soon to give up. That kidnapped girl in Utah, whose name he couldn't remember, turned up eighteen months later.

He remained in Madison another ten days, checking in with Douglas daily, driving the campus and city streets in his rental car and making excursions into the surrounding countryside. Lyle Ferguson, the Hartfield, Miller managing partner, called to say that Jack should take all the time he needed, but Jack knew that his partners would, at some point, lose patience with his sabbatical from billable hours, even given the circumstances.

The story of the disappearance of a female University of Wisconsin student was big news, locally and nationally. During the following weeks, Jack and Jenna appeared on the cable TV news shows, appealing for help in locating their daughter. They did the network news programs, too, all of the appearances arranged by the Minneapolis public relations firm on retainer to Hartfield, Miller. Jenna was particularly touched when Katie Couric teared up during their *CBS Evening News* interview, the camera close on her face. Cynical Jack told Jenna he thought this was staged. Larry King seemed genuinely sympathetic. John Walsh, host of "America's Most Wanted," whose own son Adam had been murdered by a serial killer, vowed on the air to "use the full power of this program" to recover Hope. Nancy Grace, who had her own controversial shown on HLN, declared Slater Babcock to be "guilty beyond a reasonable doubt," startling Jack, the lawyer, and pleasing Jenna. Wolf Blitzer on CNN stuck to the facts, of which there were few, and off camera shook Jack's hand, hugged Jenna, and told them his thoughts and prayers were with them.

Jack discovered that Hope was beyond the age limit to appear on the side of milk cartons—"Have you seen this child?"—and briefly considered legal action to force the Wisconsin Dairy Association to alter this policy. Lyle Ferguson reminded Jack that one of the larger dairies in the state was an important client of the firm. At first, Jack returned to Madison every few weeks. After that, it was every few months, and then less often. He would drive around, looking at the campus as if Hope might suddenly appear, coming out of the student center or driving by in the yellow Beetle, her high school graduation present. During each trip to Madison, Jack would visit with Vernon Douglas, who seemed genuinely frustrated at having no progress to report. Finally, Jack stopped coming to Madison, until today.

JACK HAS LOST track of time. How long has he been sitting here on the Harley, staring at this apartment building at 310 Hiawatha Street? Half an hour? More? He hears a car behind him and turns in the saddle to see a Madison Police Department squad car rolling up to the curb.

As Jack slips off his helmet, a female officer gets out and walks over. She wears sergeant's strips. Her nameplate says Sgt. Bradford. She could pass for a student: pretty, with short dark hair, and a trim body under her tailored uniform.

"Hello, sir," she says as Jack slides off the seat and opens one of the flaps on the saddlebag, intending to get out his driver's license and registration. As he does this, Sergeant Bradford takes a step backward, letting her right hand casually drop to the snap on the strap that secures her pistol in its holster.

"I need you to step away from the cycle, sir, and show me your hands," she says.

Jack obeys, thinking, here we go again.

"Hello officer," he answers. "Is there a problem?"

"We had a call about some man on a motorcycle watching people going in and out of this apartment building. These are student apartments, so we like to keep track of who's hanging around the neighborhood."

"Yes, of course. My daughter lived here when she was a student," Jack explains.

Without taking her hand off the pistol, Sergeant Bradford says, "I need to see your driver's license and registration, sir."

Jack finds his wallet in the saddlebags, extracts his license and the cycle registration, and offers them to the sergeant, letting her come to him. Sergeant Bradford takes them and returns to the cruiser. After a few minutes, she returns and hands the driver's license, with the learner's permit, which she doesn't mention, and the registration, back to Jack.

"Okay, Mr. Tanner. Do you have business in Madison, other than visiting your daughter's old apartment building?"

"I'm a friend of Lieutenant Vernon Douglas," Jack answers. "We're getting together today."

"*Lieutenant* Douglas? I guess it's been a while since you've seen him."

Jack realizes that it's been at least a year. Maybe the detective is retired, or deceased. "A while, I guess," he says.

"He's *Chief* Douglas now, ever since Chief Margulies retired last year."

She nods toward the Harley. "Road King. Had it long?"

"Three days," Jack answers.

She smiles. "Three days. Well don't let that bad boy get away from you." Walking back to the cruiser, she says, "So long, Mr. Tanner. You be safe now."

Jack gives her a wave, swings up onto the saddle and starts the engine, thinking, I guess I passed safe when I walked into that Harley dealership.

5: THE FIRM OF
   SMITH & WESSON

JACK CHECKS INTO the elegant old Capitol Hotel
on Wisconsin Avenue, where he always stays when in
Madison, parking the Harley in the hotel garage himself,
realizing he's become protective of his bike and uncertain
of how the valet would handle it.

His deluxe suite has a nice view of Lake Mendota. He
tosses his saddlebags on the bed, peels off the leathers,
and takes a long, steamy shower, washing away the road
grit and easing his aching muscles.

The shower finished, he finds the TV remote and
flops onto the bed. MSNBC is headlining the story of
the conviction of a thirty-two-year-old female high
school English teacher on charges of child molestation

and statutory rape for having sex with a fifteen-year-old male student. There is video of the teacher walking into the courthouse with her attorney, wearing a form-fitting black knit dress and black spike heels. She is an absolute knockout: tall, beautiful, long blond hair, blue eyes, perfect teeth, a willowy, incredibly sexy body. He thinks what every man must think when seeing this story: hey lady, you could do better than that.

The teacher reminds Jack of Susan Toth (if you add twenty years). Susan and Henry Toth are neighbors and members of a bridge group Jack and Jenna also take part in. Susan had called Jack a week after Jenna checked into The Sanctuary, a private, upscale, and discreet psychiatric "institute" (hospital) in McLean, Virginia. It is the kind of place celebrities can go and feel safe from tabloid photographers. Jack was surprised that Susan knew about this; he and Jenna had not mentioned it. His vague plan was to say that Jenna felt the need to get away and was travelling with an old college friend, or some such. But in Edina, as in most neighborhoods like it, everyone seemed to know everything. Maybe Jenna told someone in confidence, who told someone in confidence ... Didn't really matter, there was no shame in getting help when you needed it.

On the phone, Susan told Jack that the Tanner family was in her prayers, and that, if he ever needed anything, he should just let her know (let *her* know, not her and Henry). That night, at dinnertime, the doorbell rang and there was Susan, holding a casserole dish covered with aluminum foil, saying it was a tuna hot dish, a.k.a.

"Lutheran penicillin," she joked. Susan had sort of flirted with Jack over the years, in that lighthearted, nonspecific way that seems to say, I'm noticing you, you're in the cohort of men who, under the right circumstances, might interest me … Jack did the same with certain women, and he assumed Jenna did, too, with some men in their social circle. He didn't think anyone ever meant to really follow up; it was just a form of hardwired suburban mating behavior without any real mating intended, at least in Jack's opinion. Of course, there were affairs in Edina just as there were everywhere, but he didn't know of any in their circle of friends. But now here was Susan Toth on his doorstep.

Jack knew he was at another one of those forks in the road: thank her for the casserole right there at the door, or invite her into the house. There had been no sex with Jenna in a long time. What would be the harm? Two consenting adults. But without knowing exactly why—loyalty to Jenna, shyness—he took the casserole and said, that's so nice of you Susan, and how's Henry? Knowing that the mention of her spouse was unmistakable code for thanks, but no thanks.

Susan handed him the dish, kissed him lightly on the mouth and said, "Enjoy." As he watched her walk to her car, and give him a wave as she got in, he recalled reading an article in a magazine, maybe GQ or *Men's Health*, that said men had an average of X sex partners in their lives and women had an average of Y; he didn't remember the numbers, but did recall that Y was considerably greater than X. This was because women called the shots, the article explained. Basically, a man always wants it, and a woman can have it whenever she wants. So an attractive woman like Susan Toth would have no trouble keeping her extramarital dance card filled.

JACK FLIPS TO CNN. Wolf Blitzer, who showed Jack and Jenna such kindness during their appearance on his program, has a report about a college boy in Minnesota who has disappeared while walking home from a party. Will he mention the similar case of Hope Tanner, Jack wonders. Wolf does not.

Jack turns off the TV and finds four little bottles of Scotch in the minibar in the TV cabinet, reflecting that he is grossly overpaying but he needs a stiff drink. Hope is still missing and almost certainly dead. For the past eighteen months, Jenna, finally unable to cope with her grief, has been in residence at The Sanctuary. And Jack, distracted by all of this and grieving himself, has been unable to focus on anything, including his job. When the law firm had to begin "downsizing" as clients slashed budgets for outside legal counsel because of the recession, the management committee put his name on the hit list. A month ago, he was unceremoniously fired. The firm's management committee, which gave the victims the news *en masse* in the conference room, didn't even bother to call it a layoff, indicating that he shouldn't wait to be recalled.

And the man responsible for all this misery that has befallen the Tanner family is living it up in Key West.

IT'S NEARLY SIX o'clock. Jack mutes the TV and uses his BlackBerry to call *Chief* Douglas to confirm their dinner. He is transferred through three levels of gatekeepers, explaining his business to each one, before he is put through to Douglas, a sign of his high office. They have a brief, cordial chat and confirm the dinner.

Then Jack speed dials Pete Dye, who is the private investigator Hartfield, Miller employs whenever the need arises in service of its clients. "Pistol Pete" the lawyers call him, because of the big black .45-caliber pistol he wears, visible in a black leather shoulder holster whenever he takes off his suit jacket. "I'm a partner in the firm of Smith & Wesson," Dye jokes. Jack thinks that all of this is an affectation, or a marketing tool, meant to communicate the message that Dye is a serious player in the shadow world of investigation that he inhabits. It must work, because Pete Dye's hourly billing rate is equal to that of a senior partner of the law firm. Like Jack's neighbor Hank Whitby, Dye is an ex-Marine, and also a former FBI agent, with law and accounting degrees. He works out of a penthouse condo in downtown St. Paul.

After graduating from college, Jack thought about signing up for a Navy program that would have paid for law school in return for some number of years of service as a Navy lawyer. The Marine Corps had a similar program. He didn't want to ask his parents to pay his tuition, because they'd just struggled to help him through undergrad school. He decided instead do it with student loans and jobs, but now he wonders if a stint

in the service would have made him more like Hank
Whitby and Pete Dye, men of action, than like whatever
it is that he is. Probably not, because they were infantry
officers and his battles would have been fought with
paper bullets.

Jack employed Pete Dye to supplement the police
investigation into Hope's disappearance. When the
investigation wound down without result, Jack changed
Dye's assignment to providing periodic reports on the
whereabouts and activities of the lowlife scum who, Jack
firmly believes, killed Hope and, so far, has gotten away
with it. Slater Babcock's father had more than once
bought his son's way out of juvenile-delinquent-spoiled-
rich-kid sort of trouble, Dye's research revealed. But no
serious crimes were ever documented.

At Madison, Dye reported, Babcock appeared to have
straightened himself out. No incidents were reported to
the police or to the dean's office. Dye reminded Jack
that it is a very big leap from a prep-school prank such
as participating in the kidnapping and head shaving of
a rival school's lacrosse captain, or covering trees at the
headmaster's house with toilet paper, to murder.

"I'm not convinced that Babcock is responsible for
Hope's disappearance," Dye had told Jack. "Sure, there's
a first time for everything. A murderer isn't a murderer
until his first kill. Even if Babcock is responsible, maybe
it was a mistake, some sort of accident, a drug overdose
or alcohol poisoning from binge drinking, that harmed
Hope and caused Babcock to panic and cover it up until
he was in too deep to admit it. You've got to understand

that we might never find out what happened that night, unless Babcock finds Jesus and confesses."

For about six weeks after Hope's disappearance, while her story was still big news, well-intended citizens and cranks had called the Tanners and the police with Hope sightings all over the country and the world: she was seen walking with a man in a mall in Cleveland, apparently willingly; she was spotted in LAX boarding an overseas flight with a man wearing sunglasses and a trench coat who was gripping her arm tightly, and she seemed drugged; a couple vacationing in Gstaad saw her alone on a ski lift just ahead of them, then taking off down a double black diamond slope (Hope did not ski).

And so on. Dye ran down the few leads that had some chance of validity, finding all of them to be false. The worst involved a psychic with a nationally syndicated radio show who said she knew positively that Hope had been abducted by a South American crime cartel who sold girls into sex slavery. Hope was in a brothel on the Caribbean island of Curaçao, the psychic claimed, and had actually managed to call in to the program, collect, from a pay phone. How Hope got the phone number was not explained. The tape of this call was aired repeatedly for two weeks, which just happened to coincide with a network rating period. On the tape, a young woman's voice, barely audible through static and her sobbing, seemed to say, "Oh God please help me, help me mommy and daddy, they're hurting me ..."

Jack knew his daughter's voice, and that was not it. But at Jenna's insistence, and with Jack's reluctant approval, because of his wife's delicate mental state, Dye flew to Curaçao and toured the brothels. He did not find Hope, but he did locate a sixteen-year-old girl who had gone missing from her bedroom in the middle of the night two years earlier in Fort Collins, Colorado. Her stepfather had been suspected of murdering her. Dye, posing as a customer, examined the brothel's available girls, and remembered this one from photos of her that were shown on TV news programs and printed in the newspapers. Instead of shooting his way out with her, he offered the proprietor ten thousand dollars cash from his wallet for the girl. Sold. After that, Dye himself was on all the talk shows, which was very good for business.

Dye's reports showed that, after leaving Madison, Slater Babcock had traveled in Europe and Asia as an expat with an apparently unlimited expense account. At present, he owned a bar in Key West, as well as a motor yacht. Daddy was obviously still taking care of his wayward son.

"Hello, Jack," Pete Dye says, answering on the first ring.

"Hey Pete. Just checking in."

"From where?"

"Does it matter?" Jack has called his P.I. while on business trips all over the country, and overseas. Dye had never asked his location before.

"Your house is all buttoned up, your car is in the garage, no one seems to know where you are. At least no one I'm in touch with. I'm just curious about what's up."

Dye surely knows that Jack has been let go by the firm, but is diplomatic enough not to mention it. And he probably knows where Jack is at the moment, and where he's heading. That's his job and he's good at it.

"So now you're watching *me?*" There is a tone of annoyance in Jack's voice.

"I always like to know what's going on," Dye answers. "That's what you pay me for."

"Okay," Jack says. "I always wanted a motorcycle. So I bought one. I'm just taking a little ride to break it in."

"A motorcycle. What kind?"

"A Harley-Davidson Road King."

"You should have asked me," Dye says. "I've been riding since I was a kid. I would have told you that Japanese is the way to go. I've got a Kawasaki XL100 that I ride off road up in the north woods. Motorcycle mechanics fix Harleys and drive rice burners."

"I just liked the look of the Road King."

"Well, it doesn't have to last forever, does it? Just for this one trip."

So Dye does know.

"We've talked about this, Jack," Dye says. "About you not doing anything stupid, especially after all this time. You're riding a goddamned Hog to Key West, to do exactly *what* when you get there? *If* you get there."

"Maybe we shouldn't be talking about this," Jack answers. Private investigators are required to report any criminal activity on the part of their clients, or any knowledge that a crime may be committed. Jack doesn't know if he is in fact planning a crime, but he hasn't the appetite or the time to be detained for an investigation into his intentions, whatever they may be.

Dye ignores Jack's warning. "Look, Jack, go home and let me go to Key West," he says. "What'll you do, hit the kid with your briefcase? Look, I'll talk to him, maybe tell him that I've uncovered some evidence of his involvement in Hope's disappearance that the police don't know about. But that Hope's family just wants to know for certain what happened to her. Wants to know more than they want you prosecuted, so …"

Jack interrupts him. "I'll check in with you later, Pete. I'm meeting an old friend for dinner."

"Jack …"

But Pete Dye is talking to a dial tone.

AT SEVEN P.M., Jack enters the Timberlodge Steak House, located on Highway M, on the northwest shore of Lake Mendota. He and Vernon Douglas have dined there before. He finds Douglas sitting beneath a stuffed moose head in a booth near the back of the dining room.

"I suppose I should salute you now," Jack jokes as he hangs his leather jacket on a hook and slides into the booth.

Douglas grins as he half rises to shake Jack's hand, saying, "Oh, yeah, the chief thing."

"That's very nice for you, Vernon. You've certainly earned it."

"Yes," Douglas replies as he takes a sip from his mug of draft Leinenkugel. "I think I have."

Vernon Douglas, in late middle age, is still built like a college linebacker. He has been with the Madison PD for eighteen years and is its first African-American chief. He was a detective with the Chicago Police Department before that. Jack had asked Dye to check out the background and competence of the detective assigned to Hope's case. Dye's assessment: Vernon Douglas is a good man.

The waitress arrives to take Jack's drink order. He tells her he wants a Ketel One martini with three blue cheese olives. Usually Jack might order a beer, or maybe the house red. But this is the new Jack—or at least a man in search of the new Jack. So he's ordered what his neighbor Hank Whitby always gets when they're out together with the wives. Maybe it's some sort of manly elixir.

Over drinks and steak dinners, they catch up on one another's news. Douglas likes the pay and other perks of the chief's job, but gets bogged down by the heavy administrative duties that keep him from doing what he loves, which is making bad guys wish they'd never come to Madison. Jack says he is taking some vacation time, not mentioning that it is a permanent vacation from his old firm. He's decided to "recharge my batteries" by riding a motorcycle to Virginia to meet Jenna, who is visiting her sister there. Then they will ride back to Minnesota together. Jenna was against this plan at first, Jack says, but finally agreed, saying that, because it was so unlike anything they'd ever done, it might be fun.

Liars, in an attempt to seem convincing, always provide too much detail, a fact that Vernon Douglas knows as well as anyone on the planet. But he is off duty, with an old friend, and lets it slide—until, as they eat, Jack startles him by asking, with an attempt at nonchalance, "I was wondering, Vernon, if you've ever had to shoot someone."

Douglas looks hard at Jack and sighs. "I'm not going to ask why you want to know that." He cuts a bite of steak and takes a while before continuing. "Most cops never fire their weapons, other than on the range."

He finishes his beer, and continues. "As a rookie cop in Chicago, I responded to a report of shots fired in Cabrini Green. Everyone rolling responds to a call like that, but I was a block away and got there first. I saw someone lying on the sidewalk and a young man standing over him, holding a pistol. As I roared up, lights and siren, the guy turned toward me and fired three rounds at my cruiser. Two missed and one shattered the windshield. I wasn't hit. I rolled out the door onto the ground and saw the guy's not running. He fired again. I returned fire and hit him, center mass, killing him."

Douglas pauses and rubs his eyes. "He was fifteen." Then he gives Jack a look that manages to be hard and sad at the same time. "You don't forget something like that, ever—unless you're one of those psychopath flat-liners with fucked-up brain chemistry." He looks up at the moose head on the wall. "I wouldn't even want to shoot that fellow, if I didn't have to. Although, obviously, someone felt differently."

Jack checks his watch. It's already nine o'clock.

"I need to hit the hay, Vernon. I want to get on the road early, out ahead of Milwaukee rush hour."

Jack insists on picking up the check, in honor of the chief's promotion. They walk out to the parking lot together, where Douglas admires the Harley.

"I guess this'll get you wherever it is you're going," he says.

"As I said, I'm going to visit Jenna."

"Uh huh, sure you are." He grab's Jack's arm, so hard it hurts. "Listen, you're a good guy, and you don't deserve what happened to your family." He lets go and shakes his head. "What's it like to *shoot* someone? Jesus Christ, Jack! What'd you do, track that kid down and now you've suddenly grown the cajones for some vigilante justice? Don't go there. Don't go anywhere near there. Look, I hate it that the perp, whoever he is, Slater Babcock or someone else, is out there somewhere, but ...."

Jack turns away and throws his leg over the saddle and says, "What would *you* do if someone killed your daughter and got away with it?"

Douglas hesitates. "Well, I probably would hunt the scumbag down, shoot him in the kneecap just to get his attention, and then I'd do some really bad things to him."

Jack starts the cycle. "That's what I thought, Vernon."

He begins to pull away, the gravel crunching under the tires. He can see in the rearview mirrors that Douglas is saying something, but he can't hear him above the roar of the Harley's engine.

6: SOMETIMES A CIGAR IS JUST A CIGAR

'WE CARE DEEPLY about all our guests, Jenna, and that's why we're delighted when they leave, if you understand my meaning."

"Are you saying I'm ready to go home, Dr. Larrabee?" Jenna asks.

"It's my opinion that you're doing much better," he answers. "As to when you're well enough to transition to out-patient care, well, I'd say that that day will come sooner, rather than later."

Dr. Robert Larrabee is the staff psychiatrist assigned to Jenna at The Sanctuary. He is in his early sixties, handsome, with a full head of graying brown hair, tall, tanned, lean, and athletic. They sit in his office on the third floor The Sanctuary's admin building, in comfortable upholstered chairs near a coffee table on which there are insulated metal pitchers of coffee, tea, lemonade, and water.

Jenna had been sitting in that chair twice a week since arriving at The Sanctuary. The office is understated, unlike the type a man in such an important position might have, which could be intimidating to a visitor. There is no psychiatrist's couch, which, as the doctor explained when Jenna asked during her first visit, is a relic of the past. There is an antique desk, a Queen Anne, found by his wife, Julie, a collector, in a little shop in Charlottesville, he told Jenna when she asked during her second visit. Diplomas on the wall are from the College of William and Mary, the Duke University School of Medicine, and the Johns Hopkins School of Medicine's psychiatric residency program. Also on display are a group photo of the William and Mary basketball team, which includes Dr. Larrabee back in the day when he was tall enough to play power forward and the faces were mostly white, a photo of a sleek white sailboat cutting through Atlantic whitecaps off Newport News, the doctor at the helm and his wife and two teenage daughters in the cockpit, and an amateurish landscape painting, which Jenna has not asked about, fearing that her psychiatrist, or his wife, might be the artist, and not one of his young daughters.

"The truth is," Jenna says after a moment, "I feel very comfortable here—"

"Yes, we've created a protected environment at The Sanctuary. Hence the very name of the place. But it is meant to be temporary. It is important that you understand that."

"Oh, I do understand," Jenna says, not at all certain that she really does.

"How are you feeling about your medication?" he asks. For the past two months, he has been gradually reducing the strength of her antidepressant prescriptions. She is no longer on suicide watch.

"Good, good," she answers, knowing that she is both pleased and uneasy about being weaned off the meds that have insulated her from the real world.

"Have you had any of the side effects I mentioned? Dizziness, dry mouth, trouble sleeping ... ?"

Jenna considers this, brushing a strand of hair from her eyes. "Some of that. I wonder if there is anything in this life that *doesn't* have a side effect."

Dr. Larrabee smiles. "No. I don't suppose there is."

"How long will I need to be on medications, do you think?" she asks.

"That's something that your doctor in Minneapolis will be monitoring with you. It's possible you'll be on some sort of medication for life. There's nothing wrong with that. Modern psychiatry has largely turned away from Freudian psychoanalysis in favor of drug therapy. We've learned so much about brain anatomy and brain chemistry in recent years, and when we get it right, drugs work. There have been studies of the brains of psychopathic killers in prison showing that they have different brain chemistry than the normal person, and even different brain anatomy ..."

He sees Jenna stiffen and realizes what he's said. Her daughter may have been taken by one of these kinds of monsters. "Forgive me, Jenna," he says. "That was insensitive."

"It's okay."

"Anyway, years of psychoanalysis don't seem to actually help patients very much, if at all," he continues, glancing at the photo of his sailboat. "However, I do know a prominent psychoanalyst in New York. He has a very busy Park Avenue practice. He doesn't fly commercial."

Jenna laughs. As she does, she realizes that she doesn't recall the last time this happened.

WHEN THE SESSION has ended and Jenna is gone, Dr. Larrabee makes notes in her file: "Patient tolerating change from 10 mg. dextroamphetamine and 300 mg. lithium carbonate b.i.d. to 80 mg. venlafaxine b.i.d. Responded positively to humorous story for first time since admission. Is alert and participates in conversation. Flatness of personality initially observed has ameliorated considerably."

LATER THAT AFTERNOON, Jenna is sitting on a wooden bench beside a small lake on The Sanctuary's property, thinking about a call she got from Jack two days ago, saying he'd be visiting her tomorrow. She is startled by a voice behind her.

"Hi, Jenna, mind if I join you?"

She turns to see another patient, Jared Manville, standing behind the bench. He is wearing pajamas and a robe, with bare feet, and is unshaven. She has never seen him like this before; he has always been well dressed and clean-shaven.

"Please do, Jared," Jenna replies. "This is such a peaceful spot—"

Jared is a man about her age who, he's told Jenna, was a professor of art history at Dartmouth and a painter. She doesn't know why he is there; patients never talk about their particular maladies, just as prison inmates never discuss their crimes. She doesn't know if he is married, or if he is straight or gay (she feels she might be stereotyping him because he is, or was, an artist). He is tall and thin as a fence post, with an angular, off-kilter face that suggests a Picasso painting. He is intelligent and charming. Once, he invited her to his room to see his paintings. She reflexively said a polite no, not knowing if it was art or sex he had in mind, and he never asked again, so she doesn't know how good a painter he is. Or if the resume he's recounted to her is, in fact, real. One very pleasant elderly woman whose suite is next door to Jenna's seems to believe she is Marie Antoinette.

Jared grins, sits beside her, takes a dinner roll out of the pocket of his robe, and begins tossing crumbs toward a squirrel that is sitting up on its haunches, watching them.

"So, Jenna my darling," he says, "another day in the cuckoo's nest." Then he tosses the rest of the roll to the squirrel, stands up, sighs, and walks right into the lake.

By the time a frantic Jenna alerts the staff, it is too late. Back in her room, she looks into the bathroom mirror and says, "I am *not* like that. Please let me be not like that ..."

7: ARCADIA B & B

AFTER EIGHT HOURS, Jack has ridden as far as his aching body will allow this day. He glances at the digital clock below the cycle's speedometer: seven p.m. He's on I-70, heading east, approaching Columbus, Ohio. He needs gas, a meal, and a hotel.

He motors down the highway for fifteen more minutes, then leans the cycle onto the exit ramp for Grandview Heights, a Columbus suburb. Ohio State University is in Columbus. That was Hope's backup school. If only she'd chosen Ohio State instead of the University of Wisconsin. Uninvited, one of those silly old sayings pops into his mind: If wishes were fishes we'd all have a fry.

He rolls into a Citgo station. As he fills the tank, he

recalls that it was a beautiful October Friday afternoon, the leaves in full fall colors, reds, oranges, and browns, when he and Hope drove twelve and a half hours from Edina for a campus visit, on the same route Jack had just taken. Hope insisted on sharing the driving, saying, "You're no spring chicken anymore, daddy," and this became a family joke.

OSU is another one of those lovely Midwestern state universities, its imposing campus exuding a mix of wholesomeness and high purpose. Jack could picture students and faculty wearing milk mustaches strolling across the quad as they discussed the nineteenth century Lake Poets, or string theory, or where to get the best pizza. Whenever Jack visited any college or university, he wanted to stay there, retreating into the ivory tower, like a monk in a monastery. "I was good at school," Jack once said to Jenna when they attended a University of Minnesota hockey game. "I had school figured out. Everything since then has been problematic." He was being entirely serious.

Hope noticed that everyone she met here insisted on calling the place *The* Ohio State University, which she found a bit pretentious. "I don't know if I can do that all my life," she said. "Maybe I should go someplace else." When her father didn't immediately respond, she added, "Just kidding." She was admitted to Wisconsin, Ohio State, Miami University in Oxford, Ohio, the University of Minnesota, and the University of Michigan, Jack and Jenna's alma mater—everywhere she applied.

She was very methodical in her criteria: in the

Midwest, strong academics, not too long a drive from home, big campus with lots of activities in a nice university town. She picked Madison because it fit all her criteria perfectly. Jenna favored Michigan, where she and Jack had met as undergrads, but didn't push it; anywhere was fine with Jack as long as Hope was happy. But if she'd happened to choose Ohio State, well, Jack was a big college football fan and the Buckeyes had just beaten Arizona State 20 to 17 in the Rose Bowl. Hope could have gotten student game tickets. But of course he didn't mention this while she was making her decision.

The gas pump's auto shutoff clicks at just under fifteen dollars, bringing him back to the present moment. The Harley gets fifty-three miles a gallon on the highway. At that rate he'll get to Key West for about seventy bucks.

He turns out of the Citgo toward a Cracker Barrel down at the end of the strip. As he approaches the restaurant's crowded parking lot, he notices a roadside sign advertising the "Historic Arcadia Bed & Breakfast" 2.5 miles down the road. On an impulse, he decides to check it out.

Jenna liked to stay in B & Bs on road trips. He found them to be musty and frilly and overly precious. The proprietors always seemed to be former commodities traders or investment bankers or corporate execs—or lawyers, and their spouses, wanting a lifestyle change. He doesn't like Victorian architecture, antique furniture or shaving in dry sinks. Despite all this, all his B&B memories are good ones, because pleasing Jenna pleased him.

Exactly 2.5 miles down a two-lane blacktop, he comes upon the Arcadia, a three-story white Victorian, with purple gingerbread trim, set in among giant live oak and willow trees, with a back lawn sloping down to a small lake. He guides the cycle along the gravel driveway and stops in front. There is a broad porch running along the front of the house.

A man is sitting on a two-person swing near the front door, the swing's rusty chains creaking in accompaniment to the buzz of cicadas in the trees. The man appears to be in his fifties, like Jack, but with a full beard. He's wearing a red plaid shirt and jeans. A golden retriever with a grey muzzle snoozes at his feet. The man nods in greeting as Jack leans the cycle onto its kickstand, gets off and walks up the porch steps. "I was wondering about a room for one night," he says as the man rises and offers his hand.

"Garrett Kirkland," the man says as Jack returns his firm handshake. "No need to wonder. We've got one available. Got eight rooms here, as a matter of fact, with just three occupied."

Garrett eyes the Harley. "I've always thought about getting one of those bad boys," he says. "But my wife always exercises her veto. Says if I'm having a midlife crisis, I should take up woodworking, or something else that won't kill me. No offense."

"None taken," Jack says, smiling. "Can't say she's wrong."

As Garrett takes an imprint of Jack's credit card at a scarred old oak roll-top desk in the living room, he explains, without being asked, that he formerly owned a Chicago advertising agency, Kirkland Associates. His wife Marissa was sous chef at Les Nomades. "Maybe you've eaten there," he says.

"Yes I have, and it was great." The charming brick row house on East Ontario Street is one of their favorite places for dinner when in Chicago.

"Maybe you're wondering why two people give up good jobs in an exciting city to own a B & B out here in the boonies," Garrett says. "Well, when I got an unsolicited offer from a big French advertising conglomerate for a helluva lot more than I thought my shop was worth, I decided to sell. There are no hard assets with an ad agency. The inventory goes down the elevator every night, and your biggest client can call at any time and fire your ass, as happened to me more than once. So, after the wire transfer hit my bank account, I retired. Got bored after a week. We saw a for-sale ad for this place in *Gourmet* magazine. Turned out my wife liked the idea of taking a break from working in someone else's kitchen. That was three years ago."

Jack wants nothing more at this point than to freshen up and find something to eat, but to be polite he asks, "So how do you like it?"

"Absolutely hate it," Garrett answers with a laugh. "We're working harder than we did at our old jobs. Or at least it seems harder because it's mostly boring. We've got the place up for sale and are moving back to Chicago at the end of the month, whether it sells or not. I'll do some marketing consulting. Marissa has lined up a position at Charlie Trotter's."

Before heading upstairs to his room, Jack asks, "I suppose I missed dinner?"

"Too bad you didn't get here an hour ago," Garret answers. "Marissa served a Bosc pear salad, a very tasty grilled wild salmon on green lentils with thyme sauce and, for dessert, a mille-feuille of pear mousse, berries and caramel apricot sauce or grapefruit sorbet. The guests, which included three more couples who live near here, seemed to enjoy it."

"That's okay. I can go back to the Cracker Barrel."

"Cracker Barrel? No way! Marissa would kill me if I let you do that. She's still in the kitchen. She'll whip up something up from the larder. Freshen up and come down whenever you're ready."

Garrett leads Jack up a creaky wooden staircase to his room on the second floor, insisting on carrying Jack's saddlebag. There is no room key, which is one of a rural B & B's charms, Jack understands, although he has that city habit of wanting to lock up his stuff when he goes out, to prevent someone from entering the room and making off with his valuables. Of course, on the list of risks Jack is taking, this one is way down toward the bottom.

Garret pushes open the door, flips on the lights, puts the saddlebag onto a webbed suitcase stand at the foot of the bed and departs, reminding Jack to come down to the kitchen when he's ready. Jack takes in the room, which has a small connecting bathroom. It could be a model for a feature spread in *Bed and Breakfast Business* magazine, which probably does exist; there are specialty magazines for everything it seems. Chintz curtains; lace doilies on every available surface; a four-poster bed with a lace canopy; an antique oak dry sink with a flow-blue bowl and water pitcher (Jenna has a flow-blue collection, which is why he knows the term). Not his taste, but then neither is the Red Roof Inn. The bed does look comfortable, and it has a goose-down comforter, perfect for the chill evening if he cracks open the window.

Suddenly Jack is overcome with an aching loneliness. He feels the urge to pay for the room, making some excuse to Garrett (an urgent business problem, I'm needed back at the firm), and ride back home. But there is no one to go home to. He peels off his leathers, T-shirt, and boots, gets under a steaming hot shower and feels better. He puts on a white polo shirt, jeans, and Topsiders, and reflexively looks for his non-existent room key. He finds a back stairway at the end of the hall, which, he assumes, will lead him toward the kitchen.

As soon as makes his way down the stairs, the air is redolent with the warm, yeasty aroma of baking bread. If there is a more wholesome, comforting, inviting smell in the world, he doesn't know what it is. He follows the aroma down the stairs, along a hallway and around a corner into a large, well-lit kitchen. Immediately, he recognizes that this is the workshop of a master craftsman. The room is a rectangle about one third the size of a basketball court, with square footage obviously stolen from what were originally adjacent rooms. The kitchen has a high ceiling, maybe fifteen feet, white walls, black-and-white checked tile on the floor, gleaming stainless steel counter tops, a center-island butcher's block scarred by sharp knives, and oversized professional appliances: the kind of cast-iron gas range that's always lit, a restaurant-size stainless steel refrigerator with a separate freezer, prep sinks, and hanging copper pots that look like they actually get used. The works.

Marissa Kirkland is bending over in front of the oven, taking out a metal tray holding four bread pans, oven mitts on both hands. She puts the tray on the butcher's block, turns, and smiles at Jack. She is wearing a faded denim shirt, jeans, and cowboy boots. Her soft auburn hair falls to her shoulders; she blows a strand from her face. She is slim and pretty, maybe in her mid-to-late fifties, one of those women who seem to improve with age. Jack can see threads of silver in her hair and fine lines around her eyes, which are the color of lapis lazuli. She is one of the prettiest women Jack has ever run across, at any age, he thinks. And she can cook.

"Hi there," she says, shaking off the mitts so she can take Jack's hand. "I'm Marissa. You must be Jack. Garrett said you might stop by for a snack."

Garrett is a lucky devil, Jack thinks. "That bread smells amazing," he says. "I'd say it reminds me of my youth, except our family ate Wonder Bread."

Marissa is amused, which was his intent. "Sourdough, from starter I brought with me from Chicago." She flips one of the bread pans upside down, taps the bottom with the handle of a chef's knife, slides the loaf out and cuts a thick end slice, which she slathers with soft yellow butter from a dish on the counter. "Here," she says, handing the bread to Jack. "I prefer the end pieces. See what you think."

Jack takes a big bite. "Wow!" he says. "This is fantastic. It's like I've never tasted bread before."

Marissa seems pleased. "Pull one of those stools up to the counter and I'll see what I can throw together."

As Jack perches on the stool, she swings open the refrigerator door and scans the shelves, saying "Ummm … ahhh … yes …" as she pulls out various items, setting them on the butcher's block: some field greens in a plastic bag, a yellow onion, a tomato, something that looks like a withered black mushroom, eggs in a bowl, and a brick of yellow cheese.

"We'll do something light, so you can get a good night's sleep," she says as she shakes out the lettuce into a wooden salad bowl. "I think an omelet and green salad will do the trick."

"Sounds perfect," Jacks says, resting his elbows on the counter as he watches her prepare his meal. "How did you happen to become a chef?"

"Oh, I just kind of fell into it," Marissa answers as she uses the knife to slice a tomato. She continues as she slices an onion and dresses the salad lightly with olive oil and balsamic vinegar from glass carafes on the counter, then squeezes on fresh lemon juice. "I grew up in Lake Forest, on Chicago's North Shore. Dad was a commodities trader and mom had a shop selling jewelry and ceramics she made. I graduated from Northwestern with a degree in philosophy. There weren't any job

listings for philosophers in the *Tribune*, but there were
lots for restaurant workers. Both my parents were good
cooks and gourmands. They took my sister and me on
eating tours of Europe and Asia when we were growing
up. So the idea of working in the food biz struck me as
possibly interesting."

Now she is whisking three eggs in a stainless steel
bowl as butter is melting in a blackened iron omelet pan
on a gas burner. The butter is sputtering as she pours in
the eggs and uses a grater to add the cheese. She folds
the omelet over onto itself, waits a moment, then slides
it onto a big white china plate. She spoons some salad
onto the plate and grates slivers of the black mushroom
thing onto the top of the omelet.

"Black truffle," she explains. "Gives a cheese omelet
a nice finish."

"By serendipity," Jack says, watching her every move,
"an artist has found her medium."

Marissa takes a bottle of red wine from a rack under
the butcher's block, extracts the cork and pours some
into two stemmed glasses. She hands one to Jack and
lifts the other in a toast: "Bon appétit, Jack. A fruity
pinot noir, I think, goes well with eggs." She displays the
label. "Leaping Stag from St. Helena in the Napa Valley.
The vintner's a friend of mine."

She holds the glass to her nose, sniffs, takes a sip,
swirls it in her mouth, and swallows. "Very nice. A hint
of sassafras, rosemary, and cinnamon, with a light veneer
of oak. Mildly assertive, yet not pushy. I'd have to say its
presumption amuses me."

Jack takes a sip and shrugs. "Just tastes like a nice red wine to me."

Marissa grins. "Me, too! I was just putting you on with that pretentious wine blather. I've seen blind tastings where the so-called experts can't tell the difference between a fifty-dollar French and a ten-dollar California."

Jack laughs, and digs into his meal with gusto, famished. "This is wonderful," he says.

Marissa cuts another hunk of bread for Jack, and one for her, and sits on a stool beside him.

"Tell me more about your career," he says.

She spreads butter on her bread and takes a big bite. "My first job was making salads and washing dishes at a little French bistro in Lincoln Park. By the time I'd worked my way up to pastry chef at Alinea, I decided to get serious and enrolled at Le Cordon Bleu in Paris."

Jack is finished and looks like he might lick the plate. Marissa finds a rhubarb tart for him in the refrigerator and draws them both little cups of espresso from an antique copper and steel machine she says she found in Tuscany.

"So that's my story," she says. "What's yours?"

Jack has vowed to not tell his story to anyone along the way. But he owes Marissa something for the great meal, and for sharing her background. He could easily make something up. Pete Dye and Vernon Douglas obviously know where Jack is heading, and why, but no one else. He doesn't intend to share his history with strangers. But for some reason he does not understand, he feels the urge to tell Marissa Kirkland the truth, and he does.

She sits silently as he tells it all, every bit of it, feeling a sense of relief, of a burden being lifted from his back, perhaps like a Catholic in the confessional seeking forgiveness for sins of omission. When he is finished, Marissa brushes a tear from her cheek with the back of her hand, stands, gives him a hug, and says, "Oh Jack, bless you, and bless Jenna, and bless Hope. May you all be together again, in this life, or the next."

Jack is deeply moved, and manages to say only, "Thank you."

Marissa begins putting the dirty dishes into the sink, and tells him, "If you're not quite ready for bed you can find Garrett down on the dock. He usually has an extra cigar."

A FULL MOON hangs in the evening sky as Jack makes his way along a fieldstone path running down to the lake. He comes to a sand swimming beach with a long dock running out about twenty yards into the dark water. There is no wind; the lake is perfectly flat. Garrett is seated on a wooden bench connected to the end of the dock, leaning back, puffing a cigar whose end glows like a firefly in the night. Hearing creaking steps on the dock's weathered wooden slats, he turns. "Join me in a Cohiba?"

Jack lowers himself onto the bench, accepts the contraband Cuban cigar, a cutter and box of wooden kitchen matches, snips off the end of the cigar, lights it, takes several long draws to get it going. "The perfect end to a perfect meal," he says. "I think I've never eaten so well. Your wife is a fantastic chef."

"They say hunger is the best sauce, but yes, she certainly is that," Garrett agrees, exhaling a long puff of smoke as he looks up at the moon.

"May I ask how you met?" It seems to be a night for sharing personal information.

"We met in Paris. She was a student at Cordon Bleu. I was backpacking around the Continent, one step ahead of the draft, at the height of the Vietnam War. I was browsing in Shakespeare and Company, the bookstore on the Left Bank where all those writers hung out in the 1920s—Hemingway, James Joyce, Ford Madox Ford, Ezra Pound, William S. Burroughs. If you're in Paris, and you majored in English lit, as I did at DePaul, Shakespeare and Company is one of the sacred places you must visit, like a Muslim making a pilgrimage to Mecca. I'd just come from Dublin, where, of course, I retraced the route of Leopold Bloom. I wanted to be a novelist. I'd written a bad coming-of-age novel in college. It was a smarmy *Catcher in the Rye* rip off. It's amazing how the brilliant ideas you get in the shower become absolute dog poop on the page. I thought if I backpacked around Europe after graduation I might gain enough experience to overcome my background as a happy, middle-class, white kid from Winnetka who goes to college, gets good grades, and has a good time. What I found instead was Marissa. There she was, in the philosophy section, the prettiest girl I ever saw. I sidled over, rehearsing pick-up lines in my head, when she turned from the shelf, looked me over and said, 'No, I don't come here often, if that's what you're about to ask. But yes, I would like to go for onion soup and pomme fritte at Au Chien Qui Fume Cafe at Les Halles, which is what you *should* be asking if you want some company for the evening.' We've been together ever since. I did eventually find my voice in writing advertising copy."

They sit, savoring the Cohibas, which Garrett obtains from a regular guest, he explains, a salesman who gets them via FedEx from his company's office in Toronto. Canada has no trade embargo on Cuba. Jack recounts the story of JFK and his favored Cuban Antonio Y Cleopatra cigars, which he'd read about in a JFK biography, and of which Garrett hadn't heard: Just before ordering the naval blockade of Cuba, Kennedy dispatched his press secretary, Pierre Salinger, to Havana to stock the White House humidor.

Garrett loves this story. "Now here's one in return," he says. "Costco was a client of my agency. They gave us an assignment to name their house brand. We did a lot of very creative brainstorming, came up with lots of options. Value Brand. Cost Plus. Homebrand … We presented to the VP of Marketing and his staff. It seemed to go well. The VP called me later and said they liked several of the choices very much, but decided to go with something else. They named it after me! So Kirkland it is. The fact that the company was founded in Kirkland, Washington is, to me, irrelevant."

Now and then a bass leaps for a bug on the surface of the lake, making a soft splash. When his cigar is down to the yellow and black checkered band, Garrett slips off the band, pockets it and flips the glowing stub into the lake, signaling it's O.K. for Jack to do likewise with the word, "biodegradable."

They walk together back up to the house. "Sleep well, Jack," Garrett says as he opens the screen door for his guest. "Breakfast's at seven, but feel free to sleep in. Marissa will take care of you whenever you come down."

Earlier that evening, Jack had the urge to leave and return home. Now he has the urge to stay a while with these nice folks until he figures out what in the world he's doing heading to Key West on a Harley-Davidson motorcycle, and what he expects to do when he gets there.

8:   CONJUGAL VISIT

"HOW'S THE HOUSE, Jack?" Jenna asks by way of greeting as she finds her husband in the conservatory, a large, sunny, first-floor room at The Sanctuary. She gives him a kiss on the cheek. "A Ritz-Carleton for head cases," Jenna had termed the hospital when Jack brought her here just over a year ago.

Jack finds the term "conservatory" to be pretentious, even to describe this room, which does resemble the conservatory in a Newport mansion: oriental rugs over marble floors, full-length windows overlooking a large terrace, and meticulously manicured grounds, and mahogany floor-to-ceiling bookcases. They do not call this the "day room," Jack decided during his first visit, because that would call to mind prisons, nursing homes and low-rent mental institutions. The Sanctuary is anything but low rent.

"The house is fine," Jack answers. "It'll need painting this summer. It's been six years. I'll need to call the window washers when I get back (if he gets back). Your tulips came up at Easter, red, whites, yellows, and purples."

"Oh, that's nice," Jenna says. "Did you bring pictures?"

Jack is surprised. Jenna has not asked about their house, or about anything else about their life in Edina, since arriving here. "Sorry, I didn't think of it," he answers. "I will next time."

At first, he began visiting weekly, flying into Dulles every Saturday and renting a car. But it became clear that his visits were upsetting Jenna—and him as well, truth be told; he hated seeing his wife in an institution, no matter how nice the furniture was. So he started coming less often, once a month or so. Jenna has never seemed to care how often he comes. At least she hasn't said she did.

When they are together, they are reminded, Jack has concluded, that they are childless parents. Hope is never mentioned. This is the first time he's seen his wife in nearly three months. He understands that the Jenna he visits is a chemically altered version of his wife. What saves you changes you. But something seems different today. Is his poor sweet wife less tense? The light in her eyes less dimmed? Hard to tell at this point, but something ... Jenna's staff psychiatrist has counseled Jack that in time she will want to talk about the reality of their situation, and this will signal progress on the road to healing. But don't rush it.

How long will that take? Jack asked. Dr. Larrabee couldn't say. Each person is unique. Kind of like being in a coma; sometimes all we can do is wait and hope for the best. Which made Jack wonder why Jenna couldn't wait it out at home, instead of here at a cost of thirty thousand dollars a month, with insurance covering less than half that amount. With Jack unemployed, money is definitely an issue.

It is four o'clock. Perhaps twenty other visitors and patients—who are called "guests" here—are partaking of high tea set up on a long banquet table in the middle of the room. Jenna is wearing her usual Sanctuary garb, a tennis warm-up suit, this one pink velour, and running shoes. Exercise is a big part of the treatment here; Jenna does yoga and Pilates, and takes long walks around the grounds.

Jack is trying to think of more to report about life at home, even if he must make it up, but Jenna says, "That's nice, dear," takes his hand and leads him toward one of the furniture groupings near a window. "See, they're serving tea." It's the first time Jack has been here at this hour. "I love those little cucumber sandwiches, and the petit fours are to die for. Lately I can't seem to resist the sweets."

Jenna has put on some weight, Jack notices, but she still looks beautiful, despite this, despite it all. She leads him to the buffet table and hands him a plate, selecting various crustless sandwiches and pastries for both of them, as they move along the table. She pours tea for herself and coffee for Jack, remembering his preference, while having suppressed so much else of greater importance.

"This is nice," Jenna says when they are seated in uncomfortable antique-like chairs, plates balanced on their knees and their cups on a mahogany butler table with brass hinges. "I'm glad you came." She looks at him, seeming concerned. "You look tired," she says. "I hope you didn't drive all the way here from Minneapolis without stopping overnight."

Which would have been more than eighteen hours, straight through. Not likely. "I stayed in Milwaukee and Columbus," he answers. Not wanting to mention Madison.

Jack *is* fatigued. His back is stiff, and his ass is sore. He feels as if he's ridden here on a horse. The first day on the Harley was exhilarating. The second day, eight hours in the saddle to Columbus, reminded him why they invented automobiles. Today he rode seven more hours to McLean.

They continue to chat amiably for a half-hour, discussing the pleasant Virginia climate; the new wing under construction at The Sanctuary, where Jenna is in line for a larger suite when it's completed; the new chef who has added lighter spa cuisine to the menu; the "chaperoned" outings you can take to shopping malls and movies and plays … blah blah blah, as they sip their tea and coffee and eat their pastries. Again, Jack thinks Jenna is more connected than during his previous visits—or is he just imagining that, because he wants it so much?

Then Jenna surprises—no, *shocks*—him by asking, "If you didn't ride straight through, did you stop in Madison?"

What to say? At a loss, he tells an edited version of the truth. "I did. I was tired at that point, so I found a hotel and got dinner and a good rest." Thinking that might do it.

"Did you see the campus?" she asks.

Nothing to do now but see where she wants this to go. "Yes, I drove through it." Brief answers, as if on the witness stand in court. Don't elaborate, it might get you in trouble.

"Okay," Jenna says, and, to Jack's relief, is done with that subject

When Jack checks his watch, Jenna surprises him again by saying, "Why don't you come up to my room and rest up a bit before going off on your motorcycle."

So she's noticed his leather outfit and figured that it is motorcycle garb. Or maybe she was looking out the window when he drove in. He has been to her room only twice before, when she moved in, and again when he had brought from home the things she requested: certain clothing, her cosmetics case, her sewing kit (a birthday gift from Hope that she's never used), and her laptop computer. All other times, they've met in the conservatory and then walked the grounds and had lunch or dinner in The Sanctuary's main dining room (where the food is excellent), depending upon the time of day. Maybe she considers her room to be her sanctuary, Jack has always thought. He never asked to go to her room because he didn't want to upset whatever delicate balance is helping her to survive.

Jenna is free to leave the hospital grounds whenever she wishes, either on an excursion, or permanently, Jack knows. Once, at her request, he took her to a nearby outlet mall. She didn't buy anything and hasn't wanted to venture out again.

Her room is an apartment, really, with a large living room, master suite, small kitchen, and a breakfast nook. Jenna leads Jack into the bedroom, and turns down the comforter and sheet on the canopied bed.

"I think a shower and a nap before leaving is what you need," Jenna says, sitting on the bed. For Jack, this is an unexpected but welcome prospect before hitting the road again.

JACK ADJUSTS THE showerhead to pulsate and lets the hot water massage his neck, shoulders, and back. He uses a loofa sponge for a nice scrub, and then wraps a big terrycloth towel around him and pads back into the bedroom, where he finds Jenna under the covers, smiling seductively at him. Does she know somehow that this is not one of Jack's usual visits and that she might never see him again? How could she? He doesn't think that his demeanor has revealed anything about his journey. Maybe people married as long as they have been can just sense such things.

He puts away this thought, puts away all thoughts, drops his towel, slides under the covers, and embraces his wife, who is also nude. She kisses him with open mouth, touches him under the sheets and speaks softly into his ear. "You're my guy, Jack, my love, now and forever, yes you are, yes …"

Jack is overwhelmed with emotion. The old Jenna has reappeared, it seems, at least for this brief time.

The visit becomes conjugal.

Later, Jenna lies in bed, her head propped on an arm, watching Jack pull on his leathers and boots. She looks happy.

"That's a good look for you, cowboy."

Jack smiles. He's happy too.

She flips a strand of hair from her eyes. "So, you just ride into town, steal a lady's heart, and then ride out again. Is that the deal?"

Jack studies her and decides to go for it. "Do you want me to take you home?"

"You mean ride to Minnesota on the back of that motorcycle? Like I was your biker bitch?"

He laughs. "Sure, if you want. Or we can fly, or rent a car, or *buy* a car, whatever you like."

She sighs and looks away. "I can't do that, Jack. Not yet." She doesn't tell him about her last session with Dr. Larrabee. She feels she is getting better but she doesn't want to get Jack's hopes up, or hers. Not yet.

OUT IN THE parking lot, the night illuminated by
sodium-vapor lights, Jack starts up the motorcycle. As
he buckles his helmet, he looks up at the window of
his wife's suite. She is there, back lit, in the Chinese silk
robe he gave her one Christmas, looking down at him.
He pushes the Harley up off its kickstand, turns his hand
on the throttle, and rides away, wondering if he just took
a nap in Jenna's room and all the rest was just one of his
dreams.

Jenna watches the beam of the motorcycle's
headlight turn away and then the glow of its red taillight
move along the winding road leading out toward the
highway. She realizes that she is crying, something she
has not been able to do on her strong medications, which
suppressed her emotions. Her "progress," as Dr. Larrabee
terms her current status, is a doubled-edged sword. She
does want to go home. But, at the same time, she is afraid
of what she might find there.

As the taillight of Jack's motorcycle dances off into
the darkness, Jenna raises her hand and places her palm
upon the cool window glass, as if touching the night.

9: DEVIL'S DISCIPLES

AT SEVENTY MILES per hour there is no way for two
people on a motorcycle to talk, unless they have helmets
with an intercom system, which was one of the Harley
options that Jack passed up. So all he knows about the
young, pretty, red-haired, green-eyed girl sitting behind
him with her arms around his waist and her breasts
pressed into his back is what she told him when he
came across her hitchhiking at the entrance ramp to I-95
South in Fredericksburg, where he spent the night after
leaving Jenna.

Her name is Hannah, she said. She is from Fargo.
She is eighteen, but Jack wouldn't have been surprised if
she'd said thirteen. She is wearing plastic Minnie Mouse
sunglasses, a tight Jonas Brothers T-shirt with no bra,

skimpy Daisy Dukes, and pink flip-flops. She was riding on the back of her boyfriend's motorcycle, another Harley, "of course," from Fargo to Daytona Beach for Bike Week. She and the boyfriend had a fight over "whatever," and he dumped her back at a Days Inn. She still wants to get to Daytona. Was Jack headed that way?

He decided on the spot that he would make an unplanned stop in Daytona. It might be an interesting adventure, and one road orphan should help another. "Hop aboard," he said, and patted the saddle behind him. "I don't have another helmet."

"Never wear one anyway," she'd answered. "Gives me helmet hair."

Hannah swung onto the seat, wrapped her thin, tan arms around his waist, and, pressing Jack's thighs with hers, shouted "Giddy-up horsey!"

He did, and off they went.

JACK FEELS HANNAH tapping his shoulder. They've been riding for nearly two hours under a warm sun that caused Jack to unzip his leather jacket, barreling south down I-95 toward Richmond. He swivels his head and sees her pointing at a sign announcing a highway rest area coming up in two miles. He nods and gives her a thumbs-up.

In less than five minutes they are rolling into the rest area. Jack parks in front of a one-story red brick building that looks like a small elementary school. Semis, pickups, and campers are parked in a designated truck area. He turns into the car lot and parks. As he dismounts, he notices a group of motorcycles parked several rows back. He pulls off his helmet and jacket as Hannah hops off, grinning.

"Sure has warmed up," Hannah says, tugging down her T-shirt, which has ridden up to reveal the bottoms of her perky little breasts. The denim Daisy Dukes are molded to her pelvic folds; she doesn't attempt to dislodge them.

A silver-haired woman getting into the passenger side of a Hyundai is glaring disapproval as if she can read Jack's mind, which makes him wonder what the age of consent is in whatever state they end up in tonight. Cradle robber. Or maybe the old bat just doesn't like motorcycles.

Hannah crinkles her nose and says, "Boy, thanks for stopping. I sure gotta pee, don't you?"

"Morning coffee goes right through me," Jack answers.

"You go first and I'll watch the cycle," Hannah says. She indicates the saddlebag with a nod. "I mean, these aren't locked on or anything, are they?"

"Okay," Jack replies. He'd had two mugs of coffee at the Fredericksburg Ramada Inn. One of his partners, discussing the challenges of aging, quipped that you can tell a man has passed a milestone when "frequency and urgency" refers more to urination than to sex.

"Hey, I was just thinking," Hannah calls out as Jack is walking toward the building. He looks back. "We could save some money if we got just one hotel room tonight."

Huh, Jack reflects, I never got an offer like that

driving the BMW. He doesn't imagine he will take her up on it. More likely, he'd say he'd pay for her room. But he's been doing a lot of things he never imagined. And, years ago, he did see that movie, *Lolita*.

He passes vending machines and a wall containing a big highway map of Virginia, turns into the men's room and finds himself standing at a urinal beside a man in his fifties, it looks like, wearing a denim jacket with the sleeves cut off. As he approaches the urinal, Jack notices that the back of the man's jacket reads "Devil's Disciples," with a grinning devil's head beneath the ornate script. He must be one of the motorcycle group from the parking lot.

As they're both washing their hands, Jack notices in his peripheral vision that the man is wearing a golf shirt under the open jacket, jeans with a pressed-in front crease and square-toed Frye boots that look new. He has no visible tattoos. He certainly doesn't fit Jack's idea of an outlaw of the open road. The man glances over at Jack, gives him a friendly nod, dries his hands with a blower, and leaves first.

Jack walks outside and looks around. He can't see Hannah or his Harley. The building has two fronts, each facing a parking lot, so he must have gotten turned around. He walks through the open center atrium of the building and scans the front row over there. Still no Hannah or Harley. What's up with this? He notices that there is no truck parking area on this side, so it must have been the other side where he parked. He goes back through the building and over to the place where he thinks he parked. There is one empty space. He gets a feeling like you do when you've misplaced your wallet or cell phone, but worse: he's somehow misplaced a girl and a motorcycle.

Did he leave the key in the ignition? He pats his pockets. Not there. Maybe Hannah couldn't wait for him, and went to the ladies' room, leaving the key, and someone drove off with his motorcycle. When she comes out, he won't be angry, it was an honest mistake.

Jack waits for five minutes or so, and she doesn't come out. He goes inside to the ladies' room entrance, thinking to call out her name. Instead, he stops a middle-aged woman on her way in.

"Excuse me, sorry to bother you," Jack says to the woman. "Im looking for my daughter. Would you mind seeing if there's a teenaged girl in there with short reddish hair, wearing a T-shirt and shorts? Her name's Hannah."

The woman looks him over. "I suppose I could do that," she answers. But she doesn't make a move toward the ladies room. Maybe she's suspicious about the intentions of an older guy wanting to extricate a teenage girl from a rest stop bathroom.

"She's been in there quite a while, and I'm concerned she might be ill," Jack explains.

"Okay," the woman says. She disappears into the bathroom, and comes out a moment later. "No one like that in there. Sorry, mister. I hope you find her."

So he's lost another daughter. Plus his ride and all his valuables. Maybe she was kidnapped.

He goes back out to the rest stop parking area. A boy is holding a leash while a golden retriever sniffs around on the lawn, and families are picnicking on benches on a concrete pad under a shelter beside the main building. Over in the truck area, a big white, yellow and green Mayflower moving van roars to life and begins pulling out of its double space. Are Hannah and his Harley in that van, with Hannah tied up and gagged? While he's considering running after the van, shouting, it moves away and exits the lot, leaving Jack wondering what a good next move would be for a guy on foot with no I.D., cash, credit cards, or cell phone out here in the middle of wherever the hell he is. He goes back inside the building and uses a pay phone—he didn't know there still were pay phones in this cellular age—to call 911.

No more than ten minutes later, a Virginia State Police cruiser pulls up. Jack walks over and identifies himself as the person who called. As they stand beside the cruiser, Jack tells his sad tale to Sgt. William Bronson, a man in his thirties with a blond crew cut and soft Virginia accent, who doesn't react one way or another to the case of a man who should know better than to let himself be scammed by a teenaged grifter.

"Need a ride somewhere, Mr. Tanner?" Sgt. Bronson asks after he's taken down all the relevant information, including a description of Hannah, No-Last-Name.

Jack is about to accept the offer when he notices someone walking toward him from the truck lot. It's the Devil's Disciple from the men's room.

"Excuse me, but I saw a girl riding away on a Harley-

Davidson, and she threw these over there by the exit ramp" the man says, holding up Jack's saddlebag. "I figured something might be wrong." He has a New England accent, maybe Maine, or Massachusetts.

Jack takes the saddlebag, rummages around inside, and finds it filled with his clothing and toilet kit, but nothing else. Who knows why Hannah tossed the saddlebags? Who knows why she stole his motorcycle? Who knows why he picked her up? His former partner Ted Berquist used to say, "You're only as old as the women you fuck." Good old Ted. You couldn't say Ted was a gentleman, but you couldn't say he was entirely wrong, either. Did Jack really think this girl would want anything more from a fifty-two-year-old man than a ride? Well, Hannah did want more. She wanted his cash, credit cards, cell phone, and motorcycle, and she got them.

"Yes, they're mine, thanks very much," Jack tells the man.

"I'm sorry about your Harley," the man says. He offers his hand. "I'm Harold Whittaker, from Boston."

Jack takes Harold's hand. "Jack Tanner, from Minneapolis."

"Do you want a ride, Mr. Tanner?" Sgt. Bronson says with a bit of annoyance in his voice.

"My friends and I are heading to Daytona Beach for Bike Week," Harold says to Jack, indicating with a nod a group of five other men standing beside motorcycles—his fellow Devil's Disciples, apparently—looking their way. "We can give you a ride to the next town, or wherever."

Jack doesn't know what Bike Week is, but maybe

that's where he'll find Hannah and his Harley. "I'd appreciate that," he says.

Sgt. Bronson gives a whatever-floats-your-boat shrug. He reaches into the cruiser and comes out with a business card, which he hands to Jack. "You can check in with the duty officer to see if we've found your cycle."

"Thanks for your help," Jack says. The sergeant gets in the cruiser and drives away.

"Do you know that girl?" Harold asks.

"We just met," Jack answers. "She was hitchhiking. I don't even know her last name."

Harold takes a cell phone from his pocket and offers it to Jack. "I expect you've got some calls to make. Just come on over when you're done. We've got rooms booked in Richmond for tonight. Be happy to stake a fellow outlaw to dinner and a room so you can relax and get yourself organized."

Jack powers up Harold's BlackBerry as he walks toward his group. Whom to call? Pete Dye, but the phone number is in his wallet. What about Helen Abelard, the office administrator at Hartfield, Miller? She'd take care of everything: notifying his credit card companies and bank, ordering replacement cards to be FedExed, getting some cash to him, notifying his insurance company, and anything else that needs doing. Of course, he doesn't work there anymore. But he's always been pleasant to Helen. Jenna was in charge of sending her a nice fruit basket at Christmas, although the last few holidays have been missed.

Helen says she's happy to help, no problem at all.

She'll track down the info, and conference him in as needed to get the proper authorizations for his accounts. "We've all missed you," she says. Maybe she has, but certainly not his partners, who fired him.

Jack goes over to where Harold and his friends are waiting. Harold introduces him all around: "Jack, this is Tom Jarvis, Alan Dupree, Bill Standish, whom we call Miles, because his ancestors came over on the Mayflower, Langdon Lamont, and Victor Purcell."

Tom is tall, with light brown hair and the broad shoulders of a collegiate rower, which he was. Alan is short, pear shaped, with a round face and thinning hair. Miles is bald and wears round wire-rimmed glasses; Jack imagines that he wears a bow tie to work. Langdon is handsome, tall and lanky, with slicked-back sandy hair and an aquiline nose. Victor is of medium height and has a grey brush cut.

All of them wear the Devil's Disciple colors on denim or leather jackets; all are as well groomed as Harold Whitaker; all are pleased to meet Jack; all have Harold's New England accent. except for Langdon Lamont, who speaks with a Southern drawl, heavier than the state trooper's, slow and sweet as blackstrap molasses. No one indicates in any way that Jack is the naive idiot that he is. Gentlemen all.

Jack is of course wondering what kind of motorcycle gang this is. Harold saves him from asking.

"We're all from the Boston area, except for Langdon, who's from Atlanta and owns a summer place on the Vineyard. I'm an investment banker. Tom is a professor at the Harvard Business School, Alan owns companies,

Miles is in book publishing, Vic is a developer of shopping malls, and Langdon chose the right parents, so he mostly sails and works on lowering his golf handicap."

"I represent that remark," Langdon says, grinning.

"I'm a lawyer, from Minneapolis," Jacks says, and then admits, "that was my first motorcycle."

Alan smiles. "I imagine, with your hourly billing rate, you can buy another one." Jack doesn't mention that he's no longer employed.

"There's a Harley dealer in Richmond," Langdon says. "But as you can see, we prefer other brands."

Jack checks out their rides. All Japanese: a big Honda, two Suzukis, three Yamahas. They are all styled after various Harley-Davidson big-bike models, disguising their Asian provenance nicely, wide and low, with wide fenders, gleaming chrome and richly flecked paint jobs. The kick-ass Harley look, with Japan's superior technology and fit and finish. Like a Lexus in Corvette clothing, Jack thinks. And like this group of successful professionals masquerading as the Wild Bunch.

"Very nice bikes," Jack says. "How long have you all been doing riding together?"

"Harold, Alan, and I go back nine, ten years," Tom says as he extracts a cigar from his saddlebag, along with a silver cutter and a flip-top Zippo lighter bearing a crimson Harvard crest. He clips off one end, lights up, and takes a long, luxurious drag, the white smoke curling upward as if announcing a new Pope. "The other guys joined us more recently."

"I saw a program about motorcycle gangs on the

Discovery Channel," Jack says. "The Devil's Disciples seemed to be one of the main ones, along with the Hell's Angels, the Outlaws, and some others."

Miles Standish grins. "You're wondering how a bunch of WASPy Yahoos like us were admitted into one of those highly selective organizations. Like a scholarship kid being tapped for Skull and Bones?"

Langdon grimaces and walks about fifty feet away, turning his back to the group.

"I always do that just to piss him off," Miles says. "He's a Yalie and a member of that esteemed club. Whenever you speak its name, a member must leave the room."

Langdon laughs and strolls back over. "Here's the deal, Jack. Rule Number One is, everything has a price. I read in *Cycle World*, or maybe it was *American Iron*, that the Disciples decided to cash in on their rep by offering franchises."

"Very high concept," Victor says.

"So I had my lawyer look into it," Alan adds. "Surprisingly, it was legit. Initial franchise fee of fifty K, annual dues of five K each, special assessments for things like their legal defense fund. We get to wear the colors, plus we get preferred parking at Daytona Bike Week and Sturgis, and a newsletter with reviews of new cycle models and stories like the best biker bars in Arizona. They even offer discounted motorcycle insurance through GEICO."

"So far, there are eight other franchises around the country," Harold explains. "And then there are the *real* chapters, they don't say how many, on the outside and in prisons."

"There will be a Disciples hospitality tent at Daytona," Langdon tells Jack. "We dropped in the first year. We were in fact welcome. Turns out they have a finely tuned sense of irony. You gotta love that. But let's just say they party a little harder than we're comfortable with, so now we find our own happy hour."

"How often do you guys go out riding?" Jack asks.

"Schedules are hard to coordinate," Vic answers. "We get out maybe one weekend a month, cruising to Gloucester for a clam roll or up into Vermont for the fall colors. And then we do this annual ride to Daytona."

"There's also an annual gathering in Sturgis, South Dakota," Vic says.

"It's too long a ride," Harold adds. "And the other problem is, when you get there, you're in South Dakota."

Tom's cigar is burned down to the band. He drops it onto the tarmac, crushes it out with his boot, then picks it up and deposits it into a trashcan on the median, which a real Devil's Disciple probably would not do.

"Time to saddle up, Jack," Harold announces. "Ride with me," he offers. "This is a new Honda Gold Wing. Heated seat, satellite nav system, heavy-duty suspension, even an air bag. Very comfortable."

Vic chuckles. "Easy on his hemorrhoids."

Harold takes out a white helmet, offers it to Jack, and then swings up onto the saddle. "It's my wife's, but it should fit. She likes it roomy."

"Thanks," Jack says. "I really do appreciate this."

Mrs. Whitaker's helmet does fit. He finds a place for

his saddlebags, swings himself up and grips the back of the seat as Hannah did.

The others buckle on their helmets, mount up, and six engines turn over with a sound that is higher pitched than that of Jack's Road King, wherever it is. They roll out of the lot, two abreast, Harold and Jack in the third set back, and power out onto I-95 South, six *ersatz* Devil's Disciples, plus one unaffiliated tax attorney wondering where his own motorcycle is heading, what sort of charges might be appearing on his Visa and Amex Black cards, and what he might find around the next bend in the road.

10: MIRROR, MIRROR ON THE WALL

THE NAME ON Hannah's birth certificate is Teri DuShane. She is from Toledo, not Fargo. She is one of those girls who developed a woman's body early, at twelve-going-on-thirteen, attracting the attention of older men, including a nineteen-year-old cousin, a thirty-year-old gym teacher, and a fifty-eight-year-old neighbor who owned a chain of strip clubs and recruited her as a dancer when she left home at fourteen because her stepfather had begun to pay special attention to her, too. Now, at twenty, Teri has been around the track enough times to know that sex is power, that men think with their dicks, and that she can use this insight to make her way in the world.

Early on the morning of the day she met Jack Tanner, she had stood nude in the bathroom of a Days Inn located off U.S. 77 somewhere in West Virginia. She used a single-edged razor blade to cut out and arrange two thin lines of white powder from the pile of cocaine she'd poured from a plastic baggie onto a plastic room-service menu. She lifted the menu to her nose, inhaled one of the lines and shuddered as the drug dilated her pupils and elevated her blood pressure, heart rate, respiratory rate, and body temperature.

"Ahaaa," she purred. A cat with a bowl of warm milk. She rotated slowly before the mirror over the sink, arms outstretched, observing her good body. There was that skull-and-crossbones tattoo on her ass, she thought. Serves me right, washing down dexies with tequila shots, then snorting a few lines and telling the tattoo guy he could choose the tat. A rose would have been nicer, or even a barbed wire ring around a bicep. Who did he think she was, a friggin' *pirate*? However, she knew a girl, another dancer, who, after a fight with her boyfriend followed by a drunken binge, woke up with a tattoo that said, "I fucked your brother." Live with *that* Louise.

Teri checked herself out often like this to ensure that the miles of hard road she'd traveled in her young life, the drinking and drug use and sport fucking and occasional beating when she'd made a bad choice at closing time at whatever bar she'd drifted into, hadn't, by the age of twenty, eroded her good looks, which were her main assets in this life.

"Mirror, mirror on the wall, who's the best piece of

ass of all?" she recited aloud, remembering the first part of that phrase from some Disney movie she'd seen as a child. How many years did she have left before the mirror answered, "Not you, babe"?

Teri carried the menu into the bedroom, where a man in boxer shorts lay on the bed watching an episode of "Oz" on TV. Bobby Purvis had the bulky muscles and crude tats of an ex-con, which he was. "Ex" in the sense of not currently being incarcerated, but not in the sense of being considered by the State of Georgia to have paid his debt to society for a long list of crimes and misdemeanors.

His most recent conviction was for aggravated assault. Bobby was watching a football game in the Tight End Sports Bar & Grill in Valdosta. When another patron made the mistake of cheering when the Minnesota Vikings scored on Bobby's Atlanta Falcons, Bobby expressed his displeasure by hitting the man on the head with a longneck beer bottle. "Cheer about that, asshole," Bobby told the man, who was unconscious on the floor.

After serving eighteen months of his three-to-five-year sentence, Bobby decided it was time for some whiskey, and for some sex (with a woman for a change). So he walked away from a road gang laying hot asphalt on State Route 128 in Macon County. He thought he'd hole up for a while with his brother, who worked on the line at the Ford plant. He met Teri DuShane at Crazy Eddie's, a roadhouse out on Route 2, waiting for some guy who was buying her drinks to return from the men's room. Bobby took the stool next to her and asked, making a joke he'd used more than once, "What's a girl like you doing in a nice place like this?"

"Well," Teri answered with a response she'd used more than once, "they don't serve booze in church."

Then the guy who'd paid for Teri's draft Stroh's with a Four Roses shooter returned from the men's room. He was an older guy, late forties, early fifties, with a substantial gut, gray crew cut, and wad of twenties in his pocket in case he had to pay for more than drinks while trolling Crazy Eddie's for a blowjob out in the cab of his pickup. The place had been lucky for him before, but never with a pretty piece of young ass like this one.

"You're in my seat," the man said to Bobby, who ignored him as he continued chatting up Teri in search of the same thing and more.

The man tapped Bobby on the shoulder. "You hard of hearing, pal?"

Bobby turned, poked a finger into his gut and said, "Look *pal*, I just got out of the joint and if you're *lucky*, all I'll do to you is rip off your head and shit down your neck. If you're not lucky I'll fuck you *and* her. *Do you feel lucky?*"

Without hesitation, the man took Bobby for a man of his word and left the bar with his wad of twenties and needy dick in search of a safer fishing hole.

After a few drinks, Bobby confided to Teri that he was heading to Canada, Toronto, or maybe Vancouver, but if she wanted to come along with him, he was open to other suggestions. She said she'd always wanted to go to Daytona Bike Week down in Florida. Bobby thought that was a great idea; he'd trade his stolen Mercury Grand Marquis for a stolen motorcycle and head on down to the party.

"Breakfast is served," Teri said as she passed the menu over to Bobby. He took his hit and slapped her on the ass, which meant he wanted some more sex as a chaser. The cocaine and kit bag of other assorted pharmaceuticals belonged to Bobby, so she was happy to oblige.

Afterward, as they lay in bed, Bobby said, "I'm running low on cash, so I thought we'd maybe stop up at that 7-11 I noticed when we pulled off the Interstate."

TERI WAITED IN the Mercury, parked in front of the 7–11, and fired up a Kools Menthol while Bobby went in and took two quart bottles of Miller Hi-Life, a bag of pork rinds, and a two-pack of Tastycakes Creamies to the counter.

The clerk, Laurence Stemphill, rang up the order. "That'll be eight dollars and forty-two cents, mister," he told Bobby.

Bobby grinned, showing his nicotine-stained teeth, pulled a .22 Ruger from the waistband of his Levis and said no, the clerk was mistaken, his groceries were free. "You can put them, along with all the cash in the register, in a bag," Booby said, "and I'll be on my way."

Laurence Stemphill was a pimply adolescent with a buzz cut and scrawny, pale white arms protruding from his T-shirt. Bobby assumed he'd be scared shitless by the sight of the Ruger. Assumed incorrectly, as it happened, because the boy was a Neo-Nazi skinhead who'd taken the 7–11 job recently because he knew the store had been robbed twice before. Armed robberies were par for the course for 7–11s, Lawrence knew, even though they shoved the cash into safes and put up signs saying the clerks didn't have the combinations, which they didn't. Apparently, solid analytical reasoning wasn't one of the requirements to be an armed robber. Lawrence was in that 7–11 when he saw a sign saying a clerk's position was open, apply at the counter. He applied, delighted to discover a profession where they actually paid you to do easy, inside work, while waiting for a gunfight to erupt.

Laurence shrugged and said in a friendly manner, "Sure, no problem," as if the guy had asked for the key to the men's room. He punched open the cash drawer, which held no more than fifty and change, and at the same time reached under the counter for his Colt revolver, loaded with hollow-point bullets. Without hesitation, still smiling, he brought up the Colt and shot Bobby Purvis through the heart.

Hearing the shot, Teri saw through the front window that the clerk was still standing and was holding a gun, so it was Bobby who was down. Not good. Not good at all. She flipped the cigarette out the window, slid over to the driver's side, found that Bobby had left the keys in the ignition as she'd hoped, and peeled off, not wanting to wait around for the clerk to come out after her. Daytona would still be a great party, even without Bobby. But just north of the McLean exit, the damn car blew a tire and she walked away from it. She would hitch to Daytona.

Before long, Jack What's-His-Face showed up. When he left Teri alone with his cycle at the rest stop, keys (again) still in the ignition, Teri just took off on an impulse, not having planned to rip the guy off. But what the hell, if he was stupid enough to leave her with his brand new Road King … Candy from a baby.

She started it up, gunned away from the restrooms, then pulled over just before hitting the highway entrance ramp, eased the cycle down on its stand and examined the contents of the saddlebag to see what was useful and what could be jettisoned. She found a wallet, looked at Jack Tanner's driver's license photo, shook her head and smiled, thinking, guys like this are soooo easy to scam when teen pussy is dangled before them. She took out the cash, twenties, fifties and hundreds mostly, she'd count it later, and the credit cards, and stuffed it all in the pocket of her shorts. She rummaged around and decided there was nothing else in there she could use. She put the wallet back and tossed the bag over onto the grass. Might as well leave the poor jackoff with his toothbrush and underwear. After all, he *was* nice enough to give me a ride.

The guy would be reporting his Harley and credit cards stolen any minute, but maybe she could make a few quick purchases with the cards before they got turned off, a few cartons of Kools, and a steak dinner, at least, then try to sell the bike for a big discount at a bar or a truck stop.

Maybe she'd go to Philly. She'd never been there, but she heard they had those good cheese-steak sandwiches.

Or to New York, which she'd always wanted to see. Or maybe she'd go down to Daytona after all, hitch a ride with one of the outlaw biker wolf packs sure to be heading that way on the interstate, then hook up with a guy who could handle himself in a gunfight better than Bobby Purvis.

11: WE BAND OF BROTHERS

COCKTAIL HOUR IN Richmond, Virginia, a glowing red sun low on the horizon, as six motorcycles roll up the brick driveway of the Jefferson Hotel on West Franklin Street and brake to a stop under the broad front portico of the elegant century-old limestone structure. The finely tuned Japanese engines, sounding like a swarm of locusts compared to the jungle-cat growl of Jack's missing Harley, echo under the portico roof. The boys cut them off, lever down their kickstands, and stiffly ease off their saddles.

Usually, the management of a venerable ultra-luxe hotel such as The Jefferson would not be pleased by the arrival of a motorcycle gang, even one with reservations. But the Boston chapter of the Devil's Disciples always stays here on the way to Daytona Bike Week. These gang members, once they have showered off the road dust and dressed up like their real selves for dinner, fit the hotel's target demographic perfectly. They have made themselves known as gentlemen and generous tippers, so the Jefferson staff is always delighted when they arrive. Their individual preferences are on file in the computer: an extra-firm mattress, a particular brand of mineral water on ice in the room, down pillow or foam pillows, a massage appointment, a six-pack of Sam Adams or champagne or Laphroiag single malt Scotch whiskey ... These special needs are always accommodated.

"Hope these digs are acceptable," Harold Whittaker tells Jack as Harold takes a ticket from the valet parking attendant, who has welcomed him back to the property by name. "When we stopped at the battlefield, I called ahead to add you to our group. King, non-smoking."

Tom Jarvis is one of those Civil War buffs who dress in uniforms of the Blue and the Grey for battle reenactments, and have elaborate set-ups in their basements depicting troop movements in famous battles. To accommodate his passion, the Disciples always make a detour to the Fredericksburg and Spotsylvania National Military Park for a walk around what historians term "the bloodiest landscape in North America."

Jack had never studied the subject, but was truly moved by the vistas of the fields and woodlands where so many young men fell: more than 85,000 wounded and 15,000 killed. Numbers so large as to defy comprehension. Compared to this, is the loss of one daughter so tragic?

Yes, it is, to Jack. Catastrophes defy comparison to one another. If you lose a child, knowing about the carnage of a Civil War battlefield is sad, but of no comfort.

Jack eases off his helmet, puts his hands on his hips and bends backward with a groan. "Sounds perfect," he says. "It's been a long day. At this point, I could crash in a smoking room at a Motel Six."

The valet is a young man dressed in the attire of a gentleman who might have roamed the streets of Richmond when Thomas Jefferson was in the White House. As he drives off on Harold's big Honda, two other young men similarly attired swing open the hotel's ornate brass front doors.

Inside the lobby, Jack takes in the soaring seventy-foot ceiling, stained glass skylight, faux-marble columns, tapestries, stone floors, and antique furnishings. Yes, these digs will do nicely after a long day riding as a passenger on the Honda. He thinks about how much Jenna would like this hotel, and Hope, too.

After being shown to his room by a Continental soldier carrying his saddlebag over his shoulder, Jack collapses onto an upholstered armchair, pulls off his boots, kicks his legs up onto the footstool, and takes stock of his situation. Here he is in a very nice hotel room with a fireplace (the Continental soldier, with Jack's approval, has touched off a crackling blaze) in the capital of the Confederacy, with no vehicle, or cash, or credit cards, or his own means of transportation. Harold Whittaker kindly gave the desk clerk an imprint of his own card to guarantee Jack's payment, and Harold tipped the bellman for him.

A bottle of Dom Perignon is chilling in a silver bucket on the table beside his chair, a surprise that Harold, taking Jack for a man of refined tastes, must have requested. Jack takes this as a compliment, although just about any alcoholic beverage would do at this point. He pops the cork, pours half a glassful into one of the two crystal flutes, takes a sip, closes his eyes and reviews his options.

Thanks to Helen Abelard at Hartfield, Miller, overnight couriers are scheduled to deliver new ATM and credit cards in the morning, so he will be back in business. He can find the local Harley-Davidson dealer Harold mentioned and buy a new ride, or maybe switch brands. He liked the comfort of Harold's big Honda and the look of the Suziki and Yamaha, with their nice paint jobs and high-pitched engines that seemed to want to run away from the pack. Or he could cab it to the airport, fly to Miami like an adult, and figure out transport to Key West from there. Or rent a car in Richmond and drive to Key West, if he wanted to continue the road trip in a less adventurous, but more comfortable, style. Or catch a flight back to Minneapolis, an option that is always on the table.

He stares into the dancing flames in the fireplace. He can feel its warmth. He has another one of those flashbacks, this one of a snowy winter evening at home in Edina, the family gathered around the hearth when Hope was young, toasting marshmallows in the fireplace. Maybe Hope will suddenly reappear the way those two kidnapped girls did after so many years, what were their names? And then Jenna would be healed, and all this good fortune would have included his own healing, and ...

The ringing of the room telephone jars him out of this Land of Maybes. He pushes himself up out of the chair, walks over to the desk, and answers.

"Jack Tanner."

"Jack, it's Harold. Will you join us for cocktails down in the bar?"

"Sure. Sounds good."

"Great, we're all going right down. See you momentarily."

Jack rummages around in the saddlebags, extracts a pair of rolled-up khaki slacks, a green polo shirt, tan v-neck sweater, and the Topsiders. He will have to go without a blue blazer. He hadn't planned on cocktail hour with a group of Boston swells in a fancy Old-South hotel.

JACK FINDS THE boys sitting in leather club chairs in the oak-paneled bar, located off the lobby beside the hotel's main dining room. Oil paintings on the walls depict scenes of fox hunting and blue-water sailing.

Harold signals to a waitress that they're ready to order drinks. Jack asks for a draft Heineken, the others cocktails or wine; Langdon, a Southern dandy of the old school, wants a Ramos Gin Fizz.

"I like this hotel," Jack tells them. "Very Antebellum. A throwback to a time when Northerners were still welcome in the Old South."

Victor Purcell replies, "And with this recession, our Yankee greenbacks are certainly welcome. I know the owner. He's a big-time real-estate developer. Built Hilton Head, among other things."

The drinks arrive. Miles Standish, who, Jack recalls, owns a publishing house, stands and raises his glass for a toast. The others all stand too, holding their glasses high. Jack follows their lead.

Harold explains, "The first year we stayed here, one of us, I can't remember who, offered a toast as we had our pre-dinner drinks. Then the rest of us offered one, too. It's become a tradition, just like the stop at the battlefields."

Victor goes first. "To absent friends and understanding wives."

Alan is next. "To the finer things in life: English tailoring, French wines, Italian sports cars, Swiss watches, Scandinavian women, and American steaks."

Tom takes a Cohiba from his shirt pocket. "And Cuban cigars!"

Then Langdon. "To ending the estate tax."

Next is Harold, Jack's chauffeur. "To Jack Tanner, man of the law, man of the open road, and, for the moment at least, pedestrian."

Laughter all around.

Miles, the book publishing company owner, clears his throat. "Here's to we few, we happy few, we band of brothers."

"Here, here," they all say, clinking glasses. "To we band of brothers!"

"As is customary," Miles adds, "I buy dinner if any

among you can identify the source of my quotations."
He smiles at Jack. "So far, I've never had to."

After a few moments, Alan exclaims, "I have it! That
book by Stephen Ambrose, about the World War Two
infantry platoon. *Band of Brothers.*"

"That's it," adds Tom. "And the TV miniseries based
on the book. The captain says it before the Battle of the
Bulge."

"Pathetic," Miles says. "These are of course the
immortal words of King Henry V, put in his royal mouth
by the late great William Shakespeare. His St. Crispin's
Day speech on the eve of the Battle of Agincourt.
Ambrose did take his title from the work I cite. Still, I'm
looking for original source material, so my wallet is safe
for another year."

They look at Jack. His turn. This is important. A test
to see if he measures up. A guy thing. But his mind is
blank of famous quotations, of relevant sentiments, of
everything. Then something does come to mind.

He raises his glass. "No deduction otherwise allowable
under this chapter shall be allowed for any item with
respect to an activity which is of a type generally
considered to constitute entertainment, amusement,
or recreation, unless the taxpayer establishes that the
item was directly related to, or, in the case of an item
directly preceding or following a substantial and bona
fide business discussion …"

Puzzled looks from the group.

Tom, the Harvard Business School professor, grins.

"The tax lawyer quotes the United States Tax Code!"

"Showing that our annual jaunts are not deductible!" Alan delightedly exclaims.

"Unless we gin up some substantial business chatter along the way," says Langdon.

Victor gives Jack a hearty jab to the shoulder with his free hand. "Well done, Jack. I bet you can cite the chapter and verse of that section."

Jack hesitates. He's not a show-off.

"Go ahead," says Harold. "Strut your stuff."

"O.K.," Jack says. "Title 26, Subtitle A, Chapter 1, Subchapter B, Part IX, Section 274."

"Like Pat Robertson quoting the New Testament," Alan says. "Shakespeare is interesting, but you know the really important stuff. Well done, my man!"

Jack feels the glow of group acceptance, as warming as the wood fire in his room.

THE GANG IS in the Jefferson's main dining room, Lemaire, which is named, the back of the menu explains, for Etienne Lemaire, the man who served as Thomas Jefferson's Maitre d'hôtel from 1794 to the end of his presidency. White linen tablecloths, crystal glassware, heavy silver utensils, and a formally solicitous staff, as befitting what is, according to the menu, Richmond's only AAA Five-Diamond restaurant. The restaurant is full; the other diners are turned out in jackets and ties for the men, and long dresses for the ladies. Jack feels rumpled, but the Disciples lack knife-creases in their trousers, too, and no one, including the staff, seems to notice.

As they eat, the conversation ranges from signs that the economy may finally be bouncing back, to health care reform, the wars in Iraq and Afghanistan, and the rumor that the Lexus LS400 flagship sedan is finally being restyled. No one mentions the elephant at the table, that being the question: What was a Minneapolis tax lawyer doing on a Harley-Davidson in the company of a sexy young girl with felonious intent at a rest stop off I-95 in Virginia?

Jack knows that they are too polite to ask. On top of the glass of champagne in his room, and two draft beers in the bar, he has had his share of five bottles of fine wines served with dinner, and now a snifter of Cognac—quite a bit more than he usually drinks. He is feeling the relaxed warmth of the male fellowship, as well as gratitude for their roadside assistance in his time of need. Although he vowed to tell no one about the purpose of his trip, he did share it with Marissa Kirkland at the Arcadia B & B. These are men of substantial accomplishment and intelligence, whose opinion about his mission might be helpful.

When there is a lull in the conversation, Jack clears his throat and says, "Gentlemen, let me tell you a story, and see what you think."

12: MAGNIFICENT SEVEN

SEVEN MOTORCYCLES ROLL along the meandering band of I-95 South: three groups of riders, two-abreast, with Alan Dupree solo on point. Jack is positioned on the starboard side of the middle group, straddling an Alpine White BMW RX-70, purchased with his newly minted Visa card at a dealership on Jefferson Davis Highway, just south of downtown Richmond. He'd scanned the Yellow Pages over breakfast at the Jefferson and then made a morning tour of the local motorcycle dealers with the Disciples, again as a passenger on Harold Whittaker's Honda. Jack chose a BMW over another Harley or one of the Japanese models because he liked the look and has had good luck with the company's automobiles.

They were on the road by 10 a.m. It is a seven-hour run from Richmond to Savannah, where they will spend the night. The next day it will be about four hours down to Daytona Beach on Florida's Atlantic coast.

After Jack had spun out his sad story over dinner, the boys graciously insisted that they would accompany him to Key West and pass on Bike Week. They made it clear they were captivated by the righteousness of Jack's mission, by the sense of high adventure that outshone their planned week of slumming with the Daytona crowd, and by their shared desire to see how the story ended. Perhaps, by their presence, they might even influence the outcome, they suggested.

Jack protested, finally agreeing to at least spend a day or two with them in Daytona Beach; they would talk again about Key West. They promised to stay in Key West only for a Mojito or two, if that's what Jack wanted. The truth is, Jack would be glad to have the company. He knows that if he actually does confront Slater Babcock, anything can happen. If there is a body to be dealt with and it is Jack's, he would like people he knows, even if only for a few days, to handle his arrangements. He does not seriously believe it will come to that, but there is strength in numbers.

Jack raises the visor of his new helmet, white to match his bike, with a discreet BMW logo, and feels the wind on his face. He glances up to see a wedge of Canada geese heading north and wonders if the birds notice the earth-bound flock down below, heading the wrong direction for the migratory season. It's an open question whether or not Jack is heading in the wrong direction for any season. He recalls the hawk he saw floating in the Wisconsin sky, at the beginning of his trip. Natural creatures only kill what they can eat, Jack observes. Or to protect their young. They are not capable of murder.

EVEN THOUGH JACK had a big breakfast at the Jefferson Hotel—OJ, coffee, biscuits with sausage gravy, and one of the hotel's famous caramel rolls—it's nearly one p.m., and he's hungry. Great minds: right then, Alan, in the lead, points toward a sign announcing that the Five Aces Truck Stop & Cafe is at the next exit. The others, except Jack, who hasn't learned the signals, toot their horns twice to signal their assent. They lean into the exit and roll into the Five Aces parking lot.

The Five Acres dining room is packed. The only seats available are at the counter in the "Professional Drivers Section," reserved for truckers, whose rank in the hierarchy of interstate highway motorists calls for them to be segregated from the civilians, like officers from enlisted men at chow time. Tom Jarvis looks around, shrugs, and leads the way to the counter. They take stools as a waitress, who could be the twin sister of the one back at the Happy Chef in Wisconsin, comes over immediately and, without asking, fills the coffee cups at their places, hands them menus, and pulls her order pad out of her apron pocket.

"Okay if we sit here?" Harold asks her. "We're not professional drivers."

"Fine with me, darlin', if it's fine with those good ole' boys," she answers, nodding toward the other customers in the section, none of them paying attention to anything but their food. Jack sees a lot of meatloaf, chicken-fried steak, and hot roast beef and turkey sandwiches up and down the counter, everything floating in thick brown gravy and accompanied by mounds of French fries, hash browns, and mashed potatoes. He noticed that rolls of caffeine pills and Tums, boxes of Pepcid AC, and bottles of Maalox and Mylanta and Pepto-Bismol were for sale at the checkout counter, along with tubes of Preparation H; a cooler full of Red Bull stood nearby. After all the miles on a motorcycle, Jack can see the need for these products for men who make their living long-haul driving.

The gang orders blue-plate specials all around: chicken-fried steak with mashed potatoes covered with a white, floury gravy, and limp, overcooked green beans. A man who must weigh three hundred pounds, seated at the end of the counter, says to himself, loudly enough to be heard around the dining room, "Huh, looka that, buncha queers sitting in the drivers' section." Referring to the Disciples, of course, who look like what they are. Pretenders.

The big dude is dressed in bib overalls with no shirt and has what look to be prison tats on his massive arms: a swastika, a dagger with blue blood dripping off the point, and a Cupid's heart with whatever name was in the center scratched out. His long brown hair is tied back in a ponytail and he has a scraggly ZZ Top beard. Jack thinks of the movie *Deliverance*. He hears the "Dueling Banjos" theme song playing in his head. He realizes that he and his friends probably do look more like they're on their way to the Gay Pride Parade in Key West than to Daytona Bike Week.

"Bigfoot's got a big mouth," Langdon says, apparently not caring if the man hears. This startles Jack; he did not take Langdon, the genteel Southern patrician, to be a brawler.

The waitress is moving down the counter refilling coffee cups. When she gets to Bigfoot, he tells her, "I think my meal should be on the house, given that those buttfuckers are makin' me sick."

The waitress just smiles and goes into the kitchen. Bigfoot finishes, picks up his check and, as he passes the Disciples on his way to the checkout counter, says right at them, "Sure hope I don't run over any motorcycles on my way out of the lot." He must have seen them pull in.

Langdon slides off his stool, follows the man to the counter and taps him on the shoulder. What the hell is he doing? Jack wonders. The other Disciples seem unconcerned.

The man turns, regarding Langdon with puzzlement. "You need somethin', faggot, or do you just got a death wish?"

Conversations in the truckers' section pause as everyone watches this little drama play out. Langdon smiles, casually reaches into the pocket of his jeans, comes out with a pearl-handled, double-barreled derringer and pokes it into Bigfoot's big belly.

"Tell you what, you Neanderthal dickhead," Langdon drawls. "What say I accompany you outside and help you pull out to make certain that unfortunate possibility does not occur."

Jack wonders whether the sight of the pistol or the word Neanderthal surprises the guy more. After a tense moment, the room silent, the big man takes a step backward. "Fuck it, ain't worth the bother." He turns back to the cashier, a red-haired teenage girl with braces on her teeth, who didn't see the pistol, pays his check and leaves, muttering something to himself.

A man in his forties with a nametag on his shirt identifying him as Harlan, the restaurant's manager, is watching from the kitchen entrance as Langdon slides the pistol back into his pocket, walks back to the counter, where Jack, Harold, Tom, Miles, Victor, and Alan are still seated, and says, "Unless someone wants dessert, what say we hit the road."

As they slide off their stools, Vic says to Jack, "Langdon is a man of many facets. And he does have a concealed carry permit for that peashooter."

As Harold grabs the check, the manager walks over. "On the house, boys. We don't want our customers hassled like you were. But if you're ever back this way, please sit over there with the civilians."

IT'S DUSK AS the Devil's Disciples plus one arrive in Savannah. As they ride along, it is clear to Jack that this is the Old South: ante-bellum architecture, delicate strands of moss hanging down from live oak branches, and the pungent aroma of decaying vegetation. A man looking gnarled and ancient as the oaks strolls purposefully along a sidewalk on Gaston Lane Street. He sports a neatly trimmed Van Dyke and is nattily turned out in a white linen suit, Panama hat, and white buck shoes. He carries a battered brown leather briefcase, and taps the sidewalk on every stride with a brass-tipped walking stick.

Jack imagines the man and his son as attorneys in practice together, probably Vanderbilt grads. The firm's name is something like Beauregard & Beauregard, P.A., written on a shiny brass plaque bolted onto the front of an ivy-clad red brick row house. Maybe a bottle of Southern Comfort in the drawer of a scarred oak roll-top desk, to celebrate a courtroom victory, or a sunset. How much more genteel and satisfying than being in the harness at Hartfield, Miller, Simon & Swenson in that high-rise glass box in downtown Minneapolis. And in a father-son firm, you don't get fired.

The old gent glances at the passing motorcycle parade, noisy pistons drowning out the buzzing of the cicadas. He smiles and nods his head their way. If the Disciples were a bona fide motorcycle gang, and began circling and taunting this elderly fellow like Lee Marvin and his band in *The Wild One*, he might produce a derringer like Langdon's, or draw a sword embedded in the walking stick, and shoo them away.

Langdon has relatives in Savannah, he'd explained last night as they discussed their itinerary, an aunt and two cousins. The aunt, now in her eighties, is his father's sister, the cousins her sons. He has not seen or spoken with them in many years. Langdon's father, "a robber baron of the old school," became estranged from them for reasons only they knew, Langdon said. Langdon is an only child. When his father died, his entire estate was left to Langdon's mother, and a protracted court battle ensued over the aunt's claim on the estate.

"Her position was not without merit," Langdon admitted. "But our lawyer was slimier than hers—sorry, Jack—and she was left without a farthing. When mater joined pater in eternity, all that filthy lucre, much of it sheltered from the confiscatory estate tax in offshore accounts, became mine. God bless the Cayman Islands! Now I hear Aunt Lucy is in failing health, and my cousins, Jubal and Nathan, who are named for Confederate generals, have failed in a number of business enterprises, including a muffler shop franchise, a lumberyard, a used car lot, and a liquor store. How one could not make a go of a liquor store in Savannah is beyond me."

Here Langdon sips his brandy, as if reminded of it by his story. "I guess I'm getting soft in my old age, because I'm going to slip away while we're in Savannah, meet with the boys and do the right thing by the family, meaning that an appropriate amount of money will change hands." He smiled. "That being the only way family feuds ever do get resolved."

LANGDON LEADS THE motorcycle parade over brick streets, the cycles bumping along, to a small white-frame house surrounded by a black wrought-iron fence, located away from the fashionable neighborhoods and tourist attractions. Pots of red geraniums hang from the ceiling of a large front porch. There is no indication that this is anything but someone's residence.

Jack wonders if Langdon has other acquaintances in town to whom he does speak and who have invited them all to dinner, although he wouldn't guess that Langdon's friends would live in a neighborhood such as this. Here in the Old South it might be called "black bottom."

Langdon circles the house and they follow him into a parking lot covered with white gravel, so deep that Jack's rear wheel slides sideways and he almost dumps the BMW. A young boy watches from the front window of a shotgun shack across the street. A dog is barking somewhere. They dismount and take off their helmets. Jack picks up the scent of decaying vegetation and sweet magnolia blossoms in the heavy humid air.

"This is Mama Sally's," Langdon tells Jack. "Another regular stop for us. Only the locals know it. Aunt Lucy introduced me to it pre-estrangement. World-class fried chicken with hush puppies, grits, and collard greens. Pecan-crusted catfish, pork chops, and shoofly pie that is an orgasmic experience."

DINNER IS SERVED family-style at a large, round oak table, like the one at the Arcadia. It is covered with platters and bowls containing all the delicious victuals Langdon mentioned, as well as black-eyed peas, sweet potatoes, mashed potatoes, hot baking-powder biscuits with a pot of honey and a jar of peach preserves, and thick slices of country ham with a pitcher of red eye gravy, which is that evening's special entrée item. If nothing else, Jack is certainly being well fed on this trip. Maybe all he will gain from it is weight.

Mama Sally greets Langdon and the others with a hug and then is introduced to Jack. She is a slim, lovely, black woman of late middle age, wearing a starched white apron over a red silk blouse and white linen slacks. Jack had, from the name of the place, expected more of an Aunt Jemima type, and wonders if he is guilty of racist stereotyping.

"I hope you boys are hungry," Mama Sally says with a big smile. "If you're not, pretend you are, just to be polite."

The conversation over dinner is about anything but the sad history of the Tanner family, which Jack appreciates. As he takes a third helping of the golden crispy fried chicken from the communal plate, Langdon, for Jack's benefit, continues with his own family history.

"All my people are from Georgia, mostly Atlanta, where I was born," Langdon says. "Father moved us north when I was ten and began turning closed textile mills into factory outlet stores. It can be said he invented the concept, which evolved into the big-box concept, the Wal-Marts, Home Depots, Costcos, and such." He goes on to relate the additional details of a Southern Gothic kind of family history that rivals *Midnight in the Garden of Good and Evil.* Jack read that book and saw the movie and finds it all fascinating, a pleasant diversion from his own situation, all told over a great meal.

Dessert is the shoofly pie, plus hot peach cobbler with cinnamon ice cream churned in the kitchen, and strong coffee. And along with this, Miles offers another quotation: "Happy families are all alike; every unhappy family is unhappy in its own way." He adds, "I'm feeling content and generous so I'll just tell you that's from ..."

"Tolstoy's *Anna Karenina!*" Alan Dupree exclaims. "Had to read it in my comp lit class."

Miles looks annoyed just for a moment, then grins. "Okay, fair's fair, dinner's on me."

Yes, Jack thinks, draining his coffee cup and pushing back from the table, Tolstoy got it exactly right.

Bellies full of Mama Sally's good food, they ride over to the Mansion on Forsyth Park, a grand old Victorian in the historic district, now converted into a luxury hotel where, again, they are expected, and spend a restful night. Jack dreams that he is an infantry private (it is not clear in which army) in a bloody Civil War battle, and awakens without injury.

THE NEXT MORNING, they are on the road again, dropping down I-95 for the ride toward the Florida border and then through Jacksonville and the beachfront towns of the Palm Coast and into Daytona Beach. Jack has been honored with the point position, which he counts among the highest honors he has ever received.

Not far out of Savannah, they begin to encounter other

groups of riders headed south, roaring past them, way
over the speed limit, wolf pack after wolf pack of cycles
streaking toward the biggest annual gathering of like-
minded souls in the nation. They are mostly on Harleys,
Jack notes, plus a smattering of other big-shouldered
American brands like Indian and Buell and Victory, and
custom jobs of unidentifiable make. Lowriders and ape
bars and gleaming chrome and wild paint jobs no factory
produced. These are genuine outlaws, the real deals, Jack
thinks. On many of the rear seats are older women in
leather bustiers and teeny bops in skimpy bikinis; some
wear no tops at all and G-strings for bottoms. Jack is
reminded of Hannah, his felonious Lolita. A few women
ride their own bikes and look as though they could
kick the ass of any man who suggested they should be
relegated to a rear seat. All eyes front as they pass, not so
much as a glance over at Jack and Company, who, even
though they wear the colors of an actual cycle gang,
reveal their true colors by cruising at the speed limit, as
only pussies do.

The boys assured Jack they've never been hassled at
Daytona for showing up on their Japanese bikes. In fact,
a contingent of retirees from Boynton Beach showed up
last year on Vespas and was welcomed with amusement,
never having to buy their own drinks in the beer tents,
Langdon reported. The only real pariahs are those kids
zooming around on "crotch rockets," those high-speed,
low-slung racing bikes where you tuck yourself down
beneath a streamlined cowling, chest on the gas tank,
and gun it around town as if you're on the Daytona 500

race track, Miles explained. "Everyone hates those little shits," he said. "Me included."

As Jack spots the Daytona Beach exit coming up, Alan eases past him and takes the lead. Jack is grateful, because he doesn't know the way. They turn onto the exit ramp and swing east onto State Highway 92 toward the Atlantic Ocean, bikers everywhere, ready to party hearty.

The sun is descending below the yardarm. It is cocktail hour in Daytona Beach—a very different scene from the one in genteel Richmond, Jack thinks as the group begins to pass municipal light posts festooned with banners reading, "DAYTONA BEACH/WELCOME BIKERS." Clearly, the city is delighted to have the revenue Bike Week generates, Tom told Jack, but the residents would probably like it better if it came from a convention of free-spending Baptists or Knights of Columbus.

THE GROUP SWINGS off 92 and navigates along side streets around downtown Daytona Beach, impossibly congested with Bike Week traffic, then heads over the Main Street causeway across the Halifax River and onto a long, narrow barrier island, then turns left onto South Atlantic Avenue until they come up the community of Seabreeze, identified by a grey wooden sign with white lettering and a carved seagull.

Alan leads them into the driveway of a two-story white house built on stilts so that the first floor is a good eight feet above sea level. They kill the engines, lean their cycles onto their kickstands and dismount, stretching stiff backs, rotating necks, unbuckling their helmets as the hot engines tick.

"We always rent a beach house," Victor says. "Eight hundred a night during Bike Week, but it beats the hell out of a Budgetel, where the other guests are up all night shouting and fighting, or camping out on the beach, which gets even louder and funkier, and the mosquitoes bite like piranhas."

"Pricey, but not so bad divided by six," Harold adds.

"By seven," Jack says, grinning.

"The Magnificent Seven," says Alan, who is more into classic movies than classic literature, as he laughs and slaps Jack on the back.

THAT NIGHT, AS is the custom, Miles cooks steaks for dinner on a gas grill on the deck, which they eat with a salad Vic prepares, and several bottles of good cabernet sauvignon. Desert is a key lime pie. It is Harold's job to e-mail a list of provisions to the rental agent that will be waiting for them upon arrival. After dinner, they stay up late drinking Ramos Gin Fizzes, "a true Southern Gentlemen's drink," Langdon announces, which he prepares in the kitchen, while the others, who've seen this show before, sit out on the deck, finishing the wine and smoking cigars. Langdon learned the recipe during "a lost decade" in New Orleans, he tells Jack.

Jack, who'd never had a Ramos Gin Fizz, watches as Langdon, whistling "Swanee," blends gin, lemon juice, egg whites, sugar, cream, and orange flower water in a cocktail shaker, then adds soda water. He pours the creamy, frothy concoction into tall, chilled Tom Collins glasses and carries them outside on a big, plastic tray. They tell tales like Scouts around a campfire, while an electric bug catcher announces its kills with crackling zaps. Langdon makes several trips back into the kitchen to fix more gin fizzes. Jack loses count of how many he drinks; they go down easy, like milk shakes.

At three a.m., they call it quits and turn in. Jack can't remember the last time he's been this tipsy, and the difference between passing out in bed and falling asleep is a distinction without a difference.

In his dream, he has arrived in Key West:

WALKING ALONG DUVALL Street, Jack decides to grab lunch before tracking down Slater Babcock. He comes upon a place called Crabby Dick's, with an outdoor patio. He goes in and asks the hostess for a table out near the sidewalk. He's looking over the menu as the waitress comes over to take his order. She's a pretty young girl wearing a skimpy white T-shirt with a Crabby Dicks parrot logo and tight white shorts.

The nameplate pinned on her T-shirt says Bonnie—but it's Hannah, the motorcycle thief! Un-fucking-believable. She looks at Jack, and says, "Hey look, man, I'm sorry about what I did. really sorry." She smiles. "But maybe I can make it up to you."

She invites Jack to her apartment, and he says yes.

Maybe he is interested in hearing how a young girl—she was about Hope's age—went wrong. Maybe he can somehow save her ...

Hannah lives in a small, second-floor apartment above a tattoo parlor on Angela Street, around the corner and down two blocks from Crabby Dick's. When they're inside, she offers Jack a beer and then goes into the bedroom to change. He's drinking it while looking out a window that has a partial view of the water, when he hears her come out of the bedroom. He turns to find her smiling at him, in the nude. So this is how she means to make it up to him. He knows that many men, probably most men, would take her up on her offer, and call it even.

In fact, he's taking a while telling her he's not interested when she walks over to him, puts her arms around his neck and gives him an open-mouthed kiss on the lips. He is speechless—not only because Hannah's tongue is in his mouth, and he literally can't speak—but also because he's not at all certain he wants this kiss to end any time soon.

She ends the kiss, then licks her tongue into his ear and says, "Fuck me daddy ... Fuck your little girl ..."

Jack pushes her away. "What did you say?"

"Hey, take it easy. Older men always like that—the fuck-your-daughter thing. I could be your daughter's age, if you have one."

He grabs her by the arm and shouts, "You don't say that to me!"

Still smiling, she says, "You like it rough, huh? 'Cuz we can do that ..."

Right at that moment, the apartment door rattles open

and a man enters. The man looks to be in his thirties, short and thin, with the small, dark eyes of a rat, and acne scars on his face. He's wearing a wife-beater shirt that reveals scrawny arms, and dirty jeans and cowboy boots. He holds a silver revolver in his right hand.

"Hey, dude," the man says, his grin revealing nicotine-stained teeth. "You tryin' to fuck my girl?"

"No," Jack says. "I was just ..."

The man holds up his left hand, palm outward, to silence Jack.

"So what, then? You just come in to deliver a pizza and found her buck naked like this?"

Hannah goes into the bedroom and closes the door.

"Whatever you're doin' here, it's gonna cost you."

Hannah comes out of the bedroom, dressed in jeans and a halter top.

"Hey, Daryl, I kind of like this guy," she says. "Maybe we can work something out."

"What we're gonna work out, sweetie, is what we always work out," Daryl answers. "We take cell phone photos of you two in bed together, you suckin' his cock, him fuckin' your ass, whatever works. Then, if he's been a good boy, he gets to leave, without his cash and credit cards."

So he's been scammed twice by Hannah, he realizes. How dumb is that? He's no match for the denizens of the highway, not even the teenage girls.

13: BIKE WEEK

DAYTONA BEACH, DAY two, seven a.m., the beach house.

Jack awakens to the seductive aroma of bacon frying. He remembers the dream, half wondering now which of his worlds is the real one.

The bacon smell reminds him of boyhood Saturday mornings, when his father took over breakfast duties. The standing menu was blueberry pancakes with melted butter and heated syrup—one of Jack's cakes always formed into the letter "J"—plus thick-cut smoked bacon, freshly squeezed OJ, and creamy whole milk—none of that thin, fat-free, one, or two-percent stuff of today. The syrup came in a metal can the shape of a little log cabin. These cabins were rinsed and lined up on a shelf in

Jack's bedroom; he must have had a north woods village of thirty of them by the time he graduated from high school and left for Ann Arbor. He hadn't thought about any of that for decades. So far this ride to Key West seems more a trip down memory lane than a transformation of any kind. He is still good old Jack Tanner, as far as he can tell, now with a three-day growth of whiskers. But presumably he is wiser about hitchhikers.

Their beach house has three bedrooms. Jack is bunking with Tom Jarvis in what is usually Vic Purcell's spot; over Jack's objections Vic insisted on taking the sofa bed in the living room. Jack checks his watch. Someone's up early in the kitchen. Tom is on his back, snoring. Jack swings his feet onto the floor, feeling a bit dizzy—way too many gin fizzes last night. Wearing only his boxer shorts, he follows the bacon smell into the kitchen. There he finds Vic, dressed in a T-shirt advertising the Black Dog Tavern on Martha's Vineyard, worn canvas sailing shorts, Crocs, Red Sox cap, and chef's apron, whipping up a feast of Belgian waffles, bacon and link sausages, fresh fruit, and OJ squeezed on a juicer.

"Wow," Jack remarks. "Is this a beach house or a cruise ship?"

Vic turns from the waffle maker on the center island. "Welcome aboard the S.S. Purcell! I can do waffles, pancakes, eggs any way you want, bagels and lox, and espresso, regular or unleaded."

Jack perches on a stool at the center island. "I'll start with a cappuccino, but I'll make it." He notices a fancy Gaggia espresso machine on the counter near the juicer.

It's got more controls than his entry-level Krups back home.

"Let me do it," Vic offers. "You could hurt yourself with that thing."

Soon the whole gang sits around the kitchen table, feasting on Vic's spread and chatting happily, like kids in the dining hall at summer camp.

"So what's today's agenda?" Jack asks.

Alan explains, "We always start with a ride up and down International Speedway Boulevard through the city. Then we head over to the beach, and take a stroll for a little exercise."

"Exercise being defined as ogling the topless babes," adds Miles.

"The trick being to savor the view without getting stomped by the girls' boyfriends," says Vic.

"Sounds like a plan," Jack says.

Langdon pushes back from the table, patting his full stomach. "Dinner is at a seafood place we like, a short ride up the coast in Ormond Beach. Basically one does not want to be in downtown Daytona after dark. That's when the vampires come out, if you catch my drift."

Jack does. "How bad does it get?"

"The great majority of Bike Week attendees are well-behaved," Harold answers. "But there are some who come looking for trouble, and they find it. Often they're not the bikers. You get survivalist rednecks, gangbangers, Florida crackers who don't like outsiders taking over their town. And everyone's armed. Florida's gun laws are pretty much the same as Dodge City's in the days of

Wyatt Earp. Best for the likes of us to steer clear."

Vic is clearing the breakfast dishes. "Law enforcement does a good job, but they can't be everywhere all the time. There were three shootings last year, one a fatality, all after midnight. Of course, nobody saw anything. And some hillbilly ran his Ford F-150 right into a crowd on a sidewalk. Killed three people before the truck went through the plate glass window of a dry cleaner. The crowd dragged him out and stomped him to death."

"The seafood place in Flagler sounds good," Jack says.

"It's the Green Dolphin Inn on Oceanshore Boulevard," Langdon explains. "Best fried clam rolls this side of Gloucester, Mass. No reservation, shirt, or shoes required, all major credit cards accepted."

DAY THREE, TWO p.m., sunny and eighty-four degrees.

They are strolling the beach, shirtless, in shorts or bathing suits. Two days of this have filled in their cycle-rider, a.k.a. farmer, tans with a bronze tone all over, not just on their arms. Jack's beard is emerging from the I-didn't-shave-this-morning to the full commitment phase. He is feeling fit and relaxed, even happy.

A moderate wind has raised small whitecaps, good enough for the surfers and boogie boarders. As advertised, there are women lying topless on towels, or taking dips in the ocean, some of them young and drop-dead sexy, others longer in the tooth and floppier in the boobs, but a good time is being had by all. Jack, who never saw this kind of thing on Minnesota lake beaches, is almost getting used to it, to the extent that he can walk along without fear of tripping or bumping into someone.

And then, all of a sudden, there she is, the last person he expected to see, here or anywhere, except in his dreams: Hannah the felonious hitchhiker, wading out of the surf, topless, bikini-bottomed, then strolling toward a group of men and women, obviously a hardcore biker crowd, set up with coolers over by one of the lifeguard stations. Some are boisterously watching a beach volleyball game, others are just grab-assing around; all are drinking from plastic cups and beer bottles.

He stops. His companions don't notice. Is he dreaming again? He moves closer and sees it is not Hannah; it is another girl who could be her sister. He notices details: one of her nipples, and her navel, are pierced and she has a tattoo on her left buttock, a rose with thorns.

One of the bikers in the group the girl is approaching notices Jack watching her. He cuts out of the herd and comes over. He is tall, shirtless, with the carved physique of a serious weightlifter. "Like what you see, amigo?" he says. "That's Linda, and she's for rent. Five hundred for a half day, twelve hundred and she'll stay the night." Smiling as he says it. Just two guys talking business.

"Thanks," Jack answers, "but I have other commitments."

The man shrugs and heads back toward his group. *Thanks, but I have other commitments?* Jack thinks. How lame is that?

As Jack is walking away, Teri DuShane, who is standing on the ocean side of the lifeguard chair, recognizes him. She smiles, completely unconcerned. If I run into him around town, she thinks, I'll just come up with some dumbass story and he'll buy it. Probably buy me dinner, too.

DAY FOUR, NINE p.m., the Green Dolphin Inn.

The Boston Chapter of the Devil's Disciples has found five members of the Atlanta Chapter—at least the one that derives from wealthy Buckhead, there being a "real" chapter downtown—at the Green Dolphin Inn. Langdon knows one of the Atlantans; the family of Dixon "Dixie" Rutherford, Langdon explains, have been members of the Piedmont Driving Club, the city's most prestigious private social club, founded in 1887.

The Green Dolphin is an old-fashioned roadhouse, known for burgers, ribs, and the all-you-can-eat Friday fish fry. It attracts families, white- and blue-collar workers, and whoever else is rolling by on the highway. Jack notices that there appears to be no outlaw bikers in the place, which is probably why his friends make this one of their regular stops.

Langdon and Dixie are standing drinks at the bar when a woman in her forties, wearing jeans, a denim shirt, and cowboy boots, comes hurrying through the door and asks the bartender, "Who owns the cycles out in the lot?"

"They're ours," Harold answers.

"Well there's a monster truck rollin' right over the whole lot of 'em!" As both chapters of Disciples head for the door the woman calls out, "Already called 9-1-1."

Sure enough, a huge yellow truck with gigantic tires is plowing back and forth over thirteen motorcycles as the Steppenwolf song "Born to Be Wild" booms from the truck's sound system.

"Christ, it's the idiot from the truck stop that Langdon faced down," Alan yells over the roar of the truck's engine and the sound of metal being crushed. "He must have come into the bar and spotted us."

Langdon pulls out his Derringer and puts two rounds into one of the truck's huge tires, but the little .32-caliber slugs do no damage. Hearing the gunshots, Bigfoot grins, hits the brakes, and points a long-barrel revolver out of the driver's side window.

"Gun!" Miles shouts.

Everyone scatters, some running back into the bar, others taking cover behind cars, as Bigfoot begins firing off rounds, not seeming to actually aim at anyone, then roars off down U.S. 1.

Minutes later, two Volusia County Sheriff's cruisers, lights and sirens, come barreling down the highway from the other direction and squeal into the parking lot. Four deputies slide out and crouch behind the doors, guns drawn. Seeing only the wrecked cycles and people hiding behind cars, one of the deputies reaches into the cruiser, pulls out a microphone and says over the cruiser's PA system:

"Everyone face down on the ground, arms stretched out front!"

A moment of confusion, no one moving.

The deputy's amplified voice shouts: "On the ground now! Grab the dirt!"

Only when everyone is lying on the ground do the deputies ease out from behind the car doors.

"Nobody move 'till I say," another of the deputies orders. He walks over to a man in his twenties, puts his boot on the man's back, and says, "We got a call about a truck running over motorcycles, then another call about shots fired. First thing is, who was doing the shooting?"

"The guy in the truck," the man answers. "He drove off just before you arrived."

The deputy moves over to Langdon. "That right, pardner?"

Langdon starts to turn over as he answers; the deputy puts his boot hard on Langdon's back, pushing him back down.

"Didn't say turn over. I asked if that's what happened."

"Yes," Langdon answers, his face in the dirt. "We saw the guy a few days ago at a truck stop in Virginia. We didn't get along all that well."

As this deputy has been asking questions, the others have been moving from person to person, patting them down. One by one they all say, "Clear." No guns. Langdon has thrown his Derringer into a trashcan, where the deputies don't look. Later, he recovers it.

"Okay, y'all can stand up," the deputy wearing sergeant's stripes tells them.

As they get to their feet, Harold says, "Where's Tom?"

"Somebody missing?" the sergeant asks Harold.

"Got a man down!" one of the deputies calls out.

Tom Jarvis, the Harvard professor, is lying motionless on the gravel, with crimson blood pooling on the ground beneath his head.

DAY FIVE, SIX a.m., beach house kitchen.

They are the Magnificent Six now. Tom is dead. A bullet ricocheting off something hit him in the left temple, literally blowing his brains out.

One of the bar patrons got the license number of the truck. Calvin T. Laloosh, a.k.a. Bigfoot, is now in the Volusia County Jail, charged with murder in the first degree, which any competent public defender would be able to deal down to second degree, intent being hard to prove when you're high on alcohol and dexies and apparently not aiming at anyone.

Laloosh has been in trouble before, with assault convictions and firearms violations on his sheet. He did a three-year stretch in Raiford, the prison where the state's death chamber is located, offering the condemned a choice of lethal injection or electrocution—a choice Laloosh might now have to make, depending upon the skill of his lawyer. He is employed by Affiliated Van Lines, the coast-to-coast moving company, and lives alone in a trailer park in Deltona. He was arrested in his trailer without resisting and showed the Swat Team where to find his Mark XIX .50-caliber Desert Eagle semi-automatic pistol: in his pit bull's dog house behind the trailer. The dog was friendly and did not resist arrest either; he is now in the care of the Volusia County Humane Society.

None of the boys have slept. They were at the sheriff's headquarters most of the night giving statements, along with the other bar patrons who witnessed the events, and then at the county coroner's office identifying Tom's body. Harold called Kathy Jarvis in Cambridge to break the tragic news. She is flying to Daytona Beach later this morning, along with her two sons, Bob, an executive with a company in Seattle, and Tim, a partner in a New York private equity firm.

Vic has made scrambled eggs and toast but no one is very hungry. They are drinking strong espressos and dividing up the necessary tasks.

"So it's agreed," Miles says, checking the yellow legal pad on which he's been taking notes. "I'll coordinate with the funeral home in Cambridge on transportation and arrangements. Harold, you've got the family, Kathy and the boys, arriving at the airport at various times today. Alan is booking us on Tom's flight back to Boston. Vic is handling any follow-up with the Sheriff's Department. Langdon will stay in touch with the Volusia County District Attorney's Office about testifying at the trial."

"I can see about the cycles," Jack offers.

"Probably nothing there to salvage, but the insurance adjustors will want a look," Vic says.

Everyone falls silent, sipping espressos, left to their own thoughts about what has happened to their friend.

Jack envisions the "missing man" formation, as pilots do for a lost comrade, if these friends ever ride together again.

DAY SIX, NOON, Hertz rental counter, Daytona Beach International Airport.

Jack, wearing a golf shirt and khaki slacks, his riding gear packed into his saddlebag slung over his shoulder, is signing papers for a silver Taurus. The woman behind the counter looked at his driver's license photo, then at him, and he realized that with longer hair, deep tan, and the beard, he didn't look much like his old self. But she didn't say anything and processed the paperwork.

He said his sad good-byes to the fellows back at the cottage, then drove to the airport. They wished him luck and apologized for being unable to stay with him on the rest of his journey. He feels he's become as close to them in their brief time together as any friends he has, like soldiers who've been through combat together. Jack promised to let them know what happens in Key West.

When Jack was packing his saddlebag that morning, he found Langdon's Derringer tucked in beneath his boxer shorts. He thought about returning it, then put it back in the saddlebag.

14: THE UNINTENTIONAL TOURIST

AS JACK APPROACHES the entrance ramp to I-95 South heading out of Daytona Beach, he spots a girl with a backpack, hitchhiking. She is holding a cardboard sign reading "Key West," and turns it toward him, raising her eyebrows in expectation. She is pretty, with her brown hair twisted into braids and a radiant smile, in her late teens or early twenties, wearing jeans and a University of Florida "Go Gators!" T-shirt that exposes her belly.

Yeah, right, Jack thinks. Maybe she really *is* a nice college girl, like Hope, whom he should rescue from the possibility that a serial killer will be driving the next car that comes along. Or maybe the Gators T-shirt is a ruse, and she is another highway predator, like Hannah. Jack didn't opt for the extra car rental insurance. Does the basic Hertz package cover theft by renter stupidity? By honey trap?

Funny and not funny.

The girl smiles as he drives on by; he nods and smiles in return. No hard feelings. Sorry, sweetie, but I have my reasons. Maybe she is none of the above and, instead, is Yoda the Jedi Master in disguise, with the answers to the mysteries of the universe, including what he should do next. If so, he'll have to do without. Caution is his companion now.

He accelerates onto the highway, running up to eighty before he checks the speedometer, then eases back down to seventy. He paid extra for GPS and satellite radio. He hits the radio on button, finds one of those conservative talk shows on a preset channel, and settles in for the drive, with the host prattling on about how the liberals still don't get it, will never get it, are genetically programmed to not get it, blah blah blah …

FOUR HOURS DOWN I-95, Jack impulsively swings onto Exit 2D toward Miami Beach. He's been there on several family vacations and an occasional business trip. He's feeling fatigued, even after a relatively short drive in a comfortable car. He'll check into one of the nice oceanfront hotels on Collins Avenue and use it as a staging area before driving on to Key West—or as a rest stop before catching a flight home. Whichever seems right at the time. He's begun to understand the wisdom, the inevitability really, of letting go and going with the flow, as they said in the '60s. He feels that he's pretty much drifting now, as if floating in the Gulf Stream, headed to wherever the current takes him, as if someone or something else is in charge of his fate, which is a relief.

IT IS MID-AFTERNOON, sunny and hot (eighty-six degrees, according to the digital thermometer readout on the dashboard instrument panel) under a cloudless azure sky, the default Florida spring weather. As Jack crosses the MacArthur Causeway onto the island city of Miami Beach, big cruise ships are moored in line on a long pier to his right.

He and Jenna once took one of those ships, the *Royal Voyager II* it was called, to the Caribbean, stopping at Barbados, St. Lucia, Antigua, and St. Kitts, to celebrate their tenth anniversary. The ports-of-call were nice, but Jenna got seasick in some heavy weather during the return voyage. He thought the ship rather tacky, like a floating Vegas casino with shuffleboard and programmed activities ("The mahjong tournament starts on the Lido Deck in fifteen minutes! Mahjong on the Lido Deck in fifteen!"). They decided their vacations would be landlocked from then on.

At the end of the causeway he swings onto Ocean Drive, enjoying the retro angular pastel architecture of the Art Deco District in South Beach, then points north into Miami Beach proper, where it is less young, funky, and Latin, and he feels more at home. He decides on the grand Lowes Hotel, site of an NATP (National Association of Tax Professionals) convention that he attended some years ago. Fun, if sedate; you would not mistake a tax professionals' convention for spring break. Section 179 of the Internal Revenue Code allows a fifty percent deduction for convention-related expenses, a happy fact that accounted for the selection of ocean-view instead of city-view rooms, and steak instead of chicken on the banquet menu.

Jack turns into the Lowes' circular drive and stops. The young valet, wearing a white tunic with brass buttons, opens the car door and greets him with a cheery, "Welcome back to the Lowes, sir!" If the bellman thinks it odd that Jack's only luggage is a black leather motorcycle saddlebag, he doesn't show it as he lifts it out of the trunk.

Even though it's still high season, the Lowes has a room for him, courtesy of the recession. Resort business is down everywhere, especially in Florida. Jack imagines he could book a Caribbean cruise for the cost of a bus ride from Minneapolis to Milwaukee.

JACK HADN'T PACKED a bathing suit for this trip—who knew he'd be lounging by a pool in Miami Beach, an unintentional tourist?—so he buys one in one of the lobby shops: flowered Hawaiian-style boxer trunks. Not his style, but all they have in his size, at the rip-off, captive-market price of fifty-five dollars. He changes in his room, and then feels self-conscious about strolling through the ornate lobby on his way to the pool in the trunks, along with a T-shirt with a drawing of a dolphin on the front and rubber flip-flops, which he also bought at the shop. But, down in the lobby, he sees he needn't worry, no one's paying any attention to him as he strolls through.

Poolside, there are older men and women who shouldn't wear swimsuits—snowmobile suits would be more flattering: protruding potbellies, skinny, hairy legs, floppy boobs, big cabooses, and varicose veins, all held together with the chalky white skin of new arrivals from the north. Here and there are younger women with knockout bodies displayed in bikinis that would probably be against the rules at the Edina Country Club pool.

The pool area includes a village of canvas cabanas, an outdoor restaurant and tiki bar, and row upon row of reclining beach chairs around a pool big enough to be a small lake. The Atlantic, with a wide sandy beach, is right there, beyond a low metal security fence with a locking gate that opens with your room card—no riff-raff beachcombers welcome. A pretty young woman with short blond hair, in white shorts and white Lowes T-shirt, which highlights her bronze suntan, appears, toting two thick white terrycloth towels.

"Hi sir, I'm Julie," she chirps. "Would you like a lounge chair, or poolside cabana, or maybe a cabana out on the beach?"

"Just a chair by the pool would be fine."

Julie, bending from the waist in those tight little uniform shorts (how could you not give her a big tip?), places one of the towels over a chair and rolls the other into a pillow. "I can get you a drink or a lunch menu," she says. "And maybe you'd like a massage appointment?"

Jack follows her gaze over to a series of canvas tents across a lawn set up for croquet; the tents contain massage tables, two of them in use. No thanks. He lies back on the chair, orders an iced tea from Julie, slips the towel pillow behind his head, sighs, and thinks, I feel more like a conventioneer from Des Moines than an avenging angel.

Julie brings his iced tea. He thanks her, takes a sip, puts his hands behind his head, closes his eyes, and runs down a mental list what he has learned so far, eleven days from home:

Motorcycles are fun, but there is a trade-off between the exhilaration of the ride, and the possibility that you could, at any moment, be killed or injured. So the best way to enjoy it is to achieve a state of denial.

Never be tempted to own a bed-and-breakfast, unless you're married to a woman like Marissa Kirkland—and, even then, don't.

Student life at the University of Wisconsin, as at all schools, renews itself each fall with a new crop of students; past tragedies do not live on in the collective consciousness. True about life in general.

Maybe Jenna is getting better.

Do not pick up hitchhikers, especially pretty young girls.

Not all motorcycle gangs are what they appear.

Savannah is a lovely city, worth another visit—if only for the food.

Daytona Beach Bike Week is not worth another visit.

They mean it when they say that the professional drivers section in a truck stop restaurant is for professional drivers only.

On the road you can encounter random acts of kindness, as well as sudden violence—same as off the road.

The bad part about being fired from Hartfield, Miller, Simon & Swensen is not his former partners' lack of appreciation for all the hours of his life he gave to the firm. It is that he took those hours from his family.

People do not change, only their circumstances do.

Even if there is a prime mover in the universe, we're on our own, so, at least for him, the debate is moot.

You can forget, for varying intervals of time, about most any problem you might have. But when your child dies, you never forget that, even for a moment.

JACK IS HAVING a late lunch. He drove to the famous Wolfie's deli, which has the best corned beef this side of Katz's in New York, everyone says, only to find that it had closed several years earlier and the building has been demolished. Down the street he found Jerry's Famous Deli, a chain out of California he learned, which, *prima facie*, doesn't bode well. The great delis are usually one-offs. But the place certainly looks like the real thing, big and bustling, countermen hand-slicing the meats, "sky-high" sandwiches being delivered to diners in red vinyl booths, so he gave it a try and was not disappointed. The kreplach soup and Reuben are first-rate. They even have Dr. Brown's cream soda and New York cheesecake, so he forgives them the Mexican portion of the menu, which is usually found only at a California deli: tacos, quesadillas, burritos, fajitas, guacamole dip. There is no professional drivers' section at this deli, Jack notes, but maybe there should be an assisted eating area, given the age of some of his fellow diners.

After lunch, Jack drives up and down Collins Avenue, seeing the sights: the resort hotels, condo buildings, marinas with fleets of motor yachts and sailboats, the Bal Harbour Shops where Jenna liked to browse, but not buy, because she was too practical to pay the inflated prices, restaurants … Nothing he wanted to see, really. Just avoidance behavior, now that he is within striking distance of Key West, which he had come to think of as Hadleyville, the town where Gary Cooper faced down the bad guys in *High Noon*.

"COME HERE OFTEN?"

Jack can't believe he hears himself saying this clichéd line to the woman seated one stool away from him at the Lowes lobby bar. It is as if someone else said it. A new Jack Tanner, a lonely traveler hitting on whoever's handy? Or just the old Jack, lonely and looking for conversation?

She looks good for a woman her age, which is, what? In this time of plastic surgery, Botox, dental bleaching and bonding, power Pilates and Hatha yoga, personal trainers, vegan/good carb/low fat/starvation diets, spray tans, and lip augmentation, who can tell anymore? She has short, brown hair and is wearing sunglasses, a tight white V-neck T-shirt with gold glitter lettering saying "Cannes Film Festival 2008," gold lamé Capri pants on her long legs, and red slingbacks.

Jack had ordered a Corona with lime, noticed her, and for some reason decided he wanted some conversation—probably no more than that. The fact is, he is lonely. He might not have realized this if not for the bonding with his new friends from Boston. He hadn't minded being alone until he met up with them and found an easy and immediate kinship with these fellow middle-aged road warriors. Now they're gone. So why not a pleasant conversation with another solo soul, if she isn't waiting for someone?

At home in Edina, alone there, too, since Jenna went away, he came across the TV series *Cougar Town* with Courteney Cox. Out of curiosity, he watched it for about fifteen minutes, amused by the concept. This woman looks like Courteney. Maybe she is a cougar. Or maybe she's Marian the Librarian from River City, Iowa, on vacation. If so, she'll have something in common with Jack, the conventioneer from Des Moines.

"In fact, I do come here often," she answers pleasantly.

They chat. Her name is Samantha (no last name given). Turns out she is not Courteney the Cougar, or

Marian the Librarian. She is (surprise!) a working girl who advertises her "adult services" on Craigslist and is having a glass of pinot noir before keeping an appointment for a "sensual massage" for a fee of "two hundred roses an hour" with some guy—she calls him a "client"—staying at the hotel. Jack is surprised that she's revealing all this about herself. until he remembers that he's been doing the same.

In the twenty minutes until her appointment, they talk about the economy, the wars in Iran and Afghanistan, the politics of national health care reform, the lack of exciting Republican presidential candidates, and the surprising winning streak of the Cleveland Indians (she is a native of Cleveland). Why should Jack be surprised that a woman in her line of work is intelligent and well informed about the issues of the day? He guesses he shouldn't be. Maybe she's a "normal" person, whatever that is, who lost big in the market crash and is trying not to default on her mortgage. He realizes that he should not apply his own value system to other people, which is something of an epiphany for him, a lesson he's learned on the trip. To understand people, you must take them for who they are, and not for who you think they should be.

Samantha doesn't say why she's doing whatever she specifically does for a fee, and Jack doesn't ask. He doesn't tell her where he's from or why he's in Miami Beach, and she doesn't ask, the don't-ask-don't-tell rule in effect. Jack assumes she's only told him her profession in case he'd like some company later on, after the massage appointment.

He is tempted to ask her to dinner at some nice restaurant, maybe Emeril's right next to the hotel, or Joe's Stone Crab, where he's eaten before and likes the house specialty with their tangy mustard sauce, and the key lime pie. He enjoys her company. Definitely for conversation and nothing more. There are diseases to worry about.

But before he can decide, there's a chiming sound in her purse. She takes out an iPhone, scans a text message, checks her watch, slides off the stool, gives him an air kiss and says, "Ciao, Jack. You're nice."

She doesn't know it, but to Jack, "nice" at this point in time is not a compliment: it is an impediment, a measure of his failure to evolve into someone else. This good old nice Jack might as well just head back home.

THE MOON IS a silver luminescent disc above a calm dark sea as Jack strolls the beach after a dinner (alone) at Yucatan, a very good Cuban restaurant in South Beach, which the hotel concierge recommended. He did in fact call Samantha's cell phone to ask her to dinner, but he got her voicemail, twice. Must be that the client decided he wanted to book the rest of her evening.

He pauses, looking up at the starry nighttime sky. He was a junior astronomer as a young boy, getting an expensive Galileo telescope for his ninth birthday. He memorized all the phases of the moon (waning and waxing, full, gibbous, and crescent) and the constellations visible in the northern hemisphere (Leo, Virgo, Gemini, Orion …). It was a long time ago.

That's a full moon. But those stars? Not a clue, nothing that looks like a lion or a hunter or a maiden, or any other recognizable connect-the-dots shape, at least not to his adult eyes. Someone, he can't recall who, told him that your brain is like a computer hard drive. You have room for a finite amount of data storage, and when your memory bank is full, and you learn something new, some old fact gets deleted. The IRS Tax Code must have wiped out astronomy.

He is startled by a voice behind him, "Beautiful, isn't it? The nighttime sky over water."

It's a woman, standing not five feet away, looking up too, his second chance meeting with a female today. She points heavenward. "There's Cassiopeia … Ursa Major and Minor … and Hydra …" She smiles. "I'm forgetting my manners." She offers her hand, which Jack takes. "Vickie Blatchford. Sorry for sneaking up on you like that."

The voice is British, the upper-class accent they call Oxbridge. The woman, illuminated by the moonlight, is about Jack's age, barefoot, with shoulder-length auburn hair, green eyes, aquiline nose, and slender body under a blue-and-white-striped boating shirt tied at the waist and white shorts.

"Hi. Jack Tanner. Are you staying at the Lowes?" They are just outside the hotel's beach gate.

"No, I'm staying on a boat, actually."

He looks out over the water. A very large motor yacht, lights ablaze, is anchored maybe a quarter-mile offshore.

"On, not that one," Vickie laughs. "Mine is just a little sailboat, moored at a yacht club near Fisher Island. I caught a bite to eat at a nice Cuban bistro near here and decided to have a walk as a digestif."

"It wasn't Yucatan, was it?"

"Why yes, that's the place."

"I ate there tonight, too."

Is she alone? Impolite to ask.

She *is* alone, and she invites Jack to see the boat. They ride over to the Admiral Yacht Club on her rented Vespa, Vickie at the helm, Jack again a passenger on a two-wheeler. Now they sit on a padded bench in the cockpit, sipping gin and tonics. Her "little sailboat" is a thirty-seven-foot Endeavour sloop, black-hulled with a red stripe, named *Sea Sprite*, which she intends to sail to the Turks and Caicos Islands, with whatever island ports of call seem appealing along the way.

"My husband, Nigel, and I planned this voyage for three years," she tells Jack. "He's in politics. Hard for him to get away for an extended period."

Nigel Blatchford? Jack thinks he's heard that name. Maybe a high cabinet minister? Sir Nigel? So she is married.

She sips her G & T and pushes her hair back behind her ears.

"*Was* in politics, I should say. Nigel died eight months

ago, of a stroke. I can't get used to the past tense."

"I'm sorry," Jack says. "I'm not sure you ever do get used to the past tense."

She looks at him, perhaps thinking that this man might have experienced a loss too.

"We chartered this boat and paid in advance, and under the circumstances getting the money back would have been no problem. But, against the advice of friends and family, I decided to make the trip by myself. I suppose I thought it might make me feel close to him. I've sailed all my life, never as a captain, but I think I've picked up enough to handle the boat alone."

The wind has picked up, and the British flag, which Vickie brought with her, is snapping on its stern staff. "Let's go below," Vickie says. "We wouldn't want our drinks to blow away."

The boat's interior is well appointed, the main cabin all brass and mahogany, with a teak parquet deck. Vickie brings up Bach on the stereo system and refreshes their drinks in the galley. After several more, the wind still howling outside, with the music and dim lights from copper lanterns, and the warmth of the gin in his bloodstream, Jack is content. Vickie slides closer on the bench seat, touches his arm.

"Do you mind if I ask why you're here, in Miami Beach, unaccompanied? I don't mean to pry." She grins, wrinkling her nose. "But I will anyway."

"I don't mind," Jack answers. And for the third time, he tells his story. Again, it provides some level of relief to unburden himself to a chance acquaintance. He realizes that he has no friends he'd tell, and this saddens him a bit. There are, of course, people he's known a long time, but none of them are confidants with whom he'd trust his innermost secrets. Maybe this is characteristic of men. No family members in this category either—except for Jenna, who is too fragile.

When he's finished and falls silent, Vickie, tears in her eyes, kisses his cheek and tells him, "I'd very much like you to spend the night, Jack. I think we both could use the company before we go our separate ways. It's possible neither one of us will survive our journeys." This said matter-of-factly, as if the stars will determine their fates and they are mere spectators.

Which Jack, by now, is thinking, too.

15: SAME SHIT, DIFFERENT DAY

SLATER BABCOCK IS lying nude between purple satin sheets in a circular bed in the stateroom of the *Bachelor Pad*, as it cruises at a languid twenty knots in a calm Caribbean Sea, an hour out of the island nation of Nevis. Captain Henry Greenwood has the helm. The woman sleeping beside him is nude, too. He cannot recall how she got aboard and into his bed. As a memory aid, he lifts strands of her raven-dark hair from her face and studies it: smooth milk-chocolate skin, straight nose, long eyelashes, full, sensual lips. He thinks that she has something to do with one of those Caribbean medical schools for students who flunked undergrad organic chemistry in the States. He doesn't remember if she is a student, professor, or cafeteria worker. She introduced herself at a party at the Nevis Yacht Club, saying her name was Barbara and she was "with the medical college." He hadn't been curious enough about her resume to ask any follow-up questions.

Last night she wore a long, white, linen skirt and a white peasant blouse that revealed the bony ridges of her clavicle and the rolling swells of world-class breasts, and that was resume enough. He notices the skirt and blouse tossed onto a chair. He wonders what level of commitment he may have made to get her aboard, cruising toward Ft. Lauderdale, where the big annual boat show is underway, with raucous parties underwritten by the manufacturers and yacht brokerages.

Had he just offered her a ride to the show? Or, his tongue lubricated by Mount Gay rum, had he foolishly spoken some other specific or implied promise of more than a casual acquaintance, causing her to abandon her studies or students or steam tables? Would she awaken with just breakfast, or with some sort of long-term (long-term defined as more than the time it takes to reach Ft. Lauderdale) commitment on her mind? If so, it wouldn't be the first time a morning-after had taken an ugly turn.

He eases out of bed, pulls on a pair of khaki shorts, and makes his way to the galley, up three steps and aft of the main stateroom. There he finds a box of Eggo waffles in the freezer, pops one into the toaster, sees that Captain Hank has made coffee, pours himself a mug, sips the strong, dark brew until the waffle is ejected, then takes it in his hand like a slice of toast, along with the coffee mug, and makes his way up to the flying bridge.

"Ahoy there, captain," Slater says.

Hank Greenwood is a retired Coast Guard master chief, weather-beaten as an old wooden lighthouse, who hates it when landlubber assholes like Slater Babcock try to talk nautical. But the pay for captaining this honey of a boat is above average, as are the tips when he takes out charter parties, which the owner solicits to offset operating costs; with marine fuel at four dollars a gallon, a four-hour cruise can burn up nearly a thousand dollars worth of gas. Plus, he frequently gets a taste of Babcock's leftover poontang.

So, instead of answering, "Go fuck yourself," as he is always inclined, Captain Hank greets Slater with a snappy salute and a cheery, "Morning, Mr. Babcock. With this following sea, we'll make Lauderdale in about an hour."

Slater returns the salute and responds, "Make it so," quoting Captain Picard of *Star Trek: The Next Generation*, one of his favorite TV shows. DVDs of the last three seasons are aboard for viewing on the sixty-inch plasma-screen Sony in the main salon.

Slater makes his way down to the aft sundeck to sip his coffee, munch his waffle, and watch for land, hoping the humming of the Cummins twin diesels and gentle slap of waves on the hull will keep the woman in his bed asleep until he can disembark and leave her to the hospitality of Captain Hank.

16: LAND'S END

JACK HAS DRIVEN along some scenic roadways in his time: The Great River Road in Minnesota running along the bank of the Mississippi; Highway 20 through Yellowstone in Wyoming; the Pacific Coast Highway in Northern California; and, with college friends during one spring break, a wild ride in a VW Vanagon with a psychedelic paint job on Mexico's Highway 1 from Tijuana all the way to Cabo San Lucas. But none is prettier than U.S. 1, island hopping on causeways along the Florida Keys.

After three days in Miami Beach, he decided it was time to begin the endgame of this expedition. He wonders if Vickie Blatchford has set sail, hoping to find her dead husband somewhere out there in the deep blue Caribbean Sea. Is it possible that she has planned a suicide voyage, as his own might be? Might she scuttle the boat and sink down beneath the waves? He hopes not. She is such a beautiful, intelligent, and charming woman. But Jack knows how grief can change a person. Just look at him and Jenna.

He and Vickie spent the night together, lying close after unplanned (for him, at least) sex in the boat's small stateroom bunk, two weary souls taking comfort in one another's body heat and shared sadness. For the first time in their marriage, he's been unfaithful to Jenna. He wonders if she ever has been unfaithful to him. Jenna turns heads, and, over the years, it was clear that many men were interested in her. If a man wants sex, he must find a willing woman. But if a pretty woman like Jenna wants it, all she has to do is smile at a man. He does feel guilty. Should he tell Jenna about this encounter? Probably not; a confession might make him feel better, but it would certainly cause her pain, and she doesn't need any more of that. He knows that this may just be a rationalization.

In the morning, Vickie made coffee, strong and good, assuming correctly that that's what an American wanted, and tea for herself, and cheese and mushroom omelets, with English muffins and Dundee orange marmalade from a well-provisioned galley. He devoured his breakfast with relish as they chatted about casual matters: motorcycles and sailboats, books they liked, his visits to England and hers to the U.S.—anything but their sad histories or their intimacy of the night before.

She drove him back to the Lowes on her Vespa, and waved goodbye as she putted off down Collins Avenue. He showered and checked out of the hotel at ten a.m., got a map of the Keys from the concierge, and embarked upon the last leg of his long journey. By now he's given up on the idea of formulating some sort of plan before he arrives. He recalls the Woody Allen dictum that "showing up is eighty percent of life." He'll just have to show up and improvise the remaining twenty percent.

AFTER TWO HOURS, Jack sees that he is entering the Village of Islamorada, located at Mile Marker 82, which is how locations are designated along the Overseas Highway. The Lowes concierge told him about the mile markers, which measure the one hundred fifty six mile distance between Miami and Key West.

Great, he thinks. I set out on a Harley Road King, switch to a BMW touring bike, and will roll into Key West in a rented Taurus. Not exactly a triumphant arrival, but the best I can do under the circumstances.

Islamorada is a world famous fishing village, Jack knows, because a group of his Edina golfing friends once organized a fishing trip to the town. It was during a week in April, income tax season for his clients, and he couldn't go. They came back with sunburns and photos showing tarpon, sailfish, and tuna they'd boated and released. Jack regretted missing the trip. He'd done a lot of lake fishing in Minnesota, catching walleye, northern pike, bass, and a few of the elusive muskies. But he'd never gone after the really big boys you needed a fighting chair to boat. That would have been an interesting experience.

Jack decides to stop for lunch. He gets gas at a 7–11 and asks the young girl about a good place to get a sandwich. She's tanned and thin and pretty, with blond hair and blue eyes, and is wearing what must be the uniform of girls like that, including Hannah and the other hitchhiker back in Virginia: skimpy T-shirt, tight shorts, and flip-flops.

"We got hot dogs that have been turning on those rollers for a couple of days, and some sandwiches in that cooler, tuna, chicken salad, egg salad, hoagies. One of my jobs is to keep changing the sell-by dates on the sandwiches." She smiles. "So I'd say, definitely not here, mister. But just down the road, at Mile Marker 79.9, there's a marina, the Blue Marlin, that's got good clam rolls and such."

JACK PARKS THE Taurus in a sandy lot behind a rambling, two-story, white wooden building, with peeling paint, green hurricane shutters, and a rusted tin roof. The Blue Marlin Marina has obviously been around a long time and survived many a tropical storm. He walks around to the front, where charter fishing boats are lined up along three long L-shaped docks jutting out into the calm blue waters of Florida Bay, waiting for their afternoon runs. There had been good fishing that morning, as evidenced by crewmen cleaning smaller game fish at stations along the docks, with pelicans and seagulls swooping into the water as the fish cleaners toss innards into the water.

A man is having his picture taken as he stands beside a tall hoist which holds a very large fish suspend head down by its tail. A blue marlin, Jack guesses. Such a noble and beautiful animal. It should have been freed to return to the Gulf Stream, not strung up like this and then taxidermed, to hang on some rec room wall in Iowa or Indiana or wherever. Jack has the urge to go over to the hoist, lower the fish to the dock, and give the man a lecture on the sanctity of life, including the life of this fish.

Instead, he goes into the marina building for a sandwich and a beer. Inside he finds a store that sells bait, tackle, marine equipment, nautical clothing, and groceries. One wall is covered with the photos of people who've been here to fish; some are posed outside with their trophies hanging from that same hoist, others are strapped into fighting chairs on the decks of boats, their poles bent under the weight of whatever they've hooked. Some of the photos are old, in black and white; others are in color. Jack takes a look. Many of the people in the photos are celebrities he recognizes: Ernest Hemingway, Ted Williams, Dwight Eisenhower, Joe DiMaggio with Marilyn Monroe, John Wayne, Eddie Fisher and Elizabeth Taylor, Bob Hope, Mick Jagger, Bill Clinton, William Shatner, Harrison Ford …

"Help you?" a man behind the bait counter asks. The man, who looks old enough to have sold bait to Hemingway back in the 1930s, is as weathered as the marina building. He is wearing a T-shirt bearing the marina's name, and tan canvas shorts with stains on them, probably fish blood, Jack guesses.

"Can I get some lunch here?" Jack asks.

The man nods toward an inside doorway in the back wall. "Right through there," he says, then picks up a little net and begins scooping up minnows floating belly up in a tank. Maybe they're going on the lunch menu, Jack thinks.

A door in the back wall opens into a large pine-paneled room with three big fans with woven bamboo blades slowly turning on the ceiling. Jack goes in. The tables are filled with customers, many of them looking windblown and tanned as if they'd been out on the charter boats that morning.

More trophy fish are mounted on the walls, along with the heads of wild game: a bighorn sheep, a boar with long ivory tusks, an elk with a big rack of antlers, a black bear with an eternal snarl displaying pointed yellow teeth, and a moose. A sad graveyard, Jack thinks, but he's here and he's hungry, so he finds the one empty table.

Another one of those veteran waitresses comes over, hands Jack a menu, and says, without preamble, "Specials today are conch chowder, lobster mac and cheese, a grouper sandwich, breaded and fried or blackened, and baked mahi mahi." Jack orders an iced tea and the fried grouper sandwich. As he's eating, the waitress comes over and asks, "Would you mind a little company?" He sees a man and woman and a young girl standing just inside the dining room doorway.

"Sure," he says.

The family comes over and takes chairs. "Appreciate it," the man says to Jack. "I'm Larry Blaisdell. This is my wife, Marla, and our daughter, Lucy."

Jack shakes Larry's hand. "Jack Tanner. No problem at all." He nods a greeting to Marla and Lucy.

After they order, Jack learns that they are from Toronto—he can hear that Canadian "oot" for out and "aboot" for about in their speech—and are driving to Key West, just like him. Lucy is twelve and on spring break. Of course, Jack is reminded of his own family on a vacation. He thinks: Long live happy families.

They pass a pleasant lunch together and then Jack excuses himself and hits the road.

CROSSING THE CAUSEWAY onto the island of Key West, Jack decides to tour the town before choosing a hotel. He knows from Pete Dye that Slater lives in a house on Admirals Lane and that he owns a bar on Duval Street, which daddy bought for him, called the Rusty Scupper. He decides to drive past the house and the bar as if on a surveillance stakeout. He has seen digital photos of Babcock that Hope had on her computer: shots of him mugging for the camera, and the two of them in campus bars, at parties, riding one of the duck boats at the Wisconsin Dells ... Looking like a happy couple. Painful to view.

In these photos, Jack thought, Slater looked handsome and "normal." But what does normal look like?

Not like a killer? What does a killer look like? This alleged killer has sandy blond hair, regular features with a square jaw, blue eyes, a friendly smile, and the physique of an athlete. Maybe he has a beard now, or longer hair, as Jack does. There is little chance that Slater would recognize Jack, he thinks, even without the beard and hair. They've never met, and, even if Hope had shown him a family picture, he would never expect to see her father, not in Key West, not after all this time. If there were to be any confrontation with Hope's family, it would have happened long before now, Slater would think.

First, Slater's house. Jack paid extra for a GPS in the rented Taurus. He hangs a right off the causeway onto North Roosevelt Boulevard, pulls into a gas station, and enters the address of Babcock's house into the GPS. He is directed by a rather seductive woman's voice to take a left out of the gas station, proceed south along Roosevelt Boulevard, which becomes Truman Avenue after it crosses White Street, then right onto Whitehead Street, left onto Eaton Street, right onto Front Street (at this point Jack is grateful that this lady knows her way around town) and finally right onto Admirals Lane, a little semi-circle near the northwestern end of the island.

He slows as he passes number 1406, a pink cottage with a green tin roof and crushed-shell driveway, and parks in front of the house across the street. The carport at Babcock's house is empty. Wooden hurricane shutters are propped open, so Jack can see into the living and dining room. No sign of life inside.

What if Jack came back at three a.m. with a gas can and burned down the cottage, ideally with Slater Babcock in his bed? Would he be able to go back home content that Hope had been avenged, even if Slater didn't know why he was dying? Would that end the matter for Jack? Probably not. He would not have confronted the man, or found out what really happened to Hope. He checks his notebook for the address of the Rusty Scupper, programs it into the GPS, eases away from the curb and drives on. Duvall is Key West's main street and prime tourist destination, with its restaurants, bars, shops, art galleries, souvenir stores, ice cream parlors, and hotels. Jack motors slowly along, taking in the sights of this interesting little town.

The Rusty Scupper looks like a newer structure designed to look like an Old Florida ramshackle fisherman's shanty, with a corrugated green metal roof, weathered white wooden siding, and white hurricane shutters. An adjoining lot has been converted into a beach volleyball court with a thatched tiki bar hut. Jack eases the Taurus into a vacant space on the other side of the street, in front of the Almond Tree Inn. He watches customers enter and exit the bar for a while, then decides to go in for a drink and look around.

The bar has an Old Key West motif: photos of Duval Street from the early nineteen hundreds, judging by the automobiles, and of old-time fishing parties displaying their catches. Lobster pots, fishing nets with big cork floats, gaping shark jaws and more mounted game fish: big bulky tarpon, majestic sailfish and barracuda with

mouthfuls of needle-sharp teeth. The bar is packed.
The Jimmy Buffet song "Margaritaville," an anthem
for the kick-back-in-the-tropics crowd, plays loudly
on the sound system. Jack slides onto a barstool. After
a moment, the bartender, a huge man with a ponytail
and the dark skin of a native of some island somewhere,
comes over and asks, "What's your poison, sport?"

Jack orders a draft Red Stripe and scans the room.
Tourist families sit at tables munching on platters of
nachos and chicken wings and sipping drinks containing
fruit and parasols. Lined up along the bar beside him are
weathered men who look like fishing guides and tour boat
captains, and women who've clearly been here before,
judging by their bantering with the bartender, and the
men drinking shots and beers, sans parasols. All the usual
suspects for a bar like this, but not the proprietor.

And then Slater Babcock himself pushes through the
kitchen door and walks over the end of the bar. He does
have a beard now, and longer hair, and a deep suntan,
but otherwise looks like the person in Hope's photos.

"Hey boss," the bartender calls out.

"Gimme a Bloody Mary," Slater says, nodding a
hello to the customers he seems to know. He makes eye
contact with Jack, gives him a nod and a smile.

Jack nods back, seeing that Slater hasn't changed
much from his photos, except he's maybe ten pounds
heavier and has a deep tan and longer hair. He looks
like a frat boy on permanent spring break. This is the
moment Jack has anticipated all during his journey. He
looks at his beer bottle sitting on the bar. It could be

a weapon. He could knock off the end of the bottle on the bar, like they do in the movies, and jam it into Slater's face or neck. Or he could go out to his car and get Langdon's Derringer ...

"If you haven't had lunch, I recommend the hot wings and the burgers," Slater says, and Jack realizes with a start that his daughter's murderer is actually talking to him.

"No thanks, I just ate," Jack says. They are having a cordially inane conversation! He feels like he's having an out-of-body experience; he is chatting with Slater there at the bar, and also hovering above, watching the scene.

"Another time then," Slater says, and takes his Bloody Mary into the kitchen.

Jack is shaken. Jesus Christ! Are you fucking kidding me? Of all the confrontation scenarios he's played out in his mind, this was not one of them. His neighbor Hank Whitby certainly wouldn't have handled it like that. Nor would have Langdon Lamont, who faced down Bigfoot in the diner. Or even Vernon Douglas, the police chief. The long ride from Minnesota has not changed him a bit. He's still the same old Jack Tanner. So this is how his quest for closure finally ends? *I recommend the hot wings and the burgers? No thanks, I just ate?*

AS ASHAMED OF himself as he's ever been, Jack checks into the Casa Marina Resort on Reynolds Street, which he found as he drove around looking for lodging. The hotel, on the southern tip of the island, is a three-

story yellow stucco building that looks like a grand
Spanish estate. He gets a pricey Ocean Vista Room and
settles in, tours the grounds, has a massage in the spa,
then finds a lounge chair beside the pool. Thinking that
fiction might be an escape for the unhappy reality of
his life, he purchased the new John Grisham book, *Ford
County*, in the hotel store. He settles back on the chair
and begins to read it. Soon, he drifts off to sleep. In his
dream, he is the author his own desired destiny.

*A HURRICANE IS battering Key West. Where the hell
did it come from? There'd been no warning, at least none
that Jack had heard. Its name is Brenda. It's a level two, an
intensity somewhere in that middle ground between ride it
out, and mandatory evacuation.*

*The streets are deserted except for Jack, making his way
down Duvall, soaked, stormed-tossed, fighting the wind for
forward motion. It's not clear to him why he hasn't taken
shelter. A black-and-white Chevy Tahoe with Key West
Police Department markings comes rolling slowly down
Duvall toward Jack. It pulls over to the curb with a short
burst from its lights and siren. Jack looks around: who, me?
There is no one else on the street.*

*The officer, who looks exactly like Hank Whitby—who
is Hank Whitby—powers down the driver's side window
and says, "Hey Jack, what are you doing out in a storm like
this? Hop in; I'll take you to a shelter."*

*Jack does not want to be taken to a shelter with other
orphans of the storm. He knows that he is on a mission,*

even though it's not clear what the mission is. So he must make an effort to present himself to his neighbor Hank as being calm and reasonable—as calm and reasonable as a man who is out for a stroll in a level two hurricane can be.

He walks over to the Tahoe, grabbing onto a parking meter with both hands for balance, and shouts to be heard above the howling wind: "Hi, Hank. Good to see you. Jenna and Hope are at a friend's house just around the corner. I'm heading there now."

Hank stares at Jack, as if deciding whether to believe him or not, then replies, "Okay. Go directly there and stay inside."

"I will," Jack promises. "Thanks." Thanks for not diverting him from his still-unknown mission.

Two more blocks down Duvall, he reaches a bar with no sign announcing its name. This is his destination, he realizes. The building is battened down with plywood nailed over the windows. The parking lot is deserted, except for five motorcycles, which look familiar, blown over in a heap. No other signs of life.

He somehow knows that there is a hurricane party inside. He enters to find the place packed with lively partygoers. A Jimmy Buffet song, "Surfing in a Hurricane," is playing on the sound system. Jack, dripping water onto the floor, scans the crowd. Wait. Is that …

Yes, seated at a round table back near the kitchen entrance, are the Devil's Disciples: Harold Whittaker, Alan Dupree, Miles Standish, Langdon Lamont, Victor Purcell, and the resurrected Tom Jarvis. Harold notices Jack and happily gestures for him to come over. In the world of dream logic, Jack is not surprised to see them. Those were their motorcycles out in the parking lot.

Then Jack spots a young man standing at the far end of the bar with a group of three young women, one of whom looks like Hope, laughing at whatever he's saying. The man has long, sandy blond hair, blue eyes, and a beard. Jack doesn't know who this young man is, but, as he's looking at him, he realizes that this person is evil and must be killed.

Jack walks over, grabs his shoulder, and says, "Where is she?"

"What?" the man responds, turning to face Jack.

Jack grabs him by the shirt and shouts, "Tell me what happened to my daughter!"

The man raises his hands, palms out, in a gesture of peace. "Hey, look buddy, if you daughter's here at the party, I'll be happy to ..."

"You killed her!"

"Killed her? Now wait a minute ..."

"My daughter!" Jack yells. "Hope Tanner!"

The man shrugs his shoulders as if he's never heard the name before. Enraged, Jack withdraws from his pants pocket a Derringer, which he didn't know he had, presses the barrel onto the man's forehead, and says, "Admit it and I won't kill you."

"Hey, wait a minute ..."

Jack cocks the little pistol.

"Wait ... wait ... Okay, I did it. I killed her."

Through the din of the party Jack hears a familiar voice shout: "Jack! Hey Jack! Wait!"

He turns to see Pete Dye standing just inside the front

door in a combat shooting stance, his pistol pointed toward the other end of the bar at the big bartender, who is leveling a shotgun at Jack.

Standoff.

Jack resolves it by pulling the Derringer's trigger.

A metallic click. Not loaded! Then an orange-red flash from the shotgun barrel out ahead of the sound and Pete Dye firing too…

A SENSATION CUTTING through the blackness, and sounds … Jack awakens with a start, sits up and looks around in confusion, trying to clear his head. It's raining. The other guests around the Casa Marina pool are gathering up their beach bags and heading inside.

The dream is remembered. He lies back on the chaise lounge, feeling the warm rain on his body. Desperate, hopeless, Jack Tanner closes his eyes and, for the first time in his life, utters a prayer:

Please. I want my family back home.

17: HEMINGWAY WAS HERE

WALKING ALONG DUVALL on his second day in Key West, to no particular destination, Jack decides to have lunch. Then he'll pack and fly home. He doesn't know what he'll do when he gets there any more than he knew what he'd do when he got to Key West (which, he sadly knows now, is nothing). He comes upon a bar called Sloppy Joe's, which he's noticed but never gone into. It is a two-story white stucco building, with red brick pillars and the name of the establishment painted in big lettering on the top story, front and side.

Inside, the flags of many countries hang from the ceiling. The place is crowded with people having a drink and lunch at the bar and at tables; the walls are covered with memorabilia from the bar's long history, most prominently a display of photos of Sloppy Joe's most prominent patron, Ernest Hemingway. Among these photos, Jack notices, is a mounted blue marlin, similar to the one hanging from the hoist at marina on Islamorada named for the majestic fish.

Jack finds a seat at the bar, scans a menu, and orders the two house specialties, a sloppy joe sandwich and, why not?, a papa dobles—"Papa's favorite!" the menu says—to drink ("Bacardi Light rum, grapefruit juice, grenadine, splash of sweet & sour, club soda, and fresh-squeezed lime $6.75").

As he's sipping his drink and waiting for his sandwich, he scans the room and sees maybe six or eight men, all of whom look like the photo of the older Papa Hemingway: slicked-back silver hair, with a full silver beard and a ruddy face. Some of them wear T-shirts and tan canvas shorts, others wear bush jackets and long khaki pants. What the hell? Jack is reminded of a trip to Los Vegas that he and Jenna once took when an Elvis impersonators convention was in town, Elvises everywhere you looked.

A man seated at the bar beside Jack, and a woman next to him, finish their lunch and leave. When they do, Jack sees that one of these ersatz Hemingways is seated three stools down. He's wearing a tan, short-sleeved safari shirt and canvas shorts, with a length of rope for a belt, and white canvas deck shoes. Three cigars are in one of his shirt pockets.

"Like the papa doble?" the man says to Jack with a smile.

"A little sweet but good," Jack answers.

The man moves over next to Jack. "You must be wondering what's going on," he says. "Every year at this time, on July 21, which is Ernest Hemingway's birthday, and my birthday too, as it happens, Sloppy Joe's has a Hemingway look-alike contest. Attracts more than a hundred imitators. For the next three days there are other festivities, too, including an arm-wrestling contest and a running of the bulls, with inebriated fellows instead of bulls stumbling their way down Duval."

The bartender, who could enter the look-alike contest himself except that his hair and beard are red, arrives to see if they want a refill. Jack is feeling relaxed and says yes. His companion asks for another daiquiri.

As they sip their drinks, Jack introduces himself. The man, oddly, does not reciprocate. Instead, he says, "So what's your story, Jack Tanner?"

Inappropriate for someone he just met, Jack thinks.

"Oh, nothing very interesting," he answers. None of your business.

"Tell me anyway," whomever this guy is, says. "I collect stories."

THREE DAYS LATER, Jack and his new friend, whose name is Edward Hollingsworth, are out in the Gulf Stream off Key West at seven a.m. aboard Edward's boat, the *Pilar*. The boat is a twenty-eight-foot Sea Ray sport cruiser, not at all like its namesake, Hemingway's thirty-eight-foot wooden cabin cruiser, which sailed in these same waters in the 1930s, when its owner was a

Key West resident, Edward has explained.

Jack and Edward have been hanging out together continuously since they met at Sloppy Joe's. Over lots of rum drinks, Jack has for the fourth time broken his vow of silence, and has been spinning out his story, as Edward requested. Edward is a nice guy and as good a listener, and Jack is happy to have his company. However, Edward has been stingy with the details of his own life. He is a "retired businessman" who has lived all over the world; he enjoys hunting and fishing; has had four wives and has three sons; he has a house in Idaho; he has been living aboard *Pilar* for the past few years, cruising "wherever my fancy and the Gulf Stream take me." Three cats live aboard *Pilar*, too; they are all named for French novelists—Zola, Rabelais, and Balzac—and came aboard of their own volition, one at a time, at various ports of call. "They're polydactyls," Edward told Jack. "Six toes! That's special!"

Jack is just familiar enough with Hemingway lore from an American Lit course in college to know that, in addition to the name of his boat, some or all of the details of Edward's life, as he has reported them, are similar—or identical—to those of the famous writer's. And, of course, he has made himself *look* like Hemingway. So Edward is either putting Jack on for some reason, or he belongs at some place like The Sanctuary for treatment of his delusions.

No matter, Jack can use a friend, now that the Disciples are back home, someone with an upbeat personality and a certain *joie de vivre*, which can, at least a little bit, serve the same purpose for him as does Jenna's medication for her. So they'll do whatever they do for a while, he decides. He has no further business in Key West, but why hurry back to an empty house and no job? He has no more of an idea about what he'll do in Minneapolis than he had about what he'd do in Key West.

This morning, it's blue-water fishing, which Jack agreed to do when Edward assured him they'd follow a strict catch-and-release policy. That is, unless one of them hooked into "a real trophy." Then they'd have to talk.

At the moment, Jack is seated near Edward in the cockpit, as Edward navigates out to a location where he believes that there just might be some tuna running. An early morning fog has burned off; there is a light chop, not enough to make Jack seasick, which is a possibility if the wind picks up and causes *Pilar* to rock and bob any more than she is right now.

They have steaming mugs of good coffee Edward made in the galley. Jack's mood has improved from that low point at the Casa Marina pool when he awakened from his latest dream. If it didn't seem so inappropriate, given his circumstances, he might even admit he's enjoying himself, out on the deep blue sea with an interesting companion, even if he is a total head case, and not simply a big-time Hemingway aficionado.

"So maybe we should invite that kid, Slater Babcock, out for some fishing," Edward says above the wind and engine noise. "Who knows, he might hook into a big one that pulls him right in."

He's joking, of course, Jack knows. Or is he? But maybe that's not a bad idea. Edward is maybe ten years older than Jack, but he is muscular, and a former amateur boxer, he's said (more of the Hemingway résumé there; will he end up shooting himself with a shotgun to complete the act?). With Edward as his wingman, maybe Jack will be able to confront Slater in a more meaningful way than he did at the Rusty Scupper. He certainly couldn't do any worse.

"Look," Edward exclaims, pointing to the front of the boat, where two dolphins are riding the bow waves. "That's good luck, you know."

Jack hears a noise behind him. Edward swivels his chair to look and calls out, "Fish on! Fish on!" One of the four fishing rods, mounted on the stern in chrome sleeves and rigged for tolling, is bent under the weight of something big. Edward powers down the twin engines and yells, "Go for it, Jack! Grab that rod! You're in for a fight, that's for sure!"

It's a blue marlin and it does not want to be caught, so it tests Jack's resolve, as well as his arms and shoulders, for more than an hour as it dives deep, then breaks the surface to dance on its tail, as Edward expertly maneuvers the boat and keeps shouting, "Tip up! Keep the goddamned tip up or you'll lose her!" To Jack, it feels like he's hooked Moby Dick.

Edward repeatedly asks Jack if he wants him to take over the rod, just long enough to give Jack a rest, but Jack always declines, feeling that somehow fighting this fish is the most important thing he's ever done. Finally, just as Jack feels as if his arms are being pulled out of their shoulder sockets, the fish tires, and remains on the surface.

"You've got her!" Edward calls out, backing the boat slowly toward the fish. "Tip up and reel her in, steady now!"

When the marlin is alongside, and Jack has absolutely no idea what to do next, Edward puts the engines in neutral, comes down to the deck, puts on work gloves, grabs the steel leader on the line, and lifts the head of the fish up, gently. Jack thinks maybe Edward is going to kiss it.

"A beauty," Edward says, as he holds the leader with one hand and takes a pair of pliers out of the back pocket of his shorts. "Maybe six hundred pounds. Not trophy size, that's over a thousand, and I have caught just one that size, so no problem there, we'll put her back and let her grow some more."

He looks directly into one of the marlin's big round eyes and says, "I'll be baa-aack! Ha!" He uses the pliers to remove the barbless hook from the fish's mouth, then leans way over the transom and massages its belly as it gulps for air. After a while, he puts his hands on its back and pushes it slowly away from the boat. Jack watches as the fish floats motionless for several minutes, wondering if it's dying. Then it shakes itself and, with a whip of its tail, is gone beneath the shimmering surface of the Gulf Stream. Jack hopes the fish will be smarter or luckier or still too small for trophy size the next time there's a hook in the water.

"That was a very good catch," Edward says, smiling. "You know the quote, 'Anyone can be a fisherman in May'? That's from *The Old Man and the Sea*. The book was written in Cuba. You should read it if you're going to do more of this blue water stuff. In July, when the big ones run deep, anyone *cannot* be a fisherman. More than anything, including luck, it takes persistence, and most people don't have it."

He takes two cans of Foster's Lager from an ice chest under one of the bench seats, pops the tops, and hands one to Jack. "You know what the Old Man, whose name was Santiago, says as he's fighting his marlin? 'Fish I love you and respect you very much. But I will kill you dead before this day ends.' Now that's some damn fine writing, don't you think? You get that by starting with one true sentence, and then you write another, and another, and finally you have a book of fiction that's truer than real life. That's the secret to telling a good story!"

Jack nods as if he knows what Edward is talking about and drinks down half the can of Foster's in one swallow, foam bubbling down his chin. He wipes off the foam with the back of his hand and says, "It *was* a nice fish, wasn't it?"

Edward unrigs the four rods, lays them on the deck, and climbs back into the captain's chair. "Let's head back to the barn, counselor," he says. "That's enough fun for one morning, I'd say." He goes below and comes back with two long cigars. "Arturo Fuentes," he says. Let's have a victory smoke, just like good old Red Auerbach."

IT'S NOON. *PILAR* is moored at a dock at the Key West Bight Marina. Jack, bone weary after his tarpon encounter, is below deck taking a nap on the stateroom bunk while Edward is topside, cooking two grouper filets, which he bought right off a commercial fishing boat at the marina, on a gas grill, for lunch. To accompany the grouper, there is a mango and avocado salad with lemon vinaigrette dressing, a loaf of crusty French bread, and more Foster's in the ice chest. Among his other talents, Edward is a gourmet cook. He said he came to appreciate good food while living in Paris as a young man; years later, when he could afford it, he went back to study at Le Cordon Bleu Culinary School. He still has not been specific about what business or businesses he's undertaken, saying only, "Oh, this and that over the years, some of which still generate royalties."

Jack is awakened by the clanging of a ship's bell up on deck and his host's voice calling out, "Lunch!" Clang clang clang! "Lunch is served!" He sees that all three polydactyl cats have been napping with him on the bunk. At the sound of the bell, they stretch, hop off the bunk, and walk up the stairway; apparently it's their lunchtime, too.

"That Hemingway look-alike contest is tonight, isn't it?" Jack asks, as he eats a lunch that reminds him of the dinner Marissa Kirkland "threw together" at the Arcadia. "Are you entering?"

"Naw, that's for amateurs," Edward answers. "I'll say that it is kind of strange to see all those guys who look like me knocking around town."

Guys who look like *me?* Jack remembers the woman

at The Sanctuary, a schoolteacher from Maine, who thinks she's Marie Antoinette. During one of his visits, this woman stood at the door of the conservatory, dressed in an evening gown and greeting everyone as they came in for tea, giving air kisses and saying, "It was so good of you to come."

So maybe Mr. Edward Hollingsworth really does think he's Ernest Hemingway. But what would be the harm in that? Perhaps, like Jack and Jenna, he's suffered some trauma in his life and this grand delusion is his way of coping. In fact, Edward has been interested in every small detail of Hope's disappearance and the ensuing events, with a particular interest in why Jack is so convinced that Slater Babcock is responsible. When Jack finally asked Edward, as he did Vernon Douglas, what he would do in a similar circumstance, Edward thought about it for a while, and replied, enigmatically, "Oh, I never know the ending of a story until I get there and see what the characters themselves want to do. We're not there yet with your story, Jack. But I think we're getting close."

18: OUTWARD BOUND

JACK AND EDWARD get together every day for the next five days. For Jack, this time spent with the man who thinks he's a deceased writer is like attending an Outward Bound school with Edward—or maybe Mad King George—as instructor. There is more fishing, this time a full day of fly-casting for bonefish from a flat-bottomed skiff, which Edward poles around the backwaters while standing on a raised seat in the rear of the boat; there is skeet shooting at a gun range on Big Coppitt Key (Edward, as Jack expected, is an expert with a shotgun. Jack managed to hit only four or five of the clays); there is snorkeling on the reefs off Key West, which are teaming with sea life, including several sharks that glided—too closely for comfort—below them;

there is sightseeing cruise to the Dry Tortugas, a group of islands seventy miles west of Key West.

Edward wishes he could take Jack wild boar hunting at a hunting preserve he knows up near Lake Okeechobee, but there isn't time. Jack doesn't know why there isn't time, he's not doing anything but avoiding the entire purpose of his trip, but he doesn't ask, because he does not want to either kill or be killed by a wild boar. If there were more time, Edward says—this making Jack wonder what sort of deadline Edward has—he'd take Jack on a cruise to Cuba. He knows a number of clandestine spots where they could drop *Pilar*'s anchor, swim ashore, and "pick up some Cohibas, Havana Club rum, and mami chulas," the last of which, Jack assumes, has something to do with female companionship. And there is much drinking, fine dining, and cigar smoking, with Jack sometimes sleeping in his room at the Casa Marina Resort, sometimes on an air mattress aboard *Pilar*, and sometimes not at all.

From time to time, they spot Slater Babcock around town. "Hhmmm," Edward says on the first sighting, Slater playing in a beach volley ball game. "Can't tell much about what's inside a man by how he looks. Just look at me!"

ON THE MORNING of the sixth day since he met Edward Hollingsworth, Jack awakens in his hotel room, feeling like you are supposed to feel after a Conch Republic bacchanal. He showers, has orange juice and coffee in the hotel coffee shop, and decides to walk the three miles to the marina where *Pilar* is moored. The walk will help clear his head. He plans to tell Edward that he has decided to go to Slater's house that morning and, finally, to confront the man. If Slater isn't there, Jack will find him. He will have Langdon's Derringer in his pocket, loaded this time. He will do whatever is necessary to get to the truth. He'll thank Edward for his help in understanding how a man's man behaves. Edward will want to accompany him, but Jack will decline, saying this is something he must do on his own.

Of course, he could go right to Slater's house. But he wants to see Edward, just in case something happens and he is unable to see his new friend and mentor one last time.

JACK FINDS EDWARD standing on the dock beside *Pilar* as if waiting for him. "I want to talk to you about something," Jack says.

"Sure, let's go aboard and have coffee," Edward answers, and steps from the dock down onto his boat's rear deck. When Jack hesitates, Edward says, "Come on, I just made a fresh pot," and goes down into the galley.

Jack steps onto the boat and starts down into the galley just as Edward is coming up holding two coffee mugs.

"It's such a nice morning," Edward tells Jack. "Let's take a little cruise and you can tell me what's on your mind."

"I don't have time for that," Jack answers. "I've decided to talk to Slater Babcock about Hope."

"He's not at his house, or at the bar," Edward says with a smile.

Jack is confused. "How do you know that?" he asks.

"Trust me, Jack. I know. So let's put out into the Straits and have a nice chat."

Jack follows Edward up onto the bridge and takes a chair as Edward casts off the lines, takes his captain's chair, starts the engines, and pulls away from the dock.

"Let's get out a ways," Edwards tells Jack. "Then I'll drop anchor. I've got something to tell you, too."

WHEN THEY ARE ten miles out, Edward cuts the engines and pushes a button that lowers the bow anchors. "Just twenty feet under the hull here," he says. "A perfect spot."

"I wanted to let you know that it's time for me to tell Slater who I am and what I want from him," Jack says. "I'm finally prepared to confront him and find out what happened to my daughter. As soon as we're back in, I'm going to find him."

Edward looks at Jack and nods. "Okay," he says, and climbs down from the bridge. "That's good to know. Back in a second."

A moment passes as Edward goes below deck. Jack hears a commotion, then is shocked to see Slater Babcock come up the ladder from the galley, followed by Edward, holding a shotgun. Slater's hands are tied behind his back with nylon rope, and there is a strip of duct tape across his mouth. He is clearly terrified.

Edward pushes Slater down into one of the fighting chairs on the stern. "All right, Jack," he says. "You want to talk to Slater Babcock. He's ready to listen. I awoke him from a sound sleep at six a.m." Then he rips the duct tape off of Slater's mouth.

"Are you fucking crazy?" Slater shouts. "Who the hell are you people? You kidnapped me! You're in a lot of trouble!"

Jack is too stunned to speak.

"It appears to me that you are the one in trouble, Mr. Babcock," Edward says. "Allow me to introduce you to Mr. Jack Tanner of Edina, Minnesota."

"Tanner?" Slater says.

"That's right," Edward says. "I believe you once dated his daughter, Hope."

Jack finds his voice. "What did you do with her?" he demands. "You killed her, didn't you?"

Slater begins to stand up but Edward pushes him back down with the barrel of the shotgun. "Easy now," Edward says. "Just sit there for a while, boy, and we'll see where we go from here."

"Look, Mr. Tanner, I really liked Hope. I have no idea what happened to her ..."

"You're lying!" Jack shouts, all the years of anger and frustration coming out. "You slimy little fuck!"

He steps toward Slater with clenched fists, but Edward steps in front of him.

"You know," Edward says, "I don't think that the kid

is ready for an honest exchange of information." He points over the starboard bow. "Cuba is about twenty miles that way. The Guantanamo Bay Naval Base is at the southeastern end of the island. If we were having this conversation there, we might employ what our government calls enhanced interrogation techniques. But we are not there, so we'll have to improvise."

He levels the shotgun at Slater and says, "Stand up."

Slater doesn't move. Edward jacks a shell into the shotgun's breech.

"Wait!" Slater shouts, and stands up. "I didn't do anything to her. I told the police everything I know!"

"We'll see," Edward says as Jack involuntarily flinches and takes a step backward, half expecting a blast from the shotgun.

"Untie his hands," Edward tells Jack.

Jack steps over to Slater, who turns around. Jack unties the rope and steps back as Slater rubs his wrists.

"Good," Edward says to Slater. "Now open the top of that seat behind you. It's an ice chest."

Slater does.

"Now reach in, take out that meat and throw it overboard. Keep on until it's all gone."

Slater, trembling, does as he's told, tossing bloody hunks of raw beef into the water.

"You know, Jack, I've caught a lot of fish right on this spot," Edward says. "Some of them were sharks. Hammerheads, bull sharks, black tip reef sharks, tigers … Other than the great whites, the tiger sharks are the most dangerous. Seem to have a real taste for human flesh."

As the bloody hunks of meat float on the surface, Jack and Slater watch for fins to appear. "Look over there," Edward says, pointing toward the bow. Two fins are cutting the water's surface. "Just dolphins, having a romp. They don't like meat, just fish, squid and shrimp."

Jack looks at Edward and asks, "What are we doing here?"

"It's Slater who will do the doing," he answers. "We're just here observing." He looks at Slater, who has finished his job and is standing there with bloody hands.

"Good. Now jump overboard."

"What?" Slater exclaims. "You're crazy! I'm not ..."

Before he can finish, Edward fires a shell into the air above Slater's head. If this is another one of my crazy dreams, I don't want to wake up, Jack thinks.

"I mean it, young man. I want you in the water while we continue our conversation."

"No, I can't," Slater says, starting to cry. "I'm afraid ... "

Edward levels the shotgun barrel directly at Slater's chest and jacks in another shell and says to Slater, "Hard way or easy way, as they say. Your choice."

Slater is shaking and whimpering. Jack notices a wet stain spreading on the front of his khaki shorts as he turns to face the stern.

"Hold on," Jack tells Edward. "I don't want this. Not like this. It's not right." He pauses, a tear forming in his eye. "Hope wouldn't want this ..."

Slater turns back around to face them as Edward lowers the shotgun. "You may have a point, Jack," he says. "The thing is, with these enhanced interrogation techniques, the subjects either tell you the truth to get you to stop, or they lie and tell you what you want to hear to get you to stop. It takes a trained interrogator like they have at Gitmo over there to tell the difference. And even they aren't sure a good deal of the time. I think our friend here would confess to anything just to stay in the boat, wouldn't you, Mr. Babcock?"

"Yes," Slater answers, looking as if he's about to faint. Then to Jack, "But I did not hurt Hope …"

"Okay, Jack, I'd say its time to head for the barn," Edward says. "Slater, go below and clean yourself up. Stay there until we reach port. Don't worry about the cats, they're tame. Take a nice hot shower, and pour yourself a drink. You can borrow a pair of my shorts if you like, in the dresser in the stateroom. They'll be too big, but at least they're dry!"

As Edward operates the electric hoist to raise the anchor, Jack sees the chunks of meat floating on the surface of the water begin to disappear as fish begin to take them. Then he sees fins approaching the area.

ON THE WAY in, Jack sits silently in the chair on the bridge. Edward, at the helm, is smoking a cigar. When they reach the Key West channel markers, he says, "That's what revenge looks like, Jack. I've had some experience with it. It can be pretty ugly, and usually, it's unsatisfying. Contrary to what you might think, it just doesn't make you feel any better. If you're a good man, it can just add to your pain. I frankly don't recommend it."

He pauses for a moment, then adds, "If you told me this morning that you were going home without trying to see Slater again, I wouldn't have brought him up on deck. No telling exactly how that was going to go, so best to avoid it if possible."

"Would you have actually fed him to the sharks?"

"That was up to you. This is your story we're in, Jack."

"If you made him jump in, and he confessed, and you let him back into the boat, he would just have denied everything later."

Edward reaches into the pocket of his canvas shorts and comes out with a micro tape recorder. "I would have had it all on here."

"What happens now?" Jack asks as Edward slows to no-wake speed in the Key West harbor channel.

"Slater Babcock goes on being Slater Babcock, you go home, and I move on to the next port-of-call. It's time."

"But Slater will go to the police ..."

"Well, I've thought about that," Edward says, turning out of the channel toward the marina. "The thing is, I happen to know that his big bartender is dealing drugs from right there in the Scupper. Before I send him on his way, I'll suggest that he forgets about this cruise, and I'll forget that I know about the Oxycodone you can get at his place without a prescription, as well as the coke and dexies and bennies, and the Rohypnol. Ever heard of that one? They call it the date rape drug. My info is that our Mr. Babcock regularly has his bartender slip it into the drinks of young girls—many of them underage. So I think he'll develop a nice case of amnesia about the events of this fine morning." He looks over at Jack. "You should, too."

"How do you know all that?" Jack asks.

Edward smiles. "Oh, I've spent a lot of time in Key West. People tell me things, just like you did. I'm a good listener."

19: HOMEWARD BOUND

IT WOULDN'T DO for a United States Senator in these troubled economic times to be seen in the first-class cabin, especially a liberal Democrat from Minnesota, so on this flight from Dulles International to Minneapolis-St. Paul, he is in aisle seat 8A, with an attractive strawberry blond about his age in 8C and no one between them.

After the 747 achieves cruising altitude, the senator touches Jenna on the arm and asks, "You have business in D.C.?" Hoping she'll ask his, which in his self-assessment is no less than helping guide the nation through the war on terrorism, global economic meltdown, health care reform, and (alleged) climate change.

Jenna Tanner looks up from her book, *The Girl with*

the Dragon Tattoo. She'd hoped to avoid a conversation with the senior senator from her home state, not only because she didn't vote for the man, but also because he has a reputation as a skirt-chaser.

"I had some business in McLean but it's concluded," she answers, and returns to her book. That is true, and now Jenna is flying home. She has not called Jack to tell him, because she wants her return to be a surprise.

When the senator dozes off, snoring, she looks out at the clouds and thinks about how she and Jack met.

After growing up in Traverse City, a small town in northern Michigan where her father was a family-practice physician, the University of Michigan was a swirling Mardi Gras of intellectual and sensual stimulation. Jenna took to the coursework and was an honors student, eventually choosing a joint major in psychology and sociology, with the intent of becoming a social worker specializing in abused women.

The Madison campus was a strange dichotomy of Norman Rockwell football weekends and passionate social protests. Free to be herself, Jenna studied, hung out with friends, joined the Kappa Kappa Gamma sorority, dated casually, sometimes becoming involved sexually for brief periods and sometimes not.

She met Jack one evening in the law library, where she worked during her junior year. Jack was a second-year law student from Syracuse, New York. He was good-looking, if not movie star handsome, and had a nice personality. But what Jenna liked most about him was that he seemed grounded and had a clear sense of purpose about what he wanted in life (a career in law and a family), when so many young people of their generation did not. His father was a corporate tax attorney, and Jack wanted to become one, too. Like her, he wanted to have a family. They quickly became a couple and then more than a couple: lovers and best friends. When she was a senior and he was in his third year at the law school, they became engaged. When they graduated, they were married in Grace Episcopal Church in Traverse City and honeymooned in Cozumel.

No marriage is perfect but theirs was very good, Jenna thought all through the years, and she knew that Jack felt the same way. She didn't know if he'd ever been unfaithful. *Unfaithful*, what an odd term. Can't you be faithful to someone, but imperfect? She had many opportunities, with men coming on to her, but she was tempted only once; for some reason she didn't understand, she decided to attend the twentieth reunion of her Traverse City High School class without Jack, who was on a business trip to New York.

Her junior and senior year boyfriend, Steve Talbot, was there. He looked good, with salt-and-pepper hair and still lean and athletic, unlike most of the other men there. He was recently divorced. The disc jockey played their song, "Mr. Blue, " sung by syrupy voiced Johnny Mathis; they danced cheek-to-cheek in the high school gym, which was decorated that night as it was for their senior prom—"An Evening in Paris."

Steve was a real-estate developer in San Diego. They were both staying in the Traverse City Marriott. They agreed to have "just one drink" together in the hotel bar before turning in for the night. It did seem a magical night to Jenna, and it was clear that he wanted her, and it was so flattering to be wanted that way, again.

One drink became three or four, she lost count; she drank only occasionally and moderately, and she was tipsy. He "walked her home" to her room. The good night kiss was on the mouth and lingered; she took her room key from her purse, and she knew that all she had to do was to hand it him. She did not, but he took it from her hand, and she let him ...

"Never before and never again" was her thought the next morning when, mercifully, Steve had left while she pretended to be asleep. An early flight, his note said, and nothing more. Her excuse to herself was that she was drunk. Some day, when the time was right, she'd tell Jack, but that time had not yet come.

The pilot's voice announcing their imminent arrival at Minneapolis-St. Paul airport brings her out of the reminiscence. She is eager to find a taxi and give the driver the magic address: 4606 Maitland Avenue, Edina.

Home again.

THE FIRST THING Jenna notices as the taxi pulls into the driveway is that the lawn is overgrown and has dandelions, which Jack would never allow, and that the white trim and wooden shutters do need painting, as Jack told her. It's July, so she has missed her tulips—

along with so many other things, she reflects—but the columbine, aster, and salvia look healthy; the hosta are crowded and need separating.

Her good friend and next-door neighbor, Janet Davenport, is standing on her lawn, watering a bed of hydrangeas with a garden hose. Janet sees the taxi, drops the hose, and rushes over as the taxi driver is unloading her luggage. "Oh, Jenna," Janet says, crying as she hugs her friend. "Welcome home." Janet steps back and pauses, as if considering what to say next. "As soon as you get settled, we need to talk. Call me." Then she goes back to her flowers.

Jenna punches in the garage door code and uses her key to enter the house through the mudroom door. Jack will be at work, of course, but she is surprised to find both the BWM and her Subaru wagon in the garage. He must have gotten a ride in, for some reason. Her plan is to unpack, then drive over to Jerry's supermarket, stock up, and be preparing Jack's favorite dinner, which is beef Stroganoff with noodles and a strawberry rhubarb pie, when he arrives home from the office. Candlelight and a good California burgundy, will be nice, too. And there's that sheer black Victoria's Secret nightgown...

20: FINDING JACK

WHEN JACK DOESN'T come home for dinner, Jenna makes herself wait until ten p.m., thinking he must be out doing something or other, then she calls her neighbor Janet Davenport, even though it's late. Janet says that Jack hasn't been home for about a month or so; she isn't sure exactly how long he's been gone. He left without saying anything to anyone in the neighborhood, as far as she knows. She didn't mention that to Jenna out in the driveway because she assumed that Jenna knew where he was.

Jenna, alone in the big house, doesn't sleep that night. She is furious with Jack for not telling her what is going on. She doesn't need this kind of stress, not now … But then, at two a.m., in bed, with the TV on for company, she realizes that of course Jack didn't know she was coming home. How insensitive and self-centered of her to think only of herself, when something might have happened to him.

She watches the clock until eight in the morning, then calls Jack's law firm and is put through to Helen Abelard, the office administrator, whom she knows. Helen, always diplomatic, hides her surprise that Jenna doesn't know where her husband is. She tells Jenna about the phone call from Jack asking that replacement credit cards be over-nighted to some hotel in Richmond, Virginia; she doesn't recall which hotel, but if it's important, she can look it up on the FedEx invoice.

Then Helen hesitates before asking if Jenna knows that Jack "has left the firm."

No, Jenna says, she didn't know that.

"As far as I know, Jack hasn't been in touch with anyone else here," Helen says. "Maybe you should call Pete Dye. Didn't you work with him when …"

"When Hope disappeared," Jenna finishes for her. "I'm sure his number is somewhere in the house, but do you have it?"

PETE DYE IS in Los Angeles when he gets Jenna's voicemail on his cell phone that afternoon and returns her call. He tells her what he knows. because she is his client too: Jack's cross-country motorcycle trip, and his probable destination, where he must be by now, and that Slater Babcock is there.

"I'm going to Key West," Jenna says.

"No Jenna, let me," Dye answers. "My business here in L.A. is done. It really is better if I go."

"Good God, Pete, what do you think Jack is going to do? Or has done … You haven't talked to him lately?"

"I called his cell several times since we last spoke, when he was in Madison, but it always went straight to voicemail. I thought about going to Key West to find him, but he told me not to."

"And now you will go?"

"Yes," Pete Dye says. "I've just received some news he needs to hear. And you too. I tried to call him this morning and was just about to call you at The Sanctuary."

Jenna was not aware that Pete knew she'd been hospitalized, but she lets that pass. "What is the news?"

"In person is best for this, Jenna. I'll catch the red eye to Minneapolis and see you in the morning."

JENNA'S NEXT CALL is to the office of Dr. Michael Feldman, her Minneapolis psychiatrist, asking for an appointment as soon as possible.

21: FINDING HOPE

THE MORNING AFTER the boat ride with Edward and Slater, Jack is in his room at the Casa Marina Resort, packing his saddlebag, when there is a knock on the door. He opens it and is more than surprised to see Pete Dye standing there. He doesn't ask Dye how he found him here at the Casa Marina Resort: Pete Dye, Private Eye.

"Hi Jack," Dye says. "May I come in?"

FIVE HOURS LATER, Delta flight 2522 lifts off the grooved asphalt of runway 08R at Miami International Airport, bound for Minneapolis-St. Paul International, with Jack in seat 3A and Pete Dye beside him in 3B. After speaking with Dye, Jack had called Jenna from the hotel room. They cried together about Pete Dye's news about Hope, and about Jenna being home, and about Jack's mad adventure.

Dye's news is that Hope Tanner's killer is buried in a cemetery on the grounds of the South Dakota State Penitentiary in Sioux Falls. The day before his scheduled execution by lethal injection, Lyle Cutler, a fifty-five-year-old former guidance counselor at Central High School in Rapid City, told his minister that he'd accepted Jesus as his Savior and confessed to the murder of Annie Knox, a seventeen-year-old Central High student, for which he'd been convicted. He also admitted that he'd murdered four other girls over the past twelve years, including Hope Tanner. He said he wanted to tell the warden the same thing "so he won't feel badly about giving me the needle, because I deserve to die for what I've done."

After an audience with the warden, Cutler, with his lawyer present, told representatives from the governor's attorney general's offices that he frequently visited admissions offices at Midwestern colleges and universities as part of his duties as a guidance counselor. He'd been doing this for twenty-two years. He said that, beginning eight years earlier, a voice in his head sometimes told him to randomly choose and murder girls "as a lesson to all schoolgirls to obey their parents, do their homework, and not act like sluts or they'll end up like the dead girls."

It was later discovered that he had been treated for schizophrenia all of his adult life, but he had not disclosed this to his employer. He'd never been married.

He had a brother and two sisters, who, when notified by the warden of his impending execution, said that they did not wish to attend or to claim their brother's body.

After Cutler confessed to the murders, the governor stayed his execution until he was able to lead police to the places he'd buried his victims other than Annie Knox, whose body had been found in a drainage ditch in a farm field outside Rapid City by a farmer training his German shorthaired pointer to hunt.

Hope Tanner, whom Cutler identified as "that Madison college girl," was buried in the proverbial shallow grave under a live oak tree in a stand of woods about ten miles north of the campus. Cutler said that he was just driving around the campus neighborhood after having dinner following a visit to the university, when he saw a pretty girl walking alone. On an impulse, he asked her if she wanted a ride. She said no thank you, very politely, and began walking faster. He stopped the car and got out. She began to run but he was faster. Why was she running from him? He just wanted to help her. Didn't she understand that? None of them seemed to understand that. So she had to be taught a lesson, like the others. He grabbed her and forced her into his car. She was screaming but no one seemed to hear. He pulled a hunting knife out of the glove compartment and told her to stop screaming or he'd have to cut her. She did, and began to cry, which was all right. He drove out into the country, took her out of the car, made her undress, and, holding the knife to her throat, raped her. He told her to promise that she wouldn't tell anyone, and she did, but he knew she was lying, so he kept stabbing her in her neck and torso until she was quiet. Then he got a shovel out of the car trunk and buried her.

Shuffling along in handcuffs and ankle shackles, he led a team of F.B.I. agents and Wisconsin State Police to the site. Vernon Douglas was there, too. When Hope's body was found, it was transported to the Dane County Medical Examiner's Office and identified by dental records on file at the university.

When Jack did not answer calls to his house or cell phone from Douglas, and did not return voicemail messages, and Douglas could not otherwise locate him, or Jenna, he called Pete Dye. During his first visit to Madison after Hope's disappearance, Dye had made a courtesy visit to Douglas, and left his business card.

When Pete Dye told Jack that Cutler had confessed to Hope's murder, Jack asked for the details. I'll tell you if you insist, Dye had responded, but please don't, and Jack did not.

22: IN MEMORIAM
TWO WEEKS LATER

AT EIGHT A.M. on a July Saturday morning, Jack Tanner is sitting on a wrought iron patio chair in the backyard of a stately redbrick Georgian colonial at 4606 Maitland Avenue in Edina, Minnesota. He is wearing a navy blue pinstriped suit, white shirt, red tie, and black loafers. Above him, a grey squirrel with an acorn in its mouth scrabbles along a low branch on a gnarled oak tree. A bird finds its morning song somewhere higher up. Water droplets on the lawn sparkle in the sunshine; the sprinkler system had turned off a half hour earlier.

Jenna comes out of the door from the kitchen, wearing a black silk suit, white blouse, black low-heeled shoes, and a pearl necklace and earrings. She is carrying two mugs of steaming coffee. She hands one to Jack and sits beside him.

"We'll get through today," she says.

He smiles at her. "I know."

"Really we will."

"I know."

Jack has told Jenna all about the mysterious Edward Hollingsworth. Now she says, "He might have been a ghost, you know, your friend Edward. Hemingway's ghost. Or maybe a guardian angel taking that particular human shape ..."

"I'd like to think that he was one of those, and not just some delusional Looney Tunes," Jack answers. "You know what? I think he was trying to teach me something. About being a man, maybe."

"Do you remember that song by America we liked in the 70s?" Jenna asks. "About how Oz gave nothing to the Tin Man that he didn't already have?" She squeezes his hand. "You're a good man. The best I've ever come across. That guy, or that ghost or angel, and I really like Hemingway's ghost idea, didn't teach you anything about being a man that you didn't already know."

Jack looks up at the squirrel in the oak tree, and then at the window of Hope's room, as if expecting to see his daughter's smiling face through the glass.

"I wonder where he is now," Jenna says.

"I don't know. Before Pete and I drove to Miami, I stopped at the marina to say good-bye. His boat was gone. The dock master said he paid his bill that morning and left. Said he comes back every year at that time, and has been doing that for as long as the dock master's been there, which is twelve years. He left me a note. It said that if I ever wanted to get in touch with him, just put a note in a bottle and drop it into any body of water that flows to the sea, and he'll get it."

Three deer, a doe and two spotted fawns, wander into the yard and pause.

"Look at that," Jenna says. "A family."

THERE IS ANOTHER service for Hope Tanner at First Lutheran Church, the Reverend Johansen again presiding. In attendance are most of the same friends and family who came to the first gathering, as well as Pete Dye, Vernon Douglas, many of Jack's former law partners, whom he welcomes warmly and with gratitude, and, representing the Boston chapter of the Devil's Disciples, Harold Whittaker and Langdon Lamont. Jack had promised to let the boys know what happened to him, and he did. The other remaining Disciples had pressing business or family commitments, but sent their condolences, and generous donations to a charity the Tanners had named in lieu of flowers—a scholarship fund at the University of Wisconsin endowed in memory of Hope Tanner.

This time, Hope is there too, resting in a cherrywood casket, set upon a rolling metal bier in front of the altar. Sunlight through a stained glass window illuminates a display of photographs of Hope showing her growing from infancy until she is nineteen years old, forever.

Jack and Jenna do get through it: Reverend Johansen's sermon, the choir music, tender words of remembrance from Jack, loving comments from Jenna, tearful readings of prepared remarks from Hope's friends. Sometime during the service, Jack Tanner prays for the second time in his life: *Thank you for giving her back to us.*

He cannot call himself a convert. He will attend Sunday services regularly with Jenna, if she wants them to. She's said she might like that. But he still has doubt ("reasonable doubt," as jurors are instructed in the courtroom) about whether a Prime Mover oversees our lives, or whether souls survive, or if being good matters somehow in the cosmic scheme of things. But he does now understand that prayers can sometimes, somehow, be answered, and that, knowing this, his life has been unalterably changed.

AT CRYSTAL LAKE Cemetery, Hope Tanner is interred in a grave located beside two others that Jack purchased upon arriving home. The burial service is unspeakably hard, as it must be when, in a fracturing of nature's plan, parents lay a child to rest. When the service is finished, Jack and Jenna are surprised to find that there is enough left of them to survive.

Just enough.

23: ON THE ROAD, AGAIN
THREE MONTHS LATER

A PERFECT AUTUMN morning, the leaves an artist's pallet of red, gold, yellow, and orange; pumpkins on porches; apple cider time; storm windows being hung on older houses without triple-tracks; students grooved into school routines, summer vacation a memory; hunters oiling shotguns and bolt-action rifles; farmers reaping what they sowed.

A moving van is pulling away from the curb in front of the Tanner's Edina house, with all of their possessions packed inside. They watch from the front porch, holding hands. Jack has found a job on the faculty of the University of Michigan Law School, his alma mater, to teach a course in tax law.

The dean's office had sent e-mails about the position to all graduates practicing tax law in the private and public sectors. Jack was one of thirty applicants, but the only one to have been editor of the law review and a member of the Order of the Coif. Aided by a strong recommendation from the managing partner at Hartfield, Miller, and perhaps, Jack suspects, by knowledge about the Tanner family's history, he was hired.

Jenna has been doing well. They do not have "closure," they both know; Jack doesn't even comprehend what that word might mean to them. But knowing, finally, what happed to their daughter, and bringing her home, has helped them both. Jenna's doctor in Minneapolis has recommended a colleague in Ann Arbor.

It is hard to leave the home where they raised Hope and had so many good times and treasured memories, but Jack's unemployment had put a serious strain upon their finances, and it will be good to get a paycheck again. Jack had always thought about someday leaving the daily grind of corporate law practice and teaching, so he is excited to begin his new job; academia will be his refuge.

Jack and Jenna have promised friends they will return often to visit. They told that to Hope, too, at the cemetery, early that morning. And someday, they told their daughter, they will come back to stay.

AT SEVENTY MILES per hour, there is no way for two people on a motorcycle to talk, unless they have helmets with an intercom system, which Jack and Jenna do have. They are cruising along I-94, westbound, just passing the Eau Claire exit in Wisconsin. It's an eleven-hour ride from Edina to Ann Arbor. Right now, Jack is talking into Jenna's ear about motorcycles.

"So I finally chose the Harley Road King because it's less bulky than the Electra Glide, but still heavy enough for stability and comfort. But there's no matching the Japanese for reliability, so that's why I wanted this Honda Gold Wing for us, just like Harold Whittaker's."

That morning, before the moving van arrived, the Tanner's BMW sedan was loaded onto a car carrier truck. It was Jenna's idea to ship the car and for them to ride together to Ann Arbor on a motorcycle. Jack was surprised and reluctant—been there, done that—but Jenna convinced him by saying, "You've never told me much about your ride to Key West, and I really want to hear about it. What better way than during another motorcycle trip?"

WHEN JACK GOT the law school job, he and Jenna flew to Detroit and drove a rental car to Ann Arbor. After three days of looking with a realtor, they found a smaller version of their Edina house on a leafy street near the campus. They knew before they went into the house that it was the right one for them.

The house is a three-bedroom, four-bath, redbrick colonial, twenty years newer than the Edina house, but still charming, with "great curb appeal and a highly desirable location for resale," according to the realtor—a plump, pleasant, Chatty-Cathy woman in her fifties, about whose personal life the Tanners have heard way too much.

On their first tour, they were up on the second floor, which has a spacious master suite, and two other bedrooms. The realtor led them through the master, which they liked, and then into the first of the other bedrooms, which, she'd explained, was the larger of the two.

"This one will be the guest room," Jenna said to Jack. "I think we'll get lots of company, especially during the Wolverines football season, because you'll be able to get tickets."

They followed the realtor out into the hallway, but after looking at one another, not into the third bedroom. They could hear the realtor saying, "Now this one is a bit smaller, you could use it as a bedroom, or a study, and it has a very nice view of that big oak tree in the back yard, where a squirrel family lives ..."

Jenna had smiled, put her arm through Jack's, and they headed for the stairway, leaving the surprised realtor all alone in Hope's room.

ACKNOWLEDGMENTS

This novel would not have reached a final, publishable draft without the excellent editing of Arnold Dolin, a man with long experience in the New York publishing business, who challenged me to make it better all along the way. Joseph Pittman, editorial director of Vantage Point Books, did the same, asking such polite questions as, "Do you think the ending is a bit rushed?" Yes Joe, it was—when you live with a story for such a long time, it is tempting to just want it to be *over with*.

Finally, and most important, even though I'd started and stopped several novels over the years without finishing them, losing interest when imagined ideas seemed to lose their magic in the actual writing, my wife Mary continued to offer support and encouragement, even when there was no apparent reason to do so. Every writer should be so lucky.

William Wells
Naples, Florida
September 2011

CPSIA information can be obtained at www.ICGtesting.com
Printed in the USA
BVOW020856270312

286171BV00001B/3/P

9 781936 467297

TABLE OF CONTENTS

Acknowledgement v
Prologue vii

Chapter 1 1
Chapter 2 23
Chapter 3 32
Chapter 4 46
Chapter 5 57
Chapter 6 80
Chapter 7 96
Chapter 8 121
Chapter 9 139
Chapter 10 152
Chapter 11 159
Chapter 12 179
Chapter 13 190
Chapter 14 215
Chapter 15 233
Chapter 16 249
Chapter 17 267
Chapter 18 282
Chapter 19 297
Chapter 20 317
Chapter 21 335
Chapter 22 347

ACKNOWLEDGEMENT

There are no words that can help me describe my gratitude to my friends and family who have helped me turn my boyish dreams of living in the realm of knights and dragons into a verity that is told through the pages of this tale. With all great adventures there comes a time whereby recognition must be bestowed upon those who support the hero through burden and hardship. I am no hero by any means, though if I were, then I am proud to have had the support in which I have wholly received. As such, I would like to thank each and every one of my loved ones in their unrelenting encouragement, honesty, and devotion in seeing my dreams come true. I could not have asked for more. Moreover, I want to thank my beloved, who has spent countless hours scouring through pages of unbaked storytelling with the intention to strengthen that which I could neither see nor envision without the help of her expertise. I am eternally greatful. Lastly, with all my heart, I would like to thank my father, who in his wonder of literature has guided me in better understanding the value of academics, but more so who has inspired me to take a good many leaps of faith in regards to the telling of my own stories.

My hearltfelt thanks,
D.C. Andrews

PROLOGUE

My name is Cillian Tertius, son of Diadorus Tertius, and I am a builder. In truth, I no longer stand as such, for my hands have long since had the strength to mold the timbers, nor my heart the will to form the engines of war, the craft which defined my purpose in the legion; its number, that of XVI, its emblem, that of the Vined Sword. For years I have chosen to abandon the memories of the life I led in my youth. I have done so not out of shame or penitence, but rather to give my poor and abraded mind a chance to see this world absent of its errors, and of the evils that once plagued it. Now, however, at the ending of my long years on this earth, I see in all its clarity that time alone does not let one forget a good many things about our past, like the grip of a sword, the scent of blood, and the pain of loss.

And so as I sit here in my chair made of oak, the warmth of a steady hearth at my back, and a quill nestled in the arch of my hand, I prepare myself to return to a time I have long set aside, to share with you a piece of a story, one that is but a pale echo in a great tale of little disremembrance. In these pages, I will share an account of my youth, and of the part I played during the second *War of Ascension*. Though, I wish to beckon your patience fair reader, for I am old, my mind as gray as the hue of my hair. Therefore, the telling of this story will prove difficult. But I will, to the very best of my aged memory, coalesce the events that I had seen firsthand with those stories told to me by the men and women whose own tales are wholly linked to mine. With that said, I ask only one more thing of you. I ask that you do not see me as the champion of this history — this is not my intent for this work, and to name me so would otherwise distort the portrayal of my true self. In these words, I seek to bestow recognition upon the many who will come to be named, and to the untold nameless, so that the memory of their deeds will never be lost to the coming eras of this lasting peace, and so that their sacrifices are nevermore overshadowed by the great evil that brought it about.

To do this I will first need to act as an historian. But, seeing as how the *Library of the Augurs*, the place in which this vellum will surely rest, or perhaps be buried, has at present many exhaustive accounts of our long ages, I will attempt, on behalf of my foreign readers, to be as concise as I can with the history of the Anolian people, and of the events which will come to shape the foundation of my story. To that end, I will begin. But I expect, or rather I trust, that you, my kinsmen, will already be acquainted with much of these histories.

In the centuries prior to the era known as the *Great Unification*, the lands which would come to encompass the Kingdom of Anolia were once divided into twenty-three dominions, each ruled by a chieftain, or at times an overlord, whose design for sovereignty of rule came from endless war. By virtue of this practice, the people of these warring tribes saw little of firm peace, and knew nothing of genuine unity, despite that the heart of their political, religious, and social culture was, in fact, indistinguishable, as studied by our present scholars. However, at its heart our knowledge of this era is still very limited; the finer points ever lost, it would seem, to the waxing of time. We know only with certainty that the fifth century historian, Eaovis of Findor, has named this point in time as the *Age of Scarlet Rivers*, for the waters that flowed in every corner of the land were stained with never-ending battle.

The end of this era came some thousand years ago with the emergence of the brothers, Andiel and Anoarin, sons of the warlord Dioclexis II, who ruled the region now occupied by the port-city of Satricum. Under the influence of their father's lifelong view of grandeur, the two brothers set out to achieve their own designs to end the system of endless war, and to consolidate within the limits of the regions a single, unified territory that would be ruled under one controlling power. Such were the years of the *Great Unification*, twelve to be precise, wherein the two brothers led their armies on a series of brutal campaigns of dominance. These onslaughts were fruitful to their ambitions, but in turn the brothers also saw the extension of their supremacy encroach upon the borders of foreign powers far beyond their intended mark. This contact led to two more serious and prolonged wars, the first being against the pirate Kings Hiero and Hytan of Illyria, and the second against King Anthucur, the tyrant of Eraclea, who was rather quick to assimilate into his army the last coalition of those dominions whose most ardent warriors refused to be conquered. Nevertheless, the strength of Andiel's and Anoarin's will could not be undone, for the power which grew under their banners was too great a force for any army to defeat.

It is important to note that it was in these wars that our records first reveal the temperaments of each brother, and of the qualities that had begun to differentiate them. To draw upon the words of Eaovis once more, Andiel was said to be a man of many remarkable traits, the most significant of which was his ability to balance the need for violence with the dispensation of *clemencia*, or mercy in our common tongue. As such, it was in his practice to incorporate, not subjugate, the capitulated into his vision of peace, or offer banishment, and not the end of a sword, to those whose heart did not wish to take part in his vision. This characteristic proved vital in the wars of unification, and certainly in the conflicts which followed, for it is chronicled that whole armies and dominions had fallen to his earnest tongue, rather than by the sword.

Conversely, this is not the feeling we get from Anoarin during this time, even if it could be claimed that he had once shared in the same quality as his brother, especially in the early campaigns of succession. In all my years of study, I have come to learn that Anoarin's view of peace had ultimately been distorted by the wars he fought in, but more so, it would seem, from the resistance he had encountered by those fighting men who vied to be defiant until their end. Thus, it can be said that Anoarin's mercy grew ever more fickle with each confrontation, his position of rule rooted in sureties, electing execution for his captives rather than wagering upon a blurred sense of devotion from the defeated.

The difference between these temperaments, which I have briefly laid out, will greatly shape the events that I will next recount. At the end of these long and bloody wars, the two brothers stood at the head of the greatest military might in the eastern territories, and they saw, in its wake, the formation of a boundless kingdom, which they called Anolia — its name taken from our goddess of wealth and prosperity.

Peace had been established, a firm unity formed from the ashes of war. It was at this point that the lords of the conquered dominions were pressed with a final query: the appointment of their king. It can hardly be said that there was an inkling of doubt in the decision, for the chronicle states that it was immediately clear to all that Andiel should be appointed to the throne, and not because he stood the elder or the more high-spirited of the two, but for the reason that there was little justification in appointing Anoarin to a position of power, one that he would surely use to turn the land into a realm of pure tyranny just as he had so openly showed during the wars. From this point of view, among a good many others, the lords rallied with Andiel, bestowing onto him the magnate of king: the highest in the order of the augurs, chief administer of justice, and sovereign of all lords. And in this way, the era of the *Great Unification* had ended, and the age of Andiel began, A.E. as we call it, with regard to the recording of our current years.

As a result of this decision Anoarin's heart heightened with furious resentment towards his brother, for he could not fathom why it was that his position as conqueror, equal in rank to Andiel's, was flatly denounced and pushed aside by the lords he had subdued. Thus, it can be inferred, that it was at this time when Anoarin's love for his brother began to fade into nothingness, though this is only a supposition of mine based on the writings of the poet Ostilius of Ospia, whose works spoke of the rise of Anoarin's rabid desire to be king. It is unlikely, I also suppose, that Ostilius' words are completely removed from the truth, for it is shown that without delay Anoarin had turned the palace court into another theatre of war, fighting stubbornly against Andiel's rule by attempting to acquire an army of supporters among the lords that had so quickly turned their back on him.

In the spirit of the new peace, Anoarin first took the egalitarian route to strengthen his claim to the throne. He first proposed a series of radical changes in the law, the greatest of them being the redistribution of the conquered lands in a similar way to how they were previously split, promising autocratic power in civil and judicial life to the lords in vassalage. So strong was this promise that Anoarin swiftly gained loyalty amongst the wealthiest of the lords, those who cared little in the idea of military autonomy when compared to the chance to regain a greater semblance of power through wealth. Nevertheless, most of the nobility feared what would happen if Anoarin took power, and so they were incessantly opposed to his ascension, or in fuelling his stir for that matter.

Hence from the outset of his efforts, Anoarin stood peerless once again, and because of it his fury and appetite for the throne escalated to a degree of near madness. For five years he tried to win the majority favour, but by the end his methods had turned to those of befouling; secreting about in the shadows of the court with the poison of ever-new and outlandish promises, and the ceaseless blackening of his brother's claim and character. He even amassed a following among the *Inferi*, the cult of heathenish priests who saw the underworld as the cardinal dominion for all souls to rest in the afterlife. From their malignant tongues they endorsed Anoarin's position, spreading it as far as their disciples could bring it. Another year had passed in these foul ways with nothing but the air of vagrancy attached to Anoarin's name, all whilst Andiel's influence grew evermore under the heavy weight of the kingdom's growth.

From this point onward, dear reader, the tale of the two brothers dabbles in the realm of dark sorcery, but I trust that memory alone will see these next words as absolute truth. Here, Anoarin's mind succumbed to the wicked desperation of his desires, his envenomed words replaced by sharp steel. In 7 A.E., an armed conflict broke out at the unveiling of the new palace hall in the capital; the same which stands today in the region we call Tolerium. At the head of a band of pirate mercenaries disguised as his gift bearers, Anoarin sprung his assault to depose the king. Andiel's daughter, named Caia, was mortally wounded when she leapt in front of Anoarin's dagger that plunged for her mother's heart. In the end, Anoarin's attempt at the throne ended in failure. With his sell swords dead to a man, Anoarin escaped into the very shadows he once prowled, only this time, it is said, with wounds upon his flesh that no man could endure.

From here on twenty years had passed with no sight of Anoarin; so great a length of time that even the histories spend little to no effort in depicting the evil he tried to cloud upon the people in these two ensuing decades. At the very beginning, however, it is presented quite clearly that talk of Anoarin's treachery was ever alive on the tongues of every man in Anolia, these words also reaching distant shores. Be that as it may, it seems that by 27 A.E. there is no longer any mention of the occurrence within our writings. Anoarin's tale began to dissipate to the point of fabrication well before the quarter of the century arrived. I will not claim the precise reason for this happening, even though many scholars far wiser then I have explicitly stated that it was a product of Andiel's wish to bury the truth of it, a scheme that was strengthened among his most devoted lords who also wished to see away the consequences of the dark events. Yet it remains, after all, a notion that I *should* elaborate upon, for I believe that during this time there was, in fact, a change within the kingdom which aided in the fading of Anoarin's tale, one that has given direction to my life, and purpose for my craft.

As the tale of Anoarin faded, the Kingdom of Anolia prospered, swelling considerably under Andiel's desire to see his realm ripen, and to some extent, become superior in power than that of the neighbouring states long established. By 30 A.E. Anolia had reached a standing that was unmatched by any territory in her influence. Economically speaking, her wealth grew to unimaginable heights. From end to end a system of paved roadways were laid out to join each of the former dominions, some 450,000 square miles, to the capital, leaving no territory unreachable, or isolated, to the matters of the kingdom, or from the need of assistance. This was the foundation from which a near hundred villages, six walled towns, three of which were suited for the construction of a port, and two major cities, Easteria and Heraea, were established, the latter two having been organized in their regions to be a central hub for foreign and domestic trade. These advancements then saw the social life of the Anolian people flourish by leaps and bounds, and because of this the population rose equally rapidly, surrounded by no short amount of agricultural and commercial bounty. Religion was also modified, because as inclusivity among the people increased, so did the number of the divine; a good many being the lesser gods within the greater pantheon. Thus the *Sacrarium*, the sanctum of the augurs, saw the need to adopt a new central body of worship, which by Andiel's decree included each and every deity as far back as the people cared to comprise.

All of these aspects of prosperity, though they certainly encouraged the action, stand not the greatest reason in the ebbing of Anoarin's existence. It is, however, my unshakable belief that the chief cause that assisted in the ridding of Anoarin's tale was the kingdom's military reforms, or to put it more boldly, the foundation of her grand legions. Andiel inaugurated a system in which the army became a standing force, which was subdivided into twenty-three legions of volunteer soldiers that were paid and outfitted exclusively by the crown, and whose organization would better serve to guard the borders of the kingdom's vast territory. These legions remained solely under Andiel's control, a power wholly accepted by the assembly of the nobility, who wished for nothing more than to continue the cessation of war. But, Andiel himself advocated that the volunteer soldier would better serve him if he were to fight under a commander of his own choosing. For this reason, he empowered a number of his well-standing lords to oversee his legions; strictly as an extension of his *auctoritas*, or his all encompassing authority, an act which still shapes the design of the army today. Thus, the common man was not only able to adopt a life of soldiering by desire, but he also had the ability to elect to which legion he favoured to serve in, most of the crop choosing to serve the lords who had once commanded their fathers, or the nearest to their own hearth.

And so from this time onward the legions became the backbone of Anolia's mighty position, unified in its purpose to defend the realm as a single army, but altogether transforming this army into minor factions, each one bearing a unique insignia upon their armour to exemplify the regional and historical characteristics of the men who fought within them. In fact, this contributed to the strengthening of the unification as opposed to its fracturing, as one might suppose it would. Men's hearts have always gravitated towards competition, and so this allowed for harmonious rivalries to be born between the legions, and among former enemies no less, in such areas as sport and physical condition, and prowess upon the battlefield.

With these reforms the cycle of war had been brought to a close, for those who wished to lead peaceful lives absent the touch of a sword had received it, and a sense of military authority had been returned to those lords who wished to regain it. Now, there was a new subject of wonder on the tongues of the Anolian people for these years in question. So prevalent, in fact, that in the first year of the reforms, approximately 24 A.E., 125,000 men, many of whom were already under arms, were inspired to be the first to fill the ranks, followed by another 73,000 of new stock over the subsequent half decade. So, the Anolian army had amounted to numbers of great magnitude, but nevertheless they remained infinitesimal when compared to the evil that would soon come to test its might.

Now, dear reader, these next passages will form the last of the history that concerns my own account, though having reached this point I must admit that I still do not know how I should begin, or rather how best to encapsulate a time wrought with the lifeblood of twisted sorcery; devilries and horrors I have never cared to remember until the writing of this tale. But terror, to be forthright, is not what hinders my continuation, for I have shared in the same horrors of this ancient time, and the many frightful passions born from their after-effect. It is, as I believe it to be, because I will never precisely understand, and therefore accurately describe, the sentiment our ancestors felt when they had first seen *them,* the creatures of the underworld.

It began in 31 A.E with a query sprouting from the kingdom's north-western borderlands. The frontiersmen, the farmers who had taken to tilling the edges of the grasslands, had spoken of a foulness in the air, a vile scent carried by the winds beyond the ridges of the north, making putrid their sweet fruits of summer. These farmers, wishing to save their harvest, sent word to the capital of the occurrence, along with a request for an augur to be dispatched in order to find reason from the gods. But seeing the journey to be tedious, and its purpose beneath his mandate, Lord Eusebius, chief overseer of the *Sacrarium,* had sent a troupe of his pupils in his stead, instructing them to journey beyond the borders and heal the pestilence, as it had been widely deduced to be by the lords of the court. Many months had passed with no word from the augurs, or from the frontiersmen, and so it seemed to the court as though a favourable outcome had been attained, and no further thought to be given to the affair. It just so happened that at this time a second and third message of the same ilk had been received by the capital; one from the fishermen in the east, describing how the Bay of Blue Waters had been thickened with rotten fish bearing the black mark of corruption, and the next from the hunters and shepherds of the Verdant Heights, who spoke of the forests being all at once desolate of game, and the discovery of great caverns within the mountain rock that appeared to them like the dens of wild beasts, yet that were filled with the refuse of slaughter to number some thousand dwellers.

Confronted by these strange reports, Andiel immediately called for the marshalling of his legions across the kingdom. Not for war you see, but in readiness to make good on his promise, which was to send swift logistical support to any region in need of it. With equal ardour the lords followed Andiel's command, remaining faithful to their sworn principals at the founding of the kingdom. For this reason, the army put forth every effort to make certain that provisions would be dispersed onto the afflicted without delay. Time had passed with this endeavour in motion, and for a time thereafter the reports from the legions were of progress and success. Yet, by the spring of 32 A.E., a single absent report had very quickly turned the air of proud achievement into a climate of deep concern. Lord Aivas, commander of the eighth legion, which bore the emblem of the White Horse, had not reported the status of his operations in the north, news which the court should have first received, given that Aivas had been the first to be dispatched. There was also no word of Eusebius' pupils, or of their search for the unusual caverns within the Verdant Heights.

Fearing that Lord Aivas had been confronted by the Linlani, tribal warriors of the Nordic clime who were thought to have taken advantage of the pestilence in order to seize the lands upon the outermost northern territories, Anolia underwent a second kingdom-wide mobilization. Andiel, now in his aged years, marshalled the first, fourth, fifth, seventh, and nineteenth legions, 35, 000 men, to act as a show of strength, or if need be, to make war upon them. Under these conditions the Anolian army marched straight for the Verdant Heights in force, hoping to come upon the Linlani by surprise as a means to swiftly end the confrontation. However, upon reaching their mark they were confronted by neither the Linlani nor Lord Aivas' legion, but rather by a gruesome sight no man had ever seen before: a great and endless plain scorched by the fire of corruption, its surface littered with the mangled and bloated corpses of thousands, whose flesh served as meal for the Ascani creatures that feasted upon them.

The scholars of whose work I have studied are all accordant on who it was that named these creatures the Ascani. As the annals say, it was Eusebius himself who shouted in horror the name Ascanelius, the god of death, because they stood in likeness to his depiction; seen over the ages to be the children of the underworld, spawns of his onslaught. As many of you know, they took the form of a man, few of great height, like half-giants, the vast sum appearing more like the common man, yet made feral by their fiendish walk. Their skin, if in fact I can call it such, appeared like the hide of a beast, smeared with the hue of gray ash and fissured like arid clay. Their repulsive mouths were enlarged to almost double, all of them harbouring two ranks of serpent-like teeth that matched the flaxen tint of their eyes. But the greatest of their vileness, as I always thought it to be, were their spear-tipped horns, which sprouted from their barren heads, their shapes moulded and contorted in as many ways as could be imagined.

Thus the first battle against these creatures, as can be surmised, occurred in 32 A.E. at the base of the Verdant Heights, against a horde numbering some forty thousand, as supposed by King

Antios, the youngest of Andiel's sons. These creatures, having no mind for the planning of battle, charged headlong into Andiel's legions, causing the legionaries to succumb to fear and horror. As a result, the battle ended in the annihilation of 17,000 men, including all of the fifth and nineteenth legions, numbers never again to be utilized by the Anolian army. Their deaths, however, was the cost for the survivors to withdraw. As the Ascani feasted on the fallen, Andiel had escaped to the capital, wherefrom he would spend the next four years conducting the greatest war ever fought in this known world, one that epitomized men for their deeds and the gods for their cruelty, saw lands once bountiful and vivacious stripped of all their riches and metals for the arms of war, and brought men of all nations and creeds to organize into armies in the hundreds of thousands to battle hordes of equal number. But above all, this war saw the rise of dark sorcery and magic that would continue to linger on throughout the ages for the nefarious to dabble, and their essence forevermore bound to their creator, he who would come to be named as the Conjuror.

I apologize to you, fair reader, but I cannot possibly cover the details of this war here in brevity. I will perhaps, if the last of my years permit, grant onto you my vision of this time from its inception to its conclusion, with no promises of shortness, for it is already quite clear I know not how. But as it stands I'm afraid I cannot. And so now that I have given you the beginning, I believe it is time I set ink to parchment and relate to you the end of it by way of the story I had set out to tell, and of the events, both remarkable and dreadful, which will forever frame the memories of my youth.

CHAPTER 1

The Sentry of Easteria, 1023 A.E.

"Best give it here, Cillian," said a man with a coarse voice. The man rested his goatskin gauntlet upon my shoulder, forcing me to look over, shamefaced. It took me a moment to notice that it was Wymar, the aged and rugged legionary captain, who loomed over me with a dull grin hidden behind his thick, off-white beard and long greyish hair. "There's no sense in you freezing to death on your first night," he added, looking at me with his pale-blue eyes.

"Andiel be praised," I said, timidly. "I can't seem to get the damn thing started."

"I'd hurry it up then," he added, "before you end up killing us both."

I reached out and placed two black stones in his open palm, my chin sinking low as if to hide my misery caused by the night's chilling weather. The moon was already high, and only a couple of hours remained before the northern chill would be felt at its coldest. I have to admit, I learned very quickly that my years on the training grounds in the south of Anolia proved quite worthless for this wintry climate, seeing as how the sun was ever sweltering throughout the day, and at night, the air was just as hot and stifling. This night, the snow covered bedrock beneath my bedroll

1

was to be my place of rest, and as such I was rather desperate to have the warmth of crackling embers at my back.

Wymar knelt down in front of the lifeless bushel of twigs and sticks, digging his knee into the shallow snow. He raised the sleeves of his tunic to the rim of his mail vest, just below the elbow, upon which I caught sight of a black phoenix etched in ink on his right forearm. My eyes, however, were quickly drawn away, for he struck the stones with such force and experience that I was taken by surprise. Speckles of cinder then spread about, setting fire to the kindling.

"You make it seem so simple, captain," I said, rather embarrassed.

"There are many things in life that you need not force to get results, builder," he said, while gently feeding the growing flames. "But when it comes to using flint to start a fire it certainly does." He reached into the seam of his tabard and pulled out a linen pouch, whereupon he presented to me a small ball of char-cloth. "Here, use this next time," he added. "It'll be simpler. Now, keep your eyes on the flames and make sure they don't go out. Have another tend to it if you're on watch or we'll be hauling you back to Easteria in the morning with your skin as tough as stone." He stood up and stepped off several paces toward the legionary sergeant making his way toward him, catching the man's attention with the calling of his name. "I'd learn quickly, builder," he muttered as he walked off with the sergeant at his side.

I wanted to thank him, but I preferred that my ignorance, with something as simple as lighting a fire, would go unnoticed by the seasoned men near to me. Being seen as a nitwit was a fear of mine at the time. Not that I was not far from one. I was most definitely one of the youngest of the lot, a mere twenty-four years of age, which I liked to keep secret.

I spent the next hour in idleness, feeding the flames just as Wymar had instructed, but also as though my survival was bound to its bloom, which it was. I had with me my personal journal, and at times I leafed through it's pages and reviewed the basic elements of my craft, as I thought it wise to do in quiet times. Distraction got the better of me and my eyes wandered off to the pages that I held most secret: the intricate designs that I had fabricated, engines of war that I had one day desired to be utilized by the legion. This, fair reader, was my true passion, though I'm afraid the army did not care that it was, for they had taken a liking to my skill in the molding of timber, which saw my training to be that of a simple craftsman.

Nevertheless, as the hour dwindled, snow began to fall at a steady pace, forcing me to find comfort in other things, lest I wished the years of my hard work to be turned into a heap of soggy mush. Only twice before had I seen it snow in the region as light and plentiful as it was. Once during the festival of *Die Veterani,* the first day of winter commemorating those in service to the crown; and the second, when I had first arrived several weeks prior with the king's deputies, men in the legion whose task it was to bring fresh legionaries to the garrison at Easteria, or to any other garrison that that needed them. I was a replacement as a matter of fact. I, and the men who I had arrived with, were replacing those killed by the Ascani, those same creatures of Andiel's time, whose existence for the last thousand years seemed timeless to our mortal world, an endless blight to be forever checked and managed by the army. Even so, I had never seen an Ascani before, not even a dead one. For the most part the Ascani roamed in the shadows beyond Anolia's northern borders, which is the reason why us southerns, legionary or common folk, could go their entire life without laying eyes on one. I only knew of them from my grandfather's stories and those alone were enough to send shivers down my spine.

I tucked my journal in the warmth of my chest and looked to my surroundings for something to ebb my restlessness, swiftly finding interest in watching the ninety or so legionaries go about their personal concerns; some heavily entangled with their tasks, tallying and arranging bundles of provisions, others deep in slumber, or simply taken with warming themselves by their respective campfires as they took to their evening meal and rationed wine between muffled chatter.

Beyond them, I saw the port-city of Easteria, or rather its outline etched by tiny specks of torchlight. Being the center of northern trade in the region we Anolians call Norian, and bastion to all the neighbouring fishing villages near the Marble Sea, the city of Easteria remained the largest in the northeast amongst any of its imperial strongholds. From my position it rested many leagues to the east, a long way from the clearing in which her legion used as its forward lookout, one which rested high on a shelf by the mouth of the same valley that the city was set in. In fact, the valley of Easteria, as it was so called by the people, was all but ordinary, insofar as its grandeur. Two massive mountain ranges of naked rock guarded its flanks, and the gorge itself was more than a mile in width. It was blanketed by thousands of great evergreens that suddenly ceased their advance before a broad earthen plain, which spread all the way up to the walls of the city. This alone seemed to me otherworldly, because as I have already alluded to, I was accustomed to seeing the green fields of the south, the region of Norlyn, the place of my birth.

I gazed in awe for some time until a strong breeze whistled into the clearing. It battered my rosy cheeks and rustled the mail under my tabard, its chimes melding with the great many feint and miserable sighs rising among the men. I looked to the dark forest at my front, from which the wind came, and stared at the black void amid the trees. The sky above me seemed just as dark, for the moon was devoured by clouds, ridding all sense of the hour. As such, time seemed to move slowly, contrary to how I felt my nerves rising throughout my body. Yet above all these reasons to feel discomfort in my bones, it was the persistent gaze of the legionary nearest to me which made it all the greater.

"What do you look at?" he said as my nervous eyes met his. His mouth was stuffed to the brim with bread and the gleam of ale shone upon his lips. He was rough-looking and bald, sporting a grizzled beard and an eye that was fully off-white, lost by what I could have only supposed was a sword, seeing as how the scar that traversed the eye itself was deep and lengthy. "Did you hear me, boy?" he pressed. "I asked you what you look at?"

"I look at nothing," I answered meekly, trying to keep to myself. All it took was one look at his appearance to know that he was one of those brutes, an agitator. It is no secret that I looked rather boyish at this time, and so I must have certainly appeared to be easy prey in his eyes. But, I was not as green to soldiery life as he may have thought I was, and for that reason I knew exactly what game he was playing at. Still, I kept silent and continued refuelling the fire so that it would return to a luminous burn. I then, to my immediate regret, cleared my throat nervously before adding, "It's the forest, and this cold. Well, it's unsettling is all."

"Well, builder, if you put any more wood in that fire of yours it'll surely bring something far more troubling to us than the cold," he said. Here, he stood up from the boulder he was sitting on and made his way towards me, slowly, and with a slightly drunken stagger. Ale dripped from the top of the goblet that he clutched in his hand. "Who knows, it may even bring the creatures," he added with a dead stare. He took a drink, more like a gulp, and then said, "Tell me, builder, I'm curious. How is it that you do not know this? To start a fire, I mean. Are you...are you not from around these parts?"

"I'm from Nor—"

I stopped short upon hearing the cackles of the men erupt from the nearby fires.

"Ah! The south is it?" the man said as he squatted down beside me. He began measuring my worth with his eyes, as if the answer was written on my figure. "What the hell are you doing — Oh, I see! Forgive me. I spoke without thinking. You're lost, is that it? You've lost your way is that what you're telling me, boy? A wrong turn at the fork perhaps? It's a real shame. Happens quite a lot.

Me and my lads here have seen it before, haven't we?" he said as he looked to what appeared to be his followers. "Lots of you green folk with your noses under the sun get lost up here. Sad to say, but most of them just end up dead — well, we only figure they are because the Ascani drag them off into the woods. They tend to eat us, you know. Aye yeah, they cook us and everything after they kill us…sometimes even when we are still alive. But, it's nothing for you to worry about, builder. I can help you. I can show you the way back if you'd like? Back to the south." Then, all at once, he drew his knife and brought it to shoulder height, pointing its sharp end to the edge of the cliff, which was some twenty yards away. "It's just over there you see. Go on, don't be afraid, have a look."

Discomfort swelled in my chest, and I knew full well that at this point he saw me to be a green twit of raw competence, his plaything to pass the time. He asked me why I was amongst the sentry, amongst them, as if I was something of little value. I spoke of my task and of my duty to the *caelum lancea*, an engine of war similar to a ballista, but greater in its size. This engine rested at the center of the sentry, and served as an instrument of warning for Easteria — it did this by way of releasing the light from what we call a sky-torch, a red powder that was meant to burn above the clouds so that the whole of the sixteenth legion could muster at a moment's notice. In the end it did not matter that I spoke of such things, because the more I spoke, the more he mocked me, his tone bringing a greater unwelcomed seriousness in the air. On top of that, his teasing saw more legionaries gather around us, some resting leisurely against the weathered ruins that studded the clearing, whilst others held themselves upright by the reinforcement of their shields and spears. They were keen to listen to what I had to say next, oblivious to the cold and to their duties, the sight becoming more of a tavern gathering than a troupe of legionary sentinels. So, they hearkened to me and laughed at my muddled responses, and for a good while thereon their laughs seemed to embolden the brutish legionary to continue on in riling me up, to tease my inexperience and my youth.

"So which is it, builder, I'm…I'm quite confused," he laughed heavily. "Are you saying then that it's the dark that makes you shit your trousers, or the thought that you're not really a soldier, but a school boy that carries a sword at his hip. I mean with that book of yours I'd say you're just some learner who likes playing with hardwood — and probably not the same hardwood that women are after." Just then he stopped, noticing my stern, yet flustered gaze. "What was that?" he said. "It looks to me like there's something you want to say, or is that the face you make when you have to take a shit? Come now, spit it out. Don't be coy. Say! If you can't find the words, then do it with your sword, or your fists — it's up to you! But if you prefer the blade, boy, I just hope you know where to put —"

"I know where to put it," I interrupted, my voice as hot as the fire at my feet. "I'm just afraid that if I use my sword I'll miss the target, and then end up ruining that lovely face of yours. I mean it's already quite rough as it is, wouldn't you say? I wouldn't want to muck it any more."

A hush took the crowd, a silence filling the snowy air.

"Say that again?" he said, stepping towards me with an empty look. "Quite the pair you got there, builder. To say that," he added, shoving his goblet against my chest with enough force so that the ale spewed over the sides. Even through my armour I could feel the foam of the ale as it crawled down along the emblem of the sixteenth legion, a great silver sword that was entwined in brown thistle, which was elegantly sewn, as all legionary emblems were, at the center of our tabards. Then, he beckoned me to grab the cup with his eyes, and just as I did, utterly confused, he curled a grand smile and blurted, "The builder may not know how to light a fire! But he's some good sport!"

At this moment laughter rose from the crowd, and with it I felt my shoulders sink and my heart return to a steady calm. It was a rather odd feeling at first, for I was certain that moments before I was close to receiving a battering from one of my own. Instead, I now found myself surrounded on every side by a mob of men, who each in his own turn greeted me happily as though I just passed their trail of banter. I would not say, dear reader, that I was fully a part of the legion as they were, being that some were still pursuing a last laugh at my expense.

"Go on drink it!" said the brutish legionary, whose name, to my embarrassment, I have long forgotten. "Have at it! This brew will warm you nicely I promise or get you drunk enough that you won't even care." He put his arm around my neck as if I was his companion, and then he stuffed his mouth once again with a morsel of bread, which he first offered me. He was now not so brutish after all, but I recall that there was some warmth in his heart. "Laxus! Laxus!" he called out. "Come over here will you and fill his cup before the wind takes him."

"I hope you're filling it with water," said a stern voice from beyond the crowd.

I turned to the sound. As the soldiers began to disperse, rather quickly in fact, I watched the figure of a man carry his feet through the snow, nearing toward me with two brawny legionaries at his side, each bearing torches. The brutish fellow had, by this time, fled to his campfire, making it clear to me that the approaching man was a sergeant, men of rank within the legion that were often loathed for their cruelty and strict discipline in training. This particular sergeant was none other than Demetrius, the lead builder of the sixteenth legion, whose charge it was to maintain all things made of timber throughout the city. I had already convened with him earlier that day, even before I had been selected to accompany the sentry, and then more still in the hours before the departure. He was not aware that I had been selected to come along, and so at first it looked as if he was bewildered by my presence on the lookout. As he drew closer, however, his gaze very quickly shifted from a look of confusion to one of disappointment, for it was then that I realised my error. I had been idle for most of the night, and not once had I taken it upon myself to do any of the duties of my craft.

"Come with me, Cillian," he said, gently grabbing the goblet from my clutch, as if the liquid within it was acrid. He poured what remained of the ale onto the snow and tossed the cup away. Before it landed by the fire, he motioned me to follow him with a nod, which I did with my tongue firm behind my teeth.

Demetrius led me straight to the *caelum lancea*, and upon our arrival we began trailing around it, stopping only when the most senior of us lowly builders, who was at the head of the file, appeared content with its outward inspection. Inspections, as could be imagined, were a key part of a builder's duty, and they remain so today. I had never seen this type of ballista before, and for this reason the spark of curiosity and intrigue kept my eyes glued to it. I studied it diligently, taking notice that it was different to those employed in the field of battle.

To put it to vision, the bow arms at its sides extended to a length of two men, but the height of its frame reached no further than my waist even though it rested on stilts and wheels. I could never fathom why that was, since it was a two hundred year old material of war that was all but cemented to the rock. Its frame was quite captivating for me, because it was made of birchwood, a very peculiar timber that is only found within the forests on the Islands of Illyria, a claim long since abandoned by the Kings of Anolia, and has ever since been under the rule of the Kingdom of Kashtan. Its bowstring, perhaps the most intriguing addition, was made of Anolian silk, whose cost was greater than the whole of my year's wage.

"Drusus," said Demetrius to the man beside him. Demeterius was vigorously tightening one of the iron sprockets attached to the spring cord beneath the frame. "Find Nyssa for me. Tell him to come here quickly, and have him bring me his scalprum. We'll trim the timber here under the clasp, up along the stem until the breach, then we'll plug the hole with some binder. I think if we do that we'll be able to save the whole part of this stem from the rot." As the legionary Drusus moved off, Demetrius' words then turned to me, his eyes still fixed on his task. "I want you to listen to me carefully, Cillian, because even though I like hearing the sound of my voice, I don't enjoy hearing it when I have to speak about the same thing twice. Some engines have a thousand parts, others have no more than ten. Understanding where they are and how they work only covers half of what needs doing if you want to be more than just a half-witted builder. It is our task, *as builders*, to make sure that these weapons are ready to be used at all times, and in whatever the place or weather. If you leave these things unattended, they will turn on you when you need them most. I've seen it happen, and good men end up dying because of it. So, next you find yourself idle, laughing and drinking it up with the men or acting the scholar with that book of yours, I want you to take a moment and remember why it is you're here. Is that clear, Cillian?"

"Yes, sergeant," I replied.

"I may not look it, but I am happy to hear that. Now then, let me say this. I don't give two shits about your reasons for being here, nor do I care where your mother happened to give birth to you. All I want from you is your ears and your hands, and when I call for them, they better be ready to work. Listen to my instructions and apply them without fault. Some nights these tasks will be in your responsibility alone," he lectured.

After I quelled his concern with a firm nod he began, in detail, to list off the parts of the ballista while pointing at them, ensuring that I had committed each of their positions and names to memory. "Look here," he marked with his eyes. "You see the winch, aye? This one is joined by the lever at the base end. Pull too hard on it and I promise you the line will sever, as well as all your bloody fingers. Now, the claw over here—"

"Forgive me, sergeant," I interrupted, "but that's not the claw."

Demetrius gave me a stern look, making my blood quicken. "And why's that?"

"Well," I said, clearing my throat. "If I had to guess, I would say that this engine is early eighth century so, that would mean that if the lever is at the base end, then the claw is not fixed to the ladder there, but rather the builders of that time thought it best to attach the claw right over there behind the release," I said while pointing to it. "It was quite common...uhh...to the era, sergeant." I stopped abruptly, realising that I had just spoken brazenly to a man holding actual battle experience. Our eyes locked for a second, and so I quickly added, "Unless I'm wrong, of course!"

"Much quicker than the last one I'd say," Wymar said as he appeared from out of sight, his voice severing the awkward silence. His hands were resting atop the pommel of his sword, and he was chewing on something rather tough, most likely the sun-dried venison that those on sentry duty often received as a light meal from the garrison kitchen. "Or maybe it's because this one is actually listening to you, Demetrius." He moved a step closer to me and spit out a lump of cartilage over his shoulder. "Can I take him off your hands, sargeant? I need to speak with him for a moment if that's alright?"

"Aye, go on and take him before he starts spouting more of that history at me," Demetrius replied, just as Drusus returned with Nyssa. "But you better bring him back here when you're done with him — and with his gut absent of drink, if you please. I need this one to earn his pay tonight, yeah?"

"Don't worry about that. The ale is already gone," Captain Wymar replied.

I was pleased to see a friendly face, though the sentiment was quickly snuffed when Wymar snatched a torch from the nearby fire and nudged the stem into my gut. It may seem small in comparison to other facets in the strain of legionary life, dear reader, but his strike really cemented the view that my time in the legion would be an arduous endeavour. All the same, I was beginning to understand how soldiers of veterancy comported themselves. So too, did I learn, in that moment, that men of rank never bothered to announce when it was that they wished to be followed. Before I recovered my breath from the blow, Wymar had already sauntered off some distance towards the cliff's edge, leaving me to chase him like some absent minded fool.

I followed him to the precipice, some twenty yards away from the nearest campfire, my feet trudging through the unmolested snow. I stopped as he did just short of the rim, where the light of the torch proved to be nothing more than a mere speckle in the dark opulence before me. Here, I stood beside him, muted, taking in the scent of the evergreens caught in the wind, the flecks of snow falling upon my face, and the coolness of the frigid air penetrating my bones. In truth, the ambience was warm to the heart. Not only because of the sheer beauty, but also because Wymar's aura was somewhat familiar to me. He reminded me of my grandfather, Cadrius Tertius, who had once served in the ranks of the Golden Sun, the fourth of Anolia's legions. I could not help but feel a sense of admiration for the man, even if I only knew him by his position as captain.

Wymar remained silent as he rummaged through the pear-shaped pouch hanging from his belt, paying no mind to me, but intent on finding whatever item he was searching for. It got the impression that it was almost as if he had forgotten that I lingered beside him. Then, all at once, he unsheathed his dagger from his leather vambrace and began carving the rind off what looked to be an orange fruit.

"If you want some advice from an old man," he said, "I'd speak less proudly to your betters. Even if whatever you're talking about happens to be right. The men under my command tend not to have sticks up their asses, so keep that in mind until you find your place here. Be that as it may, I do give a shit as to where you are from. Unlike some."

"I understand," I said with a smirk, watching him peel the fruit. "And there's no shame in a little compassion." I then spoke freely, seeing as how he did not reply with the same old soldiery haughtiness. "I may be alone in the thought, captain, but I think a touch of kindness isn't necessarily a trait of weakness, as most of these men here seem to believe. You know, much of this kingdom was born out of Andiel's clemency, and I'd like to think some of us still share in the principals he laid out for our people, even if it's in a small habit."

"That's not what I meant when I said I care about where you're from, Cillian. I meant to say it gets quite troublesome when I have to figure out where to send the body," he said, as if what I had just uttered was the strangest thing he had heard from a legionary in a long time. "And it gets worse still when nobody else knows who you are. It's happened before. Men completely vanish from memory, as if they never existed in the first place." Right then, he presented to me a large piece of the fruit, which was skewered on the point of his knife. "Take it. It'll water the tongue."

I averted my eyes. "My thanks, captain, but...I'm fine."

"Are you sure?" he said, offering it to me once more. "It'll be awhile before we get more of these back in the city." I kindly refused it a second time. "More for me then," he added, lobbing the piece into his mouth. "So, Norlyn was it? Where your mother happened to give birth to you." He bit into another chunk, the juices dripping down into his beard. "Which part then? Riverside? Or is it that shithole village, whatever it was called, the one by the Rill?"

My smirk suddenly turned to a smile. "By the Rill. How did you — don't tell me you're from the south as well?" I bowed my head in marvel and chuckled, for all at once I had surmised the reason for his earlier kindness. "Is that why you helped me before? With the fire?"

"Look here, builder, I don't really care for the south anymore," he replied, dismissively. "I mean no insult, but I haven't given a shite about it for thirty years now — so don't go thinking that my heart suddenly yearns at the thought of helping one of its cubs. I may have been born in a piss for nothing village half-way to Heraea, but that still doesn't make me a southerner. Earth is earth no matter where you go. You've just got to live in a place long enough to call it your hearth. And the truth is, I only helped you before because of need. I've already gone through four replacement builders in these last nine months. I don't know why the gods hate you craftsmen so much, but your lot seems to drop like flies. There aren't many of you learners out there in this world with the mind for that sort of thing, so I have to do what I can, when I can, to keep you, Cillian, from going off and dying on me too — even if it's from a slight breeze. Having said that, I admire that you follow Andiel's ideals. But, you won't find much use for them out here, not if you don't learn to take care of yourself first. These lands will kill you, if the Ascani don't get around it to first."

"Yes, captain," I nodded, abashed by the lecture.

"Anyway, let's leave the lofty teachings at that for now," he went on, mouth gorged. "If I had any coin left on me I would've waggered Riverside, seeing as how the way you sound your words seem much more...well, informed then that of the common learner."

"I wouldn't be much of a builder if I didn't put some study into the craft."

"Aye, I guess you wouldn't. I just hope you've put as much study into the sword as well."

I looked out to the gorge, my eyes trailing across the expanse of the timbers. They continued far beyond the mouth of the valley, an endless sea of misshapen shadows. In the shadows I searched for nothing in particular, except the means to soothe the unease flowing through my mind. I did not anticipate to hear Wymar's remark, at least not from him, and not twice in the same night. Wymar's words were, in effect, the very same as the brutish legionary's; words that I had heard many times over.

Simply put, they were ill-opinionated utterances about my quality as a legionary, an arrogant, aged belief that was once born by the men of the legion who saw no mettle within those of the ancillary, the parts of the army detached from the infantry ranks. I was never alone to receive these verbal batterings, but there were times throughout my youth that it felt as if I was the only man in the Anolian army who was known to be incapable of using his hands if they were not gripped around the tools of a builder. I had very quickly come to despise it.

"Why are you here, Cillian?" Wymar asked in a weighty tone, breaking the silence.

I glanced over at him, not understanding his question entirely, but having some sense as to what he was suggesting by it. Nobody had cared for my reasons for joining the Vined Sword, nor did I think there would come a time when someone of note would ask that I speak them. In fact, since my arrival in Easteria, I preferred to keep my intentions to myself, being that my youthful look alone gave the impression that I would only speak words of naivety, just like what had happened with the brutish legionary.

"I see why you've already gone through four replacements," I said with a tinge of jest, in the hopes that it would hide my surprise at the question. "I suppose now this is the part when you throw me off the cliff if I speak the wrong answer. Is that it, captain?" I buried my feet into the snow and returned to a straightened face, once again hoping to veer the mood, and the prattle, upon a different path. "Is this what you do with all the newcomers that come your way? You take them aside and give them your little test of confidence?"

"You're sharp, builder. I'll give you that."

I turned back to the valley, my mind rather removed. "The king asks—"

"The king asks for nothing," he interrupted with a calm voice. "Just a moment ago you were gabbing away at the history of a bloody piece of wood, so let's skip the part of the fool. You know very well that the man chooses his legion and not the king, Cillian. Yet, the thing is, the thing *I* can't understand, is why you didn't just cross the bloody Rill and choose the Gilded Boar, or the Golden Sun for that matter. Both the fourth and sixth legions are not twenty miles in either direction of your home. It would've been simpler in travel alone, wouldn't you say?" He spit over the edge, and then brushed his lips roughly. "Yet, here you are. At the edge of the kingdom. Far away from the only possible place in which your service in the army would've meant a tad of a shite to the people around you."

"Can I not mould timber here?" I said, defensively. "My hands work all the same."

"I'm not saying that your hands are worthless, Cillian. Nor did I say that in time your worth won't be received by the men. Andiel willing, you may even do something rather remarkable in the coming years. What do I know really? I'm not a bloody priest. But truthfully, you are a long way off from the south, and you have no real cause to offer up your life for these people. You see they may be your countrymen, and they share the same blood. But take it from me, builder, it will be more than half your life before they come to respect you as their kin. Their lives will one day be in your hands. So I ask again, why is it that you're really here?"

The muscles in my face tightened. I looked over my shoulder, catching a few glances of the men closest to us. They were all northerners, seasoned men of Easteria, and as they laughed with one another around the fire, sharing bread and drink, I froze, observing the camaraderie they shared, which emphasized Wymar's words of belonging. It was at this point that I came to realise how truly different my reasons were compared to these legionaries, for it was quite clear that the heart of their purpose rested in nothing other than in the men beside them, and in the very thing we were keeping sentry over: the people of Easteria.

"It's because of my mother," I said, my tongue holding back in hesitation. If Wymar wished, he could see my time in the legion cut short for any reason he deemed, insofar as safeguarding the lives of his men was concerned. It was over; there was no secreting it any longer, there was no fooling the man with evasive words and hollow truths. For this reason, I thought it best to speak the truth, absent care for any consequence that would come out of it. "My mother's words are what saw me here," I restated. "You see she passed the month before I journeyed here. The healers said it was of some lasting affliction from her birth — I can't remember what was exactly. If it had been up to her, as most things were, then I wouldn't actually be here, in the army I mean. She always hated this choice. She never once spoke about it in front of me, but when I was a child I recall that she never stopped arguing with my grandfather, the man that she swore had planted the seed of the thought in mind with all the stories he used to tell me about his time in the fourth."

"Your grandfather was in the army?"

"He was a cook. A good one too," I said as I ran the palm of my hand down my face. "Well with him being a cook and all, you can imagine, captain, that his stories were nothing in likeness to the tales of our champions. But to a half-witted child who saw him as the father I never knew, even the smallest of his deeds strengthened my desire to join. After he passed, there was no hiding the ambition. In the end my mother was right about it all. I joined before I turned of age. That was seven years ago."

"I may not give a shite about the south, but even I know that the law of Norlyn still practices the *confirmatio*. Men under the age need the leave of their household to enlist. If your mother hated it, how was it then that she let you enlist?"

I paused, my grip tightening around the torch's stem.

"Well don't stop now, builder—"

"I lied to her," I interjected, morosely. "I lied. The thing is captain, my grandfather's coin, almost all of it in fact, had already seen me through years of study. I convinced my mother that when I'd join the army I'd become a builder, a craft that I made her believe would distance me from the ranks and the fighting, the one thing she truly thought no man in the south had any business taking part in. It was like her byword of a sort, being that the troubles of the Ascani have always been far-removed from people in the south. So yes, I lied to her for years. Even when I looked into her waning eyes I kept promising a thing that had no truth to it. I spoke the same empty words that I knew she wanted to hear."

"How is any of this a lie, Cillian? You are in fact a builder, are you not?"

A sudden heat seized me. I turned toward him, now with a vacant stare. "The lie wasn't that I was to be a builder. I never had any intention to be *far removed*. I can't speak for the men who carry a sword, but every common man in that shithole by the Rill thinks just as my mother did. Nobody there really gives a damn about anything that doesn't unease their own heart. They all see the problems of others as things to be left to their own concerns. And that, captain, is exactly why I have chosen to be here. Why I have chosen this post. The legionaries up here fight and die everyday protecting the realm against an enemy we *all* should be fighting against. As I see it, there is no point in choosing this life if I am forced to sit idle with my hands unstained because I happen to be born under the sun — believing that I need good enough reason to use all that I have learned in order to help those people in need of it. And to have the heart do it whether a tad of a shit is given or not."

Wymar kept his eyes to the valley as he ate his fruit in a manner as if he was more fixed on its sweetness than to the seriousness of my words. He turned around, gesturing that he was about to return to the men. Then, he stepped off several paces and said, "Well, that's good enough for me. Everyone has their own reasons. Just remember yours if ever there is any doubt. From here on, however, I would keep it to yourself. If you ever want to call yourself one of us I'd start by trusting in nothing else but the commands of those who will come to instruct you. Master your craft, and then perhaps in time you'll meld in with rest. Now then, that's all the storytelling I can handle for one night. Go on, Cillian. You better get back to Demetrius before he—"

Suddenly a faint thud sounded in the air, causing my body to become stiff, my legs feeling as though they had become an extension of the rock. At the same time, Wymar stopped in his tracks and slowly peered over to me, his eyes confirming that I had, in fact, heard the thud. I turned back towards the campfires and noticed the men at our rear were completely unaware of the confusion we shared, for they went about their business in the same humour as we had left them in.

"Wait there," he said, appearing to be more curious than troubled. He lowered his chin, and took to the clearing with an eager walk, letting the last of his fruit fall to the ground.

I did as Wymar commanded, but I found myself just as curious as he was. As such, I turned back to the valley with an uneasiness growing in my chest, for I knew, with conviction, that what I had heard was not some trick of the mind born from my nerves. Like a bird of prey I examined the gorge from the distant ridgeline to the edge where the thicket met with the earthen plains before Easteria, suffocating the hilt of my sword as if it somehow bettered my scrutiny of the terrain. I was lucky that it had stopped snowing, and now with the light of the moon piercing through the clouds, the forest below was immersed in a bluish shade, allowing me to see everything a little more clearly. Even so, I found nothing peculiar within the landscape, and I heard nothing more in the air but the sound of my own muffled sigh of relief.

Then, without warning, another soft, far-off thump echoed from the forest below. I could not properly tell at first, but it came from somewhere beyond the mouth of the gorge, for a flock of ravens, disturbed by the noise, shot out from their nests and into the night's sky. As my eyes honed in on the dozens of dark pellets flapping away, the warmth of my blood left me, and the longer I gazed at them the further my tongue rescinded into my throat.

I tried to call out, grunt even, but before I could utter a sound another one of these drum-like thuds sounded, only this time it was succeeded by another and another, until the lonely thumps rose to falling hammers striking a beat. Something massive was drawing near, stirring beneath the evergreens.

Just then the snap of a branch caught my attention, its crackle severing my gripping stillness. I clenched my hand tighter around the hilt as I slowly wheeled in the direction of the noise, stopping as the glow of my torch met the tree line no more than ten feet away. My heart beat like a horses' gallop, my hands trembling beyond any quiver of terror that I had ever felt before. I managed to lean forward and extend the torch above my shoulder, keeping it steady as I perused the timbers. At first glance, the trees seemed orderly and natural, each the same as the next. But then, as my eyes began to adjust to the darkness, I saw what it was that hid behind the shadow of the thicket. I saw what it was that was staring at me.

I was breathless, my heart dropping into my stomach. Each word of purpose and aim that I had just spoken with vigour quickly weakened in weight like an army in flight. The creature that looked at me was an Ascani; it's large, yellowish eyes glowed in the void, its horns curled out to its sunken shoulders, and its teeth were lined like a thousand interwoven needles. This, my dear reader, was the creature I wished to help against. And now it was standing before me, not the image of the thoughts that came from my grandfather's stories, but alive and very real. I was afraid.

Knowing that I caught sight of it, the creature carefully emerged from the thicket without breaking its stare. It did so freely, as if it knew that my tongue was anchored by horror, and could not sound an alarm. As its frame came deeper into the light, I saw that its height towered over me, whereupon I also noticed that it was armed like some warrior vagabond. A hatchet dangled at its side and a sullied leather quiver hung along its back, teeming with arrows. In its hands it gripped a bow of Linlani make, and the few pieces of armour that it wore were clearly Anolian, though their look could not have been any younger than three centuries old. Here, the creature came to a halt. It canted its head and grinned, as if to suggest that it had found its long awaited meal.

Perhaps it was the gods who had given me the strength to move, but suddenly with a furious jolt I swung all of my weight towards the men. Then, with a deep breath filling my lungs, I cried, "Ascani!"

At that the creature sprung with a shrieking cry, lunging itself toward me by kicking off the bark of the nearby tree. High it soared like a feral beast pouncing at its prey, and there in flight it lifted its bow and nocked an arrow, swiftly drawing the line to its chin. As chance would have it, the creature was stopped dead by an airborne dagger, the knife landing squarely in the center of its forehead.

"Cillian!" Wymar shouted, as he hurtled passed me. In a sudden frenzy he placed his foot on the creature's chest and stooped over it, pulling the knife from its mark. Then, he rushed over to me and snatched the torch from my hand.

"The gorge. They're something coming from the gorge," I muttered.

"I know!" he replied, pressing me to purpose. "Go to Demetrius! Set flame to the sky!"

I ran blindly in the direction of the engine, sword gripped in hand. All around me a great many voices rose in hysteria as the legionaries scrambled about, some reaching for their weapons, others desperately reequipping what pieces of armour they had removed. Meanwhile, the fiercest and vilest howls rang out amid the surrounding trees, wherefrom countless Ascani, each as horrid as the one I had encountered, poured into the clearing. They hurtled towards the soldiers, battering their battle-looted shields and clacking their teeth like maniacs hungering for slaughter. In response, the legionnaires had begun to fit themselves into tight ranks, yet the enemy's swift and surprising assault from three sides caught most of us off guard and alone. Thus, a terrible melee ensued, sword against sword, its clamour rising to a sound of murderous euphoria, heightened only by the screams of the wounded and the cries of the dying.

As I continued to make my way to the engine, a myriad of chilling whooshes cut through the air. Iron hooks, birthed from beyond the threshold of the clearing, descended upon us, their talons clasping any hard surface. One hook, as I can hardly forget, grasped the soldier beside me by the rim of his head. In a blink of an eye his body dropped to the ground, where he was then hauled off like felled timber with enough force to swipe my legs and knock me on my back. I watched in a daze as the man's body fiercely snapped about into the distance, his screams of agony ceasing only when he collided with a tree.

At that moment one of the Ascani leapt onto me. It put its hands around my throat and began squeezing ruthlessly, its nails feeling like a knife's edge as they pressed my neck. Twice I bashed the creature with the pommel of my sword, but still it remained locked in position, almost as if its desire to end my life shielded it from pain. The creature snarled and barked, pinning me deeper and deeper into the snow. Then, it leaned forward, mouth wide and dripping, searching for a taste of my flesh.

CHAPTER 2

The Ascani's teeth clacked over me. I was near out of strength, my muscles burning from the tension of keeping the beast away. In a last effort, I drove my sword under the creature's arm, the sharp point of the blade exiting its shoulder. It squealed and recoiled off my body, giving me the chance to take in a long, life-restoring breath. As I staggered to my feet I shambled back a step, dizzed by the chaos. Therewith I struck the creature a second time, bringing my sword down across its chest with what vitality I had left.

"Cillian! Get over here! Now!" Demetrius shouted, his voice at my back.

I spun around and sprinted to the engine. Half a dozen Ascani corpses were scattered around it, including Nyssa's, whose left arm was set upon his stomach. It appeared to have been torn off from as far as the base of his marred neck, from which fonts of blood darkened the snow. Drusus, the other builder, was slouched behind the ballista, his face flushed with strain as he attempted to draw the bowline to the notch with his bare hands, for the winch and its pulley were utterly destroyed. As he undertook this task, he was safeguarded by Demetrius, who battled the enemies seeking to reach the engine. I called out to let the sergeant know I was near, at which point Drusus turned to me and signalled for my assistance with an expression that suggested his hold was soon to give way.

I planted my heels into the snow, my hands clutched around the bowline. An aching tremor passed through me, and so I tightened my resolve and began heaving the line to its mark.

"Come on, boy, pull harder!" Drusus cried.

"I'm giving it all I have!" I shouted, teeth clenched. "The sky-torch! Where is it?"

"By your feet!" Demetrius answered, pressing his sword into the gut of the Ascani storming towards him. He slew another who aimed it's barbed-head spear for his back, and then two more Ascani took its place, drawing him further away from the engine.

"That's it! That's it! Just a little closer!" Drusus added.

Hastily, my eyes swept the ground beneath my feet and the little gnolls of snow that were at the base of the engine's stilts. At once, I noticed the crate which carried the ammunition, or rather I saw what was left of it. One of the fallen Ascani had collapsed onto it, and in doing so, its weight not only shattered the case, but all of the javelins as well, a good many splinters of wood dispersed about the snow. I released one hand from the line, the resistance almost doubling in an instant. Then I stretched out my arm and reached for the corpse, nudging it's leg slightly to the side, revealing but one of the sky-torches yet intact.

"Hurry! The line is nearly locked!" Drusus cried. "Hand me a torch now, boy!"

I let out the fiercest of grunts, trying to extend myself as far as I could in order to retrieve it — it was a foot away from the tip of my fingers. The arm that still held the line in place felt as if it would rip clean off from its socket, and the skin on my hand, though sheathed by a leather gauntlet, began to feel as if it were being pressed too close to a flame. "It's too far! I can't reach it!" I cried out, returning both hands to the line.

Suddenly Demetrius appeared beside me, blood gushing from the many deep lacerations on his face. He swayed a little in exhaustion, and held tight what I supposed was a grave wound upon his shoulder. With his sword still gripped in hand, he displaced the Ascani corpse and snatched the sky-torch, swiftly setting it to position. "Release it! Now—" Right then he was stopped short, his body flinging forward as if it were taken by some godly wind. A stone axe, nearly half his length, had struck the back of his mail vest with enough might and speed to fasten his torso to the engine, his guts now spewing out from his exposed ribs like a pig at slaughter. At the same time, the bowline snapped in two, and with the sound of a whiplash, the entirety of the engine burst into large pieces of chiselled timber, sending fragments shooting out like arrows in all directions.

Drusus and I were violently thrown at a distance; Drusus had been impaled in the neck and chest by many of the soaring fragments, while I, by chance, suffered no more than a few bloodied cuts and scrapes on my chin and cheeks. I did not know, however, that Drusus had been killed until I rolled onto my front side, catching a glimpse of him face down in a pool of his own viscera. It was also then when my eyes caught sight of the monstrous beast that hurled the axe. It was coming right at me, storming across the clearing to retrieve its weapon. The few brave legionaries who sought to kill it were crushed and killed by its bare fists. I was next.

I slithered like a wounded serpent toward the first glint of silver that caught my eye. Amidst the bloody frenzy, I spotted the sky-torch clutched in Demetrius' lifeless grip. Its stem was cloven at the half, though the sack which contained the sorcerer's powder, and the fuse that went with it, were yet undefiled. Here, I began to understand that the destruction of the engine was the primary aim of the Ascani, and though they had successfully demolished it, there was still a chance to warn the city if I could manage to recover the sky-torch.

As I mulled over the thought, several legionary archers rushed past me, charging towards the creature. They readied their bows and nocked their arrows, and just as the sound of their drawn bowstrings filled my ears, my mind snapped back to attention. To that end, I snagged the abandoned sword at my side and leapt to action, bolting towards the one thing that would see this horrible night come to an end.

As I approached Demetrius' corpse I was overtaken by the beast. It had reached the engine a mere moment before I did, and so I swung my sword at it like a madman, hoping that it would draw its attention toward me and away from the sky-torch that was very close to its reach. As luck would have it, it worked, but all at once the creature came at me with an outburst of fury, thrusting its fists as if it wanted to remove my head in one wallop. Again and again I avoided its attacks, and more than that, I also inadvertently evaded the three arrows that whizzed right over my shoulder. All together these arrows struck the Ascani brute in its chest. It stumbled backwards, its eyes flickered and flashed, its legs buckled under death's looming embrace. Then, a stray arrow cut through the sky and broke the monstrosity's last hold on life, striking the side of its disgusting mug. The force of this impact pushed the creature off balance, pressing me to snatch the sky-torch before the beast's full weight crashed upon the engine.

"Form barricade! Barricade!" Wymar roared, his sword high as he rallied the men.

In a heartbeat the surviving legionaries in Wymar's vicinity sprung to his command. I do not remember how I found myself standing beside him, torch and javelin in hand, but I do recall having been instinctively set to purpose by the flow of the battle, following it almost naturally. As I saw it, a little more than a third of the sentry remained, the rest either dead or cut-off from us. Wymar and I positioned ourselves behind the last of our forces as they adjoined their curved shields to form an iron curtain, otherwise known as the *Barricade*. The Ascani never saw us men as a threat, yet the sight of our barricade must have appeared formidable nonetheless. Even now in my aged years I could still feel the glory that I had felt in this moment, for whenever our shields came together there also came a great array of our legion's emblem, which was etched in colour upon our bulwarks just as it appeared upon our tabards. It may not have been my home, but to be among those who fought so desperately to save theirs made me feel a deeper sense of connection to them, one that can only be birthed within the miseries of battle.

We held our ground in the silence of anticipation, watching some hundred Ascani gather into a rabble not fifty feet before us. To our surprise, they were also still and watching, a thing that was unnatural to an Ascani war pack when faced with the opportunity to slay and feast. It was not long before they appeared high-strung by the sudden pause in taking life, some of them made hyper as they gnawed and feasted upon their spoils, the strewn limbs of the fallen.

Such a sight sent a shiver of horror down my spine, and I vividly remember the sequence of awful thoughts that invaded my mind as I held the gaze of these disgusting brutes. Images of Norlyn quickly filled my mind, and then shortly after came the thought that I would never see it again. The engine had been reduced to nothing more than a pile of firewood, and there was no doubt that the enemy would soon overwhelm us by their sheer numbers, leaving Easteria completely open to the onslaught that moved beneath the trees on the valley floor. I needed to act to thwart their ploy. I had to do something that would make good on my reasons for choosing this legion, or at the very least, make meaningful the cost of our lives.

"I'm going to light it, stand clear!" I said, slowly moving the flame to the fuse.

"Still your hand, builder," Wymar asserted, his eyes fixed on the rabble. "They'll never see it from here, and if you light it where you stand you'll kill us all." Then, he caught me glancing over at one of the trees near the edge. "It's no use. There are too many of them. They'll be on you before you get high enough to make use of it."

"I'll throw it off the edge. Surely they'll see it then!"

Suddenly the Ascani at the very center of the rabble were forcefully pushed aside. Out came a most fearsome looking creature, one whose presence seemed to establish command over all of the Ascani on the clearing. It stood shorter than most of the demons around it, though its frame was far more shapely and muscular, like that of a man's long moulded to the rigours of sport and contest. Its eyes gleamed like fiery red coals, half devoured by pestilence, and two winding horns marked the beginning of where its long, off-white hair ran down along its spine of dragon-like thorns. An iron mask covered the lower half of its visage; grilled at the mouth like the face of a blacksmith's furnace, from which its breath shot out like the steam of red-hot steel when it is doused in water.

"Cillian," Wymar voiced in a low and steady voice as he studied the masked Ascani. It was obvious to me that he was thinking about something, some deep-rooted realisation that came from seeing the spectre that stood before him. "Do you remember where we left the horses?" he went on. "Do you know how to find your way there from here?"

I thought back for a moment, to the hours before nightfall when we had gathered in advance before moving toward the lookout. "You mean that farmstead in the forest? Yes...why?"

In haste Wymar turned toward me and began unclasping my mail vest. "Listen, the man who lives there is named Nilus, one of our stable-masters. Clear this mountain and find your way to him. When you find him tell him I sent you. He'll give you a horse, but have him abandon the rest." As Wymar spoke my hands moved in assistance, removing my tabard and mail vest, tossing them to the side. He strapped my sword belt back to my waist and tucked the sky-torch into it, making sure that nothing would pierce the pouch. "Get as close to the city as you can before you light it, yeah? It'll be some hours before dawn so the night will keep you hidden. Warn them before it's too late!"

I swallowed nervously. "Captain. I don't think I can—"

"Listen here, boy!" he said sternly as he grabbed the cusp of my tunic. "You say you want to help? You say you want to show your worth? Well, builder, this is how you're going to do it! These creatures will be at the walls soon enough, and we have one chance to warn them before it happens. I'm not going to leave thousands of beating hearts to the mercy of your judgement. So go on! Just do as I ask! We'll keep them off your back. This is your task now, Cillian. See it done." He veered back toward the Ascani rabble and grasped the shoulder of the legionary in front of him. "Prepare to brace!" he hollered.

Right then a hideous, ear-piercing shriek bellowed from the throat of the masked Ascani. It unsheathed its dual swords and raised them high above its head, whereupon the whole of the Ascani war-pack charged at us headlong. In seconds the creatures collided with the legionary barricade, the crash so shocking that it wiped clean the expressionless stare off my face. The thought of leaving these men behind to their terrible fates tore at my insides, but the force of responsibility pushed me to purpose.

I quickly scanned the edge of the cliff for a spot to slip away unseen, and just as I found one the masked Ascani soared over the shield wall like a wolf, landing right in front of me. If the fiend wished to end my life, it could have, but for some reason it did not attack me. It's eyes, on the other hand, grew wide with anger as he spotted the sky-torch on my waist.

Wymar leapt between us with his bloodied sword readied at a low guard. "Go on!" he cried, while fending off the creature's swift assault.

At this point I turned away from him and darted toward my mark at the edge of cliff. The area that I had chosen to be my escape was shrouded by thick underbrush and tall boreal firs, growth which continued to skirt the rim of the cliff well beyond the limits of the eye. I lingered there for a moment, my mind teeming with all but a sensible plan in how best to find my way down. At first I looked to my left, hoping to find my next course of action in the same mountain trail that led us to the lookout. But I could not risk it, for the torchlights dotting the path made it clear that the Ascani were swarming around it. Nor was there a potential route to my right, being that the gods had not granted me the gift of flight, and thus I was unable to simply glide across the valley. Thus the weight of decision rested heavy on my shoulders, made more burdensome by my own indecisiveness.

Inside I began to feel the guilt of failure. I did not want to die, alone and under foreign stars, but I knew that if I chose to abandon my task for self preservation then it would mean that I would let the common folk of Easteria suffer the horrors of the Ascani. As such, only one path would see me off this mountain ledge, one that caused a thick lump in my throat, and infused my heart with even greater terror.

I took a half-step forward and peered over the edge with my torch extended. Below, a black misty void veiled my next mark. I had no idea how long it would take to reach the underbelly of the mountain, but I knew that the lookout, especially from the position that I stood, was no more than three hundred feet high, or so I assumed that it was because the Ascani had used their hooks to ascend the cliff. In truth, I was only reminded of this fact because I suddenly caught sight of a goreish image: the brutishly mangled corpse of that very legionary who had been mercilessly dragged off earlier in the night. His body was propped upright against a tree, fastened to it by the iron hook which pierced his skull. What was left of his flesh-torn head was tilted toward me; the glow of my torch revealing the finer details of this dreadful sight, his tongue held by a thread of its meat, and an eye that hung from its sockets like a man at the gallows.

All at once I spewed up the ale I had drank earlier that night, spilling a cone of bile onto the many rivulets of blood coursing through the snow. As I wiped the spew from my lips I spotted the rope that belonged to the hook, and therewith I grabbed it with the palm of my hand, clearing away the scarlet snow that shrouded it. For a full minute I worked the line, testing the rigidness of its frayed and knotted surface while bringing its slack to a proper position. I knew very well that the hook would tug at the man's corpse, at his face, as I made my descent. But I had no choice, for time proved to be the more relentless enemy. I passed the rope under my belt and held it as tight as I could. All I had to do was see myself to Nilus' home, and if the enemy was unaware of its position, then it meant that I still had a chance to warn the city. I hushed my thoughts of their flustering barrage, and then with some clarity of the path I placed the arches of my feet against the hard northerly rock.

"One step at a time," I thought, as I lowered myself into the dark unknown.

CHAPTER 3

After what felt like two hundred feet the sound of powerful, howling winds overtook the echoes of the battle above. I was cold to the bone, and to my increased dismay it was beginning to snow again, only now it was thick and generous. I placed one foot after the other against the barren rock, adding my own tune of heavy panting and grunting to the whistling gust. Time and again I looked down, doing so as often as my wavering courage allowed. I was eager to see any semblance of ground, preferably a clearing of a sort, and not the crown of the forest. Nevertheless, all I could see below my feet was the same dark haze, one that held dozens of suspended ropes similar to the one I desperately gripped.

"Andiel's mercy," I whispered to myself. "I must be close to the bottom by now."

On I went until a great many hoarse snarls echoed from below the veil. I glanced down and saw the flicker of some twenty lambent auras drawing nearer to the spot I intended to touch ground. Each one trailed the other in a long, ragged column, appearing like a scouting party that scrutinized the terrain for traces and tracks. I tried to keep my composure, but immediately a rush of fear and excitement overcame me. I thought that the light of my flame, whose stem was tucked underneath my arm, had been noticed, or worse, I thought that Wymar and his men had fallen, making me the last of their prey, a perfect target for their archers. With a softening breath I fell utterly silent and attentive, almost spellbound to the ebbs of their torches. I cradled the sky-torch close to my cold, numb chest. I could do nothing. Nothing but beseech *Enthera*, goddess of luck and chance, for them to pass on under me.

Alas, dear reader, she did not hear me, nor did any of the other eternal born who seemed to find joy in robbing me of an easy path. Just as I ended my plea with the heavens, I felt the tension in the rope weaken. I looked up and I saw the line rupturing not three feet above my brow, thick bonds gradually turning to single, fibrous strands. It goes without saying that I was in a panic, and so I hastened through the motions of descent, making certain that I kept as silent as possible. I will never again, throughout this tale, give thanks to the Ascani, though by means of their torchlight I had some indication of how far I was from the ground. Regardless, even if I were to hurry to the bottom and avoid death by plummeting to the base, I would still need to face a pack of Ascani by myself, a feat far more fitting for a fabled champion rather than a lowly builder.

Step after step I continued with diligent care, my eyes never once parting from the impending break in the rope. Suddenly, it snapped, and therewith I fell to the base and into a bank of heaped snow. Right away I turned upon my backside like a fish out of water, and there with my arms criss-crossed like a shield I braced for a great many swords and fangs to sink into my flesh. Except, I was met with neither the bite of blades nor the clasp of sharpened teeth, but the dead quiet of night, and the chilling sting of snow piled upon my body. Quickly, I recovered to my throbbing feet, patting my aches and pains in search of injury while making sure the Ascani, whose torches were now far away by the margin of the valley, had not suddenly turned back to the commotion of my rough landing.

A sigh of relief filled my lungs, for as luck would have it, they had not become aware of me. Even more, the sky-torch was still in good condition, save the few chips at the end of its stem. I did not notice it at first, but as I reached for my torch, I soon discovered that the flame had been snuffed by the snow, which was probably why I had escaped the eyes of that Ascani scouting party. Now, I would have to trek to my next mark in complete darkness, but of greater concern to me was that I would need to find, or fashion, another torch to complete my task. First, however, I needed to get a move on, away from a potential encounter with the brutes, and so I raced into the thick woodland before me, letting memory alone guide my feet along the quickest route to Nilus' farmstead.

As I arrived at the farm, shivering and worn, I immediately hid in the brushwood, keeping silent as I scanned the grounds for anything peculiar. This farm was not so much of a farm in the traditional sense. Rather what the sixteenth legion called Nilus' farmstead was more of a large garden that was nestled between two prominent structures; one being akin to the stone-formed dwellings of Easteria, and the other, a great wooden stable that reached as high as the adjacent trees. This was the legionary stable, and it was built to shelter over forty horses. Yet, it was within this latter structure that I found something strange: the farm was dead silent, not even the faint echo of a bray could be heard nearby. Thus, I decided not to call out, wanting to avoid alarming the man Nilus, but more so because I did not want to be torn to shreds by any Ascani waiting in ambush in the shadows of these structures.

I made my way to the rear of the stable, skirting along the edge of the forest until I had no choice but to break from its cloak. Then, I crept to the stable's massive oak doors like an assassin, where I slowly eased my way into the structure, leaving the doors ajar as they had been. As soon as I cleared the doorway, however, a vile scent filled my nostrils. The stench came from a naked man who was suspended by the neck from the highest beam. I suspected it was Nilus, but at that moment it was difficult to tell, for his face was blue and swelled, and his eyes had been altogether removed. In fact, most of his body had been mutilated to such a degree that even those who knew him would, in seeing him there, find it difficult to recognize him. He hung like a slab of meat, legs strewn to the bone as though they had been gnawed upon by rabid dogs, and the whole of his chest and back were flayed in the same way a butcher harvests meat from cattle.

I felt sick to my stomach and my whole body became weak and ever more cold by the sight. I pulled out my sword and approached the man, stepping in a pool of blood and entrails that rested beneath him. I took a breath and held my mouth and nose beneath my clothes while leaning forward to cut him loose.

Suddenly, I was taken by surprise. The voice of a young boy broke from the darkness, just beyond Nilus' corpse. "Touch my father and I swear I will gut you!" the voice said. Before I could speak a word, the boy lit a torch and planted it into the soil. All at once the bright flame illuminated the area, and as my eyes adjusted to the bright light, I discovered that the stable was emptied of all but one of the legion's horses. And, my fair reader, when I mean emptied, I mean that they were butchered to pieces and heaped into great mounds at the rear of the structure. "Drop your sword," the boy added as he emerged from the light.

I stood in place for half a moment, whereupon I carefully stepped backwards with my hands extended to the sides of my chest, as to show I meant him no harm.

"Go on! Drop it, I said!" he warned with stern, puffed eyes.

"Easy now. I'm no enemy," I said. "My name is—"

"I don't care what your name is or who you are, thief! I told you to drop your damn sword!" he blared. As he said this, he stretched his sword toward me. It was nearly his length and he held it up to the height of his chin with much difficulty. He then took a step forward and placed himself in front of the horse that was yet alive, as if guarding it.

I did as commanded, mindfully resting my sword on the ground. The boy was no more than nine, perhaps ten, winters old as I remember it, and his face and clothes were thick with blotches and smears of earth. There was a tremor in his body, not only because of the strain from holding the sword or because he was ill-clothed for the climate, but from the distress he had just no doubt endured. As such, I made no sharp gestures to heighten his anxiety, despite the voice inside my head urging me to snatch the horse and torch from him and continue on with my task.

"Listen to me, boy. I mean you no harm. All is good, yeah?" I said in a gentle tone. I wanted to calm him somehow. I wanted to get him to lower his guard and trust me. "I'm from the sixteenth — from Easteria, and we brought our horses here before the sun passed. Do you not remember?" I added, my eyes trailing over to the pile of dead horses. "What the hell happened here?"

He adjusted his stance, hesitantly, his expression still full of suspicion. "The creatures they — they came and killed them all. They killed them all and ate them...when the moon was high."

"What about him?" I asked, pointing to the horse behind him. "Why not that one?"

He took a sharp breath and glanced up at Nilus' body. His eyes began to water and his small, feeble arms trembled all the more. "That's my father's horse. We don't keep this one here with the rest. And it doesn't belong to the army," he said, as if he believed I was going to take it away from him right there and then. "He says it's mine now, and that I should look after it. Guard it."

"So it is, then," I agreed. "Tell me. What is your name?"

The boy did not answer straight away, but after my beckoning he said, "Enfredarius."

"Alright then, Enfredarius. You can call me Cillian, or builder, if you prefer. At least that is what the rest of them keep calling me," I said with a smile, hoping to ease his tension. I was not sure if it had, in fact, worked, yet I slowly pulled the sky-torch from my belt. "You see this here? Do you know what this is?"

"It's a sky-torch," he replied to my surprise, his eyes taken with a flicker of awe.

"So, you know what it's for, aye?"

"It...it sets fire to the sky."

"Right, so if you know what it is, then you must also know that if it's here with me it means that the lookout is lost." Here, I reached in the direction of the reins. "I need to warn the city, and I am going to need this horse to do it."

Suddenly Enfredarius tightened his resolve and got back on the defensive. He closed the gap between us and brought the point of his sword up to the center of my throat, holding back the tears which welled in his eyes. "Step back!"

"Enfredarius, listen to me. I know that you are scared, but you need to let me pass," I gently voiced, not wanting to invite further aggression. "There is an army of those creatures out there and they are getting closer to the city as we speak. And worse than that, the longer we stay here the more danger will come for the both of us. There's still meat on those horses back there, so soon enough they will come back here to fetch it, and then when that happens there will be more of them than I can handle alone. So please, let me go. There is no time. I do not want to have to force my way."

For a moment we locked eyes. I knew that he was only heeding whatever promise his father had demanded of him, and so I gently waved his blade away from my throat. I took a chance and moved to ready the horse by untying the reins that were harnessed to the post beside me, at which time the boy let the duress in his arms give way. He fell to his knees with a clunk, letting great big globs of earth fall from his yellow hair. He began to whimper and sob knowing he had failed to accomplish his own task.

"He heard them coming," he said abruptly, his voice gripping my attention. "My father. He heard them coming from the forest... from all around us. I wanted to stay beside him, but he hid me in the ground, covering me with the earth as best he could. Told me not to make a sound. Not to cry. Not to come out no matter what

I heard." He turned to me, eyes wide as if petrified. "I did what he asked me to do — but I heard all of it," he blurted as he began to lament. "I heard what they did to him. How they toyed with him…laughed at him…ate him."

Of all the horrors that I had seen this night, it was the sound of dread in this boy's words that gripped my heart the most. Right away, I stopped fiddling with the reins and knelt down before him, placing my hands on either side of his shoulders, embracing his arms as best I could. I had nothing of paternal wisdom in me, but I felt, in this moment, that I had words to say.

"Enfredarius, I'm sorry this has happened," I said, wholeheartedly. I watered my parched lips as I searched for how best to voice what was swirling in my mind. "Look, this entire night has been a nightmare, one that has been filled with nothing but death and sadness, and in truth, I don't know what to make of it. I don't. Call me a coward if you want, but I'm scared because of it. I'm more afraid right *now* than I have ever been in my entire life. And those things out there, the Ascani — they scare me. I thought I had the strength to be able to fight them without fear. And I thought I could do it because in my heart I wanted only to be of worth. But, I saw them…I fought them…and now I'm afraid of them. And not only them, Enfredarius, I'm afraid of this darkness…of this burden, of this responsibility, all of it. I don't want to die." I rubbed my nose and cleared my throat to stifle my oncoming tears. "But you know what? Now that I think about it. None of it comes close to what I'm truly frightened of."

"What more can you be afraid of?" he said, as he brushed away his tears.

"What I fear most is that I won't be able to do the one thing that was asked of me. The one thing that all those men I left behind are risking their lives for. And if I don't do what I was sent to do, more of us will die. Everything that you see here will happen to all those people in Easteria. So, right now, I do not care that it was commanded of me, because my heart needs to see this task done." I picked up Enfredarius' sword by the blade and I offered him the hilt. "You and I are still alive, and we have the choice. Do we stay here and hide, or do warn the city so that thousands may not suffer the same fate as your father. These are your woods, Enfredarius, and you know them better than I do. Will you help me?"

He rose to his feet, and as soon as he clutched the hilt I understood that he had mustered all that was left of his courage, both for me, and for his father. Spirited in his decision to help, his movements bold and hasty, he untied the horse and mounted it. I, on the other hand, snatched my sword, and the torch, from the ground, whereupon I opened the stable doors just enough so that the horse could pass through.

I had no sooner mounted and steered the horse to the doorway when many bestial growls rang from the surrounding woods. Among these growls were the barks of hound-like demons, the *Hircani*, fabled creatures that were said to have long ago been bred by Ascanelius for the hunt of man. They did not take the full form of a hound, but something closer in likeness to a mountain ram, bearing two great horns that often spiralled out to the tip of their elongated ears, and whose mouths always seemed to seep a greenish froth. A half dozen of these Hircani beasts had burst into the open area of the farmstead, each chained at the neck by a leash made of galvanized iron rings. They thrashed about the grounds like dogs of war aroused by the scent they tracked, pulling their masters, and the war party behind them, ever closer to where we were.

"Cillian," Enfredarius whispered with surprise, showing me his bloodied fingers.

I looked down to where the boy's fingers were near, at my leg. As I squeezed my trousers blood fizzed through my fingers, and at that moment I felt a sharp pain upon my thigh. I had done my best to roam through the forest unseen, yet it became clear that I had unknowingly left a trail of my blood for the enemy to pursue.

"Here! You steer!" I said, handing over the reins. "Stay clear of the valley. But stay to the edge!"

"What of the creatures?" he asked with nervousness.

"Go right through them," I replied with verve.

At that I spurred the horse to a gallop. The heavy doors burst wide open, slamming against the structure with a thunderous bang. I cut down the first dazed enemy in our path with the sword in my hand, bludgeoning another beast with the torch I held in the other. At the same time, the Ascani demon masters released their hold of their hounds, signalling the war pack to give chase with their guttural cackles. If not for the speed of our mount, and to be quite honest, Enfredarius' skills at the reins, we would have been grappled to the ground many times over by the Ascani and Hircani that soared at us in attack. Despite our agile escape, an Ascani archer very nearly hit his mark, for just as we cleared the open grounds and entered the backwoods, an arrow nicked the back of my calf, its iron head cutting deep.

I let out a shrill grunt, its echo quickly fading into the forest in which we vanished.

***

Enfredarius and I rode through the forest for what felt like an hour, up and down the natural slopes and twisted paths until the ground finally flattened out, and when the trees surrounding us began to separate at greater lengths. The city of Easteria was now becoming more and more visible, the lights upon its battlements had grown from tiny yellow specks to bright, amber blots. Not that we were anywhere near to it, for another league remained to be travelled at the least from where we were. And to add to the hardship, the enemy was not far at our backs, since the wound on my calf ensured a steady, bloody trail for their Hircani to sniff out. Even so, we had no time to stop and bind it, because by now the Ascani army that moved along the valley floor had passed the center of the gorge's wooded area, and so to pause for even a moment would grant these creatures more time to go on unseen.

Suddenly Enfredarius pulled at the reins and called the horse to a stop.

"What's happened?" I blurted. "Why have we stopped?"

"Over there, look," he replied, pointing to the rim of the forest. "It's open ground."

I nodded approvingly. "Right then, take it! Another half league and we'll find a spot to light it. We're almost there, keep at it—"

Just then I heard the beating of striding hooves and the snap of sundering twigs nearing from behind us. In a jolt I looked over my shoulder to see a mongrel springing toward me with its jaws wide open, this one more horrible in size than a Nordic wolf. Instinctively, I rushed my arm over to shield my throat, whereupon the Hircani's upper fangs caught my gauntlet, though its lower teeth sunk into the base of my forearm. In that same instant the horse reared high upon its hind legs, sending Enfredarius plummeting to the frozen dirt. As for me, the sheer momentum of the creature's attack propelled me a greater distance from the horse, who darted off in fright even before my back had touched the ground.

I grappled with the creature that held my arm, holding it back from ripping my tongue clean from my neck with its gaping jaws. Yet the more I tried to do so the deeper its bite buried into my arm, causing me to cry out in excruciating agony, which ultimately signalled the other creatures to hone in on us. I called out to Enfredarius as I gurgled upon the blood that streamed into my throat. I shouted with hell's fury for him to abandon me, because the strength in my arm was soon to cave in. I would have accepted my death, dear reader, knowing that the boy was alive and on his way to warn the garrison. But he did not answer me, so I could not let it end here.

Time and again my fingers raked the earth in search of my sword, but the creature's weight kept me from doing so for more than a moment. Realising that it was not near me, I quickly turned to barbarism, and so in a wild frenzy I pressed my thumb into the beast's eye with a brutality I did know I had, all the way down to the knuckle. All at once the creature whimpered as it reeled off my chest, where its frame suddenly stilled to a dead silence. As it toppled to the ground I saw Enfredarius standing behind it with my sword planted through its heart.

I was half-way to my feet when the boy rushed over and put my arm around his shoulders. He helped me stand upright, strain faced, as if my weight to him was the same as a boulder. I asked him if he was alright, noticing the gash that lined his forehead. His face and the rim of his hair were reddened with blood, and his cheeks bore the marks of deepened scrapes.

"I'm alright," he said. "And you? Are you hurt?"

"Never mind me," I replied, pulling my sword from the beast's back.

"The horse is gone. What are we going to do now?"

"The sky-torch!" I said in a panic, looking about. "Where is it?"

"Here!" he answered, as he brought it to sight.

A wave of relief passed through me. Although the stem had snapped in two and the fuse had been ripped clean-off, the torch had landed on moss covered rock, so it was still functional despite looking a little battered. Looking behind, however, I saw a number of torches barrelling towards us from all sides. I searched my mind for a plan. But I must confess, I did not know what we were meant to do, knowing full well that we could not out-run them on foot. Then, my eyes grew wide as I caught sight of a nearby tree. It was a great oak, one whose height towered over the others around it, and its branches were broad and copious, almost like a web of timber.

I spun back toward Enfredarius. "Can you climb?" I nearly shouted.

"I live in a forest," he answered. "Can you...with that arm?"

I paused for a second, painfully overturning the gauntlet on my wounded arm. The query was not if I could climb or not, but how high I would get before they would catch up to me, even if the falling snow offered some concealment to our ascent. By this time, it was clear that it was no longer my responsibility to hold the sky-torch, nor could I if I wanted to. And now that the fuse was gone, I knew what had to be done once we reached the top. I pressed Enfredarius towards the tree, cramming what was left of its stem into the band around his waist. "Hold on to this," I said. "You light our way to the top and get as high as you can. Understood?"

"Aye," he said. "But what about you?" he then asked, concerned for my safety.

I placed the torch in his hand. "I'll be right behind. Now go! Call out when you're there."

Enfredarius and I began scaling the bark and timber like tree frogs. He moved between the branches so swiftly that it surprised me, paying no heed to the Ascani that converged at the base of the tree. They squawked in hysteria, licking their blackened lips and sword-like teeth as they fought each other, and their hounds, about who was to be the first to chase after us. A few of their archers began firing their bows, but to our luck their arrows snapped against the large, tightly knit branches, many simply whizzing over our heads and into the night sky.

"Don't stop! Keep climbing!" I shouted to Enfredarius, who was several feet above me.

As I caught up with him, the pain in my arm and calf became truly unbearable. I had to stop and catch a much needed breath, but looking down as I did so with panicked eyes, for six ghoulish creatures were rapidly closing in. I raised my sword up and came down on the first Ascani who attempted to grab at my trousers, removing the better part of its arm. I watched as it crashed to the ground, taking a few of those beneath it along. Seeing its chance, another one jabbed at me. I struck the top of its head so hard that my sword remained planted in its skull, and therewith I lost my sword as the beast fell to the base.

"Cillian help!" Enfredarius yelled, as an Ascani appeared under us.

From the opposite side of the trunk the creature reached around and grabbed the boy's leg, trying to offset his balance by pulling him down with a ripping motion. I promptly overtook its attention by tugging at its horn, causing the creature to let go of its grip and spring upward toward me — perhaps I was more suitable prey. Before it could meet me face to face I pushed Enfredarius up by his heel with whatever strength I had left to give. At that moment, I was exposed. The creature managed to wrap an arm around me, squeezing me so tightly against the trunk that I thought my ribs would soon burst from my sides. I bashed its head against the bark over and over, but in a quick motion, it released me from its bone cracking hold and drove a sharpened bone-like dagger into my shoulder. A shrill cry parted from my lungs as I cupped my hand around its clenched fist, where I fiercely battled to stop it from driving the knife in any further.

"Cillian!" Enfradarius cried out again. "I'm here! I'm at the top!"

With strain I glanced upward, where I saw Enfredarius shrivel into a ball as he latched himself to the highest branch poking out from the canopy. He let out short blurts of fear as he began to take notice of the many Ascani who passed me and headed toward him. I tried desperately to give him direction, because as I have already mentioned, I knew what had to be done in order to set fire to the sky.

Meanwhile the creature I battled closed its eyes and took in the spray of my blood upon its extended tongue as though it was cool water on a hot day. Its face was flushed with mirth, and each time I tried to bury my hands around its gullet, it easily swatted them away as if the potency of my strength was that of a child.

Time was running out. I had to act. I had to move. I had to save the boy.

It was here when the beast drew me in closer while slowly opening its eyes. Its mouth grew wider and wider as it prepared for a bite. Then, without warning, a blinding red flash swallowed us. I flung from my position as if yanked from the tree by a godly force, and as I fell, I felt the burning hot ashes of sorcerer's powder freckle my body. I plummeted to the base upon my back, the frozen earth feeling like a sheet of rock. I do not recall what happened thereafter, only that in the darkening of my eyes, I caught a glimpse of the surrounding trees engulfed in flame.

CHAPTER 4

I awoke to an icy wind brushing my bare chest, and to the strong smell of smouldering wood and burning oil. My eyesight was blurred and doubling, as if I had drunk one too many cups of ale. I saw little around me but the vague figures of men moving about this way and that, whose clamour and frantic chatter were but muffled echoes in my ear. At first, I had no bearing as to where I was. I soon learned that I was no longer in the forest, but I was in Easteria, laying on a wooden cot under the awning of a teeming hospice. Countless rows of wounded men lay on linen bedding on either side of me, and they all appeared just like I did, their bodies enrobed head to toe with bloodied rags and threaded with stitches. I could hear them moan and cry at every sudden feeling of pain, these sounds causing the agony of my own wounds increase.

I arose sluggishly and propped myself onto my elbows, the exertion of which left my muscles trembling and uneasy. I blinked hard several times, adjusting my eyes to the light. Here I paused, stunned, for under the radiance of the afternoon sun lay the aftermath of a bitter siege: the grand market square before me was speckled with charred timber, and shattered kiosks set afire littered the ground. All across the stone floor there lay the remanence of the merchant wears they held. There was everything from pottery to produce, crates of fine cloths and luxury goods, each and all spread this way and that as if they were seeds ready to be sowed.

Beyond the square, town folk of every age moved up and down the roadways in a panic, sending pails and spadefuls of earth atop the stone dwellings still crowned by fire. The flames thickened the air with the scent of ash and cinder, but it was little when compared to the foul-smelling corpses of the legionaries whose bodies were left stacked like logs at the center of the square. Very near to it there was an enormous hill of slain Ascani, their numbers far greater than our dead, three hundred if I gave it an estimate. Above all, there was a seemingly endless column of legionnaires who trudged passed the hospice. I assumed they were coming from the battlements, looking utterly fatigued from battle, which I guessed had been going for many arduous hours. Their heads sunk heavily towards their filth smeared tabards, and the edges of their pummelled shields were left to drag along the dirt like a farmer's plow. To me, dear reader, it appeared like a procession of defeated warriors, yet their crimson standards were caught high in the wind, a symbol of victory in the legion.

Seeing the red upon the cloth made my mind wander from reality to the broken memory of what had led me to this place. Flashing images of the forest, of the sky torch, of the Ascani brutes chasing *us* up the trees, filled my thoughts. My heart stopped at the thought of Enfredarius, who I then realised was not among the men surrounding me in the hospice. All at once I was filled with the intent to find him, and so I achingly removed the blanket from my legs and I rose from the cot.

"Oh no you don't. Not even a chance lad!" said a soft, roused voice, who was sitting with his back to me by my bedside. As he said this, he extended his arm and placed his plump hand upon my chest, gently guiding me back down upon the bed. "Down you go now. That's it. Just let it happen," he added, while dipping his quill in a vial of ink.

"Who—"

"I wouldn't talk either," he interrupted. "The stitching on your neck will come apart."

"Where is he?" I said rather sternly, not caring to follow the man's advice.

The man laid his quill on the makeshift desk he was sitting at, and then turned to me with a damp cloth in his clutch, which he promptly placed on my forehead. He was rotund, not excessively I might add, but enough to suggest that he had a fault for food and drink. His garb was familiar to me: he wore a beige ill-fitted robe, priestly in its appearance, which I had seen a few times before as boy when the priests of the *Sacrarium* would come to sanctify the harvests and give their annual portents. That he was a priest, therefore, was unmistakable, because these men not only had a uniform method of dress, but their hair, often brown and thinly, sat upon their heads like an inverted bowl, another one of their distinguishing features.

"Who is it that you're looking for?" he said, reaching under my cot and hauling out a coffer. He left his seat to the healer who was working on the man behind him, and therewith he sat on the coffer, quite close to me, in fact, where he began inspecting my dressings. "You're going to have to be a little more specific, lad," he added, as he swirled a fine piece of lumber around his tongue. "As you can already tell, I can't help you otherwise."

My growing impatience seemed to aggravate my wounds further, and so I cradled the fresh cotton bandages around my waist, wincing at the stabbing pain in my gut. "Enfredarius," I coughed. "I'm looking for the boy Enfredarius, son of Nilus the legion's horse master. He was with me in the forest last night. He should've been brought in with me. Have you seen him? Is he here?"

"He is," the priest replied.

I smiled, my heart filled with relief. "Where then? How is he?"

The priest shot me a despairing look, and then nodded toward the corpses. "He's there."

I looked at him blankly, first because I did not believe him, but then because I had suddenly remembered that it was Enfredarius who had lit the sky-torch, from which he had taken the force of a hundred fires against his body. He confirmed what I had wanted to deny in delusion; the boy was dead, and I now knew it to be true.

A wave of sorrow came over me, the sting of remorse stabbing at my breast. I grabbed the cloth on my forehead with a trembling hand as if I were taken by a deep chill, and then slowly trailed it down over my eyes and the bridge of my nose, doing everything possible to hold back the passions whirling in my heart. Even so, a river of tears began streaming down my cheeks. I began to sob like a child, for all I could think about was how I had stripped the boy of his life by inciting him to action, by urging him up the tree, and by forcing him to do the very thing that had been asked of me. And so, over and over I pictured him at the top of the great oak, scared and all alone, his body washed over in the red burst of the sorcerer's powder.

The priest took pity on me and sought to comfort me with words of calm, absent fault and failings. All I wanted to do was keep whimpering, but for some reason I stopped myself in fear of the other men hearing me. And so after time I collected myself, whereupon I asked him to bless the boy for his deeds so that the proper divinities could guide his soul in the afterlife. It is, as you know, fair reader, that the dead are housed under the stars of those gods who symbolize the course of their life. And though Enfredarius may not have been part of the legion, his courage on that cold night in 1023 A.E. most certainly granted him the chance to be amongst those fighters who spent many long years alongside the sword. A sort of happiness overtook my sorrow as the priest performed the rite, and ever since then I have hoped that the boy had found his father in the heavens.

It was some hours that passed before I could stop thinking of Enfredarius without inviting a new wave of grief. The guilt seemed to grow each time the priest passed to check my wounds. My mind, as you can imagine, was grasping at dozens of memories and thoughts. However, there was one thought in particular that I wanted the priest to confirm, and so I had finally gathered courage to ask about the men I had left behind.

"What of the men from the lookout?" I asked, morosely, the next time the priest came by.

"The heart can only take so much misery in one day," he replied, pulling the blanket at my feet up to my shoulders. "Best you get some rest now knowing that even in all this ruin, you and that boy saved many lives, including mine if I can say so. Leave that grief for another day, alright? And let me worry about which soul is going where for now, lad. Just lay still and recover."

I took a breath and remained even-tempered, my heart exhausted at harbouring more gloom. In spite of the pain, I raised my fists to my eyes and rubbed them as if to bring clarity. He was right. I needed to lay still. As I left my mind, I began to become conscious of my body, whereupon I felt cuts, bruises, and gashes make their presence known. Each time I moved a muscle I felt like they were all being freshly received. It was at this point that I had caught sight of a ceramic medallion hanging from the priest's belt, its face etched with the image of a dove.

"You're of the Sacrarium, aren't you?" I said, realising now, dear reader, that this question was posed subconsciously, as if to remove myself from the pain I was experiencing.

"What gave it away?" he answered in a bubbly sort of way.

"That talisman on your side there. High augur of Apaliunus. God of the Sun."

"Aye, I am. Petris is the name if you were wondering."

"Why is it that you're here in Easteria? It has no temples in favour of the sun."

"Well, builder, it seems when you have a direct line to the gods it tends to make me rather sought after no matter where I happen to be. And to be a little forward, I don't really need a temple to be able to read portents and prophecies, or to make people with coin feel good about themselves. That would be like you forgetting how to build something as simple as this coffer here just because you find yourself without a hammer in your hand." He smiled, tapping the face of the coffer. "But if you want the truth, and this secret stays between you and me, I'm really only here for the food…and for the coin. I'm telling you there is nothing, and I mean nothing, that is better than a pocket full of silver and a good venison stew in your belly right before, and right after, an omen reading. I mean why limit yourself, am I right?" He turned to the side and grabbed a marl cup from the table he was working on, which I now saw was brimming with botanic medicines and food stuffs. "Here. Now that you're up, you should have a drink of this. It'll take a bit of the edge off I promise," he went on, placing the cup to my lips.

Yearning to quench my thirst, I snatched the cup from his hands and drank the contents in a few rough gasps, feeling the stitches at my neck expand with each gulp. However, in that same instant my eyes widened like full moons, and I began to cough wildly as I blurted, "Gods! What the hell is this? Is this wine?"

"Yes, why?" he said, looking at me as if I were mad. "Is that a problem?"

"Why would you give me this? My head is already spinning like a wheel as it is."

"Aye well, sorry about that," he replied. "I've always been quite shite at making tonics. Best I could do in the present moment," he then said, shrugging his shoulders.

"Is there no water?"

Petris wiped the spillage off my chin like a caring mother. "Not in these parts of the city, I'm afraid. The wells you see, and I mean all of them, they ran dry just trying to put out half these fires." He nabbed a glass carafe and poured himself a cup of the dark-red wine. "Don't worry, in a day or so they'll be back as new. Full up to the brim! But actually, now that I remember it, there will be water in an hour or so. We've already sent a cart to the docks to fetch some. Gods know you lot need it. In the meantime, however, Lord Priscus has given us his ever lordly permission to empty every brothel, tavern, and storehouse in this district — pretty much allowing all of us to drink freely to our hearts content. Well, maybe not that last one, but still isn't it wonderful, Cillian? I've had a cask of that Palagian malt to myself already, but this Falarian wine here is a first for me. I'm telling you I don't know what it is, but the smell alone...well its divine." He tilted his head back and emptied the cup down his throat in a swig, quickly becoming cockeyed by the effects of the drink. "Andiel's mercy, that's bloody fruity! Would you like to try a cup? Or maybe you'd like a vermillion more to your southern tastes, yeah? Nothing too strong on the tongue?"

I pushed myself upright to a seated position, my back leaning against the supporting pillar of the hospice, my legs brittle, feeling as though a fair wind could easily carry them off. "I think I am done with drinking wine. Better yet, perhaps instead of drink you can answer some of my questions. How is that you know so much about me, priest?" I said, between winces. "My name for starters."

He poured himself another cup with a mirthful grin, at which point I began to get a better sense for Petris' character, for his jolly, carefree nature was becoming more apparent, now that the sorrow within me had begun to fall away.

"Everyone knows your name, lad," he replied. "What did you think would happen after that feat you pulled? You know it's quite natural for people to start asking questions when they see a man slouched over the commander's horse half dead, barreling through the gates with an army of Ascani at his back. It was quite a sight if you ask me."

"You were there?"

"Aye I was, but not for long! You see those Ascani over there," he said, nodding toward the mound. "After Lord Priscus and his party carried you through the gates about two hundred of those devils managed to push their way over the walls just when the siege started. By then I was already long gone, but I heard, and I don't know if there is any truth to it, that as soon as they caught sight of you, they came after you, Cillian — like they recognized you or what not. Lord Pricus and his men fought them in the streets and brought you here afterwards. I happened to be hiding behind one of those barrels over there when he found me. Ever since then he has asked me to stay by your side at all times and keep you among the living. He's very adamant about it too. Said I'm not even allowed to take a piss without bringing you with me, if you could believe that. I figure he has some very important questions of his own to ask you."

I took in everything he said, putting together the missing pieces that brought me here. "And how is that you know of my craft?"

"Oh about that!" he exclaimed, as he pulled out my journal from the fold in his robe. "I've been reading this book of yours. I found it stashed in your tunic. I must say these works are quite impressive. Not much of an admirer in the engines of death myself, but it's still rather striking." He took a swill of his wine as he handed me the journal. "Go on, take it. It's all as it was. After all that you've been through, Cillian, I'm surprised only a corner got singed. Oh and, well...there might be a small smudge of porc gravy on the third or fourth page, but I swear it was there when I got it."

I reached out and took it with uneasy delight. I was surprised to see it whole, and fairly untouched, but I was also stung by the boyish ideas of grandeur surrounding the ambitions in this book. The contents were all but the playthings of children, but I began to see them as a token of my innocence in a new light, insofar that my designs were drawn up before my knowledge of war, or rather my true experience of it. A single night imbued me with the realities of battle, and the horrors of the Ascani, which quickly aged my mind. I no longer felt the desire to achieve the fame and praise that I had once sought after from the recognition and application of my schemes. Instead, I began to see my designs as nothing more than what Petris had so accurately named them as: engines of death.

"My thanks, Petris…for everything," I said, letting it rest at my side.

Just then he hurried to his feet and walked a short distance toward the lane adjacent to the hospice, stopping in front of a decoratively chiselled bench laden with weapons, armour, and all sorts of legionary attire. As he rubbed his large stomach with one hand he mulled over the contents, shifting them about with the other hand until he grabbed a tome of bound parchment. After that, he made his way to the table of food stuffs beside the bench and prepared himself a generous serving of bread, olives, and cheese. When he finally returned to the coffer he opened the tome across his lap and began reading it, all the while testing the limits of his hunger and the wideness of his mouth. For a few long moments he sat in complete silence as if I were a ghost to him, at times muttering a word or two as his eyes diligently tracked the words on the parchment.

"Ah, Petris," I said with confusion.

"Hmm — ah that's right!" he blurted, noticing that I was looking at him eat. He tore a piece of crumbly yellow cheese and added, "Cheese?"

"No, but I think we should inform Lord Priscus that I'm awake."

"Unfortunately that would be extremely hard, Cillian."

"Why?"

"Well, that's because he isn't here. In the city, I mean."

"When will he return?"

"I'm an augur not a cheap fortune-teller," he replied, with a full mouth. "Could be tonight. Could be tomorrow. I don't know. Your task now, lad, is to do nothing, alright? If you're not going to have any of the food, or wine, then just lay back and rest as best you can. As long as I appear to be doing something of worth not a soul will bother us, I promise. Besides, you can't even walk, so we'll need to fetch a cart to carry you too him—"

I shook my head and moved to stand. Pain shot through every part of my body, but I was determined. "I can't just stay here and do nothing, Petris. I have urgent information that the captains in the barracks need to hear. I'll be of better use to everybody if I find them as quickly as possible. And if anything should happen to me at least they can relay the details to Lord Pricus on his return. My thanks again, Petris, for keeping me alive, but really I think I've rested enough. I am indebted to you, for all of it. And I'll be sure the commander knows what you did for me."

"Wait! I can't let you just up and leave. You'll never make it."

"The barracks is not far. I'll take my chances."

"No honestly, Cillian, I can't let you leave."

I swung my legs off the bed, not really feeling them below me. The only indication that they were still attached to my hips was seeing them slide off the cot. "Trully, you've really done enough—"

All of sudden I began to feel faint, my head spinning in circles like a carousel. A great thirst seized my throat, and then all at once my muscles felt as light and brittle as the bark of a dying tree. "What...what's happening to me? My head it's...it's whirling."

"I told you lad, you'll never make it," Petris said, as he held onto me. "I've been honest about a lot of things, Cillian, but not so much with one in particular. You see the wine you drank earlier, the Falarian, well...it wasn't just delicious, but I may have put a little bit more crushed root of the *Lavia* plant in it then I should have. I thought, perhaps not soundly, that a bit more sedative would make you fall asleep faster. I'm sorry, but you were talking too much. I had to do something."

"You numbed my senses?" I blurted, wide-eyed.

"Aye, sorry about that," he replied, shamelessly. "I did say I'm quite shite at making tonics."

Petris held me gently as I all but fell back on top of the cot, the afternoon sun turning to a phantom screen of amber haze. Before my eyes the world around me quickly dimmed to black. I felt nothing, nothing but the kiss of the cold breeze upon my skin once again.

CHAPTER 5

*When I had set out to compile this memoire I had the pleasure
of speaking at length with many individuals whose stories, as I have
said in the beginning, are linked to my own. The following events
were told to me by Alia Cai, 991 A.E.-1075 A.E. I traveled back to
Easteria in 1048 A.E., and there, with the help of a dear loved one, I
had learned that Alia Cai was the last living soul that could help me
uncloud the events, which preceded my meeting with Petris. In this
next portion of the tale I will be writing, or rather reproducing, to the
best of my ability, Alia Cai's story as she heard and saw it firsthand.*

It was a beautiful, starry evening in Easteria, and at the far
edge of the city, just before the main road gave way to the legionary
barracks in front of the docks, a horse drawn cart carrying many
barrels of wines and ales halted in front of a royal tavern, its walls
made of rough-cut stone and its roof formed of a rare Phylian
timber. A small wooden plaque hung above the door, *The Vials
of Elarus* was engraved across its width. The tavern was named
as such by its original holder, a man by the name of Caelus, who
was said to have defeated the giant Elarus on the Isle of Felas a
hundred years prior during one of his sorties with the sixteenth.
He returned with six vials of the giant's blood as proof of the deed,
and for this reason, the tavern had since been the most frequented
ale house in Easteria among the men of the legion. On this night,

like every other since the breaking of the siege, songs echoed from its large stained glass windows, and its narrow rooms were filled with more than a hundred soldiers of all ranks, each and all mourning the dead in the only manner a legionary knew best: the excessive drinking of ale.

"Listen here, all of you!" slurred a soldier in a thundering voice, coarse with drink. As he spoke, he spilled golden brew all about and as he held himself up at the tavern's bar. Though his words possessed little clarity, his outburst caught the ear of every person minding their own affairs. "And hear me well all you green bastards," he added with a hiccup. "I, Sabinus, have fought these creatures on land from Ostilia to Whitetown; at sea from the Blue Waters to the Illyrian Islands; and now here…here in Easteria." The man canted his head back and drank without concern for the stiff, serious tone he had set. "But now! My brothers! Now!" he went on, drunkenly turning to the thin, large breasted tavern maid behind him. "Now what must I do! To put me face between those tits."

The air was quiet and none voiced a sound. The patrons of the tavern were absorbed by the perverse discomfort brought about by this drunken soldier. Then, without warning, the tavern maid walloped the man across his rosy cheek with a firm, open hand. The force of the slap threw him off balance, and he crashed upon the rickety floor. Everyone who bore witness erupted in unrestrained laughter, which quickly restored the tavern to a blend of a hundred different conversations.

Alia Cai was the taverns' holder, and she remained so up until her death. The spectacle just described was the standard on any given night during times of war, and while this raucous ensued, she moved between the crowded tables, pouring fresh rounds of drink into the raised cups of those who saw her approaching. When her jug was emptied, she re-filled her stock from the high-stacked barrels of spirits under the stairs that led to the second floor. On this night, she lingered there for a while, she was intrigued by the group of five men who were cramped around a small oblong table just beside the casks. In truth, she confessed to me that she was more charmed by what lay upon the table: many crooked towers of gleaming silver coins loomed over six oddly shaped dice, all of which were crudely marked with the mythical beasts and hallowed weapons of Anolian lore.

Of the men, three were unsightly ruffians; two lanky individuals dotted with pockmarks and gold piercings, and the other, their haughty leader, whose pudgy body and grease covered garbs most certainly suggested that he had never missed a meal in his life. Before him were two veteran captains of the Vined Sword. The first was Captain Meric, a young middle-aged man whose face was uniquely handsome and unscathed despite being a seasoned soldier, capable of attracting the notice of the women he constantly sought after. In fact, he was known by most as a self-proclaimed master of charm, often running his fingers through his fair, auburn hair whenever a pensive thought lingered in his mind, or more likely to keep his visage in full view of the world. The second legionary was Captain Jon, a near giant of a man with crushingly powerful arms and a physique like that of a brawny beast. He had a presence that made men of lesser stock feel uncomfortably weak. But unlike Meric, he was rather taciturn and reserved, save when the furor of battle entered his blood. He had known Meric since his early years in the army, and so he never saw himself away from him in times of battle or leisure, even if it meant watching him gamble, a thing he never participated in as he believed it was the amusement of dishonest folk. As such, he stood in silence just to the side of the group as if he were a statue, and like the rest of the legionaries in the tavern, he was clothed in his legionary uniform, which was nothing more than what was worn under our armour and tabard in battle, which was a beige, long-sleeved tunic and black, rippled trousers, tightened at the waist by a brown, iron-buckled belt.

The ruffian leader was sitting in front of Meric, his fingers interlaced as they rested on his swollen belly. He looked at him with an air of impatience. "Are you pulling at my balls, Meric?" he huffed, or at least that is what Alia swore she recalled hearing. "I don't have all night, you know. It'll be morning at this pace, so let's get a move on shall we? What's your wager?"

"No, I don't think so. I believe I'd know if I was pulling at your balls," Meric replied, eyes fixed on the table. "And patience, my dear Herelos. The moon is not yet at its highest. A moment more is not too much to ask, is it? You've been bleeding me dry since the start. So why don't you take it easy and call for another meal. It seems your appetite is making you ill-tempered."

Herelos smirked, haughtily. "Busy men in my craft hunger only for silver. As you know."

"And whole chickens, apparently," Meric muttured to Jon, wryly.

"What did you say?" Herelos said.

"Ahem!" Meric uttered, clearing his throat. "It was nothing. The ale is getting to me is all — you know how it is. Anyway, my friend, I'm ready to place my wager." He placed twelve coins in the center of the table, and therewith he reached for his cup and took a swig of wine as he winked flirtatiously to Alia, who he had noticed at this moment was eavesdropping. "Right then, I'll make this one rather simple for all of us. Twelve coins in favour of Ichias the Minotaur, with two claws, two horns, and Kaiphan's billhook. Does the dice master wish to accept the wager?"

"Are you fucking kidding me?" voiced one of the ruffians. "Of course he wants to—"

"Now, now, Marcus, let's not be crude. He's only following the rules, as we both should be," Herelos interjected. He matched the wager, taking it from the heap of coins laid out before him. "I'll gladly call your bet, Meric. But make it Centuros the Half-horse with...let's say the flail of Argos. How's that?"

"Anything to get my coin back," Meric replied.

Meric gathered up the dice and placed them in a ceramic goblet. He handed the goblet to Herelos, who gave it a hearty shake just before letting the dice roll across the table. Then, he sank back in his chair with a broad, half-toothless grin, basking in the snickers of his thugs as they swiftly collected the winnings like avarice creatures.

"My, my — seven in a row now is it?" Herelos teased.

"Eleven," Meric said, "but who's counting?"

"Andiel's mercy! Eleven?" Herelos said, with feigned surprise. "By the way am I saying that correctly? Andiel's mercy or what not...like you soldiers do."

As Meric nodded in agreement, his opponent plunged his hand into a wooden bowl filled with the remnants of his earlier meals. He brought a chicken bone to his lips, sucking and belching on the bits of gristle that were left, all the while flashing his foul looking greyish tongue and rotting teeth. "What can I say, Meric," he added, between his spirited gnaws. "Gambling is a tasteless art, but an art nonetheless." Then, he placed his elbows on the table and beckoned Meric to come a little closer. "Listen here, I'll tell you a little story, a secret more like it," he said, using the chicken bone as a pointer. "When I was your age I thought these games of odds to be nothing more than sports of chance. I learned quickly, however, that this is not the case. At least not entirely. You see, Meric, there's a rather remarkable finesse that goes into each hand. A strategy, if you will. The dice may role a certain way yes, but one has to know when their victory is certain, or when their defeat is imminent. Know that, and the coin will follow as if you were the king himself. It's all in the form I'm telling you. Don't you agree?"

"Yeah," Meric agreed, leaning in, "it's an art alright. Just like how your teeth are formed."

At once Marcus surged from his seat, gruff and heated. Alia, still watching closely, had backed away several steps from the barrels, thinking a brawl was soon to come. Meanwhile Marcus had added, "The fucking nerve on this imperial cunt—"

"Calm your arse, you fool, and sit down," Herelos barked, as he dragged his lesser back to his seat. "Are you a bloody child? Can you not see he riles you? And have you forgotten where we are, yeah? Planning on fighting the whole bloody tavern?" he added, waving his hand behind him.

He turned to Meric and gobbled down his ale as though his throat were a funnel. "Forgive my man's poor sense. He knows nothing of the pains in losing this much coin. You know sometimes I believe they forget how truly lucky they are in this world, to have food on the table when they please, to be surrounded by endless riches and lustful women, unbound by the need to labour like some poor laymen. You'd think they show some appreciation and act like civilized men once in a while. But then again, I can't really fault them for it."

"I can't imagine the stress it puts on your shoulders," Meric said, apathetically.

"It's hard for a man in my position, but I manage," he went on with a tone of self-pity. "You see there aren't many like me—" He stopped himself short, for he caught sight of a tavern maid wandering past the table. He grabbed her arm crudely and said, "Girl be of use would you and bring me some of that bread over there and lots of that aged cheese from before. And a flagon of that wonderful Falarian, yeah? And do well to make it quick before I die of hunger." He turned back to Meric. "Where was I? Oh, yeah! Life is quite difficult for me."

"You know, Herelos, a cup of water now and then would do you good," Meric said.

"Water is for the lessers, and we'll leave it for them," he replied with a demeaning air while counting his many coins. "Now then, where were we in this magnificent game of ours. Yes that's right, your silver. Would you be wanting it back? Forgive me, but seeing as how we've taken it all, I think it's about time that me and mine move on to more *wealthier* prospects...if it's all the same to you, of course."

"What do you mean?" Meric asked. He loved to play the fool when his game was weak.

"He means place another wager or fuck off," said Sagillus, the other ruffian sitting closest to Jon.

"Well, when you put it so gently like that," Meric said, drawing a coin pouch from his belt, "then I do have a last wager in me."

Herelos smiled. "My word! Would you look at that! I thought we had taken everything. And will your friend over there be partaking this time? Or will he just keep standing there pretending to be your shadow? Come to think of it, Meric, he doesn't seem to talk much, does he?"

"Words you mean? No," Meric replied absentmindedly, as he rummaged through the pouch. "But I promise if you put an axe in his hand he'll start singing until he is dead. He speaks when he wills and when it matters, no more, no less. Apart from that, he's a Linlani. You know they have no taste for these games."

Herelos' eyes widened with curiosity. "A Linlani! Here?"

"Dying breed that lot," Marcus said to Herelos. "I've heard all the stories...of the savages that come out of the far west. Killing each other by the hundreds over patches of bloody ice. Some even say they're worse than the Ascani. Barbarians, all of them."

"Aye," said Sagillus. "And me thinks the bastard's silent because it doesn't know our words. Yeah, that must be it. Whatever egg-sized brain is under that bald head of his probably falls short of his brawn. Ain't that right ya'tall cunt. Probably dim-witted too, just like one of them whores from Heraea." He expelled a lump of snot on the tavern floor that landed a few fingers length from Jon's feet. "Fucking savages," he added with a sleazy smirk. "They don't belong in these parts."

Jon looked up sharply, and therewith he slowly advanced a step.

"Clearly he understands you," Meric said, his hand laxly extended in front of Jon's frame. Here, Alia had told me that the banter was coming to an end, and that she was becoming more and more unsettled at the thought that a brawl would erupt, being that Meric's dry humour now invited fiery stares. "And it seems you're not too bright yourself, friend — insulting the very hand that saw your leathery flesh away from Ascani mouths. If I were you, I'd ask for his forgiveness now, and not when he's pulling your tongue from your throat."

"Let's have it then," Sagillus asserted, moving forward in his seat, ready to pounce. "Go on, send your mongrel at me."

"I would if not for the fear that you'd shit all over my shoes."

Sagillus grew terribly agitated. "Why don't you suck on your Andiel's beloved cock you—"

At that moment the tavern maid returned to the table with all that Herelos had called for, her hands filled with nourishment for six men. She placed the array upon the table's small width as best she could, and then took five silver coins from the pile before she walked off, oblivious to the blood boiling tensity she had strolled into.

"Alright that's enough, calm yourselves all of you," Herelos interjected, his gaze lost in his heap of bread and cheese. "Let's cool our tongues and weigh our cocks in a different way, shall we? How about we make this last wager the largest yet? What coin have you left, Meric? I'll match each piece."

"Sixty," Meric blurted, cupping his hand underneath Jon's breast. "Between the two of us."

"No," Jon asserted in his thick, foreign intonation.

"Well, that was quick," Herelos said, gathering up the dice." I guess he will not be partaking after all. So come on then let's make it quick. I'm guessing you have but twenty, perhaps thirty, coins left. But since you've lost a lot already, and because I am such a benevolent man, I can go half of that, or I can go all. It's up to you. What will it be?"

"Just wait a moment," Meric insisted, "it will be sixty."

"I said no," Jon repeated more sternly.

Seized with sudden annoyance, Meric pulled Jon downward by his tunic so that he could whisper in his ear. Meric grumbled ardently, as though he were an orator of the law, waving his free hand adamantly as if to make his argument more persuasive.

"You fail and I'll snap your neck," Jon said, reluctantly handing over his coin pouch.

"Sure, whatever," Meric voiced, as he emptied the pouch. "As long as it's not the face."

"So, are we settled?" Herelos asked, picking crumbs off his chest like berries in a bush.

"Aye, sixty silver coins as stated," Meric said, pushing them to the center. "Same wager as the last — but only now in favor of Echon the One-eyed Giant. Do you accept it?"

Herelos pushed the goblet toward Meric with the tip of his finger. "The dice are yours."

Meric hesitated for a moment. He slipped his clutch around the goblet, and instead of giving it a shake he simply let the dice fall out in a line as though he were emptying a cup of its contents. As they all came to a stop his expression erupted with rousing cheer, garnering the attention of the men close by. Herelos, on the other hand, was drowned in the shock of disbelief, his face made blue, unable to take a breath.

"Well *Enthera's* tits be bloody praised!" Meric beamed. "Have you ever seen such beautiful art, Herelos! Such a reverse in fortune!" He reached forward and began to slowly and carefully tow the great mound of silver toward him. "Andiel's mercy, Jon! Look at it all!"

"This...this can't be," Herelos mumbled in disbelief. "That's all of it! That's all I had! It's everything!" His sudden realisation caused him to grow very angry, his plump cheeks pleating like kneaded dough. "Schemes and tricks nothing more! You're a bloody cheat, a scoundrel, you...you plotted this from the beginning! The whole of this night, you bastard!"

"I played on your greed is what I did, my friend. And a word from the wise, if I may. I'd start by taking your own counsel, knowing when to win and when to lose, before you freely give it. Because clearly," Meric said, showcasing his winnings, "you're the one who needs it."

All at once the crowded room echoed with the sound of straight-back chairs screeching against the floor. On either side of Herelos, Marcus and Sagillus leapt from their seats and frantically fiddled with the break in their tunics, wherefrom they pulled out their daggers. Right away, they both made a move for Meric and the silver, but in place of success they were quickly met by Jon, who enveloped each of their clenched fists with his huge, calloused hands. He squeezed their fists with such strength that they quickly released their daggers and fell to their knees like pious monks, grunting in agony as Herelos hastily wobbled to the door like a startled stag.

The bustle had caused the tavern to go quiet as night. In the gaze of many who were drawn to the ruckus, Meric looked to Alia like a child caught in an act of misconduct, his arms stretched around the coins and his chin near flat upon the surface of the table. "Ah, well...we'll take a quarter of what he was having," he said, adjusting his hair as he exhaled with a smile.

***

In the later hours of the night, when the moon took to its descent, the tavern was reduced to light-hearted chatter, for only a small number of the sergeants from the city guard remained. Many of these men were not of the legion and their decorums, which in this regard dictated that they need not follow the rule of the witching hour. As such, they were not required to return to their sleeping quarters in preparation for morning's early instruction. In the midst of this quieted gabble, a soft, worker's hymn flew from Alia's lips as she moved about the common areas from one group to the next, clearing the night's festivities from vacant tables and renewing melted candles to fresh ones for those men all but willing to welcome night's slumber.

At a certain point, Alia found herself in the *Privata Spatium*, which was a corner room at the front end of the tavern where only men of the highest rank were permitted. In fact, all royal taverns that are charged to serve the legion have such a private room, and it is often adorned to the appetites of its patron lord. In the *Vials of Elarus* this private space was indistinguishable from the rest of the tavern, in that it was not at all sequestered, or embellished, to be deemed lordly. Rather, this room was adjoined to the common area by nothing more than two doorways on either end of a scanty partitioning wall. Crescent-shaped booths upholstered in cheap scarlet fabrics lined the shape of the room, each of them centered underneath a large window of frosted glass panes. In my later years, as I have already mentioned, I had the opportunity to speak at length with Alia in this room, and to be honest, the room itself paled in comparison to those royal taverns I had visited in cities of much lesser fortune. This one was more like a makeshift extension to the tavern, one that was hastily and frugally constructed by the original holder as a means to simply acquire the endorsement of the crown. Nevertheless I digress, it's just hard to believe, even now, that this meager space adds much to the beginning of my fate.

"Would you like me to change the candle, my lord?" Alia inquired, as she arrived at their table. She heaved her washcloth over her shoulder and began collecting plates topped with scraps and half-eaten food. "And if you want anything more to drink now would be the time to ask. I've already sealed all the barrels of ale and spirits, so if a thirst gets you, you'll have to settle for what wine I have left, or water."

"We won't be much longer," replied Lord Priscus, as he pushed aside a stack of parchment.

"It's best you leave us with a spare, my dear," added Captain Axle. "He's been saying that every night this week, yet I keep finding myself crawling into my bed when the sun's bright in my face. And that's if I'm allowed to go to bed at all."

Alia smiled and placed a fat, purple candle near the candleholder. She returned to gathering the plates, and just when she moved to leave, Priscus grabbed a hold of her wrist and turned to face her with a look of gratitude in his expression. As Alia put it, even in the late hours of night Priscus seemed to always have a pool of reserved vigour, a character trait of his that my want for sleep would later come to hate. This night, however, he appeared unusually tired and worn. It's no surprise really, because at this moment in time he had seen a little more than fifty winters come to pass, a thing made clear by the aged ruggedness of his ivory skin, and the grey streaks that lined the black of his hair and beard. But in truth the latter is all which defined his aged years, because as I remember it, when I met him myself a week later, his frame was no different than a young man's, thin and sinew in likeness to my own. Though I would be negligent if I did not mention that his was forged not as a result of lifting timber all day long, but of his countless years in rigorous battle against the Ascani.

"Is there something else you need, my lord?" Alia remembered asking.

"No," he replied, after a brief silence. "Just my thanks for your efforts. The men don't have many luxuries. But when they come here at least they have your hospitality, you know, to give them something to think about other than the sword for a night."

Alia blushed. "Andiel's mercy! If you keep saying stuff like that, my lord, I'll soon forget my place. I know where you heart lies, Priscus, so you know right well you don't need to let us common folk feel your equal. We owe you our lives, so the least I could do is pour ale in a cup for a cheap price. And yes, if we're speaking of gratitude, I should be the one thanking you. If not for your men and their free flowing coin, I would've been rid of this place soon after the debts were due. Probably would've headed south and started a brothel. It would've been simpler, and bring in coin more easily to be honest."

"Made yourself a nice fat purse then tonight? Haven't you now?" Axle grinned.

"Aye," she replied, proudly. "My girls will be happy in the morning, I can tell you that."

"Well spirits are always high around here is what I meant to say," Priscus added.

Priscus barely finished speaking when Alia caught sight of a tankard of ale on the table, a sheet of white froth cresting its rim. Its position suggested there was a third man who was not currently present at the table, a person who she immediately assumed was Captain Wymar. Alia told me that she had already known of Wymar's passing, but since she had grown accustomed to seeing him in their company, at this very seating, she haphazardly believed that at this moment he had simply sauntered off somewhere. Needless to say, my fair reader, that Wymar's seat was now occupied by his ghost, and so Alia explained to me how in an instant her mind hurtled backwards, and how her heart was taken by a blend of sadness and embarrassment, thinking that she shamed herself by thoughtlessly forgetting that Lord Priscus and Captain Axle were in state of mourning for the man.

I should take this opportunity to mention that I had only assumed with some certainty that Wymar had passed during my talk with Petris, a thing I would only later confirm to be true during my meeting with Priscus. Now, however, it is only right that I do with Captain Wymar and the men of the lookout just as I have done with Enfredarius: honour their memory. All had died that night, ninety-seven men was the final count, wherein less than a quarter of whose bodies had been recovered and laid to rest in proper fashion. Many of their names and faces I have long forgotten, and though I did not know most of them in the slightest, each and every one of them gave their lives freely for mine so that I could see the task that had been given, done. I have had my entire life to keep their story alive. But, I now leave it to you, my dear reader, to remember them, for it I must continue on with my tale.

Alia took a half-step back and bowed her head. "Forgive me, my lord, I did not mean—"

"There has been much death of late," Priscus said, as he slowly glanced at the tankard. He fixated on it as if seized by a deep thought, which ushered in a gloomy silence. "No harm done," he then added, bleakly.

"That'll be all, my dear, thank you," Axle said gently with a comforting grin. "Our thanks."

"As you wish," Alia nodded. "My comfort to you both."

As Alia drifted away to the rear of the room, continuing on with her tasks, Axle sunk into his cushioned seat and pressed his back against the frame of the booth. He brought his arms high above his head and stretched as if he had awoken from a deep sleep. As he dropped his arms, he let several fingers run along the dreadful scar that lay upon his right cheek. If I may fill in the historical bits, the mark upon his cheek was given to him by an Ascani brute some thirty-five years prior during a rather famous naval battle at the Isthmus of Pindos. In fact, it was at this very battle that he first met Priscus, who was seventeen at the time. Priscus was a squire then to his own father, King Alias. During this battle, Axle had been discovered to have a mind attuned for the strategies of war, a thing seldom seen in a young recruit. For this reason, he had been the youngest legionary in the last century to be awarded the *Vexillum Argentea*, the silver standard, a military decoration, which granted him entry into the king's military council, despite his common birth. From that moment on he was chosen by Priscus to be his *Ala Dextera*, right hand in all things, which was at this time the sixteenth legion's chief strategist and quartermaster.

"So," Axle yawned broadly. "Where were we?" His aged face was bathed in fatigue, for he was sixty-one years of age, and at this time of night was already drained from scouring through the many piles of parchment and gilded manuscripts that rested before him. If one were to simply observe him, he appeared no different than Priscus — he had fought alongside him in each one of his brawls against the Ascani, and more times than not, against the Veigurian pirates that threatened merchant vessels off the coast of Easteria. But by all accounts, however, Axle was still an elder and the one that was most certainly in need of rest.

"Latest casualty report," Priscus replied, as he opened a tome and readied a quill.

"Ah, yes of course! How could I forget?" Axle said sarcastically, as he brought the report to reading height. "Well, as it stands from this afternoon, four hundred ninety-three dead, most of them coming from the second, third, and eighth cohorts, as you already know. The number of wounded has since dropped to forty two gravelly harmed and eighty of lesser injuries, all of whom are expected to make a full recovery, or so Petris has told me. Yet, let's not forget that Petris' words in matters of healing are as good as a best guess, considering what he did to that one builder you asked him to look after, who is still in a state of winter sleep, if you were wondering. And while we're on the topic of newcomers, Demos told me he leaves tomorrow for Tolerium with those men of the new stock who have just about gone mad from seeing an Ascani for the first time. No surprise there really, but it seems today another thirteen have cracked on us, bringing the number of casualties in that regard up to a near hundred."

"Gaius is going to return here in about a month with another batch of men, so have Demos and his party wait until then. Some of those men will pick up their sword again. After that, if they still want to leave, let them. We'll pay them three months of coin and brand them *inhabilis*, root out the false among them," Priscus said, as he transcribed his commands. "I'm surprised, I did not think the count of the fallen would rise in such a short time. Wasn't it three hundred seventy yesterday?"

"Aye it was, but you know the creatures never aim to wound," Axle said. "And the current number I just told you is just the count for our enlisted men. I spoke with Severinus this morning, and according to his report a near seventy of his city guards are also dead. He hasn't even finished tallying those dead amongst the common folk yet, because everything from the wall to the market district is still in heaps and cinders, which if you ask me, makes his job as bloody complicated as a bloody labyrinth."

"Then what of our stone workers, have they finished repairing the east rampart?"

"It'll take more than a couple of days to repair an entire section of a wall, Priscus, so you're going to have to be slightly patient on that end. But if you want the truth, I'd know more of its progress if that sard of a magistrate allowed me a proper audience with his damn builders. But, he's made it very clear to me that he doesn't want the legion involved in what he's calling, *city affairs*. Say's the battlements fall under his charge or some shite, I don't know." Here, Axle made a gesture of irritation by roughly running his fingers across his head. "I mean really! If repelling a horde of Ascani isn't enough for him to realise that they can come back at any moment, and that we might need that wall fit and ready for it, then I don't know what will. I tell you what though, Priscus, I know for a fact that his builders know no more of their craft than boys fresh in instruction. So if the Ascani do come back, and the repairs aren't done, I'll pitch the bastard over the wall myself. I figure that belly of his is large enough to give us the time we need to do the work properly."

"I'll see him in the morning," Priscus said, as his eyes traced the words in the tome that lay open in front of him.

"Well in all fairness it is morning, so perhaps I should go wake his arse up."

Priscus took a pinch of pounce and sprinkled it thoroughly over his work. He then closed the book with its bronze plated jacket and handed it over to Axle, making sure the metal rings that formed its spine did not rattle too loudly. "Have the sergeants redistribute the men amongst the cohorts evenly," he said. "But, if you see Edros before I do, tell him to take half the men from the fourth cohort and the rest from the eleventh to supplement the second, their numbers are the lowest. If it comes to battle again, the eighth will form the rear guard, and what's left of the third will cover the sea until those of the lesser wounded are strong enough to hold a sword. And lastly, come first light have Marcus and his scouts press further west this time, as far as the borders of the Greenlands if they have too. If the road is clear we'll send a message to the king of what has happened here. But as it stands, I won't chance it."

"Right then," Axle said, reaching for a fresh parchment. "I'll ready a message at once."

At that moment Priscus snatched the parchment from Axle's hands. "That'll be all from you tonight. I'll handle the message, and you, my friend, are going to go to sleep. Any more written work and I fear you'll fall from weariness and be added to these lists."

Axle coughed hoarsely as he brushed the underside of his nose. "You best not be calling me old, *my* friend. And besides, if anyone is going to follow me to the afterlife it'll be you if you don't take a moment's rest yourself. Honestly, Priscus, the skin under your eyes is starting to look as black as my trousers. Leave it for tomorrow." He took a gulp of his stale brew in order to water the irritation in his throat, and then as he set his goblet down, his expression changed to one that was more heavy. "Listen here, Priscus," he said, staring at him brooding over his work. "It's clear you do not want to talk about what's muddling your thoughts, but if we are going to be here for another couple of hours I'd rather we just get to it. I've known you, what? Close to forty years now? I think I know when your mind is knotted by those conversations you tend to have in your head. And right now, I have this strong sense that the conversion is something other than these reports."

"And what would that be? Apart from all the other work that's yet to be done."

"Don't start this shite with me," Axle said, peeved. Again he sunk in his seat and sat sluggishly with his arms folded firmly. "Are we really going to play this game? You know what I'm talking about, Priscus. Don't play stupid with me — it's too late in the night for that and I'm certainly not keen. I'm not the only one who finds it to be strange. About what's going on here. I know you just want me to say it first so you can confirm it, and also make sure that you haven't finally lost your mind. Or, maybe this time you don't want it to be true."

"What is it you find strange, captain?" Priscus asked.

"Really? So we are playing then?" Axle replied in a vexed tone. "Alright then, I'm not sure. Let me see here. Oh yes, of course! That's right! Why don't we start with the fact that no Ascani, or ill-bred beast, has ever dared to attack the walls of a city, *these* walls to be precise, not for a thousand years. Or better yet, why after the same length of time would they, all at once, abandon their raids and ambushes in favour of...I don't know...gathering in numbers no short of an army's."

"Perhaps we have just witnessed the extent of their boldness. We've seen it before."

"Yeah I'm certain we haven't, Priscus," Axle said with a half grin. "I don't know who taught you how to count, but there were five thousand of them out there at least, three thousand of which we killed. That number is not some war pack looking for a meal. It was an army, and you saw as well as I did that they moved like an army. I've never seen them do that before."

"We fought them at the crossing two years ago. There were eight hundred of them then."

"Yes, there were but—" Axle stopped and took a breath. "Alright let's say for a moment that you are right, that their presence is nothing more than a show of their daring. If that were true, then I would be forced to also suppose that these creatures suddenly decided to wake up one morning and play at the strategies of war." Here, he leaned forward as if to secret his words, stealing a glimpse at Wymar's tankard. "They ambushed the bloody lookout before their assault. Not only that, but they also knew about the sky-torch, and for what purpose we use it's sorcerer's powder. No matter how you choose to see it, the two assaults were coordinated, and this Ascani army certainly knew what needed doing to keep an assault on the city of this size hidden in the dead of night. Andiel's mercy, Priscus, I can't even find my way to Nilus' farm and I'm the one who chose the ground. And there too they secured, butchering all the horses so there would be no possibility of escape. When was the last time we saw packs of Hircani being used for the hunt of man? I'm telling you this was not some brazen strike or some show of force. This was in every way a planned assault with many moving parts. And you, Priscus, you think it was all commanded. That's what you want me to say, isn't it? What you want me to confirm it. You think there is an overseer at work here, a *primorus* maybe, or perhaps a brute with half a brain."

"There are none of the *primorus* that yet live. Andiel saw to that entirely."

"And how do you know? How do any of us know? That was a thousand years ago and you know the Ascani don't age as we do. Marinus found at least a dozen of them on the lookout wearing armour from the time of King Ailenus. That's four hundred years ago." Axle hesitated for a moment, and then in a weighty tone he added, "Perhaps our fabled Andiel didn't kill them all like the stories say he did. There is still the chance that one or more survived and led the attack here. For what purpose, other than to kill us all, I honestly don't know. All I know, however, is that these creatures follow *his* will, and *his* will is bound to the *primorus*. I'm not suggesting that he's alive and walking about, but I think that if it was a *primorus*, then it's out there, somewhere, still alive."

"Why?" Priscus asked.

"Those thousands we did not kill," he said. "Well, they did not flee. They retreated."

Priscus looked at Axle with an uneasy expression. In the flicker of the waning candle light his eyes translated with little difficulty the same concerns that Axle had just voiced rationally. For this reason, he did not speak for a few seconds, almost as if his tongue was gripped by his own disquieted reflections.

I am, by all means, embellishing what Alia had supposed to overhear in this moment. Alas, I was not there to hear it for myself. But, she was certain of what had happened next, because when Priscus had finally moved to voice his views on the matter, his attention, as well as hers, was abruptly pulled to the window by the sound of a galloping horse coming to a halt in front of the tavern. Meanwhile, Axle had lowered his head to let out a held breath, and so he was unaware that something had caught Priscus' notice. "Look," he said in a more level-headed tone, at which time Priscus returned his gaze to him. "You know I'm not one for groundless conjectures or half-assed truths, so we're both just going to have to wait and get some rightful answers to this riddle when that builder wakes up. Yet something is still clearly off here, and it goes without saying that I don't quite like the feeling of it. If there is such a creature out there, we have to find it and kill it as fast as we can, because if we don't, I fear something even bigger is soon to come our way—"

Suddenly the doors of the tavern burst open, from which a burly man clothed in sullied garbs and tattered armour staggered into the common area. Without delay, and with feverish intent, he scanned the room, alternating between the many pairs of curious eyes that were fixed on him. He was holding his waist tightly as if he were wounded, stumbling around as beads of sweat and blood rolled down his pale face faster than his rasping wheezes.

"What...what's happened?" Alia asked the man, as she moved to catch him from falling.

"Your lord...where is your—"

He stopped himself short as he caught sight of the threshold to the *Privata Spatium*. He all but nudged Alia to the side and darted toward it, stopping at nothing until his iron-shod boots ceased their clatter before Priscus and Axle, who had risen from their seats just as soon as Alia called out to them in warning.

"My lord Priscus?" asked the man, with a heavy tremble in his voice. He swayed back and forth on his center as he hurriedly reached into his cape, releasing little breaths that sounded more like grunts of pain. His hand reappeared, clutched around a bloodstained scroll. "Mess—" The man reeled forward and collapsed onto the ground with a loud crash, causing every man in the tavern to dash into the room.

Priscus dropped to a knee and elevated the man's head upon his thigh. It was then that he noted that the man was no ordinary legionary, but a knight of the king's court. A man of high standing within Anolia's first legion, since he bore the mark of the Fiery Phoenix upon his tunic. You may know, dear reader, that a knight could be distinguished from the rest of his legion because his helmet was adorned by two white plumes, and the hilt of his sword was enhanced by a translucent ruby at its center, whose face was etched with the image of the *Magnus Anguis*, the great, wreathing snake.

"Alia!" Axle shouted. "Bring me some water and rags! And get one of your girls to call for a healer! His name's Petris! Quickly!"

"My lord Priscus," blurted the knight, as a wad of blood spurt from his lips.

"Quiet yourself," Priscus said, clearing the blood from the man's chin with his sleeve. Then, he turned to the sergeants peering over Axle's shoulder and said, "Wake all the men and ready the guard in full fighting order. Find captains Jon and Meric at the barracks. Both are to gather fifty mounted men at the gates, and have them wait for me there."

"This is all the clean ones I could find," Alia said, near breathless as she appeared at his side with the rags he had asked for. She knelt beside the knight, placing a bowl of water rimmed with shreds of woollen cloth by her feet. She rolled up her tight-fitted sleeves and submerged one of the rags, and hastily pulled the man's cloak aside. Here, she let out a cry, for when she pulled at his cloak, she saw that the knight's innards were bulging out from between his fingers.

"Give it here," Axle said, hand extended.

Then, without warning, the knight began to convulse. Regaining some sort of composure, Alia pressed a second rag against the knight's wound as firm as she could, while Axle retreated back on his heel and did the same with the man's squirming legs. Scarlet froth bubbled around his tongue, and his eyes grew wide. He pointed with much hardship toward the scroll he had unveiled, which was resting on the edge of Axle's seat. He muttered a few incomprehensible words while gasping for air, whereupon not a moment thereafter the whole of his body was stilled of life.

"Is he dead?" Alia voiced with a shaky breath.

There was silence in the room. Only the three of them were left, sitting around the knight's corpse in an empty tavern. Priscus rose up and pulled the cloak out from under the knight, forming a cushion to rest his head. As a gust of wind battered the glass pane, Priscus stood and reached for the scroll, bringing it to his chest as he untied the king's scarlet ribbon, which he carelessly let fall to wherever the draft guided it. He did not read the message aloud, and when he finished he simply let the parchment rest on the table as if the weight of the words strained his hold.

"I suppose it isn't good news then?" Axle said.

Priscus turned to him, deep in thought. "Gather provisions from the storehouse, enough that it can spare for a hundred men and a journey south. Have Jon and Meric gather the men, and have Petris ready that builder to move. We leave in an hour."

Axle nodded, though he was still rather unsure what was going on. All the while Priscus was looking at the scroll, or rather he was staring at it with a sort of meticulous gloom. "It seems we're going to get some answers from my brother," he added, turning to Axle.

CHAPTER 6

"Cillian!" echoed Petris' voice. "Oi, Cillian! Can you hear me, lad?"

I came steadily around from what felt like a long, dreamless sleep, and to the incessant tremble of a moving cart. Petris was holding a burning fragrance stick up to my nose, though its scent, as I clearly recall, was not one of fruits or flowers, but of scorched pine leaves and noxious smoke. Through watery eyes, I could see him hovering over me with an expression of relief on his face, which was also plastered with that same bubbly grin of his. I coughed as I waved his hand away.

"What…what happened?" I said, continuing on with the violent hacks.

"Andiel's mercy!" he said, as he turned around and snuffed the stick's burning end in a pot beside him. It was filled with grey ash, and sprouting with the many other fragrance sticks that I had supposed he had used on me. He then poured a cup of water and hastily moved to place it upon my lips after reassuring me that it was truly water.

"I really thought I had killed you, that's what. I was sure I did. By the gods, Cillian, I swear you were senseless for so long that we all had you steering for the afterlife for quite a while. I tried everything to wake you, and when nothing seemed to work one of the captains started putting coin on you never waking." Suddenly Petris perked up, his eyes widening as though he had just realised something. "Shite, now that I think of it. I took that wager."

"Why?" I said, after guzzling the water. "How long was I asleep?"

"Oh, well I wasn't really counting, but, six…maybe seven days, if you include today. Yet, I wouldn't see why you would add today, because it's more like a half-day already and—" Petris stopped as he took notice of my confusion. He cleared his throat nervously and added, "Right well, you're awake now, lad. That's all that matters."

"Seven days?" I said, astonished. "Are you playing with me, Petris?"

Petris shrugged his shoulders shamefully. "No, but I told you didn't I. I'm quite shite at—"

"At making tonics, yes I got that part. I want you to do something for me. Don't make them for me anymore, alright? Even if my life depends on it."

"I don't think I'll be making them for myself either," Petris said, averting his eyes.

A tight knot rose in my chest. I placed my palm on my forehead, gently rubbing it as if the motion would somehow relieve my thumping headache, or better yet, help uncloud the blur that muddled my memory. I took a breath and began to collect my bearings, all whilst Petris erupted in an impassioned lecture about his mixes and brews, a thing nobody asked him to talk about. In any case, I was too curious, and somewhat puzzled, by my surroundings that I cared very little to pay attention to him — not that I disliked the man by any means, but because at this time his ceaselessly joyous nature, that I would come to love in time, would have killed me outright. And so as I looked to my left and right, his voice was drowned away to a pale echo, giving me the chance to examine every inch of the cart.

I noted that I lay in the center of the cart atop a bedding that was made of various feathered cushions, each one different from the next, as if they were gathered, as I imagined, in a hurry. My chest was bare, but my lower half was tightly wrapped in linens, so much so that I could tell that underneath them, I had been stripped of everything but a thin loincloth. The cart itself, however, stole most of my curiosity. It was large enough to carry no more than a dozen men, and a third of it, as much as I could make clear, had been utterly absorbed by Petris' belongings; crates of remedial supplies, religious tomes, effigies to the gods, and without any fabrication, dear reader, plenty of cookbooks. To my surprise, I noted that the cart was the same one that had taken me to Easteria, for its high, frangible arches and sunshade made of a pleated, raisin washed toile were unmistakable to my memory. In fact, there was one particular iron rivet by the cart's tail that clicked rhythmically as the cart moved — a beat that returned to my memory as a remembrance of the bother it brought me during the previous journey. I knew that this very cart ferried legionary recruits from the southern training camps to Easteria, and for this reason I began to gather, or rather assume, that I was no longer in the northeast of Anolia.

"And that, Cillian," Petris clamoured, "is how you turn carrots into a fine tasting ale—"

"Where are we, Petris?" I interrupted.

"Valentia, I think," he replied. "At least I believe we passed into it early this morning."

"Valentia?" I said, perplexed. "We are in the south?"

Before he could answer, the cart quaked intensely as it dipped into an uneven part of the road. Petris struggled to keep himself steady, grunting several words of slight under his breath as he held on tightly to one of the arches above him. As the cart settled, Petris shifted his frame away from the point in the sunshade that I was staring at, wherefrom a single, but brilliant, shaft of light emerged from a sizable tear in the canopy. For a moment the blinding light forced my head to the side, but when my eyes became accustomed to the light I looked over and saw, between the gap of two oak planks ahead of the tear, a sight that captured every sense of otherworldly beauty. Far across to the horizon beyond, an endless sea of rolling green hills, whose fields were topped with clusters of efflorescence that gleamed many radiant colours, rested under a clear, ocean blue sky. Leagues upon leagues, these hills spread until they became one with the snow tipped ridges in the east, ones of colossal height that were made lucid by their great distance. I can tell you, dear reader, that I knew at once that I was gazing at *The Walls of Rock*, a name known for the ridges that trail for countless miles from Norian, where Easteria lies, to Valentia in the south, forming a natural border that separates these two vast regions.

"Aren't those," I began to whisper softly as if entranced by a spell of marvel.

"The *Fields of Flora*, yes," he grinned, peering through the break in the sunshade. "Splendid, aren't they? A quarter of a region named after the wife of King Agatus II." He moved to the breach with a needle and thread in hand, where he then lurched over to begin stitching a patch of fabric to the hole. I stopped him short, the sight too grand to turn away from or have shrouded. Petris smiled warmly. "You know, Cillian," he added while taking a seat, "there's quite a story that goes along with them? Along with those fields, I mean. Might even be the best tale you southerners have that has a woman in it."

Although it was the first time I saw the fields, I knew what tale Petris was making reference to, and in truth, I had heard the story many times before as a child. My mother treasured the account of the Lady Flora, and would often tell it to me as a lesson in courtship, or many a times, as a way to remember my father's love for her in the years after his passing.

"Every southerner knows the story," I said, pretending that I was not interested. But in truth I had not heard the tale in some time, so my heart yearned to have it recounted to me once more.

As such I went on in a way that I knew would indulge Petris. "Yet, I get the feeling that you want to tell me?"

"Well you see," he said, jumping at the chance, "as I remember it there was once a woman of Aeginas, the daughter of some high-lord, who had offered her hand in marriage to the then prince Agatus — you know as these noblemen tend to do. As time went on she became the Lady Flora, and as the story goes they were...let's just say...not harmonious, more so on her part, but that's beside the point. Agatus had fallen in love with her right off the ship, and to be honest, Cillian, how could he not. The damn woman was from Aeginas for Andiel's sake, the one place in this world where all the beauties are from. But that, well that was the problem. The Lady Flora knew very well Agatus' feelings, but still she refused the king's hand in marriage until he could prove his love to her in such a way that went beyond the blessings of her face. Now as you already know, the prince tried to win her love, he did this for many years, but at each endeavour she continued to decline his hand. Right so now, at this point, his father passes and the throne becomes his. But the prince cannot become king without having a queen at his side, it's the law of this land and so unfortunately she's forced to marry him. On the night before the *Matrimonium*, the sacred marriage, the king took his horse and rode off into the night, vanishing, only to return a year later looking like he had taken to the labours of the farm, hands wholly calloused, his clothes tattered, his skin dry, and you get the picture. He asked the Lady Flora one last time for her hand, and when she asked why, he did not answer, because he knew he could never say in words why his heart stirred for her. And so all he did next was ask her to follow him, right here to these fields, where for a year he had turned these green hills into a sea that glistened with a thousand colours, planting one flower for each of his reasons...or so the bloody story goes. I'm not from around these parts."

Call me what you will, fair reader, but these stories of old never cease to return me to my boyhood, and Petris' retelling of this tale transported me to a time I can now barely remember, but long to return to. Of course, I did not want him to know it. So again, I feigned disinterest by rolling my eyes. "You know, priest, all that story means is that the Lady Flora only married the king because she received a marvellous and, if you ask me, a rather outrageous gift, ridding all thoughts of true love as the tale is intended to advance."

"Andiel spare me you soldiers are the same," Petris huffed. "It's just a story, Cillian. A tale for children to grow up to think with their hearts and not only their parts. Look, the lesson here is that love is everlasting. The flowers will continue to make more flowers, and do so for all time, but each one of them is meant to represent the days you should love your partner with all your heart. And now having said that, I should remind you that you're allowed to have feelings once in a while, you know for things other than your swords and your overly-manly, soldiering attitudes."

"Excuse my attitude," I replied, "but I'm not the one who almost killed a man because my hand was heavy with sleeping powder. Anyway, if those are the fields then we're certainly on the *Via Externa*, the king's road that leads straight to the capital. Do you have a story for that?"

All at once a thump at the tail end of the cart interrupted his answer and a man thrust his head through the curtains. It was Meric, though I did not know it was him at the time. He was well kept for a soldier and fair to the eyes, but it appeared that just as he saw me he let out a great grunt of displeasure.

"Andiel's cock! Come on really! Ugh, don't move," he said to me, sorely. He poked his head out of the cart. "Oi! It's over! He's awake!" he cried, amassing a great, collective awe of malcontent from what seemed like a hundred men trailing behind the cart. "Demos! Demos! Collect all the coin and a give it to — yes you. Collect the coins and pass them around, alright? Don't start with me. Not now. Just do it."

As I listened to the chorus of long, spiritless sighs I raised myself on to the heap of cushions Petris had placed under me. I came to realise that many had wagered coin against me, including the man before me, and so at first I hesitated to ask Petris who he was. Even if I wanted to ask, Petris was already rolling his eyes as though he knew Meric very well, but in the way that suggested he was not entirely enthused to receive his company.

"Jon!" Meric shouted, repeatedly. At this point he was inside the cart, but half of his body was still jutting outward from the curtains. "Yes, you! Who else here has that name? Come here and take my horse — come on just take it! I want to talk to him." After handing over the reins, he turned and made his way to me, running his fingers through his hair as he sat by my feet with his knees to his chest. He was fairly composed, as if his previous shouting match did not happen. "So then, you're that builder everyone's calling the Night Sorcerer, hmm? I have to say man, you don't really look like an enchanter to me. What's your *more* earthly name?"

"God's Meric, give him a moment. He's only just awoken," Petris asserted.

"I only asked him his name, Petris," Meric said. "Save your wrath for the gods, yeah?"

"It's Cillian," I answered quickly.

"See!" Meric swiftly beamed. "That doesn't have a sorcerer's tune to it." I turned to Petris with a look of confusion, catching Meric's attention. "What?" he then said to Petris. "Don't tell me you haven't told him yet?"

"Like I said. He's only just awoken," Petris voiced, while extending a plate in my direction that was brimming with cheese, bread, olives, and dried meats. "Go on, have some food. But don't eat too quickly or it'll get stuck in your throat."

"Oh, you shouldn't have!" Meric grinned in appreciation as he intercepted the plate. "I'm only here for a few moments. It's very thoughtful of you, my thanks." His focus switched back to me, as did his tone, which was now accompanied by the sounds of a full mouth. "Well, builder, I really didn't want to be the one to tell you as I don't really care, but it's the name the men are giving you since some idiot convinced a good many other imbeciles that you had really set fire to the sky with your bare hands, or some shite like that. And naturally, just as all forged stories go, it spread like, no pun intended, wildfire among the men. Aside from that, I guess I should congratulate you since you're now not only a trained builder, but also a respected wizard, apparently. Still, I think Night Sorcerer is a bit meager for a name don't you think, Petris? See if it had been up to me, I would've given you a name a little more fitting like...say, the Fire Builder or...Cinder Hands — yeah I really like that last one. It doesn't matter though, nobody seemed to be on board with any of my suggestions when the rumour started."

"It wasn't me who lit the sky-torch. It was the boy—"

"Aye, Nilus' son," he said, taking a bite of the dried beef. "I was there when we found the both of you laying on the ground. It's not like we didn't see what the blast did to that boy's arm. Most of us already knew the truth of it, but good luck to you if you're going to try to change the minds of four thousand men who, I'm afraid to say, are rather invested in believing that you saved them all with some enchantment. Foolish, I know. But, when it comes to the army, it's always these types of things that are remembered." He wiped his mouth and placed the plate on his knee, turning to ask Petris a question. "So, my stout friend. Have you at least told him where we are going?"

"Tolerium." I answered, before Petris had the chance.

"He knows," Petris said, giving Meric a dirty look. "And we should get him there alive."

Meric looked down at the plate. "Oh, I'm sorry," he blurted with embarrassment. "Was this for him? Andiel's mercy! I thought it was for me. My apologies, builder. Eat up!" He was handing me the plate when suddenly he stopped short with an air of curiosity. "Wait a minute. Are you not from the south? I could swear you are."

"I am," I replied, while taking back the half-eaten food. "Norlyn. Just south of Heraea."

All at once Meric smiled, his expression gleeful. "Just south of Heraea? Is that right? God's how I adore that city like no other let me tell you. It's been years since I've been in these parts and more still since I've been to Heraea. The taverns in it's streets are grand, the ale ever flowing. And the whores, builder, *oh* the whores are beyond this mortal world. So good in fact that I've seen men die for their company and come back asking for more." Then, he stopped, taken by a thought. "Hold on, since you live so near, you must be familiar with the song. Yeah, of course you must be! The Whores from Heraea! Come you must sing it with me. A few lines off the top, yeah? It's been ages but it goes something like this... *there once was a girl named Caira—*"

Suddenly the curtains opened, wide enough to allow a wave of sunlight to wash over us. The cart dipped, as if its back wheels sunk deep into the road. In came a beast of man, Jon, whose size alone took up another third of the cart, and whose added weight seemed to apply a sudden strain on the horses that pulled us ahead. Because of his towering height he was forced on all fours like a bear, just so he could move toward us without hindrance, which he did up until he halted and sat next to Meric.

Meric gawked at him in wide-eyed disbelief. "What the hell are you doing? You're supposed to be looking after my horse."

"Horse is fine," Jon said, straight-faced. I suddenly felt like an outsider amongst a gathering of friends. He waved one hand in my direction, as if he were greeting me as a friend, which was bizarre as I have never met him before, but more so because I would have never thought to see a man of his stock do such a thing. "I want to see the Night Wizard too," he added.

"It's the Night Sorcerer, you lump of meat," Meric corrected.

At this point Meric's cheer returned, and at once he tried to sing anew. However, just as the same phrase parted from his lips, he was interrupted yet again, this time by the loud trample of galloping hooves, which approached the front of the cart. Petris barely moved to announce who he believed it was when two riders raced passed the canopy, one on each side of the cart. On reaching the tail end they halted sharply, whereupon Lord Priscus and Captain Axle burst in from the threshold, both of whom were somewhat breathless and dressed in muddied uniforms, as if they had been labouring in the field. They made their way toward me, and in quick succession, Axle overtook Jon's position, which was offered freely, and Priscus forcefully seized Meric's spot by nudging him aside.

"My lord Priscus!" I said, struggling to move to the position of attention.

Every recruit who embarks in the ranks of his chosen legion first meets the Lord for whom he will serve. In my case, I was rather unlucky. Upon my arrival in Easteria, Lord Priscus had been away from the city, and if you could believe it, he had returned on the very morning of the attack. Thus, I was meeting him for the first time, along with Captain Axle for that matter.

"Be still," Priscus said calmly, as he gently pressed his hand on my chest. He guided me back to a seated position and removed his scabbard from his belt and handed it to Petris, where he then turned to Jon and Meric ready to give orders. "About two leagues down the road there's a river, and next to it there's a clearing right by the bank. It's small and it's hidden, so be sure not to miss it. Edros and some men are already there setting up camp, but I want both of you to gather twenty or so more and see that it's done before we arrive."

Meric turned to Priscus, astonished. "But I was just about to—"

"And Jon," Priscus went on. "If you could hunt a stag or two for supper, I'm sure the men would be in your debt."

At that Jon and Meric fell to command with a simple nod, though I would be at fault if I did not mention how Meric appeared a pouty child whose toy had been taken away from him. For all that, I was glad; his eccentric air had rekindled my pulsating headache, and I desperately yearned for a few moments of quiet.

"How fair your wounds?" Priscus asked, his eyes glancing about the bandages.

"I may not look it, but I feel fine, my lord," I replied. "It's all thanks to our priest here."

"Aye, he had us worried for some time," Axle said.

"I am but two hands," Petris grinned.

Priscus advanced closer and sat rather near, hesitating a few moments before rolling up his sleeves in order to assist Petris, who had already started changing the dressings on my shoulder. "You know, Cillian, when I was a boy, my father used to tell me that courage in any man's heart is a trait that is expected in battle, inherent even, by those who take up the sword," he said, dipping a cloth in a pot of water, upon which he began bathing my wound. "Everytime I would train with him he would never let me forget it, and over the years I had no cause to disagree with him. That was until my first battle against the creatures, where I came to realise that after all his teachings my heart was yet full of fear, and that I could not even muster enough courage to lift up my sword. I learned then that no person can really know whether they possess such a quality unless faced with the hardship that brings it about. What you and that boy did for us that night, the nerve in your hearts, speaks to that. And for that, Cillian, you have my thanks."

"I hate to say it, but I was more afraid than the boy," I admitted.

"It's those that don't say they are," Priscus said, "that tend to die on us." He dressed my arm, tearing the end piece in two and binding them into a knot. "I know Petris here is going to curse me for keeping you awake, but as you've probably already figured, there's something I have to ask you, something that requires a different form of mettle, for you alone may have the answers to many questions yet unspoken."

"Yes, of course," I said. "Anything, my lord."

90

"What is it that you saw that night?" he asked in a weighty tone.

Although I expected this moment to arrive, I was surprised to find that the question made me utterly speechless. I had no clue as to where I should begin, even with the images of the horrible event flashing in my mind as clear as if I were experiencing the battle all over again. As these recollections continued to unfold Priscus noticed that I was beginning to feel flustered by them, which I was. My breath picked up it's pace as I sunk deeper and deeper into a torrent of uneasiness, whereupon I began to feel sore all over. Priscus did not press me to speak, but explained with great calm that I need only speak of what my heart could bear to relive. I was struck by his tenderness, his understanding. I understood, at least in my mind, that to keep silent would betray the great care that went into keeping me alive, but more downright, that I would forsake all those who had died in order to see me to this point. I apologized gracefully, and therewith I spoke with no end, during which Priscus, Axle, and Petris heard me attentively.

At first I spoke of Captain Wymar, whom I learned, with a heavy heart, had been a dear friend of theirs, and that I was last among them to have spoken with him. With great interest, Axle had asked me what Wymar and I had spoken about, and as I answered him, all of their faces were brightened by the warmth of his memory. Then, I told them of the horror that befell us, particularly of the masked Ascani, which very quickly created an unsettling feeling between Priscus and Axle. They each, in their own turn, asked me a wealth of questions regarding this masked creature, his features and the air of his presence, and with each response I seemed to add more clarity to what seemed to be an existing discussion about the possibility of a leader within the Ascani and among those who had attacked Easteria.

This was the first time I had heard of such a possibility, given that after Andiel's time the Ascani were never recorded to have any sense of command amid their ranks. In fact, it was Petris who enlightened us all on the history of their kind. Like every augur, he was learned of our histories, and as such, he spoke of the era of the *Primorus*; an era of which I will speak more of in the coming pages. Needless to say, the air was thick with disconcerting thoughts, much of which I knew a lowly builder like myself would never come to hear unless involved, as I was, in the events.

As the hour passed we found ourselves pulling away from troubled talk and conversing about many light-hearted matters, specifically about my training in the south, and of my craft as a builder. Priscus was intrigued to know whether the sergeants of the southern plains still drilled their recruits to near death in the practice of war, as was the case in his time. He was content to hear that the practice was the same, and proceeded to ask me more detailed questions about my craft. He was almost too interested, I found. It was not long after that Petris, absorbed by the retelling of past events, began recounting many stories concerning the adventures of Priscus, Axle, and Wymar, highlighting those that were filled with their courageous and daring acts against the Ascani, within the kingdom and upon foreign lands. Once Petris started, there was no stopping him, and so then he spoke of Jon and Meric, and their deeds equal in gallantry. It was at this point that *I* learned that Jon was not of Anolian birth, but that he was of the Linlani, tribes of men far to the west of Anolia, hidden among the fjords of the great mountains.

"How beautiful you make the world seem," Priscus said to Petris.

"It's what I do," he smiled.

"So that mark there, my lord. On your arm," I said, nodding in the direction of his forearm. "I've seen it before. It's the same as Captain Wymar's. A symbol of your laurels, is it?"

Priscus looked down at the marking as if he had forgotten it was there. He brushed his hand over it, and then clarified that it was the mark *Celeres*, our god of trust, honesty, and oaths. I had first heard talk of this mark in the days of my grandfather's tales, yet I blame the passing of time for dissociating the image from its meaning. As I knew it to be, the mark of *Celeres* was more than just an accolade of distinction within the legion, it was the utmost position of rank in our army, under the king's generalship, of course. This mark signified absolute loyalty to the realm and was awarded to twelve men by the king himself, never to be replaced in his lifetime. It was conferred onto those of exceptional quality across all social standings. Be it a lord or a commoner, these men were trusted to be the king's guardians and mentors, to defend him in times of need, and to guard him against all falsehoods that would otherwise corrupt his judgment; an ethos that was born after Andiel's great war.

"You're part of the king's council?" I asked, sounding more surprised than I intended.

"Not just him, builder," Axle said, rolling his sleeve up to reveal the same mark.

My eyes lit up in amazement. I could barely believe that I was in the presence of two of the king's chosen, and that I had met a third unknowingly. The chosen were spread out across the realm, and so to have conversed with a quarter of them is something that every admirer of fabled stories, such as myself, would consider a blessing. To my eyes, these men embodied the spirit of Anolia and her legions, and if I may deviate for a moment, fair reader, I yearned to belong to such an order — not theirs per say, but to a group of belonging. As such, I was moved to ask my own flurry of questions with child-like charisma, but before I got the chance to do so the cart suddenly stopped, the horses neighing as they do when an obstacle abruptly blocks their path. There was no danger, however, for we were surrounded by the tune of *Castra* braying from the buccina, which meant that we had arrived safely at the night camp.

"Listen here, Cillian," Priscus said, tying his sword belt back to his waist. "There was a last thing I wanted to ask you, and I want you to hear it all before you answer. Either by my choosing, or swayed by the hand of fate, there are few under my charge that take my notice. Like this mark here, there are those that stand beside me as more than just swords under my command — bound to me by neither a debt, nor burden. They are my companions if you will, holding no form of rank or position to each other, serving alongside me to be of greater use to this legion by lending me their council and their expertise."

"I don't think I fully understand, my lord," I said.

"Petris," Priscus said as he looked over his shoulder. "Hand me the book." Petris gave him a journal, my journal. "Petris tells me you're quite the builder," he added, passing it on to me. "I've seen your work for myself, Cillian, and I think that one day we can make use of it…by my side. If you wish it, you will become *sodalis*, and as such, until either of our deaths, you will stand at my side and call me lord no longer. You will lend me the knowledge of your craft whenever I call for it, and command my men in its instruction should we need it."

I took a shallow breath. All at once my confidence in my abilities fled me. "My lord Priscus, I…I am no bastion of strength like the lot of you," I said. "I have not done anything in my craft to merit such a place beside you. I have not proven anything, so I cannot accept to call myself an equal among you, for I fear that I will come to fail you when you would need me the most."

"Ours is a hard task, Cillian," Axle broke in. "Trust us when we say that we know your true worth. Because if we didn't, you would not be hearing this. Above all, what we truly desire from you is something that goes beyond your skill and talent. First, we want nothing more than a pure heart, and second, the will to put yourself behind the needs of those that need our help. Everything else will fall into place when the gods deem it right that they should do so. And if you turn out to be shite, we'll let you know. What do you say?"

My heart was beating at a gallop. I met Priscus' eyes. My mind was still awestruck at the sudden offer for the position of *sodalis*, and excitement only grew with the realisation that what was happening was truly beyond my wildest dreams. Meanwhile, Petris had parted the curtains and let in the last of the sun's rays, being that dusk was upon us. He flung the flaps atop the canopy, at which point Axle made a quick exit so that he could stretch his stiffened legs. Priscus too left the cart, none of them worried about when I would voice my answer. I sat there, alone, thinking and thinking, as if the answer in my heart was not already decided. Still, I watched as all three of them made their way to Jon and Meric, who were but a short distance away. Together they stood among the legionaries who unloaded the pack mules of their provisions, all the while speaking affably with one another. It was at this point that I understood who Priscus' companions were; Axle, Petris, Meric, and Jon.

"Cillian," Priscus shouted. "Take what time you need to dwell on your answer—"

"My lord Priscus," I blurted, catching all their stares at once. "I'll...I'll do it."

Priscus looked over to me. "We start tomorrow...if you can stand," he said, as he strolled off.

CHAPTER 7

The King's Palace, 1024 A.E.

It was the day of *Ionia*, the goddess of ends and beginnings, and from a wide, horseshoe arch in the palace corridor I watched, with my back against the stone and my legs pendulous from the ledge, as the people of the capital danced and cheered along the main road in a grand procession. I adored the spectacle wholeheartedly, for I had only once before seen the celebration for the commencement of the new annum as a young child. I had long forgotten its brilliance and magnitude; its jubilation aggrandized by the squibs and sparklers bursting like flowers over the heads of the endless number of common folk who gathered from all reaches of the realm. If I had the opportunity, I would have joined in the festivities. But sadly, my presence in the palace was not because I had sought out a bird's eye view of the celebration, but rather because I was awaiting Axle's arrival, for he had requested the day before that I meet him at the palace. Having said that, many hours had already passed with no sight of him, and so all I could do was wait patiently until I was called upon, which left me to enjoy the spectacle as the warm southern wind caressed my freshly shaven cheeks.

As midday passed, the raucous of the procession wound down to little noise, as it had, by this time, trailed off some ways away from the palace keep. The air around me, however, welcomed a new commotion, one that emanated from the corridor. Many lords and their retinues began filling the hallway, which had happened gradually and throughout the hour. During that time I never moved from the nook that I idled in. I simply scanned the groups of men that passed before me, not once seeing any sign of Axle, nor any other from my own party. I became rather irked by his tardiness, and so after another half-hour had passed, I finally pulled my journal from my belt, believing I could whittle the time more quickly with some leisurely study.

As I began to unravel the string around the clasp, my eye drifted to the marble pedestal in the center of the nook. I stood up and moved toward it with great interest, and with every intention to quell my curious nature by looking inside the thick, leather bound tome that rested upon it. I had been curious about it since the morning, though I had convinced myself not to touch it, since I was in the king's home, and I felt it was not my place to meddle in what was not mine.

But as my impatience grew at Axle's delay, so too did my curiosity. I gently ran my fingers down the book's cover, feeling the aridity of its rough surface. As I opened it a plume of dust rose from its ancient, honey coloured pages, tickling my nose to a wild sneeze. After the dust had settled, I noticed that the first page was blank, though as I moved on to the next one I observed a good many ornate legionary insignias, many of which were embroidered on the tabards of the men in the corridor, and some that I had never seen before. Right away I saw among the ranks the emblem of the Vined Sword. It was exactly in likeness to the image on my chest, which in the moment gave me pride, in a historical sense. The next several pages were filled with writings of the ancient tongue, which even today I can barely read. I quickly overlooked them all, wishing to discover what more lied ahead. As such I turned the page once more, whereupon I stopped, for the writings caught my attention.

At first glance it looked to me like a tally of goods, similar to those found in a merchant's ledger, which I soon discovered it was not. In truth, it was column after column of what appeared to be the names of men, each and all who were listed beside the date: 36 A.E. As I continued to turn the pages, carefully on account of their age, my curiosity heightened tenfold, because more and more names were ranked in the same fashion, and the date within the margin remained unchanged. I knew that these men were of the legion, but I was baffled by the significance of the year. I leafed through the breath of the tome hoping to find an answer, yet I found that not one of the two-hundred or so pages appeared differently from the next.

Again I stopped sharply, holding the last page at a curve under the weight of my thumb. I cannot properly explain what happened next, but as I peered through the page's backside an unusual chilling breeze rustled around me. All I saw through the parchment was that the form of a shadowy figure was illustrated upon the page, and it was at this point where my curiosity turned to confused distress. I flattened the page to view it, and I was struck by a vivid image. Out from a great, fiery flame came a vile looking gauntlet. It reached for the sky with contorted fingers, almost like each finger was a serpent lunging upwards to devour the sun. And its black hue was wreathed by towers of red mist, which emanated from the brakes in the armour, twisting and twirling in every direction as if taken by some enchantment, one of blood and fire, and of sorcerer's magic.

I was consumed by the image, and my sense of time and place melded together as I drifted off to my own imaginations, feeling as if I could not escape them. Then, without warning, a hard grip seized my shoulder, and at that moment I snapped to attention as I flung the book's cover to a close.

"There you are!" Axle exclaimed. By now the chatter in the corridor was very loud, and it was brimming with several hundred men who were formed into groups, each in their own conversations. "Andiel's mercy, Cillian," he added. "I told you to meet me at the palace! God's man I've been looking for you all day, and now here I find you with your nose in another book."

"I did as you asked," I said, puzzled. "I've been here since this morning."

"*At* the palace, not *in* the palace! I meant for you to wait for me outside...at the bottom of the stairs. How in the world did you get past the guards?" Axle swiftly turned his back to me and ran a hand down his face as he looked over the crowd in search of someone. "It doesn't matter now, just follow me, alright? The king is making his way to the chamber, so we best get inside before it starts. Stay close and don't go wandering off. This day is really turning out to be a storm of shite so I hope I don't have to go searching for the others now."

"Yes, captain!" I replied, stepping off to follow his lead.

At that moment several trumpets echoed in the hallway. Like the flow of a slow-moving river, everyone began to move toward the enormous, bronze plated doors that were at the very end of the corridor, a good distance ahead of us. Slowly, the doors cracked open. I did not know what lay beyond them, other than what I surmised, in the moment, to be a sizable chamber, because not once did the mass of men entering it block its threshold. As I squeezed my way through the mob, I noticed that the doors themselves were quite alike to our legionary shields, each of the panels elaborately engraved with the king's emblem, The Fiery Phoenix.

"How many times do I have to tell you that I'm not your captain anymore," he said, peering behind to make sure I was following him. "You've been *sodalis* for what...two weeks now, Cillian. It's about time you start remembering it. Unless you're having second thoughts?"

"None at all," I replied. "It's just awkward calling my betters by their proper names."

"Well, you better get used to it. I quite like being called by my name and so do the others."

"All but Meric," I said, catching up to him. "At least he prefers not to call me by mine."

Throughout our journey to the capital Meric's air toward me was that of ill-will, or perhaps in afterthought, I would define it more as indifference, but I cannot say for certain. I do know, however, that my presence among the companions seemed foreign to him, so much so that he often refused to speak to me, even when Priscus himself would ask him to convey his orders directly to me. I mused over the possibilities for much of the journey, but it was Petris, after spending much of my leisure time with him, who told me that Meric was in fact angered at hearing that Priscus had offered me the position to be a part of the *sodalis*. Perhaps you may find me foolish, dear reader, but back when I walked with Axle in the corridor, I would not have dared guess this was the reason he was sore with me, though it's best that I tell you now, since I cannot recall when I first came to learn of it. In his own way, Meric had taken terribly to Wymar's passing, and for this reason he saw me as an ill-suited aspirant that had come along to fill the void of his dear friend — and he was not searching for a new one.

"Give him time," Axle said, as if he knew Meric's grievance well. "He'll come around."

I bowed my head in observance, but immediately thereafter I thought to ask him about the book. "That book over there," I blurted, "the one that I had my nose in. There's something about it I don't understand. I mean, I know it's of Andiel's time, but is it a ledger of some kind of those who enlisted? A record immortalizing the men who served in his war?"

"Those names you saw," he replied, "they aren't those of the enlisted, but of the dead."

I picked up the pace so that I could continue to walk beside him. My eyes were made wide by his words. "Of the dead?" I said with genuine surprise. "What are you talking about? There were thousands of names in there, if not more. There were so many!"

"If you think that was a lot then I'd keep from looking to your right."

Of course I looked, swiftly wheeling my head to the side by the impulse of curiosity alone. As we continued to follow the flow of the crowd, we passed by more than a dozen archways, each with their own individual marble pedestal that upheld the same looking book. At this point my quickened steps slowed to an aimless amble, whereupon I came to a complete stop, as I was consumed by the passion of this discovery. I looked up and down the corridor, where I then learned that the entire east face of the palace, the section that overlooked the whole of the capital, was imprinted with these arches, which by my estimate, housed more than fifty of these tomes.

"Wait," I said, turning to address Axle again, "what happened in—" I stopped myself short, realising that he had long vanished from my side. Nevertheless, it was not long after that I caught a glimpse of him entering the chamber, and so like a helpless leaf riding a steady wind, I merged with the men tightening around me and walked on.

Before entering the chamber I made a last, quick stop by the grey, stone bust of *Polemos*, our god of war, and the only deity I cared to consider divine among the greater pantheon. In the earlier pages of this account I had prayed to *Enthera*, but truth be told, I detested most of the gods, if not all of them except *Polemos*, being that I had partaken in no other religious matters than in the worship of the *Honoris Bello*, a set of rituals we soldiers conducted in all things regarding battle, which was mostly a rather brief litany that would shield us from death, or at least we hoped that it would. It had always seemed to me that *Polemos* listened to my invocations, granting unto me his favour — and quite unlike the other one-sided relationships that I considered was the case between us mortals and the great celestials. As such, I paid my respect to the god of war by gently tapping my clenched fist on his shoulder, as was the legionary custom, whereupon I quickly entered the hall a little in fear of Axle's wrath.

Just as I entered the chamber I halted immediately, as if I had slammed headlong into an invisible wall. I was standing in a room of spectacular size, one that I can only best describe as being close in appearance to a theatrical arena, wholly fitted with the lavish décor of kingly grandeur. High stone walls, some fifty feet at their peak, girded the chamber, upon which splendid tapestries depicting the past histories of our legions hung in ranked rows from one end of the space to the other, each of which was illuminated by the great many paned glass windows that stood guard between them. To my left, and in the very center of the wall, I saw the throne of the king and queen resting like a crown above a grand hearth whose fire was blazing like a forge meant for the arms of war. To my right, a sight more captivating than the last. A quarter of the room was covered by tier upon tier of wooden benches upholstered in a wine coloured fabric. It was a grandstand like that in an arena, and this grandstand reached nearly all the way to the timber beams running across the ceiling; filled with hundreds of men clamouring amongst themselves. Lastly, between the king's throne and the grandstand, there was a massive, birch table, where every lord of the realm huddled around what I later learned was a huge map of Anolia and her surrounding regions. Here too, I saw Priscus, his arms wrapped tightly around the king's frame in a warm embrace.

Immersed by the sights, I wandered further in, though at the same time I began looking for my party. Out of the corner of my eye, I noticed someone waving to me. It was Axle beckoning me to come with an expression of urgency on his face. He was seated next to Jon and Meric on the second highest tier of the stand, and for some unknown reason they were more or less secluded from the large clusters of men aggregating in the lower rows. Every man in the hall, including the king, was wearing his legionary uniform, which I have already described. For this reason, half the chamber appeared to be a great big sea of red, and if it were not for their legionary emblems stitched upon their tabards, each man looked indistinguishable from the next. Still, I was captivated by the different legions present in the room, and as I made my way to the others, I took notice of the lesser known sigils such as The Winged Lion, The Silver Leaf, The Cerulean Bull, and The Black Scorpion, all of which were deemed as expeditionary forces that were garrisoned in foreign lands.

"Where's Petris?" I said curiously, while taking a seat on the tier just below Axle's feet.

"The kitchen I would expect," Meric replied, in a voice tinged with spite. He stroked his black stubble while resting an elbow on his knee. This was the first time he spoke to me in some days, and I was surprised he was sitting so close. "Aren't you two the best of friends," he added, releasing a mighty yawn. "Why don't you go look for him? Come back here in about an hour and tell us what you find."

"Enough," Jon breathed as he nudged Meric's rib.

"Quiet all of you," Axle broke in. "It's starting."

I shifted in the direction that I had last seen Priscus, and there I watched as the lords took their seats around the table, whilst the king moved to his rather plain, high-backed chair at the table's head. From our position above I was able to get a good look at him; my first time seeing him, in fact. He was an able-bodied man, callous in his appearance, but still soft on the eyes, brown-haired, and certainly younger than most of the other royals before him. His presence alone established authority, not just because of his position as king, you see, but also because when you looked at him there was a sense of power that he appeared to derive from beyond the crown. The sense of right and fairness, courage and valour, and above all he exuded so naturally a feeling which all kings of Anolia are meant to give off: the spirit of the *paterfamilias*, the father to all in the land, who we looked to for guidance on all things.

With his back to the flames the king raised his hand in order to quell the chatter. Then, when the chamber became silent, he lowered his arm and addressed both the crowd and his lords. "I now call upon my chosen scribe to begin the recording of this meeting," he said with a gentle, but resonant voice.

Barely a moment later none other than Petris himself entered the chamber, clumsily, and from a hidden door by the side of the throne. As he shuffled toward the table, he struggled to carry the two large tomes that he pressed against his hips, one of new stock and the other looking more archaic and worn from flipping through. He laid them on the table with a thud, and therewith he took a seat next to Priscus, swiftly opening the newer tome, which signalled the king to begin.

"I, Adeanus, Lord King of Anolia, declare this meeting in the year 1024 of Andiel's Era to be commenced. Let all words and all matters spoken here today bear worth for those to come after us, and let it be known that all council be spoken freely and suffer no consequence, as it is the custom of our laws." He took his seat and added, "Let us begin."

It is without embellishment when I say, dear reader, that for the next two hours shouts rang out from every lord around the table, some having abandoned their seats very quickly to cool off their tongues, others simply having been brought to their feet because their hearts were heated by the feverish energy of the discussion. Likewise, passions roared from the men in the grandstand, many shouting grunts of disappointment when they felt that their legions were being undermined by the false authority of another lord, or on occasion, the cries reveled in satisfaction when spoken of in praise. As far as I was concerned, my heart was seized with a chill, one that was accompanied by some groundless fear. It was the same fear that had seized me on the night of the lookout, for all the matters in discussion were of evil things. Many spoke of Ascani warbands that were plaguing our northern borders more than the ordinary, while more than a few others spoke of whispers and rumours of wicked sightings, visions of creatures beyond the horror of the Ascani, of witches and sorcerers, and of the *Hircani*, creatures I already knew to be real.

"Settle your tongues my lords, I beg you," Adeanus urged loudly. "None of us will get any words of meaning in if we keep howling at one another like this." Just then he turned to one of the lords who sat across the table. "Go on, my Lord Aulus. What is it that you wanted to report?"

Lord Aulus stood up, revealing his legion to be that of Horned Eagle. "Well, my king, what I have to say is no different from what the other lords have already spoken," he said in the now silent chamber. "The Ascani are most surely growing in number and their attacks are ever more frequent. Not a month has passed since the Gates of Pindus have been assaulted. They have already come at us six times in waves never lessening in number. Even now my men are fighting to keep them from overrunning the pass, and because of this a quarter of the garrison has fallen. I know it's not the time to ask, but it is my duty as your lord to request for a *supplementum* to be dispatched at once, for I fear the worst will happen if it is not given."

"If Lord Aulus moves to supplement his forces then I do as well," Lord Perris said, standing suddenly and bearing, I noticed, the emblem of the Necetian Trident, the weapon our god of the sea is said to possess. As he rose, he pointed to the lands beyond the kingdom's western borders on the very map that I had noted earlier. "My scouts upon the Fair Sea have reported seeing lone ships moving up and down the southern coast of the Linlani tribe-lands, and then as far down as the Grey Isles. These ships, the scouts say, are not like anything we have ever seen, my king. Their sails were entwined with blackish hide and their oars formed from the bones of large northern beasts. Every time we give them chase they vanish without a trace, into hazes and storms born from cloudless skies, as if some enchantment were at work. I have but forty ships, which will fair little against this enemy."

"Forgive me, Lord Perris, but it seems that you are supposing that these lone ships your men have seen — allegedly, I might add, belong to the Ascani?" said Lord Ulcar in a rather contesting tone. Lord Ulcar was old and white-bearded, and the eldest of the lords present in the chamber with some seventy-five winters behind him. He was also the commander of the White Horse, Anolia's eighth legion, which shared its history with Lord Aivas, who was the first to encounter the Ascani a thousand years prior. To be frank, it took but a moment to remark that he was a pretentious man, for he seemed to speak in the tone of a well-educated man who saw himself as all wise and all knowing, an attitude which was repeatedly made obvious throughout the gathering. And on top of his arrogance, he appeared constantly vexed, as if he were among his lessers, wanting desperately to remove himself from the setting. "And how then, if I might ask, do you know for certain that these ships aren't just mere pirates? Marauders of the Grey Isles even?" he added.

"I've fought pirates all my life and never have I seen them as I have described," said Perris.

"So again, you are sure that they are Ascani?"

"I never said I was sure—"

"Of course you didn't, and that's because you aren't, my lord Perris. *If* they were in fact Ascani, then those scouts of yours would have been the first ever to have witnessed these creatures take to the sea, which as we all know is quite ridiculous to their nature. What I *am* sure about, my lord, is the enormous cost that would undoubtedly be dispensed by the crown for this armada that you seem to desire to be built, outfitted, and sent to your charge. I am well aware that I may sound the agitator here, and I apologize my lords if I do, but we cannot simply afford to build another fleet on the whispers of god-fearing men who, by all accounts, think they saw something in the mist. However, if you truly require additional ships as you say, I can't see why *you* cannot issue them yourself by your own pocket. I mean under the king we all have oversight over our own armies, so why not build a couple more vessels to chase down this new, mysterious enemy. Thus giving us a more sound picture to your request."

"I appreciate your skepticism, my lord Ulcar, but you and I know full well that our mandate as lords of the legion goes no further than to the betterment and safety of the people themselves. All matters concerning war and its readiness falls under the king's power alone. I would do as you say if it were not the path to treason," Perris replied, straight-faced.

"Enough, both of you," Adeanus interjected. "Let's not squabble amongst ourselves. I have heard you both and I will consider both equally. But now let's hear from Lord Kaeso, and his news from the hinterlands."

Lord Kaeso was leaning against one of the chamber's pillars that overlooked the hearth, his arms folded at his belly, the shadow of the fire dancing on his cheeks. At the call of his name he had twitched slightly, as though he abruptly broke free from a hypnotic trance. At this point he cleared his throat and began speaking in a low, grim voice. "I have only one matter to report, my king," he said slowly, as though he did not know how to form his next words. "Three weeks ago," he said, "at the western edges of the Greenlands, my men and I were pursuing an Ascani warpack that had been ravaging the rim for several weeks. We tried to track them down as best we could, but for three days there was no sign of them; almost like Lord Perris' ships, they vanished. Yet, that is until we picked up their trail, one that lead us south to the town of Harthus." Here he paused, his eyes showing deeper dejection. "And if the carrion circling above didn't give it away, then the smell in the air surely did. There...in her streets...we found nothing. Nothing but rivers of fresh blood and a few hollow corpses that gave colour to the blackened soil beneath them. We looked everywhere for the village folk, and, at first, we thought the Ascani had carried them off, as they always do. One of my men, however, followed the trails of blood to the temple, and it was here we found the rest. There were hundreds stacked in its halls...of every age, and even of different neighbouring hamlets, many strewn and hung like cattle." Suddenly a host of gasps and terror-stricken whispers filled the air. "I've seen their barbarism before, my king. But, this was no simple product of their cruelty. We had not found a temple. We had found their slaughterhouse... their stores."

"Their stores?" exploded a voice in rejection. "How absurd!"

All at once my eyes honed in on the voice's bearer. It belonged to Lord Plaucus of the Stone Fortress, and right away I was somewhat uneased by his shrivelled, lanky frame. Even though I was far-off, I could feel the piercing sting of his shrewd, brownish eyes. At first glance, I can almost say that he appeared to me, in part, like a bumbling scoundrel, one who seemed to enjoy talking grandly above his peers, but never once in his life had the stomach to act upon his lofty words — an attitude that in all likelihood he adopted from Ulcar, since the two were the best of companions. As such, he gave me a sore first impression, which, if I might add, did little to distract me from his large, avian nose, a feature that topped even the strange hue of his skin, a colour akin to something sickly.

"As any man here, I am quite informed about the barbarism of the Ascani," he said, weaving his words as if his status was above everyone else. "I have seen much of it, but never have I seen or heard them eat the flesh of man, other than in the stories that are meant to scare children to bed. And to claim that they are hoarding us people as provisions is nothing more than nonsense meant to incite unwanted rumour and fear among the people. I am sure, my lords, that Lord Kaeso's over embellishment seeks to heighten our nerves. A product that I suppose comes from exertion in his many battles, and of his lengthy journeys."

"Quiet yourself Plaucus!" Adeanus responded scornfully. "I'm more inclined to believe that most here would be hard-pressed to agree with you on the matter of knowing about the barbarisms of these creatures. And now having said that, why am I not hearing this report from you? Does the village of Harthus not fall under your charge? Is it not part of the Greenlands? Tell me, my lord, are you not the commander of Andiel's Shield?"

"Of course, my king, but—"

"But what, mh? Out of all my legions yours holds the greater sum of men. Is seven thousand not enough to remove yourself from the comforts of your post? Perhaps if you had bothered to do so then the people of Harthus wouldn't have suffered such a fate," Adeanus said, with a slightly raised voice. Still seated, he forcefully pushed his chair back, it's feet scraping across the floor. He stood up with weary breath, and then he strolled off towards the hearth, appearing physically and emotionally injured by Lord Kaeso's news.

"I...I truly would have, sire," Plaucus stuttered. "If only I had received some news of these attacks or...or even sightings. I swear this is the first I am hearing news of this—"

"I have news to report," Priscus interrupted, moving to the center of the room. "That is, if the Lord Plaucus is done with his moaning, of course."

Therewith a low, collective chuckle rose from the crowd. I too added to its resonance, and as it so happens, it was the first time that I had seen something of a smile on Jon's face. I remember that I was surprised by it, because I had learned rather quickly, over the course of our journey to the capital, that he was a man of simple affections and very few words, who often kept a straight face in almost every situation he was in.

At this point Priscus began to speak, drawing us back to the discussion. "Like many of the reports said here today, the walls of Easteria have also been recently attacked. Not by any band, nor by any war party, but by a force of some thousands. It was an army — an army who sought to overtake the city in the dead of night by means of a surprise assault," Priscus said, garnering a wave of agitated whispers from both the crowd and his peers.

"The Ascani do not employ the strategies of war," Lord Aulus said, keeping an honest look.

"Aye they don't, and haven't for more than a thousand years," Priscus replied. "And that is why, my lords, I have now come to believe that each of our reports are related to a larger purpose — a greater intention. One that concerns all of us and the whole of the realm."

"Purpose?" Ulcar blurted, roughly. "What purpose?"

Priscus was leaning over the map, deep in thought. "An incursion."

At that the chamber erupted into an awful raucous of breathless chatter, prompting many of the men nearest to us to hastily make their way to the lowest tier, almost as if the word *incursion* had caught them by the belt and yanked them down the steps. At the same time, a few of the lords who were seated sprung from their seats like crickets and rushed over to the most crowded sections of the grandstand as they shouted demands of restraint to their retinues, which was then swiftly backed by the king's plea for silence.

"He never was the subtle type," Axle whispered in my ear.

"A bold claim commander Priscus, or perhaps just a stupid one," Ulcar retorted. "Incursion, really? Last I checked, my lord, our lands have been under an incursion for the last thousand years, a thing you already know quite intimately in fact." He huffed as he rose from his seat at the speed that his elderly age restricted him to, making certain that the cork brace upon his right forearm did not come into contact with any hard surfaces. Here, he faced the other lords, his face wholly awed and stupefied. "Have you all lost sense? Or have I just not been included in whatever foolish aim you are all conspiring towards? These attacks of which you speak are not uncommon or unexpected, yet you all speak of them as if they are, and now you bark that they're the prelude to war like hasty warmongers eager for it to be true. Many of you have been fighting them for all your life, but all of a sudden these threats are somehow greater?"

"What I claim, Lord Ulcar, is only what I believe to be true," Priscus said, authoritatively.

"And what if it's not, true, hm? Need I say that to spread such a false conclusion, of some Ascani invasion no less, would breed disarray in the kingdom — not to mention the sheer panic of far larger proportions that will most likely come with it."

"What has been said here weighs to the possibility."

"You are reaching far. Very far," Ulcar retorted. "So the Ascani have bound together in greater numbers and have gotten slightly bolder in their raids. What of it? It's happened before, has it not? You yourself have cut down such efforts twice before by my count, and scattered their bands to the wind more times than any man here — and yet then, you've never once uttered the calling of war." He turned his back to the crowd with his injured arm cradled like a baby, at which point he spun back around and almost beseechingly reached out as if literally snatching their stares. "Need I remind everyone of Andiel's sacrifice? Have you all forgotten about the war against the Conjuror? The Plague of Ascanelius?"

"We need no lesson in our history, Ulcar," the king interjected, his focus glued to the flames.

"Then allow me to say this, my king," Ulcar said, cooling from his high-spirited rebuttal. "A thousand years has it been that the Ascani have been nothing more than that which we have kept in check, for not one among them has the power to be the master under the god of death. Only the Conjuror was said to have such a power, a power to command his armies in war. Without that power the Ascani remain mindless beasts to no purpose but to be an everlasting plague. These creatures heed him, and only him! For this reason, sorcery has not stirred in these lands, nor any other, since Andiel's time. And so here, my lords, is where my trouble lies, for it sounds to me that some of you are suggesting a sudden visit from this shadow long since passed."

I looked over my shoulder, toward Axle, and muttered, "What is he on about?"

Axle slid forward in his seat so that his voice would not project further than my ear. As the lords around the table engaged in another clamorous exchange, he began telling me, in a sinister tone about the Conjuror, a name that by the age of my existence had long become a half-forgotten legend, and one that only those with time enough to spend with their noses in archaic books would know, even though some thought it to be more myth than history. As Axle put it, the Conjuror was the greatest and most feared of the *primorus*, those creatures of leadership that Petris had spoken about in the cart. This *primorus*, however, was different from the rest, for in the stories it was said that he was no Ascani, but a man. As legend told it, he alone was able to conjure up dark magics in order to occupy the minds of the Ascani swarms, turning great, mindless rabbles into dreadful armies, and to then utilize them in the same manner and purpose like that of the legion, a force with the sole purpose of creating Ascanelius' new kingdom.

"All those vellums in the corridor," I said, wide-eyed. "That was—"

"Aye," Axle said, taking a quick glance at the door. "Those people that dress like Petris call them the *Libri de Memoriam*. They are the list of the fallen as I have told you, those who died in the final battle that saw the last of the Ascani armies defeated, a battle that brought an end to the tale of the Conjuror."

"Well then! Lord Ulcar," Priscus said, with a heightened voice. "Let me enlighten you on the difference between chance and design. I have said what I have because any man with the mind for war could see that all these reports come from areas in the realm that hold strategic value to us, as I am certain you have already surmised, in all your wisdom. After all these years, as you put it, why would the Ascani now persist time and again on breaking through the Gates of Pindus if not with the aim to assault and destroy our forges to its south? The very ones that the bulk of our legions depend on for their armaments. It would be a heavy blow to our supply, don't you think? From the shores of Linland the enemy would not only command access to the Fair Sea, but of all the dominions around it, which then gives them the only pathway that leads right to our outermost western borders. If we look to the north, no soul now lives beyond Andiel's shield because Harthus is no more, and as such, we have no way of staging our expeditions further beyond its position, blinding our eyes to any movement along a territory half the size of Anolia herself. And of course, we have the city of Easteria, which shelters the largest port in the northeast, large enough for any sizable army to use. If the enemy were to capture any one of these positions, if not all of them, then it would give the Ascani an advantage, an opening, to invade our kingdom."

"So then, where is this great Ascani army to follow suit? The one belonging to this incursion of yours, and the one that has apparently marshalled unseen, right under our noses," Ulcar asked, growing more agitated. "Of all the lords here, not one has said anything of seeing such a force. We have not even heard a whisper from our allies in Kashtan, the east, or in the western lands. So you see, my lord Priscus, I believe you utter your words in this hall as though you were Andiel himself, clamouring for some great war to begin. You may call yourself brother to the king, but I will not humour this false narrative any longer, because for all we know this is another one of your ploys to seek out the enemy, for us to march our legions across the realm to look for some ghost of an army, all so that you can continue on and feed upon vengeance for your —"

"I believe it to be real," Adeanus said, moving away from the hearth. He sat back in his seat with a weighty thud, his back reclined upon its cushion and his chin nestled in the palm of his hand. The whole room remained silent as they watched him

113

carefully in thought. He then proceeded to raise his arm, signalling the knight behind him to open the door he guarded. "Let her in," he added.

Plaucus' face turned grim and sour at the sight of a young, black haired woman entering the chamber. "Who is this?" he said, sharply.

"My lords, this is Lera," Adeanus replied, as she moved toward the table. "The last of my hinterland scouts."

The woman marched past the guards grouped in her path with a faint limp in her step, wearing dark clothing more-fitted for an assassin than a scout. Her face was topped with several fresh bandages, and her left arm rested in a harness that was tied behind her shoulder. She appeared as battered as I did on the day that I had first met Petris, but in truth my intrigue was not affixed to her injuries, but rather captivated by her exceptional beauty. If I could make clear Plaucus' flaws, I could surely tell you, dear reader, what she looked like to me in that moment. Her skin was fair and unblemished like that of a noble maiden, her hair long and flowing, her eyes as large as moons and as blue as the sapphire waters of Felas. When she halted at her mark, anigh to Priscus and Ulcar, I got a better look, insofar that I was able to recognize that she was not of Anolian birth, but of Aeginas, a small, cloistered set of isles off the southern coast of Anolia, and as you might have guessed, the same place where the Lady Flora hailed. And so for this reason, I remained breathlessly silent and slavishly fixed, my heart violently fluttering in the hope of catching the sound of her voice.

Meanwhile, the king removed his richly gilded crown and let it drop onto the table as if it were a stone being lobbed into a pond. The clunk ushered in a heavy silence, and it seized the attention of every soul in the chamber. He rubbed the bridge of his nose as though weariness burdened him, and then invited the lords to gather around the map.

"Go on, Petris," he said, motioning him to ready the archaic tome in his possession. "Speak loudly, so that all can hear."

Right away Petris shifted himself forward along his seat until his belly was pressed up against the rim of the table. He carefully pushed aside the tome he had been transcribing in, upon which he brought the other one to his view. He opened it by its midpoint, leafing through several pages, when all of a sudden he stopped at a section that was marked by a flattened leaf. Amid the profound silence he cleared his throat, and therewith he began reading the passages before him as loud as if he were reciting one of his auguries in the *Sacrarium* itself. As he read the passages, a wave of murmurs grew in the chamber, for it was at this moment we had all been told of the existence of a long-forgotten fortress, one that had been lost to the shadows of time, a castle of a bygone era, the one they had named Northfleet.

According to what Petris had read, it was built in the years following the great war, and had stood as a symbol that marked the extent of Andiel's reach in the north. Little was known of it, and for this reason both Lera and Adeanus had stepped forward, each in their own turn, to bring clarity to the lords of the council of its significance. In fact, it was Priscus who had been the first to ask, and it was Lera who answered him. To be short, she had spoken of another growing threat to the realm, telling us that she had been the only surviving member in her band of pathfinders to bear witness to an Ascani army numbering some six thousand strong, and of which she, and Adeanus, were certain was moving in the direction of this mysterious fortress. Petris supported their claim by pulling out what looked like a topographic map of Northfleet and her surroundings, which was folded among the pages of the tome.

"Quiet! Silence all of you!" Aulus cried, extinguishing the flame of tremulous babble that grew after the news was revealed.

"Scout," Priscus said with gravity in his voice. "How old is this sighting?"

"Just over a week, my lord," Lera replied, wincing slightly as the force of her pivot kindled her pain. "Two horses died under me so I could bring this news." Then, she pointed to a location on the map, a point that I would later learn was a hundred leagues north of Easteria. "Last we saw them they were here, by the eastern coast of the Marble Sea, all of them on foot, and most setting up what looked like their camp, or as one of my brothers believed, a staging area. There was, however, a small vanguard of a few hundred, no more, that was already on the move, marching in rank and column towards the mouth of the Black Shores. We tracked them for a day, but that was when—"

"I understand," Priscus replied, nodding sympathetically. Here, he shot a glance toward us, mainly to Axle.

Lord Perris then moved closer to look at where Lera was pointing.

"Andiel's mercy," Perris said with surprise. "We don't even know if this fortress yet stands, but by the looks of it, its not far from where you last saw them. For all we know it is already in their hands, and with this report being over a week old, we have no way of knowing where the rest of them are. They could be anywhere in the region."

"I do not believe they have claimed it," Kaeso broke in. He put himself next to Perris and stood before the maps, studying them diligently with a hand combing his thick, black beard, while his eyes shifted between the charts like a hawk tracking its prey. He then stretched forward and laid the map of Northfleet atop the area where it would have been marked on the Anolian chart, aligning its corners in such a way that it filled in the void where the fortress should have been illustrated.

"Look here," he said, drawing a dozen lords to his back, including the king. "I have once ventured beyond the Black Shores, and I have seen what lies in this region. The outer territory is yet uncharted to us, but I know for the most part that its lands are similar to Easteria's. Apart from the Black Shores themselves flat ground is rare, and so if the Ascani have indeed turned west, then they will have no choice but to follow the whole of its length to where it runs no more. That journey alone is more than a month's march at the least, I would guess. If they haven't any ships they will be flanked by the waters of the North Sea to their right, and then by the mountains on their left, which run for four hundred leagues. No army of any size can traverse them, at any point, without terrible consequence. So they are locked. After that, there is still more that blocks their path to the castle even if they should find the end of the ridge."

"How do you know that?" Priscus inquired.

"I don't," he replied. "But it's drawn here on the map. Whoever it was that drew the chart of this Northfleet was sure to include enough detail regarding its surrounding terrain. Some of these markings are unclear to me, but it appears that there are no pathways to reach it from either the east or west, because if you look closely at these indications you can see that the fortress itself seems to rest in a valley, one that is hemmed in by the bay it is said to overlook to its north, and then by a great woodland at its feet in the south. So, all together, I don't think the Ascani will reach it for some time. And if what I have said is true, they can only come upon this castle by descending the east ridge. It will be their only way."

"What does it all matter?" Ulcar said. "As Lord Perris has said we don't even know that this former testament of Andiel's glory is now not just some pile of rubble. Yes, my lords, I do not deny that it is an army, and a large one at that, but such a force could never threaten incursion, or dare to think to invade the kingdom. A force of six thousand is but a drop of rain if it were to crash upon Andiel's Shield, so I don't see the need to concern ourselves with what is by now almost certainly but a heap of chalk and ruin."

"I agree with Lord Ulcar," Priscus said. "But let us not forget that castles of Andiel's time yet stand within our borders even after the lords of old have long since abandoned them for those built anew. Then, we have Easteria to consider, and all the villages around it, as they lay beyond The Shield and prone to attack. To cast a blind eye to this enemy would be a grave mistake for all of us. The last thing we want right now is a war, but more than that, to give the Ascani the very thing that Andiel had intended to bar them from, a foothold; the means to strike at us from a position of strength."

"Then why not let those Linlani barbarians deal with this, hmm?" Ulcar said. "Why must it be our blood once again? Their lands are, as a matter of fact, much closer than ours, and so I say we need only send a messenger and be done with it."

"A sound plan, I think," Plaucus said, rather pompously.

"No," Priscus replied sternly, "We do not give unto others what our swords can settle."

"What then would you have us do, my Lord Priscus? What is your plan here," Ulcar blurted, as he sat up in his seat. "I'm sorry, but did you not hear, or see, how remote this fortress is? If they can barely send an army to this place then how do you expect us to send ours—"

"That is because we are not going to send ours," Adeanus interjected. "The fires of war stir, my lords, but as it stands this new danger in the north is just another force at play on top of all the others that have been spoken of today." He stood up, slowly. "In truth, there is no certainty that we face an incursion. I will be the first to admit it, even though I said I believe it," he added, his voice getting more rigid. "But if by some chance such a thing were to come, then I want to make it very clear to all of you that I, Adeanus, did everything in my power to make sure that the Ascani never, ever, try it again."

All at once he made his way toward Petris and stood before the tome, staring at it intently for a brief second before gently closing its cover. As he turned to face his lords, he took the map of Northfleet in his hand and folded it to a square, not once disturbing the sound of the crackling flames of the hearth. Therewith he placed his hand on Petris' shoulder, eyes beaming with mettle. "Petris," he said, "write down every word I say next. I, Adeanus, Lord King of Anolia, declare this meeting in the year 1024 of Andiel's Era to be ended. Let it be known that I will now set in motion that which will see our armies ready for war, and the purging of these dark forces from this mortal world. My lord Kaeso!"

"Yes, my king," he replied, stepping forward from the flock of lords.

"Before you return to your charge I ask that you go south to the camps of Norlyn with five others of your choosing. Instruct commander Eigas and his sergeants to raise the *supplementum*, one man to match every ten now already under arms. Send word to any who would see a sword in their hand, even if you must find them among the *veterani*, those not long absent from their shields. I want them all ready to fight at my call, but be sure that none are to take the field of battle until every part of their instruction is complete. Understood?"

"Yes, my king!"

"And Lord Aulus," Adeanus continued. "You and I will return to the Gates of Pindus. My legion will relieve yours, and then from there we will combine our armies and set forth together to find the source of where these creatures are coming from."

"Aye, sire," Aulus nodded.

"As for the rest of you! You will return to your lands and prepare for my calling. Every man and sword readied and accounted for."

"Your grace!" shouted a man from the crowd. "What of the army in the north?"

"I'll handle them," Priscus broke out, inciting a low mutter amongst the crowd.

The king turned to the side, haltingly. Up until then he appeared to be full of verve, but just as his eyes met those of Priscus, his expression was suddenly that of worry. He walked up to him and gripped his extended arm gingerly. "Ever these many years you have taken it upon yourself to venture towards hardship and to where favour never ceases to betray you, my brother," he said, prompting Priscus to smile and clutch the back of his neck with brotherly love. "I'd be lying if I said it's not going to be a hard one. I hope you are sure about this," he smiled back. "After Aulus and I are done, we will come for you. All you have you to do is take refuge until I arrive, but if you find yourself getting bored, then you can rebuild the walls with their corpses."

Immediately thereafter, Pricus thieved the map lodged between the king's fingers and with it he turned to the crowd, his chest expanded and his heart filled with passion "I am Priscus, Lord of the Vined Sword, and now time has become our enemy. If no one legion of ours can fulfill this task, then I will not take with me a legion, but I will take with me whomever I can find. Any man willing to journey into the unknown, and to a fate unknown, is welcome. We will be few, and they will be many, but let it be clear, my brothers, that whatever the course we will not fail. We will find this fortress, and we will renew it to its former glory. And when these creatures crash upon its walls, they will feed not on our flesh, but on silver and iron, casting from their wicked minds any thoughts of victory. Not one piece of this world is theirs, so if the gods are willing, let us send each and every one of those bastards back to the underworld."

Right then cheers of exhilaration and chants of valour echoed in the chamber like a rising storm. The lords of the realm gathered around Priscus, some offering their hand in jubilation, many others whispering into his ear their pledges for this upcoming quest, be it provisions for the journey or men for his command. But not all were so elated by Priscus' proclamation. In this regard, I am not only referring to the Lords Ulcar and Plaucus, but also to myself, because it had only taken me moment to realise that my road now pointed due north, to a battle of no advantages, to a task of many shortcomings, and to a fortress of mystical beginnings.

CHAPTER 8

The second portion of this chapter was told to me in part by Axle Vetrix, 966 A.E.-1027 A.E. Throughout our journey to Northfleet I would often find myself in Axle's company whenever my input was required in matters that concerned my craft. At times we would share a drink by the fire, and it was in this setting, with the warmth of the hearth and the soothing taste of drink, that I would come to learn the finer details of what had happened the same night Meric's company had arrived at the village of Ortona, which will form the first part of this segment. I have done the best I could to recall Axle's words, but still I must warn you, dear reader, that I have taken the liberty to rebuild some of the fragments I have long forgotten.

"There will be some resistance for a short while, right there. Do you see it? On the stem," I said to the sergeant beside me, his knee deep in mud. He was thrusting the wheel of a rickety wagon out of a small chase in the road. "Keep your eye on the clasp, sargeant," I added. "See that it doesn't come loose again, or I promise you that we'll be carrying a lot more than just our swords from here on out."

"What would it matter, builder?" joked a legionary marching past. "A few more pieces of bedding on our backs won't kill us. And besides, if anything should happen; we'd have your magics to see us through, won't we?"

I mounted my horse with a humorous grin, knowing full well that the legionary, a man from the sixteenth no less, was snickering at that foolish title of Night Sorcerer, which seemed to follow me everywhere at this time, despite that I was half a world away from those who had given it life — excluding Meric. I said to myself early on that contesting it would be a fool's errand, and so chose instead to play along with it and bear the nonsense good humouredly. As such, I gave the man a last smirk, and then gently pulled on the reins so that I could veer the beast onto the road, where a long column of overburdened legionaries stepped to the lead sergeant's hasty cadence, four abreast. In fact, the men of the legion were often ridiculed for these forced marches, for the legion's column was many a time jokingly referred to as being a pack of mules in file. To an extent, we were, seeing as how we soldiers always handled the task of carrying our own affairs. Not just our armaments you see, but also our tools of craft, our bedding and rations, and in some cases even the weight of our winter clothing, all of which was stuffed into a goat-skin packsack. In this particular instance, our burden was slightly more arduous, owing to the fact that Adeanus had proclaimed that all beasts of transport across the kingdom were to be saved in light of this possible incursion we all feared. As such, we had been granted but three carts of the oldest stock, one of which, as you can see by the scene described above, was already falling apart.

Be that as it may, the men's faces were unruffled by this strain. We were all relatively used to it, and there were some who appeared to welcome the stress, since their hearts were brightened with thoughts of adventure — a sentiment I did not share. Yes, I wanted to help, demanded it even. Yet, there were times that I felt as if I was the only one to entertain the idea of our moving toward self-destruction. After all, we were heading towards an army of six thousand. Nevertheless, I kept up appearances, and therewith I took my leave of the sergeant, whereupon I rode toward the head of the column, cutting across the lush, sunset-burnished grassland that resided between me and the natural bend in the road some distance ahead. Then, as I came upon the head, I slowed to a trot while positioning myself beside Jon, who welcomed me back with a short nod, which he became accustomed to do whenever he saw me.

"So," Meric said, still with his same cold air. "Did you fix it?"

"A bolt had to be tightened is all," I replied. "So yes, until it becomes undone again."

In all it had been five days since we had left the capital, and of all the men I had to endure, Priscus saw it fit that it be Meric. Even here, as I remember, I still did not know what I had done to garner such ill-will from the man, and I do not joke when I say that it grew more so now that Lera had volunteered to be a part of the quest. Not because she was a woman, you see — well to a point it was, because it seemed that I, like every other man in his sight, was some hurtle barring his haughty and narcissistic charm from snatching her unbroken attention. She appeared uninterested in any of us if I am being honest. Though on the whole, not once did I think to protest his cold-shoulder, for never did I want to appear feeble in front of him, nor in front of Lera for that matter, which to my embarrassment was nothing more than my giving into the arrogance of my youth, and the naivety of my young heart.

In terms of the quest, as you must be wondering, Priscus' strategy was rather simple. In the days following the council meeting, he had set in motion his intentions to bolster our forces, as you may recall by his spirited proclamation, *with whomever he could find.* Thus, he had divided the company into two parties; the first being Jon, Meric, Lera, and me, along with a third of the two hundred and seventy legionary volunteers who nearly demanded that each of their legions be represented in this task. And the second, Priscus, Axle, and Petris, along with the remaining men. According to the plan, Priscus was to move north and secure a cohort from Plaucus' legion at The Shield by means of a written order drafted by the king, for at the end of gathering Plaucus, and

Ulcar, had angrily withdrew from the council hall before it could be told to him. My party, headed by Meric, was to travel west to the Isle of Ore just off the coast of Ortona, a rather small fishing village fifty miles south of the outermost western end of The Shield. Here, we intended to ferry to the island and take charge of the Bronze Hammers stationed there, which Lord Covirus had pledged to the quest.

"That's a shame," Meric said to me, as he flicked the peel of an orange out in front of him. He then offered a piece of the fruit to Lera with an inviting grin, which she immediately shoved off with uninterested eyes. "I thought more from all your talents."

"I carve wood, Meric," I said. "I can't just up and restore it if it's poor and ready to give way."

Meric took a large bite of the fruit. "Well it is why you're here after all, isn't it? I mean to do what you're good at, these menial tasks. You probably don't know this about me — well I don't see how you would, but when I was about, I don't know, your age around, maybe a little younger, I was in line to be a builder just like you. Aye, Andiel's promise I was — and Jon too in fact. On the day of our recruitment, it was the first thing the sergeants directed us toward. Told us to report to a rather lanky man named Libanius I think it was. I'm not sure."

"Well, why didn't you then, all those long years ago?" It was not my best jab at an insult — amateurish I know — though I knew his next words would serve to rile me up, a sentiment he knew was easy to achieve. Nonetheless, I kept myself cool-headed, because again I knew what path this was heading towards, or rather at least I knew that once again he was starting his performance of robustness in front of Lera, who just then caught me glancing at her.

"I don't remember, to be honest," he answered with a look of confusion about his face. "But it was something simple," he added, adjusting himself on his saddle. His fabricated performance prepared for what he next said, "Ah yes! Now I remember. When I was told that I would likely be a distance away from the fighting, and I mean the real fighting, I supposed then, in that moment, that the idleness and the rather childlike tasks would leave a great big gap in my spine. You know what part I'm referring to, don't you? The one that keeps all our manly bits together. Makes us who we are. I just find that fixing wheels on broken carts is not the course to greater laurels, or the path to greater adventures, if you understand my meaning. You do understand, don't you?"

I rolled my eyes, caring little for his banter. If you can call it that. "At least that big spine of yours won't feel the cold tonight. I may have just saved all this manhood you speak of should these people at Ortona shut their doors to us, and force us to sleep in the cold like we have."

"Oh! Don't worry about that, builder. I'm sure I have enough warmth to—"

Right then Jon struck Meric in the gut with his elbow. I assume he too was beginning to become annoyed by his boorish hot air, or perhaps he was just sick of hearing his voice. As Meric fought to catch his breath, Lera spurred her horse to a gallop, moving ahead of us and, halting at the top of the slope that we were moving in the direction of. As we caught up to her with the column at our backs, the light of day had begun to fade rapidly and turned the sky into a portrait of amber rays.

"We rest for the night," Jon said. "The barn over there. I think it can fit some."

I sought out the structure, but at first I did not see it, as I was taken by the sight of Ortona, which seemed from a distance to rest quietly, right up against the banks of the Silver Bay. Despite that we could see the village from our position, it was still hard to locate anything of note, because most of the village itself was obscured, cloaked in part by a soft dewy air.

The column began descending the slope in the direction of the village, and in some way I found myself riding beside Lera, close enough to bring forth a warm, rosy colour upon my cheeks, and several times, near enough that I had accidently bumped my knee against hers, which did little to calm the rising thump in my chest. Yes, fair reader, I was rather shy in the presence of a woman throughout my youth. It's not like I had any experience in matter. Anyway, since I was close enough, I thought that I would try to speak to her, introduce myself for starters. So, I turned to her, but just as I opened my mouth she also turned to me and said, "If you hit my knee again, I'll run my dagger through it."

"Yes, of course," I swiftly replied, stunned and urging my horse a little away.

By this time, we had entered the village from its south tower, and as we strolled down its muddy streets all those sweet butterflies in my gut were suddenly stilled by the eeriness which surrounded us. Everything was strangely dark, as if night had shunned its overcast over the fields and solely focused its gloominess on the hamlet's hay-topped roofs. When we found ourselves on the threshold of the market square we were met with a sullen quiet, all of us suddenly realising that the village was empty, where neither man nor beast could be spotted.

"On the left," I said, motioning with a nod. "The barges."

Meric came up from behind me and then halted at the crossroads near the market square. He stretched up in his saddle, looking about for any sign of life, and therewith toward the very end of the road where three considerably sized wooden barges, each teeming with protruding oars, briskly swayed to the slow moving current of the Silver Bay. He turned back to the column and said, "Right, well, it doesn't look like there's anyone here to guide us across, so we'll rest here tonight and cross ourselves in the morning, since I'm not up to drowning. Alright, all of you listen here, go on and see to your own matters. But be sure that you're all prepared to leave when I say."

"Where are you going?" I inquired, as I watched him move away from the group.

"It's Ortona, builder," he said. "The people in this village are known for two things. Their liking for wines and ales. And as it so happens, I do too. If you haven't already noticed there's nobody around. I'd wager that they're all in the tavern, spending lots and lots of coin that will likely be mine tonight if the gods have stopped being little sards with supplying their luck. Come along if you want, I'm sure they have women too. Maybe we can fill that spine of yours—"

Suddenly a crash caused by a door slamming upon its frame shot out from a nearby house, wherefrom an elderly man burst out onto the road with a lantern dangling from his clenched fist. For a brief instant he appeared lost and disoriented, yet just as his eyes caught sight of our company he let out a cry of relief, at which point he began to stumble towards us in haste as though he were escaping the clutches of a terrifying spectre.

"You see that, builder," Meric said to me. "Even here they know me." He dismounted and ran his fingers through his hair in preparation for the man's arrival. "It's alright there's no need to rush," he shouted to him, now about forty feet away. "You don't have to do anything. Just point me in the direction of your tavern and I'd gladly dispense some of my coin. This place sure looks like it can use some of it."

Before we knew it the man nearly jumped a few strides forward and fell to his knees in front of us, letting the lantern fall face down in the mud as he cupped his hands together as if he were some rootless beggar, his form breathless and grovelling. "Oh Andiel be praised! Thank you! Thank you! Bless the gods! Bless you all for coming! Andiel's mercy!" he blurted, as he burst into a flood of tears.

"It's only a few pieces of silver old man no need to undo yourself," Meric said.

"I don't think he's weeping about your coins," I said, as I dismounted.

"You do not know how long we've waited," the man went on.

"What are you talking about?" Meric asked, now changing his tone to a more serious one.

"Are you not the men we sent for?" the man said, as I brought him to his feet.

"Sent for?" I asked him, confused.

"The letters!" he cried, grabbing onto my arms in distress. "We sent many men with letters to the court for…for soldiers to help us!" He turned to Meric as if a prophecy revealed itself before him. "But it doesn't matter now! You're here, so you must help us! It has already been many days since they took them! We must hurry! Please! You must help us find them!"

"Who has been taken?" Meric solicited with unrest. "Tell us."

"This village is plagued! Creatures in the night have taken the children into the forest there," he replied, pointing to the great woodland at the north end of the village.

"Ascani," Jon uttered, his hand reaching for his axe.

"No! Not the Ascani," the man said, eyes widened as if they could not be opened anymore. "I cannot explain their form, but it was not them. Please, you must go now! The men of this village that have already gone after them haven't returned and the others are too weak or simply too afraid to help but — but you are strong, you are men of the legion, are you not? Warriors all of you!"

"We don't have time for this," Lera cut in, her words gripping more than a few tongues. "I say we take our chances and cross now, or we'll end up arriving at the fork long after Lord Priscus does. We can't search the entire forest in the dead of night. Clouds are moving in and it will be impossible to see in the dark. We have no idea what we'd be walking into. They could be anywhere, if they aren't already dead. We'll fair better with the sun's light and Lord Covirus' men."

"We can't just turn our backs on them," I protested.

The elder threw himself forward, hands extended toward Lera. "No, they're alive! I promise you! Every night when the sun fades we can hear their screams. I beg you, please! Let us not hear it another night," he cried, dragging his knees in the mud. Then, his expression changed as if he had another sudden epiphany. "I'm...I'm the ferryman! I'm the ferryman! You need to cross to the isle? That's why you are here, yes? I'll take you! Anywhere! You just need to help us now, for its nearly nigh—"

At that moment gut wrenching shrieks bellowed from the heart of the woodland, echoes of young children wailing and crying in fear. As the cries grew louder the howls of grief stricken mothers began to sound one after the other from every home around the market square, each more harrowing than the next. Accordingly, Jon's face was bathed with impatience, and so he sprung to action, galloping down the road at full speed with his large axe gripped in hand.

"Wait! Jon!" Meric shouted after him. He immediately mounted his horse and faced the men in the column, who were by now gathered in one, big mob. "I want twelve with me! The rest of you hold the ground and secure every inch of this village!" He took off in pursuit, spurring his horse wildly so that he could catch up with Jon.

In the short pause that followed I snatched the elder's lantern from the mud, whereupon I quickly mounted my horse with not a thought as to what I was seeking to accomplish. I was scared enough as it was, but there was some part of me that did not want to remain idle while the others went forward seeking I knew not what. And so I held the lantern out in front of me, illuminating the path ahead as I, and more than a dozen other legionaries, charged headlong toward the chilling cries that seemed to welcome the darkness of the forest ahead.

***

Priscus felt his blood curdle as the pleasantly hot day darkened to a cool evening; the very same evening in which Meric's Company had arrived at Ortona. Heavy clouds moved in from the south and cold winds blew in from the east, the chill piercing through the bones of the exhausted legionaries of his company as they marched six abreast along the *rex in via,* the king's road. Out of all the marble-paved roads in the realm, it was lengthiest, connecting the capital to Andiel's Shield by way of one continuous path of few deviations. To the men, it seemed as if they had been pressing forward upon this road for an eternity, being that they had not strayed from it in the three days since the whole of our company had been split in two. More than that, it was Priscus' intention to be the first among us to arrive at the fork, which meant they would have to endure lengthy marches that began at the crack of dawn.

On this day, however, Priscus' overzealous determination had gotten the better of him. He had aimed to push his company onward throughout the night, but as groans of weariness began to emanate from the column, he found no reason to deny the men their much needed rest. By the time the meal hour had arrived they traversed the River Rill, at which point they had reached the winter quarters of Lord Titus, legionary commander of the High Tower, Anolia's second legion. Here, Priscus was met with hapless news. As the men sluggishly passed through the south gate of this earthen fort, the few guards who roamed the grounds had rushed to inform him that Lord Titus had already departed with his legion that very morning, coincidentally to support the Vined Sword at Easteria. As Petris put it, the news was rather ill-timed, for he had convinced Priscus that he would charm Lord Titus' fierce religious zeal in securing an additional cohort for the quest. Nevertheless, the fort was void, save for the hundreds of beige tents that filled the grounds from corner to corner, each and all encircling a great, crimson coloured pavilion at the center. As a side note, this pavilion is known in the legion as the heart of command. It is customary for the men to live around it as if they were like the vessels of the heart, that which gives the legion its very life and longevity. But in any case, we will leave this for the military scholars to explain.

The men had gathered near the pavilion in a group to rest and recover, some immediately nodding off in exhaustion, while a good many others joined together around a large, iron cauldron, patiently awaiting their evening meal of a rich venison stew that Petris had set to cook.

Quite natural to his character, Priscus chose to forgo the comfort of a hot meal and a feathered bed for stacks upon stacks of dusty parchment, all of which were meant for planning their course ahead. As such, he requisitioned the pavilion for himself, seeing as Lord Titus had no immediate use of it, and dragged Axle and Petris with him. He seized the chance to further study the map of Northfleet, particularly in regards to her surroundings, being that everyday it had given them nothing but grief whenever the three of them stopped and tried to make sense of it.

For the better of an hour Priscus and Axle had been arguing over their possible courses of action, and as that hour had come to a close they had both reached a point where their extensive experience of battle drafting proved little towards the daunting task ahead of them. Axle had told me that much of that disheartening had come from them, because they could not agree on a suitable path to best journey to the fortress, or even how to find the castle itself once we were to arrive at the great woodland that shielded its southern approach, as it was drawn.

"That doesn't make any sense," Priscus said, yielding to his growing frustration.

"It's not that I'm saying you're wrong, Priscus," Axle said. "But you are."

"The south road is the only passage we can take," Priscus retorted.

"Yes, but that is if this map is even true to begin with, let alone if that path can still be seen. There's a thousand years of overgrowth that we have to consider here, which may very well have covered the trail entirely. But say we do find it. Once we enter the forest there is no turning back with our numbers. The book said that it will take us three days by foot to cross the breadth of the forest. So, I think it's safe to say that this bloody woodland is quite big. My point here is simple, and that is that we need to find some sort of a landmark, a bloody point of interest, anything really — something that we can follow in case we have no other choice but to turn back." Axle pointed to a rather long tributary that flowed along the eastern edge of Northfleet's ridgeline. "And another thing, Priscus," he continued. "Kaeso said that they would first have to follow the Black Shores to its end, did he not?"

"He did."

"And did he not say they could only come upon this fortress by the eastern peaks?"

"What are you getting at?"

"We have to start planning our route with the assumption that they have knowledge of this place as we do — even though I seriously doubt that they are aware of the same information that lies before us. When they come down from the mountain, as is the likeliest case, they will face this river here, which at one point or another they are going to have to cross. Now, as far as I can tell this river is going to work against them, because as it is drawn, here it's a rather wide one. They will not be able to cross it easily."

"Why is this of importance?" Petris asked. "Isn't it better for us that they can't."

"My point exactly!" Axle said. "Unless the Ascani have some skilled builders among them that we don't yet know about, then crossing this river will be as difficult as crossing the mountains, of course that's if this river doesn't reach their bloody ankles. If it doesn't, and let us pray to the gods that it doesn't, it will cost them more time. Lots and lots of time. For this reason I say we forget about the southern path; let us use the opportunity to enter from the west. We'll skirt along the base of the shelf. It'll cost us a day or two, I'll give you that, but we will be farther from them should they be ahead of us. At least then, we can judge whether or not you want us to fight the bastards alone, or if we wait for your brother. If it comes to battle," he said, trailing his finger along the map, "at least we can fall back and rally."

Priscus stood beside him, his eyes drifting about the map. "Are you certain of this course?"

"Certain?" Axle bluted, taken aback. "No, I've never been there before. Have you?"

"Alright that's enough from the both of you," Petris interrupted in a fatherly tone. "Look, we still have two more days before we reach the fork, so there is plenty of time to sort this out. The best we can do now is...well, I'd say fill our stomachs and sleep on it. Perhaps a prayer or two after that if there is time."

"Yes well, dear priest, unless the gods have already offered you a solution to our problem then I'd prefer we settle this before we cross our borders. I'm not sure, but it just might help us stay amongst the living for a while longer," Axle said, rather irritated. "I don't want us to walk into some trap, at least not blindly. And if it wasn't already obvious, I kind of like being alive."

"Sorry, but they haven't told me anything. It never really works like that," Petris replied, as he stepped off toward the drapes that formed the doorway of the pavilion. He rubbed his belly and added, "Right now, dear friend, I have a better way to stay among the living. And that is by having some of that delicious stew I made, which should be ready by now if you would excuse me." Here he exited the pavilion where a cool wind could be felt as he moved away.

Priscus removed his sword belt and placed it on Lord Titus' oval command table, which was made of purple heart, a light, plum coloured wood that only the very wealthy could get their hands on. I have never once seen this species of tree for myself, and, to be honest, I only know of it because Petris was rather adamant in telling me how awed he was when he had seen it for himself. It was not an item commonly found in a meager winter fort, and this one was large enough to fit more than a dozen men around its rim, a testament to Lord Titus' wealth. That being said, I do not think Titus would have been pleased about its current state if he saw it, for at this moment it was topped with not only Priscus' mud covered scabbard, but also a good many other things that I believe would cause men of wealth to be affected by — things like; dripping candles, uncapped vials of ink and used quills, iron-spined tomes, unsheathed daggers, and possibly the worst of them all, morsels of food, which Petris made worse when he returned with three full bowls of stew.

"Why is it that I get the feeling it's going to take more than a pure heart on this one," Axle said, plummeting into the seat at the head of the table. He sighed in exhaustion as Petris slid one of the bowls in front of him, stew spilling over the side. "Look, Priscus," he said, shoving a spoonful in his mouth. "I can't see another way through, only what this bloody map cares to show me. Once we pass the borders of the greenlands it'll all be new to us, and the only one that knows those parts is that scout, Lera, to a certain point. So, we'll just have to keep our wits about us with each step forward. We'll get a better sense of the path when we get closer. Make a decision then."

"Right now let's focus on getting the men we need to make this work," Priscus said. He was standing opposite Axle at the other end of the table with no evidence to suggest he was going to call it a night. Propped up by the armchair before him, there rested a saddlebag that he began to rummage through. "None of it matters in the end if we don't get there first."

"If you're looking for your brother's letter, then it's in my bag."

"Why is it in yours?"

"Unless you've forgotten, we still need it," Axle replied. "I thought it best we don't repeat what had happened at that skirmish near Easteria ten years ago. You know the time where you up and lost the plans I had drawn for the battle — the ones we needed. Knowing how many times you had gone over that one, I figured you'd do the same with this one and end up losing it somewhere. Now for Andiel's sake man, enough with the work for one night.

You're making me more nervous than I have to be. Sit down and eat something will you, before Petris here devours your share."

Petris smiled. "It does go without saying that I do call his share if he doesn't eat it."

"And I call the bloody wine!" Axle said, as he stood up. "If we are staying here awhile we might as well tap into Titus' stores, don't you think?" He moved to the rear of the pavilion like a thief, combing over Lord Titus' personal effects which were piled neatly near a single, undressed cot. Beside the cot, however, was Axle's prize, for there was a pyramid of stacked crates, about a dozen in number and very clearly out of place. "The last time I saw our friend Titus he wouldn't shut his mouth about the shipment of wine he received. A white coloured wine he had imported from Kashtan or some shite," he added, while prying the foremost crate open with his dagger. Then, he pulled out a bottle with an expression of satisfaction on his face, and returned to the table with three silver cups nestled in the palm of his hand. "Looks like the poor bastard left in such a hurry he forgot to take the lot of it with him. It's a shame he hasn't some of that southern shite that I've come to like...what was it Petris, that lighter one we had in Heraea, what was it called?"

"That wasn't wine," Petris replied, reaching out for the offered cup. "It was a spirit."

"No, I'm sure it was wine. I remember it being wine."

"Trust me lad, it wasn't. As I remember it you were too drunk to know you were gulping down something more in the same family of lamp oil than liquor. In fact, you actually did drink lamp oil by the end of that night — and a part of your beard caught on fire when you were speaking to that girl. Your face nearly went up in flames, don't you remember that? You couldn't grow hair on your chin for two years."

"It was good stuff that."

Meanwhile Priscus' eyes were glued to the letter, which he had found in Axle's bag. Axle set a cup in front of him, his tone changing to something slightly more serious as he said, "You can keep reading that letter all night if you want, but we still can't escape the fact that there's a good chance he won't give you the men. No matter what it says. It's no secret that man despises you, Priscus, perhaps even more now since you and your brother made a fool of him in front of the other lords. He might even do it just to spite you."

"It's a good thing that we have laws in this kingdom so that doesn't happen," Priscus said, eyes yet fixed. "I believe that one's called treason. And I'm sure just the thought of a royal dungeon frightens him." Here, Priscus broke from the page, his focus now caught by the glint of the silver cup. "My thanks, but none for me."

"Come on. You don't expect me to just drink with him all night, do you?"

"Aye, that goes for me too," Petris said. "But for him...in my case."

Axle gently grabbed the cup and offered it to Priscus. "Priscus, everyone is taking a rest. A little wine isn't going to harm the task. So come on, have one drink with us, and then we'll leave you to your parchements. You did everything you could for one day, and it's not like you really have anything else to do tonight."

Just then a ghastly screech was heard coming from overhead. It was quickly followed by a sundry of deep echoes, rumbles that sounded like vicious dogs growling at a distance. Voices then cried out in alarm atop the beat of signal drums, whereupon one of Titus' men burst into the doorway of the pavilion with a look of panic on his blood soaked face. Immediately, he moved to speak, but a volley of flaming arrows suddenly pierced through the canopy, three of which struck the legionary's back, the others quickly setting fire to anything their burning glow cared to consume. At this point another hailstorm of fiery arrows slammed against the pavilion, but by now Priscus and Axle had already scrambled for their swords and some shelter behind the chairs, and Petris hid underneath the table, all three of them nearly being hit several times.

When the way was clear they stormed out of the pavilion with swords in hand. They were swiftly welcomed by a stinging heat and a blinding light, for almost all of the tents and whole sections of the palisades in the western portions of the fort were lit up in flames, so much so that their brilliance allowed Priscus and the others to see clearly the battle upon the ramparts, and the several hundred Ascani silhouettes that poured over the defences and into the fort.

"Arm yourselves!" Axle shouted at the men as he dashed toward them.

"Petris," Priscus blurted. "Find a weapon and hide. Now!"

In a flash the Ascani joined together in a great cluster like a black stormcloud, funnelling tightly into the lanes between the legionary tents that were not yet aflame. As they emerged from the shadows of these tents they collided headlong with the legionary counter charge, their momentum so great that many of these creatures pierced right through the iron curtain and found themselves battling those men in the rear caught absent the protection of their armour. A brutal melee ensued, sword for sword, where Axle and Priscus were lodged in the thick of it. Petris, however, had barely made it twenty feet from the pavilion when fifteen Ascani, gone mad by their desire for flesh, had cut off his path to seek refuge in one of the tents farther to the rear of the battle.

It was Axle who saved him from their bite, cleaving his assailants by the pair and plunging his sword deep into the hearts of these foes. Not five minutes had passed thereafter when suddenly Petris cried out to Priscus from his hideaway, his head popping out of the seam, warning him that the fire was soon to engulf the pavilion, and that the map to Northfleet, and the letter for Plaucus's men, were still inside.

Hearing his words, Priscus quickly came down with his sword across the chest of the Ascani before him and then drove it's point into the neck of another creature, rapidly delivering a second blow across its back just as he parted the blade from its flesh. At this moment he turned toward the pavilion to recover everything of worth he had left behind. All around him the clamour of battle grew fiercer, and the fire heightened. Victory was far-reaching, and as he took in the unfolding chaos around him he began to realise it more clearly. The battle was very quickly turning into a perilous struggle to withstand the onslaught, because as far as he could tell, all of the horses had been scattered to the wind or butchered, and now the southern portion of the fort was set afire like a great big brazier. More than that, an endless mob of enemies joined the frenzy, continually replacing those newly slain with fresh fiends eager for battle.

Priscus turned to Axle in an explosion of purpose. At the height of his lungs he shouted his commands to him, the chiefest of them being to gather those yet alive and abandon the fort, seeing as how his men were very near to being slaughtered. Then, he seized the moment and ran heedlessly towards the pavilion, hoping that the gods were on his side, and that he could get to the parchments before the fury of the fire turned them to ash.

CHAPTER 9

Creatures in the night, the elder had said. The words repeated themselves in my mind and only served to increase my growing discomfort as I treaded forward in the dark forest. The men and I had abandoned the horses at the foot of the woodland and had rushed into the thicket, trying our best to catch up with Jon and Meric, who were some ways ahead of us, lost in part to the shadow of the trees. If not for the lantern that I had brought with me, we would not have found them. There was no pathway, not even a natural course amid the timbers, and with the moonlight incapable of breaching the thick, leafy canopy, it was starting to look as if my courage would be the only light that could pierce through the fear that surrounded my thoughts. Even so, I still wondered how long my mettle would hold firm, since we were using nothing but the distant shrills of the children as our bearing.

"Meric," I said, trying to keep my voice low when we had finally caught up to them. "Can you see anything? Do you need more light?"

"Quiet!" Meric whispered sternly.

I kept silent with the lantern out to my side, providing what light I could as I followed the man in front of me, who in turn trailed behind Meric along the narrow track that Jon was carving through the overgrowth. From the start we had been following

Jon's lead. He was heated, angry even, as he moved through the forest. Some time later I would learn that Jon's heart was made more passionate where children were involved — not to say that the rest of us were not. With this ferver, he led us deeper and deeper into the forest, where, for my part, it felt like every progressive step was an inch further into the black of pure night, and if I am going to be forthright, much further away from that tenacity one musters when plunging into unknown danger. I do recall, however, rallying a few drops of daring so that I could take to the front, but even that was short lived, because as Jon suddenly came to a stop I got a good look at what barred his path: a large, impenetrable wall of vines.

What stood before us was a great deformity in the growth of the forest. On every side plant life hung between the twisted trees like blankets out to dry, and it formed, to my eyes, a sort of shell that was so extensive that we could neither see its top, nor could we tell how far it spanned before us as the vines continued on far beyond our vision. It took most of us by surprise. But for Jon, it was just another hindrance that needed to be overcome. As such, he began to vigorously chop his way through the vines. By this point my uneasiness increased a thousand fold, because as the pieces of the growth came crashing down, rays of torchlight shot through the seams, and with them, a foul scent that immediately forced everyone to wince away.

I quickly set down the lantern and spit the taste of said smell out of my mouth. It was here when I picked up a fragment of the vine that had flown back at my feet and began to examine it. There was nothing extraordinary about it; it was odd to say the least, but at first glance I remember that I thought it was a piece of tree root that had rotted, and that would have accounted for its greyish colour. But as I brought it closer to the dim light of the lantern I discovered that the breed of this vine was foreign to the other growth in the forest. When I squeezed it firmly it shattered as easily as fractured glass, and when I opened my hand it was reduced to an ashen dust that the wind swiftly uplifted.

"Gods! What's that fucking smell?" blurted one of the legionaries. He was hunched over as if sick, clearing his lips of dripping spit. "It smells like death."

"All of you stay behind me," Meric said, while unsheathing his sword.

With that, he and Jon led us beyond the wall of growth, all of us silent and watchful. As I stepped out of the darkness and into the light my mind flashed to attention, a new sickening horror seizing my breath. My eyes grew wide like moons, for I found myself standing in a clearing, or to be more accurate, a graveyard, one that was laden with the strewn and scattered corpses of men, and the mangled, fly infested carcasses of forest beasts, most of these creatures being of young stock, like cubs, pups, foals and fawns. Some dangled from the branches above us, but most were heaped in many great knolls, each one topped with several lit torches like the candles around a sacrifice in the Sacrarium. These mounds of dead were ghastly, but they formed a pigeon-toed crescent around something far more unnatural: a sacrificial altar that was twined with innards.

Filled with fear and disgust, I took a few steps forward to observe it, because evidently my curiosity had overpowered my ability to stay still, as the others had done. I neared it ever slowly, careful about keeping my feet dry of the gut-filled, blood pools that peppered the ground. I could hardly believe that what I looked at was real, for it was more nightmarish than any terror that I had ever dreamed — even more than the Ascani themselves at this moment.

Two trunks of gnarled thorns formed the base of the altar, both twisted and contorted like the branches of an aged willow. Its surface was moulded like an oblong bowl that had been hewn from a single piece of timber, and within it, there lay the mauled carcass of a fawn, its head wholly removed and its intestines dangling from its sides like the vines we had cut through. It was no doubt a fresh kill, since it was still bleeding profusely. My eyes trailed the light of the lantern, following the path the blood flowed out. It was here that I noticed how it trickled down into a hole in the ground that was nestled between the altar's legs, a burrow of sorts which was only wide enough to enable a small man to crawl through.

"Builder," Meric muttered. "Get back here and stand beside me."

I turned around, haltingly, my gaze still glued to the altar. When I managed to break free from the trance of disbelief, I stopped dead once more at the sight of a half-gnawed, human eyeball that I was very near to step on.

"This is a lair of demons," I heard a legionary mutter.

Meric was scanning the treeline. "Quiet! Get your swords out, all of you!"

Then, without warning, a short, crow-like squawk broke from the forest behind us, forcing every man to spin around on his heel with his sword aimed in the direction of the sound. I tossed the lantern to the side and snatched a torch from the mound beside me, where I then proceeded to peer into the shadows of the timbers. It was all coming back to me again; the same fear that I had felt on the night of the ambush in Easteria. It began to overwhelm me, and my heart was racked with panic. Everything felt familiar, right down to the method in which I waved the torch from section to section, trying to illuminate every inch of the forest before me. I did so as the sound of distant twigs began to snap under advancing feet, step after step, coming straight for us upon the path that we had trailed.

I quickly looked over to Jon for an order, but the expression on his face already indicated a readiness for battle. He brought his axe to his chest and moved in front of us, closer and closer to the sound that was now but ten feet from the entrance of the clearing. He raised his axe above his head and readied a stance to strike. But just as he lifted his axe, Lera suddenly came bursting into view.

How she had crossed the forest without so much as a torch, I do not know. But it was obvious that she was blind to the strangeness that encircled us.

"So?" she said, casually unaware of the tense atmosphere she had just created. "Where are these children—"

Just then the legionary beside Meric sunk into the ground as if the earth underneath his feet had all at once vanished. His frame was half consumed by the blood-soaked earth, and as if he were trapped in quicksand, his frame continued to gradually sink deeper. All the while he was screaming in agony, shouting and barking that something was biting into his legs, into his flesh. As he flailed about erratically to the chorus of these ghastly cries, Meric and I desperately tried to pull him out. We succeeded in freeing him, but not all of him, because we were met with a fountain of blood, which spewed out from his severed waist.

"Barricade! Around me, now!" Meric cried, wiping his face of blood with his palms.

Not a second after, the wails of the children resumed, their cries echoing from the aperture beneath the altar, toward which Jon had recklessly rushed instead of forming up beside us. "Come Cillian," he said, as he peered into the hole. "Down here, children. We go after them."

"Me?" I blurted, with surprise. "Why me?"

"You have a sword don't you?" Meric said. "Go use it."

"I thought I was just a builder without a spine," I replied. "The job that is away from the *real fighting.*" I cannot remember if I spoke with spite, as you may recall the argument I described earlier, but I am reassured that if I had, Meric did not notice.

"Go on, follow him," Meric said firmly. "You're smaller than the rest of us. You'll fit."

I hesitated for a moment in disbelief, but I soon realised that Meric was in fact placing his trust in me. A dim glow of courage quickly pressed me to command. I am certain, however, that this sudden spark of firmness was neither manifested by me nor

Meric's unexpected acknowledgement, but rather by Lera, whose measuring eyes I felt upon my back. So, I bolted over to Jon, masking terrible doubt with a look of conviction upon my face.

"Tunnel," Jon said, as he retracted his upper half from the hole. "Big drop, six feet, maybe higher. I go, and you next after me."

I quickly placed a hand on his shoulder, stopping him from setting off. "Maybe I should go first. If you get stuck I can't pull you out."

Jon nodded and ceded his position to me. At this point my stomach went cold and my heart completely numb. I watered my lips with my tongue and took a knee, whereupon I plunged the torch into the hole, inspecting it diligently. "Alright then, its seems large enough for—"

I stopped short, for all at once a gnome-sized abomination of long pointy ears, big yellow eyes, and white, pallid skin sprung from the aperture with a serrated, bone dagger in its clutch. I fell backwards in a burst of surprise, my body slamming into a pool of innards. The creature was standing on my chest, and like a crazed rodent it tried to madly burrow its dagger into my breast as it screeched like a dying bat.

Right away Jon struck the creature with the face of his axe, sending it soaring across the clearing until it collided against a tree, its figure bursting into a garish display of blood and guts. At once the act incited a good many more of these creatures to spring forward. They vaulted out of fissures in the earth and shadowy recesses amid the trees, some using their hurlers to shoot stones at us from the tree tops, many others charging headlong at our legs. Meanwhile, I had barely managed to stand up when another fiend leapt at me, only this time I quickly planted my sword in its gizzards just before its saw-like teeth could sink into my thigh. I cut down another swiftly who, from the altar behind me, was plotting to strike at my back. I moved in to deliver a final blow, but forthwith the whole of my body suddenly flung forward upon the ground with a mightier slam. Here, I struck my head so hard that I was utterly dazed.

To my surprise, I managed to discover that the creature, which I had just slain, was a diversion. Unbeknownst to me, there were other varmints that had bound a thick, mud sodden rope around my ankles, unseen. In an instant they began hauling me off toward the forest with unnatural strength, a force beyond their small standing. At first I tried reaching for the binds, though my fingers were coated in viscera, so I could not grip them properly. For this reason I thought of nothing better but drive my sword into the earth in an attempt to anchor myself, but alas the action had only put more strain upon my body, because I was being stretched as if I were tied to a torture rack.

"Oi! Oi, Jon!" I cried, desperately. "Help me!"

Suddenly the strain at my ankles gave way. I fell to my stomach, and like a fish out of water I turned over onto my backside with my sword out in front of me, ready and resolved to fend off no matter what next sought to attack me. Thank the gods I did not strike blindly, because Lera was standing before me, cutting down what seemed to be a dozen creatures with stellar swordsmanship. And much to my green stupidity, I did not move, my gaze in awe as I watched her go about her dance of slaughter.

"What the hell are you looking at?" Lera shouted. "Get up and get a bloody move on!"

Amidst the confusion of battle Jon and I hurriedly descended into the aperture beneath the altar, dropping some six feet as Jon had pointed out. Next, we found ourselves at the verge of an expanded tunnel, one that was remarkably large enough to resemble the sewage works of a sizable town. By rights I thought I had truly fallen into one, being that the smell was beyond dreadful, a combination of the viscous waste and the black, slimy slurry that topped the rivulet into which we had plunged our feet — no doubt the overspill of what rested above us. I handed Jon the torch that I had brought with me while sinking my nose into my tabard, signalling him to take the lead. At this point we proceeded down the tunnel for a short while, ever slowly toward the low, resounding buzz of breathless weeping.

"Jon," I whispered, my eyes fixed on a distant lambent aura. "There's a light up ahead."

"I know," he muttered back.

We were coming near to the light ahead when another strong, sickening odour filled our noses. As we continued moving, we heard the whimpering more distinctly, and so Jon immediately quickened his step, his feet swishing the muck beneath us all about. Still, we approached the glow with some prudence, making sure our flanks were secure since at times a fiendish caw would echo from behind us. Before I knew it, the tunnel had given way to a cavern. It was more like a cove, a beast's lair of sorts, one teeming with piles of refuse and rubbish, and whose walls were partially specked with torches on brackets. As we stepped inside, the quality of the air suddenly changed as if it were filled with evil enchantments, or made putrid by the impurity which is born from their conjuring.

"Sorceress," Jon affirmed, as if he knew it to be certain. He clamped his grip around the torch's stem and slowly ventured further inside, his axe ready at his waist.

"What the hell did you just say?" I said. I was caught-off guard by the word. "What do you mean sorceress?"

"Come, Cillian," he answered. "Follow me."

Not five steps further a muffled whimper caught Jon's attention. He swung the torch just off to the side of his knee, where the light revealed the tear-sodden faces of eleven young children, each one panic-stricken to say the least and completely consumed by fear. Some were, as I recall, as young as five years, others no more than ten. They were huddled as one in a crevice against the rock face, so in Jon's mind all he had to do was put forward his open palm in assistance — but of course due to his size he did not do so gracefully. It is without wonder that the foremost in the lot, a lovely, green-eyed girl, fearfully recoiled, sinking her head into her elder brother's embrace as soon as she caught sight of Jon's appearance, which was nearly awash in the bloody grit of the creatures he had slain.

"Here, my friend. Let me try," I said, gently nudging Jon aside. I crouched and pointed at my legion's emblem "Do you see this here? Do you know what this is?" I said, reaping a few weak nods. It was the same tactic I used to get Enfredarius to trust me, and it was working. "Aye, it's the mark of the sixteenth. We are soldiers, so there's no need to be afraid of us. We are here — both of us, to help you get out of this place. Get you back to your families."

"You're soldiers?" said one of the children, the eldest among them.

"Yes," Jon added with a softened voice. "We free you now."

I extended my hand to the girl. "Right so, unless any you want to stay here longer, then I suggest we hurry on, yeah? I don't know how you've all managed to stay down here as long as you have but I am already quite set on leaving. Anyone else feel the same?"

One by one the children scrambled from the crevice like mice fleeing from a cage. The boy, the eldest I am referring to, took the lead, all the others gathering behind him. In turn, he grouped them in a tight cluster while motioning to me that they were all ready to depart. At that, Jon nodded in the direction of the tunnel, spurring us on. Yet, just as we all turned our backs to the shadows of the cavern an eerie breeze blew over us, whereupon the torches that lined the walls began to flicker violently, their orange glow all at once taking on a greenish flame.

"Where do you take my children?" hissed a female voice.

At first glance I did not see it. But then, as my eyes furiously searched through the darkness at the end of the lair, I spotted it. The gleam of two large eyes slowly emerged from the black, their shine drawing closer and closer as their bearer trailed along a winding path toward the cavern's center. I averted my eyes for a moment, signalling the children to take refuge behind me, which they did hastily and with expressions that suggested they knew very well what it was that approached us. I swallowed anxiously at their rousing fear, and when I looked back, the last of my courage fled me, vanishing at the full sight of it, or should I say at the sight of her, an entity of horror in likeness to the reports from which the lords had spoken of at the king's council. It was a thing that took the shape of a woman, but her appearance was that of a corpse, riddled with thorny spikes about her arms and legs, like those found on the stem of a rose, and bony antlers atop her head, like those of a stag.

We all stood completely still; me most of all. Jon, on the other hand, crept forward. He met the sorceress half-way along her path, halting five feet before her at the very center of the cavern. Strangely, his axe was lowered at his side, as if he had no intention to battle her, and he was rather languid in his motion, as if his vigour were being drained by her presence. Conversely the sorceress did not stop but continued to walk toward him, slowly and seductively despite her ugly frame. She carried on alluringly as she strolled around him, her eyes ogling up and down his stout physique.

"My my, what a fine form you have," she said, trailing her sword-like nails on Jon's back from one shoulder to the next. "A warrior's alacrity. But that's what you are, aren't you? Oh yes, a warrior for certain. I am sure. And a Linlani one at that it seems. Strong men built for this world, built for battle…built for war." She moved her lips close to his ear and licked the air as if flavouring his sinew. Her tongue was four sizes greater than a man's, and its tip was covered in tree bark. "Beautiful," she added with a smile. "Long has it been since I've seen such brawn upon a man. So tell me, warrior, are you terrible as well? Do you love death like I do? Do feast on the fear of your prey like I do?"

Therewith the children became more agitated and the cluster became even tighter. Looking back I could have led them out of the tunnel myself, but my mind was narrow and set on not deserting Jon to whatever fate that was in store for him. As such, there was nothing I could do but grip the youngest of them closer to me and have them hide their faces in the back of my tabard. I gripped my sword with a quiver in my hold, as Jon remained hypnotized and unstirred, absorbed by the sorceress' bewitching words.

"Fear not my children," the sorceress said. "Mother will be with you soon." Here, she halted in front of him with her head canted. "Your eyes," she went on, curling a smile upon her bluish lips. "Your eyes are like clear glass, warrior. I see right through them. I see your heart. I hear it beating, screaming, for more than what you already are — for more power. The gods have led you here, haven't they? Yes they have. So I can give you that power. And now it's all around us. It creeps in the darkness of this world, one that is born of a true king, a lasting force beyond the span of a lifetime, and then continues on for many more. Come, my strong warrior, let us bargain. Return my children to me, and I will show it to you. Become a king of the shadows, so hand in hand we will—"

All at once Jon spun around and in one fell swoop he decapitated the sorceress. A stream of clotted blood spewed from her neck, showering him in chunks of blackened sludge and pieces of rotten flesh. As her corpse fell to the ground, and her head with it, he turned to us with scarlet broth dripping from his chin. "No time," he said, prompting us to stare at him, stunned.

"Yeah right, of course," I spoke, severing the silence.

Jon came over and put two of the youngest children under his arms as if they were sacks of wheat. "Come, Cillian, others still fighting."

As he left the cavern the children came forward, no longer afraid of him, even though he looked quite worse than when first they saw him. In fact, they had all abandoned my protection for his, all of them trying to be the nearest one at his back. And apparently, I was also one of them. I had fallen behind the rest since I kept pausing in the tunnel in order to make sure we were not being followed by any more surprises in the dark. And so, by the time I cleared the breadth of the tunnel and reached the aperture beneath the altar, Jon had finished hoisting the children out. He had also climbed out himself, leaving me as the last living soul to remain beneath the earth, or at least I hoped that was the case. In any event, I could tell that the fight with the creatures above had long since turned in our favour, for the air was absent the clamour of battle, and because I could hear Meric speaking with one of the men a short distance away, giving him orders to see the children back to the village.

All the while I thought a hand would help me up, but I guess at this point in my tale I was still somewhat forgettable. There was neither a rope nor leverage to make use of, though with an eagerness to finally rid myself of this horrid place I tried again and again to climb out of the tunnel myself. "A hand would be nice," I finally called out after many failed attempts.

I bowed my head and huffed annoyingly, waiting impatiently in complete darkness. Not a moment later globules of earth landed on my head, whereupon I was greeted with an extended hand, which I blindly grabbed with a passion, as if to say, *at last*.

"It's about time," I said, worming my way out of the hole. "How could you just forget about me —"

"You're lucky I helped you at all," Lera interrupted, as she hoisted me up to my feet.

I patted my sullied clothes timidly, all the while avoiding eye-contact. With such force in her pull I thought it was Jon to begin with. "My uh...my thanks, scout." That was all I was able to say, fearing a response similar to the one when I had grazed her knee, but more so because I had done something as little as touch her hand. I thanked her, well the air, once more and then said, "I...I am in your debt."

"Did you just call me scout?" she said, perplexed.

I looked over at her as if I said something wrong. "Yes...I mean is that not what you are?"

"I also happen to have a name, *builder*. And it's Lera. Figure I should let you know judging by that look on your face. Best you start using it."

"Forgive me I just thought you'd prefer it if I'd call you... because of your— I'm Cillian."

"Yes I know," she said as she walked off. "I have ears."

Just then Meric called out to me, by my name as a matter of fact, which took me by surprise. He was kneeling by the entrance of the clearing at the head of three dead legionaries lined in a row, one of which I noted belonged to the Vined Sword. "Sarris and Pelias are taking the children back to the village — I want you and Jon to go with them," he said in a glum voice. "I'll stay here with these men until we can find a way to bring them back. I'm not leaving them in this forsaken place. If we're not back by morning, send one of the sargents to find us."

I nodded. In some ways, dear reader, I was put off by the sudden realisation that Meric was a completely different person in character. His mockeries were gone, at least for a short while, and all I saw in him was a captain in mourning for the loss of his men. I joined Jon and set off to do what Meric had asked of us, with enough speed so that the horror of this night would sooner come to a close.

CHAPTER 10

This next part of the story was told to me by Petris Ferentinus, 979 A.E - 1042 A.E. Much of what is composed in this next portion of the tale is a blend of many personal anecdotes. Over the years I have managed to piece together that which Petris had experienced firsthand with those tales that he himself had compiled from the surviving legionaries who were a part of these next events. In fact, if it were not for Petris, I would not have been able to write anything in regards to Priscus' involvement in this sequence of events you will next read. As such, I must give full credit to Petris, who helped me immensely with filling in this part of my story.

Priscus stormed toward the rear of the pavilion, hoping to overtake the spread of the fire that steadily crawled across the surface of the canopy. The doorway was entirely engulfed in red flames, its crinkle of breaking wood paling in comparison to the vast sound of wind filled flames that rose from the towers, which began to seize nearly every piece of timber and calfskin fabric throughout the fort. Suffice it to say, the fort was utterly lost. Now, with each passing moment, the structure of the pavilion grew weaker, and so when Priscus arrived at his mark, he quickly drove his sword into the fabric with an overhead strike, letting the weight of the steel fall from his brow to the end of his tabard. He grasped each side of the breach and tore it open to his size, at which point a strong gust of heat washed over him as if he had just opened the doors to a blazing furnace.

He burst inside like an ardent thief impatient to rob the contents within. But then, he came to a sudden halt. Not because the rampant fire barred his path — in fact the center of the pavillion was as of then untouched by the flames — but because he was caught in the stern gaze of an Ascani, who stared at him from the corner of its eye as it held a piece of parchment in one hand, as if to say it had been caught in the act of reading it. In Petris' words, it was here that Priscus was overcome with the realisation that this was not just any ordinary Ascani, but it was the very creature that I had crossed paths with on the lookout, the one Priscus believed had commanded the assault on Easteria: he who we had come to call the masked Ascani.

Silent, still, and somewhat unnerved, Priscus gripped the hilt of his sword as he scrutinized his peripheries, contemplating his avenues of attack, or escape. All over the fire burned wildly and its sweltering glow heightened as it began to devour more and more fuel, particularly those crates that Axle had earlier found his wine in. As the crates burned asunder, it spewed out morsels of fiery matchsticks, many setting the chairs that were closest afire, the sparks of which in turn began to creep their way toward the table, right where the masked Ascani was standing with a look of ire and madness about its eyes.

Long I often cared not to believe it, though Petris swore to me that it clutched the map of Northfleet in its hands. What makes this act unimaginable is that when the creature had returned its gaze upon the parchment, it was as if it knew full well what the drawing was, *of what Northfleet was*. This in itself was inconceivable to say the least, because in all of our history the Ascani did not care for, nor did they even know in the slightest, about the articles of the mortal realm, save for the mortals themselves fit for consumption. This Ascani, however, had the air of wit about it, which all but verified in Priscus' eyes that he was standing before an actual *primorus*.

It may be pompous to say, but if it were me, I would have lunged headlong at the beast in hopes of killing it on the spot. Thankfully, Priscus was always more level headed than I was, and so instead of attacking outright, he tried to figure out how best to retrieve the map with some off-guard strike, fearing that the creature would toss the map into a nearby flame. He sought to advance a step, but just as he did the sound of the Ascani's grinding teeth and wolflike growl ceased his movement. Then, to his surprise, it was the creature who severed the stillness between them by gently placing the map back upon the table, conveniently beside the rest of the parchments Priscus wanted to recover.

Here the Ascani pivoted to face Priscus, whereupon the two locked eyes. Slowly, it reached into its filthy sheepskin overvest and pulled out what looked to be a pale-green shred of paper. "I… Far-Skafa," the creature struggled to say in a harsh, guttural voice.

Immediately Priscus' breath was stifled and his eyes were widened in horrified disbelief. Never before had he heard an Ascani speak the words of the Anolian tongue, for their speech was that of the underworld, which they themselves rarely uttered. For this reason he looked at the beast almost as if he were bewitched, unable to break his gaze until the creature, Far-Skafa, compelled him to do so, for all at once it discarded that which it held in its hand. The fragment landed right before Priscus' feet, at which time it was very quickly made clear that it was not just some old shred of parchment, but rather something that bore weight and was much thicker in its form. So, Priscus veered his eyes to ground, and there his shock and confusion intensified greatly, for among clots of maggots and rotted flesh was the mark of *Celeres*; a piece of Wymar's forearm.

Far-Skafa shifted his head from shoulder to shoulder as if limbering up. "Your…friend—"

In a burst of madness and with a heartrending cry, Priscus lunged forward with his sword aimed at the Far-Skafa's heart. Right then the creature drew his dual-swords and threw up his guard, parrying the first attack, and then every successive blow that Priscus swung afterwards in rapid succession. Amid these frenzied attacks, Far-Skafa staggered rearward toward the bonfire at his back. He caught his footing, and then in retaliation, he soared forward like an agile feline, battering away at Priscus' sword in a concentrated effort to sever his steel and remove his head. Back and forth their blades cut through the air, their eyes ever locked in sharp and bitter hatred. For a time neither of them seemed capable of overcoming the others defence, but that is until Far-Skafa forced his weight down upon a mighty stroke, causing Priscus' own sword to inflict a shallow laceration upon his shoulder.

Priscus retreated a step backwards, his sword still braced, and his breath hot and heavy. He studied his opponent like any other, seeking the creature's weakness. His fury, however, was getting the better of him, a mistake that could very well cost his life. He stood to a straightened back, ready to fight again, though in that same instant a chime rang out from a distant buccina causing both of them to break their focus. The sound was in fact the signal from Edros, Priscus' first sergeant, who was announcing the retreat by the north gate, the only egress of the fort that was not yet completely consumed by fire.

Far-Skafa's rage rose. He charged once more like an absentminded berserker. To Priscus' advantage he swiftly took note of the creature's fanatical blindness and veered to the side. With a well-placed kick, he shoved Far-Skafa off-balance, sending him toppling over the table and into tongues of flame that were now as high as the pavilion itself. The table too had overturned, and so much of the parchment went with the creature, landing in the whir of the flames. As luck would have it, or by *ethereal intervention* as Petris had rambunctiously put it, the map of

Northfleet was untouched. It had fallen forward and had been pinned under his saddlebag, not five feet from his reach.

It was here when the opportunity to flee presented itself, and so Priscus dashed toward the upended table, snatching what maps and scrolls he first laid eyes on. There was no time to stop and think, because just when his hands began collecting the parchments a storm of fluttering embers set the table ablaze, some of these landing upon his bare forearm. He stuffed all he could in the saddlebag any which way he could, and at that he darted out of the pavilion from the breach he had made, sprinting toward the north gate alongside the last few legionaries who had managed to break free from the battle.

"Fall back! Fall back to the north gate!" Axle cried, his voice roaring over the tune of the buccina.

The hour of decimation loomed as the survivors stormed toward the northern gate, leaving their dead behind and the wounded to their fate. In one swollen mob they bolted down the roadway with a massive Ascani swarm at their backs. Arrows that were hidden by the black of night whizzed over them, several striking their marks with lethal accuracy. As men fell dead like felled trees others toppled over them, but the mob continued on at full speed, panting like dogs with burning fatigue. As they reached the north gate they came upon Petris, who was standing at the mouth of a great, makeshift bulwark made of a dozen four-wheeled carts, each brimming with horse feed. As a matter of fact it was Axle who had thought of the idea, ordering those with him to position what carts they could find in a crescent before the gate to act as a barrier for their escape.

"Through here! Through here! Quickly," Petris hollered, waving a torch above his head.

Priscus came to a stop next to Petris and began guiding each man through a rift at the center of the barrier, urging them to hurry on. "Petris! Hand me your torch!" he then cried as the queue of men lessened to the last tenth.

As the last man darted past Priscus, he plucked the torch from Petris' extended hand and began stabbing the mounds of straw, signaling to those men behind him with torches in hand to do the same with the other carts not yet alight. In a few moments the whole crescent was set ablaze, the heat so strong and ferocious that it singed the skin just being near to it. Priscus then beckoned a couple of idle legionaries to help him close the rift, for the enemy was now less than fifty feet from them and hurtling closer.

"Go, Petris! Get out!" Priscus shouted, his face straining as he pushed the cart by its wheel.

Petris nodded and quickly turned to flee, but right then he felt a hand grab hold of his sleeve, almost as if its owner wished to tear off his robe by the shoulder, or so it was the way Petris had described to me. It was Priscus as expected, who in a heartbeat yanked Petris closer toward him as to avoid the axe in flight, which was whistling right for the priest's back. It narrowly missed them both, yet the axe still managed to punch through the flaming straw and strike the timber of the cart with enough force to send a huge cluster of blazing grass atop Petris' face, burning his hair and scolding his bare skin, which scarred his visage to the end of his days. A piece of his robe had also caught fire, adding new shrieks of pain to his yelps of agony.

Priscus, realising he would not be able to carry Petris through, decided to tow him through the opening by himself. As far as Petris recalls, two more legionnaires had rushed to assist him, whereupon one of them shouted, "The others have all passed through. We are the last!"

Together they towed Petris through, and just in time, because at that moment the ends of the two center carts collapsed, filling what remained of the rift with an inferno of flaming straw and wicker. Therewith the Ascani swarm came to a halt before the wall of fire, and thereat they pushed and shoved one another to the vile beat of their sickening shrieks and want for slaughter — their thirst for blood so great that many tested the blaze for a gap, some trying to crawl under the carts, others more foolishly attempting to climb over them. Priscus knew that the fire would not hold the creatures back for long, so he swiftly lifted Petris to his feet and readied him to depart.

Here, Petris' memory was hazy, seeing as how the events just described caused him to move in and out of consciousness. He had told me, however, that Priscus had abruptly stopped as they were fleeing. At first he was confused as to why Priscus had decided to remain in the midst of what he described to be a glimpse of the underworld, but he would later come to learn that it was because Priscus caught sight of Far-Skafa. I was told that the masked Ascani was standing tall and straight amid his rabble, looking back at him through the crackling flames with eyes filled with want of retribution.

"My lord!" a voice shouted, insistently. "Let us go! Hurry!"

Priscus swiftly turned and set off from the fort without looking back. The night's sky was set alight by the hellfire behind him, but it was not long before shadows reigned once more as he and his men vanished into the black along the *rex in via*, leaving with nothing but the possessions they bore, and with the thought of survival on their minds.

CHAPTER 11

The following morning Meric's company boarded the barges under the heavyhearted gaze of Ortona's villagers. Baskets stretched full of freshly baked breads, ripe fruits, and salted fish were bundled at our feet, because the mothers of the children we had rescued thought of no better way to display their eternal gratitude than to see our provisions excessively restored. And when Cyprias, the frantic elder from the previous night, caught wind of their generosity, he persistently insisted to surmount it by taking full charge and responsibility in ferrying our company to the isle. There were many others who demanded that they should assist him, the fathers of the children for the most part. And so it was in this way that I found myself idle for the duration of the crossing, standing near the bow of the lead barge as men from foreign legions rippled the tranquil waters of the Silver Bay with loud and everlasting chatter about all things — in truth, dear reader, most of the subjects were vulgar and perverse, discussions that were, I quickly learned, a commonality among all legionaries at leisure.

I, however, had no interest in such talk, or even to converse with anyone for that matter. I kept to myself, because for the first time in a long while, I simply paused at the chance to embrace the beauty of nature's tranquility, absent the need to unsheath my sword. I remember the crossing clearly, for the morning sun on this day was bright. I gazed upon its distant crest as I took in the scent of the water and the cool mist which sprayed against my face; a feeling of renewal that I had long forgotten. Having said that, I must admit that I also remember this day because the impact of battle always had a nasty habit of turning even these pleasant moments into ones of brooding. It was not long after that my thoughts of peace were quickly overtaken by the horror of all the evil things I had so far endured, which I was starting to find was occurring more and more whenever my mind was meditative or stilled by slumber.

In truth, I have long since grown familiar with the sleepless nights, though I have never been able to understand how in one moment the world could be the most serene and peaceful place, and then become so wretchedly cruel in the next. It felt like a storm to all of us and if I could articulate it better for you, dear reader, it was as if we soldiers passed into a tempest of blood and madness only to come out of it as if said storm did not just occur. And this, I must confess, has always scared me more than death, for it appeared as though death was something so habitual to our lives that the dead themselves were often forgotten by the tide of the morrow — each name like a grain of sand, ever pilling upon each other until it eventually washes out to the endless sea of time.

As the barges drifted on I pondered on this notion for a short while, now and then stealing a glance at Lera, who had not said two words more to me since she had helped me out of the tunnel. It was of no concern to me, since by the time we reached the isle, just shy of an hour's crossing, my thoughts shifted completely. They now steered toward the faint, far-off chorus of hammers striking steel, and to the pillars of black smoke that darkened the sky at the rear of the mountain which faced the docks, the one in which we disembarked. I helped unload our affairs, and waited for Meric's and Jon's command.

"My undying thanks to you," Cyprias said to Meric, their hands locked in an endearing farewell. "Are you certain you don't want us to stay? It will be no trouble on our part. And we'll be more than happy to ferry your lot back after you're done with your business."

Meric looked at him with a warm grin. "As much as I would love to take all the credit, it was more than just me. And, my greatest thanks for your offer, but you've already done enough. I thank you for your concern, but our path is here now. We will not be coming back. It's about time you go and be with your family." Meric glanced over Cyprias' shoulder as if to speak to the men behind him. "That goes for all of you."

Cyprias nodded with gratitude, and when we finished unloading the provisions he reboarded the barges with his men in order to return to Ortona. After that an unofficial procession formed behind Meric in two misshapen columns. He led us down the pier as if we marched to battle, and then onto a dirt road whose direction was toward the mountain. We had passed alongside a great quinquereme at anchor, one whose starboard hull, I noticed, was wrapped in wooden scaffoldings, and so visibly it was under a great deal of repair. Afterwards, we marched along the dirt road for some time with heavy breath, being that the path was at a gradual slope. It swerved up along the mountain's side like the body of a snake, all the way to the legionary quarters at its summit, which I would later learn was purposely isolated from the docks and much of the isle.

Speaking of the Isle of Ore, the further we climbed the more I was able to study its terrain. I had never before seen lands this far west, and by first impressions I would say, my fair reader, that it was nothing compared to the lush southern reaches of the kingdom. It resembled, rather, like one giant labyrinth of quarries, each seemingly adjoined together by deep channels beneath the arid plain, which I can only suppose was made barren and grey by the countless years of toxic ash and soot that had settled upon it. And no matter how far the path veered away from these quarries, you were followed by the scent of melted bronze and heated iron from the forges, an aroma that quickly sickened my stomach.

"How can anybody labour here?" I voiced, brushing the underside of my nose after a sneeze. I was not in the habit of complaining.

"Cover your mouth if it ails you," Meric replied.

As we came upon the last bend in the path Meric commanded a halt, because we had finally arrived at the legionary barracks. At once I was taken by surprise. Not just because the barracks were situated on a wide shelf that overlooked the vastness of the bay, but also because it was teeming with an abundance of greenery, almost as if everything of emerald colour upon the island had taken refuge at the summit of the mountain. In fact, the entire layout of these garrison quarters was utterly the contrary to what I had envisaged given the condition of the road we had just taken to get here. I thought for sure it would be more aligned to the inside of a blacksmith's workhouse.

Twelve fortress-like structures made of stone were tightly arched like a crown around the north face of a white, marble mustering square, each of its corners adorned with the legionary standard of the Bronze Hammer fluttering in the wind. As I ventured a little closer, I saw that a curtain of immense conifers contoured the backside of the lodgings, and that the path we had used to arrive continued beyond them, its sides lined with beds of blue flora, a sight I would never again see for a legion's dwelling. It was, to put it simply, beautiful. And in my perspective the thing that truly added to this beauty was the stone rail that skirted the cliff a yard or so before the precipice, a hundred feet long perhaps, which was just as lengthy as the vegetable garden that rested before it.

"Andiel's mercy it's about bloody time," Meric said. "Any higher I would be shaking hands with the man himself." He pulled from his belt a tiny scroll bound by a scarlet ribbon, the letter that Priscus had given him. "What do you say we get what came for and then make like Aitanos and get the hell out of here, yeah? I don't know about the rest of you but the hike alone has got me wrong in all sorts of places. And I'm already bloody exhausted — not to mention the insides of my toes feel like I planted them in a swamp."

"Good to know I'm not the only one who complains," I quipped.

"We all have our moments, builder."

"Apparently it's something you both have in common," Lera said, taking a step forward. "And while we are all talking I should say that another thing you both seem to share is your lack of perception. I mean if you had any, you would've realised that there's nobody here." Here, a silence came over us, because there was, in fact, not one man of the Bronze Hammers in sight. "It's long past first light, Meric," she went on as if scolding him, "so why would they even be here? I'm not going to wager on it, but I assume that they are all further inside the island, you know for, like, task and instruction. Can none of you hear their hammers at work?"

Meric turned to Lera, baffled that he had not heard the chimes of metal work reverberating in the air. "Andiel's cock," he then blurted, realising that she was correct in her statement. "Why didn't you say something sooner? For the sake of the gods woman I know my complection and charm is unnatural to this world, making it rather hard to approach me, but you could have at least tapped me on the shoulder half way up and said two words — like *turn back*, for starters. Or even dared a third like *not that way*. Now we have to walk all the way back and —"

At that moment we suddenly began to hear echoes of weighty hammers shaping steel. As the rumbles rose we were met with another surprise, a lone legionary, bearing the emblem of the Bronze Hammer. He was not coming toward us I mean to say, but he had appeared from one of the structures to our left with a bowl in his hands and a spoonful of steamy gruel at his lips. With his red-bearded face buried in his meal he began to trudge across the square, altogether oblivious that a mob of soldiers stood in a great line before him.

"Hello there," Meric said aloud, just as the man was about to clear the center of our line.

The legionary jerked his head toward us like a curious bird and was met with a host of unblinking eyes beating down on him. Instead of appearing confused, a feeling that I would have assuredly expressed in his place, he released a loud, moan of relief, as though we were expected. "We thought you'd never come, captain," he said with a smile as he approached us. "We have been waiting for you for quite some time now."

I lost him in the brilliance of the sun for a moment, but when the glare in my eyes diminished he appeared in front of Meric. He was of stocky physique and bore a deep, criss-crossed scar across his face, like Axle's, but much worse.

"Where is your commander?" Meric asked as he searched the scroll for the commander's name. "Captain...Ein...Einarus. Aye, that appears who we are to be meeting." Here, he rolled up the scroll and then took a step forward to address the legionary directly. "Look, between the two of us, I'm tired of walking, so if you don't mind I'd like you to return to the mortal plain below and tell your captain that Captain Meric of the Vined Sword is here to speak with him, and that he's waiting at the top of this bloody mountain. I must speak with him urgently, so you know the drill, the faster the better."

"Captain Einarus?" the man replied with a raised brow. He put a spoonful of porridge in his mouth as if the situation did not call for haste. "I think I'm the wrong man for that, captain. You're going to need some sort of priest."

"Why?" Meric said, rolling his eyes. "Is he about to fall dead like I am?"

"No, captain," the man replied. "Just dead. No falling to be had."

"Dead?" I blurted.

"Oh yeah! Long time now — three, four months passed I think it was. Some aversion in his lungs turned his skin black as night, or some shite along those lines." He sponged the bridges of his wet mouth with a soiled leather rag. "Didn't you read the letter, captain? It was all in there." Before Meric could respond the man took a step back in order to speak to the crowd. "Well, I guess it's no matter since you're here now. And so, if it's all the same to you, Captain Meric, we best get a move on with the introductions and get you and your lot all squared away." He paused a moment. "Right so, can you all hear me back there? Yeah? Great! This area here is what we call the *prospectus*, the place where most of the men lay their heads. If you continue down the road behind me, there is another set of barracks by the water if that's more to your fancy. But in truth, I wouldn't be tempted to call that home. Don't let the thought of waking by the shore fool you because the air is shite no matter where you go. And trust me, over there it will surely kill you within a year, and that's if the mercenaries that are also garrisoned on this island don't get to you first. Next, I'm afraid to inform you all that our dear friend Sextus, our only decent cook and healer, has also passed to the same sickness as the late captain. And so all matters regarding food, healer's remedies, and if I may take the opportunity to announce, *entertainment*, will be forthwith handled by yours truly, Lytus Lycanus. Lastly, it's rather important I tell you now that we only have two major rules here at the *prospectus*. First, enjoy yourselves. The garden over there is open to all, so don't be shy and feel free to explore it at your leisure. We all have green thumbs. And second, if you feel the need to bathe then I suggest —"

"Andiel's mercy, what the hell are you on about?" Meric interrupted.

At the same moment, we all looked around astonished, trying to discover the source of the shouting that arose from inside the same barrack from which Lytus had appeared.

"Lytus!" it yelled, peeved. "Lytus, for god's sake are you playing the fool again?" Therewith heavy footsteps rose from inside the structure, followed by a wickedly loud sneeze, one you would imagine to come from the throat of a giant rather than a man's. "How many times do I have to tell you to save your theater practices for the arena," the voice then added as it neared the door. "You know I tire of it, and you're not very good—" The man appeared at the doorway and instantly froze, for he was taken aback by the whole of the company staring back at him. "What's all of this?"

Lytus glanced over his shoulder. "It's the replacement captain, sir. He's finally arrived!"

"What?" Meric said, thrown by the comment. "I'm not—"

"If you're not the captain we've been waiting for then who are you?" said the man from the doorway, now slowly approaching our party.

There have been few moments in my life in which the sight of an individual has taken from me the very warmth of my blood. Not because of fear you see, but because of the sheer greatness and gravitas of that person's presence. And this man, who I had only just encountered, felt to me as if he exuded the same *auctoritas*, or command, as Priscus, and who embodied the same strength, or tenacity, as Jon. As I recall he appeared no more than five years older than I was at the time, but his air was that of a mature man, quite the opposite to how I saw myself then. And he was much more handsome, his foreign-looking face squared at the chin, his cheekbones high, his brown hair short and wavy. Compared to the men before him he stood a foot and a half shorter, though his physique resembled that of an ox, seeing as he was wearing nothing more than his trousers. On these grounds alone I knew without a doubt that he was a man of Eraclea, a small tribe of men that lived at the center of the Islands of Pelagos. Eraclea was a place of endless golden pastures, which endowed Anolia's legions with their much-needed supply of grain and masses of wool. The men of this land appeared as he did, but seldom did they serve in the ranks of the legion, and so to see an Eraclean under arms was just as rare as seeing Jon, a Linlani, in the army.

Meric reintroduced himself.

"You're Lord Priscus' man?" the man said as he began to notice the variety of tabards.

"Aye," Meric replied. "At least I still think I am."

"What are you doing all the way out here? And with all these men?"

Meric raised the scroll to view. "I am here on his command — well more on Lord Iberis' orders. I have been instructed to give this message here to your commander, though your man has just spoken of his tragic death...among many other things I did not care to know."

"Excuse him. Sometimes I fear his mother not only dropped him as a child but pitched him."

"Who next commands here?"

"That would be me, captain. Or rather at least to an extent," the man replied. He cleared away the last few smudges of shaving ointment from his neck, and then slumped the russet cloth he was holding over his shoulder. His eyes drifted to the scroll, pausing for a moment to read it. "I'm Andreaus," he continued. "Captain Einarus held precedence over us in positions of command, but there was no one with rank enough except myself in the *inter sodalis* to lead after his death. I have since been the acting commander to the men here on this island. And as you've already been made aware we've been waiting for a proper replacement. I can help you as best I can, captain, though by the law I do not hold the full rank of captain, so I can't make any military decisions beyond my station."

"Well," Meric beamed, taking back the scroll he had just given to Andreaus, "today you can. Congratulations, Captain Andreaus, you've just been promoted." Meric grabbed the shoulder of a very stunned Andreaus commendatorily. "Now then, captain," he added. "How about you get dressed and then find somewhere we can talk."

***

I sat alone upon the stone rail with my legs swinging out in leisure, counting the waves below the cliff as they battered the sharp rocks covering the shoreline. The sunlight, perhaps because the afternoon was in full swing, had grown increasingly stronger and the temperature had turned from warm to pleasantly hot. On the rail I laid out a couple of items; the first being my journal, and the second, a cup of chilled wine that I had filched from the barracks moments after Andreaus had set off with Meric and Jon to the south end of the island. I knew Meric was in a hurry, we all were for that matter, since it was becoming more likely that we would arrive at the fork a day later than we had first agreed upon. In this way I found myself with nothing to occupy me once more, and so I sat in silence and reflection, my mind brimming with images of home, and with new creations of my craft.

"Why are you always looking at me?" Lera said searchingly, her voice at my back.

I pivoted at the waist. "What?" I answered, taken with confusion.

"I think you heard me, builder."

"I'm sorry, but I don't know what you talking about—"

Lera jumped over the rail like a feline. She sat next to me, fairly close might I add, nestling her rear atop the hard stone until she found a comfortable seat. "Yes, I think you do," she pressed. "I see you doing it all the time. Whenever I turn around I find you looking at me, and not just looking, but staring, no — gawking almost...as if you've never seen a woman before in your life. So I want to know, builder, have you?"

"Have I what?"

"Laid eyes on a woman before?"

"Of course I have," I huffed, as I veered my eyes away from her.

I kept my ever-increasing shyness hidden away. Not because I had a choice in the matter, but because the growing discomfort that was brought about by her inquisition quickly took its place. In all my wisdom I thought it best to keep silent, thinking, rather hopefully, that she would see some awkward fault in me and move along. In my silence, however, she just continued to stare at me with interest, as if she was simply waiting for me to confess what it was she already knew. And clearly, my fair reader, you already know that I was guilty of the act, seeing as how I did steal many gazes of her on more than one occasion. Therefore, no matter how I saw it, I was done for, finally caught. I moved to apologise, but just as I opened my mouth to sound the words she suddenly pressed her chest against mine, as if embracing me. Though I wished it so, it was not a hug or anything of the sort. It was an act to steal the cup of wine at my side, whereupon she hooked it to her lips, tilted her head back, and washed her throat until the cup ran empty.

"Yeah, I — I was going to drink that if you must know."

"Were you now?"

"It's either that or I just like sitting next to full cups of wine."

"Honestly, builder, if you were going to drink it you would've done it two hours ago when I saw you lift it back there. It wasn't even slightly cool anymore. And besides, this wine almost tastes like the grapes themselves shat in the mix. You didn't miss out on anything, I promise."

"Well first of all it was a Falarian, so you can drink it either way. And next, I have a trusted friend that says otherwise on the taste. So, I was planning on savouring it."

"What? You mean like a dog? Wetting your tongue now and again?"

"No that's not what I," I stopped. "I'm sorry, but can I ask you why you're here?"

"I thought I just told you. I want to know why it is you are always looking at me."

My cheeks flushed red, and I rekindled the part of the fool. "I told you I —"

"Yes yes, of course, I forgot. You don't know what I'm talking about," she interjected, as she let the last few drops of the beverage drip on her tongue. Therewith she let the cup fall to the ground while she spat out the granules of sediment over the cliff. "So, while I'm still here," she went on, "I have to ask you. Is it true? What the men are saying about you?"

"And what is it that they are saying about me?"

"Can you really form red sparks from your hands? And if so, can I see it?"

"Andiel's mercy," I said, letting out a baffled breath. "No, you can't see it."

"Why not? Is it because I drank your shitty wine?"

"No Lera, it's because I'm a builder not a bloody sorcerer."

"I don't understand. That's what they are calling you. The Night Sorcerer."

"Look, Lera, I apologise, but if you don't mind I haven't seen the sun so bright and the sky so blue in some time, alright. I hear it's best to take it all in when done so in silence. So, stay if you wish, but I'd rather just stop talking about senseless things if it's all the same to you."

"Right, my apologies," she said, in a tone as if to suggest that I was overreacting. She turned to the bay and fixated her sight on the waters, a deep, relaxing breath filling her lungs. There was a momentary, and I mean very brief, silence between us, for she then blurted, "So, builder, why is it that you chose to become... well, a builder?"

"Is there a reason you're asking?" I replied, my eyes closed for a moment.

"No reason. Just curious, I guess."

"Well, if it wasn't already plain, I like to build things...among other reasons."

"Aye, I get that. But what exactly is it that you build?"

"Now that you forced me to think about it, anything made of wood for the most part."

"Anything!" Lera said, surprised. "Really?"

"Yes, I wouldn't be much of a builder if I couldn't."

"So, say you want to build something big like — I don't know, a table. Can you do that?"

"If it's made of wood, then yes," I replied, slightly baffled at the question.

"A house then? Can you build a house?"

"Most are still built from wood, so last I checked, yes."

"Alright then, master builder, let's say it were—"

"If it's made out of wood, Lera, I can do it."

"I see you're getting pretty comfortable calling me by my name," she grinned, warmly.

I swallowed timidly, a vortex of bees swirling in my gut. "You asked me to." Here, my focus began to wander from her, but I decided to stake everything on the talk and become the questioner. I turned to her, rather hastily, and blurted, "You've asked quite a lot about my life but have given nothing in return." Of course I wanted her to stay, yet I rather quickly forgot to keep up the disguise that I did not. "So, let's hear your reasons," I went on, more reservedly. "Why leave Aeginas? Why did you come to Anolia to be a scout?"

"How did you know I'm of Aeginas?" she said with a raised brow.

All of my blood went to my cheeks. "I...I didn't. It was just a guess."

"Well, Cillian, it's not like there was much of a choice for me," she said, her warm mood now slightly glum. "I came to these lands alone, when I was child. No food, no shelter, no coin, just an orphan girl like all the rest, forced into a life of theft, prowling in the dark for a scrap of food when I could get it. Of course when I got older, the fastest way to get all these things without stealing was in the army. I've always wanted to fight, been around death plenty that to be part of it was nothing new to me. But if it wasn't already clear, there aren't many women in the ranks, so naturally when I joined I was placed at the backside of everything, tending to the wounded, or minding the bloody kitchens. Then years later it just so happened that King Adeanus found me beating the royal shite out of four men who tried to have their fun with me. I don't know if it was pity, but he put this sword here in my hand and had me trained as a hunter with the hinterland scouts. That was twelve years ago." She was staring out toward the bay, her eyes appearing distant as if she was gazing into memory. "Anyway," she added, snapping back to attention. "Now I mostly keep to this life because I like hunting and killing the Ascani, which I've become quite good at in these last years."

I was not expecting her life story so suddenly, or that quickly now that I come to think about it. She had once threatened to stab me in the leg if I so much as bumped into her, and when she did spew words at me they were never exactly friendly. Not that I cared really, for I figured that the past should remain fixed where it was, in *the past*. I listened attentively as she continued on, whereupon I ended her story by voicing, "You've certainly had it harder than most."

"If you say so," she replied.

"Aye, but there's something I don't understand," I said, forcing her to look at me. "After all that you have been through as a child, never knowing when your next meal would be, the solitude, all the fear surrounding it. Why is it that you said those things last night? About the children in the village? Why did you say that we should leave them? You saw how terrified they were when they came out of the tunnel. And after all, Lera, you ended up finding us on your own and in the dark. From what I've seen so far you're more than just some simple tracker, so what I'm trying to say is

172

that you could've easily led us to them from the start, even faster than Jon did."

Lera lowered her chin and grinned. It was not a merry grin, but rather one that suggested she was smirking at my naivety, as if my question was brought on by inexperience in her eyes. "And do you think I'm cruel because of it?" she asked, curiously. Do you think I have less of a heart, now that I have said what I did."

"That's not what I said. I only meant—"

"It doesn't have to be said. I am cruel, there is no lie in that. I am cruel, because I am ill."

"Ill?" I said, shifting my chest toward her as if I was healer ready to set my hands to work.

A thick and dreary tension washed over us like an ocean's wave. She was no longer looking at me, but still I noticed that there was a sort of shine in her eyes — though to me she did not appear to be sad, nor was she angered, nor had she taken offense. Instead, she seemed to be faraway, her stare still and void, almost as if her own sleepless torments were flashing before her eyes. It was the same as I had appeared during the crossing, as I have already mentioned, though her trance of woe was quite greater in its effect than mine had been.

"How many battles have you fought?" she abruptly said, slowly emerging from her trance. "How many creatures have you killed?"

"I don't know," I replied, befuddled. "Why does any of that matter?"

"Because that's your problem, builder," she replied, more sternly. "Yours and everyone who's like you. It's the way you form your words. When you talk of battle you weave your sentences together like that of a sage long in years. And aye, I get that you have proven that yours are not just vanity, being that you saved an entire city and a bunch of helpless children and all that — but all the same they're still young and lack the weight of time in battle. That is why I said those things last night, because I know something about death that you have yet to understand. You see, after all these years I have learned that there is no reasoning with the gods of death, for when their eye is on a prize, your very life, they will have it one way or the other. Yes, we found those children, and yes they were alive at the end of it. But if you want the truth, I would have rather known that those children were already dead than put the thought of chance in my heart, only to then find their corpses. This is what years in battle does to you. This is how it shapes your mind. And when you've seen as much death as I have you no longer give thought to it, or care when it happens. That's the illness I'm talking about, a numbness of the heart."

"Why then are you here?" I retorted defensively, catching her riled eye. "I don't get it. If your heart has no more room for the anguish of death, why did you come forward for this task? I'm no sage, you're right about that Lera, but I don't need to be one to know that there will be a lot more death to come. If your heart is numb to it all, why not just leave this life?"

"Vengeance," she replied.

"Vengeance?" I repeated, confused. "What are you talking about?"

"What?" she said in a condescending tone. "Did you think I left Aeginas because I suddenly thought that an adventure was in order? And let me guess, you also thought that you were the only one in all of Anolia whose life was bound to the sacrifice of others." Lera's voice was now becoming rigid, my defensive attitude had provoked her to scold my ignorance. "Twelve of my brothers, men who I have known for a third of my life, abandoned their lives for mine at the snap of a finger just so that I could bear the message about this army we move to thwart. And no, I'm not as daring as I seem, so I didn't just set off on a trip at the ripe age of six. The Ascani, after a thousand years, set foot on my homeland and slaughtered everyone in my village in the dead of night. I only survived by chance, because I was hidden under the butchered and burnt corpses of my family. You can talk about the brightness of the sun and the blue of the sky all day long, but people like me never had the chance to care for such things. So now do you get it? Why I cannot simply abandon this life? What my aim is?" Lera swung her legs over the rail to leave. The warm chatter was long gone, for I had inadvertently welcomed a new heat between us. "The world in my eyes has always been cruel, builder. Think about that next you find yourself staring at me."

"Lera wait," I let slip as she stepped off. My words rooted her in place. I remained silent for a moment. Though I felt the sensation of guilt brewing in my stomach, a deeper feeling of sympathy swelled in my heart. "You asked me before why it is I look at you," I began, my eyes peering over my shoulder. "Do you still want to know?"

Lera slowly retook her seat, only this time her back faced the precipice. I would not say she was enraptured by the mystery, but she did give me her ear.

"There is this woman known to us southerners, to those of Norlyn where I'm from," I said. "A beauty of great measure, who at the end of her life had passed into the realm of the gods with a heart filled with unwanted pain. You remind me of her."

"Right, I understand. You look at me because you think I'm pretty —"

"It's more than that," I interrupted. "This woman that I'm talking about was cast aside into the world as a child, as you were, and like you she was left to tend to her own needs with what little the earth could provide. For most of her life she knew only hunger, struggling to keep her frail body from forever becoming one with the earth. Luckily, she did survive. When she grew older she was then forced to adapt to the changing world, or rather she began to learn the skills to face the dangers of life in all its forms. She didn't join the army in her case, but she did learn how to use the bow in order to prey on the beasts of the forest. As time passed her skills grew to great heights, her arrows never missed their mark, and her belly never again crying out in hunger. This then became her downfall. After many ages her fondness towards the hunt became ravenous, and she became the maiden of death, for both beast, and man. For this reason life and death melded together until such time came when her mind could no longer tell the difference between the two. Her heart was now void, and this void numbed her soul beyond mending. Not long thereafter she died because of it, falling to this sickness just like the one you spoke of."

"Who is this woman?" Lera asked, enchanted by a tale.

"To us she is the matron of the hunt, the goddess *Emeena*," I replied. I took a second to gather my thoughts, all the while hoping that I did not appear childish to her. "Look, Lera," I added. "I know I'm just a builder whose words mean shite compared to the events of your life, but I do not think you have reached that void yet. If you need someone to talk to, then most times you can find me idling on the fringes." I stood up and gathered my journal, tucking it snuggly into my tabard. I apologised once more, and I did as if I were a boy taken by overwhelming embarrassment. "I'll leave you be," I said turning around.

Suddenly I felt Lera reach out and clutch the sleeve of my tunic. "Tell me more about your home," she said, her cheeks slightly rosy.

At this point my face was bathed in the same hue as hers, but I believe that the heat that grew in mine threatened to burn holes in my cheeks. I smiled and sat with a straightened back, where for the next hour, amid the commotion of the legionaries in the square, we spoke freely about our pasts, always keeping to tales that increased the friendly mood between us. And when Lera spoke, more than I had ever heard her do, her tongue danced like the swelling waves beneath our feet, full of newfound life and laughter, as if she had forgotten the heavy feeling that had been created between us. I do not want to seem bold, my dear reader, but I believe I had awakened something in her, a light perhaps, or a new star that was eager to cast its glow upon the darkness of the world she saw.

"You can't be serious?" Lera beamed.

"I'm completely serious," I laughed, brushing away some of the spillage of wine on my lips. Lera had nabbed a flagon for us, and we had been drinking liberally. "I swear on Andiel's life I asked for a cup of water and he gave me wine — just like this one, same taste and everything. Little did I know, however, that it was really just a cup of poison, seeing as how I was dead for a week after chugging the whole thing."

Lera laughed. "He doesn't sound much like a priest to me."

"That's exactly what I said when I first met him. He seemed more the fool."

Here I heard my name being called out from the square. I turned around, and therewith I rose to my feet with some surprise. It was Andreaus who had called out to me, seeing as how he was the only man who was walking toward us. Behind him, about a dozen yards away, I saw Meric and Jon. They were dictating orders as they stood at the cusp of a bustling host, which was the very thing that took me by surprise, for its number was beyond my expectations — I would later learn that two hundred and thirty-two additional men were secured. It was the composition of the men, however, that struck me. Firstly, there was a crowd of brawny, wedge-shaped legionaries from the Bronze Hammers. These men were out of uniform, their skin, like their garbs, was powdered in black ash as if they had been rushed to mobilize from the foundries. By the throat of the square, a hundred or so men from the same legion stood in full battle regalia, ten abreast, and as still as statues, their sergeants moving up and down the ranks in inspection. Last of all, eighty mercenary auxilia of Uthia were mustering under the command of their own captain; some loading carts with provisions, others dressing themselves in their armour.

Never before had I seen a man of Uthia, let alone one of its warriors. Because of my curious nature I committed their appearance to memory, and as I remembered it, each and all stood tall with steely frames, their eyes of blue sapphire like Lera's, for Uthia shared the same waters as Aeginas. Their skin was not as dark as the men of Kashtan, but it was made bronze by the sun, like the hue of honey. Uthian sellswords were not simply marauders in search of coin, but rather they were derived from the ranks of Uthia's army, of which Anolia was it's patron. As such, these men were clad in their foreign armour; a bronze breastplate crafted to appear like that of a muscular torso, a set of black leather greaves and vambraces, each with a series of small blade-like ridges, a shield that was shaped like a crescent moon, and lastly a head covering helmet, one that matched the colour of their cuirass, but was adorned at the very top by a crest of white feathers.

"You, builder. You're Cillian I am guessing?" Andreaus said, as he approached me.

"Yes captain, I am!" I replied as I sprung over the rail, afire with soldierly attention.

"Don't call me by my rank. You're *sodalis* to Lord Priscus."

"Yes, of course," I said with dumbfounded realisation.

"Captain Meric tells me you're quite the builder. You do well to repair wood and such?"

"I did fix the wheel of a cart yesterday," I said with a grin, thinking I was being funny. The effects of the wine were beginning to hit me, and yet I was made wholly sober, for Andreaus was staring at me as if to say that he had neither the time, nor was in the mood, to be playful. I cleared my throat and stiffened up. "Aye, I can," I added.

Andreaus stepped forward, brushing his nostrils. "Right so, how fair you with ships?"

I took in a breath with a straight face. "Well enough. I suppose."

CHAPTER 12

As told to me by Barsalus Helvius Magnus, 993 A.E - 1050 A.E.
I did not know then who Barsalus Helvius was, though this man,
a legionary of the Black Scorpion, would come to spend the greater
portion of his life alongside me. In the years after the age of war had
come to an end, Barsalus would become my most trusted student in
the craft of a builder. For this reason, over a period of many years, I
have been able to better understand what had transpired on the banks
of the Valentian, an event in our history which has since become a
fabled lesson in the struggle against evil, and the perseverance of man.
What is next to follow is this aforesaid tale, only this rendition comes
from the gatherings of a firsthand account.

The survivors of Priscus' company gathered in a cluster at
the banks of the Valentian River, the last, and largest, of the few
broadened rivers that cut through the *rex in via*. The warmth
of the late morning sun beat down upon their backs, rays of
burning light making their already drawn and sweltered faces
red. Like dogs taken with exhaustion, they fought to catch their
breaths, some collapsing to their knees to this tiredness, others
nearly drowning themselves as they took in gulps of fresh drink,
their noses near to the riverbed. Long had they been running
from the blazing fort, stopping at nothing but the dire need for a
moment's rest. In fact, they were forced to halt from more than

their exhaustion, for the path before them was barred, not only by turbulent rapids, but also because their feet were rooted in shock, a surprise born of a most unexpected sight.

"It can't be," voiced a legionary.

"Andiel spare us," said another. "Where is it? It's gone!"

Edros was at the head of the mob, his legs submerged thigh-high in the water. He turned on his heel and shouted in hopes that Priscus, who was at the rear, would hear him. "My lord Priscus!" he shouted. "The bridge it's...it's vanished!"

As Edros' words carried to the rear, the mob began to disperse in order to get a better look at what was happening. Priscus and Axle made their way to the front with Petris anchored between them, his head lifelessly slumped forward, his feet struggling to keep up with their quickened steps, his robe soaked at the neck in a ring of blood. It was here when the two of them saw what the men were agitated about, but their concern was still for Petris' safety. They laid him down upon his back, making certain that the gray, shale rock of the riverfront did not discomfort him — not that he was conscious to feel any of it. Then, as they both took in a good many life-restoring breaths of their own, they doused Petris' tongue with a splash of water and gave a last, quick inspection of the extensive burns surfacing in and around his left eye.

Petris let out a hacking cough when the water touched his throat. "Go on," he then struggled to say. "I don't...both of you. Go."

At that Priscus rose to his feet and made his way to the foot of the river, gently pushing aside the few men that stood near Edros. As he moved knee-deep into the river his face revealed the feelings that surged in his chest; anger, confusion, dismay, but most of all, betrayal. The bridge of the Valentian River was entirely gone; he was looking toward nothing more than a dozen splintered masts that poked out from the waterline. Barsalus told me that it was quite evident that the bridge had been forcefully set to ruin by the axe and not by the river's current, despite the raging waters that were known to swell the river in the warming of spring, which it was. The posts themselves had markings of a woodcutter's axe, which was in plain sight to any who were skilled in felling trees. What added more to the confusion of the whole scene was the sudden, later discovery about the dominion over the Valentian River: it fell under the charge and task of The Shield, and therefore Lord Plaucus.

"Reassurance I take it," Axle said as he moved to approach Priscus at the bank. "It's all off. First the Ascani appear south of The Shield and try to slaughter us all — and now this! Something, or someone, Priscus, does not want us to cross and make it to the fork."

Priscus remained silent for several moments, his mind in deep thought as his eyes surveilled his surroundings. As Barsalus went to take a drink of water, he was able to catch a glimpse of Priscus' expression. It appeared to him as if Priscus was studying the terrain, and for good reason I might add, being that the Valentian River had many geographical challenges apart from the river itself, and because there was no reason to assume that he and his men were free of the Ascani. The river bank, which was a little over forty yards across, was sealed amid a dense thicket, one that ran for more than two miles in every direction. And of all the few deviations the *rex in via* possessed, it just so happened that the Valentian crossing held the largest bend on the path, for the portion of the road that led to the river veered alongside the foot of a steep, wooded buff; a natural veil to anything in approach. It was clear to Barsalus that Priscus was of like mind in that there was no turning back. Crossing the river was now their only option. Their only means to put more ground between them and the creatures.

"We'd find ourselves in the Silver Bay if we try to cross this," said a voice in the crowd.

"Or drown before we do," said another. "The current is too strong!"

"Then I'd save what's left of your energy for the water if I were you," Priscus sternly said, silencing the chorus of agitated whispers. He then trudged back to the riverbank and stood before the men as they slowly gathered before him. "I want you all to listen to me," he added. "And listen well. The fire granted us an hour to spare at the most, so the Ascani are surely at our backs. Those of you who want to get out of this alive, I'd hold your tongues and do what I ask of you." Here, he removed his belt and began testing the leather by pulling at both ends. Therewith he surrendered it to Edros and added, "Everyone take off your belts, now, and give them all to Edros. We'll join them together and fashion a rope, and then tie it around each post like a waterman's line. Gnaeus, Herius, you help Edros with the rope. I'll need one man willing to cross over unclasped and secure it to position on the other side. After that we'll cross in groups of three while the rest of us form the cover."

"I'll do it," said the legionary of the Horned Eagle standing just off to Axle's side.

"My thanks," Priscus nodded. "Now, some of those posts out there are beyond repair and need replacing. Percia, Geros, Atticus, I want you to take some men and sweep the forest nearby for fallen timber, anything greater than the height of a man and sturdy enough to hold the weight. Villosus, Cassius, you take the rest and collect the largest stones that you can find beneath our feet. I want you to form a wall around us and the riverbank; in a crescent like you did with carts. Make it as high as our thighs if you can, but don't wear yourselves out. Be ready to fight."

"Aye then," Axle cried out. "I like the sound of being alive! So let's get to bloody work!"

Upon hearing Axle's stir every man in the company hurried to purpose. They removed their belts and piled them in front of Edros, who in turn began to twine them together with the help of the men around him, feeding flat ends through iron buckles with haste. Meanwhile, Priscus rushed over to assist in the surfacing of the heavy stones, much of them coming from the riverbed, others taken from the base of the buff and the forest beyond. Axle, realising his age had finally caught up with him, stood by the bank of the river dictating how best to form the defensive wall. With a new found fervour the men stacked rank upon rank of rock. The other legionaries, those tasked with the finding of timber, did well in their own right. Time and again they emerged from the forest, hoisting lengthy segments of promising wood. They stacked them in front of the sargeants for inspection and, under careful instruction, they selected the most suitable of the lot — the rest being stockpiled upon the rocks in order to strengthen the wall.

"Where the fuck is that builder when we need him," cursed one of the legionaries as he and a few others moved into the frigid water with the timber resting on their shoulders. "I swear my balls are going to turn to glass before long in this cold. I'm trained in the sword, not this, so I hope it's not too late to say that I know nothing of this craft."

"Come on. How hard can it be?" his companion boasted as they set the log upright. Then, he raised a stone above his head to drive the post into the riverbed, whereupon he struck its top end with a mighty clunk. Instead of fastening the post to the soil, the timber splintered into a dozen pieces, sending them adrift downstream.

After witnessing what had happened, another legionary, his features appearing crude and engorged by the nature of his warrior trade, pulled the soldier back to take his place. He bore the emblem of the Black Scorpion, a colour which matched his scruffy beard and thick, ragged hair. In defiance of his appearance, however, he spoke with a soft, mellow voice as he said, "It won't work that way. You can't just drive these posts into the ground with force alone. We need to dig a hole beforehand and bury about a third of it in the earth, or else they'll all shatter before you can get one to hold." He then turned to Priscus, who's attention was drawn to the commotion. At this point, Barsalus introduced himself to

Priscus and added, "If you would permit me, my lord, I can guide this work here. I have some knowledge of this craft."

Priscus agreed with a nod. Without further hindrance Barsalus began dictating the proper method of approach, which saw their task advance more easily. Even still Barsalus tells me that if I would have seen them in that moment, I would have thought them all builders. As the final post was struck to place, Edros tightened the last of the belts to the long, tawny rope coiled at his feet.

"Here, Opiter, take this end," Edros said, extending the rope to the man who volunteered to cross. "Do as I do," he added while lacing his end to the post that was erected on the bank. "Tie the knots firmly and make the line as tight you can...or we'll all be swimming down river!"

After Opiter clutched his end of the rope he leapt into the water headlong, dashing towards the first post amid the river in laborious strides. There were nine posts of worth that the rope needed to be tethered to; the first four being the ones the legionaries set to place, the rest were the remnants of the bridge. Forward he went with prudence over speed, his efforts flawless and favourable. Yet, by the time he reached the fourth post, and just when the water reached below his breast, a black feathered arrow struck the rear of his skull, its point exiting his eye. Here he fell face forward and the stream began to take him away from the company, his hand still gripped around the rope.

"Barsalus!" Priscus promptly shouted. "Grab it!"

Barsalus dropped his shield and dove into the deep end of the river, intercepting the floating corpse by the skin of his teeth. Thankfully, Barsalus was more beast than man, and so he battled the rapids with a certain confidence, even though the added weight of his mail threatened to pull him under the water. As he made his way to continue on with Opiter's task, the rattle of swishing chainmail and hair-raising shrieks echoed in approach, the sound emanating from the path behind the wooded buff. As it grew to a thunderous chime, the legionaries began forming a barricade four deep behind the wall, their shields packed tightly beside one another.

In the meantime, Priscus rushed into the river with Petris slouched upon his shoulder, straining to keep the priest's dead weight upright. He handed Petris over to Cassius and Edros, and therewith he commanded them to follow Barsalus to the other side.

"By Andiel's strength no man is to break!" Axle cried loudly, pacing crosswise at the rear of the ranks. "You will hold this bloody barricade and wait to cross at my command!"

Then, without warning, a swarm of Ascani appeared at the bend in the path. Like a black flash flood they turned around the curve and came charging across the riverbank, gnawing at the air. It was here that Priscus joined his men, and when he did Axle unsheathed his sword and pressed his shoulder up against the man in front of him. "Brace yourselves!" he roared.

Altogether the Ascani surge violently smashed into the shield wall with a thud. With that, some of the creatures in the first row fell dead to swift legionary stabs, while a good many others were crushed at the knee, for they were pressed up against the stone wall by the sheer momentum of the charge. On they came, but strike after strike Anolian swords found their mark, from which hosts of Ascani limbs burst asunder, sending globs of blood and chunks of flesh into the air, free and plentiful. Even in exhaustion the men held their ground for a long while, but the battle had begun to turn to Ascani favour. As the corpses of the Ascani began to pile upon the wall in high stacks, they allowed the enemy to climb by the half-dozen over the legionaries at several segments along the barricade. More than a few of our men in the first rank were cut down before the second and third ranks could alternate their position, which made it increasingly difficult to take a breath.

By now Barsalus had completed the task of affixing the line. He called out from the opposite bank, prompting Axle to send the second group to dare the crossing. Under volleys of black arrows the legionaries gradually traversed the rapids, and thereafter each subsequent group did so in their own turn upon Axle's command; the archers having been those first to crossover in order to provide cover with what few arrows they had left.

Here, the Ascani grew more bold in their attack. They pressed forward with all their fury and attempted to break through the barricade's center, because now the gaps in the line had widened considerably, not to mention that the line itself had been pushed some yards back from the wall. The arc began to buckle as well, forcing Priscus and Axle to run about the rear of the line and cut down the creatures passing through before they could pursue the men in the water. Their swords were quickly made red with Ascani blood, but as six more legionaries hit the ground dead the whole of the barricade suddenly collapsed, whereupon the men fought by the pair, ankle deep in the river, and outnumbered by the double.

Priscus ducked under the swing of a spiked club and brought the weight of his sword across his assailant's belly. "Axle!" he shouted as he brushed away the blanket of wet hair from his face. "Go! Go now! While there's still time!"

"And what? Leave you here?" Axle replied in the midst of battle. "Not a chance!"

"We cannot both fall here!" Priscus added. "Leave! And sever the line—"

All of a sudden a black figure appeared hurtling down towards him with immense speed, striking a well placed blow across his jaw. Priscus fell into the river upon his backside, his body taken beneath the water. He remained there, not from the blow, but because he was now firmly pinned to the riverbed by the two horrid hands that squeezed at his throat.

Of course, my dear reader, only the gods truly know what Priscus was feeling in this moment. But, as the tale goes, a tightness rose in his chest as the last of his breath coursed through him. He stirred wildly, endeavouring to release himself from the creature's hold, but his strength, ever faltering, paled in likeness to his foe's. And so little by little the echoes of the battle grew fainter in Priscus' ear while a dark haze began to devour the light in his bloodshot eyes. His time as a mortal lord was ending, his life coming to a close under Far-Skafa's gaze, which was hardened with delight.

All at once Priscus gained new strength as if the fire of *Polemos* ignited in his heart. He pressed his thumbs into Far-Skafa's eyes with a last effort, but the fiend only recoiled slightly, almost as if he were unfazed, for to him there was no strength to his action. It was then when, from the rim of his blurred sight, Priscus saw the silhouette of a man bearing down towards Far-Skafa. Naturally, there was nothing much else he could do but keep the creature's attention on him, but even with all his new found might the creature caught wind of the man's approach. In any event, Priscus' saviour managed to break Far-Skafa's straddling hold with the force of a battering ram, which sent his body soaring some yards along the riverbank.

Priscus hitched up on one arm, finally released from the clutch of death and taking in a great many deep breaths. The clamour and stench of the dead and dying came to him all at once, very intensely and sickening in its sting. He rose to his feet uneasily and he swept the riverbank in search of Far-Skafa, but at every sharp glance he could not spot the masked Ascani. He frantically looked around in search of a weapon, his eye spotting the silver glimmer of a sword under the ripples of the water, which he leapt for. Thank the gods that he did, because when he turned on his heel he saw Far-Skafa standing ten feet before him, tearing off his drenched sheepskin overvest and tossing it into the river. Here, Priscus readied his guard and held a heavy foot, at which point Far-Skafa spoke, only this time in the tongue of the underworld.

"Save that shite for your master," Priscus replied through gritted teeth.

Far-Skafa let loose a shrill cry and lunged at him with an overhead strike, his dual blades meeting the width of Priscus' steel. The force behind Far-Skafa's blow was too great for his aching body, so Priscus buckled in pain and collapsed to one knee, desperately pushing back his assailant's powerful thrusts. Again and again the creature continued to fervently thrash his swords, but by the grace of Axle's sudden appearance Far-Skafa quickly backed away, readying a new stance for which to engage both of his Anolian attackers.

Priscus and Axle threw themselves to the mercy of *Polemos*, thrusting at Far-Skafa with what strength they had left between them. Even so, Far-Skafa's stupendous dexterity and blinding blur of strikes thwarted their coordinated attacks, allowing him to heave and hurl them around like fatigued students first learning the skills of the sword. Back and forth upon the riverbank they fought, until with a last spurt of brutal force Far-Skafa got a hold of Axle's hair, twisting it roughly as he swiftly jabbed Priscus to the ground.

Far-Skafa elevated the point of his blade above Axle's chest. "You die…first—"

In that instant a white-feathered Anolian arrow whizzed over Priscus' head and planted itself in Far-Skafa's thigh. The creature shrank back in pain, whereupon he let go of his gripping hold of Axle's hair. A slew of the same arrows soared across the sky and crashed into the mass of Ascani still making their way over the mounds of corpses upon the wall, each and all adding to the heap of dead. It was here when, from across the river, the blaring sound of numerous buccina filled the air. One hundred legionaries bearing the mark of the Stone Fortress emerged from the woodland in charging haste behind their captain, who was on horseback. Rank after rank of silver helmets gathered on the opposing bank, forming hollow squares so that the archers at their centers would rain down destruction while a vanguard of infantry stormed into the rushing water, their shields high over their heads as they filed along the rope.

Amid the chaos Far-Skafa vanished into the swarm of Ascani who were now in full retreat. As more and more legionaries made the crossing, the enemy drifted deeper into the forest, a good many scrambling for their lives around the bend in which they came, a portion of them falling to the precise aim of our archers. Meanwhile, the captain on horseback appeared beside Priscus and Axle as he exited the river on his mount. In his hand he held the standard of his legion, which he used to slay the Ascani that rushed towards him.

"Sound the horn of advance," he cried. "We're going after them."

"No!" Priscus broke in, limping towards him with Axle's support.

"My Lord Priscus!" he said, eyes wide. "Athanas! Get the healer over here, quickly!"

"Recall your men, captain," Priscus said through exhausted breaths.

"But my lord...Lord Plaucus would want—"

"They're gone, leave them!" Priscus crudely interrupted, as he crumbled to his knees. He spit a wad of blood out in front of him, his teeth veiled in the scarlet viscous. "Do what I say," he added, looking up at him with a livid stare. "As for your lord, don't worry, I'll have a word with him."

CHAPTER 13

The repair of the Captain Andreaus' ship had cost us some long hours, though by the morrow of our departure from the Isle of Ore we had arrived at the fork — otherwise known as the grounds before the southern face of Andiel's Shield, or more precisely the end of the *rex in via*. It was here that news of the horrible events that had befallen Priscus' company spread like wildfire amongst the ranks of our motley army, numbering four hundred and eight at my count; ninety-four of the original company having fallen even before we had reached the first of our intended marks. The news came to us not by word of mouth, but from a harrowing sight, for upon our arrival we were greeted by rows of beaten and battered legionnaires who lay about in many makeshift hospices on the side of the roadway. And to add to our shock, a violent quarrel erupted between Priscus and Plaucus; an argument of accusation and suspicion, which at its most heated point turned into a blatant contest of curses.

Nothing was clear to me at this moment, though as the raging quarrel unfolded, Jon, Meric, Lera, and I, along with Andreaus and his men, made our way through the grounds and hospices before the gatehouse of The Shield in assistance of the wounded. The sky that had been brightened with the morning sun had now given way to many gray clouds, and from this veil came a misty rain, gradually turning the dry mud beneath our feet into a blanket of wet clay, almost like that of an earthen marsh that was thick enough to turn any easy task into a lengthier endeavour.

I will, soon enough, indulge you with the description of Andiel's Shield so as to educate my foreign readers. But first, I must speak to the quarrel that I witnessed firsthand, which seized my complete focus above the many other pressing events happening around us.

I first saw Plaucus as he approached the banister of the oaken scaffold that was affixed to the south tower of the gatehouse. And though he was high above us, I could still see the way he stiffened his limbs and clenched his hands in anger, standing very erect with his bony chest puffed out, eager to display some semblance of assertion.

"How dare you speak to me in such a way, you cur!" he shouted as he slammed his fist on the rail. "As I have said many times I know nothing of what you speak, of these war parties and of this masked Ascani creature you're on about. I have been clear on the matter, have I not? And still you push my limits. More than that, instead of informing me about this enemy, you seek to align me with it!"

"I speak only as such to swine and vermin, and to cowards like you Plaucus. A lord whose lordship is of no value to this realm," Priscus replied in equal measure, digging his feet into the wet ground as he looked up at him. "Do you know how many men have died? How many have fallen because you seem to never know what goes on in your own lands? Why don't you come down here, Plaucus, and have a look at what your falseness has done! Come here and see what your treachery has committed! And if it is not by your treachery then it is your negligence that has put the realm at risk, for not since the time of the Conjuror have the Ascani roamed ours lands as far as Lord Titus' fort, or set foot in the waters of the Valentian — you waste of a man!"

"Watch your tongue, brother of the king, for if not I will have you in chains!"

Priscus took a step forward with his hands out in surrender, "Here!" he cried in an explosion of rage — the last time I would ever see him do so in such a manner. "Go on, you murderous rat! Finish what you started and bind my hands yourself, for I'd rather spend the rest of my life in a dungeon if it sees the people of this realm free from your horseshit!"

Plaucus heaved tremulously. "Horseshit? Why you —"

On the instant of his fuming rebuttal Plaucus stopped short, because the creaking hinges of a door opening seized both his tongue and his passion. From my view I could not see the door, yet I knew that the sound arose from the shadow of the scaffold, just around the corner of the tower. "Is this truly what has become of our young lords?" a voice then said over the shuffle of light footsteps. "How far we have fallen, I'd say."

I handed Lera the bolt of bandages that I was using upon the wounded man before us, and then walked off, my curiosity drawing me closer to the quarrel. It was here that Lord Ulcar made his appearance, but in truth, fair reader, I guessed that it was him, since it was apparent to me by the haughtiness in his tone. In the time that it took him to shuffle his way to Plaucus, I took the opportunity to join Priscus at his side, a couple of steps behind him to be more exact. And there, with a hard-nosed stare, I watched the old man stop beside Plaucus, appearing as though he was his patron preparing to partake in his defence.

"Lord Ulcar?" Priscus exclaimed, surprised. "I did not know you were here."

"Well I do not see how you would have known that I was, my lord Priscus," Ulcar said with a grin. "You have only just arrived... and in a hot temper it seems." Ulcar then snapped his fingers, calling for one of the two monstrous guards of his own legion to place an overcoat on his shoulders. "But if your meaning, my lord, is that you did know of *my* being here, then I must say that it was the good Lord Plaucus who invited me to stay with him. You see, minds such as ours tend to gather when the passing of time is concerned — especially for someone long in years as I am."

"Your arm," Priscus said while pointing to Ulcar's cast. "I see it is not any fairer."

"Oh this!" Ulcar replied, looking down to his forearm as if he had forgotten that he was infirm. "I'm afraid not. I am told by the healers that I will be like this for a good while longer. As a matter of fact, this arm is part of the reason I am here if you can believe it. At any rate, it gets better as the days pass. My thanks for your concern."

"That's good to hear. But perhaps we can speak more of this later after I —"

"Yes about that," Ulcar interrupted. "I'm not one to interfere in the troubles of others, but I could not help but overhear the quarrel between the two of you. I have to say Lord Priscus that you front quite the charge here. Granted, I think we all know by now that your heart is too big for this small world, and as such you've never been one to stifle its passions. But please why don't we all cool our tongues, yeah? I'm sure we can find the truth, or the falsity, in these claims with more kind hearted words."

"The truth has already been presented," Priscus said, straight-faced. "It's all around me."

"You see!" Plaucus blurted. "He is without shame!"

Ulcar gently held up his hand to his chest, silencing Plaucus from speaking any further. "To be sure my friend, but right now we must forgive Lord Priscus' temper, for he is not simply weary from *a* battle, but from two battles, as I overheard. Both of which I do so happen to agree are rightly and undeniably suspicious, and that do deserve our immediate seeing to." He turned to Plaucus with a sort of discontent in his eyes, upon which he began to speak to him patronizingly. "I must say Plaucus, I am rather disappointed in you. Of all the lords of Anolia that have held your charge in these last thousand years, I never thought that it would be under your leadership that the Ascani would roam freely in our kingdom as they did in Andiel's time. And with that being said, I think I have to agree with Lord Priscus when he says that you never seem to know what is happening within your own lands. So, my friend, if I were you, and if you haven't already done so, I would send my scouts in search of these creatures, so that they do not cause any more damage. That would be my first priority. My next focus would be to figure out how these creatures breached these walls, if they did. Find the source, and find your answer. A sensible plan don't you think, Plaucus?"

Plaucus nodded. "Yes I —"

"Now to you Lord Priscus," Ulcar continued, directing his attention to him, "I must say that although you give an almost convincing argument of this man's quality, I can assure you there is no treachery here. I have been a guest of Lord Plaucus since last we met at the king's hall. And to my embarrassment, I have kept him by my side all this time with much talk, and no time for plotting, you see. I cannot speak for the sudden appearance of the Ascani warband, but the bridge on the Valentian was a matter already known to us since the waters of spring had finally weakened its roots some days ago; yet another issue I thought Plaucus had the sense to see to in good time."

At this point Ulcar moulded his loose robes to fashion a hooded cloak, which he used to cover his head from the heightening rainfall. Then with another snap of his fingers he summoned his guards for assistance, and therewith he moved with frailty toward the doorway from whence he came with Plaucus following close behind like a pet. "Forgive me for my leave but if I don't get out of this rain I will finally crumble. I will make sure the good Plaucus here sees that the last of these creatures wander no further. On that I give you my word. Now, however, you should see to your quest, Priscus. It has already seen the point of a sword and much delay. Only the gods now could defer it any further."

"The gods expedite it, actually," Priscus said, causing them to stop. "They bless it even by having you here with us. You see up until now I thought they had already abandoned it, but here they have sent you to impart your wisdom and clarity where its needed."

"I am but an instrument as all men are," Ulcar grinned.

"Good then I will speak no more of my untrusting thoughts and end with the king's orders," Priscus added, gripping their focus. "Do you recall, Lord Ulcar, the instructions King Adeanus put to parchment? Specifically the one that was meant for Plaucus? I only ask such a question so that you can confirm another truth for us."

"Forgive me, my lord, but I don't understand," Ulcar answered. "Apparently we are at war, so to my knowledge there were many letters written. Would you care to be a little more specific as to which you are referring."

"Aye there were, but as I said this one was addressed to Lord Plaucus; spoken aloud to all, in the allotment of one of his cohorts from the twentieth to be placed under my command. A thing that would have been told him in person if not for his hasty exit at the council."

"You want me to give you five hundred men! Are you mad?" Plaucus exploded. "First you dare insult me with charges of lies and deceit to our kingdom, and now you expect the men of my legion to follow you on this...this quest of self-destruction!"

"Andiel's mercy enough," Ulcar said, abating Plaucus' ire. "Have you not had enough? Or should we add treason to this growing list of charges?" Ulcar then turned to Priscus and nodded in agreement. "Unfortunately I was with Plaucus on his hasty exit, so I did not hear the King's orders. Nevertheless, produce the written command to me and the men will be yours. I'll have my own guards rally them."

A sudden heat gripped Priscus. "I no longer have it," he said slowly.

"What's that now?" Ulcar replied, hard of hearing.

"The scroll... it was abandoned to the fire as I fled Lord Titus' fort."

"Well," Plaucus chuckled, clapping his hands together in amusement, "isn't that a pity."

Without a second look Plaucus vanished through the doorway with an expression which suggested that there was no further discussion to be had on the matter. Meanwhile Ulcar, equally impassive, seemed to be more in a hurry to get out of the rain than to challenge an issue he thought was very well absurd. "Well there you have it," Ulcar said, his head tucked into his shoulders. "I'm sorry, Priscus, but you know our laws. Each lord does what he wills with his legion, save for the King's direct command. And since you no longer have the King's word, I cannot intervene on this matter." Ulcar then put one foot around the bend of the tower and paused for a brief moment. "I do hope you find your way my lord, and quickly too. But like I said I think for now it's best you don't stand too long in the rain," he added, while passing through the door. "You'll catch your death in it."

Priscus, faced with a sudden wave of silence, sunk his chin to his shoulder. I could not see the expression in his eyes because his wet hair was lining the side of his face closest to me, but I knew he was trying hard to pacify thoughts of anger, since his lips twitched, as if he were muttering curses to himself.

"Priscus?" I said concerned, placing my hand on his shoulder.

"See to Petris," he quickly replied, as a nearby bell began to chime its midday tune.

He drew up the sleeves of his tunic to his elbows, and walked off hastily to assist a wounded legionary being carried off by a stretcher. I, on the other hand, stood alone before the gatehouse for a few moments longer, where my mind tried to comprehend what was to come given the way things had just fallen apart. I tried to make sense of it, but I could not fathom how in a mere moment the voice of a bitter lord saw the King's words to thin air, plunging the aim of our task into deeper, unnecessary hardship.

***

For much of the afternoon I wandered about, searching every apothecary's shop and healer's kiosk for fresh bandages so that Lera and I could continue dressing Petris' numerous wounds, which were in very rough shape. Back and forth I scuttled like a mouse, from Petris' bedside to any place amid the crowded hamlet adjacent to the gatehouse that showed some promise of having what few pieces of twill and linen I was able to gather. Each new venture my pace slowed considerably, seeing as how there was nowhere else in the vicinity I could go searching without needing a horse. As such, I found myself upon the ramparts with hopes of entreating the tower guards for their healer's supplies, which I knew very well would cost me all of the fingers on my hands on top of the ridiculous sum of silver they would surely squeeze out of my pocket. And of course I was right about the price, so I would be left with nothing.

It was here, however, that I had finally come to a full stop, my clothes saturated by the rain, my eyes wide as I had come to discover how truly majestic the fortress wall of Andiel's Shield was, especially now from my view of it high upon the battlements. As promised, I will now detail this fortress so named, Andiel's Shield, so that my foriegn readers who are unfamiliar with it will have a clearer sense of the setting of this portion of the story. And with that being said, I will begin by stating that like many of the other ancient strongholds in the realm, Andiel's Shield was built to match the glory of the Anolian Empire at the closing of the Great Ascani War, which made it not only archaic, but also a relic of our Anolian ancestors. To me, I have always seen it to be a bastion in its own right, a castle if you will, though in truth The Shield differs from its counterparts because it's the only fortress in the kingdom that takes the form of a single, continuous wall that runs for twenty eight leagues from the Silver Bay to the borders of Lake Maria, separating the edges of Valentia, the southern realm, from the lush fields of the Greenlands, the northern realm. Five days it would take a man to walk across the wall from end to end, all the while traversing some two hundred wide and soaring towers that studded it's breadth, and each whose top was adorned by the legionary standard of the Stone Fortress.

On this day a heavy wind had risen alongside the rain, and so one could look up and see the standards caught high in their flutter. In terms of manpower, seven thousand legionaries formed the garrison of The Shield, each and all under the command of Lord Plaucus, as I previously noted. As it was in Andiel's time, the men of the Stone Fortress were spread out along the wall by means of chaining one company to the next at equidistance, so that no enemy could scale at any point. Never once had the Ascani set foot upon the ramparts, nor had they ever passed through the gate, of which there was only one at the very center of the wall. It is at this gate, my fair reader, where Plaucus and Priscus quarreled, and where I was now standing. The gatehouse, to say lightly, was nearly the size of a castle's keep, its bronze doors reaching twenty feet high, its towers squared and armed with the engines of war, and its rooms and halls so plentiful that a thousand men could rest their heads unconfined — not that Plaucus cared to offer his lesser men that luxury. Speaking of splendor, the men of the Stone Fortress were also guarded by the two massive, bronze plated equestrian statues of Aitas and Arillis, Andiel's two eldest sons. The statues flanked the road leading out of the gate's north end, staring upon the battlefield of the final campaign of the great war, where the two brothers had come together as equals and had finally defeated the armies of the Conjuror.

A chill inhabited every part of my body as I gazed upon their figures, feeling as if I could spend the entire day in their presence, absorbed in our history. But before my thoughts could be carried away too high into the clouds, I remembered why I was standing on the ramparts. I mingled with the last few guards that were patrolling the gatehouse and secured from them a last dressing, whereupon I hurried back to the pavilion in which Petris rested, and where I had left Lera to watch over him.

"Here," I said, tossing a bundle of scrap cloth to Lera just as I burst into the pavilion. I rushed over and knelt by Petris' bedside, quickly washing my hands in the pail of water that rested by the head of the cot. "Sorry...it's all I could find. It seems Lord Plaucus' command to stay clear of us has spread quickly, and to the common folk as well."

"Still took you long enough," Lera said. "I can't get the bleeding to stop under his eye."

"How many times do I have to tell you, there isn't much else you can do until it stops on its own," Meric broke in half asleep. He was laying on a broken cot that was nestled in the corner by the entrance of the pavilion, his body curled up under a thin blanket like an infant searching for its hidden warmth. "Look, if you can get yours hands on some honey it'll help with the binding of the wound or some shite — or find yourself some blood moss. It's green in colour and it's what Petris uses on us when we get all cut up." He turned over to face the opposite direction to return to sleep. "And for Andiel's sake I wouldn't talk so close to his damn ear. He'll wake. And then you'll have many more troubles with the bleeding if he does."

"Moss?" I said, disbelievingly. "You want me to go outside and collect moss?"

"Not just any, builder. It's a special type," Meric replied. "Any healer's shop would have it."

I lurched forward to assist Lera as she began washing Petris' face. "Well it doesn't matter now. All the healers shops are closed and everyone else is too scared to sell us anything. And I can't get anything from the armoury, lest I steal it."

My fingers brushed up against Lera's hand as I gently removed the blood soaked bandage from Petris' wound. In normal circumstances, when being near Lera, my face would have turned to a scarlet hue, though there was no time for sheepish behaviour, since a sudden squirt of blood had spurt onto my chest as soon as I lifted the cloth. The tent, however, was so ill-lit that I could barely make out where the blood was coming out from. In fact, the entirety of our accommodation, the pavillion that is, was very raw in its comfort, because as I had previously alluded to, Plaucus, in all his bitterness towards Priscus, had made certain that none in our company was to be given admission in occupying any of his legionary quarters, especially those vacant within the gatehouse. Instead, we had made our camp in haste on the fringes of the hamlet, rather deep in the fields where the wind blew more feverishly. And for this reason, the tent often shook by the battering of this wind, where cool drafts easily found their way underneath the canopy, always threatening to snuff the heart of what light we could find, two wrought-iron lanterns whose candles were all but spent.

"I'll change the dressings one last time," I said.

The light in Lera's eyes flashed as she quickly intercepted the fresh cloth that I was bringing over. "No, let me," she said, not knowing that she had completely enveloped my hands with hers. Then, when she finally realised what she had done, she cleared her throat and slowly removed her warm grip to the slow cadence of the persistent rain thumping upon the pavilion's covering. "I mean," she added, uncharacteristically timid. "You've done plenty for him already, so I'll take care of this."

"As you wish," I said, my stomach in a growing knot.

It was at this point when Priscus, Axle, Jon, and Andreaus barged into the pavilion in single file, slowly and carefully, like thieves making certain they were not being followed. In reality they were thieves, because they had stolen quite a few items from the barracks: a small squared table, three chairs, a bundle of fresh candle sticks along with their holders, and some food. They placed their bounty to order by the center mast, whereupon Priscus summoned us all to gather around the table — though Meric remained sitting upright in his cot, groggy.

"Come Cillian," Priscus said. "We have much to discuss and we haven't much time."

I did as he commanded, placing myself sidelong to Axle, who was sitting beside Andreaus at the wing of the table. He had a white feathered quill in his hand, and he was carefully guiding it's point upon a piece of parchment as though he were an artisan etching an illustration. It appeared from the corner of my eye as though he was finishing up an existing work. I moved in for a better look, and there I saw a grand illustration of a good many beautifully drawn landforms; rivers, forests, mountains passes, all of which were drafted identically to the map of Northfleet that I had seen, or rather just the natural surroundings which led to the fortress.

"It's done!" Axle said, sprinkling a helpful amount of pounce across his work.

After a moment Priscus folded the parchment to a square and stuffed the piece in his tabard. Then, rather unusually, he brought to sight the map of Northfleet; the original I mean to say, its face browned by the fire it had escaped. He flattened the map across the table and positioned four stones atop its curled corners, all whilst Jon placed his hulking frame in front of the pavilion's doorway so that no unsuspecting visitors could stumble in unannounced. It could not have been more clear that they all intended to keep this next discussion a secret to unwanted listeners, which gave me the impression that Priscus was not at all interested in discussing the reasons for it. As such I kept quiet, at which time Priscus began speaking in an earnest voice.

"Right," Priscus said, his eyes trailing to different points on the map. "From here on we'll have to continue as best we can with what provisions we have. If we go by Lord Kaeso's time frame then we have no more than thirty days to make the journey to the fortress before the Ascani make their descent from the eastern peak. If we are lucky, and that's quite the large if, the endeavour will grant us a little more time when we get there to prepare our

defences. However, make no mistake that our objective now is to get there even before they reach the peak." He placed his finger on the map and began guiding it along a northerly route. "As I see it, our best course for speed would be to take the ancient road of the *via externa*...over here, up until the borders of the hinterlands. From there, we'll arc west, close enough to Linlani territory where the plains are flat, which would then put us in a good position to move into the forest crossing at its western entrance. Another three day journey after that."

"No offence to our friend, my lord," Andreaus said. "But are you sure you want to march so close to Linlani territory. Could be dangerous, seeing as how we'd be armed to the teeth. It could cause a misunderstanding if the Linlani see us in the column. They aren't the diplomatic type."

"Linlani will not fight," Jon said. "If we don't attack first."

"He's right," Axle added, giving Jon a nod. "We'll find no trouble with the border tribes as long as we keep to the rim, and to the east side of the Argarian Woods. What I am more worried about, however, is the Ascani war packs that roam that area. Let's not forget the western plains trail all the way down to the Gates of Pindus, and since those gates are under siege, as Lord Aulus has said, then it is very likely we'll come across their reinforcements marching their way to the gates. And now that I think of it, they will be small armies over packs, judging by the numbers Aulus had claimed."

"It's just another risk we'll have to take," Priscus said. He paused for a moment and looked at each of us individually. "Look, none of us really know what we will encounter on the road, or even when we arrive at our mark. The best we can do now is simply prepare for whatever challenge we may come to face, which starting now will be our main focus. So, I want every man who is able to walk or shamble, in proper form, all weapons and armour accounted for, and rations enough for an additional two weeks. We are lucky to have what supplies Meric's group brought back,

but that supply will last us ten days at the most. So listen here, and pass this message along to the sargeants. I don't care if you have to beg, loot, or steal for more, just make sure we have enough to last the journey across the hinterlands, because there may very well be nothing to gather or any game to hunt." Priscus straightened his back. "Captain Andreaus, make sure you will delegate these orders to your men, and be certain that the Uthians are also clear to our aim. Meric will do the same for our men. And Lera, listen clearly. You're the only experienced scout among us, so I want you to study this map and remember it thoroughly, for once we pass the borders into the hinterlands you will be our guide."

"Yes, my lord," she nodded.

"And what happens if we encounter him," Axle voiced, ushering in a sudden silence. We all looked at him, confused. "I am of course referring to the creature. The masked Ascani. What is the plan if we encounter him again?"

I swallowed nervously as the image of the creature entered my mind.

"Twice now he's crossed paths with us," Axle went on. "At the fort, and at Easteria, wherefrom, I imagine, the sard's been tracking us. He calls himself Far-Skafa if anyone was wondering, and according to Priscus here, the bastard can actually speak some of our words. If you could believe it." Here a discussion broke out, where Axle spoke at length about Far-Skafa, on the suspected leadership within the Ascani, at which point it had become all too clear that this creature was in fact something similar to a *primorus*, if not one entirely.

"It doesn't matter," Priscus said, ending the discussion short. "I hate to be the one to say it, but from here on out that creature's path is aligned with ours. If that bastard still lives, then I know pretty well where we'll see him next. There isn't much we can do about it, but move as if he is at our backs."

"Not just this creature's path," Andreaus said. "Plaucus' as well." Andreaus reclined in his chair with his arms folded, the shadow of the flame's flicker dancing under his eyes. "It's not my place to speak on the man's loyalties, but you really boiled his blood to a point this morning, my lord. If by chance Plaucus is truly what you say he is, then I think our first concern will be figuring out how to leave this place without the risk of falling into another one of his snares. I don't want to see more of our men, my men, die before they even step on the other side of these walls. We need every man if we are going to complete this task, now more than ever after denying you his men."

"Plaucus wouldn't dare touch us here," Axle said. "If we are to believe that he is against us, then I'm sure his next move will be to bide his time until we are more than a day or two from The Shield. More than that, let us hope to the gods that he is not, somehow, in league with that masked creature, lest he directs him to our trail. Then again, Plaucus has always been the spineless type, especially when it comes to dealing with the Ascani. I imagine he'd more likely cower in horror at the sight of the beast rather than align himself with it, which makes this whole situation difficult to foretell."

"All the same," Andreaus said. "We need some sort of a plan of our exit."

I stepped forward, pressed by a sudden thought. "I have an idea. We can blind him."

"What? You want one of us to gouge his eyes out?" Meric said, as he stood up with a stout stretch.

"Of course not," I replied. "I mean, why don't we just leave tonight? In the dark and in the shadows. If we leave without informing him that we are doing so then it'll *blind* him to our position from the very start. He won't know where we are when he becomes aware of it, and so we can lose him on the road. And if he is as much of a coward as you say he is, then he won't dare follow us blindly, especially in open country."

"It's not that easy, Cillian," Andreaus said. "It can't be done."

"Not with that attitude," Meric said. "I think the builder is on to something."

"If we so much as move toward the gate the guards would call for him," Andreaus added.

"What about Lera then?" Meric said, pointing at her with the butt of his knife. He had begun to feast on the food that they had brought in.

"What about me?" she replied.

"You're light on your feet, are you not? And stealthy," he went on, cutting into a half-rotten apple. "You can put that skill of yours to use by sneaking your way into the gatehouse, at which point you subdue, or kill, the guards. Whatever your preference." He stuffed his mouth with a thick piece of the fruit, quickly spitting it out. "After that, when you're done and ready to go, you signal us from the tower, then you open the gate, and then all of us pass through to the other side. Simple, fast, and effective."

"You want me to subdue, or kill, over fifty men all by myself?" Lera said, dumfounded.

Meric ran his fingers through his hair. "Well, I can help if you'd like."

"We can have one of theirs do it for us?" Axle interjected. "Open the gate, I mean."

"Aye. It's already set to plan," Priscus replied, his attention drawn to the doorway.

Not a moment after Priscus finished speaking the chime of clinking chainmail rose in approach of the tent, loudly, as if the wearer were rushing to overcome his tardiness. Priscus then waved Jon away from the doorway with a short nod, and as Jon stepped to the side of the drapery, a chilling breeze blew into the pavilion from the entry. A tall, barrel-chested legionary captain entered the pavilion, at which point he placed his hand over his heart and gave a formal bow in recognition of Priscus' lordship. "Captain Cimber, my lord," he introduced himself, standing firmly at attention, like the statues I had seen. "I just now received word that you asked to see me?"

"Be as you were, captain," Priscus said. "There is no need for decorum."

Cimber relaxed his poise, arms interlocked at his back. "I hope I haven't kept you waiting."

"No," Priscus said quite cordially, as he began rolling the map of Northfleet to a scroll. "As a matter of fact, you are right on point for the hour. But first, captain," he added, handing the scroll to Axle as he gazed up and down Cimber's uniform, "I take it your instruction is going well?"

"My lord?" Cimber said with slight confusion.

"Your clothes, captain, They're completely covered in filth."

Cimber looked down to his tabard and trousers with a jolt of embarrassment. "Ah, of course, forgive me," he said, just as he noticed that he was nearly covered head to toe in blotches of wet mud. "Mud fighting," he went on. "It might seem strange, but here at The Shield we brawl in the mud when the weather turns sour — as it has. It's become sort of a tradition in the twentieth, and we use it as a form of instruction so that the men can learn how to fight in these conditions, a lesson in the endurance of battle if you will, should it ever come to it. But, my lord, if I'm being honest, I tend to have them fight each other as a means to incite their spirits with contest. It works more often than not for their spirits, and it stops them from drinking so much."

"Just because the instructions are full of cheer doesn't mean they aren't learning anything," Priscus said, gently leaning against the edge of the table. He crossed his arms and took in a breath. "If *I'm* being honest, captain, I think it's the mark of a good leader. Those of us that are in command of another's life should never forget that it is also the mind of a soldier, and not just his flesh, which needs to be seasoned. I know they are still fighting, but having your men be a part of something other than direct battle, at least from time to time, is a good way to mend those spirits that may come to break."

"Well, my lord Priscus, I cannot be that good of a leader," Cimber chuckled. "I am, after all, disobeying Plaucus' orders to stay clear of you — an order that I myself had set in motion."

"And yet here you are. Why is that?"

"It's not in me to deny the command of a lord when it is given."

"But I am not your lord."

"I respect all who hold the title, especially the one who's also the king's brother."

Priscus smiled. "Whatever your cause I am glad you're here. I only thought it right to get to know the man who saved my men at the Valentian. I think it's safe to say that without you and yours, we would've been overrun, and a lot more would've fallen — if not all of us. You have our gratitude, captain."

Cimber bowed his head with pleasure. "We saw the fire's glow from here, so we set out. All I could say is that in the end we performed our duties, nothing more. I'm just content to know that the gods allowed us to arrive when we did." Here Cimber noticed Jon standing behind him. Then, behind Jon, he saw Meric, which was starting to make him feel uncomfortable, or so his expression led me to believe. He cleared his throat. "If that was all you wanted to see me for, my Lord Priscus, I'd better —"

"There was *one* another matter that I wanted to speak to you about," Priscus interrupted with civility. He stood upright and took a short step forward, his pleasantries overtaken by an air of seriousness. "Tell me, captain, who commands the gate tonight when the moon is at its highest?"

"Tonight? That would be me, my lord," Cimber replied, mystified.

"Wonderful," Priscus said. "If that's the case then I'll need to ask something of you. I'll need you to see my force through the gate on your watch."

At that moment Cimber's courteous air turned to one of bewilderment. I will tell you, dear reader, that we were all taken aback by his direct and rather aggressive request especially given the plans we had just discussed. It brought an awkward silence that begged to be severed. Priscus did not seem to be bothered by it, neither did Axle for that matter.

"I'm not following," Cimber said. "Are you not set to depart at dawn?"

"Yes, we are," Axle said. "But I think it would be better for all of us if we left tonight."

"Preferably unannounced," Andreaus added.

Cimber's confusion increased. "Forgive me, Lord Priscus, but does any of this have to do with the disagreement this morning with my Lord Plaucus? If I'm allowed to speak plainly for a moment, then I would like to assure you that he is not what you suggest. Every man here knows that he lacks the courage of the sword, I'll give you that. But in the fifteen years that I have served under his charge, I've known him to be a man of good heart for the most part, with no treachery to be had. He means well, he's just not the same as you and the other lords."

"I am well passed my grievances with your lord, captain," Priscus answered, calmly. "My thoughts now are forward-looking and clear in their intent." Priscus advanced himself and firmly placed a hand on Cimber's shoulder, looking straight into his eyes. "Look, captain, I understand what I ask of you appears misguided. I do not mean this to be an act of deceit on your part if that's your fear. It's only a matter of seeing us press on with our task sooner rather than later. And besides, Plaucus has clearly expressed that he wants us gone as soon as possible, so in effect I'm granting his wish. All I ask is that you see us on our way. Unless that is you mean to tell me that today is the day that you deny a lord's request?"

"No...I just...I just think the secrecy is troubling," Cimber said. "Lord Plaucus —"

"All I mean is that we shouldn't bother him any further with this task of mine. Like I said, captain, Lord Plaucus wants the lot of us gone. And judging by our last encounter, I believe he'd probably think it an answer from the gods when he wakes and finds that we've already departed and stopped breathing his precious air. Don't you agree?" Cimber waved off his stare as if to drive off a bothersome thought. "So, captain," Priscus added as he removed his clutch. "Your answer?"

Cimber replied with a tentative nod, though I must say that his poise was sufficient enough to know that he fully agreed to go along with Priscus' request. He then turned to face the doorway with the intent to leave, at which point Priscus stopped him once more by asking aloud if he would be so kind as to keep Petris in good care at The Shield. It was no surprise that Pretis would remain behind, seeing as how any forced movement would surely end his life. Cimber stole a glance of the sleeping priest, nodding with heartfelt compliance. Soon after he was gone, inviting another chilling breeze in to take his place.

"Ten silver coins says he's on his way to Plaucus," Meric said.

"I don't think so," Priscus said while removing his tabard and mail vest.

"And how is it that you are so certain?" I asked him. "I'm not taking the wager, but Meric is right. He's probably on his way to inform Plaucus as we speak. I mean, you all heard what he said about the man. Took him but a second to come to his defence. And worse than that the man's loyal to a fault. This could be very dangerous, Priscus. It could mean our lives."

"There's no need to worry yourself," Priscus said, making his way to the cot that Meric had been resting on. He scrunched his tabard into a ball and laid his head upon it as he laid himself down on it. "I said what I did this morning for two reasons. The first, because I wanted all of his men to hear it. I sought to plant the seed of doubt in their minds, and since this seed came from my mouth I can assure you that right now they are all talking amongst themselves about whether or not there is some truth to it. The same applies to Captain Cimber, which then brings me to my second reason. I'm the king's brother. And the best thing about being the king's brother is that people often look at me as if I am the king himself, just as the captain just saw me. So, I wouldn't worry about losing your life over this, because apart from Plaucus perhaps, there aren't many here who would harm me even if they were commanded to do so."

"So you mean to tell me that you thought of all of this in advance, knowing it would benefit this plan of yours," I smirked, flabbergasted.

"We'll find out tonight, won't we?" he said, closing his eyes. "Get some rest. There's little time."

I looked to the others to see if they were as surprised as I was, but Meric and Andreaus had already fled from the pavilion. Jon and Axle were making like Petris, slumbering like bears in the dead of winter. Lera too had found herself a spot to rest, and for this reason I was the only one standing with his eyes opened, wondering why there was not a collective sense of worry, and if I should really be spending the last few hours of my life sleeping.

***

In the heart of night our company gathered out in the field, further out from where we had camped so that any noise would be wholly drowned in the black around us. When all was set and proper, we formed eight abreast and marched down the *rex in via*, coming once again to the gatehouse, my nerves heightened, worried still that Cimber had told Plaucus of our plan to move without his knowing. The closer we drew the more it seemed likely, for the air was filled with nothing but the sound of crickets, and both the ramparts and tower banks appeared to be unmanned by the night guard. Immediately I thought the worst, my eyes darting about like a hawk's drawn to the places that I believed Plaucus' men would all at once show themselves from.

At first, I saw nothing that confirmed my suspicions, but as we drew closer a man appeared from one of the guard rooms with a torch in hand, walking towards us cautiously as if our presence was unexpected. I knew that he was not Captain Cimber — I could not see the man's face clearly, as I was at the front of the column with the rest. He waved his flame high above his head toward the parapet, which prompted me to grip my sword. But therewith the hinges of the gate cracked open, a sound that filled my heart with a great sense of relief.

It was at this point that the man led our column, in secrecy, through the gates of The Shield. Now, the *rex in via* was no more, and so we marched headlong for a short while down a dirt road, which became one with another pathway of cobbled stone, the *via externa*, which was shrouded in a fine mist. Anigh to the bank of the adjacent river, we came upon a most unforeseen surprise. As the mist dissipated by way of our advance, the sky of silver moonlight revealed Captain Cimber standing beside an elderly man, who was cloaked by a dark covering. It was Lord Ulcar, and he was standing at the head of a caravan of wagons brimming with all manner of supplies; food stuffs, tools, weapons, and legionary uniforms. Not only that, but there were four men of his legion, and seventy of the Stone Fortress hidden in the thick brush, each and all intending to join our company — bringing our numbers to a grand total of four hundred and fifty-two, absent the wounded we left behind.

"Provisions, and men, for the long journey ahead," Ulcar said to Priscus as he neared him. "I figured after seeing your men scrounging around the fortress for supplies all afternoon, not to mention stealing from my own personal stores as well, that I'd lend a hand." He paused. "I have to say, my Lord Priscus, that stealth really isn't a strong suit of yours, is it? If secrecy was your intention then you're lucky I was there to keep it."

"I guess I was that obvious," Meric whispered in my ear.

Cimber stepped forward. "Lord Ulcar and I gathered as much as we could find; bread, drink, spare armour and steel from the armoury, and I also thought it best to add some tools in reserve for your builder there should he ever be in need of them. As for our men, don't worry about their absence here. No insult, but they will not be noticed missing. All seventy of them are green and have yet to be placed in their tower, so in effect they don't yet exist in the ranks of the twentieth. I'm sure they'll serve you well enough, but I'm afraid that when it comes to what you can devour, it will only last three weeks at the most. After that, you are on your own I'm afraid."

"This is most unexpected," Priscus said, eyes ogling the caravan.

"More unexpected than scurrying off on your toes in the dead of night?" Ulcar said. Right then Priscus raised his hand, ordering the column to a full halt. "Well," Ulcar added, "I care not for your reasons. Do what you will."

"I thought your mind far gone from this task," Priscus said, inquisitively.

"Oh no, my lord, I still think this quest of yours is quite the fool's errand," Ulcar said, as he looked to his left and right. "Still, that does not mean I would see strong men starve, or venture on to the unknown ill-equipped. I guess in your words I would say, *I'm not Plaucus after all.*"

Here, he began to move away, deeming his conversation with Priscus ended. However, just as he faded into the shadow of the road he turned around and added, "Oh yes! I almost forgot. I'm leaving with you four of my most trusted guards. That will be my contribution. I ask for nothing in return, but be sure that you let loose my horses when they are no longer needed. They've cost me quite the coin, and I'm sure their purpose will be of little use where you're going. Andiel's luck, Lord Priscus."

"You've outdone yourself, captain," Priscus said, returning his gaze to Cimber, who was in the midst of ordering his men to cede the reins of the wagons over to our men. He seemed rather leery about the unfolding events, as were we all in some respect, though I am certain that the origin of his looming doubt came from his dislike of the secretive air. "I've never thanked a man twice in the same day," Priscus went on, turning to Meric. "Meric, have the men move along."

"Provisions for the task ahead is all," Cimber replied. "This path here continues on until the river ends. It's the only road this far west that will lead you to the edge of the Greenlands without daring too close to Linlani territory. After that you'll have ten leagues to open country, and it's into the hands of the gods."

Priscus smiled. "You're a good man. Forgive me for the uneasy position I've put you in. It was not my intent." Priscus extended his arm, which Cimber clutched grateful to be of service.

It was then that I remember seeing something odd happen between the two of them. It was so subtle, it would have passed unnoticed but it appeared, from my angle that Priscus had smoothed out Cimber's tunic with his idle hand. Cimber had not noticed. "My thanks again!"

Cimber retracted from the road and placed himself in a sea of tall grass. "Let this be our part in your quest, my lord. Now, you should go, before tomorrow's light shines anew."

At that Priscus bid Cimber a last farewell as he climbed atop the same wagon in which Axle had asked Lera and I to steer. I remember him taking a seat between us as if he were Lera's father, making sure I would not become too familiar with her, which put a smile on Lera's face. At the same time, Axle, standing upright in the cart in front of us, signalled those carts ahead of him to set off, prompting the column to follow. On we went into the dark void and misty trail of the cobbled road, where men from distant lands marched abreast to those who bore the emblems of Anolia's legions. And like the armies of old who once ventured to the depths of the kingdom's reach, we advanced with our bronze and silver helmets slung around our necks, mindful of the challenges that would lie ahead, unsuspecting of the betrayal that we left behind, but otherwise starved for the destruction of the enemy, and the finding of this fortress.

CHAPTER 14

By the end of the fourth day, when the cobbled road had melded into the surrounding oceans of rich, emerald grass, our army had reached the heart of the Greenlands, the region of our kingdom that lay to the north of The Shield. None but the people of Harthus lived in these lands, for despite its perfection for the plow, there had always been the unsettling thought among the people that its distance from the rest of the realm was too great in terms of receiving her protection. Fast we had marched for five days within this region, pressing onward amid the rolling hills and verdant meadows that blanketed the paths we took, where each passing day had welcomed in new swells of fresh cloying scents and warm winds. I should say, dear reader, that although I was not of these parts, nor had I ventured through them until this moment, that this air was rather unusual, since the Greenlands melded with the frigid lands of Norwall in the east, where Easteria lies. Either way, the air was tranquil, and more than that, with no small amount of added luck, so were we, for our presence had also gone unnoticed by both the Ascani and the Linlani — not that the second had occupied our worries more than the creatures. As such, there was a collective feeling of ease that gradually spread amongst us, each and all believing as I did that we would reach Northfleet with few setbacks and surprises. Yet, like all the good things that befall us in our lives, this feeling too was not long lived. On the very last day in this leg of our journey we had finally come upon the outlying village of Harthus, the same village in which Lord Kaeso had once reported to have been plundered by the Ascani.

Never before had I seen such utter desolation of the land. Every home and place of trade had been reduced to heaps of charred stone and blackened timber. Like the base of a blacksmiths forge, we had found nothing more upon the ground than a thick curtain of black, ashen powder, which, to my eyes, sometimes seemed to be wreathing in the wind as though it were being stirred by the souls of the dead fleeing the desolation that had befallen them. Even now in my aged years I remember most clearly the scene in the nearby fields, more harrowing than the last scenery in my view. One could not walk in the tall grass without stepping upon the countless depressions that were left by those who were slain, all of them outlined by dark, carmine smears. Lord Kaeso and his men had buried those people that hung like butchered meat within the temple, but they could not wash away the imprint of the blood and viscera that was left behind. I will spare you the finer details, fair reader, for I refuse to let the memories of the sight return to me.

Oddly enough we had camped close to the village that night. And needless to say, sleep did not come easy, not only for me that is, but for Lera as well, who, for the first time, thought it best that she should spend her evening in my company, which I welcomed with less timidity. In the end it turned out to be a most pleasant night, one that was filled with playful chatter, and nothing of the Ascani.

That next morning Priscus, evidently aware that we had entered the enemy's new dominion, had quickened our already rapid pace. Truthfully, I could not tell the difference. For eight more days we had travelled a northerly path, wherein the once lush grounds of the Greenlands had then turned to a wide and woodless steppe of red and yellow tundra, and where the wind that whistled across these plains abated its warmth for cool, incessant gusts. In truth, this uncharted land resembled that of Easteria's northern borderlands, a place of few edible herbages and little game, which pretty much forced us to halve our rations in order to see our nearly emptied provisions extended.

Nevertheless, our journey from this point on had been rich in surprises, many that were almost too surreal to give weight to in the simplest of words. As we descended from the last of the barren slopes, the land had been wholly restored to a landscape of transcendent wonder, full of vivid colours one would not think to see after such sparse open country. From first light to twilight, we had marched alongside lakes of purple flora and rivers of orange lichen that appeared to extend far beyond what we could see. More than that, the sky of day was deep blue, and the waters that coursed along our path were as clear as glass, brimming with so much life that every man was able to eat twice his fill on fish alone. For this reason, we toiled from one tributary to the next for some time, until finally we came into the basin of a colossal fjord. We spent our last night on the bank of stilled blue lake, within which there were many great boulder-sized pieces of northern ice that joggled atop the waterline, bouncing up and down as though they challenged the ever-watchful ridges on their flanks.

By dusk on the seventeenth day we had finally arrived at the south edge of Northfleet's encircling forest — at least we assumed that it was, because for a dozen miles in each direction, perhaps even more, there were no more visible paths to take that were free of woodland, save the ones that were marked on the map, which we immediately searched for.

As you might have already guessed, dear reader, we had once again changed our course of action from taking the western entrance, which Priscus had originally set out to use, to the southern one; a last offhand decision that I have not a clue as to the reason. Long did we search for this mysterious hidden path. And in fact, it was Lera who had discovered it, very quickly causing no small amount of shame upon the forty men that Priscus had tasked for its search. But it was not surprising that they had trouble locating it. The forest itself was not only overgrown, but also bizarre in that it felt wholly out of place for the region. Its timbers were of many blended varieties such as thick, massive firs, slender spruces, dense heaths, and dwarfed willows, whose white, leafy canopies spread no wider than twice the length of a man. And the brush was so heavy that none could see more than ten feet passed the boundary, which, if I might add, was absorbed in the ill-boding rattle of the trees caught in the wind. Altogether, the scene was enough to spark a rustle of our own among the ranks, but not from fear you see, but from the realisation that the morrow's journey would be more demanding.

Nevertheless, our hearts were the lightest they had ever been since we had departed from The Shield. After Lera had returned to us from the last of her scouting expeditions, without incident, Priscus had ordered us to make camp, only this time a sort of small celebration was had. By the time Priscus and Axle had finished releasing Ulcar's horses, Jon and few of the most skilled Uthians had returned from a hunt with all sorts of game, and in abundance. Lytus, the bumbling legionary from the Isle of Ore, attributed himself as the most experienced cook among us, and so he prepared us a magnificent feast. Axle, with Meric of course, saw to dispersing of what wine Cimber had hid amid our provisions. Hours then passed with nothing but the mutter of merry talk and the forming of those firm bonds that are only born from good food. Later that night, Lytus graced us once again with another of his many skills. He, and his amateur band of theatrical actors, enlivened the men with a spectacle of drunken humour. They recited an entire Ovinian performance, which I must say, dear reader, was absolutely atrocious to the woman and her craft. Be that as it may, that night had fallen to rest with a smile, the greatest component for pleasant dreams.

As for me, I did not take to slumber right away. Since our departure from Andiel's Shield I had not been able to overcome the threat that was to come. It was ever on my mind in quiet hours. I had spoken my mind on the subject to Jon, who had noticed it looming upon my face like a veil. The others, however, were always seemingly at ease with our task, for the most part. Perhaps it was their experience in battle that led them to have steady minds. In truth, I do not know. All I could do was mimic their repose, and so in place of sleeping I took to refining my own preparations for the battle to come, thinking some study would do me well. Long had it been since I stopped to consider my role in this quest, and so with that in mind I sat with my back against a large rock a distance from the encampment so that the small, lambent fire that burned at my feet did not draw any attention to me, since my nose was rather deep in my journal.

"Andiel spare me," I muttered aloud with frustration. I tilted my head back and exhaled an exhausted breath towards the night's sky, which was like a canvass of the gods, for amid the stars there were sparkling streams of green and blue hue, as if they were truly like the strokes of a brush from a celestial artisan. I curled a smile in honour of the beauty and then brushed my forehead, soothing my strained memory. "Why can I not recall the simplest things?"

"Don't you ever get tired of looking at that thing?" a voice said from the shadows. It was Lera, who was emerging into the light as I turned to her voice. She was standing in front of me with two oak carved goblets in her hands, which brimmed with the last of the wine. "You know, Cillian," she went on while advancing toward me, "most men prefer to spend their time with other things like wagering coin, drinking, or having the warm comfort of a woman. Yet, you always seem to prefer that book of yours. The one you keep secret, might I add."

I slowly closed my journal, laying it at my side. "Isn't it a little late for more wine?"

"Do you want me to leave?"

"No!" I blurted. "I'm just saying it is late."

Lera sat by my side, back against the rock. She laid her cheek against my shoulder with a grin on her face, and then after tightening against me she reached up and gently placed her soft lips upon mine. Yes, dear reader, this might come as a surprise to you, but to be honest, I do not recall when the cadence of our hearts beat the same. I do remember, however, that in every hour of rest, she had sought to be near me for longer and longer periods of time — with little objection on my part of course. At times we spoke long into the evening, and we warmed each other on the coldest of nights. And this night was no different, seeing as how her kiss was long and full of desire, matching that of the night before and every night since we had, I believe, camped near Harthus. In any event, her heart had fallen for me, the lowly builder, whose acts of daring and courage were always accompanied by the tears of fear. Thankfully, she did not know that. And, even now, I think she was more in love with my stories rather than my person, considering that I was sure to have one ready every night to ease her weary mind.

"Besides," she smiled. "Do you think I'd miss one of your stories? Now that the sky shines like fair gems."

"I'm afraid I have none tonight," I replied, accepting one of the goblets.

"Hmm, that's a shame," she sighed. "Do you not know where those lights come from?" she asked, looking to the sky.

"Not in the slightest," I replied, taking a swift drink as I looked up. "But, I'm pretty sure they are more radiant now that you arrived."

"You know you can just kiss me, right?" she said, as if my words were tawdry. "You don't have to lure me in." She pressed me closer against the warmth of her chest, and in doing so she let out a brilliant smile. I could feel her fingers dig into my tunic as she again pulled herself to my lips, but here she did not kiss me.

Rather, she quickly seized my journal and retreated with it in her grip. "Let's have a look at this," she said.

"Lera, come— " I said, battling to reclaim it. "There isn't much there. It's private!"

"Like hell there isn't!" she laughed, pushing me back. "You've been looking at it more than you do me, so I want to see. Please, I've never seen what's inside!"

"It's just things of my design. Builder things. You already know that."

"Well either you start thinking about a story or I'm opening this book."

I had managed to grip the corner of the journal, but my chances to come out ahead were slipping away, because she was looking at me as if she were pleading. I let go, defeatedly, at which point she began to leaf through the pages as though she were eyeing the contents in careful study.

"Right so," she said. "What am I looking at?"

"Engines of war, mostly," I replied.

"And which of these *engines* of yours made you whine like a little girl before? Was it this one?" she asked, pointing to one of the images.

I looked at the illustration she then presented to me, which of all my designs was my most recent of works. It was a sort of bow engine, similar in the form like that of a ballista, but much smaller, a quarter of the size, I would say. I liked this design in particular because its front was fashioned by two frames that were adjoined by a thin, iron rod, which was not common to see in the building of sturdy war engines. More than that, the drawstring was hitched to each end of the rod like a traditional bow, whose latch rested on a narrow rectangular base made of one solid piece of wood. Its purpose, and what I hoped it would serve for, was to fire a shaft larger and thicker than a normal arrow, while the engine remained light enough to move between positions in a short time by no more than a single man.

"Yes, if you must know," I said. "And I wasn't whining. I was just a little frustrated."

"Why? Do you not like it anymore? I think it looks quite nice."

"It's not like it's a flower, Lera. I wouldn't use a word like *nice* to define it."

"Ah yes, I see now. You were trying to draw a flower first, but you ended up with this."

"What? No it's — it doesn't matter alright," I said, eyes drifting away from the page.

"Are you afraid I won't understand your big words or something?"

"It has nothing to do with that," I said, slightly peeved. "Look, it's just that I've built it once before, but it's been many months now that I have not had the chance to test it further. And I can't just up and build it now because it takes a month in itself to do so. I'm trying to balance the force of the tension and the weight of the frame. I know in the back of mind that it's simple, but I just can't figure it out. I was thinking, perhaps, that I could try building it at the fortress once we get there — that maybe we could use something like this to our favour. I don't know. Then, there's a chance I may never get it to work the way I want it to. Hence why I sounded like a little girl."

"If you had one now, let's say, and you were to use it on an Ascani. Would it kill it?"

"Yes, I guess. but —"

"Congratulations, Cillian. It works perfectly," she said, snapping the journal closed.

"I guess if you think of it that way then you are right."

"I know I am," she smiled. "But, if I were you I wouldn't worry too much about it anyway. To be honest, Cillian, it doesn't look like there is one thing in that book that you can build in the time that we have." She took a gulp of her wine and cleared the spillage off her lower lip. Then, she drank the last of the wine and chucked the cup off to the side without a care. "Now then, builder," she added while slowly raising herself onto my lap. "If you don't have any stories for me tonight, then you'll have to find another way to keep me busy."

"Wait, I —"

I stopped myself short, for the energy in her lustful embrace was far more vigorous than I had expected. Immediately, the connection between us mounted like a raging fire, whereupon my heart and gut were loaded with a wave of a thousand sudden flutters. I kissed her back with equal fervour as she began to undress me, as I did her. It was here that I saw, for the first time, that she wore an emerald pendant around her neck, one that was small and loose, but smooth and brilliant like sea glass, often found on the beaches of Aeginas. I do not know why, but all at once the sight of the amulet caused me a tremendous amount of unease, my desire for her passions stripped by a thought that had been looming in my mind for some time.

"What's the matter?" she said between heavy, lustful breaths. "Are you alright?"

"This pendant," I said, letting it rest on my palm. "Where did you get it?"

Lera looked down and gave it a long stare. "My father," she answered in a tone quite opposite her last. "It was my father's. Long time ago. I remember him giving it to me a day before it all happened. They made jewels out of sea glass, him and my mother. Before I was born he made one for me that he kept with him until I was old enough to tell what it was." Here she smirked, as if taken by an amusing memory. "I guess to me this pendant here is almost like your book. A secret that I cherish, something that you don't want anyone else to see, but still one that I would gladly share with you."

"Lera," I said in a glum tone. "Why are you here?"

"What?" she replied with a puzzled smirk. "To be with you. Why else?"

"I mean why are you here with us? Here in this place, on this task."

Lera slowly lifted herself off my chest. "You know why I'm here, Cillian. I told you on the Isle of Ore, didn't I? I have cause, same as you — and as any man here. Now, are we going to talk all night or would you finally like to see what's under my clothes?"

"Cause?" I said with a baffled grin. "Lera, do you think I'm here because I have cause? Save for following the duties of a soldier? If you think about it hard enough you'd see that I'm not sitting here in the dark waiting to continue on with this task because I have cause. I'm really only here because a boy sacrificed his own life to complete my task, which then, by chance, saw me in front of Priscus, who, for some reason, thinks I'm some master builder that he so happens to need by his side. I'm on this path because I was cast into it, and not because I chose to come along like you and the others. I have more in common in my being here as the Uthians do. And if you ask me, I think they are the only ones amongst us with their heads grounded on what's to come. But still I am curious, Lera. What cause do *you* have?"

"What's wrong with you?" Lera said with a hard look. "Vengeance, if for no other reason."

"Vengeance? Really?" I huffed.

"Yes, vengeance," she replied with growing anger. "Look I don't know what game you are playing at, Cillian, but have you forgotten that it was *my* party who found this army we are trying to stop, and that *I* am the only one alive among them to see it destroyed. Or perhaps you prefer to be reminded of what those creatures did to my family — what life they cast me into. So which one is it then? Which one do you prefer? Which one is more suitable ground for me to wish them all dead? So yes, vengeance, if not for my family then for my brothers." Lera then pushed me back and stood on her knees, fixing her shirt to proper form. "And besides, Cillian, you weren't just cast into this, you chose to be here like all the rest. The moment you decided to be *sodalis* to Lord Priscus you gave your word to take on his challenges."

"And when does this life of yours end? When does your vengeance end? You can't spend the rest of your life going from battle to battle, thinking it a chance to see more of them under your sword. It has to end sometime." I leaned forward, my defensive attitude increasing. "Where is it that you think we are going, hmm? Go on and tell me, because in truth I have no idea. You know ever since I joined the legion I've done nothing but follow absently in the footsteps of greater men, trailing behind them blindly, eyes closed in the shadow of their vigour from one tide to the next, never once judging what it is that I have gotten myself into, or better yet now, stopped to think how I truly feel about this task. But the worst part of it all is that I find myself not caring anymore about my own thoughts, because now I am more confused and worried about another matter."

"What other matter? What are you talking about?"

"I'm talking about you, Lera!" I blurted.

"Me?"

"Yes," I said, taking in a shaky breath. "I can't seem to figure you out. In all our time together, out here, on this bloody journey, I haven't been able to understand why it is that you always speak as if you can't wait to get to this bloody fortress. Sure, you might shout vengeance as your reason. But still never once have I heard you say anything other about your thoughts, about what we might find when we get to our mark, or even if we are going to make it there before being slaughtered by the very thing that we are moving against. You never seem to have any concerns about what could happen. You just welcome it with a smile on your face."

"We have been set to command," she said. "And this is our task. Nothing else matters."

"Oh right of course! I forget. It's because of our duty, isn't it?" I said, becoming increasingly hardened. "To be of use is it?" Here I paused for a second, stunned by my own words, which were the very same that I had been telling myself over and over since the beginning of my time in the legion. A phrase I had spoken toward myself in order to feel included, to feel valued. But I digress, dear reader. I took a breath, standing up on my knees to match her eyes with mine. Then, I grabbed her hands and cupped them as if I were about to begin praying with her. "Lera, listen to me. There is a creature out there that has been hunting us since Easteria. And for some reason, maybe by the luck of the gods, I don't know what else it could be, we marched all the way here without it, or any of them, finding us. So now, I can only assume that it has either already found its way to Northfleet, or that it has fled these lands to command that army you saw. There's talk of it, and Axle is sure that it is the latter that is more likely. Either way, that creature will show himself again, only this time with six thousand others just like it at its back. We will be slaughtered, can you not see that? And if by some chance we get to this castle before they do, then we will be trapped, and dead all the same, well before the king's army even gets there. None of this is worth your vengeance."

"You're scared to die?" she said, her eyes almost disgusted with me. "Is that it?"

"No," I answered.

"Then what is it?" she said with a raised voice.

"If your head wasn't always so concerned with children's tales and fables in the stars, then you would see what it is I am trying to tell you."

"How dare you," she exploded. "Is this your true nature, Cillian *the builder*? You soften your tongue to me only when it pleases you, and then when you have had your fill you treat me so? Do not think for one second that I am here because I have nothing better to do with my life but to fill my heart with songs and want of death. I am here because I want to be, not just for some game of vengeance you think I'm playing at. If you are too scared to face what's coming then go. Go on and leave, Cillian. Leave in the dark and abandon your charge. Abandon me, I don't care. If that's what it will take to settle your heart, so be it. I won't stop you. Though something tells me you'll only make it a league with your spine, before you will find something other to be afraid about—"

"I don't care what happens to me, Lera," I said in a low voice, looking at her sternly as tears began to well in my eyes. "I care what happens to you."

For a moment there was a dead silence between us, other than the crackling fire and the crickets chirping in the grass. My eyes turned to a pond, so suddenly, in fact, that it was almost as if a knife had pierced my flesh. I brushed my eyes with the sleeves of my tunic and looked away, stunned by my own words. "Forgive me," I then said, regaining my composure. "It's not that I don't believe in your reasons. It's just that I don't want you to die, alright. That's my fear." I took in a deep breath as I looked to the stars, thinking about what next I would say to cut the stretch of the gloominess. "You know I haven't thought about home once since we left the Isle," I said as if I had a revelation. "If the gods came up to me right now and offered me the chance to go back I think I would take it, tonight if I could." I turned back to face her. "I'd go back there. Fly across the sky on the wings of Aitanos just to see it again, even if for a last time. But now that I think about it I can't see the point. I mean I've had the pleasure of living a long life in the love of my family, but if I go back now, I'd be alone. Nobody to see me return. Call me a starry-eyed fool if you want, but I know that my heart is trying to tell me something. And I know now that something is you, Lera. All that I have left in this world is right in front of me, alive, and well, and beautiful. I want it all to stay like that. So, if I were to go back now, I'd have to take you with me, because I'm afraid that this is all going to come to an end before I want it to. Look, the path of your life is your choice. I just wanted to be the one to give you the chance to see the world without having a need to carry a sword, or at the very least give you the chance to live the life that was taken from you."

After I had spilled my thoughts, I sat back down against the rock as I had before. There were still a few tears streaming down my cheeks as I plunged my chin into my chest like a wounded child. Suddenly, I felt Lera's fingers pass through my hair as the droplets of her own tears fell upon my head. To see her with welled eyes was a surprise, because her hardened character had led me to believe she was unable to shed them. Therewith she sat on my lap, now with her back to the flames and her legs tightening against my waist.

"So much for the heart of a soldier, huh?" I said. "By the way, I should apologize again."

"What for?" she replied.

"I lied," I said, feeling her fingers trail down my face. "I lied about the lights. I know —"

At that Lera placed her lips upon mine once again, which grew more fervent in its passion than before. She put her hands underneath my shirt, and I hers, each of us grasping at the other's brawn with an ardour both of us did not know we had. Never had my hands felt the soft touch of a woman, and so I pulled her away for a moment so that my heart would not burst from my chest. There I paused, lightly cupping the arch of her chin as I traced her lips with my thumb.

"Please tell me you don't have more to say," she said, breathing heavily.

"No, I—"

It was at this moment that I retreated slightly, taken aback by the small glow of red and orange light flickering in the blue gloss of her eyes. I looked over her shoulder, confirming that the source of the glow could not have come from the fire that I had made, since it was directly at her back. Then, all at once, a fierce myriad of shouts rose up from the encampment behind us. Immediately, Lera pulled herself away from me, and together we sprung to our feet and crossed the field in haste with our swords in hand. At first we thought the enemy was upon us, but as we arrived on the scene we found the sergeants in a mad frenzy as they led their men toward our wagons, many of them were buried in scarlet fire. Priscus was already battling the flames, and he was soon joined by Axle, Meric, and Jon, who began chucking pails of earth to snuff the inferno.

Lera and I followed the mob in confusion. Like crazed badgers we used our hands as spades, digging our fingers deep into the packed earth. Nevertheless, after what seemed like an hour of exhausted labour, the fires subsided by a small degree. And so here we stood amid the inferno's brilliant shadow, defeated, listening to Priscus's echo as he instructed the men to let the fire consume its course, and to salvage what we could from those wagons not yet taken by the flames.

Just then, however, another uproar had erupted at our backs, prompting us all to turn around to see what was going on. There was a crowd of men advancing toward us, where at its center, pairs of Uthian mercenaries towed battered, half-clothed legionaries between them. There were four in total, three of which were actually dead, gone to the afterlife by Uthian spears. The legionary who was still alive was moaning in pain. His head was slumped as they dragged him closer, but still I could tell that his face was bloodied beyond measure; a stream of red dripped from his chin, and the rim of his long, blond hair was sodden with the same gore. The Uthians unhandled the man before Priscus' feet, and there he collapsed onto the ground with all his weight as if he were a corpse like the others. Then, one of the Uthians blurted a phrase in his own tongue that neither I, nor any, Anolian understood. It made no difference, however, who could understand the man, because like the spark from a flint, a bitter quarrel began to surface in the crowd between the Uthians and the legionaries, seeing as how some of our men quickly accused the Uthians of assailing and killing the men without cause.

"At ease all of you!" Priscus shouted.

"It was this one," said a strong voice with a foreign tone. It came from the back of the crowd. It was Ferix, the Uthian captain and senior, who came forward with a heavy breath as if he had just sprinted across the camp. He pointed to the legionary on the ground and reiterated, "It was this one. My man says he saw this one burn the carts."

"Lies!" one of the legionaries cried out.

Meanwhile Meric moved to set the soldier on his knees. Jon also moved to lend a hand, at which point they clutched the underside of the man's arms with an intensity that suggested they did not think him to be guilty. But just as they began to hoist him up the man leapt to his feet in an effort to escape, inciting Jon to strike him across the chin with enough force to cast a clear, near life-halting expression upon his face.

"I guess that answers that question," Axle said, taking several steps forward. He gripped the man firmly by the hair while grinding his teeth. "Who are you?" he added seethingly, looking at his chest to find that the man, as well as the rest, was absent his tabard, or a tunic for that matter. "What is your name? Who is your lord?"

"What does it matter now?" the man cackled, blood dripping from his bastardly grin. "It's all said and done, all as it should be."

"Is it now?" Axle said with a raised brow. He punched him in the gut several times, and then twisted his hair even harder. "Trust me when I tell you this boy, that I can make this a lot harder for you, even at my age. So I say again, who are you? Why have you done this?"

The man spat a crimson wad on to Axle's boot and began to laugh sinisterly. At that, Jon struck the man again and again as if his limp body were a practice totem, the sound of his anguish waning only when the sound of snapping bones overtook it.

"Enough," Priscus said, holding Jon's hand. "You can kill him after he talks."

"Oh! How merciful of you, my lord," the man grunted, mockingly. "But you can trust *me* that I won't ever talk, because it's like you say, I'll be dead soon enough." Here his laughter, and his wheezing, increased. "And so will you…all of you."

Priscus ordered the man to his feet, whereupon he suddenly surged forward and grabbed him by his throat like he would any of his enemies. He then unsheathed his dagger with ire and placed its point firmly underneath the man's eye. "By Andiel's promise I will remove one part of you until you start speaking some sort of sense to me — and about what I want to hear. I'll start with your eyes and then work my way down. Now then, tell me everything you know you miserable sard, and then I'll let the gods guide you to hell and to your brothers."

"Andiel?" the man smiled. "A name long since dead. Nothing more than a bastard of an ancient king whose shadow is insignificant to this realm." His head then crumpled to his chest as he swallowed hard in pain. "Go on and cut away, my lord. Do it if you must. But as I said none of it matters now, for your quest is done — cast in defeat and death. Nothing you do now will work to restore it, because it's just a piece you see. A piece of his plan."

The man's frame went suddenly flaccid.

"He's dead," Axle said, as he pulled the man's head back roughly.

Priscus quickly turned to the men in the crowd. "I want you all to spread the word and find out where he was camped. Search all of his belongings and then bring them to me. Ferix, have your men take me to where they had last found him. And if there are any among you who knew who this bastard was, now would be a good time to speak."

"There's no need to go searching, my lord," Andreaus said, moving into sight from the edge of the mob. "I think I've already found the hand that is behind all your words of treachery," he added with anger, casting to the ground a pile of ragged, soiled tabards for all to view. "We found them in the brush where the

Uthians captured them. Looks like the bastards were trying to bury them all."

The tabards were closest to my feet, and so I took a quick step forward and snatched one for myself. I raised it up as if I were setting it out to dry, holding it outwardly by the shoulder ends. I could not see the emblem on the tabard, for the light around me was scant and the face of the cloth was smeared with heavy clumps of dirt. I shook it about so that I could clear the obscurity, though before I was able to set it back to view Priscus yanked it from my clutch. He stared at it uneasily, as though all at once a thousand baffling thoughts swelled in his mind.

"It can't be," I muttered, seeing the emblem full well as many torches closed in.

"The White Horse," Axle said.

"Ulcar," Priscus muttered.

CHAPTER 15

As told to me by Julia Semprinus, 996 A.E.-1071 A.E, Cimber Artisianis, 989 A.E.- 1050 A.E. Of all the stories I have, and will have, to recount, this next one is high above the rest in its horror, and in its proof of celestial luck. Some years after the war, Captain Cimber left the legion in favour of a life absent the order of soldierly life, and in doing so he settled in none other than Netum, a small town on the southern borders of Norlyn. He married a young lady named Julia, a servant girl of Plaucus' court, who he had fallen in love with while he had served in the twentieth. Through Petris I had become aware that Cimber had been present on the night of what history has called "The Slaughter of the Awakening." Cimber, for his own reasons, had declined to speak to me in length of what he had seen on that night. Therefore, it was not he, but his wife Julia, who sought me out in an effort to help me understand the events. My dear reader, it is Julia's account that forms the majority of this retelling, for she had witnessed and heard all that you will next read.

"Lord Ulcar!" Plaucus cried out in hysteria as he shrank in fear near the hearth of his grand, banquet hall. The fire in the hearth was roaring, for one of Ulcar's guards had thrown a corpse upon the coals as if done so under his lord's command. Blood trickled onto the embers, causing a steady sizzling sound. "By all the gods! What are you doing!"

Ulcar was slowly and patiently walking about the hall with his hands interlaced behind his back like an overseer examining his labourers at work, which in this case were his household guards in the midst of massacring Plaucus' many dinner guests; servants, soldiers, and highborn alike. In a short time the screams and shrilling screeches died away, at which point Ulcar made his way toward Plaucus with two of his most brawny men at his back. He then paused abruptly in front of him, his eyes bright and filled with a sort of thrill for the corpses that were piled at his feet, a trait not fitting the air of how he normally comported himself.

"I beg you, Ulcar." Plaucus whimpered. "Cease this insanity at once. Please, no more!"

Right then Ulcar's guards gripped Plaucus by his arms and yanked him from underneath the mantle of the hearth. In an instant one of them hoisted him on top of his shoulders like a satchel and hurled him across the enormous, oval-shaped feasting table in the center of the hall, whereupon he crashed against the rim with a huge clamour, sending high-backed chairs, silver cutlery, and chunks of half-eaten food soaring in all directions. He howled in agony as his body struck the floor, his full weight falling on to his arm causing the bones in his left hand to shatter. Here, he writhed onto his side and began to wail in terror, stopping only, and suddenly, when a spatter of blood had spewed into his mouth from the marred neck of his servant that lay lifeless beside him.

At that moment, immessered in the nightmare, he let out another cry of horror, putting his hand to his brow as if it were the first time he had seen such carnage of death. Overcome with the idea of self-preservation alone, he turned onto his stomach and wormed his way toward the doors of the hall, his limbs shaking with a wild desperation to flee. Needless to say, Ulcar's guards caught him before he could make it several feet from where he was originally, and therewith they slammed him into his lord's seat, which had been set to face Ulcar, who was standing in deep thought by the hearth.

"Join me, Plaucus. I have words to speak," Ulcar said as he wiped away a smudge of blood from the green olive that he had raised to his lips. He ate it, spitting out the pit so casually, the air of death and the scent of slaughter having no effect on his appetite. "I'm afraid they must be said with urgency and with no small amount of privacy. So do forgive the dramatics."

"Ulcar!" Plaucus sobbed. "What is this? Have mercy on me —"

"Quiet now! Spare me of that wretched noise!" Ulcar blurted out in annoyance as he turned to one of his guards. "Go on! What are you waiting for? Sit him up straight! Nasos, Musa, you two bolt the door and keep watch. The rest of you stand guard out in the hall. I do not want any more disturbances, am I clear? And for god's sake would one of you please finish that one over there, she still lives."

Suddenly a servant girl, realising that her feigned death had been discovered, jumped to her feet and sprinted toward the doors. She was holding one of her arms close to her chest, for it hung at the elbow, threatening to detach every time her heel hit the ground. Ulcar's guards chased after her like a pack of wild dogs, pushing away toppled chairs and corpses alike from their paths. At first it seemed that she moved quick enough to evade them, but just before she was but a foot from salvation one of the guards caught the end of her robe, which, as Julia put it, ripped her pensile arm clean off, sending her face forward onto ground with a crazed shriek of pain. Still, she clawed her way forward, inch by inch in spite of the pain that came from her fingernails, which also threatened to rip off from her desperate, aggressive movements. With cries of mercy on her tongue she did not look back. Her voice then falling flat; silenced by a sword that was buried in the base of her skull.

"Check the rest while you're at it," Ulcar commanded.

Ulcar motioned for a cup of water to be brought to him. All the while he watched his guards scour the hall, each and all jabbing their swords into the backs of the deceased, including

Plaucus' servant Julia Semprinus, who by Enthera's fortune had only been grazed by the blade at her side. More than that, it just so happened that during the course of the slaughter a corpse had fallen on top of her, followed by another and another, until there were enough upon her so that her meager frame was shielded, or rather covered, by the many bodies. The guards had not noticed that she was there, and so she lay in a pool of foreign viscera with the stillness of death and the paralysis of fear, unable to do anything at all but keep herself hidden and silent with her widened eyes fixed on the events unfolding around her, those that she could see through the small gap amid the corpses.

"Now leave us. All of you," Ulcar said, reiterating his earlier command. Immediately, the bulk of the guards took their leave of the hall; Nasos and Musa barring the doors from the inside. At that, Ulcar took a sip of the water, and then splashed the rest on Plaucus' face, waking him from his hysterical blackout. "Alright then, my dearest of friends," he added, as he dabbed away swaths of blood from Plaucus' face with an already soiled rag. "Have I your full attention?"

"What — what foul heart has taken you?" Plaucus said with a drivelling whimper.

"Calm yourself, Plaucus," Ulcar replied softly. "There is no more need to be frightened."

"By all the gods you're mad!" Plaucus cried. "A...a corruption has stayed your sanity!"

Ulcar swiftly drew a bronze hilted knife from the belt of his robe and pressed its end against Plaucus' cheek. "Did I not just say before to quiet your weeping, my lord? Hmm? Do not force me to pull your tongue from your cheek. No harm will come to you, I promise...well as long as you do what I say, that is. Tonight, Plaucus, you will do more than you've ever done in the whole of your life. Tonight you are the centre of it all, the key if you will, and so now I need you to listen to me clearly, and again, with no small amount of caution." Ulcar removed the knife's edge from

Plaucus' cheek, his temper digressing. "And in truth, my friend, you will soon come to find out that it is not I that is corrupted, but you. I will show you, and cleanse all the falsities from your mind."

Plaucus shot him a bewildered look.

"Yes, my lord," Ulcar said, slowly rescinding backwards. "I know this is all confusing to you, so allow me the chance to explain —". All at once Plaucus surged from his seat with a bleating cry and with the intention of escape. "Sit down!" Ulcar then hollered, quickly returning the knife to Plaucus' throat. "Daft are we, boy? Even at my age I still know where best to kill a man. Try that again, Plaucus, and I will educate you on the matter. Do you understand me?"

In compliance Plaucus retook his seat with his chin straining upwards, fearing the blade's sharp point as Ulcar pressed it firmly against his throat as a means to give credence to his threat.

"That's it," Ulcar said, slowly pulling the knife away. "Sit down and do well to listen." Ulcar tucked his knife back in its scabbard and took a standing position as if he were a teacher moments from dictation. "First," Ulcar added, clearing his throat, "I must apologize to you. I have no doubt overstayed my welcome, and almost certainly I have bored you these past weeks with many tedious stories and lectures of old. I am afraid, however, that I must tell a last one that is of true pertinence — one that will clarify the reasoning for all this senseless necessity. Of that, my friend, I am certain. That being said, I think you will come to understand me more clearly if I begin with a simple question." Here, Ulcar narrowed his gaze. "Tell me, Lord Plaucus, do you recognize my authority? My command? Here in this great kingdom of ours? Or better yet, do you recognize your own for that matter?"

"What?" Plaucus muttered, his voice filled with the tremors of fear.

"Come now! You know better than to act a fool with me. It's a simple enough question."

"I don't understand. You are Ulcar of the White Horse, sworn lord auxiliary to the king."

"I did not ask you who I am, Plaucus. I asked you if you recognize my power as a lord."

"I don't...I don't know what you mean," Plaucus stuttered, as if short of breath.

"Well that is quite the pity if you ask me," Ulcar said, as he began to pace toward the hearth. "Not moments before you were so quick to utter that a corruption had entered my heart, and yet it amazes me that you cannot tell how it has already entered your mind, taking from you the clarity of truth that is right in front of you. You see if it were not harbouring this corruption then you would have answered my question without fault. But alas, dear friend, none of this is your fault to begin with. It's not like you would have known that this corruption was amongst us even if someone were to tell you that it was there, for it is unseeable. And it's air is more than just wicked and vile. It is also a timeless poison, one that has been festering in these lands since the beginning of this era, feeding off of all those who believe that this realm of ours is in its proper order, and that everything that we see around us, live amongst, was the product of one man's glory and vision."

"What absurdity is this? There is no such corruption of which you speak."

Ulcar suddenly jerked his head over his shoulder. His blood rising and full of passion. "Oh yes there is! The poison that I speak of is none other than Anolia herself! If you knew something about our history, Plaucus, about the record of this land before the birth of Andiel's rotten empire, then you would have the sense to see that it is really among us. It has eaten away at the greatness in the life that our ancestors lived before this bastardly perversion."

"Perversion? How can you speak so highly of the dark years?"

"Because never were they as dark as all would have you see them," Ulcar grinned, his sense now turning, very slightly, to a more ghoulish air. He began to retrace his steps, moving ever slowly toward Plaucus. "Believe me when I say that it is those who fear the magnificence of this time that cast an evil light upon it. And, if you would give me your ear for a moment, I will shed some light on the answer to the question I asked you before, for this answer lies in these so called *dark years*."

Plaucus' uneasiness began to rise. "That time was tainted! It was not just the thought!"

"Was it?" Ulcar said, lifting his eyes up to match Plaucus'. "And what made it so? Why should we defile the nature of what it truly was? Don't tell me that you above all have forgotten that this was once a land filled with wisdom and glory, a land driven by powerful lords, who held no small form of authority. It was also a time when all the earthly pleasures were bound to the strong. A time of purpose and ambition! It was then that each legion had but one lord, and that lord was also king, for no other power stood in between. Only through absolute strength did they rule in whatever manner they desired, governing their own laws and peoples, never once deferring to endless talks to see their desires achieved, or thwarted by a single man whose only power of rule comes from the jewels that sit upon his head. They all forged their charge by the sword, Plaucus. By a strength in arms and how they wished to see it, and not by what they were commanded to do. In this era, they were all warrior kings, mustering such greatness in their authority that all the other kings of this world once bowed in recognition. So tell me, where lies the darkness in such a time?"

"Is this why you did it then?" Plaucus said with a whimper. "You murdered all these people to tell me that you have dabbled in insanity? To tell me that you desire to be a lord of old? This purity that you see in the dark years is false, Ulcar. A shadow of the past drowned in endless war. You *are* truly mad if you cannot see it!"

"Endless war you say?" Ulcar said with a raised brow. "I can't believe I am agreeing with the man, but by the gods Adeanus was right. Never do you leave the safety of your walls, do you Plaucus? Where the hell have you been all your life? We've been fighting the

Ascani for a thousand years, and never once has there been even a taste of eradicating them for good. If only for a jest I would ask why you think this is so, but it is becoming more apparent that your mind is so clouded with falsities that you'd probably just answer with what history has taught you to say."

"They are the plight of Ascanelius!" Plaucus cried.

Suddenly Ulcar burst out into roaring, maniacal laughter. "The plight of Ascanelius! Really? How naïve you are, Plaucus, if you think the god of the underworld is alone in the history of this war. I really have misjudged your intelligence. It's of no concern now, however, for I think it is time I tell you that last story, don't you think?" At this point Ulcar began telling the tale of the Two Brothers, of Andiel and Anoarin, as I have done at the beginning of this account. He spoke little of Andiel, and it was evident that he spoke of Anoarin with reverence and admiration, especially when he spoke of his alliance with the *Inferi* and their dark magics. As he told the story, Ulcar erupted into an impassioned rage, and in a fit of this passion he rushed toward Plaucus, bringing the cast upon his arm up to his eyes. He exposed his knife once more, but this time used it to break the cast free from his arm in a few vigorous thrusts. The pieces of the hard fibers fell to the ground and soon revealed a large portion of the meat and flesh from his forearm strewn, as if a rabid dog had feasted upon it until the bone. "Look at it, Plaucus," Ulcar said with a crazed smile. "The creatures of this world are not *his* plight, but rather they were born to be an everlasting scourge under the visions of another. And like you see here they were once bred from the flesh of his dark sorcery, ever bound to his vitality, forever joined to the true ruler of this realm, Anoarin the Conjuror!"

Plaucus opened his mouth in horror, but before he could make a sound Ulcar silenced him by violently cupping his mouth with the palm of his hand. "History only saw him as a *primorus,* one who could gather armies at his will. But never did his own pathetic brother see that it was his own kin who was the mastermind behind it all, the very man who was cast aside by those who he had conquered. Look at my arm, Plaucus! My master has been through a great many pains to show me how to conjure them — how to use my own flesh to give them life just as he did all those years ago. I did what he asked of me with my full heart, as will you soon enough. I only regret that I could not spawn the legions he desired! Only enough to cause disarray." Ulcar then wet his lips, his tongue slithering like a snake's, his grin growing as he read Plaucus' expression. "Yes, my friend, it was me. The Ascani roaming our lands. It was always me."

"It can't be," Plaucus said, mortified

Ulcar took in a deep breath and moved a few feet backwards toward the stone column by the hearth. There he paused and allowed his thoughts to overtake him. "If you must know, I'm not the greatest of his servants," he began, speaking more to himself than to Plaucus. "I did everything he wanted! I did everything I could. I shattered the bridge and emptied the fort, yet still in the end that bastard Priscus crossed your walls." Now slightly more calm than a few moments before, he turned to Plaucus, "Be that as it may it's now no matter, for I'm sure that foolish quest of his will soon be *burning* with fresh obstacles. I'll tell you what though, that bloody sard has been quite the thorn in our side, ever since Easteria. And if it were not for him and that boy builder then the pieces of *his* plan would now be sooner coming to the end of their course."

"You lie!" Plaucus said finally. "The Conjuror is no more! Dead for a thousand years!"

"Of course it is true! Do not be daft, Plaucus! Did I not say at the council that only he could command armies in war?" Ulcar cried. Here he digressed once more, his being was seemingly taken by a newfound euphoria. "Who would've thought that after a millennium that I, Lord Ulcar, would find myself woven into the tale of the Two Brothers. Long now has it been since Anoarin had appeared before me on the darkest night, more imperial in his form than any king that I have ever seen, or imagined him to be. I tell you, my friend, I could not resist the air of his power, even if I used every ounce of my desire not to. A mere moment in his presence and I no longer harboured any fear, not even from his ghastly appearance. It was then that I knew I no longer had to worry about the coming of my own desires, that the glory of old that I had so yearned for would follow me to the grave."

"You will never see this land divided as it was."

"Oh no, my boy!" Ulcar said, propping himself up to a straightened back. "You have me all wrong! You see, Plaucus, I did not murder all these people tonight simply because I wanted to tell you that I wish to rule as the lords of old once did. A good part of me no longer has the desire for such a life. I have come to understand that my bones would be a pile of dust before I'd ever see that path come to pass. And now as I feel my long years coming to an end, I know full well that I will soon enter the afterlife leaving all as it still is. Yet, this thought no longer brings me any discomfort as I have said, because now I am certain that when I look down from the heavens I will see these lands and the rest of this mortal world burn in the fires of his coming war. And then when all is turned to ash and cinder he will take this kingdom as his own rightful charge. It will be shaped and forged in the manner of his will, which will form the foundations of his next campaigns."

"All of this is a lie!" Plaucus cried, intently. "There is no Conjuror! There is no incursion! There is no coming war!"

"Hush your tongue now and hear the last of what I have to say!" Ulcar asserted. "We all have our part to play in this story, and yours now is to help me set it all back to order, to its proper conclusion. When his armies gather in full strength, their numbers will be far greater than those of the ancient world. The first of his hordes will be here by the fortnight of the second new moon, at which point I will give unto him the last of my flesh to bolster his ranks. Your part, however, is much more simple. All *you* have to do is open the gates of your fortress when I ask it of you, and in doing so you will be spared." He then knelt down and gently grasped Plaucus' trembling hands. "He has given me his word, no harm will come to you. Do this for him and you will be birthed a king in your own right. What say you, my friend?"

Plaucus moved to speak, but neither his tongue nor his body could lift the weight of his fear. Then, after several moments in an absent gaze, the tremor upon his lips suddenly stopped as he muttered, "By all the gods, I will not!"

Ulcar's face quickly turned to a hue more fitting a crimson fruit as Plaucus began spewing curses at him just as he had done before, all of which landed on deaf ears. By the time Plaucus had finished speaking Ulcar had managed to walk off to the hearth. His teeth, now visible in the fire's glow, were clenched in anger, almost ready to shatter in his growing temper. As Julia put it, he no longer held the sensible qualities of a lordly man, but appeared to have the mannerisms of a ravenous beast whose eyes were wreathed in malice. "I thought one corpse would be enough," he then said aloud as he looked into the flame. Here, he moved his knife toward his wounded arm.

"Ulcar, what are you doing?" Plaucus said, flustered.

"You have given me your answer!" Ulcar replied. "Now you must answer to him."

At that Ulcar let out a fierce and wild shriek of pain as he thrust the blade into the opening of his wound, where he immediately started sawing off a great, big flank of flesh as if he were a butcher carving his way into the meat of a pig. Back and forth he went in a fit of lunacy, until finally the whole of his forearm had been flayed close to the bone, leaving nothing more than fonts of blood that spewed all over his robe. He then fell to his knees with an exasperated breath, holding out for Plaucus' viewing a hunk of flesh, which was promptly cut short because he tossed it into the fire with an nefarious smile cast about his face.

243

It was here that Plaucus' boldness left him entirely, because as soon as Ulcar's flesh touched the flames every source of light in the room had vanished in an instant, plunging the great hall into utter darkness. As Julia described to me, not a moment after the extinguished flames of the hearth had suddenly burst alight and, in sequence, the torches around the hall, including the candles upon the table, were lit again. Their flutter was drawn towards the hearth, as if the hearth itself had taken in a deep breath. And this breath was real, for it was visible, taken by the form of an unnatural wind, causing everything in the hall that was unfastened to tumble upon the floor. Plaucus, and Julia, were voiceless, and in disbelief of what they were witnessing. Then, the violent gale had ceased altogether, at point nothing was seeable, for the hall was ablaze with rays of scarlet light like the beams of morning's first glow, which shone from the hearth. Up until that moment Plaucus had been silenced by the overwhelming horror of the dark witchery before him, though just as he let fall his protective guard he let out a blaring shrill from his throat, his eyes locked with those of the Conjuror's, whose ghoulish figure stood before the hearth, wrapped in the ancient, black garbs of the *Inferi.*

"You see, Plaucus," Ulcar laughed, cradling his arm with a jitter. "He is real."

None could see the Conjuror's face, for it was hidden behind the shadow of his hood, his head now turning languidly toward Ulcar. There was a pause for a moment as Ulcar's eyes met with his, wherein Ulcar smiled with rapture, as if all at once he was charmed. At a stroke, however, the Conjuror dashed sidelong towards Ulcar like an arrow in flight, his feet seemingly hovering above the floor. He clutched Ulcar's throat with a hand that shot out from his oversized sleeve; the hand itself appearing like that of a corpse, mouldered in many parts to the bone. Without hesitation he hoisted him above his tall, hunchbacked frame as though Ulcar weighed no more than a feather. And as he did, the sleeve of his black robe slid down to his elbow, revealing that the entirety of his arm was the same as his hand, decayed of flesh.

"Anoarin! Master!" Ulcar screeched as he fought for air, writhing in the creature's clutch like a hen to the slaughter. "You... you swore—"

In that instant the Conjuror snapped Ulcar's neck with a slight flick of his skeletal wrist. He cast Ulcar's pendulous corpse into the hearth behind him with force enough to send it crashing upon the stone wall beyond, causing lumps of red-hot coals and balls of fiery timber to shoot out; one setting a nearby tapestry aflame, others setting fabrics and the clothing of the nearby dead alight. Meanwhile, the sound of clamorous clash of steel had sparked in the corridor behind the barred doors. I cannot be certain whether Plaucus supposed that this commotion was that of his guards battling towards his rescue, but he did look over his shoulder for a split moment toward the door, at which time he began to frantically cry out for assistance.

His pleas, however, were abruptly silenced, for just as his eyes turned back the Conjuror was before him like a creeping spectre, leaving not two feet between them. The creature came closer still, slowly bringing his hands to either side of his cowl, which had Plaucus trembling and whimpering in anticipation of the horror to come. Julia was still paralysed by fear, and all at once it became difficult for her to breathe, a force seizing her lungs, and no doubt Plaucus' too, for the air had become thick with the malice of a dark enchantment, a noxious air born of the fine crimson mists that emanated from the apertures of the Conjuror's robe. They coiled around Plaucus' body like a throng of ravenous snakes, caressing his skin until each of his senses were utterly weakened, and his blood turned to ice. It was then that the Conjuror removed his cowl, at which point Plaucus' horror, as heard through his gasps for air, grew ever greater.

What next I tell are Julia's words as she describes the horrific monster, her memory of his image engrained forever in her mind.

Of all the creatures that lurk in the night, the hideousness of the Conjuror's appearance exceeded them all in abhorrence. His face, though it took the form of a man's, bore the resemblance of a ghoul, one that was nearly naked of its flesh, wholly decrepit and decayed, and covered with the blackish scars of pestilence. Upon his head there were long strands of grey, thread-like hairs, some fluttering in breezeless air, others outstretched around his halfened ears, which were drooping quite lower from what should have been their natural position. By the same token he had no frame of a nose, and his round, obsidian eyes were hollow. Whatever flesh remained either hung from the ridges of his brows or cheeks, or from the visible bone beneath, all of which was equally rotted and purplish in colour. His teeth were ossified as well, and as you can imagine, my dear reader, they were fully visible through the hollowed sides of his jaw, where his tongue, the only feature of living-tissue, was blackish and swollen, and it's surface riddled with sores and lesions.

"What...what are you?" Plaucus shivered.

The Conjuror did not speak, but canted his head with a devilish grin. He slowly raised his arm and pointed at the second to last marble bust that was among those which adorned the columns of the hall; never once did he sever his gaze. Pressed by fear, Plaucus looked beyond the Conjuror's outstretched hand, whereupon his eyes suddenly grew wide with overwhelming shock, for the bust in his sight was none other than Anoarin himself. As Julia recalled, this bust was a gift to Plaucus from Ulcar — he had fooled him into believing it was some ancient Anolian king, and not Anoarin.

"It can't be," Plaucus said, his voice low and weighed down by renewed disbelief.

The Conjuror advanced another step, and there, with a swift lurching motion, he reached for Plaucus' shoulder. Instinctively, Plaucus reeled backwards in a fit of surprise, hurling himself to the floor upon his back. By now the clamour in the hall had turned to a great rattle, the doors shaking wildly each time it was struck by what seemed to sound like a battering ram. Plaucus quickly cast a glance over his shoulder, watching the guards Nasos and Musa as they braced the doors with all their might, as if they fought to buy the creature some precious seconds.

Plaucus wiped away the blood that had splattered in his eyes. He then spurred to action like a frenzied rat, pushing the fullness of his weight toward the doors by pressing with his heels. He chucked towards his feet anything his hands could grab, hoping to slow down, or rather dissuade, the Conjuror's persistent advance behind him. When this scheme failed, he began crying aloud as he had done before, though it seemed that no matter how loud he shouted his hollers were drowned away by the ramming of the door, and from the chimes of the clacking silver tableware his body forced about.

Meanwhile, Julia saw her chance of escape and slowly shifted her way to freedom, clawing inch by inch along the floor with one hand cupped around the gash on her waist. As luck would have it, she found her way through the swamp of dead, unnoticed. When she reached close enough to the doors her heart had suddenly been bolstered by Polemos, for in an explosion of strength and courage she jumped to her feet and pitched herself against the closest guard, who in turn was knocked off his feet, catching the Conjuror's attention.

Therewith the doors of the great hall slammed open and none other than Cimber himself burst into the room at the head of fifty legionaries, their helmets shining silver in the light of the fire, which had slowly spread to the point that a quarter of the hall was up in flames. Petris too had entered the hall with, uncharacteristically, a sword in his hand. He snatched Julia and pressed her behind him, as Cimber did with Plaucus. At the same time the legionaries gathered around the side of the table opposite the Conjuror with their shields locked tight in battle formation, the line quickly shrinking and teetering in terror at the discovery of what it was that stood before them.

"It's…It's him! It's the Conjuror!" Plaucus squawked.

At that moment the fire of the hearth crackled with a great uproar, blasting the hall with a torrid wind that brimmed with red-hot embers. In tandem the men hid behind their bulwarks; all of them except Cimber, who stirred and threw himself to battle, pouncing onto the table in front of him. As he stormed forward, ready to strike, the Conjuror's eyes flashed red. The scarlet mist remerged, more brilliantly than it had before. In a whirl it surged upwards from the end of his robe to the tip of his risen hand, whereupon it swallowed the whole of his body, and the vile grin upon what was left of his lips.

CHAPTER 16

For three days we marched in relative darkness along a narrow and marshy furrow between the trees, for when we had entered the path of the south ingress it had begun to rain ceaselessly as if the showers of spring had let fall the remainder of their burden upon us, all within a short, miserable time. Tired and dismal as we were, we trudged onward, following the path, or rather this new river, along a northerly course, which by journey's end had veered eastward to where the light of the sun had finally peered through the woodland's thick canopy. Here, we emerged from the forest, finding ourselves once again amid a terrain that seemed more the realm of the gods than a land forged for us men to dwell. In part, this landscape had a striking resemblance to that of Anolia's south, insofar that the greenery before us was bathed in summer's lustrous brilliance. I have not, however, given its sight due justice, so I will return to what I had seen in a moment, my patient reader.

First, however, I would do well to speak of the mood of the men. Throughout our journey through the forest, the men had been rather demoralised, to say the least — the mood also saturated in agitation by the Uthians who were angered that a few of our men had accused them of burning the carts. Further along in the journey the mood had changed altogether. As we had exited the forest, a great and rousing cheer rose from the ranks in a shared outcry; many of the men let sound the fullness of their relief like a mob of drunken companions, embracing one another in victory, or more simply in the achievement of conquering the forest. In truth, I was surprised at first, confused even. I had thought their morale to be completely splintered by the burning of our provisions, for not only did we suffer a loss to a sizable portion of our food and water, not to mention most of the tools to my dismay, but also much of what Cimber had given to us in spare armaments as well. More than that, the forest, having been a wilderness of little opportunity for replenishment, saw our bellies filled with nothing but wild plants and, at times, false thoughts for a proper meal to come.

It was because of these latter reasons that I was certain that the common interests that bound us together had been fractured to no repair. Though, as I have said, it appeared that in the matter of exhausted zeal I was amiss. In the spirit of their people, the Uthains mounted a triumphant howl, as if to outdo the legionary chants that had sprung. At first I thought it strange, being that they had always seemed reserved in their energy, and had mostly kept to themselves in our time together. In truth, I thought it to be a competition of sorts. But to my surprise, it was not a contest, but a welcoming. They began to take the arms of us Anolians who were drawn to the spectacle as though they were our brothers, including those of Priscus, Axle, and Jon, who were the first to approach their flock. When Lera and I were welcomed I no longer felt our company drawn apart by foreign births, and that at this point we had truly become one in our purpose, whether bound by the task, or by our call to the sword. As such, we gathered ourselves and our remaining stocks, and then took to the column once again in good spirit, only this time in a marching array of high stature, six abreast and in mixed order, hoisting high in the morning breeze what standards of Anolia and Uthia we had left.

On we went, under Priscus' guidance. We moved westward at the quick step upon a field of grass that reached no higher than our ankles, which was quite peculiar for a land that was supposed to be unkept. If I were to make a portrait of it, I would say that it had the same look as that which is found in gardens of the king's palace. As we pressed on, under a cloudless blue sky, our path was hemmed by a wide and tranquil river of clear blue water, and the face of an enormous mountain to the east. I would later discover that this peak was the same as that which the Ascani were meant to descend. It was also the furthermost point of the mountain range that veiled the entrance to the valley and the Black Shores, which meant that we were walking, unknowingly, toward a possible meeting with the creatures. Thus, to be sure that we would not stumble into a war-party waiting in ambush, Priscus sent Lera and Meric to scout ahead past the bend of the mountain. As fortune would have it, they returned quickly without cause for alarm, and so from this point forward we followed the river for another half a league, keeping ourselves not a hundred yards from the base of the peak so that if we were to be attacked we could use the sloped terrain to some advantage. Then, as the map indicated, the river split into two shallow streams; one which continued to course westward toward a wall of snow topped ridges that stood overlooking a seemingly endless woodland, and the other northward to what seemed like open country, and hopefully toward the castle of Northfleet.

North was our course. It took us another half hour just to come clear round the base of the mountain, but just as we did we found ourselves at the entrance of a broad valley, which caused an immediate firmness in my chest, because it reminded me very clearly of Easteria. I was overwhelmed by the unexpected sight before me, because never had I imagined that I would come to see such verdant beauty at the edge of the northern world. At our feet there began a near-endless sequence of very low, flat-topped hills, which then fell steadily down to a vast green meadow of grass, the very same as that which we had been walking upon. On the flanks there were two dense forests, so lush in verdure that the whole appeared like feathers on the wings of a bird. Great big follacious oaks they were to my eyes. The air too grasped my senses, for with each forward step it seemed to cool, and its scent became more and more suffused with the odour of the sea; the North Sea to be exact.

It was then that I saw it, far-off by the mouth of the bay beyond: the contour of an ancient castle, the fortress of Northfleet. I came to halt like those around me, though Lera had come up alongside me, swiftly followed by Axle, Meric, and Andreaus. Together they looked in awe at the distant fortress, yet I am only guessing that they did so because my own eyes were transfixed in said fashion. In my heart, however, I was both frightened and exhilarated. Afraid because part of me realised that I was now no more than two leagues from that which could soon become my tomb, but in the same instance I was relieved because at long last we had arrived at the start of our task, now having crossed, on foot for the most part, the same distance as half the breadth of our kingdom. But in truth, my dear reader, I was more contented by the fortress' existence, seeing as how this task of ours had already taken many lives when none had any certainty that it stood in the first place, let alone how it stood in the form that I was witnessing it presently, basking in the rays of the sun as if it were the very home of Apaliunus, lord of the gods, and patron of light and brilliance.

Even from afar I made clear the appearance of its walls, of which it had two of pale grey stone. One formed the bulwark of the castle, long in its limits and slightly contorted like the shape of a ripple on the water, and the other, seemingly twice the height of the first, appearing to me as though it girded the keep, which was very clearly embedded, in part, in the face of a great cliff that shielded the whole west side of the castle. To my aged memory, the castle itself was similar in its features to those fortresses in the southern reaches of Anolia, particularly those of Tolerium and Heraea, wherein their ramparts were adorned with a series of squared towers, all of which were void of housing and simply crowned by merlons. As we came closer I began to take note of the fortress' position. As I have already noted, Northfleet was situated at the very end of the valley by the shores of a bay, so named Eagle Bay by the men, for the two mountain ranges at the flanks continued straight off into water, but whose ends curved inward like the talons of an eagle. In terms of the fortress itself, however, much was different then when I had seen it from a distance. At first, it appeared as if it rose high above the water, though as the army came to halt before the heart of the outer wall, a forty-foot gatehouse, I was surprised to see that it rested upon flat ground. In fact, we all believed its eastern end to be one with the bay — it was a port-castle after all. Yet, this was not true. Only a small segment of the wall trailed downward onto the adjoining shore of black stones, stopping as it merged with the rocks of the cliff.

A crawl before sunset, I carefully stepped onto the castle's lowered drawbridge, whose iron chains, which would normally lead to the gatehouse's windlass, were missing. Not that it was surprising, given that this fortress was dated a thousand years. Then again, it took me a moment to realise that I was standing on timber of no less the same age, and though it was rickety, it did not seem ready to crumble at any moment, but rather it seemed still sturdy, enough to hold the weight of several men, including Jon's. Over the rail, I peered into the moat, or should I say the wide, sunken gully of dry, sun-baked earth, which was mind-boggling seeing as it had rained for some days. More than that, and much more surreal for me that is, was the stillness that commanded the walls, and the magic which seemed to bleed from the stone, for the castle was, as I saw it, untouched by the sheer abrasion of age, and in parts, faintly kept.

Suddenly, Andreaus gripped my shoulder. The force of his clutch caused a loud crackle at my feet. "Now that we know we got here first, builder, I trust your skills will fare just as well here as they did with my ship," he said with a smirk, pointing with his eyes toward a part of the battlements that was in veritable need of repair. "It looks like you have your work cut out for you."

"Aye," I replied. I was preoccupied by the pile of loose stone that rested upon the right tower of the gatehouse, which I had not seen before. "Though where to begin."

"With our supplies," Priscus said, as he walked in front of me with Axle close behind. He removed his sword belt and leaned the hilt of his blade against the nearest post. After that, he began to roll up the sleeves of his tunic while adding, "Find Edros at the rear and see to his word. I want a count of all that's left in our provisions, including the tools. And tell Meric on your way that we'll break for an evening meal once we get inside, so have him start sending out parties to gather as much as we can find before nightfall."

"Yes, but. How do you intend on getting inside in the first place?"

"By crossing through the gate. How else?" Axle replied, muddled by my question.

I looked over to the gatehouse with my own puzzled expression. "Well," I said, clearing my throat. "That won't be possible, because if you haven't already noticed we can't just pass through. That portcullis over there isn't going anywhere. There's no mechanism in place to have it opened, let alone support the weight. The rainures and gaffs for the drawbridge are all gone, and I'm almost certain that the windlass is too. Even if it were still there, we need more than a few men to climb up to the gatehouse and repair it until I can fashion some sort of proper support to hold the weight. It's either that or I can try building the whole engine as quick as I can, but it will take more than a day just to —"

"I will lift it," Jon said with confidence.

"What?" I said, turning to him. "A thousand years of rot or not. It's made so that you can't."

"Right then," Axle said, as he spun around to face the men. "Let's get a move on, shall we? I'd much prefer we don't get caught tonight with our arses out in the breeze!" Here, he addressed the men. "So then, listen well, all of you! Those of you who think you look like that giant of a man over there," he said gesturing toward Jon, "step forward and put that brawn of yours to work! The rest of you settle yourselves and keep your eyes on the look-out. Look to the trees in the east. Call out anything you see."

Rooted by Axle's words I lingered a moment, watching as Jon came toward me and the crossing with a string of bare-chested Uthians and Anolians at his back. For some reason they seemed heightened with the desire to labour, though it soon became clear to me that they were simply delighted by the chance to flaunt their brawn against Jon's, or better yet, the opportunity to triumph in a contest of strength against him.

"Wait a second," I said, dumbstruck. "You're not seriously going to have them hoist the gate open are you? That iron alone weighs triple the lot, if not more!"

"Aye, that's what we're doing," Priscus replied, readying himself as if he was going to help. "It's like Andreaus said. Luck is on our side that the creatures are nowhere in sight, but the Ascani could still be at our backs at any moment. Right now, all we need them to do is to keep it open long enough for some of us to get inside. We'll scout the area, and then after that, if there are things that need fixing, we'll do as you say."

As a matter of fact, the notion was not entirely farfetched. The portcullis, though still full, was not of the same opulence as the gatehouse which surrounded it, insofar as its size was concerned. It had the appearance of that which one might expect for a portcullis, but this one was certainly not imposing, if I put it into a single word. This realisation did not sit well in my thoughts, because this gate was the only means of entry as far as I could tell. As I looked through its hollow squares I saw no secondary gate, nor any barbican type structure. There was nothing more in sight than what seemed to be the beginnings of an open courtyard at the top of several stairs. Be that as it may, my mind was still taken with doubt at the possibility that a handful of stout men could raise it just high enough for some to pass on through, which to my great surprise they did after a short time, even before Meric could set out his search parties, or Edros and I could finish our task.

As nightfall approached Priscus, instead of entering the fortress himself as all the rest had done, decided that we captains should begin an urgent, preliminary measure of the castle's exterior, or at the very least see to the current state of its defences, since from this time onward we began to move more quickly with the assumption that the Ascani could show themselves without warning. With no time to squander, Priscus, Axle, Andreaus, and I walked around the gully to inspect the integrity of the outer wall, whereupon my blindness caused by my wonder of the fortress began to exhaust itself, seeing as I now began to notice more and more of its defects. There were several segments of the battlements that lacked the sturdiness or impregnability of their former glory. Though the castle's front wall was still intact, there were, however, quite a few fissures in the stone; some rather wide and deepened, others more narrow, from which vines permeated outwardly on the surface like veins. Beyond that, the ramparts were in good order for the most part, save for in some sections entire sequences of merlons were fully removed, while to a greater extent, three of the towers closest to the bay, and two in the west portion of the castle, appeared as though their top halves were cloven by a sickle, each one neither useable in our defence, which was a shame, but to our advantage nor were they easily scalable by the enemy.

Twice we took to our inspection, and with each pass I took note of additional areas that required mending, jotting them down in my book as they came to sight. All the while Priscus and the others kept to my front, engulfing themselves in long-winded talks about how best to prepare for our stand, which in turn aroused my eagerness to begin working on the daunting tasks ahead of me as soon as possible. By the time we had returned to the drawbridge after our third pass the sky had grown dark with weighty clouds and a hard rain began to fall, making the conditions so wretched and the earth so sodden that I was stripped from the chance to begin labouring on even the most simplest of works.

I passed through the portcullis doused and frigid, desperate for the warmth of a fire. The sting of the icy rain rattled my bones, and it felt as if every part of my body was inhabited by goose flesh. As I fought to quell a growing fit of shivers, I watched as Jon and several brawny Uthians steadily withdrew the two spires of flat-faced stones which they had used to support the portcullis' weight. Then, with the last of the stones removed, the gate shut in front of me with a loud bump and I found myself alone under the archway of the gatehouse in the company of my own thoughts.

Here I fully realised that this gate was, in fact, Northfleet's only entrance. I moiled over the discovery, but by no means in distress, for the structure, the gatehouse I mean, seemed sound in its form and all but easy to overcome. As I remember it, no more than eight men abreast could fit its width and six its height. Its roof was shaped like a half-moon, its surface paved by a roughly-hewn stone like the walls of a drinking well. The form of this stone changed as you entered the fortress because beyond this point the entry gave way to a small series of steps, as I had seen from the outside. It then led to what I would later learn to be the *atrium praeclarus*, a grand courtyard of marmoreal rock, which, like the castles of this era, occupied the majority of the castle itself.

I will say, in any case, that I could not help but direct my attention to the middling state of the portcullis, which had now become apparent to me. It was, as it appeared in my close study of it, the gravest of flaws among the ruins of the fortress that neither I, nor a flock of smiths could hope to repair in the short time which remained to us. The gods only knew how truly poor it was, though it was not as if I did not quickly come to know it myself, for each time I ran my fingers over the iron cross bars a mass of brown, flaky shavings peeled away from the surface of the metal, tinting the tips of my fingers an orange-reddish colour.

Above that, almost every rivet and bolt on the face of the gate was richly plagued with silver's rot, and at certain points there were noticeable bends in the bars, for the pins which kept them level were missing entirely.

"Just be glad it's in one piece," Andreaus said, interrupting my thoughts. He was standing at the throat of the ingress with his shoulder leaning up against the stone. "It'll hold as long as we make sure it does. Now come, Cillian, there's a certain scout who's been asking for you. Last I saw she was looking for you in the keep," he added, as he wheeled around and stepped off into the bustle of men behind him.

I took my leave of the gate, spent and wholly depleted of my strength. I made haste to find Lera, which I did soon after, and then together we took to some supper and much needed slumber, plotting ourselves in a small dimple within the rock face a short distance away from the rest of the men who were spread out across the courtyard. I closed my eyes in Lera's warm embrace, my mind on two things, whether I would be able to further explore the castle the next morning, or awakened in the dead of night ready to fight a battle.

***

The next morning I arose at the crack of dawn to the sound of an assembly call. I stretched out my hand to greet Lera, as I had done every morning, though instead of finding her warmth, my touch was met by the moist surface of a mud covered boot. Groggily, I turned my head. It was Meric's boot, and he was sitting in the place where Lera had slept with his back against the cliff, one knee outstretched and the other in his chest as if he had been waiting for me to wake for quite some time.

"You'll find a different kind of warmth in my boot," he said, fixing his vambrace to order.

"Where's Lera?" I said, sitting upright as I slowly took in my surroundings.

"Where do you think?" he replied. "Out scouting as usual. Some of us have jobs to do." He canted his head toward me with a light-hearted mirth about his face, his expression rather unusual to say the least. It was soon clear that a thought had entered his mind, one that effused a sort of warm air toward me — well in the sense that it was not immediately followed by his regular spurts of passive teasing and badgering. "You know I have to hand it to you, builder, you sure surprised me, and the rest of us for that matter."

"What about?" I asked, standing to my feet, ready to get the day moving.

"I mean after you took up Priscus' offer there was still a slight hint of doubt that you would not be up for the task of your position. And, well, there is no secret that this doubt might have been more strongly felt by a certain individual, one whose face never fails to add some, well, elegance in this occupation of ours."

"Meric," I said, looking over to him. "Is this some sort of apology?"

"No, no," he answered, now at his feet. "I'm just saying you are doing alright so far, at least from what I've been hearing on the whispers of many tongues. If I could speak a little more plainly, however, I just wanted to offer you my congratulations, man to man, you know? Honestly speaking, builder, I never thought it would be you. Well done."

"What are you on about?" I said.

"Come on now," he grinned with confusion. "You know, with Lera."

My face went red, suddenly realising that in our time together, Lera and I, had been anything but subtle. If you knew anything about the laws of the Anolian legion, my fair reader, then you would know that what Lera and I had been doing thus far was highly against the code, which was very strict in regard to relations under arms — not that many a man did not have a wife in secret, or perhaps two, at home. In a literal sense, we were breaking the law, and doing so openly as I have said. In fact, at this moment I thought Meric was fixing his way to extort me for a few coins, or worse, tell Priscus. "There's nothing —"

"Calm yourself, Cillian," he said with his hands waving off my concerns. "I like women too, enough I'd say not to bring up an age old law that has no place in the business of soldiering. There may be others that don't share our mind, however, so allow me, the master of charm, to offer you some advice. Staring up at the stars together is fine and all, but try not to swallow each other whole right on the edge of camp so everyone can see you — unless that's your fancy. And the same goes for sleeping next to each other. If you're going to do it, don't do it out in the open." Meric turned around and began walking off. "Now then, follow me would you. Priscus has asked for us. He's already started a council meeting in the keep."

I followed Meric across the courtyard with a sense of urgency in my step. As we walked, the horn rang for morning's instruction, whereupon the sergeants began their martial instructions. All the while Meric, trapped in his own world of vulgar thoughts, spoke endlessly about the comforts of women, which then very quickly turned into a rather patronizing lecture about my art of romance, lest I fail, his words not mine, at the art of long-term courtship. I pretended to listen of course, yet he was, in effect, talking to me as a friend. I just simply ignored him for the most part as I rolled my eyes at him when he was not looking.

Once we reached the end of the courtyard we halted for a few moments, because one of the sergeants had suddenly pulled Meric's attention off to the side. During this brief moment I stood at the base of the long flight of marble stairs. I had seen it the night before, though now in the sun's shine I started to see more clearly the rest of the castle. My curiosity aroused, I climbed the stair, some forty steps, all the way up until I came to a stop in front of two enormous bronze plated doors that were just as corroded as the portcullis. Right away, I saw the similarity between these doors and those which I had seen in King Adeanus' hall, for etched upon the metal slabs there were, though I could not by any means make them out, that which I supposed was the emblem of Northfleet's ancient garrison.

As I reached to touch it, Meric's grip suddenly drew me back, for without warning and without touching it, the doors opened, out from which a column of perhaps fifty men, headed by Lytus, poured out. The man bore his usual quirky smile as he led them passed the foothold, and then down into the courtyard.

"Watch yourself," Meric said, moving into the keep. "We need you."

I lingered for a minute more, because when Meric had pulled me back I had swung around to see the whole of Northfleet from a bird's eye view. Here, I noted how empty the castle truly was, now seeing that the castle itself was nothing more than a massive courtyard, one that was shielded by an outer wall. There were no markings of this fortress once having dwellings, barracks, or even a market square for trade. It did not even have a second rampart, seeing as how the place I was standing on was more like the terrace of the keep, which girded the flanks of the keep's stair like an open curtain, allowing for a singular access point to the keep itself. All I could see below my feet was a well, which in hindsight was the most important thing we needed for a seige.

I did not leave my position until Meric called out to me. As I entered the keep, a wide and high pillared hall opened up before me, which was inhabited by the boisterous commotion of the men inside moving to task and purpose; most of them stacking the remainder of our provisions in a makeshift stockpile and armoury. As interested as I was to assist, I dallied no further. At the rear of the hall I found Meric and Jon standing anigh to a crowd of senior Uthian and Anolian sergeants, about thirty men, who were all listening attentively to Priscus and Axle as each in his own turn established the order of battle.

"Well when they put it that way, it's not all that bad, is it?" Meric said satirically, as Priscus continued to speak to the men. "Of course I mean apart from the small fact that we now have a drawbridge that is quite literally just a bridge that cannot be hoisted, a gate that less than ten men can hoist up with a little bit of effort, and that our stores are down to about…I don't know what was it…three or four days at the most, *if* we force more than a few to abandon a meal or two. And let's not forget that we will be trapped inside a castle that's more akin to Adeanus' bloody villa. I mean, did you see how big that courtyard was out there? Might as well fight the bastards in the open. At least if I'm going to die, I'd want it to be quick."

"We'll have to make it work," I said, leaning against the nearest column.

"Tell that to the men who have neither a sword nor proper armour to put to good use. Ulcar's man saw to that with that bloody fire. I swear if I live to meet that old bastard one day I'll snap his neck with my own two hands, or push the sard down a mountain."

"We survive until the relief comes. That's always been the plan. Think favourably."

"Unless you have a field of grain and a running forge hidden in those trousers of yours that you aren't telling anyone about, then I'm allowed to be sullen, at least for another hour, I'd say. Enthera be praised and all that shite, but I didn't plan on turning this castle into my over glorified tomb. These walls are still full for the most part, I'll give you that. But if you ask me, as you are right now, I've got quite the sad picture of our surviving. I think our chances are still slim to none that we'll last no more than a night against what's coming."

"Would you wager your last coin on that?" I asked.

"Mine? No," he said, brushing his hair to the side. "Jon's probably. Though whose to collect the winnings if we'll all be dead." He let out a great yawn and then after a moment of silence his expression changed to a dejected stare. "You know, Cillian, I was once in a situation like this before. Well, not exactly, but as far as this feeling of despair in my gut is concerned, it is the same."

"Shouldn't we be listening to —"

"You see, builder, some years ago, about a league outside Heraea, we were coming back from a scouting mission up by the Blue Coast when we received a report, from Priscus no less, that a band of Veigurian pirates had landed on our eastern shores and had begun looting up and down the shoreline, burning and ravaging every village they saw along the way. Priscus, seeing as we were already out in the field, had tasked us to hunt them all down and put their barbarous shite to a stop. For a time we tracked them with no luck, always showing up a day behind their carnage to the same sight of burning homes and piles of charred corpses. So, you can see where the discouraging thoughts come in. It was only about a week later that we had finally come upon one of the outlying villages that wasn't engulfed in flame like the others. It was right on their path of destruction, but it was untouched. Not only that, but as we entered it, it was strangely dead and silent, much like what we had seen at Ortona. In my mind I knew that we had caught up to them, so when we entered the village we quickly began seeking them out. We searched every home, but found nothing. Well that is, until I saw it.

"What did you see?" I said, absorbed by his story.

"A light at the end of the road, in one of the houses, or some tavern by the size of it. I swear, Cillian, the god Aitanos must have entered our bones, because in a mere moment we surrounded that bloody place, swords drawn and readied to end all of them. I walked up the stairs with anticipation in my gut — like I feel now, about all of this. It festered in my blood as I put my hand on the door, hoping that some sort of a trap wasn't waiting for me on the other side. I placed my hand on the latch, and then with purpose in my heart I opened the door wide. And do you know then what it was that I saw?"

"The pirates of course."

"No," Meric replied, with a sunken gaze, eyes wide as if the shocking events were flashing before him. I saw an enemy far more daring to overcome. I saw a great big mob of large breasted women with curves upon their form that even I, Meric, drew into a heated sweat." He reached out and grabbed my arm just as I attempted to step away from him with rolling eyes. "Listen to me, Cillian," he added softly, fighting for my attention. "None of this is a lie. I'm only telling you this because the challenge of that night was no different than that which we are facing now, for even then I had neither the food nor the ammunition to last for more than a single night. If you understand my meaning."

"Andiel's mercy, man! What is wrong with you?"

"No you see, builder, when I say ammunition I really mean —"

Suddenly Jon jabbed Meric in the ribs. "Quiet," he said. "Listen."

"Be warned, all of you," Priscus said, his address rising to a more assertive tone. He and Axle were overlooking the men, slightly elevated by the lord's pulpit on which they were standing. "We've been lucky so far that we haven't crossed paths with the Ascani but now, more than ever, it can happen at any moment. And so from this point onward every passing hour will seek to hinder the tasks that we have given to you. Follow each to a point, and leave nothing to chance, or to the labour of another. Work and prepare as one. Our very lives depend on it. Is that understood?"

"Yes lord!" the sergeants cried in unison.

"Now then," Priscus added. "Let us hear from Cillian, the builder."

All at once it seemed as though a thousand heads turned to me, as if my position was already known to them. I felt a cold sweat form behind my neck, and an icy chill ran through me as every conversation in the room was silenced at once. The crowd of men in front of me was no longer just a crowd, but an immense mob which filled the hall as far back as the doors, for idle legionaries and curious Uthians, every man who was already in the keep, had gathered behind the sergeants upon hearing my name being called upon. Was it the words of a builder they wished to hear, or that of the Night Sorcerer? That I did not know. In fact, at this moment it felt as if I did not know anything, save that my blank expression was doing little to bolster the appearance of a master builder, or a sorcerer for that matter.

"Come," Axle said, gesturing for me to come forward. "Here, where all may hear you."

His calling me forward caused me to break from my nerves and move toward him — that and the force that came from Meric pushing me along. As I moved to the front of the crowd, cutting through the men and their lingering stares, I felt overcome with a weakness in my spine. You, dear reader, may be wondering why I felt so full of fear, and the answer is simple. I did not know what I was going to say to them, as I had not yet put together any semblance of a drafted plan in regards to the mending of the fortress. All I had done thus far was take notes of what needed to be done, and not how I should be doing it. In every sense I was walking blind and without guidance, even though I had in my possession a half-opened journal filled with nothing but the schemes of my war engines, which, as I have said, I could not hope to employ in our time frame. And so as I recall, my mind was buried with the thought that my skill as builder was soon to be tested on many fronts, as well as as my role as *sodalis* to Priscus, the purpose for my being here on this quest, and whether the years of long study within the craft were well deserved.

One half step to the pulpit and I was standing before the men, looking downward at them as if I were some instructor ready to give instruction, which was in that moment what I had to do. By now Priscus and Axle had ceded the center of attention to me by walking off to the side, at which point my tongue became as heavy as iron and my spine no less than brittle. The faces of a hundred grizzled veterans of foreign peoples and many legions, the old guard as I always saw them, appeared like kindling in my mind, each and all ready to erupt in flame and ruin if I should fail to deliver how best to keep this fortress standing, insofar as its structure was concerned.

"I...I...believe—" I stopped myself short, quickly digging my nose into my journal with an expression of loss about my face. I was so nervous that the words on the page melded together and I could not make them out although I was the one to write them. All the courage that I had gained since Easteria was little by little wasting away. I did not know what to do.

Then, abruptly, my eyes were struck by waves of silver shimmers; gleams more like. As I looked up with a puzzled squint I noticed Lera at the end of the hall, leaning by the door, her head hunched inside her scout's black cowl. With the silver plating on the underside of her amulet she was purposely flashing the sun's light at my eyes, clearly trying to muddle my thoughts up even more than I was already doing for myself. I could not help but grin at the sight of her smile, at which point a calmness passed over me. The tautness in my nerves were washed away, for it was then that I realised that I was not alone in this task. We were all here ready to fight; we were all here to carry the burden and face the challenge to come as one.

I moved to address the crowd, to the men who were depending on me for guidance. "Right," I said aloud with vigour as I snapped my journal to a close. I did not need it. "What was once stone, we will now make of timber!"

CHAPTER 17

Not an hour later the horn of labour sung its rousing tune and every soul within the fortress gathered in front of their sargeants with a blaze in their breast; each legionary ready to put the heart of Anolia's legions in contest against the vigour of Uthia. In the courtyard they were ranked in rows of twenty, wearing nothing more than their tunics in preparation for the heat of work, some seeking to work with the comfort of the sun's warmth upon their bare backs. I stood before them like a king atop the gatehouse with Priscus and Axle at my side, once more making clear the tasks I had laid out earlier. I was given full command of the restoration of Northfleet, and so with speed in mind these tasks were divided on the basis of skill, or any semblance of it. Altogether the tasks that Priscus, Axle, and I passed were as such. First, and above all, Meric, Lera, and Andreaus would see to the command of several small scouting parties, each one entrusted to keep their eyes on the borders of each woodland, especially the one to the east, thwarting any Ascani ploy to catch the labourers off-guard absent the defence of our walls. Next, Axle, Edros, and Ferix would see to all matters regarding our supply. Food, and to an extent weapons, as Meric had pointed out to me, were our greatest worries where supply was concerned. By this time our provisions had already been reduced by a third since our arrival. Water, however, was of ill-concern.

The water of the well was clean and ever flowing, for its ground supply came from the snow topped ridges of the west, or so the legionary who discovered this had told us.

As you can imagine I was the head of my group of newly enlisted carpenters. I was prepared for the endeavour, more confident then I had ever been before. For this reason I took under my wing many eager hearts, including Priscus, Jon, and a legionary by the name of Barsalus, who you, my reader, already know. I had learned then that Barsalus specifically had knowledge of the craft, his actions at the Battle of the Valentian River showed it. In fact, upon our first meeting, he had asked me to be his teacher, as if I were some renowned master of the art, a feeling I welcomed with humility. And so, imbued with the excitement, and desperation, to make new the ruined fragments of the past, I led those assigned to me to the border of the western forest, where the timber seemed thickest, and where the distance from the gate ran the shortest.

And so it was that for three days we laboured with fervent force and restless spirit until the revival of Northfleet had been near to completion. On the first day our sharpened axes had met the thick and rigid stems of the evergreens, cutting down no less than a hundred, and whose lengths were beyond the height of four men. Great columns of men lined the southern field so that each and every severed trunk could be hauled back to the fortress, which was done with the help of nothing more than the strength in our shoulders and the brawn in our legs. Gruelling as it was, and notwithstanding the weather, which was utterly stifling, not one man had faltered behind in his efforts. On the second day, hammers and mallets of every kind had fallen to strenuous purpose. Only a few of the fastens and nails remained from the provisions that Cimber had given us, so what timber we could not affix with iron pins, we did so with wooden pegs, or on occasion, with mighty heaps of the amber resin that seeped from the bark of the trees. Resin was, as a matter of fact, not my suggestion, but that of Barsalus, who explained to us that when heated, it turned liquid and could be mixed with charcoal to form a glue-like tar. We used it sparingly, however, on the lesser pieces of wood in the hospice we fashioned, for resin, in any form, is naturally flammable. By the end of the third day we had been able to restore entire gaps between distant merlons, restructure, and in some parts rebuild, some of the more highly ruined segments on the eastern towers and battlements, and to everyone's relief, we had reinforced the portcullis as best our labour could make possible.

Much of Northfleet's coastal edges remained as they were. The extent of their ruin was beyond our reach for repair; none could in any way see to their restoration without several weeks of prolonged labour. Our fixed efforts continued to be on the reinforcement of the outer wall, the only potential front of assault where the enemy could attack in force. An attack from the water was impossible, nor was a descent along the face of the western cliff likely. Truth be told, by this time some of the men believed that the Ascani had bypassed the fortress altogether, some had begun to think that this army in approach was not real. It was indeed strange that they had not yet revealed themselves to us, though my belief of their existence, and of their upcoming attack, remained firm. So now, on the fourth day of our labour, I took it upon myself to complete the finishing touches of our restoration, filling my time with any little task I could find that emboldened my heart more than it did the actual defences.

"Here, pass it to me," I said to the young-looking legionary beside me. I took from him his drawknife, which he was using to shave the bark from a plank. "I want you to eye my hand," I went on, as I motioned the act by quickly scraping off long strips of bark. "Straighten your back and draw the blade to your gut in short spurts. You don't have to put all your strength in it. You want the steel to do the work. Cut along the grain like I'm doing, or I promise you by the end of it you'll have nothing left of the timber, or feeling in your hands, alright?" I offered him the hilt. "Go on, give it a try."

He clutched the tool and returned to task. With the application of my guidance he proceeded to shave off long strips just as I did, which then suddenly forced him to turn to me with a childlike smile. I replied likewise with a hand on his shoulder. "I did not know it was this simple," he then said, pausing from the work. "I can't believe I was doing it wrong this whole time."

"Well, for what it's worth, I couldn't light a simple fire two months ago," I said. "We all have our time for everything. Keep on as I showed you and you'll have twenty done by midday."

The legionary averted his eyes for a moment, keeping his sunny smile. Even a blind man could tell that he wished to ask me a question, but he appeared too timid to sound the words. "It was a sky-torch, wasn't it?" he blurted as I began to walk away. "The red spark the others are always talking about. You know, the ones they say came out from your hands. It was sorcerer's powder, wasn't it? Nothing more than metal salts laced with iron shavings, things I'm quite sure are far from the stuff of enchantment?"

"What do you know of sorcerer's powder?" I asked, retaking my position near him.

"Quite a lot actually," he smirked as if reflecting on his knowledge. "Did you know that the right mixture for sorcerer's powder is quite hard to get even for learned hands. You see the elements you need are not easy to come by, which is why only some of our legions have them, and even then they won't have many." He hoisted the timber he had been working on onto a pile of finished planks. He took another, continuing to work on as he spoke. "In fact," he added, with the strain of labour on his tongue, "your legion, the Vined Sword, is probably the only one that has no more than a dozen in store. Well anyway, when you heat the metal to the right warmth it starts to burn nicely, giving you the perfect shine and colour."

"What's your name?" I asked, curiously. I have had my fair share of speaking with legionaries over the years and not many, without insult, could speak to matters that were unrelated to, farming, women, gambling, and the sword; all in that order to be precise. I was intrigued by his youth and his knowledge, which, now that I come think of it, might have been how others saw me when I spoke of my craft.

"Etorus," he replied. "Etorus of the Grey Isles."

"The Grey Isles?" I said, completely taken aback. "Aren't you a —"

"A what?" he laughed. "A thief? A brigand? A marauder? You know we seafolk aren't all raiders, rovers, or pirates. The greater part are, yes. No lie in that. But not all of us."

"A little far from home is what I meant to say," I replied with an embarrassed grin. "What are you doing here in the legion? If I may ask. I mean no insult, but I always thought the people of the Grey Isles steered clear of us Anolians like a pestilence, especially Lord Perris and his fleet. I've never heard of your people taking to the legion before."

"Trust me they don't," he replied. "I'm sure I'm the only one who was mad enough."

"What's your story then?"

"I go where the silver is I'm afraid. And here, to some misfortune, is where it's taken me," he said, with a sigh. "As far as my story goes, I'm not sure you're going to believe it. It's a little on the remarkable side, but probably not as *unique* as yours I'd imagine — you know with your ability to conjure fire and all that."

"I'd like to hear it."

Etorus laid down the drawknife and brushed off the wooden shavings from his tabard, which had the emblem of the Bronze Hammer upon it. "Well then," he said, clearing his throat. "Where to begin? This might come as a shock to you, but my father was in fact a brigand. When I was about nine he died fighting the

Kashtani sea watchers, and because of that my uncle took me in. He wasn't so noble himself mind you, but in all his pirate wisdom he thought it best that I move away from the family trade, which at that time was thieving merchant ships coming from Phylian ports. When I was young I had a way with making tonics and remedies, so from age ten I was to be an apprentice to the healers of the Sacrarium. An honourable path in life or some shite he said, but in truth I knew very well his intention was such that I bring back the knowledge of the healers to his crew. Kind of vile, don't you think? Having just lost my father. Anyway, off I went. They smuggled me across the sea in an Anolian wine ship for a month, where I nearly starved if not for a man named Attius, a legionary of Perris' legion no less, who gave me what food he could."

Here, Etorus paused, as if what next he wanted to say astonished him. "You know one would think that someone who steals coin for a living would know its value. Apparently my uncle didn't, because a year after arriving at the Sacrarium I was evicted from the temple on the grounds of what the head priest called *"a light purse in the face of the gods."* I was eleven by then, and I was cast to the streets like some unwanted dog, bouncing from one slum to the next, following the glimmer of silver and the promise of pay wherever it led me. That is until the fourteenth found me on Pindus, half dead by the side of the road. Ever since then they have put a sword in my hand and I have been following them since."

"How long do you have left in the army?"

"Ten years next week," Etorus said. "Fifteen if I take that piece of land they offered."

"You mean you're not going to go back home after your time is up?"

"To what? A life of thievery?"

"I guess not."

"You're right about that *night sorcerer*," he joked. "Unfortunately, you aren't a real sorcerer, so I guess now you can't conjure up some helpful spells for us in the battle to come. But if by some chance you *are* keeping your magics a secret, then it would be nice if you can turn that water over there into a couple barrels of cool ale. Maybe more than a couple." Etorus laughed as he slouched over the plank before him, beads of sweat dripping from his face, since by now the sun's warmth was enough to sap the spirit of even the fittest of men. "Say, Cillian, do you believe we have a chance?" he added with a more serious tone. "With the battle to come I mean? Staying alive until the king's army relieves us? I don't know if you know, but it's all the men are talking about. There's this one man in the twelfth, every night he keeps going on about how he was there at the council with the king. Says that girl, the scout, said she saw six thousand Ascani. Is that true? Six thousand of those bastards?"

I did not know how to answer him, despite having thought about that very question over and over throughout our journey, about the sheer number of Ascani we were bracing to face. Since we arrived in Northfleet I had preoccupied myself with our tasks, so I had never once allowed the angst of such a question the space to dwindle in my mind. In the end I knew the answer would make no difference even if I had given him one, seeing as how we had already built the bars to our confines and the brawn of our shield. It was, in truth, too late to think about such things. Whatever ill spirit the men now shared was no longer of cause for concern, since there was nowhere else they could go if safety was their desire.

"All we can do is believe we can," I said with a false grin. It is not like I did not believe we could not hold out. I just was not sure as many of the men were unsure - I too had not seen the Ascani army yet. "Look, the only truth —"

"The only truth right now is that if you both don't stop and take a breath, then the sun will make sure you never see the outcome for yourselves," Lera said aloud, her voice projecting from behind me. I promptly looked over my shoulder and saw her standing by a stock of freshly cut trees, great big heaps of them that reached as high as the midpoint of the wall. It was the first time that I saw her that day, and so I assumed that she had just come in from one of her scouting missions. "If you're done talking, builder, then you should come with me," she added, her arms folded as firm as her expression. "Lord Priscus wants your report. He's asked for you. Now."

"Go on, Etorus, take some water," I said, motioning my departure.

"Builder," Etorus blurted abruptly, forcing me to turn back to face him. "Before you go there was one other thing I should tell you. I said that I was good at making tonics and remedies, but what I forgot to mention is that I'm also quite good at making things turn to their opposite nature, just like what sorcerer's powder does. With that being said, if we have any more of that tree sap in our stores, then I think I can use it in another way. Might help us more in our belief."

"I'll see that it's brought to you," I said.

At that I began walking toward Lera at a quick step; she had pivoted on her heel and made her way around the bend of the timber. Fearing Priscus' impatience I picked up my pace even more on Lera's trail, whereupon I found myself halting in front of her in the middle of the stacks of timber with no other soul near to us. "Lera, what's going on?" I asked her; I sensed something was amiss. "I thought Priscus wanted my report just before nightfall —" Here, I stopped short, because all at once Lera grabbed me by the tunic and placed her lips upon mine with deep passion. "What was that for?" I smiled.

"I lied about the report," she said, her eyes fixed on my lips. "Come with me."

I have never been one to speak of what happens in the privacy between lovers, but this next part is also a part of my tale, regardless if it is unworthy of history. I remember it, my dear reader, as if I was now looking at the memory through the pane of clear glass. With secrecy Lera led me to the very top of the castle that was left unexplored. In haste I followed her through the passageways, and then into a room that I supposed was once the chamber of the garrison lord and now nothing more than an empty, dust filled space that was lit up by the sun's rays coming through the cracks in the alcoves along the north wall. In the moment that Lera barred the rickety door behind us she resumed her passionate kisses, only this time there was no reason to be secretive about it, neither was there any reason to stop us from pulling back our clothes, which we did in craze as if wanting to resume what was left out at the campfire. As Lera laid our clothes upon the cold stones to form a bed, I lit a small fire in the hearth with the few pieces of rotted wood that were scattered on the floor. It was then that I took a moment to notice more clearly the great, big fissure in the wall at the corner of the room, wherefrom I could reach out and touch the off-pour of a waterfall that flowed from the western cliff, which none of us knew resided behind the fortress. At this point it became clear to me that Lera had already scouted this room, because by the base of the fissure she had arranged a wooden pail and some rags so that we could wash away the labour of our day. Being the builder that I am, I had set up the pail in such a way that the water first flowed into it, and then as it filled it came down on us as if we were standing under the waterfall itself.

For a long while we idled in laughter under the cool water, upon which we took to the bed with the same vigour as when we had entered the room. How long we laid by the fire I do not know, only that we did so in each other's embrace with our eyes locked and full of fire, our beating hearts then falling silent to what seemed like an eternity of tranquil talk and more heartfelt stories.

***

Just as Lera had led me into the keep in secrecy, she did so on our way out. Of course our luck in staying hidden had run dry, for when we entered the lord's hall it was teeming with men sorting our provisions, completely inverse to how it was when we were first there. Once we merged with the bustle we took to the doors, at which point Meric caught sight of us.

"Where the hell have you two been," Meric said, stopping us in our tracks.

"Well," I said, flustered. "We were exploring."

"Exploring?" he replied, as if he knew that a study of the castle was not our given task.

"Why?" Lera chimed in. "Have you been looking for us?"

"As a matter of fact I have," he said with a tinge of annoyance. "Priscus has moved up the reports and he — wait a minute. You hair, both of you, why is it wet?"

"We've been exploring hard," Lera instantly replied, staring at him firmly.

With an expression of suspicion in his eyes Meric began to turn around. "Right," he then voiced. "Come along, then. They're already waiting for us."

Here, we started down the stairs, whereupon I saw Priscus and Axle just off to the side of its base, right up against the stone. They were in deep discussion with the others, Jon and Andreaus, each of them standing closely around the makeshift worker's bench that I had hastily crafted the day before with scraps of timber and damaged planks. Even though I was close enough to hear them, I could not, because opposite them, filling a portion of the courtyard, there was a martial instruction underway. One of the last matters we needed to strengthen was our unity in battle. Needless to say, the auxiliary troops of Anolia's legions were already familiar to our way of fighting, but no chances, as Priscus had put it, were to be taken. As such, the men were working at becoming one under arms with the Uthians, filling the afternoon air with the commotion of their vigorous training.

Meric, Lera, and I joined the rest of them at the table, and just as we did so the conversation shifted to our reports. Lera spoke first, quickly reporting the same announcement that she had many times before, which was that the Ascani were nowhere to be found. I spoke second, prompted by Priscus pointing his dagger to Axle's roughly constructed model of Northfleet; a small mockup that I had fashioned from pieces of stone, some of which were crowned with puny-sized standards to mark the positions of each company. I made my way across the model, speaking at length about the last of our restorations, about their progress. The last major project we had undertaken was the completion of the *ericius*, or the porcupine, which now filled the once easily traversable gully with a moat of jagged stakes. I then addressed the matter concerning the newest additions to the gate's defence, which there were two of note. First, we had placed a crescent shaped mound of earth that was topped with thorns like that of the gully in front of the portcullis, a thing we hoped would prevent, or rather slow down, the Ascani from swarming the ingress in great numbers. Second, we had constructed a series of barriers as you entered the fortress, in the event of a breach.

"And what of the drawbridge?" Priscus asked. "Has it been set to order?"

"Yes," I replied. "It's as you've asked. I pray that it works."

"With your hand behind it will," Priscus said, placing a wooden peg in front of the model to signify the crossing. "Alright then, listen here," he added after a quick breath. "Pass the word. From here on everyone is to stay inside the fortress, apart from the gathering parties. I want all the scouts focused on the east. We'll increase our search distance up until the river at the base of the peak. As for you, Cillian, I want you to tell Barsalus to report to me when the last section of the east rampart is complete — and be sure that he's relieving the labour with proper rest every half-hour. Tell his men to draw as much water from the well as they see fit. I don't want half of us falling to the sting of this heat before it all begins. That's all for now."

"If I may, my lord," Andreaus broke in, making himself seen at the head of the table. "Now that we have settled the business of our protection, perhaps we should revisit the question of our offensive abilities. And by that I mean our ammunition, and lack of weapons. I know Eraclea isn't known for its fortresses, but I'm pretty sure fifty quivers between us will do little in keeping their archers at bay, let alone slow their advance upon the walls. It seems the only plan we've managed to come up with to remedy these problems is to simply hope that we kill a good deal of them on this side of the wall so that we can loot the corpses. Aye, when it comes to arming those without swords it'll work, but plucking swords from the dead is a lot easier than collecting arrows. All I'm saying is that there has to be at least one hunter among us who knows how to fashion an arrow, right?"

"Fashioning them isn't a problem, captain," Axle said. "The Uthian captain, Ferix, has made it quite clear that we don't have the materials; no iron for the ends, and no feathers for fletchings. I haven't seen a damn bird in a week now that I think about it. I don't like it either, but we'll have to stick to looting corpses. We have no choice." He then stroked his beard and put another wooden marker on the table, only this time on what was meant to represent the midpoint of the southern and eastern fields. "What I am more worried about right now is why we haven't gotten even a slight whiff of these bastards. I know that if Petris were here he'd probably say that the gods have taken pity on us. That Apaliunus himself wished them all dead on their descent."

"I hope to the gods that it is so," Meric said with a great yawn. "I'm bloody tired."

"We'll see them soon enough," Priscus said in earnest. "If Lord Kaeso is right then they'll be here before we know it. So, let's hope Edros has our provisions in order —" Suddenly Priscus stopped himself short, because the men in the courtyard let out a great cheer. "Speaking of the man," Priscus went on, as we all watched a group of men enter the fortress with ribbed baskets stocked with large, greenish fish. Edros and his men were being mobbed with praises by those who were training in the courtyard. "Edros!" Priscus then shouted. "What news?"

Edros broke away from his group and rushed over. His expression was flushed and heated, his tunic crumpled and sodden, and his ears and nose made red from the sun. "I hope you like chard and fish, because that's all we ever find out there," he said, showing the contents of the basket to us.

"Of course, just like my absent mother used to feed me," Meric said.

Edros placed the basket at his feet. He brought one of the fish chest high for our inspection. It was plump and meaty by the looks of it, and the others in the basket were just the same. I did not know how long we would need to hold out before the relieving force would arrive, yet by the looks of it, it appeared that we would not have to do so on a hollow belly.

"The men have outdone themselves yet again, haven't they?" Edros said with a wide smile. "We cleared some forty-seven baskets just this morning, and by the gods if this sun hadn't pulled us away I'm sure we could've fished out the bay! I swear, I've never seen anything like it. There are hundreds of them just like this one over by the rocks," he said pointing to the largest and plumpest of the catch, "all of them grouped so tightly that you can snatch them right out of the water with a quick grasp." He put the fish back in its place and then rubbed his hands with the underside of his tunic. "If their numbers don't diminish by tomorrow then our supply will be all but solved. But I have to say, my lord, if we do go out tomorrow I'd ask we keep that chatty fellow Lytus away from the task. I wouldn't want that tongue of his scaring off the fish more than it already has."

"I'll help you sort them to order if you wish," I said, advancing to grab the basket.

"No need for that, builder," Edros interjected. "We'll have them all gutted, hung, and out in the sun before long. Besides, one of the Uthians knows another way to keep them from rotting by drawing salt from the sea. He's asked us to leave it all to him."

"Well, Edros, our thanks for your effort," Priscus said. "We'll make sure it lasts as —"

"Oi, you!" Meric suddenly shouted as he leapt from the stair upon which he lounged. He stormed off a short distance away into the courtyard, halting before a young looking legionary who was frantically gathering a bundle of arrows that he had seemingly, and of course mistakenly, let plummet to the ground. "What the hell are you doing?" Meric then scolded. "Did you bloody wash your hands in lard this morning? Do you know how precious these arrows are to us? What use will they be in killing the enemy now that they are all damaged?"

"Forgive me, captain!" the legionary blurted out in apology. His chin was tucked into his chest like a recruit first hearing the beration of his superior. "I did not think."

"Of course you didn't," Meric went on.

"Let it be, Meric," I said aloud, feeling a soft tenderness for the lad. "For Andiel's sake man, they're made of ash wood. They're far from damaged."

Meric huffed as he settled himself. I believe he knew in that moment that his outburst was unfounded. But, to be honest, we were all uptight about the matters that Andreaus had just spoken of. "Pick them up would you, and then see that their place isn't on the ground," he added calmly as if to excuse his temper. "And go on and get some water while you're at it. Your face looks like it's about to burst."

"Yes, captain!" the legionary answered before scampering off.

I stole a glance toward Jon, who was standing on the fringes of our captain's gathering. I was curious to see how he had reacted to Meric's sudden sergeant-like outburst. His expression, as I should have expected, was how it always was, still and blank. It was here, however, that even *his* unruffled stillness was broken, for just when Meric had returned to take his seat, a loud, shuffling sound of iron boots, followed by the calling of Priscus' name, was heard coming from the top of the stairs. The commotion came from two legionaries of the Silver Leaf, whose shouts we continued to hear as they raced down the steps with an all-consuming urgency about their faces. By the time they reached the bottom Priscus, as well as the rest of us behind him, had intercepted the men, whereupon they stopped abruptly, each with his hands on his knees while drawing in heavy, exhausted breaths.

"What is it?" Priscus said with fire. "What's happened?"

"My lord Priscus," one of the legionaries spoke up. "We've found something in the keep, in the lower chambers...where the castle melds into the rock!"

"What do you mean you found something?" Axle said, confused.

"I don't know for certain, captain," he continued while shaking his head. "I can't explain it properly, so it's best you see it for yourself. All I know for sure is that you're going to have to bring that Linlani along if we're going to find out what it is."

CHAPTER 18

Not a moment after we had received the news we found ourselves racing toward one of the doorways at the back end of the hall, particularly the one that marked the entry to the sections of the fortress that were built into the cliff. The two legionaries led us through the door, upon which we walked, in single file, down a seemingly endless spiral stair of gray, banded iron rock. It was the first time I set foot in this part of the castle. I had no awareness of its existence. Lera and I were the last in the line, and therefore the last to see that the stair opened up into a long, torch-lit corridor. We passed through the corridor in haste, stopping only when we had all entered a large chamber at its end. When I had stepped in I could hear the echoes of our steps. I should mention that the ground itself was of the same rock as the stair — well everything was in the same material being that we were well into the cliff. The wood that I had stepped on, however, was but a fragment of the debris that surfaced the ground. In fact, there lay in a great many small heaps, the reminisce of more than several splintered tables and chairs that were veiled in cobwebs, whose silky essence shone in the added torchlight that Jon had begun fixing.

As eerie as the chamber was, it was nothing compared to what we witnessed next. Beyond the debris, and to our front, there stretched across the entirety of the wall a grand curtain of creeping vines, brownish and thinly like the roots of a tree, and gathered together rather densely. They were sprouting from the ceiling, which was of concern to me in so far as I feared that the ceiling of the chamber could have been compromised, structurally speaking. It comes with no surprise that the last thing I wanted was to be buried underneath the weight of the rock.

Meric looked about cautiously as if he were studying his surroundings, but doing so with an expression about his face that suggested he was confused as to why we had been led here. "Just so you know I brought my knife," he said to the legionary at his side. "Just in case you're planning on killing us...*here* in this place."

"Why did you bring us here?" Priscus asked the men. "What is it that I'm looking at?"

"There, my lord, at the center. Do you not see it?" the legionary said as he directed his focus with a nod. He seemed hesitant to advance, and so he simply pointed forward, "There's a door, right there behind the growth."

By now Jon had fashioned several torches. One he gave to Lera, who was standing between Axle and me, and the others to Priscus and Andreaus, who were in the midst of tugging at the vines. Before any of us could react they lowered their torches to the base of the curtain, setting fire to the roots. Right away, I cried out with shock, knowing full well that the fissures in the stone, though enduring, would worsen if subjected to heat for long periods of time; not to mention that the room was a pile of kindling. I lunged to the front to put out the flames, yet for some reason Axle swept me aside with a casual, *let the fire run its course,* type of expression. As the flames caught hold of more fuel the room was suddenly engulfed in a brilliant flash of light and heat. To my surprise the inferno only lasted a few seconds, for the fire had devoured the roots in an instant, as if their substance was like that of thread. The sight before us was now nothing more than a myriad of fluttering cinders; some of which began to consume the cobwebs on the floor, the rest illuminating the oaken, marble wreathed door that was revealed to us.

"Where do you figure it goes, my lord?" a legionary asked, stunned.

"I'm not sure," Priscus replied. As he cleared away the burning roots still surrounding the door, we put out the minor flames that still burned upon the ground, which I was at the forefront. He then grabbed onto the latch after a quick inspection to locate it and pulled at it firmly. When he saw that it did not budge he pressed up against it, ramming his shoulder against it several times like a battering ram until he came to a stop, defeated. Here he turned to us and said, "None of you would happen to have the key would you?"

"Don't waste your time, Priscus," Axle said, as if the answer to what laid beyond the door was evident. "If it's barred by a key, then it's most likely a provisions room, or a storehouse of some sort." He advanced toward the door, and then as he knelt before it he waved away the black smoke and floating embers swirling near his face. "I figure this chamber here is where the garrison kept an eye on it, judging by all these damn chairs and tables about our feet. Gods know some of them even took their meals here."

"It's kind of a shite place to have one's supper. Don't you think?" Meric said.

"Aye," Andreaus agreed. "There's barely any air down here as it is."

"Right," Axle said, collecting himself to carry on. "Well, now that we know what it could be I suggest we leave before we find ourselves one with the cliff. Anyhow, our priorities are above us right now not below. If we come out alive at the end of this we'll be sure to come back and have a look."

"Wait, I don't think it's a supply room either," I said, squatting down — something had caught my eye. I sifted through the rubble before me with a rising thought in my mind. Slowly, I drew from the pile a flattened goblet and a crushed platter made of tin, studying them diligently for a moment. Therewith I peered around the room from corner to corner as if the secret to the mystery was written upon the walls. "It's a guard room," I voiced excitedly at my revelation. I stood up and handed the platter over to Priscus. "Yes, it is," I then added, moving quickly toward the door. "It's hard to breathe down here with all of us, but if it were one or two men at the most, it wouldn't have been a problem. And so that would mean that this door here was meant to keep something in, hidden away. A vault maybe, or a —"

"A dungeon," Jon said, finishing my sentence.

"Dungeon?" Meric blurted.

"Yes!" Lera said, wide-eyed. "It would explain why this room is so far into the rock."

"My lord Priscus," one of the legionaries called out suddenly. "If it is truly what they say it is, then perhaps there may be a sword or two left down there. It would do us well for the men found absent."

"I don't know if you know how a dungeon works, my lad," Meric said, "but we don't tend to keep swords close enough to those we're trying to keep them from. *If* there is in fact a sword hidden somewhere in this fortress left to be found, it would not be found here. Besides, if it is a dungeon, then the only thing we'd end up finding in there are the whitened bones of whichever poor soul yet lingers in those cells." Meric turned around and headed for the corridor. "We're all thankful that you brought us down here, but Axle's right. We are wasting time with this."

"But we are here now," I said, looking to Priscus. "Why not have a look?"

"Well it's still barred so —"

Just then Jon threw himself forward with a swift and hearty kick, snapping the latch off the door and the hinges from their sockets, which caused a loud thud to echo in the chamber. A cloud of dust had all at once overtaken us, but still I could see Jon as he clamped his fingers on the edges of the oak as if they were not human fingers, but the sharp talons of a beast. As granules of stone fell upon his back he began to grunt under the sound of snapping iron and the duress of his labour. The door, however, was no match for his brawn, for he pulled it clear from the entrance. He chucked it away, where it landed just shy of Meric's position. "Follow me," he then ordered, robbing Axle's torch, and storming into the shadow beyond.

"I guess we are following him," Axle said.

At that moment Priscus turned to us, asking for Lera's torch. He thanked the legionaries for their discovery, and then ordered Andreaus to lead them back to the courtyard to find Edros and his party, so they could secure the rooms that lined the corridor, which there were many yet uncharted. While he was dictating his commands, Lera incited me toward the opening. Looking back, it was more of a forceful nudge, as if to suggest that if something unexpected were to happen, I would be the first of us both to know. I accepted without question, my mind more curious than apprehensive. And so holding a torch out in front of me, I accompanied Jon into the darkness, just like I had done in the forest tunnels of Ortona, only this time with Priscus, Axle, Meric, and Lera at my back. They followed me closely into what I can only describe as a channel, one that seemed to pierce into the rock without an end.

As Jon continued to lead the way, creeping steadily onward, the sea scented air wasted away and a stale, musty odour took its place. It was bitter cold, and at times I could hear a faint whistling of the wind, as if the tunnel itself was breathing in the air from above. We had put some two hundred steps between us and the entry, though after what felt like two hundred more steps the tunnel began to dip into a slope, which then descended to a stairway that had been carved from the rock. This stairway led right into another large, pillared chamber, except now it was as if we were entering a crypt, for the walls and pillars were richly panelled with the same marble that contoured the door. In fact,

I then realised that the pillars were of the same marble as the courtyard's.

It was here when our single line had splintered in many different directions. Lera, Axle, Jon, and I, explored the far sides of the room while the others ventured ahead toward the room's depths. We began trailing our fingers along the crenulations of the marble with wonder, and each of us, Jon less visibly so, was enchanted by the series of frescoes that adorned the rock. Most of the images were eaten away by the passing of time, but there were some fragments that I could still make out. I knew that these images were once depictions of Anolian legionaries, since there was one particular image that revealed a row of spears floating above ranks of marching legs fitted with the same boots that we soldiers wore. The light of my flame then caught another image; it was the only one that was still untouched by the years. It depicted a crowned man sitting on an armoured mount, the silver of his spear gleaming above his head in the portrait of a large brilliant moon. Without a doubt, it was him, King Andiel, or at least that is what Priscus had told me when he was, without my knowing, looking at the image as well from over my shoulder.

"Andiel's cock!" Meric said, disgruntled. "Where the hell are we?"

"Priscus," Jon suddenly broke in. "Another door."

We all seemed to turn around at the same time, looking at him not knowing how he kept finding these passageways further into the deep, despite that there was clearly a second door as you pressed further into the chamber. We regrouped at the center of the room, pointing our torches toward Jon to reveal the discovery more clearly. The door bore signs of aging and rot, but it was in, as I remember it, the same quality as the previous one. Axle was the one who approached it first. He knelt before it with his knife drawn, ready to clear away some of the rot and dirt that surrounded the latch and key hole. Before he laid a finger on it, however, he first looked to Jon to make sure there would be no unanticipated, or forced, entries. Then, he was promptly joined by Priscus, who began assisting him in the task with his own blade.

"Careful," I said to both of them."I can't say I trust the strength of its frame."

"Ten silver that one's locked too," Meric said.

"Well," Axle said, pushing at the door. "It's locked."

"Who would've thought," Meric added, sarcastically.

"Wait a moment," I blurted, succumbing to a sudden thought. Right away Priscus and Axle stopped fiddling with the latch, and I came forward to relieve them of their unsuccessful attempts at opening the door. I ran my palm on the face of the door at head height, back and forth as if clearing away a patch of muck from a mirror. I felt the many splinters of rotted wood as they punctured my skin, but still I went on, trying to uncover what I was unconsciously being led to by my sudden realisation.

"What's the matter?" Lera asked.

"This door," I mumbled. "This door doesn't have a porthole. Neither did the one before."

"And?" Meric said. "Why is that a problem?"

"I'm not sure if you know how dungeons work, Meric," I said, turning to look at him, "but most of the time the guards are supposed to have a way to look into the cells without having to go in them first. And if it wasn't already obvious, I think any man stuck in there would have died from lack of air long before any executioner's axe. And so I'm beginning to think that this isn't a dungeon anymore."

"Everyone look, over here," Axle broke in. He blew away crumbs of wood from the section of the door he was carving into at that moment, which was above the keyhole. He then removed his leather gauntlet and watered his thumb with his tongue. Meticulously, he began washing away the blemishes and blotches of dust from what appeared to be the cloven half of a small bronze plaque. "Look at that," he added with squinted eyes. "It's…it's the mark of the legion I think. Yeah, look at that right there. It looks like a fowl of some sort. A bird perhaps, or something bigger. See the spread of its wings — and its talons just there?"

I knelt beside him to look at it more closely. Jon brought over his light. "It's a hawk…a fire hawk I think." The image etched on the bronze was like the frescos on the walls, faded and damaged to time. There was little more to go on but what Axle had already voiced. "Look at the feathers, they are shaped differently than any fowl that *I've* ever seen. The flames around are almost like the flickers of a torch."

"No legion holds the hawk as its mark," Priscus said. "Nor any that I know of in the past."

"The marks of the fifth and nineteenth legions have long since been forgotten," Axle said. "I'm not sure, but this could be one of them?"

"It can't be," Priscus said. "This fortress was built long after their demise."

"Then perhaps it's the king's phoenix," Lera said.

"Or maybe it's like a big, fat, flaming mountain pigeon. You know, those of old?" Meric said aloud, breaking the seriousness in our discussion. "I mean really, who in Andiel's name cares. Whoever they were, they aren't here now. So here's an idea, how about we stop talking about what it could be and have Jon here use his ape like strength to see what really is beyond this door. There'll be plenty of time afterwards to have this little history lesson without me, but right now I think I speak for everyone when I say that I've spent enough time lingering underground in the dark like some bloody rat. If it's all the same, I'd like to remove myself from under the weight of this cliff as quickly as I can."

I stepped away from the door, but something on the plaque suddenly caught my eye. Under the mysterious image I saw what appeared to be a letter — the letter *M* to be precise, which was partially hidden behind more incrusted dust and rot. Under the sound of Meric's vexed huff, I drew my knife toward the plaque and began to clear away the dirt with caution as if I were a gravedigger not wanting to tarnish his prize. With each flick of my wrist, clumps of grime fell off. I discovered more and more letters as I went on. "There are letters here!" I said, as I finally revealed a word. "It's of the old tongue I think! *Men...men..mentarium. Mentarium?* What the hell does that mean?"

All of a sudden Priscus yanked me back and overtook my position with a spirited leap. I lost my balance and fell backwards into Lera's frame, banging my head upon her knee. Meric, taken by the sudden commotion, rushed over to my aid, his eyes wide with confusion. He called out to Priscus, or more like he shouted at him I'd say, asking him whether his sanity had all at once left him. His words, however, fell upon deaf ears, for Pricus and Axle, appearing as though they were possessed by Ascanelius himself, took to opening the door as if their life depended on its opening. Instead of using their daggers they used their swords, like levers, driving their steel ends into any promising seam that would see the archaic hinges of the door pried open. On and on they went, each fit of effort more frenzied, and more desperate than the last. After a few moments of this craze Jon too had joined in on the action. With his shoulder pressed up against the door, the hinges began to click and crunch. And with that, they were all up against the door, pushing with fury. Then, as they each let out a last, great laborious grunt, the links snapped, sending all three of them, including the door, soaring forward into a void of black.

Just as the door hit the ground the walls shook. Every inch of dust and grit in the chamber erupted toward the ceiling, a thick cloud washing over us like an all consuming wave, causing Meric, Lera, and I to cough wildly. I covered my mouth with the rim of my tabard. Nothing around me, except Lera, was visible apart from the glow of the torches piercing through the veil of dust.

"Are you alright?" I asked her. "Are you okay?"

"Yes!" she replied with a gasp.

"I'm fine too," Meric added on his hands and knees. "In case you were wondering."

Lera and I hoisted Meric to his feet as we waved the dust away from our faces so that we could all breath in a gulp of untainted air. Just then, loud hacking coughs drew our attention toward the doorway, but as I have already said, I saw nothing beyond the aperture, for the cloud of soot before my eyes was thickest in that area. Lera and I grabbed a torch and encroached the aperture, patting ourselves down as if we were soiled rugs. As the dust gradually settled, the light of our torches enlivened the darkness beyond the door, where Priscus' frame came into sight. He was standing alongside Axle and Jon just a few feet away, each of them perfectly motionless as they stared into the wall of black before them.

"Cillian," Priscus called out. "Come here. Bring us your light."

More interested in removing the taste of grime from my lungs, I handed Priscus my torch offhandedly. *"Armamentarium,"* he said, with a tone of amazement I had never before heard him utter. "The armoury of the legion."

I felt a shiver in my bones as he spoke the words. Over the glow of Priscus' torchlight there came a glimmer of white flashes, like stars in the night's sky. As my eyes became accustomed to the glimmering spectacle, I noticed a beaming sheet of bronze and silver, the type of glisten that one would see radiating off the metals of war. I was enchanted by this shimmer, and so before I knew it my feet had carried me deep within the armoury, and as I would later realise, near the center of the chamber. By then, many of the torches affixed to the walls were set alight, upon which I found myself standing alone in front of ranks of shelving, which filled the room on three sides. They were high and wide as I recall, ascending outward from the center of the room in a sequence of half rings like the pews of an augurs' temple. A vast array of armaments, namely swords, bows, axes, and shields, were lined upon each shelf in great numbers. They were blanketed in cobwebs, but to my rising wonder they appeared to me in more than fair condition, as if untouched by the decay of this mortal world.

"Andiel's mercy," I muttered, slowly pulling a sword from the shelf. As I held the sword by its hilt, and out in front of me, I was swiftly taken by an otherworldly spirit, for the silver of the sword appeared firm and sharp, as though it had been forged just the day before. The shields too, as I saw from the corner of my eye, were whole. The bows as well were rigid and unblemished from rot, and their string's unyielding. "What sort of magic lies upon this place?" I then said aloud, unable to comprehend what I can only explain as being the magics of this world. "Nothing in this fortress makes any sense. Stone may last through the centuries, but the iron and timber of this castle still stands as if it is only a hundred years unkept. And now this, an armoury hidden in the rock, left to chance and ruin, yet all of it untouched even after a thousand years?"

"There is magic in this place," Lera said, her eyes wondering about her surroundings.

"A bygone enchantment of the old world," Priscus said, as he was inspecting his own shelf. "I've heard stories of these magics before, enchantments long dead and known only to Andiel's time. In our tongue they called them charms, ones born by the gods in the face of the Conjuror's dark sorcery. It was once said that when the armies of the Conjuror were on the verge of victory the priests of the *sacrarium* prayed to the gods for their assistance. Some say they kept silent to our calls, but there were others, smith folk, who believed that they shared their knowledge of the forge with them. Swords and spears were then made from what they called ageless steel. Weapons that would endure the passing of time until the Ascani were no more. This then is how the god's helped us fight against the plight of Ascanelius."

"Aye, my grandfather used to tell me those same stories," Axle said, waving his torch as he moved from rack to rack. He stood transfixed before a crate that was overflowing with sheathed daggers. He took one for close inspection and then said, "I used to think those children stories, but now I'm not so sure." Therewith he turned to us, his expression suggesting that he had come to an epiphany. "This is not some ordinary armoury," he added. "No garrison that I know of would store their arms all the way down here where they could not easily get to them. This is a cache, a hoard of excess. What you see here is what was left after the time of Andiel's war. Arms stored away if ever their need should arise again. It's an ancient token, don't you see? A measure to the glory of his kingdom and the power of Anolia's reach."

"Alright, calm yourself, old man," Meric said, as if Axle's words were too sensational for his taste. "Keep talking like that and you'll summon Petris to us." He was standing just off to the side of the doorway, in a wide nook that was lined with many barrels, most of them teeming with quivers of feathered arrows, others full with bundles of mighty ash-wood spears. "Besides," he added, pulling an arrow from one of the barrels, "how mighty could his empire have been? I mean look at this arrow here. If you ask me I think our beloved Andiel could've saved some of that magic steel you were talking about for some proper arrowheads, because it appears he didn't even have enough. This one's made of bloody glass. And it's not even cut properly."

Priscus walked over and took the arrow away from him. He twirled the arrowhead under the flames of his torch, and just as the silky web burned away several iridescent glimmers flashed in his eyes. "It's not glass, Meric," he said. "It's a diamond."

"Diamond!" Meric said, his eyes lighting up.

"Well, now we know why they hid it all down here," Lera said.

"To keep it away from thieves most likely," Priscus replied, handing the arrow back to Meric, whose eyes were transfixed on his new prize. "You may not like our little stories and history lessons Meric, but don't forget the part where our lands were once stripped of its ores and gems to make these weapons of war. And don't even think about pocketing that arrow. We're going to need every one."

"It's Jon you have to worry about," he said half distracted as he studied the gem.

"Are they all as such?" I said, curiously.

Lera pulled a bundle of arrows from another barrel some distance from us. It became clear that these barrels rimmed the entire armoury, leaving me to assume that there were more than three hundred quivers in the chamber, if not countless more "Aye, down to the last," she said. "And the spears too."

Meanwhile Axle was making his way over to me, emerging from the corner of the ledge I was exploring. In one hand he held a torch, which he had just used to light one of the unlit torches, and in the other, he was holding one of the newly found swords. He juggled it in his hand as he approached me, feeling it's weight and balance as if he were a swordsmith. "Solid pieces of work these swords are. There's plenty here for all of us, even the Uthians. And I take it that — oh my! Would you look at that," he said, his eyes suddenly firm upon the ground that was beyond my feet. "Well, I guess it's not a big, mountain pigeon after all."

I looked to my feet and as my eyes followed the crawl of the torchlight I saw, carved into a wide, unbroken slab of stone, the same etchings which we had first seen upon the bronze plaque. I learned then that the image on the plaque was neither a fire hawk, nor any derivation of the phoenix, but rather it was that of a great, horned dragon. As a matter of fact, this dragon was one that I had never seen before — not that I have ever seen a real one, being that such beasts have long since lived in our myths alone. What I mean to say is that the image was the first I had seen of that depiction. This creature had a long, narrow face and a mouth like a serpent's, thick with sword-like teeth. Its eyes were slender and soul piercing, and at the very top of its head there rested a crown of needles, from which a great, thorned spine flowed down to its spear-headed tail, which then coiled around its wings that were made to appear as flames.

"Cillian," Priscus said, breaking my enchanted eye. "I need you to do something for me. There's too much here for Edros' party to bring to the surface. I want you to find Andreaus and tell him what we've found here, but be quiet about it. I don't want a hundred men swarming the tunnel all at once. Tell him to bring thirty men down here."

Just at that moment we heard a booming crash as if stacks of timbered crates had all together smashed upon rock. It was followed by a series of loud grunts and hacking coughs, the tone of which made it evident that it was Jon, who was last seen venturing to the furthest of the shelves at the back of the chamber. Meric and Lera quickly came over to us, and then collectively we rushed over toward Jon, where we found him hunched on one knee over a heap of shattered coffers and toppled ledges.

"Damn it, man," Meric said, as he hurried over to help him. Jon, slightly dazed, stood upright with his assistance, clearing away the soot that tickled his nose. "Why don't you crush the whole place while you are at it? It's not like we desperately need all of these things! What…what's that in your hand?"

Immediately, Jon hoisted what was clutched in his fist for all to see. It was a legionary tabard, a crimson one at that and nearly identical to ours. He held it up by the collar, turning its face toward the light of our torches. At its center, just as it appeared upon the stone slab, the mark of the Thorned Dragon had been stitched, the colour of its threading gray like fortress.

It would be nearly twenty years later, dear reader, that I would come across the legionary history of the Thorned Dragon, which I can now safely say that Axle's hunch of its origins was, in fact, correct. This emblem was once the mark of the Anolia's nineteenth legion, the very same that had been annihilated at the Battle of the Verdant Heights in 32 A.E. According to the records, those few hundred who survived the battle, and the subsequent war, formed the garrison of Northfleet, doing so under an *oath of obligation* as it is written. In their eyes the defeat against the Ascani was seen to be a failure to the realm, and for this reason they took it upon themselves to guard Andiel's new bastion against these creatures. The nineteenth legion, as I have already mentioned at the start of this tale, would never again be reinstated, and so the men who formed the garrison of Northfleet became like their fallen brethren: ever watchful specters left to defend the fringes of the kingdom. But as the years passed so did the last of them, leaving the existence of Northfleet, and their legacy, to the pages of history.

Priscus brought his torch to the nearby shelves, revealing the stacked crates on both sides of us, about a hundred in number. In them, there were folded tabards and standards bundled atop one another like straightened towers, save for those scattered around Jon's feet. He grabbed one for himself, staring at the emblem as if he was devising a plan in his mind. "Pass these out to the men," he then voiced. "Let us bring to life the spirits of their former bearers. The last echo of the past to this once dead fortress of old."

CHAPTER 19

Night fell over the fortress as swiftly as the morning's sun had arisen. The moon above was bright and full, though a good many thickly clouds sailed in front of it like a fleet of ships, moving in the portrait of a thousand white, glimmering stars. I was in a good frame of mind, even though my bones quivered in the cool night air. I felt, at the same time, tired and sluggish, for much of that afternoon I had been tied to Edros's party, whose task it was to vacate the cache of armaments in its entirety until the chamber had been reduced to barren rock. By the time we had finished, the bustle of labour across the fortress had died to a sleepy quiet as every man had taken to resting his weary head. At first, I sought the same, though whenever my eyes closed for an hour or so I awoke with to a restless jitter that would not shake by the comfort of sleep.

In my restlessness, I loitered upon the battlements, strolling alone along the ramparts from sentry to sentry as I listened to the ebb and flow of the bay. In this peace, I began debating with myself, mulling over some unnerving thoughts, and thinking, or rather hoping, that the fruits of our labour, our restorations to the castle, were sufficient enough to hold the Ascani at bay until the king would arrive. I was the mastermind behind all of it in the end, so in effect I was trusting that I had done everything that I could to prepare us for the onslaught that was surely coming. If there was any doubt of its existence, as Etorus had alluded to, then I, by this time, did not share in the thought. And on the matter of time, it took more than a moment for me to come around, eventually finding some peace of mind in the strenuous efforts of the men, and in all that we had accomplished together.

A little while later, now a crawl past midnight, I found myself on the battlements of the gatehouse, languorously reposing on a crate by the corner merlon. I leafed through the pages of my journal, and with each turn of the page came a short, audible sigh. Of all the engines of war I had spent so many years developing, I could not bring a single one to life in the hour of our need. Time was still our enemy, despite that it was now almost a week without a sighting of the Ascani army. With all the magic surrounding this place, and the luck that came with it, I was still absent the tools needed to build them. It may seem odd to you, dear reader, to wish to build an engine whose purpose it is to take life, but that, as I liked to believe, was where my true worth lied, and not in the revival of ships and castles. From the very start, front the cliffs of Easteria, all I ever wanted was to demonstrate my worth, but on this front I would simply have to wait.

"Andiel save me," Priscus said, his voice in approach. "By the gods, you know when I first met you I did not think I would be recruiting another Petris to my side. I swear, Cillian, at times you look just like him, the only difference is I found you on the battlefield, and you're much skinnier." Priscus stood beside me and placed his palms upon the stone "I found *him* hidden in my brother's library — hiding between the shelving. I remember when he caught sight of me, he just froze like a piece of stone, that nose of his deep in a book and his mouth full of cheese. The man was so scared that all he managed to do was belch when I asked him his name."

As Priscus spoke I tucked away my handbook. I adjusted my tabard, which was of the Thorned Dragon. All but the Uthians now wore them, not because they wanted to be divided from us, but rather because tabards did not suit, practically speaking, their armour. "You know a man of your age should really consider sleeping now and again," I said.

"I could say the same for you."

"Rest isn't coming to me, I'm afraid. Not tonight."

"Well," Priscus said, clearing his throat. "Last I saw him, Jon was still walking about somewhere. If rest is what you want I can call him over and have him strike you across the chin. I suppose one of his strikes would put you to sleep. Or kill you."

"My eyes are sore for rest," I smirked, "but not of the want to never open them again."

"And if I were you I'd get right to it," he said. "The need of your craft is one thing, Cillian. But the weight of your sword will soon be greater. When battle comes I won't have you crumbling to exhaustion after the first hour." He then took in a breath, welcoming the cool breeze emanating from the darkness before him. "And one more thing," he quickly added. "Advice from a fellow man. It would be thoughtless of me not to say that if this were *my* last night among the living, I wouldn't want to spend it far away from the warmth of a loving heart. You should give your woman the same comfort. While there's yet still time."

"I'm not sure what you're talking about?" I said, off-guard and racked with tension.

"Lera, our scout," he went on. "You ought to be by her side. Unless you mean to confess to me that you're both just very good companions, ones who like to sleep so close to each other under the stars every night. I'm an old man, Cillian, but not a blind one. I think it's safe to say that you share more than a simple fondness of friendship with her. There's no need to keep it a secret. And when it comes to blind men, even one of *them* could see the same from a hundred leagues. Be lovers if you wish. There is no fault in wanting to be. And it's not like there's some law that forbids you from falling in love with someone who also carries the sword."

"But there is one, in fact," I said, nervously. "The *Lex Matrimonium*. Andiel himself wrote it before the war. I may be *sodalis* to you, Priscus, but no man in the service of the king, except those of high command, can take a wife. Not until their time in the legion is up. Actually, the punishment that comes with it is quite severe. In truth, since you are a lord, you have the power to put an end to it, and then have me banished from the army. Or put to death if you wish."

"Oh yes! Of course! I had forgotten about that one," he said, turning to me with a look as if I just reminded him about the law. "Remind me tomorrow morning about it, will you? We'll have the execution right after first light's meal. I know Jon's been itching to kill something, so this will do nicely. My thanks, builder." Here, he grinned narrowly, and then turned back to gaze upon the field. "Honestly, Cillian. It would do you well to stop reading for once in your life. Laws like that were set down in a time much different than our own, when the whole kingdom was at war. Now, I'd like to believe that the lords of this realm have come a long way from asking our youth to offer up their lives against the Ascani *without* denying them the pleasures of life that are found outside of the army. And to be forthright, Cillian, there was never really a time when any king, or lord for that matter, has had the power to govern such a thing as love. It has always been beyond us mortals to rule; left to the gods to decide its course; left to their control."

"How so?" I asked, suddenly captivated by his words.

"Well isn't it obvious?" he replied. "Take a moment to think about it. No other power in this world can change a man's heart on a whim as strongly as love, either for good or evil. And it's the only thing on this earth with enough force to keep a man fighting to his last, even when the end of his life is certain. Say I were to act on that law you spoke about, have Lera taken from you, and you from her. Do you really think either of you would simply part ways because I demanded it?"

"No," I said. "I suppose not."

"Of course you wouldn't, Cillian," he continued. "Not with a power like that beating in your heart. Even if you did not wish it, your heart will force you to fight me in order to save her from all things, and you would do so just as hard and everlasting as Andiel once did for this realm. You see his war against the Conjuror was won not only because of a strength in arms, or by arrows or spears made from gems, but because the people who fought in it trusted, and loved, him until their end. It is not always clear to the eye, but that same love can be found in all things; a mother for her child, a husband for his wife, and to some extent, even in Meric when he sees his chance at easy coin."

I smiled as he did, seeing for the first time a genuine mirth in him.

"Have you ever been in love?" I said, somewhat hesitant to have asked him. Immediately I regretted my question, for the silence that I had created between us was crude.

Priscus lowered his eyes to the stone, almost as if averting them away from me, which gave me the impression that I had been overly forward and presumptuous about our relationship. I quickly proceeded to apologize as I turned away to the eastern field, embarrassed at myself, for now I felt I had turned the mood sour.

"I was once," he said, sinking his forearms upon the merlon before him. His voice was low, almost grim, but also because it seemed he was in the act of reminiscing about a thought while his focus was preoccupied with the sound of the tide. "It was a very long time ago," he went on. "Back when I was some years younger than you are now. Her name was Neisa, the princess of Aeginas, and she was once my wife." He paused for a moment and smiled. "You see, Cillian, I wasn't always the lord of Easteria. As I think back it seems a lifetime ago we lived together with our son Aldoris, very far away from these lands on an island by the Blue Waters, close to her home. In fact, in those times I never wanted to be a lord, neither did I want to be a king. I never cared for the titles.

I used to spend my days in the legionary barracks, wanting to fight battles, while my brother spent his in the library, grooming himself in the art of politics. So, when my father passed, it was no surprise to anyone that he would be more suited to rule, a thought I supported as if I was ridding myself of the plague. But, that's not the only reason why I passed on the crown. It was also because of Neisa. A year before Adeanus became king she had come into my life. When I first saw her, she had taken my heart. She had come to the court, pleading for our help against the pirates of the Grey Isles, who at the time were marauding across the sea, attacking their merchant ships. In all my life I had never disobeyed my father, but after he refused to let me be the one to take command, I went against him. I left with her in the night. Anyway, two years later we married and had a son. This is the second time I was in love."

"What happened to your wife and your son?" I said, my curiosity exciting my discretion.

"They were taken from me," he replied. "Slaughtered by the Ascani."

My heart fell heavily as I listened to the rest of his story, from which I learned a great many things concerning his youth, and the finer details of his secret marriage to the Princess Neisa. As I remember it, and as Petris had retold it, Priscus' father had promised his union to the daughter of King Aristodemus of Velitrae, a neighbouring throne. Meanwhile, Neisa's own blood had promised her hand to the prince of a lordly house. After the pirates had been defeated, Priscus abdicated his position for the Anolian crown, as was the case for Neisa's royal standing. They began a life together among the people of the Blue Waters, and for five long years they lived in the comforts of each other's love, and that of their son Aldoris, until the day came when the Ascani raided the islands. Priscus had gone hunting that day, only to return to fires of the creatures. It was Petris who would later tell me more about what had happened that day; that Priscus, in a craze of insanity, slew every one of the creatures by himself; some say there were well over a hundred. When there were no more of them to kill, his hatred then guided him from battle to battle, to every corner of the earth where the Ascani roamed.

"That day at the council," I said. "Is that what Ulcar meant about your vengeance? Is it the reason why we are here? The reason you set yourself to this task?"

"I'm nearly sixty years old, Cillian. I have already sought, and had, my fill of vengeance. Many times over," he said. "The pain in my heart has long passed, pulled away from the darkness of its tide. You and I, and all these men, are here for another reason, something more than a desire for revenge. We are here because we can never let these creatures roam freely as if they belong to this world. They are the beasts of the underworld, and so the more we give to them, the more suffering will come to those that cannot fight for themselves. I wish that in my time there would have been others of like mind to do as I have done with my life. Perhaps then I would still be far away from these lands with my wife and son, living as a father and a husband absent the need to protect them with a sword. In the end the gods have chosen my fate to be otherwise. I'll never know why. All I can do now is remember their love, their warmth, how they were and not how I last saw them. Now, all I do is make certain that what has happened to me never happens to another. That is my path, as it is the same for some of us in the legion. So, I —"

Priscus stopped himself, as if a sound, or rather a feeling, caught his ear. He straightened his back, slowly, continuing to gaze intently toward the eastern field, his eyes scanning the blackness before him. The shift in his expression had certainly changed mine, and so I asked him what had caught his attention. I turned around to better view the point of his now fixed stare. I saw nothing but a blanket of shadow that spread across the plains, for at this point in the night a great mass of clouds had covered the moonlight above.

"Priscus, what are you looking at?" I asked nervously.

Here, I was the one who silenced myself, my tongue retreating far into my throat. At the crest of the night's shadow, some thirty feet beyond the mouth of the bridge where the light of Northfleet's torches stopped, I watched with dread as a pair of glinting, red eyes slowly emerged from the black. At first I thought it was a beast of night, a wolf perhaps. But, I very quickly realised that it was the creature: Far-Skafa the masked Ascani. Out of the shadows he came, walking toward the bridge in the same manner as I had seen him do on the night of the watchtower, upon which he stopped just shy before setting foot on the timber planks. There was no doubt that Priscus and I were in full sight, yet the creature paid no attention to us as he trailed his eyes along the battlements, looking onward to see the extent of our defences, and not at all off put by the fact that he was coming upon an occupied fortress. As if sensing our presence, he looked straight at us with the snap of his head. It was enough to send a creeping tremble up my spine, deepening my numbness. I felt the chill rising greatly at his presence, just as I feel it now as I write this.

"Cillian," I heard Priscus mutter. "Ready the signal."

Still, I stood transfixed, unable to move, for the creature's evil gaze pierced through me like a hot knife upon flesh. He was staring at me intently, as though his frame was drawn to me, and as if he recognized me from Easteria. One could tell that his hatred for Priscus was clear, though the tightening of the muscles upon his face suggested that his anger was solely aimed at me. It was then that Far-Skafa took another half-step forward, his head slowly canting to the side like a wolf does before it strikes.

I do not know what it was that forced the Ascani to suddenly change his appearance, yet his anger was suddenly overtaken by a strange show of content, that mirthful gawk that all the Ascani seem to have when the thought of blood and slaughter was soon to be had. He took a step back without breaking his gaze, continuing to do so until the whole of his body, and eyes, merged once more with the encircling darkness.

In the moments that followed an ominous stillness overtook the air that in some way managed to drown out the rush of the tide. I cursed my legs to move, wanting to act on the command that I was given — it had only been a few moments since Priscus had asked me to ready the signal. With purpose I turned to reach for the closest torch, but again my attention was stilled, now taken by the speckle of light that appeared at the far edge of the eastern field. I honed in on it. I knew very well that it was a torch, though I found myself staring at it as if captivated. Then, without warning, a second far-off glint caught my eye, this one appearing to the south, upon the path that we had taken when we had first arrived at the castle. Therewith two more followed at the cusp of the woodland in the west, and then three others along the shores of the bay. Hereafter thousands upon thousands of torches surfaced within the black like cinders resting atop a dying fire, all of them filling the whole of the valley in a grand arc.

Now I awoke — not to the sight of the Ascani army before me, or to Priscus aggressively tugging at my arm, but to the sound of the buccina, which very rapidly filled the sleepy fortress with booms of alarming cries. Under the blares of these instruments the men jumped out of their beds in a frenzy, rushing this way and that to their instructed positions across the battlements. In short order they fixed themselves in rows three deep; shields of the Uthia and Anolia one on the other. All around me the ramparts came alive with the emblems of our people, and Northfleet was once again reunited with her garrison of the Thorned Dragon, which, as I have already mentioned, was marked on all of our tabards. In fact, and though I did know it at the time, we had manned the walls so fully from end to end that it allowed for some fifty of us, who were headed by Edros, to add to the defence of the gate and the inner fortifications.

I, however, was not of the line of defense, but lingered right where I was standing. Lera, Axle, Jon, and Meric, joined Priscus and I upon the gatehouse, each of them dressing themselves with the last pieces of their armour. Right away Lera placed herself beside me and handed over my sword — I had not brought it along with me during my restless walk, despite having had fully dressed for battle, mail and all. I tightened the belt around my waist, and then adjusted the chainmail around my shoulders, not once breaking sight of the encroaching horde. As they marched ever closer, now six hundred yards away, I began to notice that their numbers were far superior than had been first spoken of at the council, some thousands more it seemed, though I must say that this assumption was built off my growing nerves, and by the roaring storm of their barks and snarls.

"That's a little more than six thousand," Meric said, equipping a quiver.

"A lot more," Lera mumbled, her face flushed with alarm.

My own heart was pounding like a nail as I sought Lera's fingers in the hopes of bringing her comfort, although if I am completely honest, I sought to quell my own growing nerves. She squeezed my hand, giving me a reassuring look that we were ready for the coming onslaught.

Upon a heartbeat the Ascani swarm abandoned their concerted march for a headlong charge. As they charged forward in attack the air was filled with the sound of their feet beating the ground, and of their enraging howls, which Far-Shaka fuelled with his own shrieks of incitement. In this wave of black I could see, more and more, the individual faces of these creatures. They need no description, dear reader, but know that they were all vile to the last, some of which I could still see clearly as I recall the event.

"Listen here, all of you!" Priscus cried out. "Jon — Meric, take the west towers and the wall as far as the rock. Andreaus, you command those on the eastern rampart all the way to the shoreline — and on your way have Ferix do the same. Axle and I will take the gatehouse and its surrounding wall! Keep them off the walls as long as you can. Not one steps inside the courtyard. Go now, hurry!"

"What about us?" I said. "What should we do?"

"Stick with me and try not to get yourselves killed," Priscus replied.

"Archers to the front!" Axle bellowed, unsheathing his sword. At once every man equipped with a bow, two ranks worth, stepped forward in unison. Upon Axle's second order they nocked an arrow and stood still at the ready, though in a much livelier display a mob of Uthians, who were positioned with Ferix on the section of wall between the gatehouse and the shoreline, hoisted their horn-tipped bows to the sequence to their own battle tactics, meaning the first rank took to a knee as the second overshadowed it. At the same time, the men in reserve within the courtyard did the same as the Uthians, though they had joined together with their spears at the throat of portcullis in a phalanx. "Archers draw!" Axle then cried, looking to his left and right.

All the while Priscus had moved forward to the precipice of the gatehouse with the standard of the Thorned Dragon clutched in his hand. He elevated himself above the rest of us by standing on top of the wooden crates that were stacked by the corner of the merlons; those very same that I had leaned on during our talk. There, he angled himself forward, placing a foot upon the stone, appearing firm and resolute like the statue of some ancient lord. The standard fluttered wildly over the silver of his helmet, his poise yet motionless as he watched the Ascani army barrel toward the fortress. There was a moment, as I looked at him, that seemed as if the withering of time was of no interest to him. But then, just when the wind had suddenly died away and the Ascani had reached a hundred yards from the walls, Priscus drew his sword, hoisting it high in the air whilst hollering, "Let us put a shine in their icy hearts!"

At that Axle cried out for a volley, and a rush of several hundred arrows whizzed into the night's sky, far up beyond the veil of the few clouds trailing above. Altogether they vanished into the gloom, but right then, in a moment that seemed as if time had slowed down, the clouds in front of the moon's face shrunk back, letting its lucent rays shine down upon the plains below. Riding these rays were the arrows, their diamond tips quickly coming alive under the moon's light, the gems shimmering so radiantly that they appeared as if the stars themselves were falling to earth. I tracked these lustrous speckles in awe, stopping only when their shine vanished as they plunged into the swarm. Here hundreds of Ascani fell to the ground in great clusters, for neither their bulwarks nor thickly guards were immune to the touch of a single arrow. Seeing this, Axle had called for subsequent volleys, and so after each shimmering storm more of the creatures thrashed to the ground.

"Prepare yourselves!" Priscus cried.

Now the Ascani line was twenty yards away from the gully. Lera and I, and the men around us, readied a bracing stance, shields locked and swords at the rim. All at once the swarm dipped into the gully, as though the whole front of their assault did not know it was there. In one formless lump they hurtled into the *ericius*, the porcupine, where more than just a few Ascani were brutally and grossly pierced like hunks of skewered meat. More than that, those creatures who took to the drawbridge were suddenly crushed under the weight of their own, for as planned by Priscus, I had weakened its support so that when the mob would reach the center it would collapse to a pit of sure death. To our luck it worked as expected, but in spite of these defences the force of their momentum was still like that of an onrushing wave. As such, those behind their first ranks had easily managed to reach the walls, seeing as how the mounds of piling corpses had paved the gully with many passages. The battle of Northfleet had begun.

"You hold them here!" I said to Lera, who was in the midst firing an arrow.

My words had caught her by surprise. It was not my aim to abandon her, I just felt as if I had been suddenly compelled to ensure that the defences were holding, especially those where Jon was stationed. I rushed along the ramparts toward the west battlements, hearing Lera's voice call out behind me. I weaved from side to side, evading stray arrows and hurled torches as they crashed down upon us, few striking their mark with precision, the majority either snapping against the stone or the rock of the cliff beyond. Fortunately, fire was not a problem, for teams of men were endlessly chucking buckets of water onto the timber as a means to keep the fire from taking hold, which was our second priority after keeping the enemy off the walls. As these men quelled the fires, so too were the healers now in the process of dragging those injured, or dead, down from the walls. Often I stopped to help them when I could, but when I had finally reached my target I slid to a knee in repose, taking a much needed breath by the two massive structures of wood that I had set out to check. Truth be told, I did not inspect them at all, because as I peered through the crack between the logs I was abruptly taken by a confusing epiphany: the enemy had not one piece of siege equipment amongst them, nothing that suggested they could scale the walls.

Suddenly two Ascani arrows struck the wood, pressing me to draw back.

"This is no time to be deep in thought, builder," Lytus said. He loosed an arrow from over my shoulder, and therewith he took another from the barrel of arrows before him. One after another he fired them with great energy and enjoyment as it appeared to me. "Come on up then!" he added. "I can't empty this barrel all by myself!"

"The Ascani!" I cried, over the heightning noise. "I don't think they can scale the walls!"

"What's that now?" Lytus replied, lending me a part of his focus.

"No ladders!" I cried again, trying to overcome the booming roar below.

"Oh!" Lytus grinned, grabbing a handful of my tabard. "They don't use ladders, boy!"

Just then my back hit the ground, because Lytus had violently pulled me away from the face of the rampart. Simultaneously, an iron hook zipped over me, and with a resonant clang it struck the stone a mere foot to the side of my head. At first it failed to catch hold, but as it rescinded back along the wall at the pace of the wielder's vigorous pull, bouncing and shimmying about, its teeth shredded the ankles of the two men in its path, narrowly missing Lytus, who dove out of its path. It was here that the hook was stilled, whereupon I could hear the growing gnarls of whatever beast approached from the other side of its iron head. I let out a breath, and just as I did so a hulking fiend surged onto the ramparts with a shrieking cry. It twirled a mighty ball-spiked mace high above its head as it scanned for its prey, which was me.

Intuitively, I reeled to the side, dodging its strike. In a single motion I reached for my sword that was resting at my thigh and planted it deep into the beast's ribs, a warm fountain of brackish blood spewed upon my face like a dense rain. Before I could wipe clean the crimson grit that coated my eyes, I found myself on my feet, feeling as if I were hoisted by the strength of three men. Of course that brawn belonged to Jon, who in a fit of haste drew my sword from the Ascani corpse and firmly pressed the hilt against my chest. He said nothing to me, but directed my attention to the sky above the horde. I wiped my eyes and looked up with apprehension, just in time to see a wave of grappling hooks soaring toward the fortress walls, their whistle sounding like a chorus of high pitched fifes playing an ominous tune.

"Brace yourselves!" a voice cried out.

Down came the hooks with such force that the rattle of their collision muffled the thunder of battle. They peppered the surface of the battlements, latching onto anything that their teeth had first come to strike, including those men who were caught absentminded. Meanwhile, Meric had rushed over to the berm of the tower, from which he overlooked Jon and I. When he caught sight of us, he came down to join us in the coming fight, but before he could reach the base of the tower, the walls were teeming with the enemy.

Like wild beasts maddened by bloodlust, the Ascani came at us, pairing off with whomever crossed their path, even though many of them were outnumbered by the groups of legionaries who advanced to meet them. To counter this defence the Ascani carelessly flung their very bodies as missiles against our shields, attempting to push us off the walls, which, in fact, had succeeded in a few places where there were too many of them already grouped in attack. For a long while we went on fighting as if to the bitter end, filling the hours that felt like mere minutes with the cries of war and slaughter. Jon and Meric fought beside me during that time, and then Lera joined us some time later, having brought with her news about Andreaus and the Uthians, who were fairing better than we were in terms of pushing the enemy off the walls. Not that I would have prefered to fight beside them rather than Lera, Meric, and Jon, being that the three of them combined had cut down more of the enemy than any of us legionaries in the vicinity, Jon alone having killed a hundred at least. Jon's efforts had also allowed us to sever the hooks from their hold. And when we felt that we had scored an advantage, and by this I mean we had pushed them off the walls insofar as they no longer had a dominant presence, we began fighting in clusters, giving each in his own turn a proper time to pause and rest. During this time the men in the courtyard steadily replaced those dead on the ramparts, and those that were found idle were tasked, once again, to be mules for the pails of water, their purpose of which I have earlier mentioned.

"Captain Meric!" echoed a legionary's voice in urgency.

Meric looked over his shoulder, realising that the man's voice had come from the courtyard. Right then, and by complete surprise, an Ascani descended on him. With a quick side-step and a ruthless strike he slit the creature's throat as if he were gutting a fish. The legionary who had called out to him was, however, not warning him about his attacker, but rather he was aiming to direct his focus to the grounds before the portcullis, where a throng of men were in an uproar. At this moment our so-called advantage was tossed aside, for without warning a ghoulish horn sounded, its echo far, but emanating from the Ascani besieging the gatehouse. As the others fought against a sudden surge of enemies, I weaved my way to the parapet to see this commotion. There, over the slumped Ascani corpses, I watched the Ascani horde before the portcullis split apart to reveal a monstrous fiend. It moved toward the gully under the spiked whips of its masters, gradually making its way closer toward the earthen mound in front of the portcullis.

"They're making for the gate!" I shouted while pivoting to Meric.

"Jon!" Meric cried in answer. "Get your ass over there now! Cillian, go with him."

Jon replied to the concern in Meric's voice with his axe. In one fell strike he cleaved several foes across their chest, sending all of their corpses soaring into the courtyard. Here, he gripped another by the throat and crushed it to jelly, snagging the grappling hook from its belt just before it hit the ground. He came over to the parapet, toward me, with hook in hand, whereupon he clamped it into the timber.

"What the hell are you doing?" I asked him, taken aback.

"Come," he replied, in the same tone as he always did. He tested the rigidity of the line by coiling it firmly around his wrist. Then, he went over to the edge of the rampart with his back to the courtyard, placing his feet in such a way as to ready a descent. "Faster this way," he then added, just as the whole of his frame vanished below the rim.

I would be lying, dear reader, if I were to say that his actions did not completely stun me. Still, I managed to ready the line to follow him, where all at once I began to recall my frightening incident with hooks and ledges from the cliffs of Easteria. I took a breath, and then muttered to myself, "At least it's not as high this time." I let my feet go, and down I went.

At this point the roars of the monstrous Ascani grew more fierce, only this time they were swiftly accompanied by the chime of rattling metal: the iron of the portcullis. I let fall my weight in the interest of speed, though instead I lost my footing as soon as my feet touched the ground. I fell onto my side and into a pond of warm fluid; the sensation immediately brought me to my feet. In the glow of the nearby brazier I inspected the sleeves of my tunic from back to front. I quickly noticed that they, as well as the rest of my garbs, were soaked in blood and crimson sludge. In a jolt of disgust my body staggered rearward on its own, my back now flush with the wall. I do not recall why it was a surprise, but I was startled when I saw the mounds of Ascani before me; heaps of dead, from which rivers of blood merged into the great, big pond that I was standing in. For hours we had chucked those slain upon the walls into the courtyard, and it was here when I had gotten a first hand view of our efforts thus far.

Suddenly Jon's sonorous cry restored me to purpose. I rushed over to the mouth of the gate, where I then saw him in front of a mob of Uthians and Anolians frothing at the mouth with the heat of battle. As they funnelled their way to the portcullis, their spears angled towards the iron, I could hear the metal bars quake. I pushed my way to the front, and therewith stopped abruptly, because I was taken by the sight of the creature, and by its savagery as it pummelled the metal with its bare fists like a captive wanting to be free from his confines.

"Press forward! Keep it off the gate!" Edros hollered, inciting the men to battle. Here, once he noticed me, he pulled me off to the side with a look of dismay upon his wet face. "Cillian!" he then bellowed. "The iron! It's not going to hold! If we don't kill that bloody thing now it's going to tear those bars right from the stone! You must tell Priscus! We need to get the archers to hit it from the tower! Do you understand me, Cillian? We don't have much —"

Right then the creature slammed its fists against the portcullis with a mighty howl, the force so vigorous that every loose bolt and rivet was sent darting into the crowd, some at such speed that they pierced through flesh as cleanly as an arrow. More than that, this thunderous percussion shook the gatehouse like an earthquake, whereupon lumps of weakened stone fell from the canopy above our heads, crushing the skulls of the men who were caught in the path of their plummet. A small fragment of said stone, nothing to warrant worry, had grazed the back of my left arm. Still, the pain propelled me a step forward, at which point I was consumed by the mob.

"Come with me!" urged one of the men. "Brace it now before it sees us to our end!"

A few fearless souls rose to the man's call. They surged forward in attack, and together they braced the portcullis with their shoulders pushed up against their shields. They blindly jabbed at the creature's stomach, yet despite their valiance nothing came of it except the enrichment of the beast's berserking rage. It struck the metal a second time, dispatching those men backwards as if they were mere leaves in a strong wind.

"Edros!" I cried, while turning back in search of him. "I'll go to Priscus! You —" I stopped short, for Edros was dead. His body sat upright against the wall with a gaping mouth and an opened skull; gore oozing down the side of his head.

As I remember, I had reached out for him as if my touch was suddenly going to restore him to life. Nevertheless, I was prevented, because all at once the sound of the iron being pummelled had turned into that which comes from metal being crushed and bent. I quickly wheeled toward the gate, where I then saw that the beast had gripped the portcullis by the spaces between the crossbars, attempting to heave the entire structure toward it. To my surprise, the creature was succeeding. The metal clicked and crackled like dry twigs, whereupon the rims of the portcullis began to gradually bend around the stone.

The sight seemed to take away our strength to act — all of us except Jon, who leapt toward the gate with an eye to counter the Ascani. With a laborious grunt he planted his feet and grasped the portcullis in the same manner as the creature, his frame standing half its size. I am not certain how I can, in words, describe Jon's appearance in this moment, for the brawn he displayed was nothing short of divine, his muscles seemingly having doubled in size. He drew up the last drops of his might and cried out sharply, matching the power of the foe before him. He did this for a short while and kept the portcullis from folding any further, yet in time the accursed strength of the creature began to overpower Jon's mortal vigour.

"Cillian!" Jon groaned, his strength leaving him. "Help me!"

I do not know from whom I managed to secure a spear, though in a frenzy to assist him I had managed to snag one that was bobbing by my waist. I lunged forward in attack, and with no small amount of luck the spear passed through an opening between the crossbars, its diamond tip striking the creature in the throat. A near cask of blood erupted from the wound as a gurgling cry of agony rose from the beast's lungs. On I pressed the spear in place as hard as I could, grinning irrationally that had succeeded in stripping the fiend of life. That is why, in the passion of this success, I did not relinquish my hold of the spear, which in bitter realisation was self-defeating, because as the beast sagged backwards my body flung upwards like the shot of a catapult. Here, I violently collided with the canopy, and then crashed upon the hard ground.

Dazed, I reeled onto my back, a wad of blood spurting from my lips. A shadow descended over my eyes, and as the light of the moon steadily faded away, I could hear the echoes of Priscus' voice ring in my ear, his shouts radiating from the gatehouse above. I could not discern what he was saying until a fire erupted in front of the portcullis — this fire a product of the weapon that Etorus of the Grey Isles had created with the resin he had asked for.

CHAPTER 20

A rush of air entered my lungs as I awoke with my cheek resting on Lera's lap. My head was throbbing to a beat, and the flaxen sunlight, because dawn had arrived, was doubling the pain around my eyes to the point that it was unbearable to keep them opened for more than a moment. I was clueless to where I was, though all around me I could hear the gut-wrenching sounds of wounded men that passed by me on stretchers. I began to feel the drops of cold water on my neck as I gradually came to. Then, as I became accustomed to the light and was able to open my eyes a little bit more, I noticed that Lera was washing my face with a damp cloth, which she repeatedly doused in a pail of water that looked to me like the swamp I had fallen into the night before. Disoriented as I was, it did not take me long to realise that Lera and I were at the top of the stairs, the ones that led to the door's of the keep. I knew that the battle was still raging on, and not because the clamour was discernible, but because we were still alive.

I stretched out for my left shoulder, though in a jolt of pain I stopped short, for it was out of place. I gave Lera permission to put it back, and so without hesitation she gripped it with one palm on each side and firmly applied pressure. The snap confirmed that she had set it back to place, which was swiftly followed by a muffled, but otherwise agonising, cry on my part. It was at this point, under

317

wide-eyed sensations of pain, that a stiffening shock seized me. I had finally taken notice of Lera's face, her complexion almost unrecognizable to me. If not for the pendant dangling at her neck I would have thought her a walking corpse, seeing as how her skin was blemished and bruised by the grit of battle. Portions of her hair were clumped like bundles of wet grass, though what made these clumps sodden was not water, but the blood of the Ascani she had slain throughout the night. And her eyes, usually filled with steely purpose and confidence, were black-shot and swollen with exhaustion. She was tearing as well, and as the droplets rolled down her cheeks they were quickly made red by the gore caught in their trail, and as such it seemed as though she was letting fall tears of blood.

"Are you alright? Are you hurt?" I said with worry, sitting up as fast as the duress in my body allowed. I placed a hand upon her cheek, inspecting every spot of blood in search of any cuts or abrasions.

"I'm fine," she said, as if too proud to speak the truth.

Here, Lera began to speak to me, though at every turn of the head there was so much commotion that my focus, and my eyes, began to drift away in overwhelming curiosity. I looked about the fortress; first into the hall and to the wounded men writhing in agony, and next to the ramparts and the courtyard, where all at once I saw the horrific outcome of the night's assault. I could not believe the sight before me; a sight that had all together stripped me of any confidence that we were going to endure. Like the leaves of autumn, corpses of both man and beast spotted Northfleet in numbers beyond counting, each laying, except for those creatures upon the mounds, in whichever contorted manner they had fallen. Parted limbs and whole bodies were slung across the breadth of the ramparts, and those that lay in the courtyard, closer to sight, were sprawled across its surface as if a second battle had taken place without my knowing. There was blood everywhere, so much of it that it coursed profusely into great pools, covering the white marble beneath almost in its entirety. More than that, scarlet rivers flowed down the inner face of the wall like hellish tapestries, silken luster appearing to be crowned by the black smoke that rose from the fires beginning to take hold on the timber, and, I would later learn, from the barricades of fire that Etorus had created to keep the Ascani from scaling the walls any further.

To say that I felt defeated would be too small a word to describe my heart. Not only did I not believe what I was seeing, but I was also starting to become enraptured by the foul thoughts of our definite demise, images in my mind of what could soon be a very real certainty. The din around me was no more, pushed aside by the voice in my head trying to make sense of it all. All this time our objective was to hold Northfleet until the king arrived to relieve us, and we were meant to do so for as long as it took Adeanus' army to reach us. That was our task. This phrase was what I kept telling myself in this moment so that my feeble heart would not altogether leap out of my chest in hopes of escaping my growing fear. I cannot explain it, but as I was brooding over these thoughts I felt as if nothing seemed to matter to me anymore, nor did anything seem to be significant in terms of what we did to prepare for this task; the collection of our food supply, the finding of the armoury, and the great labour we set out towards the restorations — none of it seemed to matter in the face of the slaughter before me. All of this carnage was the end result of a single night of war, our men depleted by a third, our enervation ever growing. *How could we possibly wait for the king? How could we possibly hope to survive if the Ascani would keep on with their attack until the last of their creatures were dead?*

"Cillian!" Lera blurted, as she lightly jabbed my wounded shoulder. "Did you hear me?"

"What?" I replied softly, coming back to lucidity. "What is it?"

"I said I love you," she said, repeating what I had first failed to hear. All the while she had been sitting on the highest stair, and I was on the one below. Her eyes were no more than a few feet over mine, but still when I looked at her, it was as if I was looking as far up as the sky. She kissed me on the bridge of my brow, very gently, and with nothing more than her love. "I realised, when I saw you on your back, that I had never told you. That I had lost my chance to," she added, with fresh tears welling in her eyes. "Many of us have fallen, Cillian. Edros, Lytus, Ferix, they're all dead. They're back there in the hall. And when I saw them bringing you there I thought you were dead too. I thought I had lost you."

"Lera I —" I stopped, gently cupping her cheek. "I'm not dead. And neither are you."

"Honestly, builder, I still don't know how you've managed it," Meric's voice suddenly broke in as he came out of the hall, though it seemed as if he had been prying. He stopped beside us and dropped three shields at his feet. Meanwhile, ranks of men began pouring out of the hall. As they rushed past him, Meric stood still, overlooking the battle. He combed his hair back by running both of his hands through it, revealing that his appearance was just as smudged by the smear of battle as Lera's, greased and bloodied. In his case, however, the gore was his, for a great, deepened claw mark ran at a slant from the key of his brow to the haft of his chin, marring the length of his face. "I hate to be the shite that breaks up your heartwarming dribble, but if I were you I'd save the romance for later and grab a shield. They're going to breach the gate soon."

"Breach the gate?" I said, surprised.

"What?" he said, grabbing a shield. "Don't tell me you thought we had scared them off?"

After several futile attempts to stand up, I did so with Lera's helping hand. The pain in my shoulder was fairly bearable — not that I had any other choice but to bear it. Meric handed each of us a shield, which, to my surprise, were marked with the emblem of the Vined Sword. In a hurry he led us down the stairs, and in the time that it took us to reach the bottom, the battle had taken a greater sour turn, from which the horns of retreat were being sounded across the ramparts. The Ascani had withered our numbers to such a low that we could no longer check their numbers upon the walls, in spite of Etorus' wall of fire. For this reason, Priscus had commanded all the remaining survivors to set fire to every inch of timber along the battlements, allowing the men a chance to abandon their posts and gather at the foot of the stair. As more men piled around me, I watched as the bulk of our forces spilled into the courtyard, bumping and rushing towards us like a herd of agitated ungulates vying to outrun the other. Here, Priscus, Axle, Jon, and Andreaus, had made their appearance beside me, whereupon the men behind them began acting on the second part of Priscus' command, which was to begin piling as many Ascani dead as they could find in great mounds at the wings of the stair.

"Stack those bastards high lads!" Axle cried. "Hurry on! Come on!"

Those tasked with heaping the dead did so with haste by recklessly flinging them on top of each other as though they were simply displacing earth. By now, the timber on the battlements had formed a veil of fire, just as dense as the ranks we formed between the mounds. All the while, the tune of wicked clarions played, and from the Black Shores to the western forest the sound of the enemy beating their feet in advance seemed to me as if their numbers had not fallen in the slightest, even though hundreds of them helped us form this last barricade.

"What do you want me to do?" I asked Priscus as he joined us.

"Get ready to fight," he replied, sticking himself next to me at the center of our mob.

"Over there! Look!" a legionary blurted, pointing his sword towards the portcullis.

At that moment a clangor of crackling iron rent the sky. The Ascani had assembled before the gatehouse in three great columns, each carrying a rope made of knotted vines, whose barbed hooks were firmly anchored between the widened seams that their battering ram, hewn from a massive tree trunk, had already pounded to ruin. They began to tug at the ropes at the cadence of their master's drums, lashing out wildly with dreadful shrieks of ecstasy every time a bolt ruptured from the portcullis, or whenever the crossbars began to bend like the twisted branches of an aged tree, which were coming apart one after the other faster than I had expected.

I realised then that my fears had not reached their peak. As I braced the edge of my shield against Priscus', a sudden touch of my hand made me turn my head. It was Lera. She looked at me with a steady calm, her eyes expressing clearly that she had accepted her fate, as if to say death to her was good and fair if it happened at my side. Of course, dear reader, I felt the same. There is nothing more I could tell you of my feelings, but that I had abandoned the idea of defeat in favour of not daring to draw back, or advance for that matter. Instead, I vied to hold my ground with her at my side, until the very end.

We all stood in anticipation, waiting for the Ascani to breach the gate. The archers, what was left of them, had positioned themselves on the mounds and upon the stairs overlooking the infantry, readying what few arrows remained. Altogether we massed a bare two hundred strong, including the wounded who thought themselves fit enough to join the barricade. As Axle ordered the barricade to stand at the ready, I quickly looked to my left and right, just in time to see a swell of red-stained swords and Uthian spears come down upon the rim of the shield wall. It was only then that I noticed Axle and Andreaus lined beside Priscus, and that Meric was standing beside Lera and Jon; all of whom, perhaps coincidentally, bore the mark of their respective legions upon their shields.

I was convinced that this would be the end of my short life.

Then, without warning, a rumble erupted from the gate as the portcullis suffered through the last of its ancient hold. In many fragments the metal broke away, which were propelled backwards through the Ascani horde like a farmer's plow. Immediately, the creatures began to funnel into the courtyard, easily overcoming the palisade that we had fashioned. The corpses in the courtyard had slowed them down, though in a stampede the black mass barrelled headlong towards us, sparking a chorus of muttered curses and foreign prayers among the ranks, which then brought the barricade to a teeter as the men shuffled about on their heels in fear.

Hearing this uneasiness fester, Priscus broke his readied stance. He struck the face of his shield with his sword, stopping only when all eyes and shaky breaths veered toward him. In this moment he appeared as he always did, stout and brave, as well as a lord who knew that his life was as equal to the rest. There was no fear in him. With his sword gripped high and his chest expanded he turned to the men and roared, "Garrison Hold!"

Therewith every man let sound a spirited cry. We braced for the shock, whereupon in a frenzy the Ascani crashed into our shield wall with a deafening clunk. The force of the collision pushed the whole of our frontline backwards several paces, but at the same time they had hurled straight into a wall bristled in silver thorns. Many were impaled like needles in a pincushion. In short order we pressed back with terrible fury, steadily recovering the form of our barricade, which allowed the archers to better mark their targets, and the spears at our backs a better chance to strike the enemy. Relentlessly, we jabbed and slashed our swords from the breaks in our defence, the clash of steel and pummelled shields filling the air. Before we knew it the sun was already midway to its highest point. Now, the stink of fresh blood began to fuse with the odour of the festering corpses at a count that I could not venture to guess. Furthermore, the veil of flames had spread onto portions of the ramparts, turning the bundled dead into pyres of cooking flesh; a terrible scent that has lingered in my nose throughout all my long years. On they kept coming, trying to penetrate the iron carapace from all directions. With each thwarted attempt they became increasingly maniacal in their want for blood, and as such they began pitching their own, dead or alive, over us as if they were hurling stones, all whilst a good many others sought to snake their way underneath our bulwarks as a means to gnaw at our feet.

"By your feet!" I yelled to Priscus. I raised my sword and brought it down upon the skull of the Ascani reaching for his legs. Another appeared at mine, slithering passed the ridge of corpses. I thrashed back and forth in a frenzy, severing the tip of its nose and fingers. Then, the Uthian behind me surged forward and pushed his blade through its ear. "We can't hold them for much longer!" I then added, returning my attention to the front.

"Keep at it, boy!" Axle blared. "Hold tight, and break them here!"

Most of the hours that we fought were a blur to me, dear reader, and so I cannot say for certain when it was that Priscus had commanded us to form the Iron Carapace, calling for all those in the subsequent ranks to raise their shields above their heads to stop the Ascani, and their arrows, from plunging into us. Though we could not see the enemy, save for the eyes of those directly pressed up against our shields, we could still feel the weight of their push. However, a few moments after Priscus had spoken something peculiar had happened. The weight of their push had lessened abruptly, as if all those in front of Priscus and I had backed away. It was here when a gauntlet broke passed the barricade like a thrusted spear, grasping the rim of Priscus' shield. There was no time to retaliate, for in a heartbeat his shield swung open like a door, upon which the gauntlet appeared again and clutched his neck, violently drawing him out from the ranks.

Priscus hit the ground a distance away, rolling onto his back atop a sheet of Ascani dead. In spite of my better judgment, I leapt forward on impulse, my shoulder inclined against my shield as I smashed my way towards him. The creatures before me tumbled out of my way, and with each forward step I could hear Lera and Axle curse at me for breaking from the barricade — I should say that their curses were born of worry, and not insult. As I think back, they were right to be worried, for just as I reached Priscus, some fifteen feet from the barricade, I had found myself in front of Far-Skafa. In the process of meeting him I had managed to deflect his swords from reaching Priscus' chest. The act enraged him, and so in retaliation he charged at me, twirling his blades at such speed that I could not anticipate the direction of his forthcoming strikes. I brought my shield up to shoulder height, ready to defend myself. But then, all at once, Far-Skafa was still, for Priscus had thrown himself into battle, placing himself between us with a readied poise, one which reminded me of Wymar upon the sentry of Easteria.

I slowly began to retreat, my eyes locked with Far-Skafa's. At this point it was all too clear to me that he recalled my face from the cliffs of Easteria, and to be honest, dear reader, it seemed that it gave him some sort of pleasure, as if he was pleased to see that his two most hated enemies were conveniently presented to him for slaughter. Meanwhile, I wanted to rejoin the others, but we could not, being that as I glanced over my shoulder I came to see that there was no chance of reaching them. We were completely enveloped by the enemy, who had formed a ring around us like that of an arena.

"Priscus," I nervously mumbled. "We're surrounded."

"Keep your mind on him," he muttered. "Stay focused. The rest won't attack."

"And why's that?" I said with more unease, eyeing the wall of snapping teeth around us.

"Because our flesh has already been claimed," he replied, rooting himself more firmly.

Far-Skafa took a step forward, shifting his neck from side to side as if he were limbering up for the coming fight, a thing which seemed to be his prompt for battle. He removed his sheep-skin overvest by ripping it clean off, revealing his ghoulish muscularity and devilish vitality. Here, he pointed one of his blades to Priscus, and then said very forcefully, "Your life, this place...all mine now."

"Cillian," Priscus whispered to me, still looking straight ahead at his nemesis. "Do me a favour, will you?"

"What is it?" I said with confusion, thinking this was no time to be asking for favours.

"Help me kill this grilled faced bastard."

Just then in an explosion of wrath, Far-Skafa set-off after us. Together we pressed our attack, each of us trying to land the mortal blow while making sure to keep to the center of the ring and away from its pike-prickled edges. A single error would cost me my life, our lives, since Far-Skafa was proving to be the far better swordsman. I tried to overpower him with brute force, yet with each ensuing strike his dual blades fell heavier upon my sword. Not a minute after we began exchanging blows I fell to a knee, narrowly dodging a strike that would have otherwise taken my head off. How careless I was to unite steel with sickly flesh, and as such Far-Skafa slammed his fist into my gut, forcing a gush of air and dribble from my mouth. I quivered back in pain, unable to regain a proper footing. Few of our strikes managed to graze their mark, yet those that did were gravely repaid with more accurate slashes.

Priscus was thrown to my side, trails of blood running off his chin. "Strike high!"

Priscus pounced forward and swung his aim at Far-Skafa's legs, whilst I, breathless and out of strength, aimed my strikes above the breast. The creature's eyes flashed as he fell back, almost as if he was flustered by our coordinated attack. This newfound upper hand, however, was the last we would ever attain. At the swift turn of his heel, he lunged back at us with a straightened leg, where his boot slashed across Priscus' cheek, sending him reeling off to the side with his hand cupped around his jaw. At that same moment I, once again, rashly beset Far-Skafa with the intent to catch him off guard. He had lurched downward opposite my sword and brought his blade across the mail upon my back. I was not cut, but still my eyes widened and a hoarse grunt bellowed from my throat, for the blow felt as though it had left its mark. More than that, he had snatched a handful of my hair and twisted it roughly. He began pummelling my face with the point of his iron mask, leaving scars that are still visible on my face. As blood bubbled at my lips he pulled me around as if I were his spoils of the hunt, which heightened the snarls of the Ascani onlookers. I stumbled under his hold, knowing full well that I needed to get free, otherwise his swords would soon find my heart. Like a mouse caught in a trap I wiggled and wormed, despite the increasing force in his battering fists. By the end of this great passion of defiance I began clawing at his face; my hand then finding a firm clutch on the top rim of his iron mask. I tensed my muscles and wrinkled my nose, and then I tore it off with a savage cry.

Far-Skafa cast me aside as high pitched shrieks left his throat. As my back hit the ground time seemed to come to a halt; held in place by the gruesome sight that lurked within the corner of my eye. He turned to me with hunched shoulders, his head canted to the side like that of a ravenous beast whose eyes were filled with sheer hysteria. It was at this moment that I fully saw the horror that hid behind the mask. From ear to ear the flesh below his cloven nose was torn, gashed, and mangled as if it was eaten away by plague, it's entirety framed in the portrait of his teeth, which were as thin as fishing hooks.

Before I knew it he was standing over me. He pressed his foot on my shoulder and brought the point of his sword to my neck. I could see a portion of his tongue squirm at the base of his chin as he attempted to steady his breath. *"Argul...Irgul...Anoarin,"* he hissed.

I did not know what Far-Skafa's phrase meant, nor did I want to understand it. All I wanted was to keep his focus on me for as long as I could, because as long as his attention was fixed upon me he had all but forgotten about Priscus, who very swiftly caught him at his blindside, sacking him off his feet. The creature, as luck would have it, landed upon the point of an Uthian spear, which pierced his thigh. In spite of this wound, they grappled about crazily, each of their fists finding a good many well placed hits. Then, Far-Skafa cudgelled the side of Priscus' head with a clenched palm, sending him once again on his back. He mounted Priscus like a horse, his hands squeezing at the man's neck, whose face was very quickly turning a shade of blue and purple. I wanted to help him, but the aches of my wounds felt like chains that were rooted to the marble.

I looked at Priscus slowly wither. I was mortified. From my belt I pulled out my dagger, and with the last of my strength I was able to pitch it over to him. Priscus saw it land beside him. He grabbed the dagger and skewered Far-Skafa's eye, forcing the beast to recoil. Here, Priscus nabbed Far-Skafa's mask and bashed it across his jowl, dispatching pieces of flesh and slivers of teeth into the air. He continued to bludgeon him again and again in a frenzy, and as Far-Skafa careened to the side his foul jaw came apart in small chunks. For Priscus, this was not enough. With a final grunt he jammed the mask downwards with such force that the whole of Far-Skafa's face caved in like the rind of a squashed fruit.

Far-Skafa, the *primorus*, was dead.

The weight of relief fled my lungs, though danger still lurked around us. As we fought, the Ascani had been tamed under Far-Skafa's presence, but now that their leader was no longer among the living I was certain that we were soon to be swarmed by the mass thirsting for a chance at our flesh. Our minds, Priscus and mine, were connected, for before I rose to a knee he had hastily tottered to my side with his sword gripped and prepared — the man was utterly worn out, his age finally showing through his stare as the rage of battle began to bleed away its former passion. Be that as it may, he firmly plotted his stance as if he sought to take on the whole of the horde single-handedly, or at least kill as many as he could before any could get to me.

I tried to speak to him, endeavouring a last word, but in place of words scarlet bubbles were all that surfaced from my parting lips. This was it. Hell would soon be upon us. I remember clearly the images that crossed my mind: flashes of the people who shared a place in my heart. I saw the face of the man who stood before me, and the faces of the men who stood behind me. I thought of my father and my mother, and of my grandfather, and the comfort of their past love. And most of all, I saw Lera. Not just her face you see, but of everything from the very beginning; all of the things that we shared, all of the things that made my heart heavy and my innards flutter. And so, my dear reader, I simply closed my eyes and smiled as the Ascani ring burst asunder.

Then, without warning, my eyes reopened as if awaking from a nightmare. The Ascani, now not ten feet from us, had come to a sudden halt, their heads perked upwards to the sky like curious hens. Upon the air there came a far-off sound, one of drums beating heavily in the fields outside the fortress. I had never before seen these creatures in a state of inquisitiveness, and as the thumps grew louder they also became, if I dare say, anxious. Both man and beast were gripped by the sound, and as such the struggle at the carapace began to gradually ebb, bit by bit until the battle in the courtyard had come to a complete stop.

"My lord Priscus! My lord Priscus!" an archer repeated in jubilation. He was standing at the top of the stair with his bow pointed to the southern field. Even from afar I felt the shine coming off his smile. "Banners!" he then cried out even more ecstatically. "Crimson banners!"

Like the synchrony of an actor's cue one hundred peals of the buccina rent the black-fumed sky, and with this tune came the stomp of iron boots and the jangle of chainmail, their thunder more powerful than the battle cries of a thousand throats chanting in unison. The legions of Anolia had finally arrived.

The Ascani in the courtyard, perhaps because their chances for fight and slaughter were better sought outside the castle, suddenly turned their backs to us. They headed back to the portcullis, where the swarm had become wedged, simply because the throat of the gatehouse proved too narrow for the enormity of their numbers. Nevertheless, our zeal for battle had been restored at its utmost, and so Priscus, seeing the chance to regain a foothold in the castle, ordered the pursuit. The men broke off from the barricade with a bloodlust of their own, and together they stormed forward, lashing their swords and spears upon Ascani backs viciously. By the dozen they fell dead over and over again until our own ranks swallowed us to the rear, and to safety.

As the men fought on under Andreaus' command, Axle rushed over to Priscus, his expression ripe with irritation "Set yourself apart from the rest of us if you must," he berated while inspecting my wounds. "But for Andiel's sake man, could you not drag our builder with you."

"I'm afraid I'm with the captain on this one," Lera said, her own anger directed at me. She tore a piece of fabric from one of the standards at our feet and bandaged my leg. "Always the bloody hero, aren't you?" she added, tightening the knot firmly as if to make her anger known.

"If it wasn't for him we'd both be dead," Priscus said, nodding at Far-Skafa's corpse.

"One thing less to worry about," Axle said, quickly helping me to my feet.

"Just so everyone knows. I would've helped with that," Meric said, appearing with Jon at his side. "I simply didn't have the chance." He came very close to me and pressed a half-charred standard against my chest. "Can you walk?" he asked. He did not wait for me to reply, but instead he turned his back to me and said, "Come along now, Cillian. The battle isn't over. First it's best we let Petris know that we're still alive so they don't start bombarding this place. We'll fight our way to the top of the gatehouse and signal him with the standard from there."

"Petris?" I blurted out in confusion, as if I did not grasp the name. "But how could he —" I stopped myself short, for all at once the clearest of recollections seized my thoughts. The image was that of our departure from The Shield, the night when Priscus spoke with Cimber by the side of the road, and of the moment when he had strangely adjusted Cimber's tabard. "The map?" I muttered. "The map of Northfleet from the book! That's what you hid in Cimber's tabard? That's why Axle was drawing a second one."

"Aye," Axle replied, getting ready to move. "Not the wisest of choices at the time, since we thought then Plaucus our turncoat, and not that bloody sard Ulcar. First we considered entrusting the map with Petris, perhaps hiding it where the bastard keeps his biscuits, which would certainly be the first place his hand would go to when he would awake. But like all things of worth it was best not to leave it with him. The plan then was for Petris to convince Plaucus in giving up the men he denied us and then have them meet us on the road. So, we took a gamble and thought of no better person to safeguard the path to our rescue then with Cimber, the only man in the Stone Fortress who could help Petris with the convincing. Luckily, it worked."

"But what of the king's army?" I said. "Isn't that what we were waiting for all this time?"

"Well, yes," Axle said. "But in war, Cillian, you have to have more than one plan in action if you want to survive. And this plan, judging by the time of its arrival, got here first."

"Yeah and the second thing to come won't be the king's army but our deaths if we don't stop talking in the middle of a battle," Meric said.

Suddenly the clashing of steel caught our attention. The Ascani by the portcullis, some hundred yet remaining, had stayed behind in favour of battle, catching our men in pursuit alone and out of rank. Without so much as a word Priscus rushed off towards the melee, motioning Axle to follow him. I, on the other hand, was forced to a limping sprint by Meric, who pushed me towards the eastern wall and to the nearest steps that led to the battlements; Jon and Lera having already dashed off ahead of us, carving a path through the enemy. They all fought hard up the steps and across the ramparts while I followed closely with the shaft of the standard resting upon my shoulder. When we had reached the gatehouse I stood in awe, as I had done the night before, glaring through the flames at the thousands of Ascani still alive. This time, I should write, that there was triumph, and not fear, in my gaze, because beyond the black swarm of the Ascani I saw the legion of the Stone Fortress marching in advance of their foes; six cohorts, three thousand glistening helmets filling the southern plain in the Anolian order of battle.

Though my standard was already caught high in the wind, I waved it more vigorously from side to side. The Thorned Dragon upon the cloth swirled and eddied as my shouts of joy and pride reigned in the air, their resonance mimicking what could have very well been the beast's roar. As the legion of the Stone Fortress came to a halt its center split apart, whereupon three men made their appearance on horseback. Their figures were only speckles to my squinting eyes, but even so there was one amongst them that I could identify without fault, a man whose rounded waist and priestly garbs I could never confuse.

"Petris!" I cried aloud, tears of joy swelling in my eyes.

This was then the moment that the horns of Anolia's army blared for a last time. The sea of silver helmets dipped, and the whole of the army barrelled across the field. The two armies clashed headlong, upon which the thunder of war sounded in the beaten grass.

"Andiel's joy, builder!" Meric beamed, patting his forehead against mine. His happiness was overwhelming, more so than when his full-pursed wagers were won in his favour. "By the gods, look at them all! He brought half the twentieth with him! Can you see that? That's what happens when the lady of luck fancies you — and by you, I obviously mean me." He turned his back to the battle, toward Jon, and then took in a deep breath, finally relieved. "I'm glad one of us saw through Ulcar's shite in time.

Now, Jon, before you punch me in the gut I need you to listen to me, alright? If you do what I say we can make lots of money off this. First we'll use all the silver you have left. If we win we'll then use mine, but if we lose we'll —"

Meric suddenly stumbled forward as if faint, prompting me to grab onto his arm in order to keep him from falling over. His knees, however, gave way and he fell into my open arms. I held him upright as best I could, yet his weight proved too heavy for my depleted strength, and for my aching shoulder. I called out for help, a desperate plea took its tone. Jon had already taken the side opposite mine, where he anchored Meric's flaccid arm on his neck, relieving the heft off my frame. Meric began to cough wickedly, blood coated spittle darkened his teeth. We looked about his body for a wound, which Lera had found by pulling his tabard away from the center of his belly, revealing a great, wide gash upon the mail.

"Meric. Why the hell would you keep this silent?" I said, taken aback. I quickly rumpled the end of my tabard with trembling hands and pressed it tightly against his open wound. He was now veering in and out of consciousness, barely able to keep himself from collapsing. "Lera, cover our front," I yelled. "Jon! Let's get him to the keep! Quickly!"

"You know, Cillian," Meric muttered with a grin as we began to hoist him up. "If I have ever taken the piss out of you it's because I knew you could handle it. You...you aren't half-bad if I dare say, and you have more than just an empty head on your shoulders, almost like me. If this is to be the end of my life then I just wanted to tell you that I never meant anything by the jesting. It's a problem of mine. I just can't help bugging the newcomers, especially those that look as charming as I do."

"Gambling and women are your problems, Meric," I said.

"Oh yes!" he smiled in realisation. "They are, aren't they?"

"Quiet," Jon said firmly. "Blood flow faster when you talk."

"Alright then my friend," Meric whinced. "On your lead. Get me out of —"

Just as we brought Meric to a stand his body rocked violently, his chest pressed forward. A gust of air shot out of his lungs as if he plunged into icy water, his haggard face turning ghostly white. At the moment his body had rocked forward, shattered rivets of mail and chunks of his guts were flung in Lera's direction, whilst gushes of blood splattered against our faces. As we all broke our hold of him, our eyes swept down to Meric's stomach, where the head of a harpoon, it's form like that of an eagle's talon, jut out from a gapping rift of mangled entrails just above his navel. I peered over my shoulder and saw that the hook was attached to a rope.

Meric's red, tear-filled eyes drifted over to Jon. I had never before seen fear in him, but at this point in time he was staring at Jon as if he were a frightened boy seeking help and comfort from a hallowed brother. Tears of blood rolled down his face, and from his mouth came only blurts of guttural sounds. Then, he forced out a single word and said, "Jon."

Right then the slack in the rope snapped with a huge crack, and therewith Meric's frame was ripped from our frozen clutches. As he flew backwards his legs struck the merlons of the gatehouse, which contorted his figure as if he were made of nothing more than sculptor's clay. As we looked onward completely stunned, Meric had vanished from our sight, leaving behind a broad trail of his viscera along the blackened timber and scorched stone.

CHAPTER 21

I had hardly come to understand what had just happened when Jon let sound a heart-rending wail, a cry that betrayed every trait in his Herculean frame and appearance. His battle-worn face, drowned in a mire of sorrow, was reduced to that of a child caught in the immobility of horror. As the tears continued to well in his eyes he staggered toward the stone and timber that Meric had collided with, his jaw shivering intensely at the sight of the entrails dangling upon them. He had reached out for them as if touching them would see Meric return, but something within him ceased his movement. It was his anger that stopped him, his outcries now growing more feverish and frantic. He gripped his axe and wrung the stem, and then in the blink of an eye he vaulted over the merlons of the gatehouse.

I reached after him, nearly vaulting over the wall myself if not for Lera's stilling shout. Here I peered over the merlons and gazed at the grounds before the gate in search of Jon, fearing that he had fallen to his death, or worse, that he had been made lame by the sheer height of the drop. To the contrary, I found him emerging from the corpse filled gully, bereft of sanity. In turn, I was surprised to see that Priscus and Axle had managed to press the Ascani from the castle, the battle in the courtyard now shifting just beyond the gate. As their melee was underway, Jon moving through the thick of it, the battle upon the plains was rising in our favour. The bulk of the Ascani were being pushed back to the shoreline by the men of the twentieth, but the rest, perhaps some thousand, had been caught with the eastern forest on their flank.

I turned to Lera and motioned my desire to join them by way of Jon's method of descent.

"Have you lost your mind?" she blurted. "That drop is twenty feet at least. We'll break all the bones in our legs, Cillian. You can barely walk on your own as it is!"

"It's ten — perhaps less," I said. The corpses of the Ascani were stacked upon the face of the wall beyond the half, seeing as how they were plotting to use their dead as scaling ladders. I knew a jump from our height would not kill us, that is unless we unwittingly fell upon the point of a sword.

"What is it with you and plunging from high places?" she said.

"It's faster this way!" I said, suddenly realising that my words sounded like Jon's.

I quickly grasped Lera's arm, and then stormed toward the rim like a wounded stag. As one we leapt from the ramparts and ascended into the air. Promptly, we plummeted some ten feet onto the mound of Ascani corpses, our bodies spiralling right into the fray at its base. Here I rose swiftly, my senses aroused by battle. As I reached for my sword I noticed that my scabbard was missing, and as misfortune would have it, so did the massive brute that caught sight of me. Apart from the red colour of Far-Skafa's eyes, I had never seen any other Ascani to that bore the same pigment. The eyes of this creature, however, seemed to gleam red as it charged at me with blind fury, lashing at the air with its axe. I shuffled and wheeled, recoiling from the creature's strikes by the skin of my teeth, for the battering I had received by Far-Skafa had begun to catch up with me in its fullest, my body feeling as though it was suddenly taken by a spell of frailty. Even with the creature on my mind, I had no intention to be halted by the fighting. My aim was to find Jon and sedate his ceaseless craze, knowing well that his rage would lead him to his own ruin. As such, I kept looking for an escape. But, the Ascani's persistence kept me from daring to get the upper hand.

Suddenly I was at the edge of the gully. As I ducked in time to dodge a head severing strike Lera had rolled into action, saving me from stumbling backwards and into the only part of the ditch where the stakes were ready and waiting. While sprouting from her roll she hewed the creature's leg clean off, and as it fell to its one good knee, she grappled its horns and twisted them to their opposite ends as if wringing water from a cloth. It's eyes no longer having the red hue that I had witnessed beforehand.

"Here," she said with a heavy breath, nudging the hilt of her sword against my rib.

"What about you?" I said, grasping it.

"I got these," she replied. She then broke off into the battle with a half-stemmed spear in one hand and a dagger in the other, leaving me stunned and unable to voice the desperate call for caution that my thoughts shouted.

My frame of mind shifted as Jon's figure appeared to me in the corner of my eye, even more berserking than last I had seen him. It is without excess when I say that he himself had reduced the enemy by a hundred in that short time, leaving behind their mangled corpses as a trial. I began to move rapidly in his direction, penetrating deeper across the chaos, where steel flashed about wildly, and Anolian arrows flew overhead like hailstones. Needless to say, my dear reader, that the earth beneath my feet was marked by the visage of death, wherein the dead lay in equal number to the blades of grass that once coated the field, which was now nothing more than a sludge-like, boggy swamp that slowed my pace to a near crawl.

After a good many gruelling moments I had come at last to the rim of the fray, where to my dismay I had lost sight of Jon. The trail of corpses continued on, yet there was no way for me to find its end because it had merged with the distant cohorts who were battling the Ascani at the shoreline. It was not all ill luck, for I had inadvertently stumbled into the vicinity of Priscus, Axle, and Andreaus, who were in the company of three others; Plaucus, Petris and Cimber — Plaucus was laying in a lord's litter at this time, his body wounded and wrapped in bandages, some bloodied, others fresh. I saw that Priscus was in the midst of a deep exchange with him, their hands joined together in such a way that any who saw it would think that Plaucus was in the midst of his final words. The tone of their chatter was anything but joyous, nor did it seem that it was one of quibbling and quarrelling. It seemed, however, one of fear and alarm, which was made clear by Plaucus' eccentric gestures.

"Cillian!" Petris cried as our eyes met. In truth, I barely heard him call out to me, because a fresh, reinforcing cohort was marching past us at the cadence of its musicians. It was only when I saw him rushing towards me that I realised he was shouting my name.

I ran to meet him halfway, whereat I grabbed the sleeves of his robe to further tighten my hugging embrace. Petris' friendship, though still at its dawn, felt as if it had the weight of a lifetime behind it, and so to see him in the flesh warmed my heart to its fullest. Yet, once my smile faded I found myself standing before him in silence. I wanted to tell him how happy I was to see him, to see the recovery of his eye wound, but my tongue would not dare voice any words of elation. Rather, it was stilled by the manner in which Petris proceeded to stare at me, grim and worried, as if ill news were caught in his throat, though he did not know how to profess it.

I returned his gaze. How is it that news of Meric's death had so quickly reached him? Had Jon been the harbinger? I did not know. It was not my desire to reconfirm Meric's passing, and by coincidence I did not have to, because just as I moved to speak, Priscus, Axle, and Andreaus joined around us, each of their faces bearing the same look of uneasiness as Petris. From my perspective it was all too clear by their expressions that they were bearing the distress of Meric's death. As such, we remained a few moments in gloomy silence. But, truth be told, the longer it went on, the more I began to feel that they shared something more than just the pain of loss, something more akin to dread.

At this point Axle stepped forward and spoke in a pressing tone. "Forget it for now! We'll deal with it when the battle is over. I can hardly believe it to be true, and of that my heart is certain, but right now we need to finish this quickly before Plaucus' nerves drive the whole of his army to shite and ruin."

"We can't just push it aside," I said with a raised brow.

"Cillian, now is not the time," Axle affirmed.

I forcefully wedged my way past the group, garnering their scrutiny. I recall, vividly, the ire that filled my heart. Meric was dead, and so perhaps Axle was right that there was nothing more to be done on the matter. Still, Jon was yet in the thick of the battle, and as I have already mentioned, he cared little for his own life. I was so fixed on finding him that I understood Axle's words to mean that we should let Jon do what he pleased — I know now that this is not what he implied.

"Where are you going?" Petris said, confused as to what I was doing.

"I have to go after him," I said. "We have to find him."

"Clear your head," Priscus said, firmly. "There is nothing to be done about him now."

"Aye, he's right lad," Petris added. "There will be time enough afterwards to deal —"

"There isn't any time!" I interrupted, as I looked for an idle horse. "You don't get it, Petris. Jon saw it happen in front of his eyes and it has driven him mad. He's out there right now searching for him! We need to find him and stop him now, because if we don't he'll continue rampaging on until he's dead, or until he recovers Meric's body."

"Meric's body?" Petris said, as if caught off-guard.

"Yes," I replied, while turning on my heel. I was off-put by Petris' tone of surprise. I turned to look at them and was met by a collective gawk of bewilderment. "His body," I went on, speaking as if I was repeating something they already knew about. "Jon went after Meric's body. He —" Here, I stopped talking, since it became clearer to me as I spoke that none of them were aware of what I was saying. Immediately, a sour taste filled my mouth. If they did not know about Meric's death, then I had just brought to light the news of their dear brother's passing in the most unpleasant of ways.

The air rushed out of Petris' lungs. "I can't believe it. Meric's dead."

Then, a voice cried out in approach, breaking the morose silence. "My lord Priscus!" It was Cimber astride his mount, coming towards us at a furious gallop. He came to halt beside Priscus, struggling to keep his horse still. "The Ascani! They're fleeing towards the eastern forest!" he said, sticking into the ground the standard of the Stone Fortress that he was carrying. "The castle has been secured! My Lord Plaucus' injuries have pressed him to seek rest inside the keep. He wishes you to take full command of the twentieth."

Priscus straightened his back and erupted with a flurry of commands, steering those present, the nearest sargeants, towards points of need across the battlefield. Axle followed suit, who in turn spurred Andreaus to action. Petris and I were the only two who remained fixed as the rest of them moved about. In my regard, I did not move because I was trapped in my own head, a confusing thought now busying my mind with sudden realisation.

"Wait," I said slowly as the bustle around me continued. My voice was almost a whisper, yet it was loud enough to halt the bustle and look to me. "I don't understand. If not for Meric. What is it then that has you all so concerned?"

All at once an enormous crackle of thunder cut across the sky, bringing the whole of our army's advance to an abrupt halt. I first looked at Petris, and then up at the sky, unable to comprehend how thunder could be born with the absence of a single cloud. As I stood, speechless, I began to feel the sun's rays upon my face fall short of its morning's warmth, despite they were present and bright. We were all nervous for what was coming next. Little by little, the blue sky above us began to darken to a grey hue as heavy, storm-like clouds appeared from nothing. Foul scented winds then followed, their force mounting to such strengths that the waters of the bay stirred to waves of great height, and the trees of the forests swayed so violently that many threatened to collapse, others precisely doing so. Amid the crackle of the timbers and the crash of the waves a myriad of sonorous rattles broke from the clouds, turning the winds to an unimaginable tempest, a gale which hurled man and beast, and all the sludge of the battlefield, this way and that, as if each were of the same heft.

Then, the strangest of things came to pass. The raging tempest folded inward upon its heart, swishing and whirring into a point of convergence not thirty feet before us, whereupon a medley of demon-like voices shot from its core. As far as I could tell through the break in my fingers, its core appeared to crackle like lightning absent its silver spark, which drew in the flames of nearby pyres, as if the flames themselves were being summoned by them. It was only when the maelstrom began to ease that the colour of the flames vanished, brilliant red swirls taking their place. Like converging rivers the swirls melded together, forming what looked like some sort of a oblong doorway, whose edges were spinning so quickly that it formed yet another current, one which kept our heads firmly planted in the mud.

Suddenly, the whirlpool ceased its rotations, and therewith all things became still and silent. Dazed, and utterly disoriented, the two cohorts of legionaries in our vicinity staggered to their feet at a terror stricken pace, cautiously forming a grand circle around the aberration. In that time, I was laying on my stomach with short, quivering breaths filling my cold-scorched lungs. I was staring at the crimson doorway, my eyes ardently enchanted with awe and fear. I brushed the silt off my face and rose to a knee, doing so with the help of Lera, who was now at my side.

"Stand behind me! All of you!" Priscus shouted. Axle, Andreaus, and Petris ran towards him with a few dozen men at their backs. As they took to defence, Priscus placed himself before them with a stance as steady as the grip of his sword.

Petris, however, broke-off from the rest and shambled his way behind me — we were close at hand. He was completely dishevelled, and he was breathing rather heavily as if he had just dashed across a great distance. There was horror in his eyes as well, as if Ascenelius had come for his soul. "It's him," he muttered in fear. "It's him, Cillian. It's the Conjuror!"

At the mention of that name a chorus of terrible gasps broke from nearly every mouth that surrounded the scene. A hooded figure, dressed in black, shapeless robes, like that of an augur, began to emerge from the swirl. As it passed through the doorway the outline of its body burned like the edges of torched paper, but none of the flames seemed to latch upon the fabric. Like a frail, old man suffering from a limp, the figure made its way towards us with its head fixed towards the ground. A scarlet mist seeped from the extremities of its mail gauntlets, one of which was clutched around the neck of an ill-clothed man whose hands were bound by knotted rope, and whose head was covered by a grey, blood-splotched shroud. Nearer and nearer the figure came with the flaccid body of its captive being dragged across the corpses. Then, it halted before Priscus, at which time it did nothing more than stand before him in a grim and lifeless silence, its head still slumped.

Something deeper than fright had come over all, seeing as how none moved a single muscle. Priscus alone, in all his mettle, dared to confront the hellion before him, and so he closed the gap by several steps, his sword firm by his waist. "Who are you?" he said sternly.

The dark figure did not speak, but replied to Priscus by slowly raising his head to view, which amassed another ensemble of sharp and shivery moans. The figure was no man at all, but the ghoulish remanence of a corpse — the Conjuror. From Julia Semprinus' words I have already told of the harrowing abomination which was his appearance, and just as I have already noted, his face, and his person, was truly that of the underworld.

The Conjuror stared at Priscus for a few seconds, and then with a malignant grin, his eyes shifted downwards to the man sealed in his grasp. He reached over and clenched the top of the cowl, at which point the hooded man began to squirm in defiance to the cadence of his dispirited and feeble gasps. At a creeping pace the Conjuror pulled the shroud from the man's head, revealing him to be none other than King Adeanus of Anolia.

Throats that were filled with blares of surprise soon turned to laments of disbelief, for at first sight Adeanus appeared unrecognisable, even to those of us that were near to him. His look was all but short of a battered corpse, his face slashed and bruised, his eyes puffed and swollen. The bridge of his nose was splintered like log and a river of blood trailed down his neck, joining the untold number of fresh lacerations across the whole of his body. One of his ears was also severed at the root, which was encrusted by a film of curdled blood and rot.

All at once a great passion to recover their king surged amongst the men, and so the enclave of legionaries charged forward in attack. In that same instant, however, Priscus let cry a resounding command for them to halt their advance, a response to the Conjuror's increasingly constrictive hold of the king's throat. Here, Priscus then commanded the men, at the Conjuror's unspoken demand, to withdraw back to their positions and not interfere, which they all did except us companions.

"Priscus? Is that you?" Adeanus said, blood gurgling out of his throat. He was looking about hysterically in search of him, and though Priscus was not five yards away, he could not see him, for his eyes were so bloated that he was effectively blind. "Brother? Are you there—" he said, stopping short because of the Conjuror's tightening grip.

Priscus' eyes lit up with anger. "Release him!" he demanded. "Release him now or I'll—"

A breath-robbing pain spread over the king's face as the Conjuror responded with an even greater clasp of his neck. Every muscle in Adeanus' body went limp, and his eyes seemed as if they were moments from parting from their place, a sight which filled my stomach, and my heart, with an intense hunger to charge forward and end the king's torment. Still, Priscus continued to unleash his ire through his clenched teeth. He brought his sword up to his chest and added, "I said unhand him now! Or I swear by Andiel's fury I will forever finish what he started."

The Conjuror had all the power. He continued to retort with uttermost violence, which grew with each of Priscus' threats. We all saw that the king was suffering dearly because of it, but for Priscus, his desperation to help his brother appeared to make him sightless. And because of this, the Conjuror become irritably impatient, and so as his hunched shoulders broadened, his back now straightened like a lofty spire, he hoisted Adeanus high above the height of his shoulder as if he weighed nothing. There in suspension, the king's body writhed uncontrollably, his legs squirming like a skewered fish, his toes scraping at the mud.

It was at this point that Priscus looked on in hollowness, as though the vigour in his recent threats had suddenly died away by the realisation of the suffering man before him. I do not claim, dear reader, to know what past memory had entered his mind, though I am certain that in this moment the feral sounds of his brother's desperate want for air had altogether returned him to those events. He let his sword fall to his side and said, "What is it that you want?"

Never before had I heard the sound of fear or despair in Priscus' voice, let alone seen him relinquish the point of his sword to an enemy and in the face of the Conjuror no less. I was awestruck, dazed even, for to me Priscus had always stood as an equal to those champions whom I so highly revered; a shield against the Ascani and their masters, unfaltering in his spirit to fight against them. Now, I found myself looking upon a man whose endless miseries brought about by war had at long last pierced through his rugged guise, a man who would do anything to save his brother.

I stood upright, how quick I do not know, yet hastily enough to stumble faintly. I fell back an inch into Petris' gripping embrace. "I'm alright," I said under my breath.

"That's good to hear lad," Petris said, while sneakily concealing my hand behind my back and placing the hilt of a sword into my palm. "I don't need to be an augur to know that you're going to need this. Be ready."

Meanwhile, Axle crept up to Priscus' backside like an assassin, slowly and carefully, unwanting of the Conjuror's attention. He reached out to him with an open hand and an expression illuminated with heedfulness and concern, for he too had noticed Priscus' look of defeat and anguish. "What are you doing, Priscus?" he murmured. "Do not lower your sword or he'll end you both." He watered his lips and inched his way closer. As soon as he was near enough to be clearly heard he began to talk with a pleading inflection in his voice. "Please listen to me. I cannot begin to understand the pain in your heart — but make no bargains with this demon. There is nothing in that creature's heart but malice and lies, Priscus, and if all the stories of him are true, then remember what he did to this world...of the destruction. If you weave your words with his, their blight will turn against you, and his war will start again. So I beg you, turn away from him. Trust us to find another way to free your brother, and let us take this chance to drive a sword through what's left of this bastard's heart. Are you hearing me, Priscus? Turn away from him!"

Priscus did not answer. His stare was utterly fixed and void. He moved forward another step and repeated, "What is it that you want? What do you want from me?"

Suddenly, the Conjuror loosened his hold and gasps of air entered the king's throat. With the same treacherous grin he lowered the king to his feet, turning him around so that he faced us, placed as though he were being used as a shield. Still, the creature did not speak, but his tight hold of Adeanus' spine was sufficient enough to show that he threatened to continue terrible punishment if any of us should move or respond in a way that displeased him. It was at this point that the Conjuror's grin widened to a smile as his idle hand broke away from his side. He brought it to shoulder height, where all but one of his boney fingers had curled into his palm.

My blood went cold, ice trailing along my spine. A numbness formed in my chest, far more intensely than ever before. The Conjuror's stiffened finger was pointed at me.

CHAPTER 22

Time seemed suspended as his finger seemed to pierce through my heart. My body was stiff, and so all I could manage to do was look about, confused. I was searching for answers within the hundred pairs of eyes that fell upon me. *Why was it that the Conjuror wanted me?* I was just a builder, and otherwise indistinguishable from all those around me. *Could it be that my actions at Easteria had drawn his attention and wroth?* But I was reminded that the Conjuror was not there and so, to put it bluntly, I stood there dumbfounded with none of my thoughts bringing fresh clarity.

It seemed that I had also forgotten how to speak, for I felt my lips quiver whenever I tried to. The air around me was so thick with my crippling fear that it made me speechless, and for this reason my heart thumped loudly in my chest. As my fingers danced around the sword's hilt, Priscus slowly turned to his side, towards me. He stared at me in such a way as though his heart ached with the weight of cruel decision, one which was clear enough to suggest that he was mulling over the idea of giving in to the Conjuror's demand.

"Priscus," I managed to voice. "I—"

"Not you, Cillian," Lera said, her words cutting through the thickness more easily than mine did. "He wants me."

I turned to look at her, surprise mixed with misunderstanding. I felt her presence like that of a haunting shadow at my back, upon which I saw her standing directly behind me, which is why it appeared that the Conjuror's finger was aimed at me. At first I could not believe it, and as these everlasting moments went on I refused to believe it. As I broke through the shock, anger grew within me. The very thought of offering Lera up to the Conjuror tore at my insides, as if rabid beasts were feasting upon them. Her eyes welled as I searched her face intently for answers, the weight of this anger falling heavier on my shoulders with each passing minute. My blood turned to liquid fire. I could not — I would not, give her up. I was far removed from encouraging the idea. Apprehensive as I was, I mustered the courage to face the Conjuror; first stealing a glance at Priscus, who was increasingly sapped by the emptiness of his grief, which was now intertwined with bewilderment. He was as clueless as I was.

Now, dear reader, I must deviate a moment and tell you of another matter, one that, I believe, I will never be able to effectively convey. As my eyes met with the Conjuror's a sudden clarity seized my thoughts. My mind, as if taken by some enchantment, jolted back to the day of the king's council, whereupon a series of vivid memories flashed before my eyes, much of them being of Ulcar and the other lords speaking about the upheaval across Anolia. In truth, it was almost as if I was witnessing that which the Conjuror wished me to see, and what I saw was the truth: the real reason for our presence in Northfleet.

Many years after I had heard Julia Semprinus' tale, I was able to confirm what I had now come to piece together. We had walked right into the Conjuror's grand scheme. All the while I had believed that our task in Northfleet was meant as a preemptive strike to stop the Ascani from gaining a position in the north, but this was not the true purpose — far from that which *we* had fabricated. It was never about the fortress itself, or who had control over it. Rather, it was always about Priscus, and the aim to have him out-of-the-way. In fact, the castle was but a guarantee, one that was meant to play upon Priscus' nature, and one that would make certain that he was separated from his brother, thereby severing the heart of Anolia's strength, which was the very thing the Conjuror despised: the love between brothers.

The Conjuror looked at me with nefarious satisfaction, as if to suggest that he knew what it was I was thinking, and that the crux of his plan, though stumped in part by Ulcar's failings to slay Priscus on our route, had been an overall triumph to his liking, which it was. What is worse, however, is that he seemed to be pleased with my anger. Somehow I had caught his attention by thwarting his attack at Easteria. And, it was becoming more likely, by that rapt grin of his, that I was caught in his scheme for revenge. But why Lera? How is it that he knew well my connection to her? The answer is to come in the pages that follow. But still, dear reader, what better way to end my life then to tear out my heart.

"No!" I said firmly, shielding Lera with my body and placing the sword in her grasp as if to keep it hidden. "This is another one of his tricks! As was it all from the start! Can't you see it? The attack on Easteria, and the attacks upon our borders. It was all nothing more than a scheme to divide us — to divide you Priscus from your brother." I stretched a hand outwards as if my body language would help me sound more convincing. "This creature has no desire to keep your brother alive, Priscus. If we give him what he wants he'll just kill him all the same. He's already won a battle in a war that he has been plotting for these last thousand years, so he's not going to hand him back! He's going to kill him! He's going to kill both of them!"

"He's right!" Axle broke in. "Listen to him, Priscus! If your brother is here before us then it means the legions he was commanding are lost. Do not bargain with him!"

"What other choice do we have?" Andreaus broke in. He spoke calmly, as if the decision on who to let live was clear and uncontested. "Never in my life did I think I would come to say this, but I say we give this creature the girl and let us be done with this. We can't just sit here and abandon the king's life!"

"Aye," Cimber said with a heavy heart. "I say we bargain."

"What the hell are you talking about? Have you all gone mad?" Axle said, flabbergasted. "We all know the bloody story! We all know what the bastard wants! For Andiel's sake listen to me! If we turn her over to him now it'll be over for all of us. Everyone in the kingdom! This sard of an ancient fiend is after what the people of this realm once denied him, and now he's all but cut off the head that holds the crown. And when he does take the crown he'll kill you next, Priscus. And then with you out of his way the land will be divided and leaderless. So, for the last time, I'm going to ask you to put that fucking head of yours back on your shoulders and snap out of it. Drive your sword into that creature's heart and end it all before it's too late. Do not forsake all that we have fought for. Don't give him anymore blood!"

"Look at him! All of you!" Andreaus shouted. "How can we not help him?"

"Quiet yourself, captain!" Petris said. "It is not your place to choose."

"And neither is the decision yours, priest," Andreaus replied, in the tone of a broken man. He was hurting inside, and for good reason. Still, you may think him cruel for his words, dear reader, but it would be unjust if I did not convey his heart in this moment. Andreaus was a man whose sword was as sharp as his bond, and it so happens that it was Adeanus himself who had given him his sword when he had joined the Bronze Hammers. His devotion to him was strong, like iron, and thus I say with faith that there was no cruelty meant in his remarks. There was just as much validation in his reasons as there were in mine, which was love.

"More will die if we do," I said, my stance as it was. "The war will start again!"

"Then we'll fight that war when the time comes, builder. Just as we have all these years," he replied, turning to Priscus. "My lord, save your brother. Save the king!"

As we argued amongst ourselves, Priscus' eyes were locked with his brother's not caring to even shift them over towards us to quell our fighting, or even bother to stop us from speaking on the matter of whose life should be offered.

"Forgive me, Cillian," Andreaus said, advancing towards Lera with his sword out at his side. "We all know where your heart lies, but I can't just stand by and watch my king suffer any longer. Her life, as mine, as all of ours, was forfeited the moment the emblem was put on our chest. She is a part of the legion as the rest of us, and so her life is owed to the realm. And the king is that realm." He reached out to grab her. "I'm sorry, but there isn't any other way."

"Stay your hand, captain!" Axle blurted, stopping him in his tracks. I never thought Axle to be one to turn his sword against a brother in arms, but he did, perhaps inadvertently. If a clash of swords were to happen he was ready for it. "We will not trade a life for another," he went on. "I would not offer hers. I would not offer yours. I know you well enough, Andreaus, to know that you are not in the habit of siding with the evil of this world, no less with the master that controls them. Do not force me to take action, brother."

"Calm your hearts!" Petris cried. "We'll find another way! We must!"

"No need," Andreaus said, lowering his sword. "It seems it's already been decided."

I peeked over my shoulder just as the clunk of steel plunging into the mud filled my ears. I did not know that when Andreaus had moved towards us, I had shifted myself, and Lera, so that our backs faced the Conjuror. Lera had let fall the sword and was slowly backing away from me, her head down and defeated, her eyes no longer glassed, but dripping pools of tears.

"What the hell are you doing, Lera?" I said, stupefied.

"He's right, Cillian," she replied. "There isn't any other way. I owe him my life."

"What?" I added. "Your life is your own. Come back here! Now!"

Suddenly, the air stirred as if it were being inhaled by the lungs of a great giant. Cries of fear from the surrounding legionaries made the re-emergence of the Conjuror's whirlpool known, from which the sprinkle of blood-fused sediment spotted my now pale face. My gaze was fixed upon the whir, many tongues of crimson mist twirling about the edges. I traced their twists and turns with my own look of despair, high above at first, and then down to their radiant ends, where something bizarre gripped my focus. I noticed that these radiant swirls were emanating from the Conjuror's idle hand, or more to the point, I noticed that it was the flesh upon his thumb that nourished his magic spell, giving it brilliance and life.

"Here!" Lera shouted above the gale. "Take it!

As I jolted back to the sound of her voice I caught her soaring amulet with my chest, taking my eyes off her for a mere second. In that time she had begun to move closer toward the Conjuror, trudging through the mire in reverse as her long hair moved wildly from the strong winds emitting from the whirlpool. At the same time, Priscus stepped off to the side with neither fault nor qualm in his action, leaving a clear path for Lera to tread freely to the Conjuror's welcoming hand. His face was lit up by the maelstrom, the glow of the mist highlighting his anguish. Still, he remained irreparably hardened on doing what was needed to retrieve Adeanus.

"You can't!" I yelled, stepping-off after her. "Come back! Lera! He'll kill you —"

Right then Andreaus and Cimber each seized one of my arms, as if they were both dungeon guards snatching a fleeing captive. I tried to worm free with a desperation I did not know I had, but even with the gale battering their faces their hold felt like shackles made of rock and iron. What manner of hysteria gripped me I do not know, but I begged and weeped for Petris to help me. He was frozen in place with fright, not knowing what to do, and Axle, who rushed to my rescue, had been stopped by a wall of shields that had been set in place by those men who saw their opportunity to side with Andreaus and save their king.

"Don't let her do this!" I cried out to Priscus. My words were dimed by the wind, and their echoes seemed to fall on his deaf ears. "Don't do this Priscus! This is not in your heart! This is not who you are! I know your brother is all that you have left in this world, but think back — think back to your wife and your son! Think of the pain in your heart when they were taken from you! Because that is my pain now, Priscus. I beg you! My lord! I beg you please don't do this! Kill this creature and be done with it!"

Whether Priscus heard me or not I will never truly know, but I knew he had read my lips at the very least, or rather that he had guessed the words, because he immediately looked away from me as though he was burned by the guilt that passed through my words. Not that I cared about his guilt. I was unrelenting in my screams, caring very little to be seen as I had once feared at the beginning of this tale. And so I continued to call out to him with the tune of a weary heart, intensifying with each of Lera's continued steps.

"Cillian stop!" Lera shouted, as she came to a halt. She was now not three feet from the Conjuror. She clenched her jaw to stop herself from weeping, or lamenting her decision. Then, she raised one hand as if motioning a farewell.

At this point my tongue, instead of thrashing about with continued pleas, stopped in despair, in disbelief, in grief at what happened next. A barrage of silver glints, poking out of the rim of her sleeve, had filled my eyes. It was a dagger, my dagger to be precise, which I had forgotten that I had retrieved from Far-Skafa's corpse. She had lifted from my belt without my notice when I was pressed up against her. Here, my eyes grew wider than ever before, because suddenly I knew what she was intending to do, believing it was the only path to ending this nightmare.

"I love you," she mouthed, lowering her arm to her side.

Then, without warning, her eyes blazed with fury. She let fall the dagger from its secrecy, snatching the hilt in a heartbeat before it could fully part from her hand. She then spun around with a high and terrifying cry, leaping toward the Conjuror so quickly that it appeared the creature could not move in time to intercept. She held the knife with both hands, descending from her pounce like a wild beast, its point plummeting straight for the heart.

In an explosion of rage the Conjuror thrusted the king a foot to the side. He lurched forward in a spasm and planted his feet into the mud. Framed in the brilliance of the whirlpool behind him, he instantly brought his idle hand to the height of his chin, where sparks of red mist began to flicker around the chunks of flesh dotting his fingers. The black of his eyes were consumed by red ichor, and at this moment a sudden strong wave of wind burst out of his palm, it's force beyond the power of the natural world. It first collided with Lera, who slammed onto the ground, and then it struck all those caught in its path, propelling nearly all to fall backward.

I was cast to the ground like all the others, the hind part of my right thigh receiving a small cut by the head of a spear jutting out from the bed of corpses I fell on. By then, however, any pain to my flesh could not match that of my heart, and so seeing as I was unbound by gripping holds I faltered to my feet, foaming at the mouth as I aimlessly cried out to Lera in the veil of ashen dust before me. I stumbled toward the crimson glow in search of her, but by the time the brilliance fully resurfaced it was already too late. The Conjuror had appeared in the fullness of his form with not one, but two, figures writhing in his clutch as if they were being presented to me like butchered slabs of meat at a market auction. I froze, watching blood and saliva erupt from Lera's mouth.

Her eyes drifted to mine from over her shoulder, their colour nothing other than that which comes from crushing strangulation. I tried to take action, but I soon found myself trapped in the same predicament as Priscus, where any act of defiance resulted in her increased agony. It was at this moment that I had felt the most powerless than I have ever been in all the years of my life. This powerlessness was accompanied by a wave of heated wind, whereupon there came a long and clacking sound from the Conjuror's throat, phrases of the ancient tongue. It was no enchantment as I had feared it to be, but rather a flurry of claims and threats, which grew bolder as he glared at us in such a way as to announce our failure to help either Lera and Adeanus. Then, he ceased these threats by looking to Priscus, his head canted to the side with that same nefarious grin on his face, which was also teeming with intentions.

"Priscus," Adeanus blurted out, suffocatingly.

At that the Conjuror flicked the hand that clutched Adeanus towards his chest. In one turn of his wrist, he snapped the king's neck as if it were a dry twig, the sound of crushed bones sparking a semblance of renewed life in Lera's eyes. He continued to squeeze the king's neck until the tips of his fingers met, and then, with a flinging motion, he hurled the corpse far out to his side. As our eyes were pulled to the king's corpse, the Conjuror turned and merged with the whirlpool, the tail of his robe, and Lera's drooping legs, the last of what my eyes saw of them.

At that moment Priscus let sound a horn of agony and anguish. He raised his sword, dashing full tilt towards the whirlpool. I cried out as well. Not to stop him, but to go after Lera. As the aperture gradually wound down to a close I surged forward after him absentmindedly. Far into the whirlpool I followed him, until the feeling of the air and wind was suddenly no more. All that remained around me was a void of black shadows floating in breezeless space, absent light, absent Priscus' figure. A dullness entered my bones, a hypnotic tiredness descended over my eyes.

I fell to my knees in this chasm of black and succumbed to the weariness.

***

I awoke suddenly as if the spark of life had all at once returned to me. The heat of a feverish sun burned upon my back, my legs inundated in the rushes of cool sea water, my cheek pressed down against a blanket of white, marbled sand. Seagulls chirped overhead, and a faint rustle of foliage flapped at a distance in front of me. I stretched my hands out to my sides, my fingers boring into slivers of broken seashells. I stood up, dazed and sore, as if I had been lying stiff for a decade. I cleared away the sand caked upon my parched lips and looked up to the sky with squinted eyes, for the radiance of the sun burned my vision to a sheet of ivory and gold.

"What's happening? Where am I?" I mumbled, cupping my hand over my eyes. Suddenly the shadow of a figure appeared before me, and with it came the jangle of jewels upon chains and the perfumed scent of rich oils. "Lera?" I asked, inquisitively. "Is that you?"

"I'm afraid I'm not this Lera, my dear," said a man's voice in a foreign tone.

By now my eyes had adjusted to the light and the whole of this man's body was clear to me. In tandem, a host of shapes had formed behind him, a large crowd spanning far-off to the background of tropical timbers and lush canopies. This strange man was dark-skinned, as were they all, but only few were dressed as he was; garbs of orange and purple silks that were garnished with gold sashes and precious gems. The others appeared to be their prisoners, who were shackled at the hands and feet, each and all led by heavily armed guards.

"Who the hell are you?" I said, defensively.

"Me?" the man replied with his fingers interlaced at his chest. "Well, who I am is of little concern to you, my wandering friend. I'm just here to welcome you."

"Welcome me?"

"Why yes!" he said, signalling the man nearest to him who was holding a bludgeoning club. "To Kashtan!"

The club met with the side of my head. The light of the sun vanished.

CPSIA information can be obtained
at www.ICGtesting.com
Printed in the USA
LVHW020304220221
679596LV00004B/158